R. E. LEE

A BIOGRAPHY

By

Douglas Southall Freeman

VOLUME III

CHARLES SCRIBNER'S SONS

NEW YORK   LONDON

Charles Scribner's Sons
Macmillan Publishing Company
866 Third Avenue, New York, NY 10022
Collier Macmillan Canada, Inc.

Library of Congress Catalog Card Number 77-83150

ISBN 0-684-15484-6

First Macmillan / Hudson River Edition 1988

10   9   8   7

Printed in the United States of America

R. E. LEE

Books by
DOUGLAS SOUTHALL FREEMAN

GEORGE WASHINGTON

LEE'S LIEUTENANTS

THE SOUTH TO POSTERITY

R. E. LEE

Charles Scribner's Sons

CONTENTS

CONTENTS

ILLUSTRATIONS

Between Pages 274 and 275

General Lee with certain officers of his personal staff and of the general staff of the Army of Northern Virginia

Lieutenant General Richard Stoddard Ewell

Lieutenant General Ambrose P. Hill

Lieutenant Colonel Walter H. Taylor

Little Round Top after the Confederate attack of July 2, 1863

The manner of men that Lee commanded

What Lee left behind at Gettysburg

The pontoon-bridge and ford at Jericho Mills

The toll of Cold Harbor

The type of railway on which Lee had to rely for supplies

Part of the interior of Fort Stedman

The mess-kit and the field-glasses used throughout the war by General Lee

General Lee on Traveller

Title-page and inscription in General Lee's prayer-book

What the war did to Mrs. Lee

"The Mess," used by Mrs. R. E. Lee as her Richmond home from approximately January 1, 1864, until late in June, 1865

ILLUSTRATIONS

MAPS

viii

ILLUSTRATIONS

ILLUSTRATIONS

x

ILLUSTRATIONS

R. E. LEE

CHAPTER I

The "Might-Have-Beens" of Chancellorsville

"It is a terrible loss," Lee wrote Custis in the first shock of Jackson's death.[1] So deep and personal was his grief that when he talked of him with General W. N. Pendleton, days afterward, he wept unabashed. "Great and good" were the adjectives he used, again and again, in speaking of the dead "Stonewall."[2] To one officer he said, "I had such implicit confidence in Jackson's skill and energy that I never troubled myself to give him detailed instructions. The most general suggestions were all that he needed."[3] For the remainder of his life his references to Jackson always had a tone of affectionate warmth, and in his official report of Chancellorsville he praised him with the superlatives he was wont to reserve for the men in the ranks alone: "The movement by which the enemy's position was turned and the fortune of the day decided was conducted by the lamented Lieutenant-General Jackson. . . . I do not propose here to speak of the character of this illustrious man, since removed from the scene of his eminent usefulness by the hand of an inscrutable but all-wise Providence. I nevertheless desire to pay the tribute of my admiration to the matchless energy and skill that marked this last act of his life, forming, as it did, a worthy conclusion of that long series of splendid achievements which won for him the lasting love and gratitude of his country."[4]

In the spirit of this encomium he steadfastly viewed the death of his greatest lieutenant as the act of Heaven. "Any victory would be dear at such a price," he said, adding quickly: "But God's will be done."[5] To his brother Charles Carter Lee he wrote, "I am grateful to Almighty God for having given us such a man."[6] He looked to that same God to raise up some one in

---

[1] Jones, *L. and L.*, 242.
[2] Lee to Mrs. Lee, May 11, 1863, *R. E. Lee, Jr.*, 94; *O. R.*, 25, part 2, pp. 793, 812, 821.
[3] *R. E. Lee, Jr.*, 94.   [4] *O. R.*, 25, part 1, p. 803.
[5] Jones, *L. and L.*, 242.   [6] May 24, 1863; 31 *Confederate Veteran*, 287.

Jackson's stead, while he sought to save the morale of the army, and especially that of the Second Corps, from impairment because of the loss of the man whose body was sorrowfully borne to Richmond and thence to Lexington.[7] In his general order announcing the passing of "Stonewall" he said:

"The daring, skill and energy of this great and good soldier, by the decree of an all-wise Providence, are now lost to us. But while we mourn his death, we feel that his spirit still lives, and will inspire the whole army with his indomitable courage and unshaken confidence in God as our hope and our strength. Let his name be a watchword to his corps, who have followed him to victory on so many fields. Let officers and men emulate his invincible determination to do everything in the defense of our beloved country." [8]

Jackson's example, he said in the letter to Charles Carter Lee, "is left us," and Jackson's spirit "I trust will be diffused over the whole Confederacy." [9] To Hood, he wrote, "We must all do more than formerly. We must endeavor to follow the unselfish, devoted, intrepid course he pursued, and we shall be strengthened rather than weakened by his loss." [10]

This was the utterance of a humble spirit. Lee never dreamed of claiming what military critics have since been disposed to assert —that Chancellorsville was perhaps more nearly a flawless battle, from the Confederate point of view, than any that was ever planned and executed by an American commander. Facing an army two and a half times as large as his own, better equipped in every way and supplied with more numerous artillery, Lee had been on the defensive at the opening of the operation and had been threatened in front and on the left flank by a well-planned and admirably executed advance. In the face of his opponent's superiority, Lee divided his army, wrested the initiative from Hooker, again divided his force and overwhelmed the XI Corps. On the 3d he drove the enemy back to the lines, and on the 4th,

---

[7] Much to his regret, Lee did not feel that he could spare the Stonewall brigade to accompany Jackson's remains as a guard of honor (*Jones,* 154).

[8] *O. R.,* 25, part 2, p. 793.

[9] 31 *Confederate Veteran,* 287. [10] May 21, 1863; *Hood,* 52.

the least successful day of the operations, he forced Sedgwick to retreat. He took a great risk in leaving so small a force at Fredericksburg and he seemingly took still longer chances on May 2 when he detached Jackson and faced Hooker with only two divisions; but except for the capture of the Fredericksburg Heights on the 3d, the situation was entirely in his hands after May 1. In a week's fighting, and through the campaign made possible by the successes of that week, he so changed the military situation that the Army of the Potomac did not again undertake a march on Richmond for precisely one year. It was undoubtedly the most remarkable victory he ever achieved and it increased greatly his well-established reputation both in the eyes of the enemy and of the South.[11]

Lee did not make a single serious mistake in judging the plans of the enemy or in parcelling out his forces to checkmate Hooker. Almost alone among the Confederate commanders, he insisted from the first that the main attack was to be delivered on the left, and though he could not leave sufficient men under Early at Fredericksburg to prevent the capture of the heights, he at least protected himself against surprise from that quarter. His handling of Anderson and McLaws on May 3 was tactically as excellent as his general plan was brilliant.

If any criticism is to be made of the operations that Lee could personally control, it was that he failed to organize the attack earlier on May 4 at Salem Church, when he had Sedgwick almost surrounded on three sides by the columns of McLaws, Anderson, and Early. A battle on so extended a front was, as Alexander justly said, an all-day undertaking,[12] but the signal was not given until 6 P.M. It was another instance where Lee seemed temperamentally unable to hasten a slow lieutenant, in this case, McLaws.

The claim that Lee should have brought Anderson to the vicinity of Salem Church during the night of May 3, though advanced by competent authority,[13] is, once again, the counsel of perfection. On the evening of the 3d, when he had been compelled to send off McLaws to cope with Sedgwick, Lee could reasonably assume that after having beaten the enemy that day, he could drive him on the morrow with four divisions, but it was

---

[11] *Fitz Lee*, 257.　　[12] *Alexander*, 357.　　[13] *Alexander*, 356.

asking too much even of him to demand that he attack Hooker with only three divisions. It was not until he saw how the Federal positions had been strengthened on the night of the 3d-4th that he reasoned he must reconcentrate his whole army by disposing of Sedgwick entirely, before he could hope to carry the fortified Federal line. Then, but not until then, was he justified in assuming the defensive for one day with a force further reduced. He cannot fairly be condemned for failing to detach nearly two-fifths of his troops on the evening of the 3d in the face of the main Federal army, so long as there was a chance that he could follow up the victory of that day and drive Hooker into the Rappahannock on the morrow.

Little has been written, but much might be said, of Lee's bold action in refusing to detach Stuart for pursuit of Stoneman's 10,000 cavalry.[14] In this, Lee applied the lessons he had learned on the way to Second Manassas and on the march from South Mountain to Hagerstown and back again. He would not again willingly be blinded by the absence of his mounted forces, least of all in a country where observation was as difficult as in the Wilderness. Deliberately he risked his communications in order to have the main body of his cavalry with him. How well that cavalry served him and how, in particular, Fitz Lee contributed to Jackson's march around the Federal right flank, is a notable part of the history of the campaign. It is hard to conceive how the flanking operation could have been undertaken with the same speed or with like assurance had Stuart been galloping across Midland Virginia in pursuit of Stoneman. The contrast between what Lee knew and could do at Chancellorsville, when Stuart was present, as compared with his groping through Pennsylvania when Stuart was absent two months later, is proof enough of the wisdom of his course. Hooker, on the other hand, was handicapped from the outset by his lack of cavalry. With an adequate force covering the Federal right, Jackson's movement on May 2 would have been a failure, if, indeed, Lee would have had the temerity to undertake it. Chancellorsville saw a definite decline in the strength of the Confederate horse, but witnessed a notable increase of skill in its employment.

[14] For the strength of Stoneman, see O. R., 25, part 1, p. 1067.

4

Remarkable as was the victory, it was bought at an excessively great cost. The toll of general officers was very heavy. Four brigades lost eight successive commanding officers.[15] Total Confederate casualties numbered 13,156, of whom 1683 were killed, 9277 were wounded, and 2196 were prisoners of war.[16] These losses, Lee told the President on May 7, reflected the difference in the strength of the opposing armies. The killed and wounded, he explained, were "always in proportion to the inequality of forces engaged."[17] Hooker's losses, then of course unknown to Lee, reached 16,845,[18] a far smaller percentage of his total strength.

The disparity of numbers to which Lee attributed his heavier casualties was due, in part, to the absence of Pickett's and Hood's divisions of Longstreet's corps. That fact raises a question which goes deeper than the strategy of the field: Had all Longstreet's corps been present, would Sedgwick have been destroyed? Could Hooker have been trapped in the gloomy woods before he had time to extricate himself and recross the Rappahannock? *Prima facie,* if the 62,500 that Lee commanded during the operations were able to win so stunning a success, it is reasonable to assume that the addition of 12,000 fine veterans would have magnified his victory. Consequently, in any fair appraisal of Lee's generalship, the question becomes one of whether Lee erred in permitting Longstreet to remain in Southside Virginia to collect supplies when his bayonets were so badly needed on the Rappahannock.

The reasons that prompted Lee to trust Longstreet's discretion, and not to demand his early return to the Rappahannock, have already been given.[19] The army needed provisions. If it were to assume the offensive, it had to accumulate a reserve. If this could be done in no other way than by employing two crack divisions as commissary troops, then, up to a certain point, the work was

---

[15] *O. R.,* 25, part 1, p. 1008.

[16] The figures were compiled by Alexander, *op. cit.,* 360–61. Guild, in his official report, put them at 10,281, but did not include the prisoners of war and gave fewer killed by 102 and fewer wounded by 577 than Alexander later showed. Among the wounded were many whose injuries were so slight that Lee reprobated their inclusion among the casualties (*O. R.,* 25, part 2, pp. 798–99). Of material booty, 13 guns, 19,500 small arms, and 17 stands of colors were captured. Eight Confederate guns were taken on the Fredericksburg heights by Sedgwick (*Taylor's General Lee,* 175; *O. R.,* 25, part 1, p. 818).

[17] *O. R.,* 25, part 2, p. 782.

[18] *O. R.,* 25, part 1, pp. 185, 191.   [19] See *supra,* vol. II, p. 499 *ff.*

worth doing. But time was pressing. Lee had set May 1 as the date beyond which one army or the other could not defer an offensive, yet it was not until April 27 that he inquired how soon Longstreet could rejoin. Longstreet, to be sure, was slow in collecting the supplies and failed to take advantage of his opportunities of meeting the Federals on even terms. His stay in Southside Virginia did no credit to him. Even in his military autobiography, which certainly did not understate his achievements, he was quite content to dismiss his expedition with a few anecdotes. Longstreet's slowness, however, does not exculpate Lee. Essentially a field commander, Lee was not successful in directing operations at a distance from him, except when dealing with Jackson. In the case of Longstreet's expedition, as in several other instances, he was too much disposed to trust the discretion of an absent lieutenant. A careful reading of the correspondence between him and Longstreet raises the suspicion that he permitted Longstreet to browbeat him. He took all the risk on his own front while Longstreet did nothing to justify the detachment of 12,000 of the best men in the army. Lee cannot be excused for this. His yielding to Longstreet on August 29, 1862, may have limited the success attained at the second battle of Manassas, and like compliance certainly was a factor in preventing a victory at Gettysburg; but it is possible that Lee's acceptance of Longstreet's unsoldierly excuses in March and April, 1863, cost him and the South still more dearly. Lee himself expressed to Hood his belief that if his whole army had been with him at Chancellorsville, Hooker would have been demolished.[20] He might have said more. Had Longstreet reached him in time for him to assume the offensive before Hooker seized the initiative, the result might have been a swift march northward and a Gettysburg fought in May instead of July, with the added leadership of Jackson and with the strength of the men who fell at Chancellorsville.

Failure to recall Longstreet earlier must, therefore, be written down as the darkest "might-have-been" of the Chancellorsville campaign, and as one of the great mistakes of Lee's military career. The public, not foreseeing the consequences, did not think

[20] *Hood,* 53.

6

so. The few who had any inkling of the facts were disposed to blame the War Department rather than Lee.[21]

Precisely two years had elapsed since Lee had taken the decisive step in mobilizing the Virginia volunteers. Two years of desperate contest, lacking one month, lay ahead of him. He was thus midway his military career as a Confederate commander when Jackson died. Much he had learned of the organization and administration of an army, much of conciliating rivals, much of arousing the best in men, much of creating the morale of victory. In the hard school of combat he had mastered the art of the offensive so fully, both in strategy and in tactics, that little seemed left for him to acquire. But his military education was not yet completed. On a hill near a little town in Pennsylvania, the bell of a quiet seminary was calling him again to school to learn a new lesson, written red in blood.

[21] 1 R. W. C. D., 315.

CHAPTER II

THE REORGANIZATION THAT EXPLAINS GETTYSBURG

WHO was to lead Jackson's corps and to act in his stead? "I know not how to replace him," Lee confessed to his wife.[1] Among the infantry officers of the Army of Northern Virginia there were only four men whom he seems to have considered for corps command—A. P. Hill, R. S. Ewell, R. H. Anderson, and John B. Hood. Of these four, Lee regarded A. P. Hill as the best division commander he had, and from the time of the Maryland expedition had placed him next in line for a corps.[2] Among the officers who had led Jackson's "foot-cavalry" from Front Royal to the Potomac and back again to triumph at Port Republic and at Cross Keys, the man who had been closest to Jackson in those operations had been Major General R. S. Ewell, now able for the first time to walk after having lost a leg at Groveton. There was strong sentiment for his appointment as the "logical successor" of Jackson.[3] "Dick" Ewell, as he was universally called, was then forty-six. After his graduation from West Point he had served with cavalry until 1861. He always insisted that in fighting Indians on the plains he had "learned all about commanding fifty United States dragoons, and forgotten everything else." Odd in appearance and in speech, he was quick-tempered but generous and kindly, and notoriously profane until he underwent a change of heart during the war.[4] Professing to have some strange malady, he slept most irregularly and subsisted on a peculiar diet of wheat. An excellent tactician and a rapid marcher, he was fond of personal participation in battle, and more than once, during the Valley campaign, he had temporarily turned over the command to a subordinate in the absence of Jackson, had gone among the skirmishers, had satisfied his appetite for a fight, and then had returned with the fervent hope that "old Jackson would not

[1] May 11, 1863; *R. E. Lee, Jr.,* 94; *cf.* Jones, *L. and L.,* 242.
[2] See *supra,* vol. II, p. 418.
[3] *Mrs. McGuire,* 215; *Pendleton,* 272.   [4] *Eggleston,* 156.

8

catch him." His temperamental fondness for desperate adventures had made him an ideal lieutenant to Jackson, whom he much admired but early suspected of being insane. After he had once heard Jackson seriously assert that he never took pepper with his food because it made his left leg weak, Ewell had been satisfied that "Stonewall" was mad. He had confided to one of his friends that he "never saw one of Jackson's couriers approach without expecting an order to assault the north pole." His soldiers idolized him, despite his hard marching, which seems to have been based on his professed maxim that "the road to glory cannot be followed with much baggage. . . . We can get along without everything but food and ammunition." [5] Few jokes in the army were more cherished than that of Ewell's insistence during the winter of 1861–62 that he could find food where his commissaries affirmed the country had been swept clear. He went off on a foraging expedition and subsequently returned with one lean cow of leathery flanks. When asked how far he thought this would go in feeding the army, he was nonplussed and admitted that he had forgotten he was heading a brigade! He was thinking in terms of his fifty dragoons on the prairie.[6]

As for R. H. Anderson and John B. Hood, Lee regarded both as "capital officers" who were improving in the field, though neither had so great reputation as either A. P. Hill or Ewell. Lee believed they would make good chiefs of corps, if it was necessary to use them, but he did not prefer either of them to their seniors.[7]

Outside the infantry then with the Army of Northern Virginia, only two other men could reasonably have been considered at the time. One was D. H. Hill and the other was "Jeb" Stuart. D. H. Hill was a most tenacious fighter. Few division commanders could get more from a given number of men. That had been demonstrated at South Mountain and at Sharpsburg. But the North Carolinian was critical and outspoken and not the type of lieutenant with whom Lee worked most satisfactorily. Besides, he was in command in North Carolina, where the civil authorities imposed in him a measure of confidence that made them willing

---

[5] *O. R.,* 12, part 3, pp. 890–91, 892.

[6] This sketch of Ewell is drawn from R. Taylor, *op. cit.,* 36–38. General Taylor served with Ewell in the Valley and was one of his closest friends.

[7] *O. R.,* 25, part 2, p. 811.

to trust him with fewer troops than they would have demanded for defense under almost any one else.[8] Hill, moreover, was in an odd state of mind at the time, insisting on explicit orders and asking that the district commanders under him report directly to the War Department.[9]

Stuart was held by some to have exhibited qualities on May 3 that marked him as the best man in the army to be retained permanently in the command he had assumed on the night of May 2, after both Jackson and A. P. Hill had been wounded.[10] There is a hint in one of Lee's dispatches indicating that Stuart thought Lee had not been satisfied with his handling of the infantry that day because Lee had not publicly commended him;[11] but as Stuart recommended some one else for succession to Jackson's corps,[12] it is hardly probable that he regarded himself as in line of promotion for that post. So far as the evidence shows, Lee did not consider him. This doubtless was because he regarded Stuart as indispensable where he was. Neither Wade Hampton nor Fitz Lee, who were the senior brigadiers in the cavalry, had then shown much of Stuart's extraordinary skill in intelligence service, which was perhaps his most useful contribution to the Army of Northern Virginia. Even had they been ready for promotion, it is hardly probable that Lee would have considered them. He would never willingly have supplanted Stuart, because he believed a general of infantry could more nearly take Jackson's place at the head of the Second Corps than any one else could perform for the army the service that Stuart was rendering. It must, however, remain a tantalizing subject of speculation what the result would have been if Lee's choice had fallen on Stuart, for Stuart would have fought furiously at Gettysburg, and no new commander of the cavalry would have ventured on the raid that deprived Lee of part of his cavalry during that campaign.

A. P. Hill, Ewell, Anderson, Hood, D. H. Hill, Stuart—the choice narrowed down to A. P. Hill and Ewell. In reality, it was hardly a choice, because Lee had long considered the corps too large to be handled by one man in the tangled country through which the army operated. He had long desired to

8 *Alexander*, 367 n.   9 *O. R.*, 25, part 2, pp. 811, 832.
10 *Alexander*, 360.   11 *O. R.*, 25, part 2, p. 792.
12 *O. R.*, 25, part 2, p. 821. This letter does not state whom he mentioned.

increase the number of corps and would have done so earlier had he been able to decide upon suitable commanders.[13] He determined now to make the best of the dark necessity and to reorganize the army into three corps. Longstreet, of course, was to remain at the head of the First Corps; to Ewell, as Jackson's lieutenant, the Second Corps was to be entrusted, and for A. P. Hill a Third Corps was to be created. On May 20 Lee submitted the proposal to the President, and commended Hill and Ewell to his consideration.[14]

In its consequences this was one of the most important resolves of Lee's military career. At the most critical hour of its history it placed two-thirds of the army under new corps leaders. A. P. Hill had never commanded more than one division in action, except for the confused hour after Jackson had been struck down. Hill, however, was devoted, prompt, and energetic, and, though both Longstreet and Jackson had put him under arrest, he deserved promotion. If he did not thereafter display even a spark of the genius of Jackson, he never was guilty of any irremediable blunder. With Ewell, the circumstances of promotion were unusual. Lee took him at the valuation of others, rather than on his own knowledge of the soldier. The selection was sentimental and therefore inevitable. Ewell had served directly under Lee only for the period from June 26 to July 13, and from August 15 to August 25, 1862—in all, something less than a month, and then always subject to Jackson's guidance. Lee esteemed him as an "honest, brave soldier who [had] always done his duty well," [15] but he did not know the full extent of the physical disability resulting from Ewell's loss of a leg, and still less did he know the working of a mind to which he was entrusting the lives of more than 20,000 men. Some of those who had served with Ewell in the Valley were aware that he would not initiate a plan if he could possibly subject it in advance to the criticism of others.[16] Lee had never had an opportunity of discovering this lack of self-confidence in Ewell, nor was he aware that Ewell's experience with Jackson had schooled him to obey the letter of orders and not to exercise discretion. This had made him a better

---

[13] *Hood,* 53; *O. R.,* 25, part 2, p. 810. [14] *O. R.,* 25, part 2, pp. 810–11.
[15] *O. R.,* 25, part 2, p. 810. [16] *Cf. R. Taylor,* 37.

rather than a worse commander under Jackson, whose Army of the Valley had been small enough for "Stonewall" to keep all its operations under his eye; but it was to prove a heavy handicap to Lee, who had become accustomed to march with Longstreet and to leave Jackson to use his own sound judgment in handling the other corps. Lee did not realize how difficult it would be for a man of Ewell's temperament to adjust himself quickly to a system of command that usually placed an immensely greater responsibility on Lee's principal lieutenants than Jackson had ever entrusted to his subordinates. Gettysburg was to show the results of A. P. Hill's inexperience and of Ewell's indecision in the face of discretionary orders.[17]

The promotion of A. P. Hill and of Ewell being promptly authorized by Mr. Davis,[18] Lee decided to apportion his troops equitably among the three corps he proposed to set up. The army consisted at the time of eight divisions, including the two of Longstreet's that had been sent to Southside Virginia. Jackson had commanded four—A. P. Hill's, D. H. Hill's,[19] Early's, and Trimble's, the last led at Chancellorsville by Colston. Longstreet had McLaws's, Pickett's, Hood's, and R. H. Anderson's. To rearrange these two in three corps of three divisions each, Lee had to take one division from Longstreet and one from Jackson's old corps, and had to form a new ninth division. He decided to transfer Anderson from Longstreet and A. P. Hill's former division from the Second Corps and to give these two to A. P. Hill for his new Third Corps. As A. P. Hill's division had consisted of six brigades, Lee separated two of these from their former comrades. He made up the ninth division with these two and with the brigades of Pettigrew and Davis which he received from North Carolina in return for brigades he had previously detached.

Lee, it will be recalled, had already promoted Rodes to D. H. Hill's old division, and Edward Johnson he had assigned to the division formerly commanded by Trimble. Colston, temporary

---

[17] Longstreet, who was not friendly to A. P. Hill, thought Ewell that officer's superior. Ewell, he said, was Jackson's equal in execution, but far inferior in independent command. "neither was he as confident and self-reliant" (*Washington Post*, June 11, 1893, p. 10). In that same article, Longstreet stated that he had recommended to Lee that Jackson, instead of Kirby Smith be sent to the Trans-Mississippi. Lee had admitted the choice would be excellent but said he wanted Jackson with him.

[18] *Cf. O. R.*, 25, part 2, p. 824.

[19] Which had been under Rodes at Chancellorsville; see *supra*, vol. II, pp. 558–59.

commander of that division at Chancellorsville, he now relieved. This arrangement necessitated the selection of two new division commanders, one to succeed A. P. Hill and the other for the new division. After some rather confused correspondence with the War Department and the President, who was anxious to promote the ablest men, Lee named Harry Heth for one of Hill's divisions and W. D. Pender of North Carolina for the other.[20] Numerous promotions to succeed brigadier generals killed or disabled at Chancellorsville, or found incompetent, had likewise to be made.

The result was an almost complete reorganization of the army, as follows:

The First Corps was reduced to three divisions—McLaws's, Pickett's, and Hood's, in none of which was there any change.

The Second Corps, now Ewell's, included Early's, Johnson's, and Rodes's divisions. The four brigades of Early were unchanged. Johnson's division was under a commander who had served a very short time with Jackson and had never been with Lee except for some minor co-operation in the West Virginia campaign of 1861. Three of the four major units of this division were under new brigadier commanders—George H. Steuart, James A. Walker, and John M. Jones—and the fourth, Nicholls's, continued under its senior colonel because Lee was unable to find a man to succeed Nicholls.[21] Here, then, was a different, a revolutionized command for the famous old division that included the Stonewall brigade. It was hardly surprising that all the field officers of that brigade tendered their resignations.[22] The third division of the Second Corps, under Rodes, contained one new brigade that had never fought with the Army of Northern Virginia.[23] One of the other brigades was led by a colonel.[24] Taken as a whole, the Second Corps, as reconstituted, was a difficult command for any man and especially for one like Ewell, who

[20] *O. R.*, 25, part 2, pp. 810–11, 827; *O. R.*, 51, part 2, p. 716.

[21] *O. R.*, 25, part 2, p. 810. General Nicholls had been badly wounded at Chancellorsville and had been incapacitated for field-duty because of the amputation of a foot.

[22] *Pendleton*, 273.

[23] That of Brigadier General Junius Daniel—Second, Thirty-second, Forty-third, Forty-fifth, and Fifty-third N. C., *O. R.*, 25, part 2, p. 813.

[24] E. A. O'Neal. This was Rodes's old brigade.

had been absent from the Army of Northern Virginia for nine months.

The Third Corps, that of A. P. Hill, comprised Anderson's, Heth's, and Pender's divisions. That of Anderson was in good hands, and its command had not materially changed. But Heth's division was led by a soldier who had joined the Army of Northern Virginia only in February. Two of the four brigades of this division were strangers to the army. The third division of the Third Corps, Pender's, had a new commander, and one of its brigades was under an officer who had just been promoted.

While this reorganization of the infantry was in progress, the battalion formation of the artillery was perfected, and the general reserve artillery was divided among the three corps.[25] The officers remained much the same, though there were numerous promotions. The battery personnel was not changed, but new contacts had to be formed with unfamiliar divisional chiefs. There was, inevitably, a temporary lack of complete co-ordination with the infantry.

Weakened by the hard winter, the cavalry, too, had to be enlarged. With the patriotic co-operation of Major General Samuel Jones, commanding in southwest Virginia, Lee procured from that quarter a new and large brigade of horse under Brigadier General A. G. Jenkins, but neither this officer nor his men were accustomed to the type of cavalry fighting in which the rest of Stuart's command was experienced. Another cavalry brigade was also brought from western Virginia under Brigadier General John B. Imboden. This officer had been on irregular, detached duty, and many of his men had recently been recruited, some of them from the infantry service.[26]

In short, the reorganization affected all three arms of the service. It involved the admixture of new units with old, it broke up many associations of long standing, and it placed the veteran regiments of a large part of the army under men who were unacquainted with the soldiers and with the methods of General Lee. The same magnificent infantry were ready to obey Lee's orders, but many of their superior officers were untried and were nervous under new responsibilities.

[25] O. R., 25, part 2, pp. 838, 850; O. R., 27, part 2, p. 346; *Alexander*, 370.
[26] O. R., 25, part 2, pp. 789–90, 795, 805, 819, 837; 3 C. M. H., 610.

Even in Longstreet's corps, which remained intact except for the transfer of Anderson's division to Hill's Third Corps, there was a difference, little observed, perhaps, but exceedingly ominous. Where other troops had undergone a change in the personnel of their commanders, the First Corps was to discover that it had suffered an unhappy change in the outlook of its leader. Longstreet's service in Southside Virginia had been inconspicuous, if not discreditable, but it had given him a taste of independent command, and had greatly increased his opinion of himself as a strategist. On his way back to the army, which he rejoined on May 9, he had stopped in Richmond and had been much flattered by an interview with the Secretary of War, who had asked his advice on the unpromising situation at Vicksburg. Longstreet had proposed that he take two divisions of his corps, reinforce the army under Bragg, and take the offensive against Rosecrans. The secretary had not approved the plan, but Longstreet had returned to the army, secretly swollen with the idea that he was the man to redeem the falling fortunes of the Confederacy.[27] Jackson's death increased this feeling of self-importance. The grave "Stonewall" had eclipsed Longstreet in public opinion and had held first place in the esteem of Lee, careful though Lee was never to show favoritism. Now that Jackson was no more, Longstreet seemed to feel that it was his prerogative to devise as well as to execute, to dictate the strategy as well as to direct the tactics, to be the commander's commander and to guide his errant faculties by his superior military judgment. Nothing quite suited him— least of all the appointment of two Virginians to the rank he held. D. H. Hill or McLaws, he grumbled to himself, would have been better than either Ewell or A. P. Hill, but neither was of Lee's own state and consequently both were passed over.[28]

Two untried corps commanders, three of the nine divisions under new leaders, seven freshly promoted brigadier generals of infantry, six infantry brigades under their senior colonels, a third of the cavalry directed by officers who had not previously served

[27] For his visit to Seddon, see *The Annals of the War Written by Leading Participants, North and South, Originally Published in the Philadelphia Weekly Times* (cited hereafter as *Annals of the War*), 415–16.
[28] *Cf. Longstreet*, 332.

with the Army of Northern Virginia, the artillery redistributed, the most experienced of the corps commanders inflated with self-importance, above all, Jackson's discipline, daring, and speed lost forever to the army—such was Lee's plight when the establishment of the new corps was formally announced on May 30, though the reorganization was not then complete.[29]

To explain this reorganization is largely to explain Gettysburg. Nothing happened on that field that could not be read in the roster of the army, the peculiarities and inexperience of the new leaders, the distribution of the units, and the inevitable confusion of a staff that had to be enlarged or extemporized to direct troops with which it was unacquainted. But for the larger experience of the men in the ranks and the broader knowledge of war acquired by Lee and some of the other leaders, the army was back where it was at the beginning of the Seven Days' Battles. If the next general engagement came quickly, it would certainly be the Gaines's Mill of the second period of the war in Virginia. Full co-ordination would be almost impossible.

Lee had made what he considered to be the best selections from the officers available and he realized some if not all of the risks he took in subjecting the reorganized army to the early test of a great battle on alien soil. Even had he been wholly conscious of the danger he faced, the option of delay for the training of his new subordinates was denied him. Was he to upset the enemy's plans for the summer campaign and force him to relax the tightening grip of Grant on Vicksburg? Then he must strike quickly. Perhaps his state of mind was most fully disclosed in a few sentences of a letter he wrote Hood while the reorganization was under way. "I agree with you," he said, ". . . in believing that our army would be invincible if it could be properly organized and officered. There never were such men in an army before. They will go anywhere and do anything if properly led. But there is the difficulty—proper commanders— where can they be obtained? But they are improving—constantly improving. Rome was not built in a day, nor can we expect miracles in our favor." [30] There it is: absolute confidence in the men who shivered and sweltered, endured hunger and tramped

---

[29] *O.R.*, 25, part 2, p. 840. [30] May 21, 1863; *Hood*, 53.

cheerfully over hard roads on bare feet, lay wounded and un-complaining or, like stoics, faced death on strange fields; absolute faith in the ranks, and consciousness of the limitations of the command, but, along with that, the patience and the hope of an intrepid soul.

CHAPTER III

THE ARMY STARTS NORTHWARD AGAIN

WHILE Lee was reorganizing the Army of Northern Virginia after the death of Jackson, he could not forget the enemy across the river or the Federal forces that were gathering in ominous strength on other fronts. During the two weeks following the battle of Chancellorsville, Hooker made a few moves of no consequences, but he seemed to be receiving reinforcements as if the Washington government were determined to utilize his army for the major eastern offensive of the year.[1] Around Vicksburg, the front of the Federals was slowly advancing, while General Joseph E. Johnston seemed powerless to divert Grant. In Tennessee, Rosecrans was defying Bragg. In North Carolina, a force appeared to be preparing for another drive against the railroads, and from Hampton Roads a small army was threatening the lower end of the Peninsula of Virginia.

In what manner could the dwindling Confederate armies best be employed against the hosts that were concentrating as if to cut the South into bits that could be devoured at leisure? Longstreet maintained that Bragg should be strengthened to club Rosecrans; Secretary Seddon favored the dispatch of two of Longstreet's divisions to the Mississippi; Lee explained that, in his opinion, the Confederacy had to choose between maintaining the line of the Mississippi and that of Virginia.[2] If he could procure sufficient troops and could draw General Hooker away from the Rappahannock, he proposed to assume the offensive and to enter Pennsylvania. He believed that the best defensive for Richmond was at a distance from it; he did not think it desirable to fight again on the Rappahannock, where he could not follow up his victory. Neither did he wish once more to carry his army into the ravaged counties near Washington. A defeated foe could easily retire within the defenses of that city, as Pope had done.

[1] O.R., 25, part 2, pp. 791–92.　　[2] O. R., 25, part 2, p. 790.

18

Even had Lee been willing to give battle in Virginia, he did not think he could subsist his troops there,[3] whereas, if he marched into Pennsylvania he would find provisions in abundance.[4] By crossing high up the Potomac he could move into the rich Cumberland Valley, draw the enemy after him, clear Virginia of Federals, break up their plan of operations for the summer, and perhaps force the enemy to recall the forces that were troubling the south Atlantic coasts and threatening the railroads.[5] Contact with the realities of war, moreover, might increase in the North the peace movement which seemed to be gathering strength.[6] "It would be folly," he said subsequently, "to have divided my army; the armies of the enemy were too far apart for me to attempt to fall upon them in detail. I considered the problem in every possible phase, and to my mind, it resolved itself into a choice of one of two things—either to retire to Richmond and stand a siege, which must ultimately have ended in surrender, or to invade Pennsylvania."[7] Of all the arguments that weighed with him, the most decisive single one was that he could no longer feed his army on the Rappahannock. He had to invade the North for provisions, regardless of all else.[8]

While he was developing this plan, he was summoned to Richmond for conference. He spent May 14–17 there and reviewed the military situation with the President, the Secretary of War, and the Cabinet.[9] Davis was much troubled at the time by calls for troops at Vicksburg and sought the advice of Lee, who urged that Johnston attack Grant promptly;[10] but when it came to a final choice between advancing into Pennsylvania or detaching troops from Lee to do battle on the Mississippi, the President and all members of the Cabinet except Postmaster-General Reagan favored a new invasion of the North.[11]

[3] *Cf.* Heth in 4 *S. H. S. P.*, 153: "It is very difficult for anyone not connected with the Army of Northern Virginia to realize how straitened we were for supplies of all kinds, especially food."

[4] *Marshall*, 182 *ff.*, and William Allan's notes of a conversation with Lee in *ibid.*, 250–51; *Long*, 269.

[5] *O. R.*, 25, part 2, pp. 791–92; *ibid.*, 27, part 2, p. 305; 2 *Davis*, 438.

[6] *O. R.*, 27, part 2, pp. 302, 305; *Cooke*, 270–71.

[7] 4 *S. H. S. P.*, 154.   [8] *Cf. infra*, pp. 49–50.

[9] 1 *R. W. C. D.*, 325; *Mrs. McGuire*, 214; *Reagan*, 121. Some of the considerations that prompted Lee to advocate an advance into Pennsylvania were developed subsequent to this conference.

[10] *O. R.*, 25, part 2, p. 843.   [11] *Reagan*, 121–22.

Back on May 18 at his old headquarters near Hamilton's Crossing, Lee began to develop the details of his new adventure. He met with opposition from one man only—Longstreet. The commander of the First Corps was still enamored of his own theory that the proper course was to reinforce Bragg and attack Rosecrans. It is impossible to say how far his ambition influenced his proposal or to what extent his plan stirred his ambition. Perhaps he dreamed of supplanting Bragg and of winning the decisive victory. In any case he held with tenacity to his opinion and argued for it stubbornly.[12] Lee heard him, as always, with patience, but did not see how any good could possibly result from dividing the Army of Northern Virginia, perhaps for months, in the face of the enemy. The Confederacy was witnessing around Vicksburg at the time an example of the impotence that followed a dispersal of force.

Finding that his own plan had no chance of adoption, Longstreet unwillingly yielded, but insisted that if a campaign was to be undertaken in Pennsylvania, it should be offensive in strategy but defensive in tactics. If Lee would move into Pennsylvania and not attack the enemy, but attempt to force Hooker to give battle, Longstreet conceded that the results might justify the venture. He even assured General Lee "that the First Corps would receive and defend the battle if he would guard its flanks, leaving his other corps to gather the fruits of victory." [13]

The event was to show that it would have been better if Lee had stood Longstreet before him and had bluntly reminded him that he and not the chief of the First Corps commanded the Army of Northern Virginia. Had he done so, he either would have had a different lieutenant general in the fateful days of July, or else his senior lieutenant would have been in a different state of mind. Apparently, however, it never occurred to Lee that Longstreet was trying to dictate. So little was such an idea in his mind that when Swinton affirmed, some years later, in his *Campaigns of the Army of the Potomac*,[14] that Longstreet had told him Lee had promised to maintain a tactical defensive in Pennsylvania.

---

[12] *Annals of the War*, 416–17.   [13] *Longstreet*, 334.

[14] *Swinton*, 340: "General Lee expressly promised his corps commanders that he would not assume a tactical offensive. . . ." Swinton added as a footnote, "This and subsequent revelations . . . I derive from General Longstreet . . . in a full and free conversation."

Lee refused to believe that Longstreet had ever made a statement to that effect. The idea, he told Colonel William Allan, was absurd. Lee "never made any such promise and never thought of doing any such thing." [15] At the time, moreover, he promptly rejected a proposal that Seddon conveniently put forward, without any knowledge of the discussion at headquarters, for placing Longstreet in command between the James and Cape Fear. "The services of General Longstreet," Lee said simply, "will be required with this army." [16] Longstreet in his vanity mistook Lee's tact and politeness for acquiescence in his plans and went about his preparations for the move in the proud belief that he had carried his point and that the campaign was to be conducted in accordance with his ideas.[17] It was characteristic of him to be energetic and enthusiastic when he approved the course of his commanding general, but to be apathetic and full of misgivings when his superior acted contrary to his views. This graceless quality was stronger than ever during the months immediately following Jackson's death, when he magnified his own office. He had nobody but himself to blame for misinterpreting politeness as

[15] Allan's memorandum in *Marshall*, 252. Allan quoted Lee as referring to "a reported conversation with Longstreet, in which the latter was reported to have said that General Lee was under a promise to the lieutenant general not to fight a general battle in Pennsylvania." There is, of course, a material difference between a promise "not to fight a general battle" and a promise to hold to a tactical defensive, but as Lee had read at least a part of Swinton, there can scarcely be room for doubt that the "conversation" of which he spoke is that in which Swinton quoted Longstreet as contending that Lee had promised him to adhere to defensive tactics.

[16] *O. R.*, 25, part 2, p. 811.

[17] *Cf.* Henderson: Longstreet made "no attempt to explain on what grounds he considered himself entitled to dictate conditions to his superior officer. He had no mandate from the government as Lee's adviser. He was merely the commander of an army corps —a subordinate, pure and simple; and yet he appears to have entered on the campaign with the idea that the commander-in-chief was bound to engage the enemy with the tactics that he, General Longstreet, had suggested" (*Journal of the Royal United Service Institution*, October, 1897). Longstreet, in his later writings, was careful to refrain from asserting that Lee had *promised* him not to pursue a tactical offensive in the North. He referred to "an understanding" in *Annals of the War*, 417. In 3 *B. and L.*, 246, he employed this extraordinary language: "I then accepted his proposition to make a campaign into Pennsylvania, provided that it should be offensive in strategy but defensive in tactics"; and in *From Manassas to Appomattox*, 331, he said: "All that I could ask was that the policy of the campaign should be one of defensive tactics. . . . To this he readily assented as an important and material adjunct to his general plan." At no time, however, did he ever deny that he had told Swinton that "General Lee expressly promised his corps commanders that he would not assume a tactical offensive. . . ." Inasmuch as Longstreet could not deny what Swinton attributed to him, yet would not assert over his own signature that Lee had made him any such promise, it is not necessary to seek for confirmation of Lee's statement that he made no commitment regarding his course of action in Pennsylvania.

compliance. Yet the episode is a warning to students of war that tact is sometimes dangerous in dealing with self-assertive subordinates.

Unaware that there was any menace to the cause in the mind of Longstreet, Lee's misgivings were not of him, but of the safety of Richmond, the strength of the army, and the possibility of manœuvring Hooker out of his strategic position on Stafford Heights. A Federal force reported to number 5000 had gone to West Point at the head of York River, thirty-seven miles from Richmond.[18] Troops of unreported roster were still in the vicinity of Suffolk. Lee was satisfied that an offensive across the Potomac would impel President Lincoln to abandon any plan for a general forward movement from the coast, but he considered it likely that a dash might be made on Richmond, and he could not afford to leave it defenseless, though he was most anxious to recall to the army the brigades that had from time to time been detached from his army and sent southward.[19] How could he protect Richmond and at the same time make his army large enough for a distant offensive?

Gathering sufficient strength for the offensive was a matter of provisions, of horses, and of additional men, not a question of morale, for the victory at Chancellorsville had raised the spirit of the army to the highest pitch.[20] As for food, Longstreet's activities in eastern North Carolina had not resulted in the accumulation of any surplus at the advanced base. Whatever had been collected in the North state during the spring had disappeared in the commissary warehouses. However, raids into transmontane Virginia had yielded a goodly stock of cattle. Lee planned to requisition some of this from General Samuel Jones just before he moved,[21] and he reasoned that if he could drive beef on the hoof with him until he reached Pennsylvania, he would find abundance of everything there.

Little could be done in procuring horses from the South.[22] The

---

18 *O. R.*, 25, part 2, p. 797.

19 *O. R.*, 25, part 2, p. 834. In addition to Pickett's and Hood's divisions, Lee lost Ransom's, Cooke's, and Evans's brigades (*O. R.*, 25, part 2, p. 833).

20 *Cf.* W. S. White in *Richmond Howitzers Battalion*, 185: "Lee's army has the greatest confidence in him, and if we are defeated it will be at terrible cost to the enemy" (June 10, 1863).

21 *O. R.*, 25, part 2, p. 846.   22 *O. R.*, 25, part 2, pp. 812-13.

animals with the army were in a slightly better condition now that grass was springing, but they were still thin. They looked much as they had during the Chancellorsville operation when a Federal officer had said that they and the wagons were like a "congregation of all the crippled Chicago emigrant trains that ever escaped off the desert."[23] There was nothing to do but to use these mournful beasts until they could be recruited by the sleek horses enjoying the lush grass of the fat Cumberland Valley.

The reinforcement of the cavalry with Jenkins's and Imboden's brigades was under way.[24] When the army moved into the Valley and the Federals were cleared out, Jones's brigade, which was still serving there, would be available, also. The mounted troops would then number seven brigades, enough to cover the advance, if properly disposed. Any material increase in the infantry, though it seemed imperative, was almost a forlorn hope. Hood was returning with his full division and Pickett was at Hanover Junction with three of his four brigades, but all Lee's powers of persuasion had not sufficed to prevail upon President Davis to release the fourth brigade of Pickett or the three brigades that had been sent southward during the previous winter.[25] Unless he could procure them at the last moment, he would not have for the campaign as many as 75,000 officers and men of all arms— about 60,000 infantry, 4700 artillery and 10,200 cavalry.[26] Except for the cavalry recruits, most of these troops were tried veterans of Chancellorsville and of the campaign of 1862, men who had never failed Lee. As he reviewed some of them toward the end of May[27] his confidence in them was greater than ever. "The fact is," to quote Harry Heth, "General Lee believed that the Army of Northern Virginia, as it then existed, could accomplish anything."[28] If the detached brigades were returned, Lee was willing

---

[23] *Marginalia*, 48.   [24] See *supra*, p. 14.

[25] *O. R.*, 25, part 2, pp. 831, 833, 842.

[26] *O. R.*, 25, part 2, p. 846. This return certainly included Jenkins's and Imboden's cavalry and it probably included Jones's brigade also, though the return read "Not reported" opposite the entry "Valley District." If Jones's 1500 horse were not included, this would raise Lee's total strength to nearly 76,000, but it would credit Stuart with 11,-700 cavalry, which are certainly more than he had. The fullest analysis of Lee's strength at this time was given by Early in 4 *S. H. S. P.*, 244, and by Taylor in 5 *ibid.*, 240, but as they wrote before the publication of the *Official Records* their figures are perhaps subject to revision.

[27] *Malone*, 33; E. A. Moore, 177–78; Captain R. E. Parks in 26 *S. H. S. P.*, 10.

[28] 4 *S. H. S. P.*, 160.

to trust the army for its part in the great gamble of a second invasion of the North, even though the odds against it were dangerously long. But how could he recover those absent brigades so long as Richmond seemed to be threatened by raiders?

The final difficulty in the way of an advance, that of manœuvring around the Federal right flank and wresting the initiative from Hooker, could only be measured by the attempt. There was, however, the risk that Hooker might anticipate Lee and either move his army from Aquia Creek to James River by water, or cross the Rappahannock and offer battle before Lee could start, or else throw his bridges and start an advance on Richmond as soon as Lee weakened his forces at Fredericksburg. The gossip in the camps was that Lee had said he believed he would "swap queens," Washington for Richmond,[29] but he never hoped to capture Washington and he never intended to expose Richmond if he could prevent it. He was not sure what his adversary was planning to do, and he could not find out. For it no longer was as easy a matter for Lee's spies to penetrate the Federal lines as it had been under the lax administration of Burnside. Whatever else Hooker had failed to do, and however much he had disappointed the expectations of the North, he had reorganized his outposts and had placed an almost impenetrable screen around his army. For the first time on Virginia soil, thanks to the improvement in the Union cavalry and in the intelligence service of the Army of the Potomac, the Federals knew more of what was happening on the south side of the Rappahannock than Lee knew of what was taking place north of the river.[30]

In the face of these uncertainties—the safety of Richmond, the return of detached units, and the possibility of a sudden move by Hooker—Lee had to prepare for the defensive while hoping to be able to take the offensive. On May 11, Stuart had been

---

[29] *Cooke,* 274.

[30] *Cf.* Lee to Stuart, May 23, 1863: "As regards the enemy, it is difficult for me to determine his intentions" (*O. R.,* 25, part 2, p. 820); Lee to Stuart, May 31, 1863: "I am unable yet to determine what are the plans or intentions of the enemy; reports are so contradictory" (*O. R.,* 25, part 2, p. 844). See also Lee to Davis, May 30, 1863 (*ibid.,* pp. 832–33). In contrast, see the report, May 27, 1863, of George H. Sharpe, chief of the bureau of information of the Army of the Potomac (*O. R.,* 25, part 2, p. 528). This document is correct in nearly every particular as to the location of the Confederate units and the plans of Lee. It seems to have been derived chiefly from deserters, whereas Lee thought most of the enemy's information was coming from Negroes (*cf. O. R.,* 25, part 2, p. 826).

ordered into Culpeper to observe the enemy;[31] on the 19th, as soon as Lee had returned from Richmond, the artillery had been put on the alert.[32] The next day Pickett had been ordered to prepare to march to the front when called.[33] By the 23d Lee was satisfied that Hooker was making ready for another move. Stuart was directed to concentrate and await developments.[34] Four days later there were indications of a decline in the strength of the Federal forces in front of Fredericksburg.[35] This was taken to be a sign that Hooker was about to advance again by some of the fords on the upper Rappahannock. McLaws was accordingly instructed to have his troops in condition to cross the river in a counter-demonstration, and Hood, who had come up in rear of the Confederate left, was told to move to Verdiersville, close to the fords of the Rapidan.[36] "I wish I could get at those people over there," Lee said that day, as he looked wistfully across the river.[37]

The apparent imminence of another battle on the south bank of the Rappahannock, where victory would be as barren as costly, made Lee more anxious than ever to launch his projected offensive in Pennsylvania. He was willing to take the other risks if he could be reasonably sure of the safety of Richmond and could recover his "lost brigades." The difference between a hazardous defensive and a practicable offensive resolved itself into the difference between the strength he then mustered and the strength he could command if those brigades were returned to him. Yet it was so easy for Hooker to engage Lee while the forces at Suffolk and at West Point marched on Richmond! By May 30 Lee was almost persuaded that the time had passed when he could take the offensive, and as he was desirous of building up a force for the protection of the Richmond front, he urged on the Secretary of War that troops be called to Richmond from the Carolina coast, that the fortifications be strengthened, and that local-defense units be organized.[38]

Three anxious days passed at the end of May, with the troops

31 *O. R.*, 25, part 2, p. 792.   32 *O. R.*, 25, part 2, p. 808.
33 *O. R.*, 51, part 2, p. 711.   34 *O. R.*, 25, part 2, p. 820.
35 *O. R.*, 25, part 2, p. 827.
36 *O. R.*, 25, part 2, p. 839; *ibid.*, 51, part 2, pp. 717-18.
37 R. H. McKim: *A Soldier's Recollections*, 134.
38 *O. R.*, 25, part 2, pp. 827, 832-33, 834, 839, 844.

disposed either to start a march up the Rappahannock or to meet Hooker if he crossed the river.[39] Lee could not wholly forgo hope of the offensive, even in the face of all the obstacles, but he had to admit to the President, "If I am able to move, I propose [to] do so cautiously, watching the result, and not to get beyond recall until I find it safe."[40] Then, unexpectedly, on the very day that this letter was written, June 2, there came a telegram from Richmond announcing that the troops previously at West Point, supported by a force from Gloucester and Yorktown, were marching northward.[41] The destination of these Federals was not clear, but it was manifest that if they were moving away from that city no immediate advance on Richmond was contemplated. Lee saw in this his opportunity. Now, if ever, he must seize the initiative and forestall the offensive he believed Hooker was preparing. With Richmond no longer in serious danger, he could hope that the President would authorize him to call Pickett's division and Pettigrew's brigade from Hanover and start his manœuvre around the Federal flank in the hope that he might enter Pennsylvania.

There was no certainty that the President would authorize the movement of the troops from Hanover Junction, but orders were forthwith issued by Lee for an advance by part of the army the very next day. Ewell was called to headquarters and given his instructions. Longstreet was present during the conference, on Lee's invitation, and promptly took the floor to argue his thesis of a strategic offensive and a tactical defensive. He insisted that if the army was to take the offensive at all, it should do so south of the Potomac, preferably in the vincinity of Culpeper Courthouse.[42] Lee, as usual, seems to have let Longstreet present his view fully, with few remarks on his own part, but with no intention whatever of sanctioning another battle that could only exact a heavy toll of the Army of Northern Virginia on a field whence the Federals could easily withdraw to the Washington defenses.[43]

On the morning of June 3 the enemy showed no sign of

[39] Cf. Hood's instructions, O. R., 25, part 2, p. 845.
[40] O. R., 25, part 2, p. 848; cf. Lee to Stuart, June 2, 1863, O. R., 25, part 2, p. 850.
[41] O. R., 25, part 2, p. 847.   [42] Longstreet, in 3 B. and L., 248–49.
[43] It is possible that this interview with Ewell occurred before June 2, but that seems to be the most probable date.

attacking,[44] and McLaws's division was set in motion up the Rappahannock for Culpeper. The march was conducted without any Federal demonstration. That night Heth's division of A. P. Hill's corps relieved the pickets of Rodes's division of Ewell's corps,[45] and on the morning of the 4th Rodes started toward Culpeper. Still there was no activity on the Stafford Heights. Emboldened by this, Lee withdrew Early and Johnson on the 5th and left only A. P. Hill on the Fredericksburg line. Scarcely had the last of Ewell's regiments wound their way over the hills than the Federals began to lay a pontoon bridge over the Rappahannock on the old site opposite Deep Run. It was done so ostentatiously as to raise suspicion from the first,[46] but it was followed by a furious cannonade and then by the crossing of a small force of infantry. Lee reasoned that Hooker was either attempting to feel out the Confederate strength, or else was attempting to divert attention from some move on his own part, but he deemed it prudent to halt Ewell's march in case Hooker should develop a general offensive, and he disposed Hill's forces to hold the line temporarily. On the 6th, the Federals not being strengthened, Lee became satisfied that Hill could cope with the troops in his front and he ordered Ewell to resume his advance. That afternoon, having delivered to Hill detailed instructions drawn up the preceding night, Lee broke up headquarters at Hamilton's Crossing—for the last time, as it proved—and took the road his men marched.[47] Hill's orders were to resist the enemy, to conceal the movement of the army, to fall back down the line of the Richmond, Fredericksburg and Potomac Railroad, if attacked in superior force, and to call up Pettigrew's brigade and Pickett's division from Hanover Courthouse if necessary. In case the Federals disappeared from his front, Hill was to cross the river and pursue.[48]

Had Lee made an orderly appraisal of the situation when he

---

[44] For once, Lee was entirely misled as to the intentions of the Federal commander. That officer was then out of favor in Washington and, though he had not been so informed, was not to be allowed to fight another battle. The policy of the Federal administration in dealing with the Army of the Potomac at the time was the passive one of waiting developments.

[45] O. R., 51, part 2, p. 720.

[46] O. R., 27, part 3, p. 859.

[47] O. R., 27, part 2, pp. 293, 347.

[48] O. R., 27, part 3, p. 859.

stopped by the roadside and bivouacked on that night of his new march toward the enemy's country,[49] his chief causes of concern would have been the reorganization of the army, and the brevity of the time that had elapsed since it had been effected. The process of selection and commission had been slow. It had been only four days before the march began that the Second Corps had been formally set up under Ewell and the Third under A. P. Hill.[50] The battalions of ordnance had not been allotted the corps until June 2,[51] and on the 4th the general artillery reserve had been broken up and the corps chiefs of artillery assigned.[52] The troops were the same magnificent fighting men, but the groupings, in large part, were new. Too many untried general officers were facing northward for the most difficult campaign the Army of Northern Virginia had ever undertaken. Granting that delay in launching the offensive was impossible, the risks involved in ordering the army into the enemy's country before the recently named commanders had accustomed themselves to handling large bodies of troops with their small staffs were immense and ominous.

[49] O. R., 27, part 3, p. 347.   [50] O. R., 25, part 2, p. 840.
[51] O. R., 25, part 2, p. 850.   [52] O. R., 51, part 2, p. 720; O. R., 25, part 2, p. 859.

CHAPTER IV

Manœuvring to Enter Pennsylvania

Arriving on the morning of June 7 at Culpeper Courthouse,[1] near which two of Longstreet's divisions and all three of Ewell's were encamped, Lee was more than ever convinced that his army must be reinforced if it was to execute successfully his plan of invasion. He telegraphed Davis a suggestion that a brigade from Richmond be moved to Hanover Junction to relieve Pickett, so that commander could bring Longstreet's third division forward. The brigade from Richmond could be replaced by one from the Suffolk front, whence nearly all the Federals were said to have departed. Lee urged, also, in a letter to the President, that Beauregard's troops from Charleston, S. C., either be sent to reinforce Johnston in Mississippi or to unite with the Army of Northern Virginia.[2] At the same time he ordered Imboden's cavalry, which had not yet joined Stuart, to organize a raid into northwest Virginia, and he instructed Brigadier General A. G. Jenkins to prepare his brigade of horse from southwest Virginia for co-operation in the Shenandoah Valley, whither he was hoping soon to be able to send a part of the army on the second stage of the proposed advance into Pennsylvania.[3]

The remainder of the cavalry, scattered around Culpeper, had been made ready by the drama-loving Stuart for a general review, which he asked Lee to witness the next day, June 8. The spirit of the son of a Revolutionary cavalryman prompted Lee to agree. General Hood, also, was invited to witness the scene and "to bring any of his people." He responded by marching on the field with his entire division. This was a little more than had been bargained for, but it was accepted in a spirit of hospitality. The only condition the hosts imposed on the Texans was that they were not to yell "Here's your mule," which was deemed a special insult to cavalrymen who prided themselves on their steeds and on their ability to keep their saddles. If the infantry insisted on challenging opprobriously the horsemanship of the

[1] O. R., 27, part 2, p. 347.
[2] O. R., 27, part 2, pp. 293–94.   [3] O. R., 27, part 3, p. 865.

troops, Wade Hampton laughingly threatened to charge them.[4]
Terms of peace and amity having been concluded between the
two arms, the Texans spread themselves at ease in front of the
cavalry, who had been drawn up in two lines on a vast field, east
of the town.

At the appointed hour Lee arrived with his staff and most of
his general officers. Stuart, much bedizened, met the commanding
general. Some of the young ladies of Culpeper had decorated
"Jeb's" saddle with flowers and had put a wreath around the neck
of his mount. Lee was much amused. "Take care, General
Stuart!" he said banteringly. "That is the way General Pope's
horse was adorned when he went to the battle of Manassas."[5] Not
long before, at a review of the Second Corps, Lee had ridden so
fast that only A. P. Hill and one member of his staff had remained at his side when he drew rein.[6] Lee had enjoyed the
experience, and now he put Traveller at the gallop, past the long
front of the first line of gaunt cavalrymen. They were clad in
tattered butternut or gray, but they made a gallant showing with
their burnished sabres. Three miles Lee rode, by flags that bore
the names of many battles. Then he turned and galloped three
miles back along the second line without a pause.[7] Many were
the aching sides and panting steeds when at last he halted on a
little eminence above which a large Confederate flag was flying
on a high pole.

Now it was the cavalrymen's turn. Wheeling into column at
the sound of the bugle, they galloped past at the charge, Stuart
riding at their head with his blade at *tierce point*. It was just
the sort of scene devised in feudal times to make men forget the
butchery of war in admiration of its pageantry, and it must have
made Lee's heart beat faster, but it aroused only the contempt
of some of Hood's footmen, who had no high opinion of the
valor of cavalry. "Wouldn't we clean 'em out," one of the Texans
remarked, half wistfully, "if old Hood would let us loose on
'em?"[8]

As his climax, Stuart placed on a hillock near Lee his famous
horse artillery—the guns the dead Pelham loved so well; and

---

[4] Cooke: *Wearing of the Gray*, 317. [5] D. H. Maury, 239.
[6] E. A. Moore, 177–78. [7] Pendleton, 277–78.
[8] Cooke: *Wearing of the Gray*, 317.

then, while the pieces blazed away with the smoke and roar of blank cartridges, he led a sham charge against the batteries.[9] It was great fun to "Jeb" and to many of his men, but certainly not to the horses or to some of General Lee's guests, who, as the worthy Pendleton complained, "had to sit on our horses in the dust half the day. . . ."[10] Lee had been known to profess that he was only qualified to be a colonel of cavalry, or perhaps a brigadier if he had good subordinates,[11] and he did not weary. "It was a splendid sight," he wrote. "The men and horses looked well. . . . Stuart was in all his glory."[12] But he was not too much occupied with the spectacle to notice that the trees of the Richmond saddles were very hard on the backs of the horses, and that the Richmond-made carbines were very inferior. He sought forthwith to correct them.[13]

Early the next morning, June 9, Lee received a hurried report from Stuart announcing that the enemy's cavalry, with some infantry, was pouring across Beverley and Kelly's Fords, on both flanks of the Confederate outposts.[14] Lee suspected that the move was simply a reconnaissance, and he wrote Stuart where he could get infantry in case he needed it, but urged him to conceal the presence of Confederate foot if it was possible for him to do so.[15] Soon it became apparent that the Federal horse coming from the direction of Kelly's Ford had outwitted Stuart's troopers on that road and were moving to get on the flank and in the rear of the Southern cavalry defending the approaches southward from Beverley Ford. Well it was, then, that Stuart had concentrated his men for the review the previous day, for he required every one of them. The action centred around Fleetwood Hill, a long ridge running with the meridian just north of Brandy Station on the Orange and Alexandria Railroad, seven miles northeast of Culpeper Courthouse. Hour after hour, in charge and countercharge, the opposing cavalry contended for this high ground. Lee left the management of the field to Stuart and, of course, had no fear

---

[9] *Cooke,* 278; *R. L. T. Beale,* 67.   [10] *Pendleton,* 278.

[11] *Jones,* 148. All these accounts confuse the reviews of June 5 and 8.

[12] Lee to Mrs. Lee, June 9, 1863, misdated June 8 in *R. E. Lee, Jr.,* 96.

[13] *O. R.,* 27, part 3, p. 873.

[14] *O. R.,* 51, part 2, p. 722. Kelly's Ford, it will be remembered, was four and one-half miles below, and Beverley Ford something less than two miles above Rappahannock bridge.

[15] *O. R.,* 27, part 3, p. 876.

of a serious disaster, because he had sufficient infantry at hand to hurl the Federals back across the Rappahannock if the Confederate mounted troops were worsted; but in the afternoon, as this battle of Brandy Station developed into the greatest cavalry engagement of the entire war,[16] he ordered an infantry brigade to report to General Hampton,[17] and he rode forward in person to survey the situation.

As he approached the field Lee was shocked to meet his own son, Rooney, being borne to the rear with a severe wound in the leg, received at 4:30 P.M.[18] Fortunately, the wound was not considered mortal, and Rooney seemed much more concerned over those who had fallen in the fight than over his own condition.[19] While Lee was doing what he could to make his son comfortable, the battle ended in a retreat of the Federals by the routes they had followed in their advance. It was by every count, as Lee's adjutant wrote his sweetheart, "a grand cavalry fight," and the result probably bore out that officer's estimate: "Altogether, our cavalry is justified in claiming an advantage, though neither side can be said to have gained a great deal. It was nearly an even fight." [20] The Confederate losses were around 485;[21] those of the Federals approximately 930.[22]

Lee did not regard this action as a serious threat to the continuance of his operations,[23] but he had to contend with a more serious obstacle in the attitude of the administration. In dispatches from the War Department a new concern for the safety of Richmond was observable, together with an extreme reluctance to forward the troops he believed necessary for the adequate reinforcement of the army. This state of mind on the part of the administration had led him on the 8th to offer to return closer to Richmond if the government so desired,[24] and it could not be

---

[16] Often called, also, the battle of Fleetwood Hill.   [17] *O. R.*, 27, part 2, p. 564.

[18] *R. E. Lee, Jr.*, 96–97; *O. R.*, 27, part 2, p. 771.

[19] *R. E. Lee, Jr.*, 96–97; cf. *Jones*, 398.

[20] Walter H. Taylor, June 11, 1863; *Taylor MSS.*   [21] *O. R.*, 27, part 2, p. 719.

[22] *O. R.*, 27, part 1, pp. 904, 905. Stuart's report is in *O. R.*, 27, part 2, p. 679 *ff.* Lee briefly mentioned the action in *ibid.*, p. 305. H. B. McClellan gave a full account in *op. cit.*, 257 *ff.* He also furnished a large map, though that in Stuart's report, *loc. cit.*, p. 686, is adequate. Von Borcke wrote a small book on the engagement, in collaboration with Justus Scheibert: *Die Grosse Reiterschlacht bei Brandy Station.*

[23] Longstreet contended in *Annals of the War*, 418, that if Lee intended to assume the offensive at any time during this campaign, he should have done so on June 9.

[24] *O. R.*, 27, part 3, p. 868. Cf. *ibid.*, 874–76, 880, 882.

ignored for the future. On the other hand, he could not escape the general logic of an offensive-defensive nor overlook the strategic advantage he had already gained through the failure of the Federals to attack A. P. Hill at Fredericksburg.[25] As he read the Northern newspapers with care, he was confirmed in his belief that the projected campaign in Pennsylvania would strengthen the arguments of the Northern peace party, which was already contending that the South could not be conquered by force but might be won back to the Union by a generous peace. His resolution held: he would send one corps forward and await developments. If that corps did nothing more, it would at least clear Milroy from the Valley and probably would force the Federals to abandon altogether the line of the Rappahannock.[26]

The plan of advance had been worked out before the vanguard had left Fredericksburg. It called for the co-operation of Jenkins's cavalry in preparing the way for a march to Winchester by Ewell, who had been selected for that task because he had a full corps of three divisions and also because he knew the country thoroughly. If Ewell was unmolested, he was to mask Winchester and was to continue over the Potomac, through Maryland and into Pennsylvania.[27] Longstreet was then to advance northward on the eastern side of the Blue Ridge, so as to cover the advance of A. P. Hill. When Hill was also in the Valley, Longstreet was to follow him, and the cavalry were to hold the mountain gaps until the advance into Pennsylvania had called all the Federals north of the Potomac.[28] It was, of course, a bold plan, but in view of the nature of the terrain and the speed with which the movement could be made, it was no more dangerous than other manœuvres Lee had successfully executed.[29]

Had there been any strong demonstration on the morning of the 10th by the Federals across Beverley Ford, Lee would perhaps

---

[25] O. R., 27, part 2, p. 294. [26] O. R., 27, part 2, p. 295.
[27] O. R., 27, part 2, p. 295. [28] Longstreet, 335.
[29] For a most excellent statement of the reasons why Lee's extension of line was comparatively safe, see Maurice, 198–99. It must be remembered, in addition, that the Rappahannock afforded Lee fairly good cover, so long as the fords were held, until an advance toward the Valley had reached Warrenton Sulphur Spring Ford. That point was only twenty-five miles, two days' easy marching for Lee's fast-moving infantry, from Chester Gap into the Shenandoah Valley. The distance from Culpeper Courthouse to Chester Gap, via Sperryville and "Little" Washington, was forty miles, or three days' marching. Once in the Valley, of course, Lee could hold the gaps and advance in complete safety.

have deferred the start of Ewell; but as the enemy remained quietly in his camps, Lee let the orders stand, and the reconstituted Second Corps started on its way.[30] It was noticed that Ewell was in fine health and spirits and, despite his wooden leg, rode his horse "as well as anyone need to." [31]

As Ewell's men turned westward toward the Blue Ridge, Lee sat down to write the President on the subject that had been so much in his mind during the days since Chancellorsville—the promotion of the peace movement in the North. A most important letter it was for two reasons. It showed Lee alive to the danger that the Southern cause would be lost because of the superiority of Federal resources. Similarly, it disclosed Lee's simple reasoning on politics, with which he had little acquaintance. He pointed out that the intransigeant attitude of the Southern newspapers was discouraging those Northerners who were arguing that the South would return to the Union if the Washington government made peace. Then he said:

"Conceding to our enemies the superiority claimed by them in numbers, resources, and all the means and appliances for carrying on the war, we have no right to look for exemptions from the military consequences of a vigorous use of these advantages, excepting by such deliverance as the mercy of Heaven may accord to the courage of our soldiers, the justice of our cause, and the constancy and prayers of our people. While making the most we can of the means of resistance we possess, and gratefully accepting the measure of success with which God has blessed our efforts as an evidence of His approval and favor, it is nevertheless the part of wisdom to carefully measure and husband our strength, and not to expect from it more than in the ordinary course of affairs it is capable of accomplishing. We should not, therefore, conceal from ourselves that our resources in men are constantly diminishing, and the disproportion in this respect between us and our enemies, if they continue united in their efforts to subjugate us, is steadily augmenting."

He went on to explain that the strength of the Army of North-

[30] O. R., 27, part 3, p. 886; R. H. McKim: A Soldier's Recollections, 143.
[31] Pendleton, 277.

ern Virginia was declining, and he argued that an effort should be made to divide the North by encouraging the peace party. Continuing, he said:

"Nor do I think we should, in this connection, make nice distinctions between those who declare for peace unconditionally and those who advocate it as a means of restoring the Union, however much we may prefer the former.

"We should bear in mind that the friends of peace at the North must make concessions to the earnest desire that exists in the minds of their countrymen for a restoration of the Union, and that to hold out such a result as an inducement is essential to the success of their party.

"Should the belief that peace will bring back the Union become general, the war would no longer be supported, and that, after all, is what we are interested in bringing about. When peace is proposed to us, it will be time enough to discuss its terms, and it is not the part of prudence to spurn the proposition in advance, merely because those who wish to make it believe, or affect to believe, that it will result in bringing us back to the Union. We entertain no such apprehensions, nor doubt that the desire of our people for a distinct and independent national existence will prove as steadfast under the influence of peaceful measures as it has shown itself in the midst of war.

"If the views I have indicated meet the approval of Your Excellency, you will best know how to give effect to them. Should you deem them inexpedient or impracticable, I think you will nevertheless agree with me that we should at least carefully abstain from measures or expressions that tend to discourage any party whose purpose is peace.

"With this statement of my own opinion on the subject . . . I leave to your better judgment to determine the proper course to be pursued." [32]

This letter was as ingenuous as it was sincere. So great was Lee's faith in the Southern people that he believed they would be willing to resume the war for independence in case peace negotiations produced no better terms than a return to the Union.

[32] *O. R.*, 27, part 3, p. 882.

With less knowledge of the state of mind of the North, he thought that, in like conditions, a powerful element would be willing to concede the independence of the South rather than have the war resumed. Unless this happened, he could see no other outcome of the struggle than the ultimate defeat of the Confederacy by the more powerful Union. This was twenty-two months before Appomattox.

Following the dispatch of this letter there came a period of confusion as to the intentions of the Federals. The War Department reported a raid up the Mattapony River, near Richmond, and an expedition from Suffolk on the south side of the James.[33] Lee believed the former of these movements was a foray to destroy crops,[34] but the concern of the administration was so deep that Lee was forced to approve the detention of Corse's brigade at Hanover Junction when Pickett's division at last moved to rejoin Longstreet.[35] Before the exact state of affairs below Richmond was determined, A. P. Hill reported on the morning of June 14 that the enemy had withdrawn from the south bank of the Rappahannock and seemed to be evacuating Stafford Heights, but Lee hesitated to call the whole of Hill's new Third Corps to Culpeper until he was sure that none of it would be required to reinforce Richmond or Hanover Junction. Nor was he certain as to the disposition of the main body of the Army of the Potomac.[36] He could only surmise that Hooker knew of his movements and was covering the approaches to Washington.[37]

The loss of time sustained by reason of this uncertainty might be serious enough, Lee feared, to defeat the full execution of his plans.[38] By the morning of June 15, however, the situation began to clear. Acting under authorization given on the 9th, Hill had started Anderson's division for Culpeper in the confident belief that the Federals were really leaving the line of the Rappahannock.[39] Ewell reported that he had cleared Berryville, and was preparing to attack Winchester, which he had found more strongly fortified than he had expected.[40]

---

[33] For details of these affairs, see *O. R.*, 27, part 2, pp. 777–84, 788–90.
[34] R. E. Lee to G. W. C. Lee, June 13, 1863, *MS.*, Duke University.
[35] *O. R.*, 27, part 3, p. 885; *cf. ibid.*, 886, 925–26.
[36] *O. R.*, 27, part 2, p. 295.
[37] *O. R.*, 27, part 2, pp. 306, 315.   [38] *O. R.*, 27, part 2, p. 295.
[39] *Cf. O. R.*, 27, part 3, pp. 869, 890.   [40] *O. R.*, 27, part 2, p. 295.

Ewell had been ordered not to delay his march for a siege of Winchester. Consequently, Lee assumed that Ewell on the 15th was already en route to Hagerstown. This would necessarily mean that the Army of Northern Virginia was spread out from some point north of Winchester to the lower Rappahannock. For a time there would be no force between Winchester and Culpeper except a few cavalry outposts. It was to meet just this situation that Lee had planned to advance Longstreet east of the Blue Ridge. On the 15th in a personal conference with that officer,[41] followed by written orders later in the day, Lee outlined very simply the details of this operation: Longstreet was to start northward, with Hood's division, and was to be followed by McLaws and then by Pickett, three brigades of whose division had now reached Culpeper. Longstreet was to march to Markham, just east of Manassas Gap in the Blue Ridge, and was to demonstrate, if he saw fit, against any Federal force he might encounter. Three brigades of cavalry were to operate on his front. His trains, if Longstreet so desired, could move by Chester Gap into the Valley, where they would be safe from Federal raiders.[42] Two brigades of cavalry were to be left behind to guard the fords of the Rappahannock and to cover the march of the Third Corps as it passed westward up the right bank of that stream.[43] By this move Lee hoped to confuse the enemy as to his plan of action and also to facilitate the advance of Hill. The Federals would hardly attempt to advance far southward against Hill if they found a large force potentially in their rear. Should an attempt be made to destroy Longstreet, he could easily retire to Ashby's or to Snicker's Gap, and hold it against the enemy. In case of a Federal advance northward to head off Ewell in Pennsylvania, Longstreet could readily move into the Valley, occupy the gaps, and hasten by unhindered marches to Ewell's support. If all went well, the original plan of having Hill pass in rear of Longstreet could be executed without danger, and Longstreet's corps would then act as rearguard. There were thus to be four successive movements —Ewell's advance toward Hagerstown, Longstreet's march to the east of the mountain passes, Hill's tramp up the Rappahannock

41 *O. R.*, 27, part 3, p. 890. 42 *O. R.*, 27, part 3, p. 890.
43 *O. R.*, 27, part 2, p. 315.

and thence along Ewell's route, and Longstreet's final withdrawal through the mountains and to the Potomac. These stages of the elaborate manœuvre are marked, in order, by the numerals on the sketch shown opposite.

On the evening of the day that Longstreet left Culpeper, Lee received good news: Ewell had driven Milroy from Winchester the previous night and had captured some 4000 prisoners, the greater part of Milroy's force.[44] The whole of Ewell's corps was now free to advance to the Potomac. Two of Hill's divisions were on the road to Culpeper, and the third was ready to leave Fredericksburg.[45]

It was now time for Lee to move in person. By the 17th, having sent Rooney to his wife's home with many affectionate messages,[46] Lee broke up headquarters and rode to Markham.[47] On his arrival, he found that Stuart had been engaged that day in hot actions with the enemy's cavalry at Aldie and Middleburg,[48] but had not established contact with the Federal infantry. From Hooker's failure to face him, Lee continued to assume that his adversary was moving toward the Potomac. Reports from some of the scouts on the 18th and 19th confirmed this, though it was not clear whether Hooker would make for Harpers Ferry, enter the Valley, or cross the river somewhere in the vicinity of Leesburg.[49] Stuart's scouts insisted that the enemy infantry were encamped east of the mountains, inactive. Major John S. Mosby had captured a dispatch in which Hooker's chief of staff had notified the commander of the cavalry corps that "the advance of the infantry is suspended until further information of the enemy's movements," but Hooker had added in a later paragraph: "If Lee's army is in rear of his cavalry, we shall move up by forced marches with the infantry." The same dispatch spoke, also, of a cavalry raid toward Warrenton. It mentioned, further, that pontoons were being assembled at the mouth of the Monocacy, which enters the Potomac directly east of the Catoctin range. All this important information was dated from Fairfax Station, June

---

[44] O. R., 27, part 3, p. 890. For Ewell's report of the battle of Winchester, see O. R., 27, part 2, p. 442 ff. Lee briefly summarized the action in O. R., 27, part 2, pp. 313–14.
[45] O. R., 27, part 3, p. 890.
[46] R. E. Lee, Jr., 97; Jones, 398; Jones, L. and L., 245.
[47] O. R., 27, part 3, p. 900.
[48] O. R., 27, part 2, pp. 295, 687 ff.   [49] O. R., 27, part 2, pp. 295, 296.

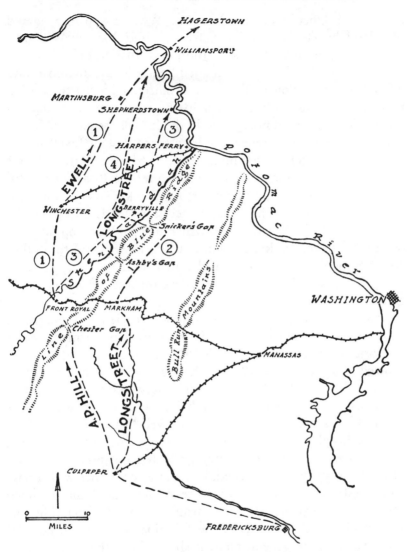

Successive preliminary stages of the advance into Maryland and Pennsylvania by the Army of Northern Virginia, June, 1863.

17, 10:30 P.M., and when received was nearly forty-eight hours old.[50]

In addition to this uncertainty, Lee had to contend with an

[50] Mosby: *Stuart's Cavalry in the Gettysburg Campaign* (cited hereafter as Mosby, *Stuart's Cavalry*), 65–66; *O. R.*, 27, part 2, pp. 176–77.

unexpected difficulty on the Potomac. When Ewell had entered Maryland, he left Early at Shepherdstown and Rodes at Williamsport,[51] and was advancing with Johnson's division only. Lee reasoned that if the Federals remained south of the Potomac and offered no opposition to Ewell, that officer, with his three divisions, could accomplish as much in the collection of supplies as the whole army could hope to do in the face of the enemy. It was desirable, therefore, to relieve Rodes at once, so that Ewell would have his whole corps with him. Lee accordingly started Hood's division for the Potomac on the 18th to relieve Rodes. Unfortunately, a threatened movement against Snicker's Gap compelled him to recall Hood. This made it necessary for Lee to await the arrival of Hill's leading division, which he could send on, in place of Hood,[52] to relieve Rodes. Time would be required to do this. All operations were being slowed down by the scarcity of food, though Lee was keeping every wheel turning in the effort to gather provisions.[53]

Anxious as Lee was that Ewell should be left unhindered to gather supplies from Pennsylvania, he must have reinforcements in position to move to Ewell's support the moment Hooker showed signs of crossing the Potomac. It was desirable, of course, to await the arrival of Hill's rear division, which was just west of Culpeper, but if Hooker moved before Hill was massed, Lee's intention was to hurry Longstreet to Ewell.[54] Lee had, therefore, to shape his plans for quick execution in an emergency. In doing this the handling of the infantry presented no special problems, but as the cavalry was detached, Lee had a conference with Longstreet and Stuart to arrange for the movement of the mounted forces. There was not then, nor was there at any later time, the least doubt in his mind as to the function of the main body of the cavalry in the general plan: it should keep the enemy as far to the east as possible, protect the lines of communication, and supply information as to the movements of the enemy.[55] To do these things the cavalry should of course operate on the right flank of the army as it advanced. For the time Lee believed

[51] *O. R.,* 27, part 2, p. 550. Lee thought the division at Williamsport was Early's (*O. R.,* 27, part 3, p. 905).
[52] *O. R.,* 27, part 3, p. 905.
[53] *O. R.,* 27, part 2, p. 295; *ibid.,* part 3, pp. 905–6.
[54] *O. R.,* 27, part 3, p. 905.   [55] *Longstreet,* 340.

that two brigades should be left to hold the passes of the Blue Ridge till the infantry were safely across the Potomac. The remaining three brigades should accompany the army.[56] Jenkins's and Imboden's cavalry, which had not been part of Stuart's former command, could be employed to cover Ewell's advance.

But Stuart had a more ambitious plan. The Richmond newspapers had expressed disappointment over his showing at Fleetwood and had called on him to perform some great feat that would restore his reputation.[57] Probably inspired by this, Stuart proposed that when he left two brigades in the mountains he should take the three others, move to Hooker's rear, and annoy him if he attempted to cross the river. Should he find that Hooker was intent on going into Maryland, he could break off and rejoin the army. Longstreet approved this proposal, and Lee assented, in principle, but he told Stuart that when he discovered that Hooker was actually passing the river, he "must immediately cross himself and take his place on our right flank as we moved north."[58] There the matter ended for the time.

On the 19th Lee passed through Ashby's Gap to Millwood, three miles northeast of White Post, and the next day established headquarters at a point a short distance beyond Berryville on the Charlestown road, where he determined to wait until the whole of Hill's corps came up.[59] Longstreet was put on the alert to start for the Potomac and, through a misunderstanding of his orders, withdrew on the 20th from the mountain gaps and established himself west of the Shenandoah.[60] By ill fortune the enemy selected the 21st for a general cavalry advance on Stuart and drove him back into Ashby's Gap by nightfall.[61] As the Federals had infantry support, there was danger that they might seize the

[56] *Marshall*, 201.   [57] *O. R.*, 27, part 1, p. 41.

[58] *Marshall*, 201. There is some doubt as to when this interview occurred. Marshall said that Lee told him it took place when he left Stuart near Paris, and Marshall made that June 21 (*loc. cit.*, 201). Mosby stated that "it is well understood that Stuart rode that night to see General Lee at his headquarters" (*op. cit.*, 72). But it is apparent from Lee to Davis (*O. R.*, 27, part 2, p. 296), that Lee was at Millwood on the 19th, and from his dispatch of the 20th to the President, *loc. cit.*, he was certainly at Berryville on the 20th. Pendleton (*op. cit.*, 279) noted that Lee heard him preach on the 21st at the same place. There may have been two interviews, one on the 19th and one on the 21st, but if Lee had seen Stuart on the night of the 21st, as Mosby affirmed, it is a little odd that Lee should have given Stuart explicit instructions in writing a few hours thereafter. See *infra*, p. 43.

[59] *Marshall*, 198–99, but see note *supra* concerning Marshall's error as to the date of these movements.

[60] *O. R.*, 27, part 2, p. 357.   [61] *O. R.*, 27, part 2, pp. 357, 691.

pass and might pour into the Valley on Longstreet's rear when he began his march toward the Potomac. McLaws's division had to be sent back to prevent this.[62] At daylight on the 22d, however, it was found that the Union infantry had withdrawn and that the cavalry was retiring eastward. Stuart followed vigorously.[63]

The presence of Union infantry so far north and its failure to attempt to force the gap was the strongest sort of evidence that the enemy was making for the Potomac east of the Blue Ridge. Additional information began to filter in during the day indicating that the Federals were preparing to cross the river, though Lee was still not satisfied as to the exact location of the main force.[64]

Provided the army could be subsisted, it was still, of course, the policy of wisdom to detain Hooker south of the Potomac, while Ewell, undisturbed, continued to collect supplies in Pennsylvania. So long as Hooker remained where he was and did not give battle, Lee could have many of the benefits of invasion with none of the risks and losses. But the enemy was too close to the Potomac for comfort. If Hooker could steal even one march on Lee he might get across the river and perhaps interpose between Ewell and the remainder of the army. Lee had already had one unhappy experience with a division of force on the north side of the Potomac, during the Sharpsburg campaign, and he had no desire to repeat it. Besides, the whole of Hill's corps was now closer at hand, and there was no reason for waiting.[65] It was safest, on every count, to move to the Potomac without further delay. If this were done, Ewell could be permitted to continue his march toward the Susquehanna, because the remainder of the army would soon be within supporting distance. Anderson's division was ordered to the river; Ewell was instructed to move on if ready. He was to proceed in two columns. One was to advance by Greencastle and Chambersburg toward Harrisburg. The other was to march by Emmitsburg and Gettysburg toward York,[66] east of the mountains that formed a barrier to the Cumberland Valley. This second route was chosen so as to keep the enemy at a distance from Lee's lines of communications.[67]

---

[62] O. R., 27, part 2, p. 357. Cf. ibid., part 3, p. 914.
[63] O. R., 27, part 2, p. 691.
[64] O. R., 27, part 2, p. 297, part 3, p. 913.　　　　[65] O. R., 27, part 3, p. 914.
[66] O. R., 27, part 2, p. 443; part 3, p. 914.　　　　[67] O. R., 27, part 2, p. 307.

Before giving the order for the movement of Longstreet, Lee had to decide finally the question of the disposition of the five brigades of cavalry with Stuart. Jenkins was already in advance of Ewell in Pennsylvania; Imboden was in Hampshire County, where he had been operating against the line of the Baltimore and Ohio Railroad.[68] The remaining five brigades were in or near the Blue Ridge. As Lee reflected on Stuart's proposal to take three of these brigades and operate in rear of the Federals during their advance northward, he became apprehensive. If Stuart did this, he might be delayed in crossing the river east of the mountains and might not be able to perform his principal mission, that of covering the right of the army in Pennsylvania.[69] In order that Stuart might understand fully that this duty in Pennsylvania was the all-important thing, Lee instructed Major Charles Marshall, in answering a communication from Stuart, to cover the point.[70] Soon Marshall submitted this:

"Headquarters, June 22, 1863.
"Maj. Gen. J. E. B. Stuart,
    "Commanding Cavalry.
    "I have just received your note of 7:45 this morning to General Longstreet. I judge the efforts of the enemy yesterday were to arrest our progress and ascertain our whereabouts. Perhaps he is satisfied. Do you know where he is and what he is doing? I fear he will steal a march on us, and get across the Potomac before we are aware. If you find that he is moving northward, and that two brigades can guard the Blue Ridge and take care of your rear, you can move with the other three into Maryland, and take position on General Ewell's right, place yourself in communication with him, guard his flank, keep him informed on the enemy's movements, and collect all the supplies you can for the use of the army. One column of General Ewell's army will probably move toward the Susquehanna by the Emmitsburg route; another by Chambersburg. Accounts from him last night state that there was no enemy west of Frederick. A cavalry force (about 100) guarded the Monocacy Bridge, which was barricaded. You will, of course, take charge of Jenkins' brigade, and

[68] *O. R.*, 27, part 3, pp. 905–6.   [69] *Longstreet*, 340.   [70] *Marshall*, 201–2.

43

give him necessary instructions. All supplies taken in Maryland must be by authorized staff officers for their respective departments—by no one else. They will be paid for, or receipts for the same given to the owners. I will send you a general order on this subject, which I wish you to see is strictly complied with." [71]

Lee read this letter and approved it,[72] but he had to take into account two contingencies: Was Longstreet in position to entrust his rear to two brigades only; and, secondly, where could Stuart most readily cross the Potomac without disclosing the movements of the army? Might it not be well for Stuart to go east of the Bull Run Mountains, perhaps through Hopewell Gap, and then pass by the rear of the enemy, thus creating a doubt as to the objective of the army? Might not that be better than crossing west of the Blue Ridge or heading for the Potomac between the Blue Ridge and the Bull Run Mountains? Probably because he knew Stuart's propensity for daring, spectacular raids, Lee decided to refer the question of Stuart's best route to Longstreet, along with the question on which Longstreet would properly have to pass—that of whether two brigades were sufficient to hold the passes. He sent the letter to Stuart under cover of a note to Longstreet, with instructions to forward the message to Stuart if he saw fit to do so.[73]

The next day, June 23, the information as to the enemy's movements was somewhat conflicting. Stuart reported that on the night of the 22d his cavalry outposts had advanced as far as Aldie. He seemed to be troubled by the statement, in a captured dispatch, that a column of cavalry was moving southward to Warrenton, whereas the Army of the Potomac was supposed to be making northward. Later in the day he sent word that Major

---

[71] O. R., 27, part 3, p. 913.   [72] Marshall, 202.

[73] Lee's note to Longstreet, unfortunately, has been lost, but its substance can easily be reconstructed from this passage in Longstreet's note to Stuart: "General Lee has inclosed to me this letter for you, to be forwarded to you provided you can be spared from my front, and provided I think that you can move across the Potomac without disclosing our plans. He speaks of your leaving, via Hopewell Gap, and passing by the rear of the enemy. If you can get through by that route, I think that you will be less likely to indicate what your plans are than if you should cross by passing to our rear. I forward the letter of instructions with these suggestions. . . . P. S. I think that your passage of the Potomac by our rear at the present moment will, in a measure, disclose our plans. You had better not leave us, therefore, unless you can take the proposed route in rear of the enemy" (O. R., 27, part 3, p. 915)

Mosby had gone east of the Bull Run Mountains and had found the enemy's infantry quietly waiting in his scattered camps. On the other hand, Lee's scouts affirmed that the Federal corps which had been at Leesburg had withdrawn, and that the enemy was laying a pontoon bridge at Edwards' Ferry on the Potomac, six miles east of Leesburg.[74]

Now, if the information as to preparations for a crossing at Edwards' Ferry were correct, that would mean two things— first, and obviously, that Hooker's design was to cross east of the Catoctin Mountains, and, secondly, that if the Army of the Potomac was concentrating on Edwards' Ferry, its long columns would be spread some distance southward on all the roads, making them impassable for Stuart. It followed, therefore, that if Stuart operated far in the rear of the enemy, he would almost certainly be compelled to cross the Potomac east of Edwards' Ferry in order to perform his major duty of covering the right flank of the army after it entered Pennsylvania. This was a geographical fact that will be apparent from the sketch on page 46, which gives the general direction but not the exact routes of columns converging on Edwards' Ferry.

Hooker, of course, would require a long time to move his immense army cross the Potomac. There was, consequently, no reason why Stuart could not ride around him, pass the river east of Edwards' Ferry, and reach the right flank of the Confederate column in Maryland before Hooker would be dangerously close. Stuart's march to Frederick by this route would be only some forty miles, whereas if he rode in Hooker's rear as far as the vicinity of Centreville, and then turned back, crossed the mountains and passed in rear of the Confederate army via Shepherdstown, he would have to cover eighty miles to Frederick. But the wisdom of a crossing east of Edwards' Ferry in passing over the Potomac was contingent on Stuart's being able to disorganize the Federal wagon trains and confuse the crossing without being materially delayed. If he lost his way, or became confused among the moving Federal columns, or stopped to indulge his fondness for fighting, he might be late. It was necessary, therefore, to make it plain to Stuart that while he could cross the Potomac

[74] *O. R.,* 27, part 2, p. 297; Mosby, *Stuart's Cavalry,* 78.

45

east of Hooker's army, he must put his major mission first and must not attempt a ride around the Federal army if he were hindered in the attempt.

But suppose Stuart was right in saying the enemy was inactive; suppose Hooker had no intention of making early use of the

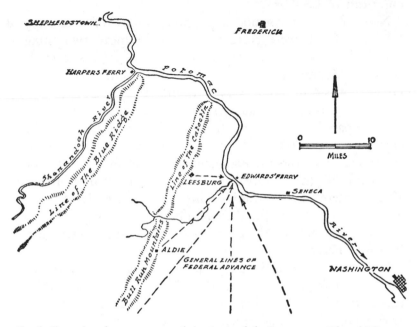

Sketch illustrating the convergence of the Army of the Potomac on Edwards' Ferry, June 23–24, 1863.

pontoon bridge at Edwards' Ferry; suppose there was significance in the report that a Federal column of cavalry was moving southward to Warrenton—what then? If the enemy was simply waiting, it was much more important that Stuart should be with the army on its advance into Pennsylvania than that he should remain east of the mountains in Virginia with his whole force, merely watching Hooker. And if the enemy was not moving northward, but was aiming at Warrenton, there was no reason why Stuart should waste his strength and wear down his horses in futile battles in dealing with diversions. He had better conserve his men and mounts, withdraw west of the Blue Ridge as soon as the army was beyond the Potomac, and then perform his major mission. Once the army of invasion was in the enemy's country, all such columns as that which was reported to be moving on Warrenton would be recalled by Hooker. Meantime the two brigades left in the mountains would have to deal as best they could with raids on Warrenton or the lines of communication.

In view of all this, only part of which was known to Stuart, Lee prudently decided, in answering Stuart's dispatches of the day, to cover the operations of the cavalry in the contingencies that might develop and to explain once again that its main function was to cover the right of the army in Pennsylvania. Lee directed Marshall to do this in further instructions. Marshall demurred on the ground that Stuart had been told in person and in the dispatch of June 22 precisely how he should act, but Lee insisted, and Marshall prepared a letter[75] in which he said:

"If General Hooker's army remains inactive, you can leave two brigades to watch him, and withdraw with the three others, but should he not appear to be moving northward, I think you had better withdraw this side of the mountains tomorrow night, cross at Shepherdstown next day, and move over to Frederickstown.

"You will, however, be able to judge whether you can pass around their army without hinderance, doing them all the damage you can, and cross the river east of the mountains. In either case, after crossing the river, you must move on and feel the right of Ewell's troops, collecting information, provisions, etc.

"Give instructions to the commander of the brigades left behind, to watch the flank and rear of the army, and (in the event of the enemy leaving their front) retire from the mountains west of the Shenandoah, leaving sufficient pickets to guard the passes, and bring everything clean along the Valley, closing upon the rear of the army.

"As regards the movements of the two brigades of the enemy moving toward Warrenton, the commander of the brigades to be left in the mountains must do what he can to counteract them, but I think the sooner you cross into Maryland, after tomorrow, the better.

[75] Marshall. 207.

47

"The movements of Ewell's corps are as stated in my former letter. Hill's first division will reach the Potomac today, and Longstreet will follow tomorrow.

"Be watchful and circumspect in all your movements." [76]

It is possible that Marshall was less careful than he should have been in drafting this letter because he was confident that Stuart had been fully told what to do; but the meaning is plain enough when the dispatch is read in the light of the information Lee and Stuart then possessed. Lee did not intend to require that Stuart cross into Maryland "immediately east of the mountains," as has been so often claimed. In the situation that actually developed, Lee undoubtedly intended to give Stuart discretion, after midnight of June 24, to pass around the Federal rear, which meant crossing the Potomac east of Edwards' Ferry. The one proviso was that Stuart must not be so hindered in following the routes as to be delayed in performing his principal service in the campaign, that of covering the Confederate right in the enemy's country. This was the all-important thing; Stuart was not to attempt to pass around the enemy's rear if he met with hindrance or delay. In case he did, he was to withdraw west of the mountains and follow the army into Pennsylvania. [77]

Even when these orders had been issued to protect the flank of the army when it moved into Pennsylvania, Lee still looked about to see what further measures he could take to strengthen himself for the test that awaited him in the enemy's country. In the hope that Corse and Cooke might be spared to reinforce him, he urged the War Department to send them forward. [78] One other possibility presented itself—the employment in his support of Beauregard's troops whom he had suggested, while still at Culpeper, that the President send either to Virginia or to join Johnston in the West. [79] He now proposed formally that

[76] O. R., 27, part 3, p. 923. This dispatch was sent direct to Stuart, and not through Longstreet, as the commander of the First Corps was then west of the Shenandoah, out of touch with Stuart and under orders to move the next day to the Potomac (O. R., 27, part 3, p. 358; O. R., 51, part 2, p. 726).

[77] For a survey of the "Stuart-Gettysburg controversy," see Appendix III—1.

[78] O. R., 27, part 3, pp. 925–26. Cf. ibid., 944.

[79] Supra, p. 29; O. R., 27, part 2, pp. 293–94. Lee had raised the question, less definitely, with the Secretary of War about the same time (O. R., 27, part 3, p. 869, letter of June 8).

Beauregard come to Virginia in person, if with only a small force, and establish himself at Culpeper Courthouse. This, he argued, "would not only effect a diversion most favorable for this army, but would, I think, relieve us of any apprehension of an attack upon Richmond during our absence. . . . If success should attend the operations of this army, and what I now suggest would greatly increase the probability of that result, we might even hope to compel the recall of some of the enemy's troops from the west."[80] Lee's plan, in short, was to utilize the inner lines of the Confederacy in playing on Lincoln the game that had so embarrassed the Richmond authorities when McDowell had been threatening an advance from Fredericksburg while McClellan was in front of Richmond. If the President approved his idea, Hooker would have to detach troops to combat Beauregard. In that way, the powerful and united army of Hooker might be weakened and divided long enough for Lee to strike a staggering blow. Lee had already suggested to General Samuel Jones that he undertake a diversion in western Virginia.[81]

On the morning of the 24th, while the long columns were slowly moving under the June skies down the Valley toward the crossings of the Potomac,[82] Lee rode from rear to front with his staff. On the road he overtook Colonel Eppa Hunton, who was leading Garnett's brigade of Pickett's division in the absence of its sick brigadier. For half an hour he travelled with Hunton

[80] Lee to Davis (*O. R.,* 27, part 3, p. 925). Longstreet contended, *op. cit.,* pp. 336–37, that this was a part of Lee's plan from the first, but that Lee had to deal cautiously with the Richmond authorities, and, as they were slow to forward even the brigades that belonged to the Army of Northern Virginia, "he did not mention the part left open for Beauregard until he had their approval of the march of the part of his command as he held it in hand." The candor of Lee's correspondence with President Davis does not justify this assertion. Lee doubtless had the general idea in mind, but if he had developed it fully, he would almost certainly not have delayed proposing it until two days before he crossed into Pennsylvania. Longstreet, who gave no dates, was probably confused as to his chronology.

[81] *O. R.,* 27, part 3, p. 906. For Jones's explanation of the reasons why he could not do this, see *O. R.,* 27, part 3, p. 942.

[82] The fullest itineraries of the march from Culpeper into Pennsylvania are in Kershaw's, Anderson's, and Nelson's (Kemper's) reports, *O. R.,* 27, part 2, pp. 366 *ff.,* 613 *ff.,* part 3, p. 1090–91. Early (*ibid.,* 464 *ff.*), and Rodes (*ibid.,* 550 *ff.*) supplemented Ewell's partial report of his movements (*ibid.,* 442 *ff.*). R. H. McKim (*A Soldier's Recollections,* 143 *ff.*) gave the various advances of Ewell, but his statements do not wholly agree with those in Ewell's report. Major W. M. Henry, commanding the artillery with Hood's division, First Corps, had a complete itinerary (*O. R.,* 27, part 2, pp. 427 *ff.*), though he does not seem to have remained constantly with the infantry. A vague but useful account of Hood's position day by day is to be found in J. C. West: *A Texan in Search of a Fight* (cited hereafter as *J. C. West*), 75 *ff.*

and talked of the adventures that awaited them on the other side of the river. Hunton, though second to none in desperate valor, was apprehensive of the outcome and frankly stated that a disaster in Pennsylvania might make withdrawal to Virginia difficult. Lee had his own misgivings, but in the presence of his subordinates he was always cheerful and confident. To Hunton he appeared most enthusiastic as he explained that an advance into Northern territory was necessary because provisions and supplies of every kind had been very nearly exhausted in Virginia. The invasion, he said, gave promise of success and would either end the war or allow the army rest for some time to come.[83]

After arriving opposite Williamsport, Lee received from the President a letter in which Mr. Davis endorsed Lee's views on the encouragement of the peace party in the North. In answering this on the morning of June 25, Lee reverted to his proposal that Beauregard be moved to Virginia, if only with a skeleton command. Already, he said, Federal apprehension for the safety of Washington was causing the Federals to recall troops for its defense; all the Federal force at Suffolk was reported to be evacuating, and General Buckner stated that Burnside's corps was being sent back from Kentucky. "I think," Lee said, "this should liberate the troops in the Carolinas, and enable Generals Buckner and Bragg to accomplish something in Ohio. It is plain that if all the Federal Army is concentrated upon this, it will result in our accomplishing nothing, and being compelled to return to Virginia. If the plan that I suggested the other day, of organizing an army, even in effigy, under General Beauregard at Culpeper Courthouse, can be carried into effect, much relief will be afforded. If even the brigades in Virginia and North Carolina, which Generals Hill and Elzey think cannot be spared, were ordered there at once, and General Beauregard were sent there, if he had to return to South Carolina, it would do more to protect both states from marauding expeditions of the enemy than anything else. . . ."[84]

83 *Autobiography of Eppa Hunton*, 86–87.
84 *O. R.*, 27, part 3, p. 931. Lee was so convinced of the value of this movement that he wrote Davis a second letter on the subject later in the day, from the Maryland side of the river (*ibid.*, 931–33).

Then he quietly announced to the President what had doubtless been apparent to him as a possibility from the time he had found that he would have to undertake his expedition, if at all, with only the troops then at his disposal: "I have not sufficient troops to maintain my communication, and, therefore, have to abandon them."[85] The army would have to take the great risk of living off the country. Imboden had supplied some beef; Ewell had been told that the ability of the rest of the army to follow him into Pennsylvania would depend on the supplies collected,[86] and he was collecting beef and flour.[87] But that was all that had been assured Lee. Much food must be bought. The crossing had been set for a time when there was reason to expect that the Potomac would be low and fordable for weeks,[88] but if provisions should fail and the river rise, what would happen to the army? Moreover, the artillery ammunition that could be carried with the army was just sufficient for one heavy battle.[89] Lee hoped that if the operations were favorable, he could bring up more ammunition under a cavalry escort, and that the abandonment of communications would not be complete,[90] but that was a long chance in a campaign that Lee now hoped to continue north of the Potomac until fall.[91]

He did not magnify his possible achievements as he closed his letter to the President. "I think," he said, "I can throw General Hooker's army across the Potomac and draw troops from the South, embarrassing their plan of campaign in a measure, if I can do nothing more and have to return. I still hope that all things will end well for us at Vicksburg. At any rate, every effort should be made to bring about that result."[92]

He had omitted nothing, so far as he then knew, to reduce the inevitable risks. To summarize:

The two corps then with him were to advance to Chambersburg in support of Ewell's advanced columns and, at the fitting moment, were to move toward the Susquehanna and destroy the rail communications with the West. On this second stage of the advance, Hill was to follow a route east of the mountains to keep

---

[85] *O. R.*, 27, part 3, p. 931.
[87] *O. R.*, 27, part 2, p. 443.
[89] 4 *S. H. S. P.*, 99.
[91] Allan in *Marshall*, 251.
[86] *O. R.*, 27, part 3, p. 914.
[88] *O. R.*, 27, part 2, p. 299.
[90] *Marshall*, 219.
[92] *O. R.*, 27, part 3, p. 931.

the enemy at a distance, and Longstreet to move directly north on Harrisburg.[93]

Jenkins's cavalry brigade was to move in front of the army, Imboden on the left,[94] and Stuart with three brigades on the right, operating in the direction of Baltimore so as to force an enemy-concentration as far eastward as possible.[95] Jones and Robertson were to cover the rear until the enemy was across the Potomac and were then to join the main army, keeping to its right and rear.[96]

Reinforcements, if sent forward, were to go by train to Culpeper, march thence through Chester Gap and northward down the Valley to Winchester, where they would receive orders.[97]

To relieve pressure on Vicksburg, and to brighten the prospect of success by the Army of Northern Virginia, Lee had made four proposals—that General Samuel Jones advance on the enemy in western Virginia, that Bragg and Buckner move against the diminished Federal force in Kentucky, and that Beauregard, stripping the south Atlantic coast, move to Culpeper Courthouse and threaten Washington from the south, while the President undertook a peace offensive, directed against the morale of the North.

All these efforts were to be co-ordinated. The supreme endeavor of the South to win its independence was now to be made. So far as the Army of Northern Virginia was concerned, the hour had come. In the midst of a heavy rain[98] on the morning of June 25, the bands struck up "Dixie," [99] the cheering division began to move, and the man who carried his nation's hope turned Traveller's head into the Potomac.[100]

[93] See note 29, p. 60, *infra.*   [94] *O. R.,* 27, part 3, p. 924.
[95] *Longstreet,* 340.   [96] *O. R.,* 27, part 3, pp. 927–28.
[97] *O. R.,* 27, part 3, p. 926.   [98] *F. W. Dawson,* 91.
[99] *Hood,* 54.
[100] *Manuscript Narrative of the Campaign of 1863* by General A. L. Long, lent to the writer, with great kindness, by the late A. R. Long, of Lynchburg.

CHAPTER V

Lee Hears a Fateful Cannonade

LIKE the three witches who on another day "so foul and fair" met Macbeth on the heath, a group of ladies under dripping umbrellas awaited Lee on the Maryland side of the Potomac—not to hail him as thane of Cawdor, but to wish him victory on his second invasion of the North. Their spokesman, whom Captain Dawson in a most ungallant phrase charged with having a "face like a door-knocker," stepped forward as Lee rode up.

"This is General Lee, I presume?"

Lee admitted his identity.

"General Lee," she went on, "allow me to present to you these ladies who were determined to give you this reception."

Lee thanked her and introduced General Longstreet and General Pickett, whose flowing locks fell back from eyes that never failed to see all that was comely in the other sex. Then came flowers and fair words and, at length, a wreath the ladies desired to put around the bowed gray neck of Traveller. Lee balked at this. Garlands were well enough for Stuart, but for the mount of an infantryman commanding an army of invasion on a desperate venture—well . . . he was extremely indebted to the ladies for their courtesy, but would they excuse him? Marylanders of the persuasive sex who had braved rain and radicals to do honor to a "rebel" were not so easily put off. A parley ensued, with the ladies insistent and Lee resolute. It was compromised at length by giving the wreath to a courier to carry for the General.[1]

The holiday spirit of this welcome persisted. After Lee's column stopped in a hickory grove on a hill three miles from Williamsport, Colonel Taylor spoke up. "General," he said, "this gentleman has brought me some raspberries, and I have asked him to take snack with us." Lee turned quickly and saw Leighton

---

[1] *F. W. Dawson,* 91.

Parks, the little boy who had visited him in Maryland the previous year. He smiled: "I have had the pleasure of meeting your friend before," he answered. Then he stopped, lifted the youngster and kissed him. He had the lad eat with his mess, and then took him into his tent, put him on his knee and talked to him until General Hill demanded the same privilege. After Hill, Longstreet insisted on a chat and confidentially whispered that he had a pony he thought could carry the boy's weight if he would join his staff. At length when Lee resumed his duties, Hill told an orderly to "bring the captain's horse," and after it developed that the youngster could not mount so high, Lee lifted him into the saddle. "Give him time," he said, "and he'll do for the cavalry yet." [2]

The friendly spirit of the invasion was somewhat the same the next morning, June 26, when Lee left his camp[3] and rode through Hagerstown en route to Chambersburg, whither Hill's and Longstreet's columns were moving. Although it was raining again,[4] another company of ladies surrounded him, and one of them asked for a lock of his hair. As the General's grizzled coverage was beginning to thin, he made that his excuse. Besides, he said, he was sure they would prefer a ringlet from a younger officer. There was General Pickett—surely he would be glad to give her one of his curls. This did not appeal strongly to Pickett, who had left his heart in Virginia, nor did the proposal impress the young lady.[5] Those who had seen the General at the time of the first invasion of Maryland remarked that he had aged perceptibly in ten months,[6] but Southern sympathizers did not lionize him less on that account, and even one Northern girl who persisted in waving a Union flag was heard to say as he passed, "Oh, I wish he was ours"[7]—a remark that must have been the text of many a quip among irreverent and envious young staff officers.

From Hagerstown he rode northward and entered Pennsylvania for the first time since the beginning of the war. Hill

---

[2] *Leighton Parks, loc. cit.* See *supra*, vol. II, p. 355. Doctor Parks was rector of St. Bartholomew's, New York City, 1904–25.

[3] A. J. L. Fremantle: *Three Months in the Southern States*, New York edition of 1864 (cited hereafter as *Fremantle*), p. 236.

[4] *Fremantle*, 235.   [5] *F. W. Dawson*, 91.

[6] *Leighton Parks, loc. cit.*   [7] *Marginalia*, 21.

had gone ahead and as Lee rode toward the public square in Chambersburg, Hill came down the street and met him. Another throng was awaiting him, and a man with a camera was stationed in a window, only to have his picture ruined by soldiers who insisted on being included in it. Posterity will not readily forgive them their forwardness, for if the artist had not been interrupted he doubtless would have taken a photograph of high historical interest.[8] However, if the good people of Chambersburg could not have a picture, they could at least have a look, and they eyed Lee critically, if with awe.

"What a large neck he has," one civilian whispered.

"Yes," said a nearby Confederate, "it takes a damn big neck to hold his head." [9]

Lee moved on and established headquarters in a little grove out from the town on the road to Gettysburg, a picnicking place, known as Shatter's Woods and later as Messersmith's Woods.[10] "A Confederate flag marks the whereabouts . . .," an Austrian visitor wrote. "There are about half a dozen tents and as many baggage wagons and ambulances. The horses and mules from these, besides those of a small escort, are tied up to the trees or grazing about the place." [11]

Here the atmosphere was not that of merrymaking, but of preparation for battle. Lee's first concern, on the 27th, was to assure the safety of private property. Before he had left Virginia he had talked on the subject with General Trimble, and had expressed himself strongly against the retaliatory acts that were being urged on him in many letters. "I cannot hope," he had said, "that Heaven will prosper our cause when we are violating its laws. I shall, therefore, carry on the war in Pennsylvania without offending the sanctions of a high civilization and of Christianity." [12] It had been in this spirit that he had issued orders on June 21 governing the seizure of supplies for the army while in the enemy's country. He had then directed that all

[8] Jacob Hoke: *The Great Invasion of 1863* (cited hereafter as *Hoke*), 160–62. Hoke stated that Lee arrived about 9 o'clock. If he was correct as to the hour, Lee left Williamsport much earlier than the time, 11 A.M., at which Fremantle had been told he had started north.

[9] W. H. Stewart: *A Pair of Blankets,* 94.   [10] *Hoke,* 169.

[11] Fitzgerald Ross: *A Visit to the Cities and Camps of the Confederate States* (cited hereafter as *Ross*), 43.

[12] 26 *S. H. S. P.,* 119.

the necessities of the army should be met by formal requisition on local authorities or by purchase and payment in Confederate money. Where Confederate notes were refused, the quartermasters were to issue receipts, setting forth the name of the owner of the seized property, the quantity and the fair market value.[13] These instructions had been measurably respected by Ewell's troops, but now that the whole of the army was in a district where Lee expected it to remain for some time, the regulations were reiterated in General Orders No. 73 for the guidance of the individual soldiers. After thanking the men for their fortitude and loyal performance of duty, Lee said:

"Their conduct in other respects has, with few exceptions, been in keeping with their character as soldiers, and entitles them to approbation and praise.

"There have, however, been instances of forgetfulness on the part of some, that they have in keeping the yet unsullied reputation of the army, and that the duties exacted of us by civilization and Christianity are not less obligatory in the country of the enemy than in our own.

"The commanding general considers that no greater disgrace could befall the army, and through it our whole people, than the perpetration of the barbarous outrages upon the unarmed and defenseless and the wanton destruction of private property, that have marked the course of the enemy in our own country.

"Such proceedings not only degrade the perpetrators and all connected with them, but are subversive of the discipline and efficiency of the army, and destructive of the ends of our present movement.

"It must be remembered that we make war only upon armed men, and that we cannot take vengeance for the wrongs our people have suffered without lowering ourselves in the eyes of all whose abhorrence has been excited by the atrocities of our enemies, and offending against Him to whom vengeance belongeth, without whose favor and support our efforts must all prove in vain.

"The commanding general therefore earnestly exhorts the

[13] O. R., 27, part 3, pp. 912–13; General Orders No. 72, of June 21, 1863.

troops to abstain with most scrupulous care from unnecessary or wanton injury to private property, and he enjoins upon all officers to arrest and bring to summary punishment all who shall in any way offend against the orders on this subject." [14]

These orders were written, no doubt, with an eye to the encouragement of the peace movement in the North, for mercy disarms hate; but they were drafted in sincerity and they were enforced with vigor,[15] despite some grumbling in the army and some protests at home.[16] No officer below the rank of general was allowed to go into Chambersburg without a special pass from Lee, which he was slow to give.[17] By daily reminders and by careful example—as when he stopped on the road opposite a pasture to put up bars that some negligent soldier had left down[18] —he succeeded in protecting property from damage and women from insult. There were no charges of rape and few of plundering. The chief difficulty of the officers was in keeping hot, bareheaded soldiers from snatching civilians' hats as they marched through the crowd-lined streets of the little towns. "This was repeatedly done in the presence of officers, who invariably tried to have the offending person pointed out, that the stolen property might be restored and the offender punished, but in the similarity of the men and the necessity for the column to keep moving on, not a single one was detected"—so testified a Northern writer.[19]

Regardless of hats, the army had to be ready for action. By the 27th Ewell was well advanced in two columns, one as far as Carlisle on the road to Harrisburg,[20] and the other, which consisted of Early's division, within about six miles of York. Ewell's orders were to take Harrisburg if his force was adequate, and Early was under instructions to cut the railroad between Harrisburg and Baltimore and to destroy the bridges at Wrightsville and Columbia.[21] Longstreet's and Hill's corps were encamped around Chambersburg and Fayetteville, in excellent

---

14 *O. R.*, 27, part 3, p. 943.
15 *Our Living and Our Dead*, vol. 3, pp. 672–73; *Hoke*, 175–78; *Fremantle*, 242 ff.
16 *Fremantle*, 238, 245; *DeLeon*, 257–58.   17 *Fremantle*, 242.
18 *F. W. Dawson*, 92; *Our Living and Our Dead*, 3, 673.
19 *Hoke*, 178.   20 *O. R.*, 27, part 2, p. 443.
21 *O. R.*, 27, part 2, pp. 464–65, 466.

health and full of confidence, far better shod and clad than when they had entered Maryland in 1862.[22]

The general advance of the army was to be on Harrisburg, in order to draw the enemy out and to cut communications between East and West. The execution of the plan depended primarily on the arrival of Stuart's cavalry, for it manifestly was dangerous, if not impossible, to move freely so long as nothing was known of the position of the Federals. Presumably, Hooker was still in Virginia. Otherwise Stuart would surely have notified Lee. But the uncertainty hampered operations.[23]

While waiting for Stuart, Lee checked his maps carefully by all the information he could get from Southern sympathizers,[24] and he had a lengthy interview with Major General Trimble, who had been chief engineer for one of the nearby railroads and knew the country well. Trimble told him there was scarcely a square mile east of the mountains in Adams County that did not offer good positions for manœuvre or for battle. Lee was pleased at the assurance: "Our army," he was quoted long afterwards by Trimble as saying, "is in good spirits, not overfatigued, and can be concentrated on any one point in twenty-four hours or less. I have not yet heard that the enemy have crossed the Potomac, and am waiting to hear from General Stuart. When they hear where we are, they will make forced marches to interpose their forces between us and Baltimore and Philadelphia. They will come up, probably through Frederick, broken down with hunger and hard marching, strung out on a long line and much de-moralized, when they come into Pennsylvania. I shall throw an overwhelming force on their advance, crush it, follow up the success, drive one corps back on another, and by successive repulses and surprises, before they can concentrate, create a panic and virtually destroy the army."

Trimble expressed his belief that this could be done, because the morale of the troops had never been higher. "That is, I hear, the general impression," Lee answered. Then, as Trimble rose to go, Lee laid his hand on the map and pointed to a little town east of the mountains, Gettysburg by name, from which roads

---

[22] *Leighton Parks, loc. cit.; Welch,* 58: "I have never seen our army so healthy and in such gay spirits."

[23] *O. R.,* 27, part 2, pp. 307, 316. [24] *Leighton Parks, loc. cit.*

radiated like so many spokes. "Hereabout," he said, "we shall probably meet the enemy and fight a great battle, and if God gives us the victory, the war will be over and we shall achieve the recognition of our independence." [25]

Bidding the stout-hearted Trimble adieu, Lee turned to the further study of his map and to the administration of the affairs of the 40,000 men who waited in their camps for his word to go forward. Much he had to do, also, for the civilians who came to him freely with the troubles the invasion brought to their households. He dealt with them as considerately as he could, seeking always to promote peace sentiment. One woman who visited headquarters with a request that he make provision for the hungry in Chambersburg remained long enough to ask for his autograph.

"Do you want the autograph of a rebel?" he asked, in surprise.

"General Lee," she retorted, "I am a true Union woman, and yet I ask for bread and your autograph."

"It is to your interest," he answered, "to be for the Union, and I hope you may be as firm in your principles as I am in mine."

Lee told her that his autograph might be a dangerous souvenir for her to possess, but when she insisted, he gave it to her, and turned the conversation to the cruelties of war. His only desire, he said, was that they would let him go home and eat his bread in peace. [26]

The 28th came, and still no word of the enemy, of Stuart, or of the cavalry that had been left behind to guard the passes of the Blue Ridge. Outwardly, Lee continued calm and cheerful, but inwardly his apprehension rose, and he began to wonder if the absence of reports from Stuart meant that the Federal commander was contemplating an attack on Richmond while the Army of Northern Virginia was above the Potomac. [27] However, taking "no news" to mean "no danger," [28] that day he ordered

---

[25] Trimble, in 26 *S. H. S. P.*, 121, said he was confident that he quoted Lee almost verbatim. He wrote, however, probably twenty years after the events and when he was an old man. A copy of the map that Lee used in this campaign is reproduced on a reduced scale as Plate CXVI., No. 2 in the *Atlas* of the *Official Records*.

[26] *Hoke*, 197–99, quoting Lee's interviewer, Mrs. Ellen McLellan, widow of William McLellan of Chambersburg.

[27] *Marshall*, 217.   [28] *O. R.*, 27, part 2, p. 316.

Ewell to pursue his advance on Harrisburg, with Longstreet and probably Hill to follow on the 29th.[29]

As the day passed without other incident, Lee's wonder at the silence of Stuart increased, and when he retired for the night, it must have been with amazement that an officer who was in the habit of reporting so promptly and so regularly should have sent no messenger since the army had crossed the Potomac on the 25th. Stuart had been told plainly that if he found Hooker moving northward, when he was himself sure of the safety of the mountain passes, he was to move into Maryland and take position on Ewell's right. That was Stuart's chief mission and a fundamental of the whole plan of operations, for it was an essential precaution of invasion to keep a heavy cavalry screen between the army and the enemy.

After 10 o'clock on the night of the 28th there came a rap on Lee's tent pole, and when Lee answered, Major John W. Fairfax of Longstreet's staff[30] entered and announced that Harrison, one of Longstreet's scouts, had arrived and had brought the startling news that Hooker was north of the Potomac. It seemed so incredible, in the absence of all confirmation, that Lee was skeptical. "I do not know what to do," he said to Fairfax, "I cannot hear from General Stuart, the eye of the army. What do you think of Harrison? I have no confidence in any scout, but General Longstreet thinks a good deal of Harrison." [31] Fairfax had no opinion and went his way. Later in the evening, Lee decided to talk with Harrison and sent for him. The scout duly reported —a stoop-shouldered, bearded man about five feet, eight inches tall, dark and wiry, well dressed in civilian clothes, but dusty and very tired.[32] The spy said that he had left Longstreet at Culpeper

---

[29] There is some confusion as to Hill's order. He said (*O. R., 27*, part 2, p. 606) that he was to move eastward and northeastward to cross the Susquehanna and to seize the railroad connecting Harrisburg and Philadelphia. Longstreet, *op. cit.*, 348, stated that Hill misconstrued his orders on the 28th-29th, but he also noted (*ibid.*, 340), in another reference, that Hill was to follow Ewell's "eastern column," Early's, along the route Hill mentions. Lee simply reported (*O. R., 27*, part 2, p. 316), that "orders were . . . issued to move upon Harrisburg." The most probable explanation is that the original orders for Hill to follow Early were suspended during the wait at Chambersburg and that, when he received instructions to move east of the mountains, Hill assumed this advance was in accordance with his former orders.

[30] *Longstreet*, 347.

[31] John W. Fairfax to Mrs. James Longstreet, Oct. 12, 1904—*Fairfax MSS.*

[32] For a description of this mysterious man, see Longstreet in 3 *B. and L.*, 244. In his last version of Harrison's arrival, General Longstreet charged (*From Manassas to Appo-*

and had gone to Washington, where he had frequented the saloons and had picked up much gossip. Hearing that Hooker had crossed the Potomac, he had started for Frederick, walking at night and mingling with the soldiers during the day. At Frederick he had found two corps of infantry, one to the right and the other to the left of the town. He had heard of a third corps nearby but had not been able to locate it. Having learned that the Army of Northern Virginia was at Chambersburg, he had procured a horse and had hurried northward. On the way to Chambersburg, he had ascertained that two more corps were close to South Mountain. Incidentally, he had heard that General Hooker had been replaced by Lee's old comrade and friend, Major General George Gordon Meade.[33]

Lee heard Harrison through without a tremor,[34] but he was profoundly concerned by the intelligence the spy brought. Hooker on the north side of the Potomac, close to his rear, and not a cavalryman at hand to ascertain whither he was moving! There could hardly have been worse news. Lee had not fully carried out his design of abandoning his communications with Virginia. There had, as yet, been no reason for doing so. Although he did not consider his line to the Potomac open for all purposes, he still believed that if a strong cavalry escort were supplied, he could bring up ammunition from Virginia as long as the Federals were east of South Mountain. But if the Army of the Potomac was already at the foot of that ridge, the new commander would almost certainly cross, move westward and destroy the Confederate communications.[35] Not only so, but if the Federals got into Cumberland Valley, they might force Lee to conform and thereby rob him of the initiative, which he must retain for the type of campaign he hoped to conduct. The situation instantly became

mattox, 347) that Lee refused to see the spy and discredited his report. Colonel Fairfax, loc. cit., was of the same opinion, but Colonel Marshall mentioned casually in his narrative of Gettysburg (op. cit., 218) that he saw Lee sitting and talking with Harrison. General Sorrel said, op. cit., 161, that "the general heard him with great composure and minuteness." Evidently Lee sent for Harrison after Major Fairfax left. The scout may have returned with Sorrel.

33 In his first account of this famous incident (3 B. and L., 250), General Longstreet did not mention the troops that Harrison met near South Mountain, but Marshall's statement of what Lee told him of Harrison's report (op. cit., 219) indicates that Longstreet was correct when he remarked in From Manassas to Appomattox that Harrison had encountered Federals near the mountains.

34 Sorrel, 161.   35 Marshall, 219.

one of gravity—and because of Stuart's unexplained absence, the army was blindfolded.

Almost as soon, therefore, as Harrison had finished his story, Lee determined on his course of action. The advance of Ewell on Harrisburg must be abandoned; the Second Corps must be recalled; Longstreet's and Hill's orders to march northward must be cancelled; the whole army must be concentrated at once and must be moved east of the mountains so as to compel the Federals to follow and thereby to abandon their threat to Lee's rear.[36] As there was no way of ascertaining when Stuart would arrive, Imboden's cavalry, which was operating to the westward, must be called in, and the two mounted brigades that had been left behind in the passes of the Blue Ridge must be brought up immediately.

Orders flew fast.[37] A messenger hurried off to Carlisle to recall Ewell.[38] Another took the road back to Virginia with orders to Robertson and W. E. Jones to hasten forward.[39] By 7:30 A.M. Lee had so far developed his plan that he saw there was danger of delaying the movement by crowding too many troops on the road from Chambersburg eastward, so he modified Ewell's orders and directed him to march directly from Carlisle toward Cashtown or Gettysburg.[40] Hill was to use the road that led over the mountains from Chambersburg to these towns, and he was to be followed the next day, June 30, by Longstreet, who was to leave one division to guard the rear until the arrival of Imboden's cavalry.[41]

The day of the 29th had broken dark and stormy,[42] and Lee's feelings were gloomy. As he prepared to mount for the day he saw a former staff officer of Jackson's who had just come up from Virginia, and he eagerly inquired of him if he had any news of Stuart. The officer replied that he had met on the road

[36] *O. R.,* 27, part 2, pp. 307, 316. [37] *Long,* 275.
[38] *O. R.,* 27, part 3, p. 943. [39] *O. R.,* 27, part 2, p. 321.
[40] *O. R.,* 27, part 3, p. 943. This letter to Ewell is dated "June 28, 1863—7.30 A.M." but there is a note in Lee's letterbook that the text was copied from memory. In the copying, the date was wrongly given. As Doctor McKim has shown in 37 *S. H. S. P.,* 212, the paper was certainly written on the 29th. Mosby's efforts to prove the contrary in his *Stuart's Cavalry* are unconvincing.
[41] *O. R.,* 27, part 2, p. 317. Longstreet hinted in *Annals of the War,* 419, that he suggested this movement, but Lee's orders make it plain that he had acted before he saw Longstreet on the 29th.
[42] *Marshall,* 225.

two cavalrymen who had said that on the 27th they had left Stuart in Prince William County, Virginia. Lee was surprised and visibly disturbed.[43] Repeatedly during the day he inquired

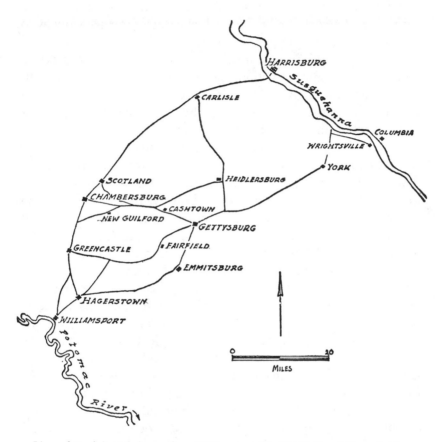

Lines of Confederate advance from Williamsport into Maryland and Pennsylvania, June–July, 1863.

for additional news of the movements of the cavalry.[44] Not a word further did he hear. All Jenkins's troopers were with Ewell; Early had the only other organized unit, White's battalion. Why Jones and Robertson were delayed, Lee did not know. Imboden, who might at least have supplied men for a reconnaisance, was

[43] 33 S. H. S. P., 139.
[44] Long MS.; 4 S. H. S. P., 156; Taylor's General Lee, 187.

63

two days' journey away. So completely was Lee stripped of cavalry that the foraging actually had to be done by men mounted on horses from the artillery or the wagon train. But this did not compass the whole of Lee's embarrassment. Not only was he entirely without cavalry for an advance against an enemy who might soon be hanging on his front, but he also was deprived of the presence of Stuart himself, on whom he had been accustomed to rely for information that he had come to value as consistently accurate.[45] A Federal visitor found him restless and concerned during the day,[46] but later he recovered his poise completely and jestingly told Hood, who came to call: "Ah, General, the enemy is a long time finding us; if he does not succeed soon, we must go in search of him."[47] When he went out to walk in the road for exercise, during the afternoon, his outward calm was as complete as ever and he announced quietly to some officers who attended him, "Tomorrow, gentlemen, we will not move to Harrisburg, as we expected, but will go over to Gettysburg and see what General Meade is after."[48] When asked for his opinion of the latest change in the command of the Army of the Potomac, he answered that he thought the Federal cause benefited by the promotion of Meade, but that this was counterbalanced by the difficulties Meade would encounter in taking charge of the forces in the midst of a campaign.[49] He said then, or soon thereafter, "General Meade will commit no blunder in my front, and if I make one he will make haste to take advantage of it."[50] As Lee spoke, Heth's division of the Third Corps was moving to Cashtown, east of the mountains.[51] The advance was slow on account of the rain, and cautious because of the absence of all information concerning the position of the enemy.[52]

Still with no news from Stuart, Lee speeded up the march on

---

[45] H. B. McClellan, 336–37.

[46] Hoke, 205–6. It is certain that Hoke's informant, Doctor J. L. Suesserott, was guilty of unintentional exaggeration when he wrote in his old age that Lee "with his hands at times clutching his hair, and with contracted brow . . . would walk with rapid strides for a few rods and then, as if he bethought himself of his action, he would with a sudden jerk produce an entire change in his features and demeanor and cast an enquiring gaze on me, only to be followed in a moment by the same contortions of face and agitation of person."

[47] Hood, 55.

[48] Longstreet, 383 n., quoting Doctor J. S. D. Cullen.

[49] Long, 274.

[50] Eggleston, 145–46.

[51] O. R., 27, part 2, pp. 606–7.

[52] O. R., 27, part 2, pp. 307, 317.

the morning of June 30. Hill went on with Pender to Cash-town,[53] and two divisions of Longstreet's corps started on the same road from Chambersburg. Pickett remained behind, according to Lee's plan, to protect the rear until Imboden's arrival; Law's brigade was left on duty at New Guilford;[54] and Anderson of Hill's corps, who was encamped at Fayetteville, east of Chambers-burg, was directed to move on July 1.[55] Lee himself left with Longstreet's troops on the 30th, and about 2 P.M. went into camp at a deserted sawmill near Greenwood, where he intended to wait until the next morning.[56]

Thus far on the road no enemy had been encountered. Such information as Lee could get from officers and men who had come up from the rear was to the effect that Meade was still at Middletown, about midway between Frederick and Boonsboro, and had not struck his tents to move.[57] Late in the evening of the 30th, however, General Hill, who had ridden on to overtake his troops at Cashtown, sent back word that Pettigrew's brigade of Heth's division had gone on that day from Cashtown to Gettys-burg to procure shoes. Near Gettysburg, Pettigrew had found Federal cavalry, and some of his officers reported that they had heard the roll of infantry drums beyond the town. Having only his brigade with him, and no cavalry support, Pettigrew had not felt justified in advancing farther and had returned to Cash-town.[58] Lee could hardly believe this report,[59] and even if it were true he could do nothing until morning.

Dawn of July 1 broke with a gentle breeze, and was sunshiny and clear, except for occasional showery clouds.[60] Anderson's divi-sion passed Greenwood early to join its corps, which had spent the night between Cashtown and Gettysburg. Despite the uncer-tainty, Lee was cheerful and composed, and called to Longstreet to ride with him.[61] The men of the First Corps were confident, and as they swung into the road, doubtless every one of them shared the view Lee's adjutant general had expressed in a letter

---

[53] O. R., 27, part 2, p. 607. [54] O. R., 27, part 2, p. 358.
[55] O. R., 27, part 2, pp. 317, 358, 607, 613.
[56] O. R., 27, part 2, p. 358; Ross, 43; Annals of the War, 419–20.
[57] 4 S. H. S. P., 157.
[58] 4 S. H. S. P., 157; O. R., 27, part 2, pp. 317, 607, 637.
[59] Colonel William Allan, quoted in Marshall, 250.
[60] Cooke, 301. [61] Longstreet, 351.

two days before: "With God's help we expect to take a step or two toward an honorable peace." [62]

About six miles east of Chambersburg, the head of the First Corps found Johnson's division of Ewell's corps pouring into the road from the northwest, in obedience to Lee's order for a quick concentration. It was a welcome assurance that the greater part of the army would be together for any adventure that lay beyond the mountains; but Johnson's men and their wagons blocked the road, over part of which, first and last, six divisions and the trains and reserve artillery of all three corps had to pass.[63] Lee directed Longstreet to halt the First Corps and let Johnson have the road.[64]

After a short wait, however, Lee proposed that they ride ahead, and, with their staffs, he and Longstreet began to climb the mountain, past the toiling troops of Johnson.[65] As they ascended there was audible, above the tramp of horses and the familiar clatter of bayonets against canteens, an occasional distant rumble—artillery! At first Lee imagined that it was simply a brush with cavalry, but his lack of information irritated him. Ordinarily, in Virginia, no sooner would he hear the challenge of distant guns than a courier would ride up with a dispatch from Stuart explaining what was afoot, but now—where was Stuart and what did the firing mean? Lee could not altogether conceal his impatience and admitted frankly that he had been in the dark since he had crossed the Potomac.[66]

As they approached the crest of the divide, the sound of firing came insistently from the east.[67] Lee could restrain himself no longer. Bidding Longstreet farewell,[68] he quickened Traveller's pace and hurried on to Cashtown, where he met A. P. Hill,[69] sick and very pale.[70] Hill knew little, except that Heth's division had gone ahead under instructions not to force an action, if it encountered the enemy, until the rest of the army came up.[71] Soon Hill galloped off to see for himself what the cannonade meant.

Hearing that Anderson's division was in the town, together with the reserve artillery of the Third Corps, Lee thought that

---

[62] Walter H. Taylor, June 29, 1863; *Taylor MSS.*
[63] *Alexander*, 381.
[64] *Longstreet*, 351–52.
[65] *Longstreet*, 352.
[66] *Long*, 275.
[67] *O. R.*, 27, part 2, p. 348.
[68] *Longstreet*, 352.
[69] *Taylor's Four Years*, 92.
[70] *Fremantle*, 254; *Cooke*, 301–2.
[71] *Taylor's Four Years*, 93.

Anderson might know something further, and he sent for him. As he waited, he listened intently to the sound that drifted sullenly over the rolling hills. He continued to listen for a moment after Anderson came up. Then he said, more to himself than to the General: "I cannot think what has become of Stuart. I ought to have heard from him long before now. He may have met with disaster, but I hope not. In the absence of reports from him, I am in ignorance as to what we have in front of us here. It may be the whole Federal army, it may be only a detachment. If it is the whole Federal force, we must fight a battle here. If we do not gain a victory, those defiles and gorges which we passed this morning will shelter us from disaster." [72]

Anderson had no information that Lee had not already received. After a few more words, he left Anderson and started onward again toward the sound of the guns, the opening guns of Gettysburg.

[72] Anderson, quoted in *Longstreet*, 357.

CHAPTER VI

THE SPIRIT THAT INHIBITS VICTORY

OVER the hills from Cashtown, along a road he had never travelled before, Lee galloped toward Gettysburg like a blinded giant. He did not know where the Federals were, or how numerous they might be. Ewell—and doubtless Hill also—he had cautioned not to bring on a general engagement with a strong adversary until the rest of the infantry came up,[1] but with no cavalry to inform him, he could not tell what calamity he might invite by advancing at all, or what opportunity he might lose by advancing cautiously. Never had he been so dangerously in the dark.

Louder and nearer was the sound of the artillery. Soon, to his regret and surprise,[2] infantry volleys in a spiteful staccato added their treble to the bass of the guns. Smoke was now visible on the horizon, swept by the breeze into a long cloud. At 2 o'clock, when he still was about three miles from Gettysburg, he came into the open country and found Pender's division deployed.[3] In the distance, action was visible. He turned into a grassy field on the left of the road and found a position that commanded a good view. Quickly putting binoculars to his eyes he studied the gray and green panorama before him. A cultivated ridge, long and wide and broken only by a few rail fences and patches of woodland, led down to Willoughby Run. Beyond that little stream the ground rose to another ridge on which stood conspicuously a Lutheran seminary with a cupola. Over this ridge to the east at an elevation about fifty feet below that of the ground on which Lee stood, was Gettysburg. South and southeast of the town, dimly discernible, were dangerous-looking hills and ridges.

Lee's eyes could not have lingered long on their vague outlines, because his glasses must have fixed themselves quickly on the

[1] O. R., 27, part 2, p. 444.   [2] 43 S. H. S. P., 56.   [3] O. R., 27, part 2, p. 656.

smoke that was rising on either side of the Chambersburg road where it crossed Willoughby Run. Evidently there had been an attack and a repulse. The artillery was blazing away, and Heth's division was apparently forming on a front about a mile in length. Two of Heth's brigades were in bad order. Beyond them, across the run, where the smoke from the Union batteries was swelling, must be the Federal infantry—and how strong? That was the question Lee's anxious mind instantly fashioned: Was it a heavy force or merely a detached unit, sent to guard the Gettysburg crossroads? The guns did not seem very numerous, but the infantry fire came from a front at least as long as Heth's. That was ominous.

Soon Lee's presence on the field became known, and officers began to bring him news. Heth had sent forward two of his brigades, Archer's and Davis's, during the morning. They had pushed forward vigorously and had driven the enemy back. Later the Federals had attacked them in heavy force and, about an hour before Lee arrived, had compelled them to retire. Part of Archer's brigade had been cut off, and Archer himself had been captured.[4] Heth was now resting his men in line of battle preparatory to attacking again with his entire division, and Hill had directed Pender to support him.[5]

Finding their opponents out of range, the Federal infantry had halted and had ceased firing. The artillery exchange was slowing down. As Lee rode closer to the lines he was still so uncertain of the strength of the opposing troops and so anxious not to bring on a general engagement until his whole army was concentrated, that had there not been a sudden stir north of Gettysburg about 3 o'clock he would probably have forbidden an advance. The enemy began to move out troops in that direction; the right of the Federal line that faced Hill was drawn in; firing commenced briskly. Soon from the woods above Gettysburg a long gray line of battle emerged. It was Rodes's division of Ewell's corps, marching under orders to join Lee at Gettysburg. Having heard the sound of Hill's engagement, Rodes had taken advantage of the cover on the ridge and was coming up almost on the right flank of the forces that had been engaged with Hill. It could not have

---

[4] *O. R.*, 27, part 2, pp. 607, 638.   [5] *O. R.*, 27, part 2, p. 638.

happened more advantageously if this chance engagement had been a planned battle!

The Federals rallied quickly to this new threat. As they deployed to meet Rodes's attack, he had to change direction somewhat to the right. In doing this his left brigade, Doles's, shifted to confront a column that had started northward from the town as if to turn Rodes's left. Doles thus became detached from the rest of the command. O'Neal's brigade on his right thereupon lost direction and was scattered. The attack against the flank of the troops facing Hill had, therefore, to be delivered by two brigades, Daniel's and Iverson's, with Ramseur's in reserve.[6] The details of all this could not be seen, of course, from Lee's position, but it was soon apparent that Rodes was having hard fighting, in the face of stubborn resistance, and was not advancing rapidly.

General Heth rode up to Lee. "Rodes," said he, "is heavily engaged; had I not better attack?"

"No," said Lee, reasoning that little was to be gained and much was to be risked by committing himself to the offensive with only part of his forces. "No, I am not prepared to bring on a general engagement today—Longstreet is not up."[7]

But the very gods of war seemed to wear gray that hot afternoon. Rodes had not been long in action when smoke began to rise still farther to the eastward and guns from that quarter added their roar. Early's division of Ewell's corps had arrived on Rodes's left and was driving the Federals who had been threatening Doles' flank. At precisely the right place, and at exactly the right moment, a third blow was being delivered. Everything was working perfectly. The hard-beset Federals formed a right angle now, their left running from south to north, and their right from west to east. Opposite their left was Heth, with two of his four brigades unscathed and with Pender's fresh division in reserve. At the angle in the line Rodes was hammering hard. On the Federal right, Early's veterans were thundering. With Pender it would be easy to outflank the Federal left, and with Early to turn their right.

As quickly as the situation changed with the arrival of Early,

[6] *O. R.,* 27, part 2, pp. 553–54.   [7] Heth in 4 *S. H. S. P.,* 158.

Lee's decision was reversed. So fair an opportunity was not to be lost. The orders flashed quickly—let Heth go forward; bring up Pender at once. It was a miniature Second Manassas! Before night Confederate independence might be closer to reality.

The men in the ranks were as willing as their commander. With a rebel yell that echoed weirdly over the Pennsylvania hills, Heth's brigades swept eastward. Shifting their advance somewhat toward the right, Pender's troops moved across the ridge, joined with Heth, and charged irresistibly over Willoughby Run. Rodes pressed on; Early swept everything before him. In forty-five minutes the battle was over. The Federals were routed and had been hurled back toward the ridges south and east of Gettysburg. The town was in Early's hands. Nearly 5000 bewildered prisoners were being herded on the field. Almost as many dead and wounded lay on the ground. A doubtful morning had ended in a smashing victory. The campaign of invasion could not have had a more auspicious opening.[8]

Riding hurriedly forward across Willoughby Run and up the next ridge, Lee halted near the point where the Chambersburg turnpike comes down from the ridge.[9] Here he had a closer view of the ground to which it was to be assumed the enemy would retreat. Half a mile away, at his feet, lay the town of Gettysburg. South of it was a high cleared hill that seemed to dominate a series of ridges that spread from it to the east and to the south. Toward this hill, in confused and demoralized masses, the defeated Federals were retreating. On the hill were blue infantry reserves and artillery. Some of Hill's guns were at once ordered up by Lee to open on these troops.[10] If more than this could be done—if the ground could be seized at once and the Federals driven from it—the Confederates would control the whole position. Could this be accomplished without bringing on the general

[8] *O. R.*, 27, part 2, pp. 316, 606, 637–38. Perhaps the clearest general narrative of the day's fighting is that of Cecil Battine: *The Crisis of the Confederacy* (cited hereafter as *Battine*), 186 *ff.*

[9] *Marshall*, 227–28. A favorite myth is that Lee climbed the next day to the cupola of the seminary, though it was being used for the wounded, and there, under the protection of the hospital-flag, directed the battle. Colonel Taylor, who knew Lee's every movement on the field, denied this as a wholly false charge (*Taylor MSS.*). There is not the slightest evidence that Lee was ever in the seminary. The story doubtless originated in the fact that he went on the 2d to the cupola of the almshouse on the other side of the town.

[10] *Taylor's General Lee*, 190; J. J. Garnett in *Brock*, 268–69.

engagement that Lee was anxious to avoid until the entire army was up? Hill, who was unhappily sick, reported that the Federals had fought with unusual tenacity[11] and that his own men were exhausted and disorganized.[12] Prisoners had been taken from two Federal corps—the I and the XI—and they stated that the whole Union army was moving on Gettysburg.[13]

Ewell, then, must undertake the advance. As Lee did not know the condition of Ewell's men or the strength of the hill from the northern approach, he did what he always did with his corps commanders in like circumstances: he issued discretionary orders. Sending Ewell an account of what he saw, he told him it was only necessary to "push those people" to get possession of the hill, and he suggested that Ewell do so, if practicable, without committing the whole army to battle.[14]

Soon after this message was sent by Major Walter H. Taylor, General Longstreet rode up. General Lee pointed out to him the enemy's position, and while he was engaged with other military duties, Longstreet made a careful survey of the front with his field-glasses. The two were, at the time, on a long hill, Seminary Ridge, that fell away to the east and then rose again to the road that led from Gettysburg to Emmitsburg. East of this road was rolling land parallel to Seminary Ridge and about three miles in length. At its southern end was an eminence of some 600 feet known as Round Top. Northeast of this, at a little distance, was a second hill, slightly lower, styled Little Round Top. At the northern end of the ridge was a high cleared position, on part of which was the burial ground of the town, which gave its name to the hill and to the ridge—an ominous name, fated soon to be all too apt, Cemetery Hill, Cemetery Ridge. From where Lee and Longstreet stood, they could see that the high ground continued eastward and southeastward from Cemetery Hill, reaching another height called Culp's Hill. The whole of the opposite ridge was, therefore, a fishhook with the shank running from south to north and with the point to the southeast. Round Top was at the end of the shank of the hook, the loop, so to speak, where the line might be joined. Cemetery Ridge was the shank, Cemetery

---

[11] *Fremantle*, 254. [12] *O. R.*, 27, part 2, p. 607.
[13] *O. R.*, 27, part 2, pp. 317–18.
[14] *O. R.*, 27, part 2, p. 318; *Taylor's General Lee*, 190.

Hill the beginning of the bend, and Culp's Hill the point. Gettysburg was directly north of the bend. It was a most formidable

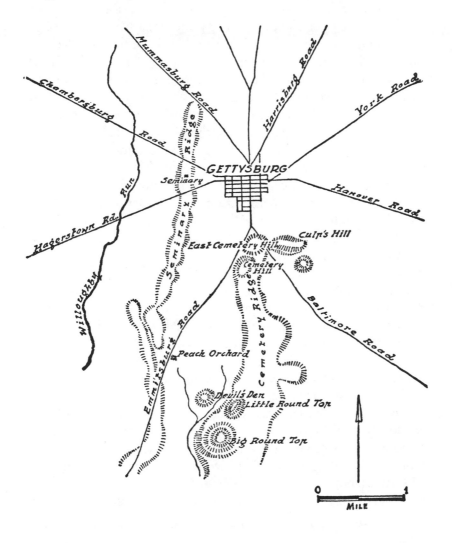

position, distant an average of about 1400 yards from Seminary
Ridge, which, in turn, afforded excellent ground for a defensive
battle.

Longstreet studied the terrain closely by the side of the chief
with whom there had not been a ripple of disagreement since

they had entered Pennsylvania;[15] but when Longstreet put down his glasses and turned to Lee, it was to assert his innate self-confidence and his faith in the plan he had formulated, ere he left Virginia, for offensive strategy and defensive tactics. Without waiting, apparently, for Lee to ask his opinion, he declared the field ideal for the course on which he had set his heart. "All we have to do," he later quoted himself as saying in substance, "is to throw our army around by their left, and we shall interpose between the Federal army and Washington. We can get a strong position and wait, and if they fail to attack us we shall have everything in condition to move back tomorrow night in the direction of Washington, selecting beforehand a good position into which we can put our troops to receive battle next day. Finding our object is Washington or that army, the Federals will be sure to attack us. When they attack, we shall beat them, as we proposed to do before we left Fredericksburg, and the probabilities are that the fruits of our success will be great." [16]

This was rather remarkable language for a subordinate to address to the commanding general, ten minutes after his arrival on the field of battle, and when he had not been advised of the strength of the enemy. It was, moreover, a proposal that involved great risks. Meade presumably was moving from the direction of Washington, but how close he was and how fully concentrated, Lee did not know and could not ascertain in the absence of his cavalry. The Southern army had been compelled to advance cautiously to Gettysburg, and had been more than fortunate in finding and in driving the enemy there. To have led the army blindly around the Federal left "would have been wildly rash." [17] The surest hope of victory, the best defensive, was to attack the two corps immediately in front, as soon as a sufficient force for

[15] Cf. Fremantle, 249: "It is impossible to please Longstreet more than by praising Lee"—June 30.

[16] 3 B. and L., 339. Besides this version, written about 1884, Longstreet inspired or dictated an earlier account, probably in 1876, published in Annals of the War, 421, and wrote a third, circa 1894, in his From Manassas to Appomattox, 358 ff. It is impossible to reconcile the three. They form a progression in General Longstreet's defense, which developed into an attack on Lee's management of the campaign. For manifest reasons the earlier versions, of course, are followed in this narrative, though a few verifiable incidents that do not appear in his previous articles are cited from Longstreet's final apologia.

[17] Maurice, 208. See also note 46, p. 82, infra.

the purpose could be brought up. To delay and to manœuvre was to gamble with ruin.

Lee therefore answered Longstreet at once: "If the enemy is there, we must attack him." [18]

Longstreet retorted sharply: "If he is there, it will be because he is anxious that we should attack him—a good reason, in my judgment, for not doing so." And he proceeded to argue his point.[19]

Lee said little more but displayed not the slightest intention of changing his plan of attacking the enemy at the earliest possible moment, before the whole of the Army of the Potomac could be brought up.[20]

At some stage of the discussion Colonel A. L. Long returned from a reconnaissance Lee had ordered him to make in front of Cemetery Hill. Long reported that the position seemed to be occupied in considerable force, with some troops behind a stone fence near the crest, and with others on the reverse slope. An attack, he said, would be hazardous and doubtful of success.[21] About the same time, Lieutenant James Power Smith arrived with a message from Ewell. He probably had passed Taylor as the latter was hurrying to the commander of the Second Corps with Lee's orders to take Cemetery Ridge if practicable. Ewell, said Smith, desired him to inform the commander that General Rodes and General Early believed they could take Cemetery Hill if they were supported on the right, and that "it would be well if Lee occupied at once the higher ground in front of our right, which seemed to command the Cemetery Hill."

"I suppose," Lee answered, "this is the higher ground to which these gentlemen refer," and, pointing to the front, he handed Smith his field-glasses. "You will find that some of those people are there now." [22]

---

[18] *Annals of the War*, 421. Here is a very striking example of the manner in which General Longstreet changed his story as he grew older. The language here quoted is from his initial account. In 3 *B. and L.*, 339, he has Lee say: "No, the enemy is there, and I am going to attack him there." In *From Manassas to Appomattox*, 358, he wrote: "I was not a little surprised, therefore, at his impatience, as, striking the air with his closed hand, he said: 'If he is there tomorrow I will attack him.'"

[19] *Annals of the War*, 421.   [20] *Annals of the War*, 421.

[21] Long in 4 *S. H. S. P.*, 66.

[22] 33 *S. H. S. P.*, 145; 43 *ibid.*, 57. Ewell evidently referred to East Cemetery Hill; the "higher ground" was Cemetery Hill proper.

After Smith had looked, Lee went on. "Our people are not yet up, and I have no troops with which to occupy this higher ground."

Then he turned to Longstreet with a question that officer had not previously given him opportunity of asking: Where on the road were the troops of the First Corps? But Longstreet was angry because his counsel had been rejected, and he was not disposed to be communicative. McLaws's division, he said, was about six miles away, but beyond that he was indefinite and non-committal.

Lee urged him to bring his corps up as rapidly as possible, and turning to Smith gave him this message to Ewell: Smith was to tell Ewell that Lee did not then have troops to support him on the right, but that Lee wished Ewell to take Cemetery Hill if it was possible. He added that he would ride over to see Ewell very shortly.[23]

Longstreet did not like this either. Although the troops about whose position he was so vague were those on whom Lee would naturally rely for an assault on the western flank of Cemetery Hill, Longstreet argued—then or before this time—that if Lee intended to attack, he should do so immediately.[24]

Lee explained again his reasons for not making the attack at once and expressed regret that the non-arrival of Imboden at Chambersburg had forced him to leave Pickett's division there. A general assault must wait until the arrival of at least McLaws's and Hood's divisions of the First Corps.

Longstreet had no more to say, thinking that Lee might later change his mind and make no attack,[25] and presently "Old Pete" rode off. It was now about 5:30 P.M. Firing had ceased along the whole front. Major Taylor had returned and had reported the delivery of Lee's message to Ewell,[26] but there was no sign of any

---

[23] 33 *S. H. S. P.*, 145; 43 *S. H. S. P.*, 57. There are slight differences in the order of Lee's remarks in these two accounts by Smith, but the variations are not material.

[24] This part of the interview is not narrated in either of Longstreet's earlier accounts, but it is of record that he complained later in the evening to Doctor J. S. D. Cullen that "it would have been better had we not fought at all than to have left undone what we did." (See Cullen's letter in *Annals of the War*, 439.) In his third version (*op. cit.*, 359), Longstreet stated that he objected to deferring the attack. The sequence of the various parts of this conversation between Lee and Longstreet is in some doubt. Longstreet affirmed that he made his protest before the message was sent to Ewell and he may be correct in this, but it could hardly have been long before Smith left.

[25] *Longstreet*, 359.   [26] *Taylor's General Lee*, 190.

effort on the part of Ewell to storm Cemetery Hill. To ascertain precisely the state of affairs on the front of the Second Corps, Lee rode over to Gettysburg and soon found Ewell and Rodes together. In the arbor back of a little house north of the town on the Carlisle road, he sat down with them to hear their reports.[27]

Their statements showed all too plainly that the new organization of the Second Corps was operating very clumsily. Two of Rodes's brigade commanders had failed badly in the attack that Lee had witnessed. Colonel Edward O'Neal of Alabama had stayed with his rear regiment while the other three had been almost useless in the fight. General Iverson had been misled by a foolish report that one of his regiments had raised the white flag and had gone over to the enemy.[28] Rodes had lost nearly 2500 men and found himself, at the end of the action, on ground from which he did not believe he could advance directly on Cemetery Hill.[29] Early had a better position, but after his first successful onslaught, his progress had been held up by panicky reports from an inexperienced brigadier that troops were advancing on the York road against his left flank.[30] Worse still, Ewell had been irresolute. He had been thrown off his balance, early in the day, by the receipt of discretionary instructions to march either on Gettysburg or on Cashtown, as circumstances might dictate. Accustomed to explicit orders, he had complained then of what he termed the ambiguity of Lee's directions and had for a time been undecided what to do.[31] After he had reached Gettysburg he had remained passive in the streets awaiting orders. So contrary was such a halt to the traditions of the fast-moving Second Corps that one of the staff officers of the dead "Stonewall" had said sorrowfully to his mates, "Jackson is not here!"[32]

Early had already established by his positive manner a singular domination over the mind of Ewell and he had promptly urged that Hays's brigade, which had an excellent position, should be allowed to advance at once and take Cemetery Hill, but Ewell had hesitated.[33] The fiery Trimble, who had joined Ewell and

[27] 4 S. H. S. P., pp. 257, 271; 3 C. M. H., 403.
[28] O. R., 27, part 2, pp. 444–45, 553–55.   [29] O. R., 27, part 2, p. 555.
[30] O. R., 27, part 2, p. 469; 4 S. H. S. P., 255–56.
[31] 26 S. H. S. P., 122.   [32] 33 S. H. S. P., 144.
[33] 4 S. H. S. P., 254. For Hays's statement that he believed the hill could have been taken, see Annals of the War, 436.

was acting as a volunteer aide, had at length lost all patience and had pleaded, "Give me a division and I will engage to take that hill." When Ewell had declined, Trimble had said, "Give me a brigade and I will do it!" Still Ewell had refused. "Give me a good regiment," Trimble had cried, "and I will engage to take that hill." After Ewell had again withheld consent, Trimble is alleged to have thrown down his sword and to have left Ewell, swearing he would not serve under such an officer.[34] Ewell had explained to Early that he wished to wait until the arrival of Johnson's division, before he attacked, but by his delay he had lost an opportunity of seizing easily the position on Cemetery Hill that was the key to victory.[35]

All this had been before 4 P.M. A little later, when Johnson had arrived half a mile north of Gettysburg, in rear of Rodes's division, Ewell had inquired of Early where he thought Johnson should be placed. Early had advised that Johnson seize Culp's Hill at once, but Ewell had continued irresolute and had insisted on making a reconnaissance.[36] False reports had continued to come in from straggling cavalrymen of enemy movements in rear of his left flank; Ewell had "seemed at a loss as to what opinion to form." [37]

These provoking details, of course, were not related to Lee when he went into conference with Ewell and Rodes, but it was manifest that Ewell had abandoned all intention of attacking that evening. Equally must it have been plain to Lee, despite his lack of close acquaintance with the man, that Ewell's new responsibilities had sapped his powers of decision.

Soon Early arrived, by Ewell's order, and the conversation turned to the operations of the next day.

---

[34] R. H. McKim, in 40 *S. H. S. P.*, 273. General Trimble, 26 *S. H. S. P.*, 123, did not mention this exchange, though he stated that Ewell "moved about uneasily, a good deal excited. . . . He . . . was far from composure."

[35] 4 *S. H. S. P.*, 257. For the statement of Generals Hunt and Hancock that the hill could readily have been taken prior to the arrival of Hancock at 4 P.M., see 3 *B. and L.*, 284; 5 *S. H. S. P.*, 168. Colonel Bachelder (*ibid.*, 172 *ff.*), expressed the opinion that the position was not secure against attack until 6 P.M.

[36] 4 *S. H. S. P.*, 255–56, 257. Johnson had marched twenty-five miles that day (*C. R.*, 27, part 2, p. 503).

[37] Early in 4 *S. H. S. P.*, 256. It should be added that while Early recorded these evidences of Ewell's indecision, he seems not to have been aware of their relation to the failure of Lee's campaign, and, in the article here quoted, he argued lengthily that the inaction of the Second Corps, after the first success, was not responsible for the loss of the battle.

"Can't you, with your corps, attack on this flank tomorrow?" Lee asked.

Ewell said nothing; Early took the floor. Anxious as he had been during the afternoon to engage the enemy, he argued now that the approaches were very difficult. The Federals, he said would certainly concentrate in front of Ewell during the night, inasmuch as the divisions of the Second Corps were the only troops in close proximity to them. An attack, he contended, would be most costly and of doubtful issue. The ground was more favorable to an attack south of Gettysburg, Early maintained, and if an offensive there resulted in the capture of the Round Tops, which he pointed out through the gathering dusk, the Confederates would dominate the entire field.

Ewell and Rodes acquiesced in this view. After some discussion, Lee inquired: "Then perhaps I had better draw you around towards our right, as the line will be very long and thin if you remain here, and the enemy may come down and break through?"

Again it was Early who answered, not Ewell, and it was pride, not tactics, that shaped his reply. He felt that his men had won a victory and that they would consider their success empty if they were ordered to give up the ground they had gained. Besides, he could not move his seriously wounded. Lee need not fear, he asserted, that the enemy would break through. The Second Corps could hold its own against any troops that might be sent down from the hills to attack it. Early did not think then or thereafter that his answer carried with it any implication of unwillingness to have Ewell's men do their part in the battle; but if the old commander of those troops, sleeping in his newly made grave at Lexington, had heard Early, he would have risen wrathfully in the cerements of death at the suggestion that the Second Corps could remain inactive when victory lay just over the crest of Cemetery Hill.

Lee must have been disappointed at Early's answer and must have been puzzled to note a moment later that Ewell, though he had been schooled under Jackson and had fought in the Valley, contented himself with merely agreeing that Early was right. Lee pondered their proposal, his head bent low. An attack

79

on the right . . . Hill's corps badly battered. . . . "Well," he said at length, more to himself than to them, "if I attack from my right, Longstreet will have to make the attack." Then he raised his head: "Longstreet is a very good fighter when he gets in position and gets everything ready, but he is so slow."[38] Lee had expressed the same opinion of Longstreet to Custis[39] and he voiced it privately after the war,[40] but he probably would not have made such a statement in the presence of other officers if he had not been thrown off his guard by the perplexities that developed when first Longstreet and then the commanders of the Second Corps balked at an offensive, the chosen and tested tactical method of the Army of Northern Virginia.

Early went on to explain that if an attack were made on the right, the Second Corps would follow up the success and destroy the enemy's right. Lee was not wholly convinced that the chiefs of the corps were correct in their stand, but, tentatively, he accepted their view and left them, ere long, with the understanding that the attack was to be made on the right as early as practicable the next morning, and that the left wing was to press the enemy and pursue any advantage that might be gained.[41]

After Lee returned to Seminary Ridge and received the reports of reconnaissance made during the late afternoon, he became dissatisfied with the decision he had reached in council with Ewell and he sought an opportunity of reviewing his whole problem. Anderson's division was now up, and Hill's corps was complete. So was Ewell's. Longstreet should be able to have McLaws's division on the ground by daylight, along with all Hood's, except Law's brigade, which would arrive from New Guilford during the forenoon. The time of the arrival of Pickett's division would depend on when Imboden reached Chambersburg. So much for the infantry. As for the cavalry, Jenkins's brigade was close at hand, and word had been received—at last!—from Stuart. He was at Carlisle, whither messengers had been sent to hurry his

---

[38] Early in 4 *S. H. S. P.*, 274. Early was challenged for attributing this language to Lee, but in 5 *S. H. S. P.*, 274, he insisted that he had used Lee's words.

[39] Personal statement of W. Gordon McCabe.   [40] 5 *S. H. S. P.*, 193.

[41] For other accounts of the conference, see *Long*, 292–93; Walter H. Taylor in 4 *S. H. S. P.*, 83 and in *Four Years*, 96–97. See also *Early*, 271, and Early in *Jones*, 31 ff., and in *O. R.*, 27, part 2, pp. 469–70.

march.[42] He would not, however, be available until late on the 2d. Lee, therefore, would have about 50,000 infantry and some 2000 of Jenkins's cavalry available early on the morning of July 2. All the reinforcements he could hope to receive thereafter, if he delayed the battle, would be Stuart's weary horse and about 7000 infantry. If, then, he was to take the offensive, his first judgment expressed to Longstreet when they met on Seminary Ridge was confirmed—he must strike as soon as possible, and before the whole of the Federal army arrived in his front.[43]

But was it wise to attack at all? What alternatives were there? He could take Longstreet's advice and move around to the right, interposing his army between Meade and the approaches to Washington. Secondly, he could await attack where he was. Thirdly, he could retreat by the route on which he had advanced.

As he had come through the passes west of Gettysburg, it will be remembered that Lee had admired their strength and had told Anderson that he could withdraw, if necessary, and defend the gorges. But now that he had nearly the whole of his army east of the mountains he realized that any attempt to evacuate his troops and his wagon train, in the face of a foe who had not been crippled by his blows, would be difficult and dangerous.[44]

He could not afford to await attack, living off the country, because the enemy could easily seize the gaps in the mountains and confine his foraging parties to a very narrow area.[45]

The only alternative to a direct attack before the enemy was fully concentrated was, therefore, to move to the right, turn the

---

[42] O. R., 27, part 2, pp. 308, 697; 37 S. H. S. P., 96.

[43] The strength of Lee at Gettysburg has been a subject of much discussion. The Count of Paris computed that Lee fought with 62,000 to 63,000, against 80,000 or 82,000 (6 S. H. S. P., 12). Early (ibid., 13 ff.) maintained that the battle-strength of the Army of Northern Virginia was 59,500, and that after the arrival of Lockwood's and Stannard's brigades on the morning of July 2, Meade had 82,208. Taylor (5 S. H. S. P., 246) gave Lee 67,000 at the climax of the battle and insisted that Meade had 105,000. Colonel William Allan estimated Lee's strength at 60,000 (see 4 S. H. S. P., 41). Battine (op. cit., 281) put the Confederate infantry at 57,000 and the Federal at 67,000. Alexander (op. cit., 368–70) took the Confederate figures for May 31, 76,224 and accepted Livermore's deduction of 7 per cent for the infantry and artillery and of 15 per cent for the cavalry. This would give Lee 61,417 infantry, less the casualties of July 1, and 8751 cavalry, a total force of 70,168. On the same basis, the strength of the Federals, excluding casualties of July 1, would be 105,990. Putting the Confederate losses on July 1 at 5000, and allowing 7000 for the Pickett's division and Law's brigade, Lee would have had 49,000 infantry and artillery on the morning of July 2 according to Alexander's computation. The writer's estimate is about 1000 higher.

[44] O. R., 27, part 2, p. 318.   [45] O. R., 27. part 2, p. 318.

flank of Meade and get between him and Washington. But if this were undertaken at once it would have to be done in the absence of the greater part of the cavalry. It would entail a wide flanking march against an enemy of whose position he was still uncertain and could only learn through Jenkins's inexperienced troopers. Such a march, moreover, would necessitate a continuous concentration, with no chance of foraging for the army. If Lee considered such a move a second time, after having dismissed it in his conversation with Longstreet, he definitely abandoned it later in the day as impracticable, and in this decision he has since been sustained by nearly all military critics. Marshal McMahon attempted somewhat the same movement seven years later, without his cavalry—and came to Sedan.[46]

Strategically, then, Lee saw no alternative to attacking the enemy before Meade concentrated, much as he disliked to force a general engagement so early in the campaign and at such a distance from Virginia.[47]

Tactically, what was the best plan? Manifestly, Ewell was not disposed to undertake an assault on Cemetery Hill from the north. If Ewell, Early, and Rodes were agreed that it could not be done, then manifestly it would not be done. But an attack on the right, opposite Cemetery Ridge, to be followed up on the left, as tentatively agreed upon in conference with Ewell—was this the wisest course? Late reconnaissance reports did not discourage an attack on the right;[48] but would Ewell be able to co-operate effectively? Or would the Second Corps simply be left idle while the rest of the army fought? Lee's doubts increased on reflection. It seemed better to shorten the line, to concentrate heavily on the right and to throw the three corps

---

[46] G. F. R. Henderson: *The Science of War*, 290. For detailed explanations of the impracticability of the move, as proposed by Longstreet, see Early in 4 *S. H. S. P.*, 60, and 5 *ibid.*, 285; William Allan in 3 *B. and L.*, 355; *Maurice*, 206–7; 2 *Davis*, 447; Hunt in 3 *B. and L.*, 293; Long in 4 *S. H. S. P.*, 123. Meade in 3 *B. and L.*, 413, was the only critic who agreed with Longstreet. He said that Longstreet's proposal was "sound military sense" and the step he feared Lee would take, but added that he prepared for it by putting the Army of the Potomac in condition to move from the heights if Lee tried to interpose between him and Washington. It should be noted that Colonel McIntosh in 37 *S. H. S. P.*, 140, affirmed that Lee's retreat after Gettysburg showed that Lee was wrong in saying he could not withdraw through the mountains. McIntosh, however, overlooked the difference between pursuit by an enemy badly crippled after three days' fighting and pursuit by a fresh army, damaged only by the action of July 1.

[47] *O. R.*, 27, part 2, p. 318.   [48] *Cf. O. R.*, 27, part 2, p. 446.

against that position, rather than to operate on a long exterior line.

Having reached this conclusion, Lee sent a message to Ewell, telling him that the ground looked favorable on the right and that, if he could do nothing where he was, he should move during the night and reinforce that flank.[49] In answer to this message, Ewell rode over late in the evening. He explained that two of his lieutenants had reconnoitred Culp's Hill at the point of the fish-hook and had found it unoccupied by the enemy. If allowed to stay where he was, Ewell believed that Johnson could capture that eminence, which overlooked Cemetery Hill.

This at once changed the outlook. For, obviously, if Ewell could take Culp's Hill and thereby keep the Federals from using Cemetery Hill for an enfilading fire on the troops that were to attack Cemetery Ridge, the Second Corps could be profitably employed where it was. Lee therefore cancelled the orders for Ewell to move to the right and directed him to take Culp's Hill as soon as practicable.[50]

Longstreet was with Lee during the evening[51] while this change in plan was being matured. Lee gave him no positive order to attack at any particular point the next morning, yet Longstreet must have known that Lee wished the First Corps brought up as rapidly as possible. He must have understood, also, that Lee intended to attack as soon as it arrived, in the hope of driving the Federals from their position before the whole of the Army of the Potomac was concentrated in his front. In dealing with Longstreet—as with Jackson until his death—it was not Lee's custom to give explicit orders on the field of battle:[52] he had been

---

49 O. R., 27, part 2, p. 446. Marshall, op. cit., 232, said that after his interview with Ewell, Early, and Rodes, Lee contemplated a movement around the left flank of the enemy, but evidently he confused the orders to Ewell, which plainly anticipated an attack by the Confederate right, with Longstreet's proposal for a turning-movement.

50 O. R., 27, part 2, p. 446; Longstreet, 360. There is some doubt whether Johnson was actually preparing to take Culp's Hill when Ewell received orders from Lee to move to the right, but the weight of the evidence is strongly that Johnson's movement came later. Ewell's report, loc. cit., certainly indicated that no order cancelling any such operation, on the basis of Lee's instruction, had been sent Johnson. For the details, see Taylor's Four Years, 96; Alexander, 386, and Early in 4 S. H. S. P., 261–63.

51 He stated, Annals of the War, 422, that he "left General Lee quite late on the night of the 1st."

52 Cf. Longstreet in Annals of the War, 422: "General Lee never, in his life, gave me orders to open an attack at a specific hour. He was perfectly satisfied that, when I had my troops in position, and was ordered to attack, no time was ever lost."

83

content to outline his plan and to express his wishes in the belief that his corps commanders would arrange the details more accurately than he would be able to do. He simply followed his established practice when he refrained on the night of July 1 from giving Longstreet direct orders to have his men at the front by a given hour. It never occurred to him that Longstreet would make his commander's usual deference an excuse for delaying a movement he disapproved.[53]

The plan was discussed at Lee's headquarters, and seemed to be fully understood. As Longstreet had to bring up his troops and deliver the major blow, whereas Ewell's men were already at hand for their lesser part in the enterprise, Lee decided to time Ewell's movements by Longstreet's. Toward midnight, a courier went off with orders to Ewell not to attack until he heard Longstreet's guns open.[54] "Gentlemen," said Lee to some of his weary officers, by way of final announcement, "we will attack the enemy as early in the morning as practicable."[55]

Then, under a pale moon that gave a weird light to the field,[56] Lee retired to a small house east of Seminary Ridge, and just north of the Chambersburg pike, for a few hours' rest. In the nearby orchard his staff made their bivouac.[57] On the ridges about headquarters and in the fields outside the anxious town, most of the Confederate soldiers were already asleep. To the westward, Hood and McLaws had halted their weary columns. From the south, Federal corps were marching fast over shadowed roads. Groaning wagon trains were bringing up shell and food for the Army of the Potomac. But the issue did not depend solely on valor, strategy, tactics, logistics, and the weight of numbers. Half-

---

[53] This is one of the most controverted points in the Confederate dispute over the causes of Lee's failure at Gettysburg. The charge that Lee ordered Longstreet to attack at sunrise, and that Longstreet disobeyed positive orders in failing to do so, rests on the testimony of General W. N. Pendleton. He stated in a lecture long after the war that Lee told him on the night of July 1 that he had given Longstreet orders to this effect (*Pendleton*, 286). President Davis accepted Pendleton's statement (2 *Davis*, 441). There is no doubt that General Pendleton so understood General Lee, but there is no supporting evidence that Lee directly gave the order to Longstreet. Longstreet's denial appears in *Annals of the War*, 422, 437. Taylor in his *Four Years*, 100–101, and in *Annals of the War*, 311, sustained Longstreet's claim. So did Venable in 4 *S. H. S. P.*, 289. Long also had no knowledge of positive orders, but was satisfied Lee intended to attack early (4 *S. H. S. P.*, 288). For the general argument that Lee purposed to take the offensive as soon as practicable on July 2, see Early in 4 *S. H. S. P.*, 269, 387–88; 5 *ibid.*, 279–80.

[54] O. R., 27, part 2, p. 446.

[55] *Long*, 277. Cf. Long in 4 *S. H. S. P.*, 67, 288.

[56] White in *Richmond Howitzers*, 202.   [57] *Marshall*, 233; *Long*, 277.

determined already, by Ewell's irresolution, the battle was being decided at that very hour in the mind of Longstreet, who at his camp, a few miles away, was eating his heart away in sullen resentment that Lee had rejected his long-cherished plan of a strategic offensive and a tactical defensive.

CHAPTER VII

"What Can Detain Longstreet?"

LEE was up and at breakfast before daylight on July 2, and soon he had his officers scurrying off to make reconnaissance for the attack. Captain Samuel R. Johnston of the Engineers was sent at 4 o'clock to examine the ground over which the assault was to be made.[1] Colonel Long and General Pendleton were directed to see that the artillery was well placed.[2]

Then Lee rode out to a post of observation on Seminary Ridge to answer for himself the question on which the probability of defeat or success most hung—the question of how heavily the Federals had reinforced their troops on Cemetery Ridge during the night.

Eagerly Lee put his glasses to his eyes and studied in the growing light the long hillside in front of him. He could not have asked for a better prospect than that which greeted him. The Federals were still on Cemetery Hill, but so far as he could see, nearly all the ridge south of the hill was bare! The two corps that had been defeated the previous afternoon had not yet been strengthened. Ewell had intercepted a message during the night showing that Sykes's V Corps had been four miles east of Gettysburg at 12:30 A.M. and was to march at 4 o'clock. As this dispatch had been addressed to Major General H. W. Slocum, commanding the XII Corps, it was to be assumed that Slocum's men were close at hand also.[3] But neither corps was up yet—and if Longstreet was ready to attack, the ridge could be taken and the remnant of the I and XI Corps destroyed.

Lee turned and looked for Longstreet's veterans, who, by this time, should be shaping their gray lines along the slope from

---

[1] 5 S. H. S. P., 183. [2] Long, 280–81; O. R., 27, part 2, p. 350.
[3] For the capture of the dispatch from Sykes to Slocum, see O. R., 27, part 2, p. 446; for the text, see ibid., part 3, p. 483. No report seems to have reached Lee at sunrise on the morning of July 2 that the III Corps had arrived (see O. R., 27, part 1, p. 369).

86

which they were to advance. But they were not there, not a man of them. Although their commander had been ordered the previous afternoon to hasten his march, when one division was then only about six miles away,[4] there was not a sign of the approach of the leading brigade.

Was the opportunity to be lost because of Longstreet's slowness? Would the V and XII Corps reach Cemetery Ridge before McLaws and Hood arrived opposite them? What could be done? Could Ewell attack meantime, and if not, would it be wise to revert to the plan formulated and rejected the previous day, and to bring the Second Corps to the right, in case Longstreet delayed so long that the full strength of the army would be required to drive from the heights the Federals who would soon occupy them? Feeling that the golden minutes were slipping through his fingers, Lee hurried Major Venable off to Ewell to inquire what his prospects were, and to tell him that the question was whether all the troops should be transferred to the right.[5]

Soon after Venable had ridden off, General Longstreet arrived on the ridge.[6] The head of his column was not far behind, but the start had been most leisurely and the two divisions were spread out for a long distance on the Chambersburg road. Longstreet not only was late but was in a bad humor besides. As soon as he saw that the Federals were still in position on Cemetery Hill, he renewed his argument for a turning movement to get between the enemy and Washington. The fact that Lee had informed him the previous afternoon of his intention to attack Cemetery Ridge did not deter him from again insisting that his own plan was better.[7] Lee listened courteously, but continued unshaken in his belief that a battle had become in a measure inevitable, and

---

[4] 33 *S. H. S. P.*, 145.

[5] Venable in *Annals of the War*, 438. General Early (4 *S. H. S. P.*, 291), cited Venable's statement as proof that Lee had become satisfied on the morning of the 2d that Longstreet was averse to attacking and that he had to devise a substitute plan, but it seems almost certain that Longstreet did not arrive until after Venable had left. Ewell's reference to his orders in *O. R.*, 27, part 2, p. 446, indicated that he confused the message Venable brought him with the instructions Lee gave later in the morning

[6] For the evidence as to the time of Longstreet's arrival at Gettysburg on the morning of July 2, see Appendix III—2.

[7] *Annals of the War*, 422; 3 *B. and L.*, 340. In his third narrative of the battle, *From Manassas to Appomattox*, 362–63, Longstreet said nothing about his advocacy of his own plan on the morning of the 2d. He there represented himself as ready to execute orders Lee was not ready to issue.

that an instant offensive might yield so decisive a victory as to justify the risks.[8]

As Longstreet argued and Lee waited for the arrival of McLaws and Hood, Federal reinforcements began to file into position on Cemetery Ridge. Minute by minute their strength increased until it soon was apparent that instead of occupying the ridge without resistance, Lee had to reshape his plans so as to take it in the face of the enemy's opposition, and with the least interference from Cemetery Hill. As he studied the terrain, he observed that there were two excellent positions on the Emmitsburg road, which ran for part of its length on high ground between the two main ridges. One of these positions was directly west of Round Top and the other at a peach orchard on the farm of J. Want. Lee reasoned that if he extended his right until he was opposite Round Top, he would get beyond the Federal left. Then, by advancing up the Emmitsburg road, he could seize the peach orchard, plant his artillery there and cover an attack on that section of the ridge occupied by the foe. In this way he would be able to escape an enfilade from the guns on Cemetery Hill for much of the distance of advance. If his move up the ridge did not drive the Federals from that position, he might have to make a frontal attack on the upper end of the ridge. This might be subject to enfilade from the hill, but if, meantime, he was astride the lower end of the ridge he would have an enfilade of his own against the left flank of the Federals who were opposing a direct attack from Seminary Ridge. If Ewell could advance and seize Cemetery Hill, he could stop all Federal flank fire.

To ponder this plan, Lee left Longstreet and walked alone among the trees. As he paced back and forth, engrossed in his thoughts, still more Federals arrived on Cemetery Ridge and disappeared behind the fences that covered its sides. More eyes and more field glasses were fixed on them now, for numbers of Lee's officers were coming up to report. Hill was there. So was Heth, his head bound up from a wound received the previous day. The foreign observers were intent witnesses. Two of them were perched in a tree, studying the Federal position.[9] Soon General Hood arrived, ahead of his troops, and sought out Lee.

[8] *O. R.*, 27, part 2, pp. 308, 318.   [9] *Owen*, 244; *Ross*, 49; *Fremantle*, 257.

"The enemy is here," Lee told him, "and if we do not whip him, he will whip us." Hood interpreted this to mean that Lee was anxious to attack forthwith, but Longstreet, who must have overheard the remark, hastened to say privately to Hood, "The General is a little nervous this morning; he wishes me to attack; I do not wish to do so without Pickett. I never like to go into battle with one boot off." [10] This was an admission that Longstreet, in the face of Lee's known wishes, desired to delay the action indefinitely, for there was no certainty concerning the hour of Pickett's arrival.

At length, when General McLaws rode up to report his column nearby, Lee sent for him and explained his tactical plan of extending the Confederate right across the Emmitsburg road, beyond the Federal left flank so that he could sweep up the ridge. "General," he said, "I wish you to place your division across this road," indicating the place on the map, and then pointing to it across the open country. "And I wish you to get there if possible without being seen by the enemy. Can you do it?"

"I know of nothing to prevent me," said McLaws, "but I will take a party of skirmishers and go in advance and reconnoitre."

"Major Johnston of my staff," Lee continued, "has been ordered to reconnoitre the ground, and I expect he is about ready."

"I will go with him," McLaws said.

Longstreet, who had been stalking up and down, came up at this juncture and broke in, "No, sir," he said to General McLaws, "I do not wish you to leave your division." Pointing to the map, he said, "I wish your division placed so." He apparently thought Lee intended a frontal assault on Cemetery Ridge, for he indicated a line in a direction perpendicular to that Lee had traced.

"No, General," said Lee, quietly, "I wish it placed just opposite."

McLaws observed that Longstreet was "irritated and annoyed," but he did not presume to ask the reason. Instead, he repeated his request to reconnoitre with Johnston. Longstreet peremptorily refused. Lee said nothing further, and McLaws, somewhat bewildered, went off to put his division temporarily under cover.[11]

What was Lee to do in the face of such temper and antagonism?

---

[10] *Hood*, 57.
[11] McLaws in 7 *S. H. S. P.*, 68. McLaws quoted Lee as styling Johnston "major," but actually Johnston did not attain that rank as an engineer until March 17, 1864.

Had he been Jackson, he would of course have relieved Long-street of command without further ado and would himself have directed the operations of the First Corps. But that was not Lee's method of dealing with his lieutenants. Never in his whole career did he order a general officer under arrest. It was his practice to make the best of their shortcomings, to reason with them when possible, and to appeal to their better impulses. In this instance, if he felt any resentment, he did not show it. Instead, he assumed that Longstreet would do his duty. He simply ignored the insubordination. And, indeed, had he been stirred by any other impulse, what could he have done with a battle imminent? He had no one to replace Longstreet. Already two of his three corps were under new commanders. Had Long-street been relieved, the First Corps would have passed under the control of General McLaws, whose lack of dash at Salem Church was a warning of what might be expected if heavier responsi-bilities were placed on him. Costly as were Longstreet's delay and stubborn self-opinion, it was better to shove him into battle, knowing that he would fight well when actually engaged, than to risk the lives of 15,000 good troops under a less capable leader.

Lee's handling of an awkward situation seemed justified by the immediate reaction. Soon after the colloquy, Colonel Alex-ander came up and reported that the artillery of the First Corps was arriving on Seminary Ridge. Longstreet at once gave him instructions, in Lee's hearing, to place the batteries where Lee wished them stationed.[12]

In the expectation that Longstreet would recover his balance and dispose his troops for an immediate attack, Lee now left him and rode over toward Gettysburg to see the situation on Ewell's front. Captain Justus Scheibert, the Prussian observer, who had been with Lee at Chancellorsville and had noticed his quiet demeanor on that field, remarked after the war that "in the days at Gettysburg, this quiet self-possessed calmness was wanting." Lee, he said, "was not at his ease, but was riding to and fro, frequently changing his position, making anxious inquiries here and there, and looking careworn." [13] Longstreet also insisted that Lee "lost the matchless equipoise that usually characterized

[12] 3 B. and L., 358.   [13] 5 S. H. S. P., 92.

him." [14] There were those who disputed this and maintained that Lee was "never quicker in his perception or clearer in his judgment." [15] But if there was any relaxation in Lee's self-mastery, who could have wondered greatly at it in the remembrance of what he had encountered in the way of obstinacy, tardiness, and irresolution since he had reached Gettysburg? Something was amiss with the reorganized army, especially with the corps command, the most important part of the whole military mechanism.

It must have been about 9 o'clock when Lee reached Ewell's headquarters in the outskirts of Gettysburg.[16] He found that Ewell was out reconnoitring his front with Colonel Venable, whom Lee had sent to him earlier in the morning. General Trimble was at hand, however—for he had not executed his threat to quit Ewell—and when Lee asked to be taken to some point from which he could get a good view of the enemy's position, Trimble conducted him to the cupola of the almshouse. Thence, as he looked, Lee could see that the Federals on Cemetery Hill had improved their ground greatly during the night. "The enemy have the advantage of us in a short and inside line," he said to Trimble, "and we are too much extended. We did not or could not pursue our advantage of yesterday and now the enemy are in a good position."

Descending from his lookout, he soon met Ewell and repeated to him what he had said to Trimble. As he encountered other officers, his language was the same. Trimble noticed how Lee kept repeating the words, "we did not or could not pursue our advantage." It seemed to Trimble that Lee was expressing in this manner his regret that his first plan of crushing the advanced guard of the enemy had not been executed. More probably this was Lee's diplomatic manner of suggesting that, though the Second Corps had failed to do all that it might have done on the 1st, it must not fail in decision and co-ordination now.[17]

[14] *Annals of the War,* 433.   [15] Wilcox in 6 *S. H. S. P.,* 123–24.
[16] Trimble in 26 *S. H. S. P.,* 125; *Longstreet,* 363; *Long,* 281, and Long in 4 *S. H. S. P.,* 67. Longstreet (*Annals of the War,* 422) stated that Lee remained on Seminary Ridge only a short time after sunrise, but he corrected this in his last version. He is confirmed in this correction by other witnesses. Doctor Cullen stated (*Annals of the War,* 439) that he saw Lee and Longstreet together on Seminary Ridge after sunrise and that they were still there when he returned, some two hours later.
[17] 26 *S. H. S. P.,* 125. Trimble added that Lee held a consultation and determined to move Ewell to the extreme right. In this, however, it is manifest that Trimble confused the events of the evening of July 1 with those of the morning of July 2.

Lee found no change in Ewell's position, except that Johnson's division was in line of battle far to the left, opposite Culp's Hill. Nothing had happened to better the prospects of an attack on the left.[18] Colonel Long, who came to Ewell's post in a short time, after having made a careful survey of the artillery positions from the centre to the left, had discovered no opening.

Lee was hoping that Longstreet would soon open the attack, and as the minutes passed in silence all along the front,[19] he began to get restless. After a time he reiterated his orders to Ewell: The Second Corps was to make a demonstration when Longstreet attacked and was to assume the offensive if it found an opportunity.[20] Then, visibly chafing at Longstreet's continued delay in advancing, he started back with Long toward the centre, in order to make a closer reconnaissance of Cemetery Ridge. When he reached a point where he could get something of a view of the high ground, he found that the enemy was rapidly strengthening his position, and that the chances of a successful attack were fast slipping away. "What *can* detain Longstreet!" he exclaimed toward 10 o'clock. "He ought to be in position now." [21]

As Lee rode on toward Seminary Ridge he came to one of the gun positions of Colonel R. Lindsay Walker, chief of artillery of the Third Corps. Observing Major W. T. Poague with Walker, he reprimanded him sharply for not hurrying with his batteries to the right. When Poague explained that he was attached to the Third Corps, not to the First, Lee apologized and asked eagerly, "Do you know where General Longstreet is?" Walker replied that he thought he knew where Longstreet was and offered to guide Lee. "As we rode together," Walker has recorded, "General Lee manifested more impatience than I ever saw him exhibit upon any other occasion; seemed very much disappointed and worried that the attack had not opened earlier, and very anxious for Longstreet to attack at the very earliest possible moment. He even, for a little while, placed himself at the head of one of the brigades to hurry the column forward." [22]

---

[18] *Cf.* Venable in *Annals of the War*, 438.   [19] *Cf. Cooke*, 310.   [20] *Long*, 281.
[21] *Long*, 281. Taylor, in *Four Years*, 99, verified Long's statement that Lee was disturbed over Longstreet's tardiness.
[22] 5 *S. H. S. P.*, 181.

When Lee at last located Longstreet it was 11 o'clock or later.[23] One glance was enough to show Lee he had been disappointed in his expectation that Longstreet would act to carry out his wishes. The commander of the First Corps had done nothing except to dispose his artillery and to deploy McLaws's division closer at hand.[24] Although most of Longstreet's troops, by his order, had delayed their start until after sunrise, their march had been only four or five miles, and the last of them had now been at hand, or close in rear, for more than three hours. During all that time the Federals had been visibly increasing in number on Cemetery Ridge. And Longstreet had been content to wait in the face of the known wishes of the commanding general that he attack as early as practicable! It was incredible but it was the fact, and it left Lee no alternative to ordering the attack it was manifest Longstreet was endeavoring to delay. Lee therefore told Longstreet in plain terms what he wanted him to do and directed him to move against the enemy with the troops he then had on the field.[25]

Still assuming, despite the delay, that his positive orders would be carried out, Lee did not wait to see them executed, but rode off again to make a further reconnaissance, this time on the right, where a small Federal column was reported to be holding a position in the woods near Anderson's front.[26] Soon, however, he met General Pendleton and learned that the enemy had been driven out by Wilcox's brigade, which had extended its front and was ready to co-operate in the attack Longstreet was to make.[27] By this time, noon had passed. Still seeing nothing of Longstreet's

[23] *Long,* 281–82, said that Lee searched until 1 o'clock for Longstreet, but he was certainly mistaken in this. Longstreet (*From Manassas to Appomattox,* 353) affirmed that it was 10 o'clock when Lee returned and 11 o'clock when he gave the order for the advance, but there are abundant witnesses that Lee was at Ewell's headquarters about 9 A.M. The incidents that are known to have occurred before Lee's return could hardly have consumed less than two hours. In *Annals of the War,* 422, Longstreet stated that Lee returned from the Confederate left at 9 A.M.—an impossibility.

[24] *Cf.* Fremantle, 257. Longstreet (*From Manassas to Appomattox,* 363) indirectly gave as his chief reason for delay the alleged fact that the "engineer who had been sent to reconnoiter" had not returned. His reference is either to Captain Johnston or to General Pendleton, more probably to the former; but Johnston had completed his reconnaissance early and had reported to Longstreet at 9 A.M. (5 *S. H. S. P.,* 183). General Pendleton had already communicated both to Lee and to Longstreet his opinion that the enemy's positions on the right could be stormed (Pendleton's report, *O. R.,* 27, part 2, p. 350).

[25] Longstreet, *op. cit.,* 364–65, with the intimation that Lee had only decided at 11 o'clock where the attack should be delivered.

[26] In rear of the house of H. Spangler.   [27] *O. R.,* 27, part 2, pp. 350, 607–8.

deployment, Lee turned his horse's head once more and sought Longstreet out. He found that the columns had at last begun to move to the right. The reason for this further delay, it developed, was that although Lee had specifically ordered Longstreet to move with the troops then on the field, that officer had seen fit to wait about forty minutes for Law's brigade to come up.[28]

Longstreet's mood now changed: he was determined to carry out orders literally and thereby to put on the commanding general all the responsibility for the failure he anticipated. At the outset, when the march commenced, he remembered that Lee had told him Captain Johnston was to conduct the column to the right, by a route which he had reconnoitred. If Johnston was to do it, let him do it! "As I was relieved for the time from the march," Longstreet later wrote, unabashed, "I rode near the middle of the line."[29] Captain Johnston had received no orders from Longstreet and, of course, had been given none by Lee after he had been placed at the disposal of Longstreet. He only knew that he was expected to conduct the column by a concealed route, if possible, to the positions he had reconnoitred early in the morning. He set out, quite unconscious that the commander of the First Corps had temporarily delegated to him the leading of the troops who were to open the decisive attack in what might be the most important battle of the war.[30]

Lee rode with Longstreet, as he often did when he wished to hurry him along. The afternoon was now at its hottest, and the soldiers were suffering for lack of water,[31] but now, as always, they wound their way cheerfully along the by-ways and over the fields. It was not theirs to know—such are the crimes of war— that some hundreds of them were to be slain needlessly before the fiery sun had set, because the pique of one man had thrown away the advantage that an early assault would have given them

---

[28] Longstreet claimed (*op. cit.,* 382) that he delayed because Lee had ordered him to attack with his two divisions, which would not be complete until the arrival of Law. He completely overlooked the fact that in his official report (*O. R.,* 27, part 2, p. 358), he had said: "Previous to his [Law's] joining, I received instructions from the commanding general to move, *with the portion of my command that was up,* around to gain the Emmitsburg road, on the enemy's left." See Early, 5 *S. H. S. P.,* 182; *Taylor's Four Years,* 97–98; *Long,* 283.

[29] *Longstreet,* 366.

[30] Major Johnston in 5 *S. H. S. P.,* 183–84.

[31] Nearly all the regimental reports mention the extreme heat (*cf. O. R.,* 27, part 2, p. 401). For the lack of water, see *ibid.,* part 2, p. 354.

in wrestling with an adversary who was crowding the unseen ridge with his brigades. As they tramped along, an officer came up from the right and reported to Lee that the enemy was moving troops toward Round Top, the great natural bastion on the left of the Federal line. From the nearest high ground, Lee focussed his glasses on that eminence, but soon lowered them. It was true, as reported: The enemy was extending his left. "Ah, well," said Lee, "that was to be expected. But General Meade might as well have saved himself the trouble, for we'll have it in our possession before night." [32] The record of the army seemed to justify words that otherwise would have been boastful.

About half-way down the front, at the lane leading into the farm of E. Pitzer, General Lee turned his horse to the left and bade farewell to Longstreet, into whose unwilling hands he committed the opening attack. Riding along the lane and through the woods, he joined Hill on the eastern edge of Seminary Ridge, opposite the Codori house.[33] Thence, north and south, he could survey the Federal position. Save for the dispute of skirmishers and the occasional crack of a sharpshooter's rifle, it was, at first glance, as calm a scene as ever had met the gaze of a phlegmatic farmer who had paused on the hill to rest a complaining plough horse. But the landscape took on a sinister cast when field glasses searched it. There in Gettysburg, a mile and a half to the left, Rodes's division was waiting. Along the ridge, the blue of Federal uniforms blended into the green of the foliage, and the yawning barrel of many a fieldpiece could be seen in the shade. Behind the stone fences was a constant stirring, vague but ominous. Directly south of Lee's position, the peach orchard was now crowded with something besides trees. Still farther to the south, shimmering in the heat that radiated from jutting boulders, were the wooded heights of Round Top, still apparently deserted, in spite of the report that the Federals were occupying it. To the left of that eminence was Little Round Top, where the Federal signal station was working busily. How far the infantry line extended toward these towering positions, it was impossible to discern, but the occupied front was long and bristling—a very

[32] Polley: Hood's *Texas Brigade*, 155.
[33] *Longstreet,* 365–66, 380 n.; *Fremantle,* 259–60. The Bachelder map for July 2 shows the spot.

95

different sight from what it had been when Lee had observed it at dawn.

It was 2 o'clock when McLaws's troops filed past Wilcox's brigade on the right of R. H. Anderson's division of the Third Corps.[34] Soon Longstreet's men would be in position south of Hill, outflanking the extreme left of the Federal line, as Lee hoped. Then they were to attack astride the Emmitsburg road. If their advance reached a point opposite Anderson's division, without driving the Federals, Hill understood that he was to attack frontally. As the battle swept northward on Hill's front, Ewell was to await a favorable opportunity and, if he found it, was to storm the sides of Cemetery Hill. It was a difficult plan, and of such doubtful issue that there was small wonder that Lee's face took on "an expression of painful anxiety." [35]

As Lee waited, Heth came up, to bear his commander company in the hour of contest;[36] Long remained at hand; Hill did not leave; the ubiquitous Colonel Fremantle was watching vigilantly, lest he lose a single scene of the pageant he had crossed the ocean to observe. Now Lee would watch Round Top through his glasses; now he would chat with Long or with Hill; but most of the time he sat alone on a stump, waiting and waiting for Longstreet to send his infantry forward. Soon the artillery opened, along a wide front, like the drums of a stirring overture to an opera that told of the struggle of demigods and heroes, and then, as if to remind the angry deities that human love and mortals' hope were stakes in the coming combat, a band in Rodes's division, from a ravine on the left, began to play lively polkas and waltzes.[37]

But the drama did not open immediately. Some of the performers had been delayed once more in reaching the stage. When the head of the First Corps was within a mile and a half of the ground where Hood's division finally deployed, Captain Johnston notified Longstreet that if the troops continued along the road, they would pass over the crest of a hill where their presence would be disclosed to the enemy. At the same time, Johnston pointed out a shorter, concealed route across a nearby field. But

34 O. R., 27, part 2, p. 617.
35 W. F. Dunaway: Reminiscences of a Rebel, 89–90.
36 4 S. H. S. P., 159.   37 Fremantle, 259–60.

Longstreet insisted that Johnston go on. When the head of the column reached the top of the hill, whence the signal station on Little Round Top could be seen, Longstreet halted it and, after a conference with General McLaws, decided to countermarch and seek a better route. Hood, however, was so close on McLaws's rear that the two divisions overlapped and became confused when the attempt was made to retrace their steps. Much time was lost while Hood went on by one route and McLaws by another. Longstreet subsequently explained this curious incident by saying that he did not feel at liberty to interfere with McLaws's advance, as Lee had told him Johnston was to lead that column, but he considered himself free to move Hood, of whom Lee had said nothing.[38]

As the column approached its destination, Longstreet asked McLaws how he proposed to attack. McLaws replied that this would depend on what he found when he reached his position. "There is nothing in your front," Longstreet answered. "You will be entirely on the flank of the enemy." But no sooner was McLaws in sight of the ridge, about 3:30 o'clock, than he perceived that the Federal line extended far beyond his right.[39] It was manifest then that in all the time that had elapsed after Lee had signified his intention of attacking on the right, Longstreet had done nothing to verify the reconnaissance made early in the morning. Because of the lack of information, the Confederate right had to be extended still farther, and Hood had to be deployed beyond McLaws with his right flank directly opposite Round Top. All the while, Longstreet's apathy was so pronounced that even his own adjutant general subsequently confessed it.[40]

Soon Hood learned from scouts sent out by Law that he could

---

[38] There is confusion, if not a direct conflict of testimony here. In his official report (*O. R.,* 27, part 2, p. 358), Longstreet wrote: "Engineers, sent out by the commanding general and myself, guided us by a road which would have completely disclosed the move. Some delay ensued in seeking a more concealed route." Similarly, in *Annals of the War,* 422–23, Longstreet put the whole blame of the delay on Johnston. That officer, however, gave a very different version of the march in 5 *S. H. S. P.,* 183–84, and McLaws still another account in 7 *ibid.,* 69–70. In his last narrative, *op. cit.,* 366, Longstreet modified his earlier statements and passed over the incident in a few words. He contended in his final publication that he moved with alacrity and promptness after having received his orders.

[39] McLaws in 7 *S. H. S. P.,* 69–70.

[40] *Sorrel,* 164: "As Longstreet was not to be made willing and Lee refused to change or could not change, the former failed to conceal some anger. There was apparent apathy in his movements. They lacked the fire and point of his usual bearing on the battlefield."

work his way around the southern end of Round Top and take it in flank and rear.[41] Law insisted that this would be a far less costly line of advance than up the Emmitsburg road, as Lee's orders contemplated. Hood agreed and sent back a messenger to acquaint Longstreet with the facts and to ask permission to turn Round Top. But Longstreet's strange mood hung over him. Willing as he had been during the morning to delay all action, in the hope of forcing Lee to adopt his strategy, he was stubborn now in adhering to the absolute letter of his instructions. Quickly he sent word back to Hood: "General Lee's orders are to attack up the Emmitsburg road." Right or wrong, it was Lee's battle, not his, and he did not propose to modify the commanding general's plan, no matter how the situation had changed. Again Hood asked permission to flank Round Top and to avoid a costly struggle on its stony sides. Again Longstreet refused in the same words. A third time Hood besought him to permit the easier move; a third time Longstreet refused and sent one of his staff officers to repeat Lee's orders.[42] "If [Lee] had been with us," Longstreet wrote, thirty years later, "General Hood's messengers could have been referred to general headquarters, but to delay and send messengers five miles in favor of a move that he had rejected would have been contumacious." [43] He had forgotten, apparently, when he wrote, that he had left Lee opposite the Pitzer house, and that Lee was then less than two miles off, easily available.

Of all this, of course, Lee knew nothing. During the whole afternoon, he received only one message and sent only one.[44] He had no intimation of the difficulties Longstreet had encountered on the march or of the situation that Hood had found on the flank. His first assurance that the troops were in position came about 4 o'clock when Hood's right brigade, that of Law, went

[41] Law in 3 B. and L., 321–22; Hood, 57–58.
[42] Hood, 58–59; John W. Fairfax to W. H. Taylor, March 31, 1896, Fairfax MSS. In 1910, William Youngblood, one of Longstreet's couriers, published in 38 S. H. S. P., 312–18, an account of an interview in which he alleged Lee, Longstreet, and Hood participated. He stated that Hood then reported that he could turn Round Top, and that Lee declined, saying he believed the position could be taken by direct assault. Longstreet and Hood, in their narratives, make it plain that the information regarding a turning movement against Round Top reached Longstreet after he had left Lee, and that he did not forward it to him.
[43] Longstreet, 368.   [44] Fremantle, 259–60.

forward under a floating cloud of smoke.[45] The troops were so far off that even with his glasses Lee probably could see little of their movements, though the speedy outburst of firing from the vicinity of Round Top showed that the Confederate right was clambering over the rocky shoulder of that eminence. The advance was difficult, but progress was steady.[46] Soon, on the left of Law, Robertson's brigade became heavily engaged. As it pushed toward the rocky position known as Devil's Den, north of Round Top, G. T. Anderson and Benning threw the remaining units of the division in support. But instead of moving up the Emmitsburg road, with their right flank on the ridge, as Lee had hoped, Hood's men were forced to fight their way directly toward the ridge and, where they could mount it, to turn to the left. It was desperate going, and the volume and direction of the fire showed they were encountering the stiffest resistance.[47]

By this time, from the northeast, there swelled the roar of Ewell's artillery. Evidently he had heard Longstreet's guns and was making the demonstration required by his orders; but of the effect of his cannonade Lee could tell nothing. No infantry fire was audible from that direction.[48] On Lee's right, however, the battle was now drawing closer to him and was partially visible through the smoke. About 5:30 McLaws's right brigade, under Kershaw, advanced skillfully against a very difficult position in its front. Behind him Semmes's brigade moved quickly. Then, on McLaws's left, Barksdale's Mississippians followed their leader across the field, his white hair streaming in the afternoon sun. Their charge was against the peach orchard, and their advance was made with a dash and precision that won the praise of soldiers who had witnessed some of the most desperate assaults of the war. Directly before them was a strong picket fence, the crossing of which was expected to cause the Mississippi troops much trouble, but the impact of their charge broke down

---

[45] Cf. J. C. West, 94–95.

[46] Law in 3 B. and L., 324–25; Oates in 6 S. H. S. P., 173.

[47] Hunt suggested (3 B. and L., 300) that Lee mistook the position in the peach orchard for the Federal main line, but Lee's report, as already indicated, shows that his advance was made on the supposition that if the Union troops could be driven from the high ground along the road, this elevation could be used advantageously by the artillery to cover the assault on the stronghold of the ridge (see supra, p. 88).

[48] Ewell's guns opened on Johnson's front about 5 P.M. See Ewell's report, O. R., 27, part 2, p. 446.

the fence in an instant, and they were soon beyond it, working havoc among the red-breeched zouaves who had defended it.[49] A few minutes more and nearly everywhere Longstreet's men were gaining ground. Law's troops were over the shoulder of Round Top, fighting like demons around the foot of Little Round Top. Devil's Den was taken; Robertson and G. T. Anderson were hammering by the side of Law's weary Alabama soldiers. Back of the Rose house, half a mile northwest of Devil's Den, the resistance of the Federals was stubborn, and the Confederate line had not advanced more than a quarter of a mile east of the Emmitsburg road. At the peach orchard, Barksdale's men were in a fair way of driving the Federals out, despite heavy reinforcements and a wicked artillery fire.

If the advantage was to be pushed, Hill must now take up the fight. As the general direction of the Emmitsburg road is from the southwest to northeast, Hill's right division, that of R. H. Anderson, would have to cover a much greater distance than had been traversed by McLaws's division in reaching the road. The ground, moreover, was cleared and exposed to a sweeping artillery fire. On the highway, opposite Anderson, the Federals had an infantry force and some guns. East of the road, the ground dipped to a little ravine and then rose to Cemetery Ridge.[50] The whole stretch from Anderson's position to the opposite ridge was 1400 yards—all of it directly under Lee's eyes. But Anderson's four brigades were chafing at the delay and ready for the attempt, though the afternoon sun was waning fast and the hour was now past 6. At the word of command, the soldiers with whom Wilcox had so gallantly held the line at Salem Church two months before, sprang to the charge, followed quickly on their left by Perry's brigade. They brushed aside the skirmish line; they reached the road; in a quick exchange of volleys, they drove the Federals back. Then down the slope they dashed to the ravine and, under a steadily increasing fire, began to mount the heights, only to be met by a new Federal line, advancing to meet them. Here, for nearly half an hour, Wilcox's men met charge after charge, though separated on their right from McLaws.[51] Perry's men, on Wilcox's left, fought with

[49] Captain G. B. Lamar, Jr., quoted by McLaws in 7 S. H. S. P., 73–74.
[50] O. R., 27, part 2, p. 618.   [51] O. R., 27, part 2, p. 618.

equal valor. Neither had any support, as Anderson's division had been deployed in a single line.[52]

While these two brigades of Hill's corps were fighting to hold their ground east of the Emmitsburg road, Wright's Georgians moved forward on the left of Perry. Before he reached the road, which was defended by a small Federal force, Wright observed that Posey's brigade, which was to cover his left, was not advancing. He halted his men and sent back word to Anderson, who assured him that Posey would follow. Wright thereupon ordered the advance to continue. His troops hurled back the Federals in the road, crashed through their main line, captured a number of guns, and then almost without a pause, dashed up the ridge. While Lee looked on with admiring eye, they reached the crest and found themselves among the Federals' massed artillery. Firing fast, they forced the Federals from the high ground, which was narrow at this point, and drove them down into the gorge to the east. The grip of the Federals on the ridge was now broken. If Wright could get support enough to extend the position he had so gallantly captured, the day would be won!

It was not to be. Perry's brigade had given ground on the right; on the left, Posey had not succeeded in reaching the road.[53] Soon Wright found the Federals massing heavily for a counterattack, and he had to make his way back from the ridge as best he could, with heavy losses. Wilcox was forced to retire about the same time. The valor of the attacking brigades had been above reproach, but the divisional command had been negligent, orders had been confused, and Mahone's brigade had not stirred.[54]

Had Ewell been able to achieve more? Lee had heard nothing from him during the afternoon. The artillery fire from that quarter had diminished after 6 o'clock, and in the din of the action it had been impossible to tell whether the infantry of the Second Corps had been engaged. Just before darkness fell on the field, Rodes's men deployed west of Gettysburg and moved to the

[52] O. R., 27, part 2, p. 631.
[53] O. R., 27, part 2, pp. 623–24. Wilcox in 6 S. H. S. P., 102–3, pointed out a minor error in Lee's report where it was stated that Posey participated in the attack. Posey's own report (O. R., 27, part 2, pp. 633–34) explained that he failed to advance because the troops on his left, Mahone's brigade, did not support him.
[54] Cf. O. R., 27, part 2, pp. 608, 614, 618, 624; 27 S. H. S. P., 193 ff. See infra, Appendix III—3.

southeast, but they halted and ere long withdrew. Lee did not know that this was the last phase of a tragedy in faulty co-ordination. At 6 o'clock, when the Confederate artillery had been almost silenced by the overpowering Union guns, Ewell had ordered Johnson's division forward against Culp's Hill. The sun set before the troops began to climb the steep incline from the crest of which the Federals awaited their attack, but Johnson's advance was steady, despite the tangle on the hillside. As Johnson fought his way upward, Early threw two brigades into action against East Cemetery Hill. Their attack was furious and as the distance they had to cover was short, they were soon within the Federal lines. But here, as with Wilcox and Wright, when they looked about for support, Early's men found none. Rodes's division, which was expected to join in the attack, moving on the right of Early, had been slow in deploying and had more ground to cover. Once the column was stopped while a report was sent to the division commander. Rodes himself was concerned because he had no assurance of support on his right. When at length he was in position to attack, Early was giving ground. The whole of the three days' battle produced no more tragic might-have-been than this twilight engagement on the Confederate left. For Early's right regiment had been within 400 feet of the flank of the Federal batteries commanding the approaches to the hill from Rodes's front. Had Rodes's 5000 been at hand to support Early for even an hour, the Federal guns could have been captured and turned on the enemy. Cemetery Hill would have been cleared, and the ridge to the south could have been so enfiladed that the Federals would have been compelled to evacuate it. As it was, Early's men fell back in bitterness of heart; Rodes took an intermediate position. On the whole left wing of the army Steuart's brigade of Johnson's division alone held the position it had stormed, and that command occupied only some rude trenches that had been abandoned by the enemy.[55]

[55] Ewell's report (*O. R.*, 27, part 2, pp. 446–47) gave the main facts; Early's report (*ibid.*, 470) is elaborated in his autobiography, *Early*, 278, and in 4 *S. H. S. P.*, 277; Rodes's account is in *O. R.*, 27, part 2, p. 556. Lane in his report (*ibid.*, 666) explained his efforts to support Rodes. General Lee's report (*ibid.*, 319) contained a mild censure of Rodes for failing to advance. Marshall (*op. cit.*, 237) said: "If General Rodes had prepared his troops to advance on the right of General Early the latter would not have been compelled to withdraw from a successful attack, and the position on Cemetery Hill

It was now night, sultry and oppressive,[56] and the moon had risen above the grim ridge the Confederates had attacked.[57] The skirmishers kept up an intermittent fire, but the hot guns of the weary artillerists were silent at last. The dead and wounded covered the ground, many of them where burial or succor could not be given. The casualties among the general officers had been high. Hood had been wounded in the arm,[58] Pender had been very seriously injured by a shell and was doomed to die.[59] Barksdale had been killed in the brilliant charge of his brigade; Semmes had received mortal hurt; Colonel Isaac C. Avery, who had been leading Hoke's brigade of Early's division, had been killed; J. M. Jones and G. T. Anderson had received lesser wounds.[60] On Cemetery Ridge the Federals believed that Longstreet himself had been slain and that his body was within their lines.[61]

"The whole affair," Colonel Walter Taylor wrote subsequently, "was disjointed. There was an utter absence of accord in the movements of the several commands."[62] It was a failure, yet not altogether a failure, and not a failure that reflected on the valor of the men in the ranks. They, at least, had done their full part, however much their leaders had erred. In the face of the most stubborn resistance the Army of the Potomac as a whole had ever offered, Hood's men had achieved the seemingly impossible in taking Devil's Den and in threatening Little Round Top, Wright and Wilcox had reached the main Federal positions, and Early had been within sight of victory.

Troops that had achieved this much, despite Longstreet's delay and Ewell's failure to co-ordinate his attacks, could be counted on to do still more if the whole strength of the army could be employed the next day. Lee's confidence in his men, at the end

---

would have been held. The capture of that hill would have enabled General Early to have enfiladed the Federal troops opposed to those of General Longstreet, and the effect of such fire at that time might have changed the result of the day."

[56] E. R. Rich: *Comrades Four*, 75.   [57] *Cooke*, 317.   [58] *Hood*, 59.

[59] *O. R.*, 27, part 2, p. 310, contains Lee's tribute to him. *Welch*, 72: "He was as brave as a lion and seemed to love danger." See, also, *Our Living and Our Dead*, 1, pp. 137-38, 2 *ibid.*, 176.

[60] *O. R.*, 27, part 2, p. 320.

[61] Colonel R. M. Powell of the Fifth Texas had been mistaken for Longstreet (3 *B. and L.*, 320).

[62] *Taylor's Four Years*, 99.

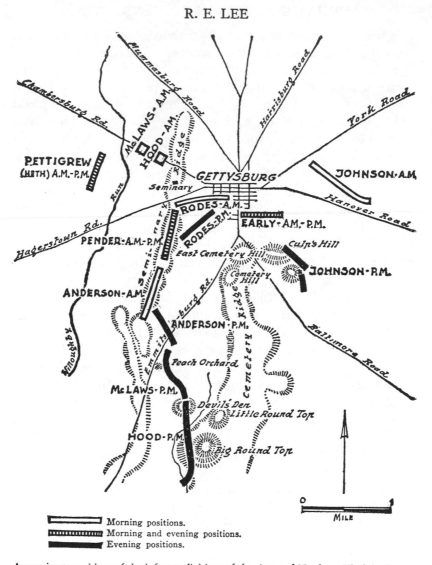

Approximate positions of the infantry divisions of the Army of Northern Virginia, 8 A.M. and 9 P.M., July 2, 1863. Johnson's evening position, except for that of Steuart's brigade, is not certain. Hood's division had advanced farther but withdrew during the evening to the indicated front.

of the second day, was as great as it had ever been. Then, too, favorable ground had been gained. The right seemed well anchored. Steuart's gains on the left might be enlarged. The ridge traversed by the Emmitsburg road had been taken. Above all, the peach orchard was in Southern hands, and, as Lee saw it, could be utilized to cover an assault on the position that Wright had shown was not impregnable.[63]

Enough troops were at hand for a supreme effort on the morning of the 3d. Pickett's division had arrived within striking distance during the afternoon and its commander had been told by Lee to rest his men for the morrow.[64] Johnson's division was comparatively fresh; so was Pender's; Smith's brigade of Early's division, and Mahone and Posey of the Third Corps had not suffered heavily.[65] Imboden's cavalry was in support. And Stuart, the wandering, much-missed Stuart, whose absence had caused so much embarrassment, had arrived on the left, with two of his brigades, before sunset.[66] Two more brigades of cavalry would be up before daybreak. Jenkins, also, would be available again. The casualties of July 1 and 2 would thus be made good, temporarily, by reinforcements.

For these reasons—because the morale of the army was still superb, because much ground had been taken, because admirable artillery positions had been won, and because reinforcements had arrived—Lee determined to renew the battle on the third day.[67] He ordered the artillery made ready to open all along the line as early as possible[68] to cover the advance, and he directed Ewell to renew his attack at daylight.[69] Longstreet did not ride to Lee's headquarters to report, contrary to his custom, but, still sulking, contented himself with sending a verbal account of what had happened on his front.[70] Lee replied with orders for Longstreet

---

[63] O. R., 27, part 2, p. 320; McKim in 40 S. H. S. P., 281–82; Battine, 226 ff.

[64] O. R., 27, part 2, p. 320; Walter Harrison: Pickett's Men (cited hereafter as Walter Harrison), 88.

[65] Cf. Hunt in 3 B. and L., 369.

[66] H. B. McClellan, 332. For the movement of Stuart's cavalry in Pennsylvania, see Appendix III—4.

[67] President Davis (op. cit., 2, 448) thought Lee should have retreated at the end of the second day's fight. Hunt (3 B. and L., 369) was of opinion that the situation justified Lee in renewing the action.

[68] O. R., 27, part 2, p. 351.

[69] O. R., 27, part 2, p. 447.

[70] Annals of the War, 429; Longstreet, 385. Speaking that night to Captain Ross, Longstreet said: "We have not been so successful as we wished," and expressed the belief that this was due to the wounding of Hood and the death of Barksdale. Ross, who was an experienced soldier, added his own opinion in recounting this conversation: "Perhaps," said he, "if the attack had been made a little earlier in the day it would have been more successful" (Ross, 54).

to attack the next morning.[71] That assault would be decisive: Either Meade would be beaten and the road to Baltimore and Philadelphia would be opened, or . . .

[71] In *O. R.*, 27, part 2, p. 320, is Lee's own statement to this effect. It never was contradicted by General Longstreet in any of his writings until the appearance of *From Manassas to Appomattox*, in which (385) he said Lee did not give or send him orders "for the morning of the third day."

CHAPTER VIII

"It Is All My Fault"

A LIGHT haze obscured the scudding clouds and dimmed the pale stars in the early morning of July 3, but the thermometer gave warning of another torrid day,[1] and a roaring cannonade swept over the ridges to tell that Ewell, in obedience to orders, was preparing to attack.[2] Lest delay again occur to prevent co-ordination of the assault, Lee rode immediately to the headquarters of the First Corps, far down on the right. On the way he saw nothing of Pickett's division, which he had ordered up from its bivouac on the Chambersburg road. Neither did he observe any evidence of preparations for the offensive. When he reached the ground where Longstreet had spent the night, he discovered the reason. "General," Longstreet began, "I have had my scouts out all night, and I find that you still have an excellent opportunity to move around to the right of Meade's army, and manœuver him into attacking us." In fact, Longstreet had already directed his troops to start to the right, despite Lee's orders for a renewal of the assault on Meade's position.[3]

Weary as Lee must have been of Longstreet's endless contention for the acceptance of his own plan, he listened patiently, and then, once again, told Longstreet that he intended to attack the Federal army where it stood with the three divisions of the First Corps— Hood's, McLaws's, and Pickett's. But Longstreet was not to be silenced. He argued that he had been a soldier all his life, and that he did not believe any 15,000 men could be found who would be capable of storming the ridge. More than that, he insisted that he could not deliver the assault with his full corps. Hood and McLaws, he said, were facing superior forces. They could not attack

[1] *John H. Lewis*, 77; 33 *S. H. S. P.*, 126.
[2] *Ross*, 60; *O. R.*, 27, part 2, p. 447.
[3] *Annals of the War*, 429; *O. R.*, 27, part 2, p. 359. For Lee's statement that Longstreet did not start his movement against the Federal left centre as early as had been anticipated, see *O. R.*, 27, part 2, p. 320.

where they were, he maintained, and if they were withdrawn and employed against Cemetery Ridge, the Federals would pour down from Round Top and get on the flank and in the rear of his corps. His argument was warm and lengthy.

Lee believed that his plan was practicable and that a general assault along the right held out the highest promise of success. His army had never yet failed to carry a Federal position when he had been able to throw his full strength against it. Only when his assault had been delivered with part of his forces—as at Malvern Hill—had he ever failed. But now, in the face of Longstreet's continued opposition, he probably reasoned that if Longstreet did not have faith in the plan it would be worse than dangerous to entrust the assault to his troops alone. Lack of confidence is half of defeat. So, as happened only too often, Lee put aside what he regarded as the best plan and, out of consideration for a subordinate, improvised a second best. He would leave Hood and McLaws where they were and would shift the front of the attack more to the centre. For McLaws's division he would substitute Heth's of A. P. Hill's corps, and in place of Hood he would use two brigades of Pender's division to co-operate with Longstreet's fresh division under Pickett. This would give Longstreet substantially the same effective strength as if he attacked with the whole of the First Corps. It seemed a reasonable thing to do in the circumstances, but, as the event proved, the shift of the attack to the right centre subjected the assaulting column to a fire on both flanks.[4]

This arrangement called for the movement of the two brigades of Pender three-quarters of a mile to the right, and as that would take time, Ewell was notified that Longstreet's attack would be delayed until 10 A.M.[5] To make it certain that Pender's brigades

[4] This conversation between Lee and Longstreet has been the subject of much debate. Taylor (Four Years, 102–3), Venable (ibid., 108 n.), and Long (op. cit., 288, 294) were all of opinion that Lee ordered the assault to be made by the whole of the First Corps. Longstreet flatly denied this in Annals of the War, 431–32, but in From Manassas to Appomattox, 386, he admitted that this was Lee's first intention. He went on to explain that he prevailed on the General to make the substitution. The language of Lee's report (O. R., 27, part 2, p. 320) bears Longstreet out. The conflict of testimony, like that over the origin of the left-flank movement by Jackson at Chancellorsville, is probably due to the fact that the witnesses who say that Lee ordered the entire First Corps to make the assault probably heard only the early part of the interview. It is possible, though not probable, that Lee's consent to make a change in the column of assault was given subsequently to this conference.
[5] O. R., 27, part 2, p. 447.

should have experienced leadership in the assault, Lee directed that General Trimble be summoned from the left and put in charge of them.[6]

The change of plan did not satisfy Longstreet, whose chosen maxim of manœuvring to compel the enemy to attack was violated by Lee's aggressiveness. "Never was I so depressed," Longstreet subsequently confessed, "as upon that day." [7] He argued that the guns from Little Round Top would enfilade his line, and, though he finally subsided, he was not wholly reassured when told by Colonel Long, whose judgment of artillery was usually excellent, that the fire of these guns could be suppressed.[8]

When the discussion was over, Lee rode with Longstreet back toward the centre to study the ground more closely and to see that the artillery was well posted for its indispensable part in the attack.[9] Longstreet remained listless and despairing. Even the men in the ranks observed that he kept his eyes on the ground and had gloom written on his countenance.[10] Despite his dark humor, however, Longstreet had made one wise decision. He had entrusted the placing of his corps of artillery to one of his battalion commanders, Colonel E. P. Alexander,[11] perhaps the best artillerist in the Army of Northern Virginia. Alexander had advanced seventy-five of the eighty-three guns of Longstreet's corps to good ground along the Emmitsburg road, from the peach orchard northward for about 1300 yards.[12] All these pieces were in advance of the infantry positions, and some of them, on Longstreet's left, were within 650 yards of the enemy. Five guns of Poague's battalion of Hill's corps were also in advance. The other

---

[6] O. R., 27, part 2, pp. 320, 608; Trimble's diary, 17 *Maryland Historical Magazine*, 8. After the fall of Pender, the division had been temporarily under the command of Brigadier General James H. Lane. Trimble had been designated for command in the Valley, but had not taken command and had ridden, unassigned, into Pennsylvania (O. R., 25, part 2, pp. 801–2, 812, 830).

[7] *Annals of the War*, 430.

[8] *Long*, 288. Alexander, who was not partial to Long, remarked (*op. cit.*, 416) that it was astonishing that Long's statement passed unchallenged; but if the discussion was confined to the possibility of an enfilade from Little Round Top, the only Federal artillery there was Gibbs's Ohio battery, which did little during the day (O. R., 27, part 1, p. 662). The left of the massed Federal artillery, Ames's New York unit, was half a mile north of Gibbs and in rear of the stone house of George Weikert (O. R., 27, part 1, p. 901).

[9] O. R., 27, part 1, p. 320; *Annals of the War*, 431–32.

[10] *History of Kershaw's Brigade*, 235.

[11] *Annals of the War*, 429–30; 5 *S. H. S. P.*, 44, 202.

[12] The left of Longstreet's artillery was almost directly opposite the northeast corner of the Spangler wood (*cf. Alexander*, 418).

pieces, however, were under cover along Seminary Ridge, and a full battalion was in rear, unable to find position. Even those on the ridge were at a distance of 1400 yards from the enemy. Very little was done to produce a converging fire or to blanket the Federal guns on Cemetery Hill.[13] Altogether, about 125 guns would be available to protect the attack of the infantry.

As Lee passed among them the artillerists were at ease, waiting for the struggle they knew was coming. Some of their officers slipped out where they could see the enemy's lines and could speculate on the ranges and on the prospects of the battle. Seeing Major James Dearing on the ridge within range of the enemy, Lee sent word to him to retire. "I do not approve of young officers needlessly exposing themselves," he said, "their place is with their batteries."[14] Then he rode on. His face was anxious and careworn, but his manner was as self-possessed as if he were back at Culpeper, watching Stuart's troopers in the sham battle with their own horse artillery. Tomorrow might see the army's banners in victorious pursuit of Meade's shattered divisions on the road to Baltimore, or, if the charge failed, the next day's sun might find the defeated Army of Northern Virginia struggling back to the mountains, a triumphant enemy at its heels. Yet Lee did not believe it would be so. He had to consider the alternative, of course, but despite Longstreet's misgivings, he had unlimited confidence in the prowess of the army. Where Wright had gone the day before, with little artillery support, he was confident three divisions could go now—and could stay. Nor was he shaken by the concern of some of the officers. When he met General Wofford, that officer proudly told him that he had nearly reached the crest of the ridge the previous afternoon. Lee asked him if he could not go there again.

"No, General," said Wofford, "I think not."

"Why not?" Lee inquired.

"Because, General, the enemy have had all night to entrench and reinforce. I had been pursuing a broken enemy, and the situation now is very different."[15]

[13] *Alexander*, 417–19; *O. R.*, 27, part 2, pp. 456, 610, 672; McIntosh in 37 *S. H. S. P.*, 135. For the armament of the batteries, see *O. R.*, 29, part 2, p. 637.

[14] 34 *S. H. S. P.*, 329. A similar incident, during the bombardment, involved a young North Carolina lieutenant (3 *N. C. Regts.*, 382).

[15] Wofford in A. Doubleday: *Chancellorsville and Gettysburg*, 187–88.

Lee was determined that nothing should be lacking in infantry preparation. Twice he rode the whole length of the line with Longstreet and then went over it again without him.[16] When at last he was satisfied, the morning hours were gone, the sun was high, and the heat was burning. From the sky the last cloud had been driven.

On the left, unknown to Lee, Johnson had been assailed and had begun a counteroffensive before Ewell had received Lee's notice that Longstreet would not attack until 10 A.M.[17] Johnson was wearing himself out and would be unable to co-operate when the great assault was launched. Co-ordination had failed again!

The two brigades of Pender's division were now in rear of Spangler's wood; Pickett's division had silently moved up and was in position west of the Emmitsburg road, behind Alexander's guns. In front of Heth's division, almost midway between the armies, the skirmishers were carrying on a sharp struggle, and Hill's artillery was wasting much of its scanty ammunition. This fire died away shortly after noon, however, and silence fell over the field. The only omen of what was about to come was a twin beacon of flame where the skirmishers had been engaged— a wooden dwelling house and a large barn ignited by the Federals because they were in the line of fire.[18]

While these buildings were burning, Lee rode out in front of the right of Pettigrew's command with Longstreet and with Hill to arrange the last tactical details.[19] Beneath them, Seminary Ridge fell away unevenly and then rose again to the Emmitsburg road. On the right of the front of assault the road was 300 yards from the ridge. Between the highway and the enemy's position there was a little swale that afforded some shelter. But on the centre and left the road was only 135 yards from the ridge, and the ground rose almost directly, without cover.

The objective that Lee chose for the coming assault was a small grove of umbrella-shaped chestnut oaks,[20] known locally as Ziegler's Grove but described by the Confederates simply as the "little clump of trees." A close examination of this ground through strong glasses showed that a post-and-rail fence ran south to

[16] *Annals of the War*, 431–32. [17] *O. R.*, 27, part 2, pp. 447–48, 504–5.
[18] *Alexander*, 420; *O. R.*, 27, part 1, pp. 454, 465, 467; part 2, pp. 663, 666.
[19] 7 *S. H. S. P.*, 92. [20] 5 *N. C. Regts.*, 104.

north along Cemetery Ridge and that in rear of this stones cleared
from the ridge had been piled up in a crude wall about two and
a half to three feet high. This stone wall turned east at a right
angle and ran in that direction for eighty yards before it turned
north again. Within this angle the stone fence was about two
feet higher than on the south-and-north stretch below.[21] The
intervening fields between Seminary Ridge and the stone wall
were crossed and recrossed with fences, and the Emmitsburg
road was bordered on either side by a stout barrier of plank and
posts.

Narrow the objective was, compared with the front of attack.
The lines therefore would have to converge. How could this best
be assured? Pickett's was to be the right division in the attack,
with Kemper's brigade on the right in the first line and Garnett's
on the left. Armistead was to be in support. Heth's division,
under Pettigrew, was to form on Pickett's left, its four brigades
from right to left being, in order, Archer's, under Colonel B. D.
Fry, Pettigrew's old brigade under Colonel J. K. Marshall, Davis's
and Mayo's (Brockenbrough's).[22] The two brigades of Pender's
division under Trimble were to be in support of Heth—Scales's on
the right, led by Colonel W. L. J. Lowrance, and Lane's on the
left. On the extreme right, in rear of Pickett's right flank, Wilcox
was to be placed to meet any counterattack against the flank.
The line, then, was to be as follows:[23]

Mayo   Davis   Marshall   Fry   Garnett   Kemper
*   Lane   Lowrance   Armistead*
*   Wilcox*

Fry's was thus the centre brigade and its direction would be
straight ahead. Pickett's division, and the three left brigades of
Pettigrew were directed to dress on Fry as soon as they were in
the open.[24] The distance that Pettigrew would have to cover
was considerably greater than that of Pickett, if measured from
their respective positions to the ridge; but as Pickett's right would

[21] 2 *N. C. Regts.*, 43; 5 *N. C. Regts.*, 106.
[22] From this point, Heth's division will be mentioned as Pettigrew's, after its field
commander in the charge.
[23] *O. R.*, 27, part 2, pp. 359, 608, 650, 659.   [24] *Longstreet*, 389; 7 *S. H. S. P.* 92.

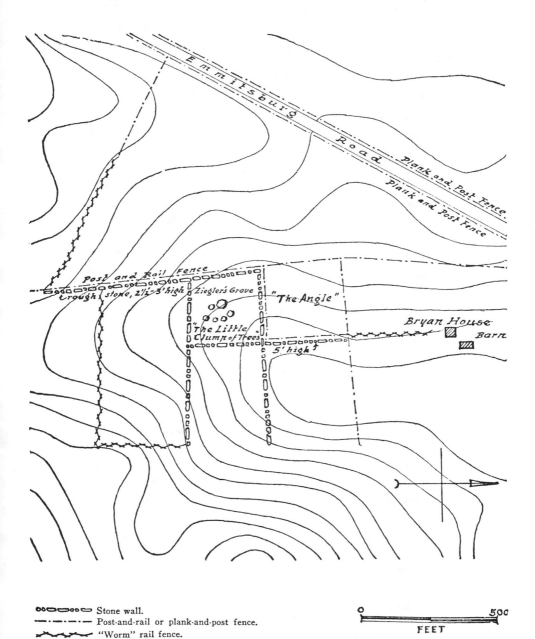

Stone wall.
Post-and-rail or plank-and-post fence.
"Worm" rail fence.

Objective of the Confederate assault of July 3, 1863, on the right centre at Gettysburg, showing the contour (intervals of 4 feet) and the nature of the obstructions.

have to swing much farther to the left than Pettigrew's left would
have to move to the right, the two divisions were expected to reach
their objective at the same time. The artillery was to cover the
charge by a concentrated bombardment of the enemy's position.
The infantry were not to start until the artillery fire had done its
fullest execution and had silenced the enemy's batteries, if this was
possible. Meantime, the columns of assault were to be kept under
cover and were not to be shown the field over which they were
to charge, but the officers were to go to the crest, examine the
ground, and prepare the men for what awaited them.[25] Longstreet was to be in general command, with authority to call on
Hill for Anderson's division if he required it. Hill was anxious to
employ his whole corps in the charge, and besought Lee to permit
him to do so, but the General refused. "What remains of your
corps," he said, caution blending with confidence, "will be my
only reserve, and it will be needed if General Longstreet's attack
should fail." [26] The orders must stand. When everything was
ready, Longstreet was to have two cannon fired in quick succession as a signal for the bombardment to open. To him, also, was
given the responsibility of deciding at what moment the infantry
should start and when the batteries should limber up and follow.

Was the plan understood? It was. Had aught been omitted
in preparation? Neither Hill nor Longstreet knew of anything—
at least Longstreet did not think to tell Lee that he had not
inquired whether the artillery still had enough ammunition for
a long cannonade. Lee folded up his map, the three rose from
the fallen log where they had seated themselves, and, mounting
once again, they rode each to his station.[27] The commanding
general was still confident; Hill was alert but had none of the
immediate responsibility of the assault on him; Longstreet was
close to black dismay. "He knew," Longstreet subsequently said
of Lee, "that I did not believe that success was possible; that care
and time should be taken to give the troops the benefit of positions and the grounds; and he should have put an officer in charge
who had more confidence in his plan." But of this he said

25 *Longstreet*, 390.   26 41 *S. H. S. P.*, 40.
27 7 *S. H. S. P.*, 92.

nothing to Lee.[28] For the supreme effort of all his warring, Lee had to act through a sullen, despairing lieutenant.[29]

There was a momentary flurry as a troop of Federal cavalry rode into the rear of Hood's division, but this was quickly over. A battery of horse artillery was put into the Emmitsburg pike to protect the flank against further incursions by mounted troops, and the last preparations were complete.[30]

The time had come to give the order for the bombardment. Longstreet could not bring himself to do it. Instead, he wrote Colonel Alexander: "If the artillery fire does not have the effect to drive off the enemy or greatly demoralize him, so as to make our effort pretty certain, I would prefer that you should not advise Pickett to make the charge. I shall rely a great deal upon your judgment to determine the matter and shall expect you to let Gen. Pickett know when the moment offers." [31] Then Longstreet went off in the woods and lay down—to think of some method of assisting the attack, as he affirmed, but as Colonel Fremantle thought, to go to sleep.[32]

Alexander was of the bravest of the brave, but he was unprepared to assume the responsibility he felt his chief was trying to unload on him. As soon as he received Longstreet's note, he replied, in substance:

"I will only be able to judge of the effect of our fire on the enemy by his return fire, as his infantry is little exposed to view and the smoke will obscure the field. If, as I infer from your note, there is any alternative to this attack, it should be carefully considered before opening our fire, for it will take all the artillery ammuni-

---

[28] *Longstreet,* 388.

[29] In 2 *Land We Love,* 44, a "Prisoner of War" stated that he saw Longstreet in company with Lee and Pettigrew not long before the charge and heard him say, "If it can be done, my troops can do it, and I will lead them." There is no confirmation of this incident in any other account and it does not accord with Longstreet's own portrayal of his state of mind.

[30] *Longstreet,* 390.

[31] *Alexander,* 421. Longstreet (*op. cit.,* 390–91) passed rather lightly over this and made it appear that he sent these instructions to Alexander at the same time that he directed Colonel J. B. Walton to open the bombardment, but Walton had the signal guns fired immediately after receiving his orders and Alexander affirmed that he got the note from Longstreet "some half-an-hour or more before the cannonade began" (*op. cit.,* 420). The conclusion is unescapable that Longstreet wrote Walton after the receipt of Alexander's first reply, mentioned below.

[32] *Longstreet,* 391; *Fremantle,* 263. Fremantle affirmed that Longstreet actually fell asleep.

tion we have left to test this one, and if result is unfavorable we will have none left for another effort. And even if this is entirely successful, it can only be so at a very bloody cost." [33]

Aroused to receive this message, Longstreet drafted an answer as follows:

"Colonel: The intention is to advance the infantry if the artillery has the desired effect of driving the enemy's off, or having other effect such as to warrant us in making the attack. When that moment arrives advise Gen. Pickett and of course advance such artillery as you can use in aiding the attack." [34]

This paper reached Alexander at a time when General A. R. Wright was with him. "What do you think of it?" he asked Wright.

"The trouble is not in going there," his fellow-Georgian answered. "I was there with my brigade yesterday. There is a place where you can get breath and re-form. The trouble is to stay there after you get there, for the whole Yankee army is there in a bunch." [35]

Alexander sought out Pickett, who was calm and confident, and then sent back this brief note to Longstreet:

"General: when our fire is at its best, I will advise General Pickett to advance." [36]

The silence on the field was now almost complete. Directly opposite the Confederate line a little group of Federal officers

---

[33] *Alexander*, 421. Alexander stated (4 *S. H. S. P.*, 104) that he did not possess the original of this reply but was sure that his memory of its language was substantially correct.

[34] *Alexander*, 421. General Alexander had the original of this dispatch. Some idea of the accuracy of General Longstreet's account of the battle may be gathered from comparing the actual text of the message with his summary of its contents, given in *Longstreet*, 391. Alexander, he said, "was informed that there was no alternative; that I could find no way out of it; that General Lee had considered and would listen to nothing else; that orders had gone for the guns to give signal for the batteries; that he should call the troops at the first opportunity or lull in the enemy's fire." General Longstreet wrote this approximately eighteen years after General Alexander had printed the original of Longstreet's dispatch in 4 *S. H. S. P.*, 105.

[35] *Alexander*, 421–22.   [36] *Alexander*. 422.

were sitting about on the ground, after a late breakfast, smoking
and wondering whether Meade had been correct when he had
said early in the morning that if Lee attacked at all that day it
would be against the centre, because he had tried on both flanks and
had failed.[37] The Federal infantry were huddled behind the
stone wall that ran along the ridge, or were blistering in the tall
grass in front of the wall, where the first line had been formed.

The Southern infantry were idling under cover. They had ceased
their usual banter, because the rumor had spread among them
that they were to be called to charge over the rim of the hill
that cut off their view of the Federal position,[38] but in the memory
of old triumphs, and in their unshakable faith in the leadership
of Lee, they were as confident as ever they had been. All Pickett's
fifteen regiments were Virginians, some of them among the
earliest volunteers. They were fresh and had done no severe
fighting since Sharpsburg. Trimble's ten regiments, Pender's
former command, were from North Carolina, as good troops as
that state had sent to the front. Two of Pettigrew's brigades were
of A. P. Hill's famous old "light division," Virginians, Tennesseans, and Alabamians, but both these units were small and both
were under colonels. One of them, Mayo's, was in bad condition.[39]
Pettigrew's two remaining brigades were Davis's Mississippians
and his own North Carolinians. They were new to the Army of
Northern Virginia, but they had caught the contagion of its
morale. Wilcox's old brigade of five Alabama regiments had been
tested on many a field.

Thus, in the forty-seven regiments of the column of attack, about
15,000 men, there were to be nineteen regiments from Virginia,
fourteen from North Carolina, seven from Alabama, four from
Mississippi, and three from Tennessee. If Perry were employed
in support, three Florida regiments would be added; if Perrin
were called in, he would lead the five South Carolina regiments
that had been McGowan's and previously Gregg's famous brigade.
And if Wright were needed, his Georgians would be ready again.
Every Southern state east of the Mississippi was, or might be,
represented in the assault—the Army of Northern Virginia at its

[37] John Gibbon: *Recollections of the Civil War*, 145, 146.
[38] 32 *S. H. S. P.*, 184.   [39] 5 *N. C. Regiments*, 125.

best, a cross-section of the Confederacy, city dwellers and the sons of great planters, men from the tidal waters and from the hungry mountains, scholars and illiterates, the inheritors of historic names and the unrenowned sons of the poor. Hungry, athirst, dirty, they waited under the noonday sun whose fiery course was to decide whether America was to be two nations.

One o'clock in the stately house in Richmond where Davis, sick and anxious,[40] looked up expectantly for a telegram from Lee whenever a knock came at his door; noon along the Mississippi, as Pemberton with heavy heart was penning a letter asking terms of General Grant for the surrender of Vicksburg; tea time in London, and a sealed letter on the desk of John Bigelow, telling Secretary Seward he was satisfied that Lee's invasion of Pennsylvania had been made in concert with J. A. Roebuck's proposal in the House of Commons that Her Majesty's government enter into negotiations with foreign powers for the recognition of the Confederacy.[41] Almost on the hour, the silence of the fields around Gettysburg was broken by a gun on the Emmitsburg road. Before men had time to shape the question that rose in every mind, the echo of another cannon swelled from the same position. It was the agreed signal for the opening of the bombardment.[42]

Instantly the gunners all along the line sprang to their loaded pieces, and in another moment the roar of the massed batteries shook the ridge. Orders were to fire in salvoes,[43] and as the guns were discharged together, the concussion told of a coming terror that would make men long for the lesser dangers of Gaines's Mill and of Sharpsburg. Two or three miles away, waiting teamsters heard the windows rattle as if assailed by a sudden storm.[44] The firing was a little high for the stone wall behind which the Federal infantry were huddled, but as the exploding shells struck

---

[40] For Davis's indisposition, see *O. R.*, 27, part 3, p. 956.

[41] John Bigelow: *Retrospections of an Active Life*, 2, 26.

[42] *O. R.*, 27, part 2, p. 434; 5 *S. H. S. P.*, 50. The signal-guns were fired by Miller's battery on the northwestern edge of J. Smith's apple orchard. Alexander (*op. cit.*, 422), said it was "just 1 P.M." by his watch; General John Gibbon (*O. R.*, 27, part 1, p. 417), General William Harrow (*ibid.*, 420), and General Alexander S. Webb (*ibid.*, 428) gave the same hour. Colonel J. B. Walton endorsed Longstreet's order to open fire as "received 1:30 P.M.," but in 5 *S. H. S P.*, 50, he stated that the instructions reached him shortly after 1 o'clock.

[43] *O. R.*, 27, part 2, p. 352.

[44] D. E. Johnston: *Story of a Confederate Boy*, 205–6.

the ridge they hurled the earth into the air and shattered rocks that flew in fragments as deadly as the iron itself.[45] Soon the Federal batteries opened, eighteen guns from the very grove Pickett was to charge, and up and down a line that lengthened until a front of fully two miles was blazing in answer.[46] On their high trajectory, round shells could be plainly seen for the whole of their flight, but the rifled shell were visible only when they tumbled.[47] Soon the smoke and the dust obscured the target and darkened the sun. Save for the odor and the long, sulphurous strata above the denser clouds, the scene resembled the centre of some furious thunderstorm.[48] Now the Confederate shell found a caisson, and as its contents exploded with a roar and a flash of flame, the artillerists raised a yell that was plainly heard by the Federals. Now, in return, a Union missile struck in the waiting ranks of the infantry, and the stretcher-bearers rushed in to carry out the wounded, the men who never saw the other side of the hill.[49]

Twenty minutes of this maddening bombardment, and the ammunition of some of the Confederate batteries was half gone, with no diminution in the Federal fire. Alexander felt, by this time, that there was little hope of silencing the enemy's fire and he reasoned that unless the infantry moved soon, the artillery would not be able to cover its advance. He scratched off this note to Pickett:

"General: If you are to advance at all, you must come at once or we will not be able to support you as we ought. But the enemy's fire has not slackened materially and there are still 18 guns firing from the cemetery." [50]

Behind Alexander's position, between the artillery and in the infantry, Longstreet rode at a walk, looking neither to right nor to left.[51] In front of Armistead's and Garnett's brigades, the

---

[45] Gibbon, *op. cit.*, 147.   [46] *Alexander*, 423.   [47] Gibbon, *op. cit.*, 147.
[48] D. E. Johnston, *op. cit.*, 205–6; J. H. Lewis: *Recollections from 1860 to 1865*, p. 77. This latter small work contains one of the most graphic of all accounts of the charge. It is singularly accurate in detail.
[49] 32 *S. H. S. P.*, 34.
[50] *Alexander*, 423. He had been wrongly told that Ziegler's Grove was a cemetery.
[51] 32 *S. H. S. P.*, 192.

chaplains came out and, kneeling, offered prayers amid a knot of bareheaded boys.

"This is a desperate thing to attempt," Garnett said to Armistead.

"It is," stout-hearted old Armistead answered, "but the issue is with the Almighty, and we must leave it in His hands." [52]

Presently, after a shell had hit a nearby tree, Armistead calmly pulled off a splinter and exhibited it to the men. "Boys," said he, "do you think you can go up under that? It is pretty hot out there." [53]

There was a confident answer, but presently, when a rabbit sprang from the bushes and leaped rapidly toward the rear, a gaunt Virginian voiced the feelings of thousands when he cried: "Run, ole hahr; if I was an ole hahr I would run, too." [54] The wounded were more numerous; a fragment of a bursting shell had struck down Colonel W. R. Aylett of the Fifty-fourth Virginia. [55] It was harder waiting under that fire than it would be in making the assault. [56]

Suddenly, through a rift in the smoke, Alexander saw Federal batteries withdrawing from the vicinity of the little grove. At the same instant the Federal fire began to fall off. It was now or never. On a bit of paper, Alexander scrawled to Pickett:

"For God's sake come quick. The 18 guns have gone. Come quick or my ammunition will not let me support you properly." [57]

A messenger dashed off through the smoke with the paper.

Pickett, at that moment, was in receipt of Alexander's previous dispatch. He read it and without a word passed it on to Longstreet, who had dismounted. Longstreet scrutinized it, but gave no order.

"General," said Pickett, anxiously, "shall I advance?"

Still no answer from Longstreet. He turned and looked away, and then, as if the effort cost him his very heart's blood, slowly nodded his head.

[52] F. W. Dawson, 95–96.
[53] W. H. Stewart: A Pair of Blankets, 101.
[54] F. W. Dawson, 96.
[55] Stewart, op. cit., 101.
[56] 32 S. H. S. P., 34.
[57] Alexander, 423.

Pickett shook back his long hair, and saluted. "I am going to move forward, sir," he said, and galloped off.[58]

About that same time, a shell fell close to the ordnance train, which was parked near at hand. Fearing for the safety of all the ammunition the army had to replenish the gaping caissons, General Pendleton ordered the wagons to the rear[59] and, a little later, recalled four of the nine eleven-pounder howitzers that Alexander had not been able to employ in the bombardment but had intended to use in following up the advance. Major Richardson, left in charge of the other howitzers, moved them also, to get them out of the line of fire.[60] Alexander must have been notified promptly of this, for when Longstreet rode to him after Pickett had left, Alexander told him that the howitzers were gone and that the ammunition of all the batteries was running low.

"Go and stop Pickett where he is," Longstreet said sharply, "and replenish your ammunition."

"We can't do that, sir," Alexander said. "The train has but little. It would take an hour to distribute it, and meanwhile the enemy would improve the time." [61]

"I do not want to make this charge," Longstreet said slowly and with deep emotion. "I do not see how it can succeed. I would not make it now but that General Lee has ordered it and is expecting it." With that he stopped, but he did not send word to Lee of the state of his ammunition. Lee received no intimation from any source that it was nearly exhausted.[62]

The Confederate artillerists paused now, for the infantry had to pass through the batteries. The Federal guns continued for a few minutes and then they, too, reserved their fire. Three hun-

---

[58] *Annals of the War*, 430–31; *Longstreet*, 392; *Alexander*, 423–24.

[59] *O. R.*, 27, part 2, p. 352.

[60] Alexander in 4 *S. H. S. P.*, 108, and in 3 *B. and L.*, 363; also Alexander, *op. cit.*, 420. Longstreet, who wrongly stated the number of these guns as seven in *Annals of the War*, 431, had so magnified them by the time he came to write *From Manassas to Appomattox* that he described them there (392), as "the batteries [Alexander] had reserved for the charge of the infantry" and affirmed that they "had been spirited away by General Lee's chief of artillery." Alexander made no complaint because, as he said, "had these guns gone forward with the infantry they must have been left upon the field and perhaps have attracted a counter-stroke after the repulse of Pickett's charge" (*op. cit.*, 420).

[61] *Alexander*, 424. In 4 *S. H. S. P.*, 103, Alexander explained that 130 to 150 rounds were carried with the guns and that the ordnance train did not have more than 100 per gun, probably not more than sixty.

[62] Lee in *O. R.*, 27, part 2, p. 321; *Marshall*, 240.

dred yards behind Alexander's batteries, the infantrymen realized that their time had come.[63] Soon Pickett galloped up, as debonair as if he had been riding through the streets of Richmond under the eye of his affianced. "Up, men," he called, "and to your posts! Don't forget today that you are from old Virginia!" [64] Almost at the same moment, on the crest, Pettigrew called to Marshall, "Now, Colonel, for the honor of the good Old North State, forward." [65]

General Garnett, buttoned to the neck in an old blue overcoat, and much too ill to take the field,[66] mounted his great black horse and rode out in front of his column as it sprang into line.[67] Kemper on his charger took position in advance of his willing regiments.[68] Armistead, who was to support these two brigadiers, turned his horse's head and came up to the color-sergeant of the Fifty-third Virginia. "Sergeant," he cried, "are you going to put those colors on the enemy's works today?"

"I will try, sir, and if mortal man can do it, it shall be done!" [69]

Then Armistead took off his hat, put it on the point of his sword and shouted in a voice that had never failed to reach the farthest man in his brigade, "Attention, Second battalion, the battalion of direction! Forward, guide centre! March!" And turning his horse, he went on ahead of them, his white head a mark for the bullets that were soon to fly.[70]

Now the skirmish line was in open; now Garnett and Kemper rode out.[71] Behind Kemper was Colonel Eppa Hunton of the Eighth Virginia on his horse, and behind Garnett was mounted Colonel Lewis Williams of the First, both of them too sick to walk but neither of them willing to be left behind. All the other officers, by Pickett's orders, were afoot.[72] And now the front brigades, except Davis's and Mayo's, were emerging from the

---

[63] 32 *S. H. S. P.*, 185. This account, frequently cited here, was written by Colonel Rawley W. Martin of the Fifty-third Virginia, who participated in the charge and was captured, wounded, after the assault failed.

[64] D. E. Johnston, *op. cit.*, 205–6.   [65] 2 *N. C. Regts.*, 365.

[66] He had arrived about 9 A.M. (*O. R.*, 27, part 2, p. 385).

[67] 33 *S. H. S. P.*, 28–29.

[68] D. E. *Johnston*, 211.   [69] 32 *S. H. S. P.*, 186.

[70] W. H. Stewart, *op. cit.*, 101; J. H. Lewis, *op. cit.*, 79; *F. W. Dawson*, 96. Stewart stated that the Third was the battalion of direction, Lewis, the Second.

[71] *Alexander*, 424.

[72] 31 *S. H. S. P.*, 230, a valuable paper by Captain Robert A. Bright of Pickett's staff.

woods.[73] The front was oblique because of the greater distance Pettigrew had to cover,[74] and there was a gap between Garnett's left and Fry's right. Once clear of the woods, at a word of command, the whole line was dressed until it was almost perfect in its formation.[75] Nineteen battle flags were in sight, their red deepened by the sunlight,[76] and the array seemed overpowering, but, as the smoke had lifted, those who looked on the right could see that the flank of Kemper was separated by almost half a mile from the left of McLaws—as if inviting an enfilade fire in its advance, or a counterattack should it fail.[77] From the left, the sight was one to make men catch their breath. Far beyond that flank, in Gettysburg, Rodes's soldiers called out to the Federal surgeons: "There go the men who will go through your damned Yankee line for you!"[78] Lee saw it all, and the sight that stirred him most was that of the bandages on the heads and arms of some of Pettigrew's Carolinians. They had been wounded in the battle of July 1, and had been mustered back into the ranks by their commander, along with all the cooks and extra-duty men.[79]

Davis had come out of the woods by this time, as had Mayo's brigade, lagging on his left. Soon the supporting line was visible, too—Armistead on the right, then Lowrance, then Lane on the left—and twenty-five more battle flags were visible. Armistead's left overlapped Lowrance's right at the start, but this was quickly rectified, and the whole swept forward at common time, Armistead's men with their arms at right shoulder.[80] Each unit moved as if the distance had been taped and marked for a grand review.

Two hundred yards forward and scarcely a shot. Kemper, moving sharply toward the left, was across the double fence at Spangler's lane. Garnett's men, with scarcely a stir in their alignment, were negotiating the post-and-rail fence in their front and were sweeping through a lesser obstruction as if it were not there. Then, as if awakened from a dream, the Federal artillerists opened—not with the weakened fire that the supposed with-

[73] 5 *N. C. Regts.*, 125.   [74] 5 *S. H. S. P.*, 39–40.   [75] 32 *S. H. S. P.*, 34.
[76] *F. W. Dawson*, 96. The number, of course, does not include those of Mayo's and Davis's troops or those of the supporting infantry brigades, which had not yet come from the woods.
[77] 7 *S. H. S. P.*, 83. For the lifting of the smoke, see 5 *N. C. Regts.*, 125.
[78] Lieutenant F. A. Haskell in *Gibbon, op. cit.*, 167.
[79] 5 *N. C. Regts.*, 104.
[80] *Walter Harrison*, 91; *J. H. Lewis*, 79.

drawal of eighteen guns had led the Confederates to anticipate, but with the full fury of massed guns. The blast was concentrated on Pickett, because Pettigrew was not yet within effective range.[81] The shells tore gaps in the line; flags began to go down; behind the advancing ranks, dead and writhing men littered the ground. But the charge continued at the same measured pace, with scarcely the fire of a single Southern musket.

Soon the skirmishers were brought to a stand at the post-and-plank fences along the Emmitsburg road.[82] They disputed this barrier with the Federal skirmishers, who held their own until the main Confederate line was within one hundred yards. Then the enemy fell back. Openings were made in the stubborn fence, but as the men made for these, they crowded together and offered a mark that the Federal gunners reached again and again.[83] Once beyond the second fence on the eastern side of the road, Pickett's men were halted, and the line was drawn again with care.[84] Armistead was close behind now, the flanks of Garnett's and of Archer's brigades had met,[85] and Pettigrew's two right brigades, though they had been forced to cross a number of farm fences,[86] had kept their formation admirably. Davis had caught up, but Mayo's brigade was falling behind more and more.[87] All Pettigrew's units were now under artillery fire[88] and were suffering heavily.

Up the hill now and at double time! Kemper swings still farther to the left, up a little swale, and his flank is bare to the enemy's bullets. More colors go down;[89] hundreds of men have fallen. Still the formation is excellent, and the front is heavy enough to cover the 250 yards that separate the Confederate right from the wall. Here is the Federal advanced line already, hidden in the tall grass. It fires and flees.[90] A flash of flame, a roar, and the Federal infantry behind the stone wall has opened with their volley.[91] From the right, a small Union command is

[81] J. H. Lewis, 79; O. R., 27, part 2, p. 644.

[82] 32 S. H. S. P., 191. This is the account of Captain John Holmes Smith, a most useful narrative of the charge.

[83] 32 S. H. S. P., 188.

[84] Gibbon, op. cit., 151.

[85] O. R., 27, part 2, p. 647.

[86] O. R., 27, part 2, p. 651.

[87] 5 N. C. Regts., 125, 130, 134.

[88] O. R., 27, part 2, p. 644.

[89] 32 S. H. S. P., 190.

[90] O. R., 27, part 2, p. 386.

[91] 32 S. H. S. P., 190; J. H. Lewis, 80.

tearing Kemper's flank.[92] Garnett, still on that rearing black horse, is shouting to his men; the rebel yell rolls up the ridge in answer to the Federal challenge; Garnett is charging bayonets; the Union artillery has stopped its blasts on the right but is still pouring canister into Pettigrew.[93] Only a hundred yards for Pickett now, hardly more for Pettigrew. Fry's brigade has almost been absorbed by the commands on its right and left.[94] Armistead is on the heels of Garnett and Kemper; Lowrance and Lane are fighting across the field in the rear of Pettigrew through bursting shell.[95]

"Fire!" cries Garnett, and his men for the first time pull trigger.

"Fire!" Kemper echoes, and his troops send a volley against the wall at the same instant that their high, furious yell breaks out. Armistead had ridden back so that his line can fire,[96] and his horse is down. There goes his volley; on the left, where the stone wall is farther up the ridge and higher, the Federal infantry have opened on Pettigrew.[97]

Twenty-five yards—only twenty-five to the barrier in Garnett's front. The grimy faces of the Federal infantry can be seen where the smoke lifts for an instant in front of the wall. But the lines are all in confusion now. Fry's men are mingled with Garnett's, Marshall's right is piling up on Garnett's left. Garnett is down, dead, and his horse is racing back toward the Confederate lines, a great gash in his shoulder;[98] Kemper has fallen; the line is melting away on the right and on the left. Still the dauntless men rush upward. The Virginians and some of the Tennesseans and Carolinians are at the stone fence, and on their left the rest of Marshall's brigade is rushing into the open ground at the angle and fighting on to the wall, eighty yards farther eastward.[99] Armistead is up now, at the low barrier, his sword is high, and his hat, pierced by the point of his sword, is down to the hilt of his blade. His voice is ringing out above the din "Follow me!" Over the wall then, with the bayonet, and on to the crest of the hill![100] About 100 men of five brigades follow him into

[92] O. R., 27, part 1, p. 373.
[94] 5 N. C. Regts., 107.
[96] J. H. Lewis, 80.
[98] 33 S. H. S. P., 28–29.
[100] O. R., 27, part 2, p. 386.

[93] Cf. Haskell in Gibbon, op. cit., 155.
[95] 5 N. C. Regts., 127.
[97] O. R., 27, part 2, p. 644.
[99] 5 N. C. Regts., 107–8, 151 ff.

the mêlée, with butt and thrust, but they fall at every step.[101] In the angle, Marshall's men press on. The enemy is all around them. Where are the thousands who marched in that proud line

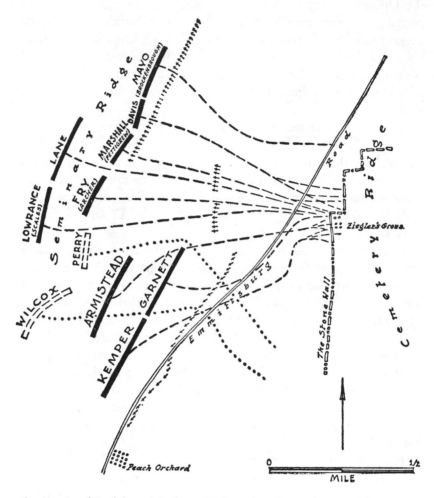

Convergence of Confederate brigades on Ziegler's Grove ("the little clump of trees") in the advance of the right-centre, July 3, 1863.

from the woods? Where are the flags and where the supports? The right is in the air; they are bluecoats firing over there, not Confederates. And on the left—more Federals. The place

[101] O. R., 27, part 1, p. 428.

is a death-trap—are there no officers to tell one what to do? In the front are the enemy's batteries; Armistead lies yonder among the guns, forty yards within the wall, his left hand on a cannon, his right still grasping his sword. Davis has reached the wall and has recoiled, broken; Mayo's men have failed; the left has melted away. Lowrance and Lane are in the angle, but they are only a fragment.[102] Are there no reinforcements to drive the victory home? Wilcox is advancing on the right and that is Perry's little brigade beside him, but they have lost direction. Instead of following Kemper's turn they are moving straight on— to annihilation if they continue.[103] A few batteries have advanced, but their fire is weak and erratic.[104] No support; no succor! In the angle and beyond the wall, there is nothing to do but to struggle with those thickening masses of Federals. Here and there an officer is calling out "Steady, men";[105] pistols are being used against muskets;[106] Captain M. P. Spessard yonder has stopped to take a last look at his dying son and then has sprung over the wall, and is fighting with his bare sword in a hand-to-hand struggle with Federal infantrymen.[107] That color-sergeant is using his flag staff as a lance;[108] the flag of the Eleventh North Carolina has gone down again and again, and now Captain Francis Bird is carrying it and rallying his men;[109] the survivors, unconsciously crowding around the standards, are stumbling over the bodies of the dead; every minute sees the struggling remnants thinned.

From the right there is a rush and a volley; on the left the Federals loose an overwhelming blast of musketry;[110] in front, they stand stubbornly behind the wall at the angle and on the crest.[111] The column is surrounded—there is no escape except in abandoning the heights, won with so much blood and valor. Every man for himself! Uplifted hands for the soldier whose musket has been struck down, a white handkerchief here, a cry

---

102 *O. R.*, 27, part 1, pp. 428, 464; part 2, pp. 647, 651, 660.

103 Wilcox did not receive his orders to advance until twenty or thirty minutes after Pickett had charged, and as he moved forward in support, he could not see Pickett's lines and was overwhelmed with gunfire (*O. R.*, 27, part 2, p. 620; 4 *S. H. S. P.*, 117; *Memoir of Capt. C. Seton Fleming*, 79 *ff.*).

104 *O. R.*, 27, part 2, pp. 352, 435; *Alexander*, 425, 428–29.

105 Haskell, in Gibbon, *op. cit.*, 161.

106 *Ibid.*

107 *O. R.*, 27, part 2, p. 387.

108 4 *S. H. S. P.*, 93.

109 1 *N. C. Regts.*, 590.

110 *O. R.*, 27, part 2, p. 644.

111 Haskell in Gibbon, *op. cit.*, 162.

of "I surrender," and for the rest—back over the wall and out into the field again.[112] The assault has failed. Men could do no more!

Down the ridge toward Alexander's guns the Virginians made their way; straight across the field the men of Pettigrew's and of Trimble's divisions retired. Only a few kept the semblance of formation. Three hundred of Garnett's brigade, escaping by what seemed a miracle, slowly and sullenly came down to the Emmitsburg road and on to the batteries.[113] Men who could still walk hobbled along, some of them with two rifles as crutches; those whose legs had been broken or whose feet had been shot off dragged themselves toward the lines.[114] On the whole field, only one or two battle flags were to be seen. The vengeful Federal artillery fire followed these retreating flags, but it was uncertain and scattering, for on the hill, too, ammunition had been almost spent. A few Union soldiers came out in pursuit and aimed hungrily at the Confederates, but there was no immediate counter-stroke. The repulse had been too costly. At last the survivors reached Alexander's guns and staggered on to the cover of the low ground west of the batteries. And there, there they found Lee astride Traveller.[115] From the spot where the Virginia monument now stands, he had witnessed—who presumes to say with what emotions?—as much of the charge as was visible through the smoke and dust. As soon as he had seen that the assault was failing, he had ridden out to rally the men and to share the ordeal of the counterattack, if one was to come.[116] In person he had ordered Wright to support Wilcox, should the Alabamians be pursued.[117] His one thought now was of those who had come back, dazed or wounded, from the ridge. With Longstreet and some staff officers he circulated among them.[118] For every one he encountered he had a word of cheer—"All will come right in the end—we'll talk it over afterwards—we want all good and true men just now."[119] A few would pass on bewildered, but most of them brightened

112 *J. H. Lewis*, 83; Haskell in Gibbon, *op. cit.*, 163–64.
113 *O. R.*, 27, part 2, p. 387.   114 *Cf. Fremantle*, 265, 266.
115 *Fremantle*, 268; *W. W. Chamberlaine*, 72; *Long*, 295–96.
116 Alexander in 3 *B. and L.*, 366–67; *Alexander*, 425.
117 *O. R.*, 27, part 2, p. 625.
118 *Longstreet*, 395; 32 *S. H. S. P.*, 34.
119 *Fremantle*, 268.

when they recognized him, and some, even of the badly wounded, stopped to cheer him.

All his self-mastery had been mustered for this supreme test, and he seemed to overlook nothing. When the roar of a Federal cheer swept down from the left, Lee thought that perhaps Johnson on the other flank had gained some advantage and he directed Lieutenant F. M. Colston, Alexander's ordnance officer, to ride and see what it meant. Colston started, but his horse balked, and he began to belabor him with a stick. "Don't whip him, Captain," Lee called, "don't whip him. I've got just such another foolish horse myself, and whipping does no good." [120]

He was still expecting a thrust by the enemy, and where he met a man whose wounds were light he told him, "Bind up your hurts and take a musket." One coward, who pretended to be injured, he ordered some nearby gunners to pull from a ditch and set on his feet. When Colonel Fremantle rode up to see the dreadful climax of the drama, Lee greeted him: "This has been a sad day for us, Colonel, a sad day; but we can't always expect to win victories."[121] And in the next breath he cautioned the Britisher to seek a safer place.

A little way off Lee saw Pickett, who had remained in the field watching his flanks and seeking support during the charge,[122] and he hurried over to meet him. "General Pickett," he began, "place your division in rear of this hill, and be ready to repel the advance of the enemy should they follow up their advantage." At least one officer noticed that Lee said "the enemy," instead of his usual "those people," but Pickett was too nearly frantic with grief to remark Lee's language.

"General Lee, I have no division now, Armistead is down, Garnett is down, and Kemper is mortally wounded."

"Come, General Pickett," said Lee, "this has been my fight and upon my shoulders rests the blame. The men and officers of your command have written the name of Virginia as high today as it has ever been written before."

120 *Fremantle*, 268; *Alexander*, 426. Figg, *op. cit.*, 146, explained that the horse did not balk but was unwilling to be separated from Alexander's mount with which he had been paired on the march.

121 *Fremantle*, 268.

122 Captain R. A. Bright, in 31 *S. H. S. P.*, 231 *ff.* There is no foundation whatsoever for the story that General Pickett did not direct the charge. He remained throughout the action at his proper place in rear of the column of attack.

Some of the survivors crowded around the riders then, and Lee repeated, "Your men have done all that men could do; the fault is entirely my own." [123]

At that moment he noticed a litter being carried through the batteries. "Captain," he said to one of Pickett's staff, "what officer is that they are bearing off?"

"General Kemper."

"I must speak to him," and he touched Traveller. When he overtook the litter, the bearers halted, and Kemper opened his eyes. Lee took his hand and pressed it. "General Kemper," he said, "I hope you are not very seriously wounded."

"I am struck in the groin," Kemper answered, calm amid his suffering, "and the ball has ranged upward; they tell me it is mortal."

"I hope it may not prove so bad as that; is there anything I can do for you, General Kemper?"

In great pain Kemper lifted himself on one elbow: "Yes, General Lee, do full justice to this division for its work today."

Lee bowed his head. "I will," he said. And the soldiers carried Kemper on.[124]

Presently General Wilcox came up, in a battered straw hat. He had brought out his men by following the swale under the Federal line, but his losses had been heavy,[125] and as he tried to explain the condition of his brigade, his emotion overwhelmed him. Lee shook his hand. "Never mind, General, all this has been my fault—it is *I* that have lost this fight, and you must help me out of it the best way you can." [126]

Then he turned once again to speak to the men from the ranks. Whatever their plight, he had comfort or cheer or exhortation. Some Federal prisoners had been captured in the skirmish along the Emmitsburg road, and one of them, who probably had been wounded as he made his way to the rear, was lying on the ground. The stout-hearted fellow cried out "Hurrah for the Union" as Lee passed. The General heard him, stopped his

---

[123] Bright in 31 *S. H. S. P.*, 234. C. T. Loehr, *War History of the Old First Virginia Infantry Regiment* (cited hereafter as *Loehr*), 38.

[124] 31 *S. H. S. P.*, 234. Alexander, *op. cit.*, 426, gave a slightly different version of this meeting, but Bright was present through it all and wrote before Alexander.

[125] *O. R.*, 27, part 2, p. 620; *Alexander*, 425; 5 *N. C. Regts.*, 109.

[126] *Fremantle*, 269.

horse, dismounted and approached the bluecoat, who was satisfied that Lee intended to kill him. Instead, Lee looked down sadly at him and then extended his hand. "My son," he said, "I hope you will soon be well." [127]

Ere long the last of those who had survived the slaughter on the ridge passed wearily up the hill. Captain Bird, who had taken the falling flag of the Eleventh North Carolina, had brought it off the field, though eight men had been hit while carrying it, and the staff of the battered colors had been struck twice while he held it.[128] Captain Spessard, who had fought so splendidly, had managed to escape from his assailants.[129] Trimble had been struck in the leg but had been carried to the rear.[130] The carnage had been as frightful as in front of the stone wall at Fredericksburg. From Pickett's division only one field officer had found his way back to the lines. All the others had been killed or had been wounded and captured. Garnett had taken in more than 1300 men and had lost 941. Pettigrew's brigade had but a solitary staff officer to rally the remnant, and of his whole division only 1500 or 1600 returned.[131] The Thirty-eighth North Carolina could muster a bare forty, under a first lieutenant,[132] and Company A of the Eleventh North Carolina, which had crossed the Potomac with one hundred, had only eight men and a single officer.[133]

Yet the fighting spirit of the men had not been destroyed. Wright's and Posey's soldiers had been ready to go into the charge to support Wilcox, when Longstreet had restrained Anderson with the assurance that the attack had failed and that a further attempt would simply be a waste of life.[134] Colonel Fremantle, mingling with the gunners of an advanced battery, found the men anxious for the Federals to attack, and when they saw Lee they assured their visitor, "We've not lost confidence in the old man: This day's work will do him no harm. 'Uncle Robert' will get us into Washington yet; you bet he will." [135] Sergeant Charles Belcher of the Twenty-fourth Virginia, bringing back his colors from the ridge, had called out to Pickett, "General, let us go it

---

[127] *Long,* 302. The Federal who narrated this incident did not state that he was a prisoner at the time, but Lee would hardly have encountered him otherwise.

[128] 1 *N. C. Regts.,* 590.

[129] *O. R.,* 27, part 2, p. 387.

[130] *O. R.,* 27, part 2, p. 660.

[131] *O. R.,* 27, part 2, pp. 644, 645.

[132] 2 *N. C. Regts.,* 693.

[133] 1 *N. C. Regts.,* 590.

[134] *O. R.,* 27, part 2, pp. 614–15.

[135] *Fremantle,* 270–71.

again";[136] and in all the anguish and disappointment there was, as Colonel Fremantle attested, "less noise, fuss or confusion of orders than at an ordinary field day." [137] Two divisions were mere fragments,[138] and the stream behind Seminary Ridge flowed red because so many men knelt to bathe their wounds.[139] But the Army of Northern Virginia still had terror for the enemy. The attempts at a counterstroke were abortive, except on the extreme right, where General Farnsworth led a futile charge at the cost of his life.[140] On Cemetery Ridge, where twenty fallen battle flags lay in a space one hundred yards square,[141] so deep had the attacking column hacked its way toward the heart of the enemy that when supporting Union batteries came up and caught their first glimpse of the herded prisoners, the officers ordered a retreat. They believed the Confederates had stormed the ridge and they could not credit the evidence before their eyes that the men who had defeated them on so many fields were disarmed and helpless.[142]

Lee remained with Alexander more than half an hour, now in the open and now behind the edge of the ridge, where the group of horsemen could look over the crest without attracting the fire of the enemy.[143] Slowly, then, when it was all over, he rode back toward headquarters. If he saw Longstreet again, after encountering him while he was attempting to rally Pickett's survivors, there was not the slightest touch of crimination. Longstreet, in fact, having fortified himself with rum,[144] was somewhat confused in mind. Although there is not the slightest suggestion that he was drunk, he was doubtful whether or not he had ordered McLaws to leave his exposed position.[145] The few batteries that had attempted to follow the charge were gradually withdrawn, and after nightfall Alexander skillfully brought all his guns back to Seminary Ridge.[146] The infantry were recalled from the right

---

[136] *Loehr,* 38. [137] *Fremantle,* 268.
[138] Such was the spirit of Pickett's division that the survivors grumbled much, later in the day, when Lee assigned them to the tame duty of serving as provost-marshal's guard (32 *S. H. S. P.,* 38).
[139] 32 *S. H. S. P.,* 37.
[140] 3 *B. and L.,* 393 ff., Longstreet, 395–96; *O. R.,* 27, part 2, p. 360.
[141] *O. R.,* 27, part 1, p. 440.
[142] Haskell in Gibbon, *op. cit.,* 167–68. [143] *Alexander,* 426.
[144] *Fremantle,* 267. [145] 7 *S. H. S. P.,* 88.
[146] *Alexander,* 426.

to a shorter line. They accomplished the manœuvre without material interruption by the enemy.[147]

Lee had no complicated strategic problem to solve now, no alternatives to ponder. Retreat was the only course left open to him. The army had sustained such heavy losses it could not consider a renewal of the offensive. The greater part of the artillery was almost powerless for lack of ammunition. Federal troops would certainly attempt to seize the gaps in the mountains and to interfere with the evacuation of the wounded. Subsistence could not be had in the narrow area Lee could control. Orders were therefore issued before the day was out to prepare for the withdrawal as soon as the wounded and the wagon trains could be cleared.[148] Lee left to Longstreet the completion of arrangements for the retirement of the First Corps. As he did not intend to move the Second Corps until last, Lee did not visit Ewell that night, but he rode over to A. P. Hill's headquarters to discuss with him the arrangements for the Third Corps, which was to head the column of retreat.

After a long conference over the map,[149] Lee walked Traveller back through the moonlight and the sleeping camps about 1 A.M. When he reached his own headquarters, where his exhausted staff officers had already sought repose, he was so weary that he could hardly dismount. With an effort he reached the ground and stood for a moment, leaning heavily on his horse. "The moon shone full on his massive features," wrote one of the few witnesses, "and revealed an expression of sadness that I had never before seen upon his face."

Presently General Imboden, who had been ordered to await him on his return from Hill, addressed him in a sympathetic voice: "General, this has been a hard day on you."

"Yes, it has been a sad, sad day for us," Lee answered mournfully, and relapsed into silence, thinking of the failure of the charge that might have won the battle and perhaps have decided the war. Then, after a minute or two, he straightened up and broke out with an excitement of manner that startled his companion: "I never saw troops behave more magnificently than

---

147 O. R., 27, part 2, p. 360.
148 O. R., 27, part 2, pp. 299, 360; *Alexander*, 435.   149 3 B. and L., 420

Pickett's division of Virginians did today in that grand charge upon the enemy. And if they had been supported as they were to have been—but for some reason not yet fully explained to me, were not—we would have held the position and the day would have been ours."

Another pause, brief this time, and then he exclaimed in a voice that echoed loudly and grimly through the night, "Too bad! Too bad! Oh, too bad!" [150]

[150] 3 *B. and L.,* 421.

CHAPTER IX

WHY WAS GETTYSBURG LOST?

WOULD Meade attack? Every man in the Army of Northern Virginia put that question to himself on the morning of the 4th of July, and no man knew the answer. If the Federals had the strength to take the initiative, they would find the Confederates frightfully extended, bleeding, and almost without ammunition. Should the Union commander for any reason withhold attack, another dawn would find Lee on his way back to Virginia, moving as fast as he could without endangering his wagon-train.

As the anxious hours passed without any sign of a Union offensive, the plans for the withdrawal took form. Instead of following the long route back to Chambersburg and thence to Hagerstown, the army was to go southwestward to Fairfield and westward to Greencastle. Stuart was to send a brigade or two of cavalry to hold the passes west of Cashtown on the Chambersburg pike, so that the Federal horse could not advance by that line and get ahead of the slower-moving Southern infantry before it reached the Potomac. The rest of the Confederate troopers were to use the Emmitsburg road and protect the rear and left flank of the army. The wounded were to leave as soon as practicable. Hill was to follow. Then Longstreet was to take up the march and was to guard the prisoners. Ewell would cover the rear. All the wagons not used in transporting the wounded were to form a single train, placed midway the column. To prevent all misunderstandings, Lee issued these orders explicitly and in writing.[1]

A hundred troublesome details absorbed the weary commander of the defeated army. In an effort to relieve himself of the burden of 4000 unwounded prisoners, he dispatched a flag of truce proposing an exchange, but Meade prudently declined.[2] Engineers

[1] *O. R.*, 27, part 2, p. 311.   [2] *O. R.*, 27, part 1, p. 78; *Early* 276.

were sent back to select a line in rear of Hagerstown, in case the
enemy pursued vigorously;[3] the wounded were painfully assembled with great difficulty, and an artillery force was provided to
supplement the escort, which consisted of Imboden's cavalry.[4] A
brief report was prepared for the President.[5]

To add to the difficulties of the retreat, a torrential rain began
to fall ominously about 1 P.M. and delayed the start of the ambulance train.[6] Final preparations had to be made in a blinding
storm. When at last the wounded were on their way, in rough
wagons that were as torturing as the rack,[7] fully 5000 sulkers and
sick contrived to march with them. Lee could not readily prevent
this, but he was most solicitous that no panic or sense of demoralization spread among the troops. When "Sandie" Pendleton
brought the daily report of the Second Corps, he said to Lee
encouragingly, "General, I hope the other two corps are in as
good condition for work as ours is this morning." Lee was fond
of "Sandie," but talk of this sort was apt to create dangerous im-
pressions, so he looked steadily at young Pendleton and said
coldly, "What reason have you, young man, to suppose they are
not?"[8] To sustain the morale, he moved about as calmly as
if the withdrawal of the army in the face of the foe were a simple
summer's-day field manœuvre. He had little to say, but when he
rode past the camps of the Texans and was welcomed with their
loyal cheer, he was not too much absorbed in his own sombre
thoughts to raise his hat in acknowledgment of their greeting.[9]
In the afternoon, while the storm raged, Lee, without a tremor
visible to any one, surveyed from one of the ridges the tragic
scene of the defeat;[10] and when, in the evening, he stopped at
Longstreet's bivouac on the roadside, his remark was the same as
that with which he had met Pickett on the field after the fatal
charge: "It's all my fault," he said, "I thought my men were invincible."[11] Longstreet had lost his sullenness in the face of the
disaster to the army, and though he and Lee did not talk of the
battle, Longstreet calmly voiced his sobered opinion to Colonel

---

[8] 3 C. M. H., 420.   [4] 3 B. and L., 422.   [5] O. R., 27, part 2, p. 298.
[6] 3 B. and L., 423; Fremantle, 274; Sorrel, 171; O. R., 27, part 2, pp. 966–67.
[7] 3 B. and L., 424.
[8] O. R., 27, part 2, p. 1048; Pendleton, 295.
[9] J. M. Polk: Memoirs of the Lost Cause, 18.
[10] Fremantle, 254; Ross, 71.   [11] W. M. Owen, 256.

Fremantle. The assault had failed, he said, because it had not been made with a sufficient number of men. He made no reference then to the rejection of his plan of moving by the right in an effort to get between the enemy and Washington.[12]

The next day, July 5, was sixteen daylight hours of purgatory. The rain was falling as heavily as ever; the men were muddy, wet, and hungry.[13] So slowly did the other corps drag themselves along the blocked road that it was 2 A.M. before Ewell left the field of Gettysburg, and 4 P.M. by the time he reached Fairfield,[14] which was less than nine miles from his starting point. Even then, some of his wagons were lost.[15] Ewell was so outraged by this that he wished to turn back and get immediate revenge, but Lee refused to countenance such a foolish adventure. "No, no, General Ewell," he said, "we must let those people alone for the present—we will try them again some other time."[16] The rain continued during the night of July 5–6,[17] but as the leading corps was then through the mountains it was able to move, unabashed, at greater speed than it had ever made before in putting distance between itself and its old adversary. "Let him who will say it to the contrary," one Texas recruit confided in a letter to his wife, "we made Manassas time from Pennsylvania."[18]

At 5 o'clock on the afternoon of the 6th, Longstreet's corps, which was then the van, succeeded in reaching Hagerstown.[19] Lee rode with it and found to his vast relief that the ambulance train had arrived at Williamsport that day with the wounded. But the elements had again lone battle against the South: the pontoon bridge below the town had been broken up by a raiding party, and the Potomac, swollen by the rains, was far past fording. The army, its wounded and its prisoners, were cut off from Virginia soil. More than that, a mixed force of Federal cavalry and artillery had appeared in the rear and had threatened the capture of the wagons and their pain-racked loads. The teamsters had been organized, however, to support Imboden, two regiments of infantry that had been returning from Winchester had been rushed up, and the attack had been held off until Stuart had

[12] Fremantle, 274.
[13] Malone, 38; White in Richmond Howitzers, 210.
[14] O. R., 27, part 2, pp. 448, 471.   [15] Fremantle, 277.
[16] White in Richmond Howitzers, 211–12. [17] Fremantle, 280.
[18] L. C. West, 96.   [19] O. R., 27, part 2, p. 361.

arrived with his cavalry. The Federals had then been repulsed.[20] Despite this success, the situation was worse than serious. The raging river was so high that some days, perhaps a week, would pass before it was fordable. The country roundabout had already been foraged; few supplies could be collected. Meade, in Lee's opinion, was certainly pursuing in the hope of attacking before he crossed the Potomac. Any long delay would involve another battle in Maryland, and a disaster with the river at flood would mean annihilation.[21]

Lee's first thought was for his wounded. He gave orders that all the ferry-boats in the vicinity should be collected so that he might use them in transporting the sufferers to the south bank.[22] The wagons must wait until the river subsided or until the pontoon bridge could be reconstructed,[23] and if Meade attacked, the army must prepare to give battle once more to the Federals.[24] Fortunately, the engineers had found and had laid out an admirable defensive line. It extended from Downsville, which lies three miles south of Williamsport, northward in front of that town to the Conocoheague. Both flanks were well covered.[25]

The men in the ranks were not conscious of the danger they faced, or else they defied it. They were in sight of their own country once more and their morale seemed unimpaired, thin as were the ranks.[26] "We are all right at Hagerstown," one of Lee's staff officers wrote his sister reassuringly, "and we hope soon to get up another fight."[27] Another young soldier maintained, "The army is in fine spirits and confident of success when they again meet the enemy."[28] Lee himself reported the condition of the army good "and its confidence unimpaired."[29] The bands began to play again,[30] and the soldiers renewed their jests. Some of the men were not so mindful as Lee had commanded in respecting the

[20] O. R., 27, part 2, pp. 322, 107 ff.; Worsham, 168; Long MS. Long noted that "the teamsters of the train acted with great gallantry on this occasion. They were armed and acted as infantry."

[21] O. R., 27, part 2, pp. 309, 322–23.

[22] O. R., 27, part 2, p. 322, ibid., part 3, p. 983.

[23] 3 B. and L., 422.   [24] O. R., 27, part 2, p. 300.

[25] Long MS.; G. B. Davis: From Gettysburg to Williamsport, 3 M. H. S. M., 461–62.

[26] Alexander in 3 B. and L., 367.

[27] Walter H. Taylor to his sister, July 7, 1863, Taylor MSS.

[28] R. H. McKim: A Soldier's Recollections, 181. Cf. Jones, L. and L., 253: "I never saw the soldiers of the Army of Northern Virginia more anxious to fight or more confident of victory than they were at Hagerstown. . . ."

[29] O. R., 27, part 2, p. 299.   [30] 2 N. C. Regts., 399.

property of the Maryland farmers, and had to be given stern orders not to forage or to steal horses.[31] Finding one battalion of artillery burning fence rails, Lee sent for the major and asked if a copy of General Orders No. 73 had reached him. The officer admitted that he had received those famous instructions against damaging the property of civilians. "Then, sir," said Lee, "you must not only have them published, but you must see that they are obeyed." [32]

In the press of duties in front of Williamsport, Lee found the loss and suffering of his men brought home to him. On June 26, his own son, Rooney Lee, wounded at Brandy Station, had been taken from his bed at "Hickory Hill," Hanover County, by a Federal raiding party, and had been carried to Fort Monroe, where he was held as a hostage for the good treatment of some Federal officers who had been threatened with death as a measure of retaliation. Lee's warmth of feeling for Rooney made the capture of his son a deep personal sorrow, and he hastened, busy as he was, to send comforting words to the soldier's young wife.[33]

Not for a moment, however, did Lee let his concern for Rooney or his uneasiness for his troops shake his equanimity. No trace of resentment was there in his dealings with the men who had failed him. He greeted Longstreet cordially as "my old war horse." [34] In fact, for months thereafter Lee showed more than usual warmth to Longstreet, as if to make it plain that he did not blame him and did not countenance any whispering against Longstreet that might cause dissension in the army.[35] When Captain Ross, the Austrian observer, came to call, Lee talked of Gettysburg as if all the fault had been his own. He told Ross that if he had been aware that Meade had been able to concentrate his whole army, he would not have attacked him, but that the success of the first day, the belief that Meade had only a part of his

---

[31] *O. R.*, 27, part 3, pp. 982–83, 987.   [32] 37 *S. H. S. P.*, 142.

[33] *O. R.*, 27, part 2, pp. 796–97; *Fremantle*, 287; *Mrs. McGuire*, 224; *R. E. Lee, Jr.*, 98 *ff.*; personal account of the incident given the writer by Honorable Henry T. Wickham, then a boy at "Hickory Hill"; *Jones*, 399; *Jones, L. and L.*, 277–78. Fortunately, Rooney Lee stood the journey without relapse. By Aug. 2, 1863, Lee heard from a returning surgeon that his son was walking about on crutches. Later in the summer, a Federal general in Libby prison sought through Reverend T. V. Moore to arrange a special exchange between Rooney Lee and himself, but Lee opposed such special exchanges and wrote Mr. Moore that he could not seek for his son a favor that could not be asked for the humblest soldier in the army (*Jones*, 184).

[34] 3 *B. and L.*, 428.   [35] See *infra*, p. 168.

army on the field, and the enthusiasm of his own troops had led him to conclude that the possible results of a victory justified the risks. He added that his lack of accurate knowledge of the enemy's concentration was due to the absence of Stuart's cavalry.[36] In writing to the President, he was full of fight and urged once more that Beauregard's army be brought to the upper Rappahannock for a demonstration on Washington.[37] "I hope," he said, "Your Excellency will understand that I am not in the least discouraged, or that my faith in the protection of an all-wise Providence, or in the fortitude of this army, is at all shaken. But, though conscious that the enemy has been much shattered in the recent battle, I am aware that he can be easily reinforced, while no addition can be made to our numbers. The measure, therefore, that I have recommended is altogether one of a prudential nature." [38]

This was written on the 8th of July. The next night an officer who had escaped from the Federals at Gettysburg arrived with news that the enemy was marching on Hagerstown.[39] This confirmed Lee's belief that Meade intended to attack him north of the Potomac,[40] and he prepared accordingly. His cavalry were thrown out as a wide screen and the infantry were moved into the lines prepared for them.[41] In person he supervised the posting of Longstreet's men; he issued a stirring appeal to the army to meet once more the onslaughts of the enemy.[42] He did not lose grip on himself, but to Colonel Alexander, who observed him on many fields, Lee never appeared as deeply anxious as on July 10.[43] The wounded and the prisoners were not yet across the river; supplies sufficed only from day to day because the flood waters made it impossible to operate some of the flour mills; forage was

---

36 *Ross*, 80. It was at this time that Lee explained to Scheibert his theory of the high command and his belief that the commanding general should not attempt to direct the battle tactically. See *supra*, vol. II, p. 347.

37 *O. R.*, 27, part 2, p. 300. President Davis and Adjutant General Cooper had already vetoed this proposal, which Lee had advanced before he entered Pennsylvania (see *supra*, p. 47). Unknown to Lee, however, Mr. Davis's answer had been taken from the courier by Captain Ulrich Dahlgren and had been forwarded to General Meade. The assurance this letter gave him that he had nothing to fear in the way of an advance from Virginia on Washington is alleged to have been one of the reasons for Meade's decision to remain at Gettysburg and to receive Lee's final assault there (*Alexander*, 367; 8 *S. H. S. P.*, 523; *O. R.*, 27, part 1, p. 75 *ff.*).

38 *O. R.*, 27, part 2, p. 300.

39 This officer was Lieutenant Thomas L. Norwood of the Thirty-seventh North Carolina (*O. R.*, 27, part 3, p. 991).

40 *O. R.*, 27, part 2, p. 353.

41 *O. R.*, 27, p. 300; *ibid.*, part 3, pp. 994–95.

42 *O. R.*, 27, part 2, p. 301.

43 *Alexander*, 439–40.

getting very scarce, and the horses were subsisting only on grass and standing grain.[44]

The Federals had been approaching cautiously,[45] but by the 12th they grew bolder[46] and appeared in considerable strength around Boonsboro and Sharpsburg.[47] Lee's mind wavered between hope and anxiety. "Had the river not unexpectedly risen," he wrote his wife, "all would have been well with us; but God, in His all-wise providence, ruled otherwise, and our communications have been interrupted and almost cut off. The waters have subsided to about four feet, and if they continue, by tomorrow, I hope, our communications will be open. I trust that a merciful God, our only hope and refuge, will not desert us in this hour of need, and will deliver us by His almighty hand, that the whole world may recognize His power and all hearts be lifted up in adoration and praise of His unbounded loving-kindness. We must, however, submit to His almighty will, whatever that may be." [48]

Lee's prayers seemed answered on the 13th. Jackson's handy-man, the resourceful Major J. A. Harman, had torn down old warehouses and had constructed a number of crude boats that had been floated down to Falling Waters, where some of the original pontoons had been recovered.[49] With these a crossing had been laid—"a good bridge" in Lee's thankful eyes,[50] a "crazy affair" to the more critical Colonel Sorrel.[51] The river at Williamsport was still deep but fordable, at last, by infantry. Lee determined not to delay a day in reaching a wider field of manœuvre on the south shore of the forbidding Potomac. To expedite his movement he decided to use both the ford and the pontoons—Ewell to cross by the former route, and the trains and the rest of the army by the bridge.[52] Longstreet demurred at this withdrawal, because there was a chance of fighting a defensive battle on ground to his liking, but Lee overruled him and personally directed the preparations for the crossing.[53]

[44] *O. R.*, 27, part 2, pp. 300, 301, 327; *Longstreet*, 429.
[45] Meade believed that Lee had taken up a succession of strong positions (C. A. Page: *Letters of a War Correspondent*, 35).
[46] Pearson, *James S. Wadsworth*, 231.　　[47] *Long MS.*
[48] *R. E. Lee, Jr.*, 101–2; *cf. O. R.*, 27, part 2, p. 301.
[49] 3 *B. and L.*, 428.　　　　　　　　[50] *O. R.*, 27, part 2, p. 323.
[51] *Sorrel*, 171.　　　　　　　　　　[52] *O. R.*, 27, part 2, p. 323.
[53] *Longstreet*, 429; *O. R.*, 27, part 3, p. 1001.

That afternoon, as if to defeat the whole difficult enterprise, rain began to descend heavily. By nightfall the river seemed to be pouring from the skies.[54] As Ewell's road to Williamsport was hard-surfaced, his progress was steady, but at the ford there was much confusion.[55] Nerves grew raw under the strain.[56] A new road had been cut to the bridge at Falling Waters and under the downpour this soon became so heavy that the wagons began to stall. Instead of the swift march for which Lee had hoped, there was a virtual blockade.[57] Hours passed while drenched and wretched thousands stood wearily waiting for the trains to move on. All night the laboring teams struggled through the mire, and soldiers strained at the hub-deep wheels. Lee sat on his horse at the north end of the bridge, encouraging the men until even his strong frame grew weary.[58] "The best standing points were ankle-deep in mud," Longstreet recorded, "and the roads half-way to the knee, puddling and getting worse. We could only keep three or four torches alight, and those were dimmed at times when heavy rains came." [59] Toward morning the report was that Ewell's column would soon be in Virginia; but at Falling Waters dawn found the rear of the wagon train still swaying uneasily on the pontoon bridge. Longstreet and Hill were yet to cross, with every prospect of being attacked while on the march. Leaving Long-street to direct the movement on the north side of the river,[60] Lee went to the southern shore to expedite the clearing of the bridge, and there he waited while the survivors of Longstreet's corps tramped through the rain. It was the last time Lee ever passed over that stream as a soldier.

[54] *Alexander*, 440; *Malone*, 38; W. H. Stewart: *A Pair of Blankets*, 113.

[55] *Cf. O. R.*, 27, part 2, pp. 448–49.

[56] Major Venable was sent to the ford to report on conditions there. When he came back to headquarters he announced with disgust and in a loud voice that things were going badly at Williamsport. Lee rebuked him hotly for speaking of such an important matter in a tone that could be heard by every passing soldier. The General's manner was so severe that Venable went off in a huff. Busy as Lee was, he observed that he had offended his loyal subordinate, and when he went to his tent to drink a glass of buttermilk, he sent for Venable to join him. The major came but refused to be mollified by the General's oblations. At dawn the next day, when Lee's staff was with him on the south bank, Major Venable, still smarting under Lee's reprimand, lay down and went to sleep. Seeing him exposed to the storm, Lee took off his own poncho and quietly put it over the officer. Needless to say, when Venable awakened and found what Lee had done, he forgot his pique and set down the episode in the book of his remembrance as another example of the thoughtfulness of his chief (*Long*, 301).

[57] *Longstreet*, 429.　　　　　　　　　[58] *Cooke*, 333.

[59] *Longstreet*, 429.　　　　　　　　　[60] *Longstreet*, 429–30.

Finally the rear brigade of Longstreet's corps reached the bridge-head. Only Hill and the cavalry remained behind. Lee's anxiety was not wholly relieved, for, while he was grateful that so large a part of the army had escaped, he believed it certain that Meade would attack Hill. When Colonel Sorrel rode up and reported that Longstreet's last file had passed, Lee bade him return and urge the Third Corps to make the utmost haste and not to halt unless compelled to do so. Soon Sorrel came back and announced that the road was clear. Hill, he said, was only three-quarters of a mile from the bridge.

"What was his leading division?" Lee inquired.

"General Anderson, sir," Sorrel answered.

"I am sorry, Colonel; my friend Dick is quick enough pursuing, but in retreat I fear he will not be as sharp as I should like."

At that moment the echo of a heavy gun rolled up the river gorge. "There!" the General exclaimed. "I was expecting it—the beginning of the attack!" [61]

But instead of halting or stampeding at the sound, Hill's tired troops continued their steady tramp across the bridge. Ere long General Lee learned that only the rear division, Heth's, was in contact with the enemy, and that it was holding its own. At one time Heth dispatched an officer to request that Pender's division be sent back to reinforce him, but when ordered to continue his movement, he contrived to reach the river with no other loss than that of the stragglers and sick whom he had not been able to push on ahead of him.[62] "As the bulk of the rearguard of the army safely passed over the shaky bridge," one observer testified, "as it swayed to and fro, lashed by the current, [Lee] uttered a sigh of relief, and a great weight seemed taken from his shoulders. Seeing his fatigue and exhaustion, General Stuart gave him some coffee; he drank it with avidity, and declared, as he handed back the cup, that nothing had ever refreshed him so much." [63]

[61] *Sorrel,* 171–72.

[62] The total number left on the Maryland shore was put at not more than 500, though General Kilpatrick, who commanded the Federal cavalry that attacked Heth, insisted he captured an entire brigade. Heth's heaviest loss was in the person of General Pettigrew, who was mortally wounded in a brush with a small cavalry detachment that was allowed to approach the lines in the belief that it was Confederate (*O. R.,* 27, part 2, pp. 303–4, 310, 323–24, 640 ff.; *Long MS.; Lee's Dispatches,* 105–6). Lee put a mild censure in his report on the withdrawal of Fitzhugh Lee's cavalry without notice to Heth, though, as usual, he did not name the responsible officer (*O. R.,* 27, part 2, p. 323).

[63] *Cooke,* 333.

The final operation had been more harrowing, in the opinion of General Lane, than even the first stages of the retreat from Gettysburg.[64] Men had become so weary that they had fallen asleep in the rain and mud whenever the column had halted.[65] One South Carolina colonel who had been in all of Lee's campaigns, pronounced it the severest march his men had ever made.[66] Heth had required twelve torturing hours to cover seven miles.[67] But the retreat was over! The Potomac stood between the battered Army of Northern Virginia and the disappointed Federals. Many were the regrets that the Confederates had been "allowed to escape." Loud were the protests that Meade had not pushed his pursuit vigorously.[68]

As the army manifestly must have rest, Lee moved it on the 15th to the vicinity of Bunker Hill.[69] His expectation was to advance into Loudoun County, but the swollen Shenandoah prevented an early crossing.[70] Forced to remain temporarily where he was, Lee sent out men and horses, threshed wheat, carried it to the mills, ground it, and, with the beef captured in Pennsylvania, contrived to give a sufficient ration to the hungry army.[71] Thousands of the cavalrymen were dismounted because their horses had not been shod and had become lame. Robertson's brigade had been diminished, chiefly on this account, to a bare 300.[72] Lee collected horseshoes as rapidly as practicable, reduced transportation once more, procured corn for animals that had not tasted it since Gettysburg, and did what he could at so great a distance from Richmond to refit the troops.[73]

Before Lee could make more than a start in the never-ending work of reorganization, Meade crossed the Potomac east of the Blue Ridge and advanced his cavalry to the passes into Loudoun. Fearing that this might presage an attempt to keep him in the Valley while the enemy moved on Richmond, Lee promptly made counter-dispositions and placed Longstreet in Manassas and

[64] O. R., 27, part 2, p. 667.   [65] O. R., 27, part 2, p. 667.
[66] O. R., 27, part 2, p. 374. This was Colonel James D. Nance of the Third South Carolina.
[67] O. R., 27, part 2, p. 640.
[68] O. R., 27, part 1, pp. 92–94; 2 Meade, 134; H. D. Sedgwick: Correspondence of Maj.-Gen. John Sedgwick, 2, 132; H. G. Pearson: James S. Wadsworth, 235 ff.; H. H. Humphreys: Andrew Atkinson Humphreys, 203–4.
[69] O. R., 27, part 3, p. 1106.   [70] O. R., 27, part 2, p. 324.
[71] O. R., 27, part 3, p. 1049; Welch, 60.   [72] O. R., 27, part 3, p. 1106.
[73] O. R., 27, part 2, pp. 302, 611, 653–54, 676; ibid., part 3, pp. 1011, 1015.

Chester Gaps before the enemy could take them.[74] With the waters lowered somewhat, a pontoon bridge was then thrown over the Shenandoah, Longstreet's remaining troops crossed, passed through Chester Gap, and reached Culpeper on July 24. Hill followed. Ewell, who was left in the Valley in the hope of picking off a force at Martinsburg, then moved to Madison Court-house, where he arrived on July 29. A force left at Manassas Gap had an affair with the enemy, but drew off with no great difficulty and rejoined the main army. The enemy shifted to War-renton, and from that base on the night of July 31–August 1 sent a cavalry column and some infantry across the Rappahan-nock. The Confederate horse promptly opposed this advance; but as the Federal movement might be the initial step in a manœuvre to catch him between the Rappahannock and the Rapidan, or else to resume operations in front of Fredericksburg, Lee decided to transfer his whole army south of the Rapidan. This was accomplished by August 4, on which date the Gettys-burg campaign may be said to have come to its conclusion, with the opposing troops holding almost the very ground whence Jackson had started the first stage of Lee's offensive a year previ-ously.[75] The rapid changes of position during this last phase of the campaign were made with little loss and in good spirit. There was, however, the inevitable reaction that follows open cam-paigning, and among the North Carolina conscripts some deser-tions occurred.[76] To disappointed civilian eyes, the morale of the troops seemed lower than usual.[77] Even Major Walter Taylor, who was more familiar with the temper of the tired men, had al-

---

[74] O. R., 27, part 2, p. 324; ibid., part 3, pp. 1020, 1024–25, 1026–27.

[75] Lee's official reports of these movements will be found in O. R., 27, part 2, pp. 305, 310, 312, in O. R., 29, part 2, p. 624, and in Lee's Dispatches, 106–8. Longstreet's report is in O. R., 27, part 2, p. 362; Ewell's in ibid., 449; Early's in ibid., 472–73; Hill's in ibid., 609. For the correspondence see O. R., 27, part 3, pp. 1031, 1035, 1037, 1039, 1040, 1049, 1051, 1075. See also Early, 284 ff.; 1 R. W. C. D., 390 and 2 ibid., 6.

[76] G. W. Beale, 120–21; O. R., 27, part 3, p. 1052; 2 R. W. C. D., 4. In The Ameri-can Issue, Virginia Edition, Feb. 21, 1925, an amusing incident of the march to Cul-peper was reported. One of Lee's veterans, on passing his home, presented the whole family to the General. The soldier's mother, Mrs. Simms, produced a bottle of old blackberry wine and hospitably asked the General if he would refresh himself. Lee de-clined but suggested that his staff officers might be glad to taste her vintage. When Mrs. Simms offered it to them, they approved it so heartily that the rearmost had to content himself with wistfully smelling the bottle. The "cup that General Lee declined" has been preserved and was long in the possession of Reverend Doctor B. W. N. Simms, of Waxahatchie, Texas.

[77] T. A. Ashby: The Valley Campaigns, 244–45.

ready been compelled to admit that the army was better satisfied when on Southern soil.[78] By the second week in August, this reaction was past, and the spirits of officers and men were high again. "This is a grand old army!" Taylor wrote proudly, soon after Lee's headquarters had been established at Orange and the two armies had become inactive.[79] "No despondency here," he exclaimed, "though we hear of it in Richmond." [80]

Disappointment was, indeed, general at the capital, and there was much questioning throughout the South.[81] Lee refused to accept this as justified, and remarked that little value was to be attached to popular judgment of victories or of defeats. He told Major Seddon that after Fredericksburg and again after Chancellorsville, he had been greatly depressed because he could not follow up either success, but the country had been jubilant over the outcome of both battles.[82] "As far as I am concerned," he said of one series of hostile complaints, "the remarks fall harmless," but he felt that censure of the army did harm at home and abroad.[83] When General Pickett filed a report in which he complained of the lack of support given him in the charge, Lee returned the document. "You and your men have covered yourself with glory," he said, "but we have the enemy to fight and must carefully, at this critical moment, guard against dissensions which the reflections in your report would create. I will, therefore, suggest that you destroy both copy and original, substituting one confined to casualties merely. I hope all will yet be well." [84] In

[78] Cf. W. H. Taylor, July 17, 1863: "Our men, it must be confessed, are far better satisfied when operating on this side of the Potomac. . . . They are not accustomed to operating in a country where the people are inimical to them, and certainly every one of them is today worth twice as much as he was three days ago. I am persuaded that we cannot without heavy acquisitions to our strength invade successfully for any length of time." (Taylor MSS.).

[79] Lee was at Culpeper from July 23 to Aug. 4, on which day he moved to Orange Courthouse (cf. O. R., 29, part 2, p. 624).

[80] Walter H. Taylor, Aug. 8, 1863 (Taylor MSS.).   [81] De Leon, 257.

[82] 4 S. H. S. P., 153.   [83] Lee to Davis, July 31, 1863; Lee's Dispatches, 108–9.

[84] O. R., 27, part 3, p. 1075. General Pickett either complied with this request or else gave strict instruction that the MS of his report should not be printed, for it has never appeared. When Arthur Crew Inman issued Pickett's war letters in 1928 under the title Soldiers of the South, he even omitted, at the instance of Mrs. Pickett, part of a letter of July 4 in which General Pickett expressed some of the criticisms he made in his report (op. cit., 61–62 n.). It is plain that Pickett's complaint was that his attack was not properly supported by Pettigrew and by Trimble. Major Walter Taylor was of the same mind. In a letter of July 17, 1863, to his brother (Taylor MSS.), he attributed Pickett's repulse to the strength of the Federal position—"a sort of Gibraltar"—and to the action "of the division on his left," which, said Taylor, "failed to carry the works in its front and retired without any sufficient cause, thereby exposing Pickett's flanks."

preparing his own report the following January, he struck from Major Marshall's draft all specific criticism.[85]

Despite Lee's example and influence, criticism of the Confederate operations at Gettysburg was not silenced in 1863 and has been expressed at intervals ever since. Where confined to the actual military details of the campaign, this criticism is easily analyzed, for no other American battle has been so fully studied, and concerning none is there more general agreement on the specific reasons for the failure of the losing army.

The invasion itself was, of course, a daring move, but, in the circumstances that Lee faced, politically and in a military sense, it probably was justified. The first mistake was in connection with Stuart's operations. To recapitulate this point, Lee intended to allow his cavalry commander latitude as to where he should enter Maryland. He is not to be blamed for giving Stuart discretion, nor is Stuart justly subject to censure for exercising it. But the *Beau Sabreur* of the South, by pushing on after he had encountered resistance east of the Bull Run Mountains, violated orders and deprived Lee of his services when most needed. He should have turned back then, as Lee had directed him to do should he find his advance hindered by the Federal columns. Stuart erred, likewise, in taking with him all the cavalry brigades that had been accustomed to doing the reconnaissance work of the Army of Northern Virginia. General Lee, for his part, was at fault in handling the cavalry left at his disposal. He overestimated the fighting value of Jenkins's and of Imboden's brigades, which had little previous experience except in raids, and he failed to keep in close touch with Robertson and Jones, who remained behind in Virginia.[86] Once in Pennsylvania, Lee's operations were handicapped not only because he lacked sufficient cavalry, but also because he did not have Stuart at hand. He had become dependent upon that officer for information of the enemy's position and plans and, in Stuart's absence, he had no satisfactory form of military intelligence. It is not enough to say

[85] *Marshall*, 181; Marshall quoted by McIntosh in 37 *S. H. S.* ., 94–95. *Cf. infra,* 233 and Appendix III—1.

[86] It was not, apparently, until after the retreat from Gettysburg had begun that Lee had a just estimate of Imboden's troopers. He then told Stuart "they are unsteady, and, I fear, inefficient" (*O. R.,* 27, part 3, p. 985).

with General Early, in exculpation of Stuart, that Lee found the enemy in spite of the absence of his cavalry.[87] Had "Jeb" Stuart been at hand, Lee would have had early information of the advance of the Federals and either would have outfooted them to Gettysburg or would have known enough about their great strength to refrain from attacking as he did. The injudicious employment of the Confederate horse during the Gettysburg campaign was responsible for most of the other mistakes on the Southern side and must always remain a warning of the danger of permitting the cavalry to lose contact with an army when the enemy's positions are unknown. In its consequences, the blunder was more serious than that which Hooker made at Chancellorsville in sending Stoneman on a raid when he should have had his mounted forces in front and on the flank of the XI Corps.[88]

The second reason for the Confederate defeat manifestly was the failure of Ewell to take Cemetery Hill when Lee suggested, after the Federal defeat on the afternoon of July 1, that he attack it. Had Ewell thrown Early forward, without waiting for Johnson, he probably could have taken the hill at any time prior to 4 P.M. or perhaps to 4:30. Ewell hesitated because he was unfamiliar with Lee's methods and had been trained in a different school of command. Jackson, who had always directed Ewell's operations, had been uniformly explicit in his orders and had never allowed discretion unless compelled to do so; Lee always trusted the tactical judgment of his principal subordinates unless he had to be peremptory. Ewell, moreover, was of a temperament to take counsel, and was puzzled and embarrassed when told to capture Cemetery Hill "if practicable." Lee could not be expected to change his system for Ewell, nor could Ewell be expected to change his nature after only two months under Lee.

The third reason for defeat was the extent of the Confederate line and the resultant thinness. Lee's front on the second day, from Hood's right, opposite Round Top, to the left of Johnson, was slightly more than five miles in length. Communication between the flanks was slow and difficult. Co-ordination of attack

---

[87] Cf. 4 S. H. S. P., 269–70.

[88] In 1896, General C. A. Battle, in a public address, asserted that Lee ordered Stuart before a court of inquiry for his absence during the Gettysburg campaign, but this was not the case. The court was convened to hear evidence regarding the loss of certain wagons in Fitz Lee's brigade (Taylor MSS.)

was almost impossible with a limited staff.[89] Lee should have held to the decision reached late on the afternoon of the 1st and considered again on the morning of the 2d. He should have abandoned all attempts against the Culp's Hill position. By concentrating his attacks from Cemetery Hill to Round Top, he would have increased the offensive strength of his line by at least one-third. In doing this, he would not have subjected himself to a dangerous enfilade from Cemetery Hill, because he had sufficient artillery to put that hill under cross-fire from Seminary Ridge and from Gettysburg. Lee finally discarded the plan of shortening his line on the representation of Ewell that Johnson could take Culp's Hill—an instance where the advantage that would certainly have resulted from a concentrated attack was put aside for the uncertainty of a *coup* on the flank.

The fourth reason for the defeat was the state of mind of the responsible Confederate commanders. On July 2, Longstreet was disgruntled because Lee refused to take his advice for a tactical defensive. Determined, apparently, to force a situation in which his plan would have to be adopted in spite of Lee, he delayed the attack on the right until Cemetery Ridge was crowded with men, whereas if he had attacked early in the morning, as Lee intended, he probably could have stormed that position and assuredly could have taken Round Top. Longstreet's slow and stubborn mind rendered him incapable of the quick daring and loyal obedience that had characterized Jackson. Yet in the first battle after the death of "Stonewall" it seemed the course of wisdom to substitute the First for the Second Corps as the "column of attack" because its staff and line were accustomed to working together. Longstreet's innate lack of qualification for duty of this type had been confirmed by his period of detached duty. He was never the same man after he had deceived himself into thinking he was a great strategist. It was Lee's misfortune at Gettysburg that he had to employ in offensive operations a man whose whole inclination was toward the defensive.

But this indictment of Longstreet does not relieve Lee of all blame for the failure on the second day at Gettysburg. His greatest weakness as a soldier was displayed along with Longstreet's,

[89] *Cf.* Alexander in 4 *S. H. S. P.,* 110.

for when Longstreet sulked, Lee's temperament was such that he could not bring himself either to shake Longstreet out of his bad humor by a sharp order, or to take direction of the field when Longstreet delayed. No candid critic of the battle can follow the events of that fateful morning and not have a feeling that Lee virtually surrendered to Longstreet, who obeyed only when he could no longer find an excuse for delay. Lee's one positive order was that delivered about 11 o'clock for Longstreet to attack. Having done this much, Lee permitted Longstreet to waste the time until after 4 o'clock. It is scarcely too much to say that on July 2 the Army of Northern Virginia was without a commander.

The conclusion is inevitable, moreover, that Lee allowed operations to drift on the morning of the 2d, not only because he would not deal sternly with Longstreet but also because he placed such unquestioning reliance on his army that he believed the men in the ranks could redeem Longstreet's delay. If Longstreet was insubordinate, Lee was overconfident. This psychological factor of the overconfidence of the commanding general is almost of sufficient importance to be regarded as a separate reason for the Confederate defeat.[90]

The mind of Ewell was similarly at fault on July 2. Although he had then been given his direct orders by Lee in person, Ewell either did not comprehend the importance of the task assigned him or else he was unable to co-ordinate the attacks of his three divisions, two of which were under commanders almost as unfamiliar with their duties as he was. Ewell's attacks were those of Lee at Malvern Hill, or those of McClellan at Sharpsburg, isolated, disjointed, and ineffective. Had Early and Rodes engaged when Johnson made his assault, there is at least a probability that Early could have held Cemetery Hill. If he had done so, the evacuation of Cemetery Ridge would have been necessary that night, or else Pickett's charge could have been driven home with the help of a shattering Confederate fire from the captured eminence.

Fifth and most fundamental among the reasons for Lee's failure at Gettysburg was the general lack by the reorganized army of co-ordination in attack. Some of the instances of this on July 2

[90] See *infra*, p. 155.

have already been given. To these may be added the failure of
A. P. Hill's corps to support the advance of Wright and of Wilcox
when the attack of the First Corps reached the front of the Third.
General Wilcox maintained that Anderson's division was badly
handled then and that the captured ground could have been retained if Anderson had been on the alert.[91] Wilcox may have
been in error concerning some of the details, but the impression
left by the operations of Hill's corps is that they were not unified
and directed to the all-important object of seizing and holding
Cemetery Ridge. An even greater lack of co-ordination was apparent on the 3d. It was imperative on the last day of the battle
that the three corps act together with absolute precision, for every
one must have realized that another repulse would necessitate a
retreat. Yet the reorganized army did not fight as a single machine. Longstreet could have had Pickett on the field at dawn
and could have attacked when Ewell did; but he was still so
intent on carrying his own point and moving by the right flank,
that he devoted himself to that plan instead of hurrying Pickett
into position. When Longstreet would not attack with his whole
corps, Lee made the mistake of shifting his attack northward,
and of delivering it with parts of two corps. Pickett and Pettigrew advanced together almost as well as if they had belonged
to the same corps, but there was no co-ordination of their support.
The men at the time—and critics since then—seem to have been
so intent on watching the charge that they have forgotten the tragic
fact that after the two assaulting divisions reached Cemetery
Ridge they received no reinforcements. Probably it was the course
of wisdom not to have rushed Anderson forward along with
Pickett and Pettigrew, but there has never been any satisfactory
explanation why Wilcox's advance was delayed or the whole of
Anderson's division was not thrown in when it was apparent
that Pickett and Pettigrew would reach the enemy's position. It
was probably to this that Lee referred, on the night of July 3, in
his conversation with General Imboden.[92] There were risks, of
course, in hurling all the troops against Cemetery Ridge, and
leaving none in reserve, but Lee had done the same thing at
Gaines's Mill and at Second Manassas, and in both instances had

[91] See Appendix III—3. [92] See *supra*, p. 134.

driven the enemy from the field. Similarly, the advance of the left brigade of Pettigrew's division was ragged and uncertain from the moment it started, yet nothing was done by Hill or by Longstreet to strengthen that flank or to create a diversion. On the front of Ewell that day there was no co-ordination of his attack with Longstreet, or even co-ordination of his own divisions. Two of Ewell's divisions waited while Johnson wore himself out on Culp's Hill during the morning, and then, in the afternoon, those two in turn were repulsed. Ewell was ready to assault when the day was young, but Longstreet was not then willing. When Longstreet at last was forced into action, Ewell was half-crippled.

Lack of co-ordination was displayed in the artillery as well. So much has been written of the volume of the fire delivered against Cemetery Ridge that few students of the battle have stopped to count the batteries that were not utilized. Colonel Jennings C. Wise has computed that fifty-six of Lee's field-pieces were not employed at all on July 3, and that eighty of the eighty-four guns of the Second and Third Corps were "brought into action on a mathematically straight line, parallel to the position of the enemy and constantly increasing in range therefrom to the left or north." [93] Nearly the whole value of converging fire was neglected. Furthermore, the Confederates lost the greatest opportunity of the battle when they did not dispose their artillery to blast the Federals from Cemetery Hill. That eminence stands at the northwestern turn of the long Federal line, the "bend of the fish-hook," and is open to attack by artillery on an arc of more than 200 degrees from the northeast, the north, the northwest, and the west. A concentrated bombardment on the 2d would have driven the Federals from the hill and would have made its capture easy. Once in Confederate hands, it could have been a *point d'appui* for an attack on Cemetery Ridge. A short cannonade of Cemetery Hill on the 3d, more or less a chance affair, played havoc with the Federal batteries stationed there and indicated what might have happened under a heavier fire.[94] It is almost incredible that this opening was overlooked by the chief of artillery of the army or by the gunners of the Second and Third

[93] 2 *Wise*, 666–67.   [94] *Alexander*, 417–18, 426–28.

Corps. There are only two possible explanations. One is that General Pendleton devoted himself to reconnaissance, chiefly on the right, instead of studying the proper disposition of the guns. The other is that the lines of the two corps chanced to join in front of Cemetery Hill, so that liaison was poor. Neither Colonel Lindsay Walker of the Third nor Colonel John Thompson Brown of the Second seems to have realized to what extent the hill was exposed.

Southern critics of Gettysburg, admitting all these mistakes, have been wont to say that while each error was serious, the battle would not have been lost if any one of the blunders had been avoided. There is a probability at least as strong that few of the mistakes would have occurred if Jackson had not died and a reorganization of the army had not thereby been made necessary. Then it was that Lee was compelled to place two-thirds of the troops under corps commanders who had never directed that many men in battle; then it was that the sentimental demand of the South led him to put at the head of the reduced Second Corps the gallant Ewell who had never served directly under Lee and was unfamiliar with his discretionary methods; then it was that new division commanders were chosen; then it was that the staff, which was always too small, was divided among generals who were unacquainted with the staff personnel, with the troops, and even with the field officers; then it was that Longstreet, by the ill-chance of war, was cast for the rôle of the irreplaceable Jackson and became the appointed leader of the column of attack, the duty of all others for which he was least suited. Read in the light of the aftermath, the story of the reorganization of May, 1863, thus becomes one of the major tragedies of the Confederacy and explains why the death of Jackson was the turning-point in the history of the Army of Northern Virginia.

Such, in brief, were the principal Confederate mistakes at Gettysburg and some of the reasons for them as they appear to the student after seventy years.[95] How did those errors appear to Lee? What was his judgment of the battle and of the campaign?

[95] The "Gettysburg controversy" of 1876–79 evoked much bitter but intelligent criticism of the campaign in 4, 5, 6, and 7 S. H. S. P. The material there has never been invalidated. General Trimble supplied a good critique in ibid., 26, 116, and McIntosh in

Said he: ". . . the loss of our gallant officers and men . . . causes me to weep tears of blood and to wish that I never could hear the sound of a gun again." [96] More than 23,000 Southerners had been killed, wounded, and captured by the enemy from the beginning of the campaign at Brandy Station to the return to the lines on the Rapidan (June 9–August 4). [97] Five guns had been lost, approximately fifty wagons and more than thirty flags.[98] Lee believed, however, that the enemy had paid a price in proportion,[99] and he was far from thinking that the invasion had been fruitless. Much of what he hoped to achieve had been accomplished—the enemy had been driven from the Shenandoah Valley, the hostile forces on the coast of Virginia and the Carolinas had been reduced, the Federal plan of campaign for the summer had been broken up, and there was little prospect of a resumption of the offensive that year by the Union forces in Virginia.[100] He was no more prepared to admit a crushing defeat than Meade was to claim one,[101] and perhaps he shared the philosophical view later expressed by General Early that if the army had remained in Virginia it would have been forced to fight battles with losses as heavy as those of Gettysburg.[102] As criticism spread, Lee was quick to absolve his men of all responsibility for failure to attain the full objective. The army, he wrote Mrs. Lee on July 15, "has accomplished all that could be reasonably expected. It ought not to have been expected to perform impossibilities, or to have fulfilled the anticipations of the thoughtless and unreasonable." [103]

ibid., 37, 112 ff. Battine, *op. cit.*, is more tactical than strategical in his approach. Curtis's paper in 3 *M. H. S. M.*, 356 ff. and Livermore's in 13 *ibid.*, 487 ff. are authoritative. Alexander's account, *op. cit.*, 363 ff., is admirable in every way.

[96] Jones, *L. and L.*, 278; cf. *O. R.*, 27, part 2, p. 1049.

[97] The loss in the infantry and artillery at Gettysburg was 20,486, including prisoners not listed by the Confederates but reported by the Federals. At Winchester, the casualties numbered 252; in the minor engagements, they were 316, and among the cavalry, 1817 (*O. R.*, 27, part 2, pp. 337, 346, 712 ff.). Estimating the number captured at Falling Waters on July 14 at 500, the total is 23,371.

[98] *O. R.*, 27, part 1, p. 85; *ibid.*, part 2, p. 354; *ibid.*, 51, part 2, pp. 758–59.

[99] He was correct in this. During the same period from June 9 to Aug. 4, the Federals had lost about 3500 killed, wounded, and captured at Winchester, 200 at Berryville and Martinsburg on the Confederate advance toward the Potomac, and 23,049 at Gettysburg. The casualties in the cavalry engagements raised the aggregate to 28,129 (*O. R.*, 27, part 1, pp. 168 ff.; *ibid.*, part 2, p. 442). Apparently no detailed Federal return was ever made of losses at Winchester.

[100] *O. R.*, 27, part 2, p. 302. Cf. *R. E. Lee, Jr.*, 108, July 15, 1863.

[101] Cf. Meade to his wife, July 8, 1863: "I never claimed a victory, though I stated that Lee was defeated in his efforts to destroy my army" (2 *Meade*, 133).

[102] *Early*, 286.   [103] *R. E. Lee, Jr.*, 108.

In his preliminary report of July 31 he said: "The conduct of the troops was all that I could desire or expect, and they deserved success so far as it can be deserved by heroic valor and fortitude. More may have been required of them than they were able to perform, but my admiration of their noble qualities and confidence in their ability to cope successfully with the enemy has suffered no abatement from the issue of this protracted and sanguinary conflict." [104] He hoped that the final reports would "protect the reputation of every officer," [105] and he was determined not to blame any of his subordinates. "I know," he said, "how prone we are to censure and how ready to blame others for the non-fulfilment of our expectations. This is unbecoming in a generous people, and I grieve to see its expression." [106] He felt that he had himself been at fault in expecting too much of the army. His confidence in it, he frankly confessed, had carried him too far[107]—an opinion that was shared by some of the men in the ranks.[108] Overlooking all the tactical errors and all the mistakes due to the state of mind of his subordinates, he went straight to the underlying cause of failure when he said it was due primarily to lack of co-ordination. On July 13, in a long letter to President Davis, he summed up his views:

"[The army] in my opinion achieved under the guidance of the Most High a general success, though it did not win a victory. I thought at the time that the latter was practicable. I still think if all things would have worked together it would have been accomplished. But with the knowledge I then had, and in the circumstances I was then placed, I do not know what better course I could have pursued. With my present knowledge, and

---

104 *O. R.,* 27, part 2, p. 309.
105 Lee to Davis, July 31, 1863, *Lee's Dispatches,* p. 109.
106 Lee to Davis, Aug. 8, 1863, *O. R.,* 51, part 2, p. 752.
107 "I alone am to blame in perhaps expecting too much of its prowess and valour."—Lee to Davis, July 31, 1863 (*Lee's Dispatches,* 110). *Cf.* Lee to Margaret Stuart, July 26, 1863: "The army did all it could. I fear I required of it impossibilities" (Jones, *L. and L.,* 283). *Cf.* also *Longstreet,* 401, quoting General Lee, on the authority of Fitz Lee, as telling Captain Sidney Smith Lee that "he was controlled too far by the great confidence he felt in the fighting qualities of his people, and by assurances of most of his higher officers."
108 *Cf.* J. C. West, *loc. cit.:* "I think General Lee never would have attacked the enemy in their position in the mountain side except for the splendid condition of his army, and his confidence in its ability to accomplish anything he chose to attempt." This was a contemporary letter.

could I have foreseen that the attack on the last day would have failed to drive the enemy from his position, I should certainly have tried some other course. What the ultimate result would have been is not so clear to me." [109]

After reflecting fully on the outcome in the comparative quiet of his camp at Orange Courthouse, he decided that he should ask to be relieved of the command of the army. In the course of a deliberately written letter to the President he said:

"The general remedy for the want of success in a military commander is his removal. This is natural, and, in many instances, proper. For, no matter what may be the ability of this officer, if he loses the confidence of his troops disaster must sooner or later ensue.

"I have been prompted by these reflections more than once since my return from Pennsylvania to propose to Your Excellency the propriety of selecting another commander for this army. I have seen and heard of expression of discontent in the public journals at the result of the expedition. I do not know how far this feeling extends in the army. My brother officers have been too kind to report it, and so far the troops have been too generous to exhibit it. It is fair, however, to suppose that it does exist, and success is so necessary to us that nothing should be risked to secure it. I therefore, in all sincerity, request Your Excellency to take measures to supply my place. I do this with the more earnestness because no one is more aware than myself of my inability for the duties of my position. I cannot even accomplish what I myself desire. How can I fulfill the expectations of others? In addition I sensibly feel the growing failure of my bodily strength. I have not yet recovered from the attack I experienced the past spring. I am becoming more and more incapable of exertion, and am thus prevented from making the personal examinations and giving the personal supervision to the operations in the field which I feel to be necessary. I am so dull in making use of the eyes of others I am frequently misled. Everything, therefore, points to the advantages to be derived from a new commander, and I the

[109] *Lee's Dispatches*, 110.

more anxiously urge the matter upon Your Excellency from my belief that a younger and abler man than myself can readily be obtained. I know that he will have as gallant and brave an army as ever existed to second his efforts, and it would be the happiest day of my life to see at its head a worthy leader—one that would accomplish more than I could perform and all that I have wished. I hope Your Excellency will attribute my request to the true reason, the desire to serve my country, and to do all in my power to insure the success of her righteous cause.

"I have no complaints to make of any one but myself. I have received nothing but kindness from those above me, and the most considerate attention from my comrades and companions in arms. To Your Excellency I am specially indebted for uniform kindness and consideration. You have done everything in your power to aid me in the work committed to my charge, without omitting anything to promote the general welfare. I pray that your efforts may at length be crowned with success, and that you may long live to enjoy the thanks of a grateful people." [110]

Lee said nothing to any one of this letter, though its language indicates that it was written with an eye to its possible publication in case the President saw fit to relieve him of command. There is not a hint in any other contemporary paper that he had asked to be relieved, though there had been a rumor, about ten days before, that he had resigned. [111]

He had not long to wait for the President's decision. In a reply to General Pemberton, who had sustained a far worse defeat, Mr. Davis had said on August 9, "My confidence in both [you and Lee] has not been diminished because 'letter writers' have not sent forth your praise on the wings of the press." [112] On August 12 or 13, Lee received from Mr. Davis a long answer in which the chief executive deplored the clamor of the times and then continued:

"But suppose, my dear friend, that I were to admit, with all their implications, the points which you present, where am I to

---

[110] O. R., 51, part 2, pp. 752–53.   [111] 1 R. W. C. D., 389.
[112] Pemberton MSS., kindly loaned the writer by John C. Pemberton, of New York, through Mrs. H. Pemberton Rhudy of Philadelphia.

find that new commander who is to possess the greater ability which you believe to be required? I do not doubt the readiness with which you would give way to one who could accomplish all that you have wished, and you will do me the justice to believe that if Providence should kindly offer such a person for our use, I would not hesitate to avail of his services.

"My sight is not sufficiently penetrating to discover such hidden merit, if it exists, and I have but used the language of sober earnestness when I have impressed upon you the propriety of avoiding all unnecessary exposure to danger, because I felt our country could not bear to lose you. To ask me to substitute you by some one in my judgment more fit to command, or who would possess more of the confidence of the army, or of the reflecting men of the country, is to demand an impossibility. . . ." [113]

That ended it! Lee had to go on. Perhaps it was fortunate for the South that his request to be relieved of command did not become known, for the mere suggestion of such a possibility might have created discontent akin to mutiny in the Army of Northern Virginia. There probably was no exaggeration in the statement of one veteran, years afterward, that "the army would have arisen in revolt if it had been called upon to give up General Lee." [114]

The discussion of Gettysburg, however, did not end with this private exchange of letters. It continued into the winter and to the close of General Lee's life. To Longstreet's credit be it said that he did not criticise his chief at the time or argue in public the alleged virtues of his plan of operations which he continued to believe superior to Lee's. In a letter to his uncle, three weeks after the battle, he expressed willingness to assume his share of the responsibility—all of it, in fact.[115] He claimed at a later date that Lee asked him after the campaign, "Why didn't you stop all that thing that day?" [116] Subsequently, also, he maintained that Lee

---

[113] *O. R.*, 29, part 2, p. 640.
[114] C. Irvine Walker: *Life of General R. H. Anderson* (cited hereafter as *Irvine Walker*), 149–50.
[115] James Longstreet to Doctor A. B. Longstreet, July 24, 1863: *Annals of the War*, 414–15.
[116] *Philadelphia Times,* July 27. 1879, p. 8.

told a staff officer of the First Corps in the winter of 1863–64 that if Longstreet had been permitted to carry out his plan, instead of making the attack on Cemetery Ridge, he would have been successful. In east Tennessee, again, Longstreet showed a friend a letter in which Lee was quoted as saying, "Oh, General, had I but followed your advice, instead of pursuing the course that I did, how different all would have been." [117] But in the face of charges that these statements were torn from their context, and in spite of a challenge to produce the originals, Longstreet remained silent. [118] Not until General Lee had been dead for years did General Longstreet make the remarkable assertion that he "would and could have saved every man lost at Gettysburg." [119] It was still later that Longstreet wrote that Lee was "excited and off his balance" at Gettysburg "and labored under that oppression until enough blood was shed to appease him." [120]

Since the publication of the official reports and of the narratives of the leading Confederate participants has shown the full measure of Longstreet's sulking, it has often been asked why Lee did not arrest him for insubordination or order him before a court-martial. The answer is quite simple: When Lee said, "It is all my fault," he meant exactly what he said. He undoubtedly considered himself to blame for the result. He was in command. If his orders were obeyed, the fault was with his plan; if his orders were not obeyed he was culpable for permitting them to be disregarded—so he must have reasoned. Even if this had not been his feeling he still would not have rid himself of Longstreet, for the simple reason that he had no one with whom to replace him. Grave as were Longstreet's faults, and costly as his peculiarities proved to be at Gettysburg, he was Lee's most experienced lieutenant and, after Jackson's death, the ablest, once he could be induced to go into action. Had he been removed, any successor then available would have disclosed other faults perhaps more serious. Lee displayed not the slightest difference in his manner toward Longstreet after the campaign: he was as friendly as ever

---

[117] *Longstreet*, 400.

[118] 5 *S. H. S. P.*, 192, 279; *Taylor MSS.* It is highly significant that in 3 *B. and L.*, 349, Longstreet himself gave a different version of what Lee was alleged to have said in this letter. He there quoted Lee as saying to him, "If only I had taken your counsel, even on the 3d, and had moved around the Federal left, how different all might have been."

[119] 3 *B. and L.*, 349.   [120] *Longstreet*, 383–84.

and, as always,[121] determined to make the best of his subordinate's idiosyncrasies.

Lee made little comment on Gettysburg during the war. In talking with General Heth, who was one of the few generals in the army whom he called by his first name, Lee expressed conviction that the invasion of Pennsylvania was sound policy, and said that he would again enter that state if able to do so. He also remarked to Heth, when the *dicta* of the arm-chair strategists were under discussion, "After it is all over, as stupid a fellow as I am can see the mistakes that were made. I notice, however, that my mistakes are never told me until it is too late, and you, and all my officers, know that I am always ready and anxious to have their suggestions." [122]

When the war had ended, General Lee was still reticent in writing and speaking to strangers about Gettysburg or about any other of his battles, and never went further than to say to them that if the assault could have been co-ordinated success could have been attained.[123] In conversation with close friends, he would sometimes be more communicative. In April, 1868, he discussed with Colonel William Allan the invasion of Pennsylvania, explained in some detail his reasons for taking the offensive, and then, according to Allan's contemporaneous memorandum, went on:

"He [Lee] found himself engaged with the Federal Army . . . unexpectedly, and had to fight. This being decided on, victory would have been won if he could have gotten one decided simultaneous attack on the whole line. This he tried his utmost to effect for three days, and failed. Ewell he could not get to act with decision. Rodes, Early, Johnson, attacked, and were hurt in detail. Longstreet, Hill, etc., could not be gotten to act in

[121] Longstreet in *Washington Post*, June 11, 1893, p. 10. [122] 4 *S. H. S. P.*, 153, 159–60.

[123] Lee to William M. McDonald, April 15, 1868: "As to the battle of Gettysburg, I must again refer you to my official accounts. Its loss was occasioned by a combination of circumstances. It was commenced in the absence of correct intelligence. It was continued in the effort to overcome the difficulties by which we were surrounded, and it would have been gained could one determined and united blow have been delivered by our whole line. As it was, victory trembled in the balance for three days, and the battle resulted in the infliction of as great an amount of injury as was received and in frustrating the Federal campaign for the season" (*Jones*, 266–67). *Cf.* also Lee to B. H. Wright, Jan. 18, 1869, printed in Jones, *L. and L.*, 452–53, without the name of the addressee, which, however, appears in Lee's Lexington letterbook: "The failure of the Confederate army at Gettysburg was owing to a combination of circumstances, but for which success might have been reasonably expected."

concert. Thus the Federal troops were enabled to be opposed to each of our corps, or even divisions, in succession. As it was, however, he inflicted more damage than he received, and he broke up the Federal summer campaign." [124]

Discussing the battle with Governor John Lee Carroll of Maryland, Lee is quoted—though at second-hand—as saying that the battle would have been gained if General Longstreet had obeyed the orders given him, and had made the attack early instead of late. Lee was also credited with saying in the same conversation, "General Longstreet, when once in a fight, was a most brilliant soldier; but he was the hardest man to move I had in my army." [125]

The literal accuracy of various parts of these statements may be questioned, but it is certain that in the last years at Lexington, as Lee viewed the Gettysburg campaign in some perspective, he concluded that it was the absence of Jackson, not the presence of Ewell or of Longstreet, that made the Army of Northern Virginia a far less effective fighting machine at Gettysburg than at Chancellorsville. Not long before his death, in a long conversation with his cousin Cassius Lee of Alexandria, the General said that if Jackson had been at Gettysburg he would have held the heights that Ewell seized.[126] And one afternoon, when he was out riding with Professor White, he said quietly, "If I had had Stonewall Jackson with me, so far as man can see, I should have won the battle of Gettysburg." That statement must stand. The darkest scene in the great drama of Gettysburg was enacted at Chancellorsville when Jackson fell.[127]

[124] Allan's memorandum in *Marshall*, 250.

[125] 5 *S. H. S. P.*, 193. The "governor" to whom this was reported to have been stated by General Lee is identified from a letter of General Fitz Lee's in the *Taylor MSS. Cf.* a somewhat similar comment by Lee on Longstreet's slowness quoted by Colonel McIntosh on the authority of Colonel Marshall in 37 *S. H. S. P.*, 106.

[126] *R. E. Lee, Jr.*, 415. The reference would seem to be to the attack of Early on the afternoon of July 2, but it is possible that Lee was misunderstood and that he had in mind the opportunity of seizing Cemetery Hill that was lost on the afternoon of July 1.

[127] H. M. Field: *Bright Skies and Dark Shadows*, 303–4, quoting Professor White. This remark affords an excellent illustration of the manner in which Lee's undramatic observations were sometimes swollen into bombast. Lee's statement to White was simple and characteristically cautious in wording, but in 12 *S. H. S. P.*, 111–12, the language has been "dressed" to this: "If I had had Stonewall Jackson at Gettysburg, I should have won there a great victory, and if we had reaped the fruits within our reach, we should have established the independence of the Confederacy." The version given by Jones, *op. cit.*, 156, was almost as rhetorical: "If I had had Stonewall Jackson at Gettysburg, we should have won a great victory. And I feel confident that complete success there would have resulted in the establishment of our independence."

CHAPTER X

Can the Offensive Be Resumed?

(bristoe station)

"We must now prepare for harder blows and harder work." [1] In that spirit Lee faced the enemy after his return to Virginia. Unchanged in bearing or in determination so far as any one could see,[2] he wrestled again with the food shortage that had been one of the chief reasons for the invasion of Pennsylvania. Weakened by 23,000 men, he was back in a devastated country and was forced to rely once again on Northrop for the army's food. Because of this, he realized that he might be compelled to retreat nearer to Richmond,[3] but he was not willing to relinquish the initiative to General Meade if he could take it himself. For he still held that the offensive-defensive was the true strategic policy of the South, even if prolonged invasion of the North was impossible.[4]

As soon as the army settled down on the Rapidan, Lee undertook from his headquarters on the fine plantation of Erasmus Taylor[5] to bring the army up to offensive strength again. His

---

[1] Lee to Margaret Stuart, July 26, 1863; Jones, *L. and L.*, 283.

[2] *R. E. Lee, Jr.*, 103; *Mosby's Memoirs*, 374. *Cf.* G. M. Neese: *Three Years in the Confederate Horse Artillery* (cited hereafter as *Neese*), 204; "General R. E Lee passed our camp today; he rode along the road unaccompanied by any one and seemed as unconcerned as an old farmer going to his daily toil."

[3] *Cf.* Davis to Lee, Aug. 2, 1863; *O. R.*, 51, part 2, p. 749.

[4] *Cf.* Lee to Davis, Aug. 22, 1863, "As soon as I can get the vacancies in the army filled, and the horses and men recruited a little, if General Meade does not move, I wish to attack him" (*O. R.*, 29, part 2, p. 661). *Cf.* same to same, Aug. 24, 1863, *ibid.*, 664. Scheibert, *op. cit.*, 76, quoted Lee "after Gettysburg" as saying to him, "I see clearly that it is no longer possible for us to achieve peace by taking the offensive; in this civil war, the more we conquer, the more we stir up hatred; that is why, as far as possible, I am confining myself to the defensive and sparing my men." Maurice (*op. cit.*, 216), doubtless on the authority of Scheibert, affirmed that delay became Lee's main object after Gettysburg and fortification his favorite method. But there is overwhelming evidence to show that the statement to Scheibert could not have been made until some months after the close of the Gettysburg operation, unless it was intended simply to describe the policy Lee was following for a brief period.

[5] *R. E. Lee, Jr.*, 109; *Sorrel*, 179. Lee recorded the unfailing hospitality of the Taylors and remarked that though he had paid Mrs. Taylor two visits for the purpose of prevailing upon her to desist from sending him food and dainties, she continued to do so,

first results were encouraging. The return of stragglers and of lightly wounded and the arrival of 3000 men loaned him temporarily from the army of Major General Samuel Jones raised Lee's effective strength to 58,000 by August 10,[6] for all of whom the resourceful Colonel Gorgas soon provided arms to replace those lost at Gettysburg and on the retreat.[7] Although there were among the conscripts further desertions that Lee sought vigorously to check,[8] rest continued to raise the morale of the troops.[9] But the limitations of man-power were soon apparent. Mr. Davis had to admit that he saw no prospect of increasing the army to its former strength;[10] the soldiers were almost barefooted;[11] the supply of rations was menacingly short; the railroads were scarcely able to haul what the commissaries found;[12] the equipment of the cavalry was in embarrassing disrepair [13] and the horses received so little grain that they recovered slowly.[14] Soon Jones's troops had to be ordered back to him,[15] and the ranks were further reduced by a series of furloughs Lee thought it prudent to grant.[16] The inflow of conscripts and of returning wounded did little more than offset this. The end of August found the army stronger by only 2600 than it had been on the 10th.[17]

Thus circumstanced, Lee could not take the offensive, though he hoped soon to be able to do so. Nor was it certain that a march against Meade was the best contribution the Army of Northern Virginia could make at the time to the general strategy of the South. On August 24, at a time when there were some indications of a possible advance by the enemy,[18] President Davis asked Lee to come to Richmond to discuss with him a new and

---

[6] O. R., 27, part 3, p. 986; ibid., 29, part 2, p. 636. On July 30, with the cavalry not included, the effectives had numbered only 45,396 (O. R., 27, part 2, p. 1065).

[7] O. R., 29, part 2, pp. 628, 631. Cf. ibid., 647.

[8] O. R., 29, part 2, pp. 641–42, 645–46, 647, 649–50, 676, 692; Lee's Dispatches, 122–23.

[9] Long MS., Sept. 5, 1863: "Our army has been greatly benefitted by a month's quiet and rest. Our ranks have been continually filling. Our discipline and drill is now better than it has ever been." Welch (op. cit., 75) noted that in 1862, when men were sent to the hospital, they were expected to die, but that they received excellent treatment in 1863.

[10] O. R., 27, part 2, p. 1041; O. R., 51, part 2, p. 749.

[11] Welch, 77.

[12] Welch, 29, part 2, pp. 625, 628; O. R., 51, part 2, pp. 742–44.

[13] O. R., 29, part 2, p. 648; IV O. R., 2, 718–20.

[14] Jones, L. and L., 288; O. R., 29, part 2, p. 643.

[15] Aug. 24, O. R., 29, part 2, p. 665; Lee's Dispatches, 124.

[16] O. R., 51, part 2, pp. 754–55.

[17] O. R.. 29, part 2, p. 681.   [18] R. E. Lee, Jr., 110.

menacing situation,[19] in the development of which he had greatly missed Lee's counsel.[20] Lee left Longstreet in charge and went immediately to the capital, where he remained with one or two days' intermission, until September 7.[21] He discussed with the President the means of preventing desertion[22] and of procuring more corn for the animals attached to the army,[23] and he had to advise on a large and critical problem of general strategy. The strong army with which Grant had captured Vicksburg, while holding off Johnston, was being unwisely dispersed by the Federal administration and gave no immediate concern; but in Tennessee, where conditions had been fairly stable for many months, the enemy under Rosecrans had forced Bragg in July to abandon Tullahoma and to fall back on Chattanooga. That able Federal commander was now manœuvring to force his opponent from the city. Buckner was facing Burnside at Knoxville, with every prospect that the Confederates would be compelled to evacuate that place, also. If Knoxville and Chattanooga were yielded up, the Confederates would lose the most direct line of communication between Virginia and the Mississippi valley. That was not all. When Vicksburg had surrendered, the Confederacy had been cut in half. If the enemy were to follow this by breaking Bragg's front and marching through Georgia, the eastern half of the Southern republic would itself be split in twain, and nothing would be left the government at Richmond except the two Carolinas and that part of Virginia below the Rappahannock, a fragment that could not long survive.[24] Even this area was threatened, not only from the north but from the coast as well. Charleston, S. C., was under formal siege. Battery Wagner had fallen, Fort Sumter was a mass of defiant ruins, the city had been bombarded. The Federal blockade had tightened everywhere. At Wilmington alone did the fast British merchantmen find a ready port for the munitions shipped to the Confederate Govern-

---

[19] O. R., 51, part 2, p. 759. [20] O. R., 51, part 2, pp. 741–42.

[21] R. E. Lee, Jr., op. cit., 110, dated from Orange, on Sept. 4, a letter in which the General described briefly an inspection of the enemy's position from Clark's Mountain on Sept. 3. As Jones (2 R. W. C. D., 32) stated that Lee was in Richmond Sept. 3 and 4, it seemed probable that the letter in R. E. Lee, Jr., was misdated, but a check of the original, kindly made by Mrs. Hanson Ely, confirmed Sept. 4 as the correct date.

[22] O. R., 29, part 2, p. 692. [23] O. R., 51, part 2, p. 761.

[24] H. M. Cist: The Army of the Cumberland, 168 ff.; 1 Grant's Memoirs, 578 ff.; 1 Sherman's Memoirs, 344 ff.; R. S. Henry: The Story of the Confederacy (cited hereafter as Henry), 290 ff., 306 ff.

ment, and at Wilmington there was a menace of land operations that would flank the defenses of Cape Fear River.[25]

In this crisis, the darkest the embattled South had yet known, what course held out the strongest promise of relief? That was the question President Davis discussed in long, private conferences with the commander of the Army of Northern Virginia, whose strict conception of the subordination of the military arm to the civil government kept him from offering suggestions regarding other armies than his own, except when his views were sought by the President or by the Secretary of War. Lee did not believe the danger to Wilmington imminent enough to justify the government in weakening its scanty forces elsewhere.[26] Charleston he trusted the enemy would never get,[27] though he found the administration apprehensive of its safety and anxious to send troops there to strengthen General Beauregard. The main choice, as Lee saw it, then, lay between attacking Meade and attacking Rosecrans. Which should be done? As Bragg could not take the offensive without additional troops, should he give ground or should he be reinforced from the Army of Northern Virginia, with all the consequent risks to Richmond? Longstreet had long been anxious to go to Tennessee and to co-operate in an attempt to drive Rosecrans from that state;[28] Lee's inclination was to assume the offensive against Meade. The President, it seems, at first leaned so strongly to this view that Lee ordered the army to be made ready for an advance, on the assurance of the quarter-master-general that sufficient corn would be forthcoming for the horses.[29] On September 2, however, the Federals entered Knoxville, the enemy's movement against Chattanooga developed, and the situation became so alarming that Davis concluded he must reinforce both Beauregard and Bragg from the Army of Northern Virginia. With some misgivings[30] but, as Davis has recorded "with commendable zeal for the public welfare and characteristic self-denial," [31] Lee acquiesced in the movement of two brigades to Charleston, S. C., and in the dispatch of the rest of one corps to Tennessee. The President was anxious that Lee assume com-

---

25 *O. R.*, 29, part 2, p. 670 *ff*.   26 *O. R.*, 29, part 2, p. 703.

27 *O. R.*, 29, part 2, p. 661.   28 *Annals of the War*, 443–44; *Longstreet*, 433.

29 *O. R.*, 51, part 2, p. 761.   30 *O. R.*, 29, part 2, p. 720.

31 2 *Davis*, 428.

mand on that front himself,[32] but left the question open while Lee hurried back to the Rapidan on September 7[33] to prepare the troops for movement. Lee had decided to designate the First Corps, less Pickett's division, for the adventure in the West, and as he found Longstreet most anxious to go,[34] he was confirmed in his opinion that it would be best to remain personally in Virginia, to detach Longstreet, and to leave the direction of affairs in Tennessee to officers familiar with the troops.[35]

The plan was that Longstreet should proceed by way of the Virginia and Tennessee Railroad to the vicinity of Chattanooga, join with Bragg in an attack on Rosecrans, and return promptly to the Army of Northern Virginia.[36] The troop movement was to be made as quietly as possible, and Longstreet's destination was to be kept a secret. Believing that Rosecrans was manœuvring to effect the evacuation of Chattanooga, as in reality he was, Lee urged that he be attacked without delay.[37] Within twenty-four hours after he reached Orange, Lee had McLaws's and Hood's divisions of Longstreet's famous veterans on the road.[38] Pickett was to follow. When Longstreet came to headquarters to say farewell, Lee bade him God-speed. "Now, General," he said, "you must beat those people out in the West."

"If I live," Longstreet quotes himself as having answered, "but I would not give a single man of my command for a fruitless victory."

Lee assured him, in parting, that the President was prepared to follow up a success,[39] and as Longstreet rode off, Lee turned back to his own problem. He was left to direct an army that was now reduced to 46,000 officers and men,[40] an army that seemed strangely different without the familiar divisions of the First Corps. Fortunately, everything had been quiet during Lee's absence in Richmond[41] except for the escape of General Averell

---

[32] O. R., 29, part 2, p. 700–701.   [33] Ibid.

[34] Longstreet was so desirous of trying his hand in Tennessee that he offered to take the troops near Richmond, to assume Bragg's command, and to turn over his corps to that officer (O. R., 29, part 2, p. 699).

[35] Cf. O. R., 29, part 2, pp. 700–701, 702. Lee wrote Longstreet, Oct. 27, 1863: "I think you can do better than I could. It was with that view I urged your going" (O. R., 52, part 2, p. 549).

[36] Longstreet, 436; O. R., 29, part 2, pp. 720, 726.

[37] O. R., 29, part 2, p. 709.   [38] O. R., 29, part 2, p. 709.

[39] Longstreet, 437.   [40] O. R., 29, part 2, p. 709.

[41] Pendleton, 301.

after a mischievous raid in western Virginia.[42] Partly because the men were at leisure, and partly to remind them that the Army of Northern Virginia still had might, Lee staged a picturesque review of the Second Corps on September 9, and one of Hill's troops two days later. As on the historic eve of the battle of Brandy Station, he rode the full length of the line and then, surrounded by his staff officers and a company of ladies, he watched the men march past. "By their steady and firm step and soldierly bearing," one participant recorded, they showed "that they were not disheartened, but ready to go wherever their trusted and beloved commander might point the way."[43]

Despite the stimulation of these reviews, the course of events in Tennessee made Lee fear that Longstreet might not arrive in time to be of help.[44] Before the First Corps reached Richmond news came that Bragg had been forced to evacuate Chattanooga and had retreated to the Chickamauga River. The same day, September 9, a powerful Federal column compelled the capitulation of the Confederate troops holding Cumberland Gap where the Virginia, Kentucky, and Tennessee borders meet.[45] This closed the Virginia-Tennessee Railroad and necessitated the movement of Longstreet's corps by the difficult route through Atlanta.[46] There were, besides, vexatious discussions as to the particular units Longstreet should take with him.[47] At length he set out from Richmond, with affectionate assurance to Lee that if he could do nothing in Tennessee, he would ask to be sent back to Virginia.[48] Longstreet was confident enough, and expectant of new honors, for there were broad hints from the War Department that he would be named to succeed Bragg,[49] but Lee was apprehensive, especially as the news of the transfer of the corps, which was to have been a military secret, became generally known, to his deep disgust.[50] Lee could only urge speed and greater speed in attacking Rosecrans.[51]

[42] O. R., 29, part 2, pp. 632, 650, 709.
[43] Morgan, 170. Cf. Jones, L. and L., 283; Pendleton, 302; McHenry Howard: Recollections, 227; Worsham, 179–81; R. E. Lee, Jr., 106–7; Grayjackets, 229.
[44] O. R., 29, part 2, p. 720.   [45] 2 Davis, 427, 428 n.
[46] O. R., 29, part 2, pp. 720, 726, 738; Longstreet, 436.
[47] O. R., 29, part 2, pp. 706, 708, 710, 713.
[48] O. R., 29, part 2, p. 713; Taylor's General Lee, 222.
[49] Colonel John W. Fairfax to James Longstreet, April 16, 1898, Fairfax MSS.
[50] O. R., 29, part 2, pp. 719–20; R. E. Lee, Jr., 416; 2 R. W. C. D., 32, 33, 36.
[51] O. R., 29, part 2, pp. 730, 742–43.

There were reasons for concern, also, on the line of the Rapidan. The activity of the Federal cavalry indicated that an attack might be brewing.[52] General Sam Jones, alarmed by the capture of Cumberland Gap, began to call on Lee for reinforcements.[53] Deliberately keeping up a bold front,[54] Lee sent back all his surplus supplies to Gordonsville, in anticipation of an enforced withdrawal.[55] He had already cautioned Davis to strengthen the Richmond fortifications and to expedite the erection of arsenals farther inland.[56] Similarly, he advocated haste in the completion of the railroad that was to link Danville, Va., with Greensboro, N. C. With the Virginia and Tennessee already severed, and the enemy threatening the Petersburg and Weldon Railroad, a new line of rail communication was necessary. Otherwise, the Army of Northern Virginia might no longer be able to draw supplies from the South.[57] And that would mean ruin.

Then, in a dark hour, the telegraph clicked off the announcement—as glorious as it was unexpected—that Bragg with Longstreet's help had struck Rosecrans at Chickamauga on September 19-20 and had thrown him in retreat on Chattanooga. A new crisis had been passed. Hope rose in every Southern heart. If the victory could be followed up, the whole gloomy prospect of the war might be transformed. Lee immediately announced the success to his troops [58] and wrote his warm congratulations to Longstreet. "My whole heart and soul," he said, "have been with you and your brave corps in your late battle. It was natural to hear of Longstreet and [D. H.] Hill charging side by side, and pleasing to find the armies of the East and West vying with each other in valor and devotion to their country. A complete and glorious victory must ensue under such circumstances. . . . Finish the work before you, my dear general, and return to me. I want you badly and you cannot get back too soon." [59]

[52] O. R., 29, part 1, pp. 134–35; ibid., part 2, p. 720; 12 S. H. S. P., 323–26.
[53] O. R., 30, part 4, p. 647; cf. ibid., 30, part 4, p. 678.
[54] O. R., 29, part 2, p. 749.   [55] O. R., 29, part 2, p. 731.
[56] O. R., 29, part 2, p. 711.   [57] O. R., 29, part 2, p. 736.
[58] O. R., 29, part 2, p. 746.
[59] O. R., 29, part 2, p. 749. Lee's gratification over Chickamauga was marred by the report that General Hood and General W. T. Wofford of Longstreet's corps had been killed. This report was later proved to be unfounded (O. R., 29, part 2, p. 753), but for the time it caused Lee great distress. "I am gradually losing my best men," he said, "—Jackson, Pender, Hood" (O. R., 29, part 2, p. 743; 2 Gulf States Historical Magazine, 292–93).

But after Gettysburg and Vicksburg, Fortune's smiles on the South always quickly turned to frowns. Jubilation over Chickamauga lasted only a few days. Then it was found that what had happened so often in Virginia had been repeated in the West: The Army of Tennessee had exhausted itself in winning a battle and did not follow up its success. Rosecrans withdrew in safety to Chattanooga, and the Confederates were slow to follow. Disquieting reports arrived of friction between the dyspeptic Bragg and his high-spirited subordinates. Longstreet's self-confidence began to evaporate, and he called loudly for the leadership of which he was later so critical in his review of Gettysburg. "Can't you send us General Lee?" he pleaded with the Secretary of War. . . . "We need some such great mind as General Lee's. . . ."[60] General Leonidas Polk wrote directly to Lee, asking him to come West and reap the fruits of victory.[61] Lee was a long time in receiving this letter and then tactfully avoided a criticism of Bragg,[62] but he was conscious of the shortcomings of that officer and fearful that he would lose his advantage by laying siege to Chattanooga. His own view was that Bragg should cross the Tennessee River below the town, attack Rosecrans' communications, and compel a retreat.[63]

While Bragg's movements were still in doubt, Lee received reports from spies on September 28 that the XI and XII Corps of the Army of the Potomac had been withdrawn and had been sent to reinforce Rosecrans.[64] The time of the departure of the two corps was given as of September 25, but Meade's army still appeared so strong that it was October 1 before Lee was satisfied that Meade had been forced to part with these units.[65] Meantime, however, Lee notified the President of the suspected movement and urged that Bragg act before the reinforcements reached his adversary.[66]

Until he learned that the Federals were weakened, Lee had been bluffing Meade, while himself expecting an attack, and he

---

[60] *Polk,* 2, 275.
[61] *O. R.,* 30, part 4, p. 708.
[62] 2 *Polk,* 276–77.
[63] Jones, *L. and L.,* 284.
[64] *O. R.,* 29, part 2, p. 754.
[65] *O. R.,* 29, part 2, pp. 756, 757–58, 766. The spies' reports were accurate as to the time and extent of the detachment (*O. R.,* 29, part 1, p. 148).
[66] *O. R.,* 29, part 2, p. 754.

had been scouring Virginia for reinforcements.[67] Now that the odds against him had been reduced, as he thought, by about 12,000,[68] Lee began to consider the advisability of seizing the initiative once more. There were ample arguments against such a course. The ranks were thin and the men were poorly clad and worse shod. Lee himself was far from well. About September 20 he began to have violent pains in the back which were attributed at various times to lumbago, to sciatica, or to rheumatism.[69] Although they were not so diagnosed, they probably were the first positive symptoms of angina pectoris, the results of the strains of the summer on a heart weakened by his illness in the spring.[70] In the light of his experience at Gettysburg with the defects of the reorganized army, it was dangerous for him to take the field in poor physical condition, because he might be called upon to direct operations in person. But there were strong reasons why, in his opinion, an advance was desirable, even though the nights already were chilly and the forests along the Rapidan were flying the warning colors of approaching winter. A movement against Meade would certainly prevent the detachment of additional troops to the West. That was the all-important consideration. If, furthermore, Meade could be driven back to the Potomac and held there during the winter, northern Virginia would be spared the distresses of Federal occupation, the railroads would be more nearly safe from raiders, and the campaign of 1864 would open where Lee would have ample ground for manœuvre without exposing Richmond.[71] As the condition of the horses was somewhat improved, his belief in the strategic

67 *O. R.*, 29, part 2, pp. 727, 739, 742, 748, 749, 750, 752, 758; *ibid.*, 51, part 2, p. 769; *R. E. Lee, Jr.*, 110. Meade had contemplated an advance and had been satisfied he could drive Lee back, but had not felt that he could follow Lee to the Richmond defenses with the forces he had (2 *Meade*, 142).

68 *O. R.*, 29, part 2, p. 769. Actually the reduction had been around 16,300 (*O. R.*, 29, part 1, p. 148). Meade still had 80,700 effectives (*O. R.*, 29, part 1, p. 226), and Lee had less than 50,000 (*O. R.*, 29, part 2, p. 764). Long (*op. cit.*, 303–4) was wrong in saying that Lee had nearly 60,000 and that the two armies were nearer an equality than they had previously been.

69 *O. R.*, 29, part 2, p. 781; *Longstreet*, 573; Lee to Leonidas Polk, Oct. 26, 1863, 2 *Polk*, 276.

70 For a discussion of the nature of General Lee's illness, see vol. IV, Appendix.

71 Lee filed only a preliminary reticent report of the Bristoe campaign. His correspondence of the period is scanty. His principal reason for undertaking the campaign is given only in a letter of Oct. 26, 1863, to Longstreet in which he said he had made "a move upon General Meade to prevent his detaching reinforcements to Rosecrans" (*O. R.*, 52, part 2, p. 549). The other reasons are, of course, readily inferred from the general military situation.

wisdom of an offensive-defensive led him once again to take risks for the sake of possible gains.

The "leaks" from Richmond during Longstreet's southward movement prompted Lee to proceed with much secrecy in making his plans. Apparently he did not even notify the President of his intentions, though the fact that he would advance and the probable time of his start were known even to clerks in the War Department.[72] Meade was north of Culpeper on a ridge that would serve as well for defense as for attack[73] and had two corps extended to the Rapidan.[74] In this position the enemy could not be assailed to advantage by a frontal attack. Hence Lee determined to manœuvre him from his position and to thrust at him when he found a favorable opening. This would necessitate a roundabout march, at a distance from the enemy, if the movement was to be a surprise. To cover his advance, Lee directed General Imboden to move up the Shenandoah Valley and to protect the flank of the army by occupying the mountain passes.[75] Then Lee divided his cavalry, which had been reorganized into two divisions under Wade Hampton and Fitz Lee, respectively.[76] Fitz Lee was to remain on the Rapidan to cover the army's rear until Meade retreated. Hampton's division, led by Stuart, was to move on the right of the column.[77] Supplies were to be sent up the Orange and Alexandria Railroad to Culpeper, as soon as the road was opened by Meade's withdrawal.

When the time for the advance arrived, Lee's "rheumatism" in the back was so severe that he could not mount a horse, but he determined not to delay operations on that account. The two corps of Ewell and Hill crossed the upper Rapidan on October 9 and made their way through the hills toward Madison Courthouse, which was reached on the 10th.[78] The appearance of Federal cavalry in front of Stuart that day showed that the movement had been discovered and that Lee could not hope to catch Meade off his guard.[79] Lee, who was riding in a wagon,[80] was not surprised when Union horse was encountered, because an injudicious

[72] Cf. 2 R. W. C. D., 62.
[73] O. R., 29, part 2, p. 758.
[74] O. R., 29, part 1, p. 410.
[75] O. R., 29, part 1, p. 411; ibid., part 2, p. 780.
[76] O. R., 29, part 2, p. 707 ff.
[77] O. R., 29, part 1, p. 410.
[78] O. R., 29, part 1, p. 405-6.
[79] O. R., 29, part 1, p. 374.
[80] O. R., 52, part 2, p. 549.

announcement that he would cross the Rapidan had appeared in one of the Richmond newspapers.[81]

Stuart easily disposed of the prying cavalry outposts on October 10,[82] and cleared the road for the advance of the infantry toward Culpeper on the 11th. When the army reached Stone House Mountain,[83] five miles from that town, Lee learned that Meade had evacuated his position and had put the Rappahannock between him and his pursuers. All his stores had either been removed or destroyed.[84] It was necessary, therefore, to undertake a new turning movement to reach the Federals. Before this could be started the army had to be rationed, a process that had to wait on the arrival of the railroad trains, because the country, stripped bare by the invaders, could furnish nothing.[85]

While the hungry columns rested by the roadside, Lee rode into Culpeper. His back was better and he could keep on his horse, though every motion gave him pain.[86] When he reached the town, the old men, the cripples, the women and the children turned out to greet him. As they thronged about him, one petticoated super-patriot informed the General that during the occupation of the place by the enemy certain young ladies of Culpeper had gone to General Sedgwick's headquarters and had been entertained there with band music, "Yankee band music." Some of those who were accused of this act of near-treason were in the crowd, and while they doubtless would have been glad to scratch out the eyes of the informer, they trembled as Lee put on an air of mock severity. He teased them with a dark look for a moment and then he said: "I know General Sedgwick very well. It is just like him to be so kindly and considerate, and to have his band there to entertain them. So, young ladies, if the music is good, go and hear it as often as you can, and enjoy yourselves. You

---

81 *O. R.*, 29, part 1, pp. 405–6. As a matter of fact, the Federals did not learn of Lee's movement from the press but by direct observation on the front he had occupied. His departure from the Rapidan had been reported to Meade a few hours after it had occurred, but Meade had not been sure whether it presaged a retreat or a turning-movement (*O. R.*, 29, part 1, p. 276).

82 *O. R.*, 29, part 2, pp. 410, 440; *H. B. McClellan*, 377.

83 *Early*, 303.

84 *O. R.*, 29, part 2, pp. 407, 410; *Taylor's Four Years*, 115.

85 *O. R.*, 29, part 2, p. 410. For the use of the railroad to bring up supplies, see *ibid.*, 444.

86 *O. R.*, 52, part 2, p. 549.

will find that General Sedgwick will have none but agreeable gentlemen about him." [87] That settled it: youth was vindicated. The fate of the super-patriot, after Lee's departure, is not in the record.

Meantime, on the 11th, the cavalrymen were having a most exciting day. Stuart had flushed the Federal horse early in the morning and had been pursuing with his wonted dash. Every few hours he sent back to Lee to report his situation, for he had learned his lesson in Pennsylvania and did not intend to permit himself to get out of touch with the commanding general again. Late in the afternoon, when Lee had left Culpeper and had established camp for the night on the road near the village of Griffinsburg, one of Stuart's staff officers rode up with the news that Fitz Lee had encountered Federal cavalry units and was driving them northward from the line of the Rapidan in the direction of Brandy Station, while Stuart himself was pressing another column back toward the Rappahannock.

General Lee was with Ewell when this message arrived, and he received it, said the officer who brought the report, "with that grave courtesy which he exhibited alike toward the highest and the lowest soldier in his army."

"Thank you," he said. "Tell General Stuart to continue to press them back toward the river."

Then he smiled and added: "But tell him, too, to spare his horses—to spare his horses. It is not necessary to send so many messages."

Turning to Ewell, he said of the staff officer and of another who had preceded him only a few minutes, "I think these two young gentlemen make *eight* messengers sent me by General Stuart." [88]

Stuart, in obedience to this kindly hint, may have spared his horses in sending more reports to Lee, but he did not withhold the spur in following the enemy. True to his expectation, Fitz Lee joined him near the scene of their famous cavalry action of June 9, and together they fought a second battle of Brandy Station, almost as interesting as the first because of the soldierly co-ordination of horse artillery, cavalry, sharpshooters, and dis-

[87] *Long,* 306, on the authority of General Henry J. Hunt.
[88] *Cooke,* 346–47. Cooke was one of the officers.

mounted cavalry. By nightfall they had driven the enemy over the Rappahannock.[89]

Lee's task on the morning of October 12 was to outflank Meade and to intercept him on his retreat up the Orange and Alexandria Railroad. In its essentials the problem was analogous to the one he had solved successfully fourteen months previously by sending Jackson around Pope's rear. Now, however, he could not hope to repeat this manœuvre on a large scale, because of the weakness of the army and of the transport; but he was willing to undertake a shorter turning movement, in the hope of forcing Meade into a position where the Federals could be attacked advantageously.

The only roads available to Lee for this purpose led to Warrenton, so he chose that town as his immediate objective. Dividing the army into columns of corps, Lee set out from the vicinity of Culpeper early on the morning of October 12, his front and right flank covered by Stuart's cavalry. Ewell's corps was to move by way of Jeffersonton and Sulphur Springs. Hill was to take the longer, better-protected route via Woodville, Sperryville, Washington, Amissville, and Waterloo Bridge—a winding way, but one for which there was no substitute.[90]

While the cavalry skirmished on a wide front with the enemy, Ewell's infantry, which Lee accompanied in person, marched undisturbed by Rixeyville to Jeffersonton. Although thousands of men were barefooted[91] they did not complain or straggle. With their faces to the north, they were as confident as ever. As the column approached Jeffersonton, the village where Lee had given Jackson his orders for the march around Pope, the cavalry encountered a Federal outpost, scattered behind hills, fences, and the wall of the cemetery. The Eleventh Virginia was dismounted and was sent forward, but it was not strong enough for the task. Lee thereupon ordered Stuart to deploy a regiment on either

---

[89] Stuart's clear report is in *O. R.*, 29, part 1, pp. 440 *ff.* *Cf.* H. B. McClellan, 377 *ff.*

[90] *O. R.*, 29, part 1, pp. 406, 410, 444. Probably because he did not wish to disclose his line of advance to an enemy whom he might have to meet again on the same terrain, Lee nowhere mentioned in his report the line of Hill's advance. Neither Hill nor any of his subordinates filed any report of operations prior to Oct. 14, but it is possible to reconstruct Hill's route from J. F. J. Caldwell's *History of . . . McGowan's Brigade* (cited hereafter as *History of McGowan's Brigade*), 114, and from the report of General Irvin Gregg who noted (*O. R.*, 29, part 1, p. 366) that the 1st Maine Infantry encountered infantry, believed to be Hill's, between Amissville and Gaines's Crossroads. There are several references to a crossing at Waterloo Bridge.

[91] *O. R.*, 29, part 1, p. 408; *ibid.*, part 2, pp. 784-85.

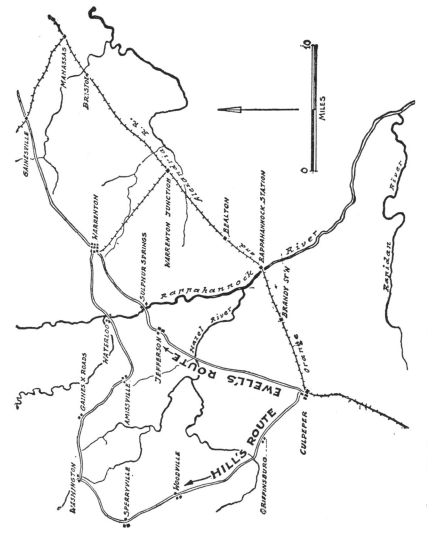

Routes of Ewell's (Second) and A. P. Hill's (Third) corps from Culpeper to Warrenton. Oct. 12–13, 1863.

side of Jeffersonton and to force the enemy out. In a few minutes there was a sharp clash, then the Federals gave way and scattered, with Stuart's men hunting them down in fast pursuit.[92]

From Jeffersonton the Warrenton road turns to the northeast, crosses a ridge and descends to the valley of the upper Rappahannock at Warrenton Sulphur Springs, the scene of Early's anxious adventure that August night in 1862 when the rising waters cut him off on the left bank of the stream from the supporting troops of Jackson.[93] When the advance reached the familiar ground around the ford, it discovered the enemy on guard, with dismounted cavalry in rifle pits and with some artillery in position. Stuart at once advanced his own dismounted men, and Lee's former military secretary, General A. L. Long, brought up a battery from the Second Corps artillery, of which he was now chief. The Federal gunners were quickly driven off, but when the Twelfth Virginia Cavalry rode up to the bridge, it found the planking removed and came under a hot fire from sharpshooters. Without hesitating, the Twelfth turned about, made its way to the ford below the bridge and dashed across. The Federal rearguard at once withdrew, the cavalrymen replaced the planking, and two divisions of infantry, passing quickly over, once again stood north of the Rappahannock. It was now nearly dark, and Lee called a halt.[94]

Early on the morning of October 13 the remaining troops of Ewell's corps crossed at Sulphur Springs and moved on Warrenton. Their march was not rapid, because Lee knew that Hill had a longer route to pursue, and he did not desire to be in the presence of the enemy until the two corps were reunited. It was afternoon when he reached Warrenton, where Hill joined him

[92] O. R., 29, part 1, pp. 444–45.   [93] See *supra*, vol. II, p. 294.
[94] O. R., 29, part 1, pp. 406, 410, 417–18, 445; *Long*, 306–7; H. B. McClellan, 385–86. The position of the Army of Northern Virginia was unknown to General Meade during the day of Oct. 12. After crossing the Rappahannock he suspected that Lee might still be at Culpeper, awaiting battle, and sent back three corps and a division of cavalry toward Brandy Station (O. R., 29, part 1, p. 10; *ibid.*, part 2, pp. 296, 297). This left him only the I and III Corps north of the river. It was contended by Long (*op. cit.*, 307), and by others who drew their information from his book, that this situation presented an opportunity that Lee lost. Actually, however, the two corps of the Army of Northern Virginia were so far apart that Lee could not have struck Meade north of the Rappahannock on the 12th, even if he had known of the division of Meade's forces, which was not ordered until 10:30 A.M. As soon as Meade heard of the arrival of Lee at Sulphur Springs, he directed the troops on the south bank to return at once. This order was issued at 9:15 P.M. (O. R., 29, part 2, p. 298), and was executed promptly.

about dark, too late to undertake a farther advance that day, especially as the entire army had to be rationed from the wagon train, now that Lee no longer was in touch with the railroad.[95]

During the day Lee had received messages from Stuart through Fitz Lee, announcing that enemy troops were still at Warrenton Junction, but were burning stores. Before nightfall a courier arrived with a dispatch, dated 3:45 P.M., in which Stuart stated that a Federal wagon train was moving from Warrenton Junction as if following infantry toward Warrenton. Stuart's note indicated that he was close to the enemy. He said, in particular, that he would dispatch further information very soon, as one of his officers was making a reconnaissance at that moment.[96] Then, curiously enough, the flow of messages stopped. As the day ended and the troops went into bivouac around Warrenton, Lee became apprehensive and waited long after his usual hour of retirement for further news. Had Stuart been cut off? Was the enemy approaching Warrenton?

About 1 o'clock a staff officer came to Lee's tent and announced that a spy in Stuart's service, Goode by name, had arrived with a strange tale. Lee went out to the campfire to hear what the man had to report. Goode was much concerned: Stuart, he said, had found the enemy moving northward along the Orange and Alexandria Railroad and had started back with two brigades of cavalry toward Auburn, on the way to Warrenton. As Stuart had approached Auburn he had discovered another heavy Federal column moving northward past Auburn toward Greenwich. Stuart had taken his men out of the road and had hidden them in a wood behind a hill north of Catlett's Station-Auburn-Warrenton road; but he was between two forces of the enemy and

---

[95] O. R., 29, part 2, p. 410; History of McGowan's Brigade, 114. The late junction with Hill is undoubtedly the explanation of the slow advance on the 13th, which has mystified some of Lee's biographers. Cooke (op. cit., pp. 354-55) was so much surprised at Lee's slowness that he expressed doubts whether Lee really desired to intercept Meade. Fitz Lee (op. cit., 315-16) contended that if Lee had advanced five miles beyond Warrenton to Auburn or fourteen miles farther to Bristoe, he could have caught Meade on the move. In explanation of the omission from Lee's report of all mention of Hill's movement to Warrenton, it should be noted that Lee was much averse to the publication of his reports, which President Davis in some instances had given to the press. Writing to the Secretary of War, April 30, 1864, Lee said that these publications should be avoided as he would have been very glad to receive such information regarding the enemy as the published correspondence between the War Department and General Joseph E. Johnston gave the Federals (O. R., 33, 1330-31. Cf. O. R., 11, part 3, p. 636).

[96] O. R., 51, part 2, pp. 776-77.

might be discovered at any time. He had sent Goode to inform General Lee of his plight and to ask that a force be sent to make an artillery demonstration west of the Auburn-Greenwich road. If this were done, Stuart might open with his own artillery and create so much consternation among the Federals that he could effect his escape. On the map, Goode pointed out the situation as follows:

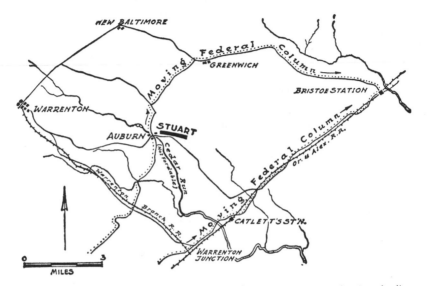

Hypothetical position of Stuart's cavalry, night of Oct. 13–14, 1863, showing the lines of march of the Federal columns. Stuart's exact position is indeterminable.

Lee went back into his tent to consider what had best be done to relieve Stuart. While there he could plainly hear Goode's voice, as the spy chatted with staff officers around the camp fire. There was a standing order in the army against the discussion of confidential matters by spies with any one but the officer to whom they were sent. Goode's apparent disdain of this very necessary regulation angered Lee. Going to the door of the tent he said in a loud, wrathful voice that he did not want his scouts to be talking in camp. Scarcely had he turned back when Major Venable entered and told him that Goode was fairly trembling at the General's rebuke. The man had not been talking incautiously, Venable said, but had simply been trying to explain where the

178

artillery could be placed to save Stuart from discovery. Lee re-
pented instantly of his stern treatment of the faithful Goode.
Going out to him, he gave orders that a supper with hot coffee
should be prepared for the man, and he was not content with his
amends until he had placed Goode on his own camp stool in the
headquarters mess tent and had seen him well supplied with
food.[97]

This done, Lee ordered General Ewell to make the desired
diversion at dawn, and prepared the army for a general advance
against Bristoe on the Orange and Alexandria Railroad. About
daylight there came the sound of a brief cannonade from the
direction of Ewell's approach, followed quickly by a more distant
salvo, evidently from Stuart's guns.[98] Soon Stuart himself rode up
to Lee and reported triumphantly that he had broken through
the enemy's lines and had escaped with negligible loss. He had
spent an anxious night, he said. His troopers had been compelled
to remain in the saddle. At the bridle of each animal hitched to
the wagons and to the guns, a dismounted cavalryman had stood
to stifle every impatient neigh of the horses and each inquisitive
bray of the mules. Once, during the long vigil, some of Stuart's
officers had proposed that they abandon the guns and the train
and cut their way out, but Stuart had refused. His own judgment
had forced him to reject another idea with which his imaginative
mind had toyed—to move out into the road, to turn the enemy's
wagon train westward in the darkness, and to fall in as if the
two lean brigades in gray were part of the Federal army. When
daylight had come a fog had obscured the ground, and as soon
as he had heard Ewell's guns he had opened with his own batteries against Federal infantry who had leisurely been boiling
coffee, in a most tantalizing manner, within sight of the hungry
Confederates. Then he had rushed off.[99]

[97] Venable's account in *Long*, 309-10.   [98] *History of McGowan's Brigade*, 115.
[99] *O. R.*, 29, part 1, pp. 447-48; *Long*, 308; *McCabe*, 418; *Cooke*, 351 ff.; H. B.
McClellan, 387 ff. The Federal reports will be found in *O. R.*, 29, part 1, pp. 238 ff.
General Stuart and apparently all other Confederate narrators of this amusing episode
assumed that the Federals were moving northward from Auburn to Greenwich all through
the night, but it is apparent from the report of Brigadier General Henry Prince (*O. R.*,
29, part 1, p. 314), that his division, which formed the rearguard of the III Corps, reached
Greenwich at 3 A.M. The II Corps did not follow him on that road but halted at Auburn
tor daylight and then turned into the road to Catlett's Station, as explained in Warren's
report (*O. R.*, 29, part 1, pp. 237-38). Caldwell's division crossed Cedar Run after 2
A.M. and took position facing Warrenton, with its rear to Stuart. Had Stuart reconnoi-

From Stuart's report it was apparent that part of the Army of the Potomac was close at hand, but as the enemy had direct roads there was little prospect that Meade would soon be overtaken. The army set out for Bristoe, however, in high spirits—Hill by way of New Baltimore and Greenwich, Ewell by Auburn and Greenwich.[100] The march was long and the pace was fast.[101] Lee was stirred by the zeal of the men, and when he came to write of the advance, he told the President, "I think the sublimest sight of the war was the cheerfulness and alacrity exhibited by this army in the pursuit of the enemy under all the trials and privations to which it was exposed." [102] A North Carolina soldier in Hill's corps atributed the speed of the march to less lofty motives than pure patriotism. According to him, on reaching Greenwich, "we found the camp fires of the enemy still burning and evident signs of their departure in haste. . . . Guns, knapsacks, blankets, etc., strewn along the road showed that the enemy was moving in rapid retreat, and prisoners sent in every few minutes confirmed our opinion that they were fleeing in haste. It was almost like boys chasing a hare. Though the march was very rapid, not a straggler left the ranks of our regiment, every man seeming in earnest and confident in the belief"—then he admitted the real reason—"that we would soon overtake and capture a portion of the Federal army before us with their wagon trains." [103] Shoes for bare feet, blankets for shivering shoulders, sutlers' delicacies for hungry stomachs—these were the spurs that hurried the regiments on.

At Greenwich, Ewell gave Hill the direct road to Bristoe Station, and as he was familiar from boyhood with the ground,[104] he conducted his own corps forward by farm roads a mile and more to the right of Hill's line of advance. Lee rode with Ewell at the head of the Second Corps, accompanied by General Pendle-

---

tred, he would have found the right flank of this division close at hand. By passing beyond it he could have crossed the Auburn-Greenwich road and could have gone on to Warrenton before daylight. The darkness was, however, a dangerous obstacle to any such adventure as this, and Stuart's decision to wait until daylight doubtless was the correct one. The map that accompanied Warren's report, printed in O. R., 29, part 1, p. 1018, makes plain Stuart's error in assuming that troops were marching up the Auburn-Greenwich road all night.

[100] According to Warren's map (O. R., Atlas, Plate XLV, No. 6), part of Ewell's corps first struck the Auburn-Greenwich road about two miles north of Auburn.

[101] History of McGowan's Brigade, 115. [102] O. R., 29, part 1, p. 408.
[103] 2 N. C. Regts., 440. [104] O. R., 29, part 1, p. 246.

ton.[105] About mid-afternoon, as he approached the railroad, Lee was greeted with a heavy outburst of firing on the left, infantry and artillery—Hill evidently engaged hotly with the enemy. Proceeding at once across country to ascertain the nature of the engagement, Lee did not arrive until the action was over. Then he learned the grim details of as badly managed a battle as had ever been fought under the flag of the Army of Northern Virginia.

This is what happened: As his corps approached Bristoe Station, where Jackson had reached the Orange and Alexandria Railroad in August, 1862, A. P. Hill observed a large force of the enemy on the near side and many more troops on the far side of Broad Run, a fordable little stream that courses from north to south until it reaches the railway, and then turns to the east. As Hill's advance was from the west, the stretch of Broad Run above the railroad was almost directly in his front. He accordingly deployed Heth's division facing the stream, with the intention of crossing at once and pursuing the enemy.[106] Only two brigades had been put in position—Cooke's on the right and Kirkland's on the left —when they received orders to attack immediately. The enemy across the run was moving hurriedly off at the time, and Poague's battalion was being advanced to shell the column.[107]

Just as Cooke started forward, a sharp fire broke out on his right, from the direction of the railroad cut, which ran from southwest to northeast. Throwing forward two companies to feel out the enemy, Cooke halted and sent word to Heth of his predicament; but as Anderson's division was coming up, Hill felt that he could repulse any troops on Heth's flank, and he sent peremptory orders for Cooke to advance at once across the run, whither all the Federals in sight had now fled.[108]

"Well," said Cooke, who had shown his fibre when he had stood almost unsupported at Sharpsburg, "I will advance, and if they flank me, I will face my men about and cut my way out." [109]

Scarcely had he started than the whole of the railroad embankment on his right began to blaze with musketry. The embank-

[105] Pendleton, 304.
[106] O. R., 29, part 1, pp. 426, 430; 2 N. C. Regts., 440–41.
[107] O. R., 29, part 1, p. 426.   [108] O. R., 29, part 1, pp. 426, 430, 435
[109] 2 N. C. Regts., 441.

ment formed an ideal breastwork, and behind it, on rising ground, Federal artillery was soon visible.

Then it dawned on the Confederates that while they had been intent on pursuing the troops across the run, another Federal force had advanced up the railroad and had taken position where

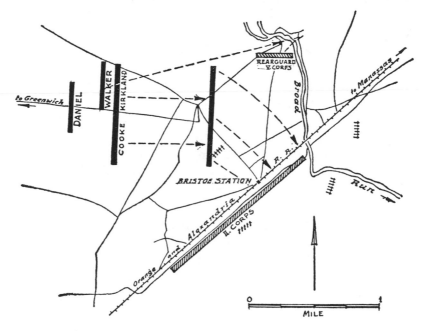

Manœuvres of three brigades of Heth's division, Third Corps, Army of Northern Virginia, in action of Oct. 14, 1863, at Bristoe Station.

it could sweep Heth's flank. It was as fine a trap as could have been devised by a month's engineering. Cooke's brigade, of course, could do nothing but retreat forthwith or else pivot on its right and attack the enemy behind the railway embankment. As Cooke was badly wounded, almost at the first fire, his senior colonel made a quick choice and ordered the charge. Kirkland conformed, swung his left around, and made for the enemy in the cut. He, too, was wounded, but his men kept on. They reached the embankment and plunged over it, only to be driven back speedily or captured. Cooke's men gallantly approached the embankment but came under a heavy enfilade and failed to reach

182

their objective. The two brigades fell back and in doing so uncovered a Confederate battery that had been placed, unknown to them, on the right of the road in rear of Cooke.[110] The enemy promptly advanced and seized four of the guns, which he hauled off. Walker's brigade, which had gone across the run, made a quick return and attempted to recover the lost artillery, but it was too late.[111]

Within forty minutes—before Anderson's division could get in position on Heth's right, and ere the Second Corps reached the field of action—the battle was ended and night was falling. Two Confederate corps had been within striking distance and so disposed that if Hill's attack had been delayed even half an hour, the Federals moving along the railroad could have been roughly handled and perhaps cut off. As it was, two brigades had borne the brunt of the action. Both had been wrecked. Cooke's fine regiments had lost 700, and Kirkland's 602.[112] In the Twenty-seventh North Carolina, which had been most severely exposed to direct and to enfilading fire, the casualties numbered 290 in an effective strength of 416, and all except three of the thirty-six officers were killed, wounded, or captured.[113] The total losses reached 1361.[114]

The army was indignant. "There was no earthly excuse for it," Colonel Walter Taylor protested, "as all our troops were well in hand, and much stronger than the enemy." [115] Said Sloan, "A worse managed affair than this fight . . . did not take place during the war." [116] When the reports reached President Davis, he endorsed on Hill's, "There was a want of vigilance." [117] Lee said little, but the next morning, when he went over the ground, and listened as Hill sorrowfully told his story and manfully took all the blame upon himself,[118] his look was glum and disappointed,[119] and he silenced Hill with words that were, for him, the worst of rebukes: "Well, well, General, bury these poor men and let us say no more about it." [120]

110 *James A. Graham Papers*, 162.
111 *O. R.*, 29, part 1, pp. 427, 431, 433, 435, 437.
112 *O. R.*, 29, part 1, p. 433.   113 *2 N. C. Regts.*, 443.
114 *O. R.*, 29, part 1, p. 433.   115 *Taylor's Four Years*, 116.
116 *Sloan*, 74.   117 *O. R.*, 29, part 1, p. 428.
118 *O. R.*, 51, part 2, p. 811.   119 *W. W. Chamberlaine*, 83; *Cooke*, 356.
120 *Long*, 311. The Confederates all reported that it was the III Corps they had chased across the run. *Cf.* Hill in *O. R.*, 29, part 1, p. 426. As a matter of fact, the re-

During that same morning of October 15, the cavalry reported that the enemy had retreated beyond Bull Run and was entrenching there.[121] Should Lee follow? He was confident that if he did so he could turn Meade's position and either force him north of the Potomac or compel him to take refuge in the fortifications around Washington.[122] But the army, of course, was not strong enough to besiege Washington, and if it attempted to hold Meade on the Potomac, or close to that stream, it would be compelled either to march into Loudoun or draw a line close to Bull Run. There was perhaps enough food in Loudoun to supply the army temporarily, but the roads into that country were rough with stones, and the October nights would be cold. The quartermaster's corps had not issued enough shoes before the advance. The men's footgear was in wretched condition.[123] If he could avoid the necessity, Lee was anxious to save his soldiers from new hardships. Besides, a move farther northward would carry the army to such a distance from Richmond that it could not be available in case the Confederate capital were attacked from the east.[124] Remaining where he was, in front of Manassas Junction, seemed to Lee as difficult as advancing into Loudoun, except for the exposure of the troops. He could draw no provisions from the naked country roundabout, and though he was on the railroad, it could not supply him. Meade had destroyed the bridge over the Rappahannock and had blown up one of its piers. This could not be repaired in time to serve the army. Everything would have to be hauled by wagon from the rail-end on the south side of the river.[125]

Were the possible benefits worth these risks and hardships? Lee was disposed to answer in the negative,[126] but while he was

tiring corps was the V (cf. O. R., 29, part 1, p. 277). The defending force along the railway cut was the II Corps, of which Webb's and Hays's divisions received the weight of the attack. The losses in the II Corps, including the few casualties that morning at Auburn, were 546 (O. R., 29, part 1, p. 250). For the small part played in the action by Anderson's division of Hill's Corps, see O. R., 29, part 1, p. 429. Wilcox's troops had not come up when the battle was fought. The commanding officers of the Second Corps filed no reports, but Early, op. cit., 304, gave a curious account of the slow and confused advance of his division.

[121] O. R., 29, part 1, p. 411.
[122] Taylor MSS., Oct. 15, 1863; R. E. Lee, Jr., 111; O. R., 29, part 2, p. 794.
[123] O. R., 52, part 2, p. 550.
[124] O. R., 29, part 1, pp. 407, 408, 409; ibid., part 2, p. 794; Pendleton, 305; R. E. Lee, Jr., 111.
[125] O. R., 29, part 1, p. 406.   [126] O. R., 29, part 1, pp. 406, 407.

debating, he began the destruction of the railroad in order that Meade could not utilize it in pursuing the army back to the Rappahannock.[127] For this work of tearing up the railway, Lee employed, among other troops, Lane's North Carolina brigade, which had long specialized in this art under the tutelage of "Stonewall" Jackson.[128] The rails were first detached from the cross ties. Then the ties were dug from the road bed and were piled in square pens at convenient intervals. Thereupon the rails were placed on top the pens, which were then set afire. When the centre of the rails became red hot and the ends began to sag, soldiers would take the rails, run with them to the nearest tree, post, or telegraph pole, and quickly wind them around the upright. The rails thus twisted were called "iron neckties" and, of course, could not be relaid.[129] This work, begun on the 15th, was continued the next day, while wrecking detachments destroyed the nearby bridges.[130] On the 16th a heavy autumnal rain saturated the ground and swelled the streams.[131] The army could hardly have moved had Lee desired it to do so; and had he found it necessary to put the shivering men on the march, Lee could not have led them, for his condition, which was now pronounced lumbago, was so painful that he was confined to his tent.[132]

Satisfied on the 17th that he could accomplish little by staying in Meade's front,[133] Lee started the army back toward the Rappahannock on October 18, and left the cavalry to watch the enemy.[134] He was not certain how soon Meade might attempt to follow him[135] and, to retard the enemy, he continued to destroy the railroad southward until he reached a point from which he believed it would be possible to transport the much-needed rails to the south bank.[136] The march was depressing because of the devastation of the country. "Never," wrote Walter Taylor, "have I witnessed as sad a picture as Prince William County now presents. 'Tis desolation made desolate indeed. As far as the eye can reach on every side, there is one vast, barren wilderness; not a fence, not an acre cultivated, not a living object visible; and but

127 O. R., 29, part 1, p. 407.   128 2 N. C. Regts., 479.
129 2 N. C. Regts., 479, 663; Taylor MSS., Oct. 17, 1863.
130 O. R., 29, part 1, p. 407.   131 Ibid., p. 407.
132 Pendleton, 304.   133 O. R., 29, part 1, p. 408.
134 O. R., 29, part 1, p. 411.   135 O. R., 29, part 1, p. 408.
136 O. R., 29, part 2, pp. 794-95.

for here and there a standing chimney, on the ruins of what was once a handsome and happy home, one would imagine that man was never here and that the country was an entirely new one and without any virtue save its vast extent." [137] "Not a living thing,"

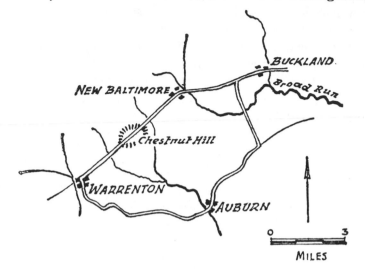

Terrain of the "Buckland Races," Oct. 19, 1863.

another officer exclaimed, "save a few partridges and other small birds! No horse or cow, no hog or sheep, no dog or cat,—of course, no man, woman, or child!" [138]

By noon of the 18th the army reached the Rappahannock, for its march was swift; but because of the slowness of the engineers, the pontoon bridge was not ready, and the tired columns had to wait.[139] Seeing near the river a farmhouse that had been spared, probably because some Federal commander had maintained his headquarters there, Lee rode up to look at it. He was shocked at the deliberate vandalism he beheld there. "Not a soul remained," the faithful Pendleton chronicled. "Drills, however, and ploughs of most valuable kinds had been piled together in the yard by the Yankees and burned; wagons, carts, and an elegant carriage had been cut to pieces and smashed up with axes; and the negro cabins were in general reduced to ashes." [140]

[137] *Taylor MSS.*, Oct. 25, 1863. [138] *Pendleton*, 304.
[139] *Taylor MSS.*, Oct. 25, 1863.
[140] *Pendleton*, 304–5; *cf. O. R.*, 52, part 2, p. 550.

At length the pontoons were in place, the bridge was laid, and Lee crossed to the south bank with half the army. The other forces followed the next morning.[141] The whole movement was completed without interruption, except for the action that won the alluring name of the "Buckland Races." This affair was on October 19. The Confederate cavalry, which had been on picket duty in the vicinity of Bull Run, had fallen back in two columns, one toward Warrenton under Stuart and the other toward Bristoe under Fitz Lee. Stuart made a stand on Broad Run in the vicinity of Buckland and was holding off the enemy when he received a dispatch from Fitz Lee stating that he was on his way to support Stuart. If Stuart fell back down the Warrenton road, Fitz Lee said he could himself assail the Federals' flank and perhaps rout them. Stuart promptly retired until he reached Chestnut Hill, about two and a half miles above Warrenton. Hearing then the guns of Fitz Lee, he turned on Kilpatrick's cavalry, who correctly assumed that they were in a trap and retreated in great haste, pursued by Stuart. Not until Buckland was reached did Stuart halt the chase. The fact that fleeing Federals and following Confederates were so close together on the stretch of seven miles gave the contest the nature of a race. Hence the name bestowed on the action.[142] Lee was much pleased with the affair, which yielded 250 prisoners and much booty, but he promptly forbade Stuart to undertake a raid to the Potomac during the temporary demoralization of the enemy.[143]

While the "Buckland Races" gave a saving touch of humor to the withdrawal, they did not relieve the expedition of failure. Lee had asked, in effect, whether the offensive could be resumed, and the answer, all too plain, was that it could not be with the limited forces he had, and with his *matériel* as poor as it then was. If he could get more men—or even more shoes and feed for his horses—it might be different; but without these, for hunger or for plenty, for worse or for better, the Army of Northern Virginia must remain temporarily on the defensive, in a stricken land.

141 *Taylor MSS.*, Oct. 25, 1863.
142 *O. R.*, 29, part 1, pp. 382, 387, 391–92, 451–52.   143 *O. R.*, 29, part 2, p. 794.

CHAPTER XI

A Surprise and a Disappointment

(RAPPAHANNOCK BRIDGE AND MINE RUN)

BACK on the south side of the Rappahannock, the Army of Northern Virginia, which had been in good spirits during the Bristoe expedition,[1] was satisfied that the year's bitter fighting had at last been ended.[2] Meade was somewhat of the same mind. He believed that Lee had advanced to Bristoe Station in order to destroy the railroad and thereby to hold off the Army of the Potomac while he sent more troops to Tennessee—"a deep game," Meade said, "and I am free to admit that in the playing of it [Lee] has got the advantage of me."[3] But Lee was not so sure that all was over for the winter. He presumed that Meade would advance again. "If I could only get some shoes and clothes for the men," he said, "I would save him the trouble."[4] On the possibility that supplies might be forthcoming for a limited offensive, he kept his pontoons on the Rappahannock, close to the piers of the old railroad bridge at Rappahannock Station. Simultaneously, he fortified a bridgehead on the north bank of the river. In doing this, he had a defensive as well as an offensive object in view, for as long as he was able to maintain the pontoon bridge he would be in position to divide Meade's forces and could throw a flanking column over the river in case his adversary attempted to cross the Rappahannock, either above or below him.[5]

Two weeks and more passed without important incident. The Army of the Potomac advanced to Warrenton, halted there for some days, and then began to feel its way slowly toward the Rappahannock;[6] but Meade did not appear to threaten a general

---

[1] *Taylor MSS.*, Oct. 15, 1863.
[2] *Welch*, 81; *Taylor MSS.*, Oct. 17, 25, 1863.   [3] 2 *Meade*, 154.
[4] *R. E. Lee, Jr.*, 111; cf. *O. R.*, 29, part 1, p. 408; *ibid.*, part 2, p. 800.
[5] *O. R.*, 29, part 1, p. 611. For Lee's headquarters at this time in "a nice pine thicket," see *R. E. Lee, Jr.*, 111.
[6] *O. R.*, 29, part 1, pp. 610, 611.

advance. During the respite thus afforded him, Lee experienced some concern over the unsatisfactory handling of affairs in western Virginia.[7] There was, too, the usual futile effort to get reinforcements, especially of cavalry;[8] and some correspondence passed with the War Department over a proposed transfer of troops to South Carolina, a movement against which Lee protested with the reminder that "it is only by the concentration of our troops that we can hope to win any decided advantage."[9] For the rest, Lee was content to give the men a vacation from marching and to remain at headquarters near Brandy Station,[10] as quietly as was possible, for he was in constant pain, and for five days at the beginning of November was unable to ride.[11] He had set November 5 for a review of the cavalry corps and had invited Governor John Letcher to witness it, but he was afraid he would not be able to endure this ordeal. Fortunately, though, he felt better that day[12] and was able to participate in a ceremony that delighted the spectators and made the heart of Stuart proud.[13] Several of Lee's nephews and his youngest son were among those passing in front of the commander, who had a secret parental delight in noting that Rooney's old regiment, the Ninth Virginia, made the finest showing.[14]

Ever since the famous review of June 8, 1863, on that same historic field near Brandy Station, there had been a tradition in the army that pageantry was always followed by action. Once again this was vindicated. On the very day of the ceremonies the outposts reported the enemy advancing to the Rappahannock, and by noon on November 7, Federal infantry was in front of

[7] O. R., 29, part 1, p. 409; ibid., part 2, pp. 799, 800, 803–4, 814, 816.
[8] O. R., 29, part 2, pp. 800–801, 807–8.
[9] O. R., 29, part 2, p. 819; Taylor MSS., Oct. 25, 1863.
[10] Taylor MSS., Oct. 25, 31, 1863.
[11] R. E. Lee, Jr., 113, 114.   [12] R. E. Lee, Jr., 114.
[13] Malone, 43; W. B. Hackley: The Little Fork Rangers, 88.
[14] R. E. Lee, Jr., 114. While this review was under way, a civilian from Alexandria approached the General and presented him a box, with a statement that he had been requested to deliver it to the General by persons he professed not to know. When Lee opened it he found in it a pair of very handsome gold spurs (R. E. Lee, Jr., 114). These spurs are now in the Confederate Museum, Richmond, Va. It developed, years after the war, that the spurs had been contributed by Baltimore ladies with the assistance of W. A. Jarboe, of Upper Marlboro, Md., that they were kept for some time at the Cartwright plantation in Saint Mary's County, and that they were smuggled across the Potomac by a Confederate spy, Captain Charles Caywood of Charles County, Md. (Washington Post, April 9, 1899, p. 22, col. 4; ibid., April 16, 1899, p. 22, cols. 1–4).

the *tête de pont,* while a large column was moving to Kelly's Ford. As the ground on the south bank of the river at this ford was somewhat similar to that at Fredericksburg, in that it offered no deep defensive position from which to dispute a crossing,[15] Lee intended to permit Meade to cross and then to attack him in superior force by holding part of the Federal force at Rappahannock Bridge.[16] The Confederate troops were well disposed for this purpose. Ewell's corps extended from Kelly's Ford to a point beyond the bridgehead, Hill was on the upper stretches of the river, guarding the fords, and the cavalry covered both flanks.

When, therefore, Lee learned during the afternoon that the enemy had crossed at Kelly's Ford, in front of Rodes's division, he felt no particular concern. Johnson's division was ordered to reinforce Rodes, Anderson was brought up close to the left of the railroad to support Early, who commanded the crossing, and the rest of Hill's corps was put on the alert.[17] Early had only Hays's brigade on the north side of the river, in the works covering the pontoon bridge, and no units resting directly on the south bank; but without waiting for orders he advanced the rest of his division as soon as he heard that the enemy was concentrating in front of the *tête de pont.*[18] Lee overtook Early on his way to the bridge and rode forward with him to a hill overlooking the position on the north bank.

Early hurried across the pontoon bridge, which was in a protected position, and Lee busied himself with disposing two batteries of artillery that were at hand. After half an hour or more, Early returned and reported that the enemy was gradually approaching the bridgehead under cover of a range of hills, and that the defending force was entirely too small to man the works. On the arrival from the rear of the head of Hoke's command, the leading brigade of Early's division, Lee ordered it over the bridge to support the troops already in position, but he declined to send more men to the north side. He believed that seven regiments would suffice to defend the bridgehead, inasmuch as the enemy could not advance on a longer front than the two brigades held.[19]

[15] *O. R.,* 29, part 1, pp. 610, 631. [16] *O. R.,* 29, part 1, p. 612.
[17] *O. R.,* 29, part 1, p. 612. [18] *O. R.,* 29, part 1, pp. 619, 620–21.
[19] *O. R.,* 29, part 1, pp. 612, 621. Hoke's brigade consisted at the time of only three regiments, as the fourth, under General Hoke, was on detached service in North Carolina (*O. R.,* 29, part 1, p. 612). General Martin McMahon stated in 4 *B. and L.,* 87, that

Soon after Hoke's brigade crossed, the Federals planted artillery where it could deliver a cross-fire on the bridgehead. Answering this challenge, the Confederate batteries quickened their fire, and Lee moved up to a hill nearer the river in order that he might observe the fight more closely.[20] He soon discovered that the Southern gunners were accomplishing nothing because of the length of the range, and he ordered the fire halted.

In a short time dusk fell. A heavy south wind was blowing and carried away from the river the sound of the action. Soon the Federal ordnance ceased its practice. Shortly afterward flashes of musketry could be seen, but these were not long visible.[21] This stoppage of fire convinced Lee that the Federals were merely making a demonstration against the bridgehead, probably to cover their advance at Kelly's Ford; and as the enemy had never made a night attack on a fortified position held by the infantry of the Army of Northern Virginia, Lee concluded that the action in that quarter was over for the day. If the enemy came too close, he believed it would be possible for the troops on the north side to return to the south bank under cover of the batteries.[22] Leaving General Early in charge, Lee rode back to headquarters, where he received the unwelcome news that the enemy had captured parts of two regiments at Kelly's Ford, had laid a pontoon bridge, and had sent a large force over to reinforce the first units.[23]

In this situation, of course, the logical course was to carry out the plan previously prepared for this contingency—to hold the bridgehead, to demonstrate there, and to move the greater part of the army eastward to engage the troops that were facing Rodes and Johnson at Kelly's Ford. But before Lee could execute this plan, Early sent him almost incredible news from the *tête de pont:* After darkness had fallen, the enemy had massed in great strength, had stormed the bridgehead and had captured the whole force on the north side, except for those who had swum the Rappahannock or had run the gauntlet over the pontoon bridge!

the colonel commanding one of the brigades told him, after being captured, that Lee had asked if more troops were needed on the north side, and had been assured that the position could be held "against the whole Yankee army."

[20] It seems probable, though it is not absolutely certain, that Lee's first position was on the hill a quarter of a mile south of the river and west of the railroad, and that his second position was on the hill in the bend of the stream and close to the pontoon bridge.

[21] *O. R.,* 29, part 1, p. 621.   [22] *O. R.,* 29, part 1, pp. 613, 622.

[23] *O. R.,* 29, part 1, pp. 612, 631–32.

Fearing an attempted crossing, Early had set fire to the south end of the bridge and had lost the pontoons.[24]

Lee's defensive plan collapsed as he read Early's dispatch. If the bridgehead was gone, it would be futile to demonstrate on the left while attacking on the right at Kelly's Ford. Meade would laugh at the helpless Southern troops opposite the old railroad bridge. Moreover, the Army of Northern Virginia could not safely remain where it was, on a shallow extended front, with the Rapidan River behind it. Pope had nearly been caught there, with the positions reversed. Lee saw that he must move back, and at once. Within a few hours after Early had reported the disaster at Rappahannock Bridge, the troops had been routed out from their huts, the wagons had been packed, and the army was retiring to a line that crossed the Orange and Alexandria Railroad two miles northeast of Culpeper and barred the road from Kelly's Ford by way of Stevensburg.[25] Lee was, of course, concerned over this hurried movement, but he did not let it upset his poise. As he prepared to leave his headquarters near Brandy Station, he went to Major Taylor's tent and found that officer stretched out in front of a roaring fire. "Major Taylor is a happy fellow," he commented cheerfully, and went on his way.[26] There was no sleep for Lee that night, and he was glad to see his faithful staff officer snatching rest while he could.

As the army formed line of battle in its new position on the morning of November 9, there was some expectation that Meade would attack, but when he let the day pass without following up his success at Rappahannock Bridge, Lee again put the columns in motion and, on November 10, was back on the south side of the Rapidan, whence he had started one month and one day previously for Bristoe Station.[27]

The troops were much chagrined at the necessity which threw them back from the Rappahannock. The affair of the bridge was, Taylor insisted, "the saddest chapter in the history of this army,"

---

[24] *O. R.*, 29, part 1, p. 622 *ff.*

[25] *O. R.*, 29, part 1, pp. 610–11, 613, 616. The line taken up extended from Mount Pony northward to the John Bell plantation, west of the Orange and Alexandria Railroad, and thence northwest to a point about three-quarters of a mile east of Chestnut Fork Church. See the sketch in *O. R.*, 29, part 1, p. 614.

[26] *Taylor MSS.*, Nov. 15, 1863.

[27] *O. R.*, 29, part 1, pp. 610–11; *Taylor MSS.*, Nov. 15, 1863.

showing "miserable, miserable management." [28] Sandie Pendleton, son of the chief of artillery and one of Jackson's former staff officers, was burning for Lee to attack Meade and "let us retrieve our lost reputation." He went on: "It is absolutely sickening, and I feel personally disgraced by the issue of the late campaign, as does every one in the command. Oh, how each day is proving the inestimable value of General Jackson to us." [29] A young North Carolinian, less close to the saddles of the mighty, probably voiced the sentiments of the army when he said, "I don't know much about it but it seems to me that our army was surprised." [30] Early was intensely humiliated, though he did not feel himself responsible.[31] Lee called for prompt reports both of the attack at the bridgehead and of the capture of the skirmishers at Kelly's Ford; but when the documents were received he could only say that sharpshooters had not been properly advanced in front of the bridgehead, and that Rodes had erred in placing two regiments on picket duty, instead of one, at Kelly's Ford.[32] "The courage and good conduct of the troops engaged," he said, "have been too often tried to admit of question." [33]

The morale of the army was not impaired by this unhappy affair.[34] The men went cheerfully to work building new huts, and contrived to make themselves comfortable after a fashion.[35] Lee sought once more to get shoes for those who were barefooted[36] and began a long correspondence with the commissary bureau concerning the rationing of the army.[37] Supplies were so scanty and the operation of the Virginia Central Railroad so uncertain that he was compelled to serve warning that he might be forced to retreat nearer Richmond.[38] As he could not leave the army to go to the capital to discuss these matters with Mr. Davis, he requested the President to visit the army, and, during

---

[28] *Taylor's Four Years*, 116; *Taylor MSS.*, Nov. 7, 1863.

[29] *Pendleton*, 305.   [30] *James A. Graham Papers*, 166.

[31] *O. R.*, 29, part 1, pp. 622, 625; *Early*, 316.   [32] *O. R.*, 29, part 1, pp. 612, 613.

[33] *Ibid.*, p. 613. Meade, for his part, was disappointed that Lee declined battle between the Rappahannock and the Rapidan (2 *Meade*, 156).

[34] *Taylor MSS.*, Nov. 15, 1863: "The loss of two brigades does not weaken us much numerically and not at all morally."

[35] *Cooke*, 360.   [36] *O. R.*, 29, part 2, pp. 830, 835.

[37] *O. R.*, 29, part 2, p. 837; see *infra*, p. 251, n. 77.

[38] *O. R.*, 29, part 2, pp. 832–33.

a period of rainy weather from November 21 to November 24, conferred with him on the situation.[39] Lee's most immediate concern was for the horses, which were almost without forage. He anticipated the loss of many of them from starvation during the winter, and he did not believe that without food they could survive more than two or three days of active operations. The country round about had been stripped almost as bare as the devastated area north of the Rappahannock.[40]

But whether men or mounts survived or perished, Lee had to guard his front against the powerful, warm, and well-fed enemy that might again descend upon him. A little tributary of Mine Run, known as Walnut Run, fifteen miles northeast of Orange Courthouse, was fortified to cover the right flank. Ewell's corps was extended from that point westward to Clark's Mountain, where the old lookout was re-established. In Ewell's absence on account of sickness, this part of the line was entrusted to Early, with particular instructions to study the defensive possibilities of Mine Run.[41] From Clark's Mountain westward to Liberty Mills, a distance of approximately thirteen miles, Hill's camps were spread.[42] The cavalry covered both flanks, and as Lee thought it probable Meade would make his next advance from Bealton to Ely's and Germanna Fords,[43] Hampton's division on the lower Rapidan was enjoined to maintain a ceaseless watch for an advance in that quarter.[44]

For more than two weeks after the line of the Rapidan was manned, Meade showed no sign of any disposition to assume the initiative except for minor cavalry demonstrations.[45] Then, on the night of November 24, one of Lee's spies reported that eight days' rations had been issued the I Corps, and another scout told of suspicious movements by Federal horse in Stafford County.[46] The next morning Stuart's cavalry was put on the alert,[47] and the

[39] Taylor MSS., Nov. 21, 23, 25, 1863; Jones, L. and L., 295; 2 R. W. C. D., 101. On Sunday, Nov. 22, the President and General Lee attended service and heard General Pendleton preach (Pendleton, 306).

[40] O. R., 29, part 2, pp. 830, 832.   [41] Early, 317.

[42] O. R., 29, part 1, p. 830; McCabe, 424–25.

[43] O. R., 29, part 2, p. 832.   [44] O. R., 51, part 2, pp. 783, 785.

[45] Taylor MSS., Nov. 14, 15. 1863.   [46] O. R., 29, part 2, p. 846.

[47] O. R., 51, part 2, p. 787.

army became expectant of a new battle.[48] "With God's help," wrote Major Taylor, "there shall be a Second Chancellorsville as there was a Second Manassas." [49]

Lee's belief was that his able adversary, in making another thrust,[50] would attempt, on crossing the Rapidan, to advance through the Wilderness of Spotsylvania in the direction of the Richmond and Fredericksburg Railroad.[51] He had already suggested to General Imboden in the Shenandoah Valley that he join with Mosby's Rangers in operations against the Federal line of communications,[52] and he now prepared to move quickly to the northeast in order to interpose between Meade and his objective. For once the roads favored him, and he had three fair highways almost to Wilderness Run and two nearly to Chancellorsville.

A heavy fog limited vision from the Confederate signal stations early on the morning of November 26,[53] but this lifted as the day wore on, and disclosed the enemy moving in force through Stevensburg toward Germanna Ford.[54] As this was precisely what Lee had expected Meade to do, orders were issued for the Confederate movement to begin during the night.[55] Care was taken to cover both flanks,[56] and a route was selected for the wagon train that would place it where it could either reach the army quickly or retire southward toward the line of the Virginia Central Railroad.[57] At 3 A.M. on the morning of the 27th, Lee left his headquarters near Orange Courthouse and started for Verdiersville.[58] The weather was excessively cold, and icicles formed thickly on the beards of the officers,[59] but Lee was in high spirits, now that there was a prospect of battle.[60] He was quite unconscious of the inward grumbling of his staff that he had started ahead of every one else and would arrive at his destination ere more seasonable sleepers were astir.[61]

[48] Taylor MSS., Nov. 25, 1863; Richmond Dispatch, Nov. 30, 1863, quoted in McCabe, 426.

[49] Taylor MSS., Nov. 25, 1863. Part of this letter, misdated Nov. 26, 1863, appears in Taylor's Four Years, 120.

[50] R. E. Lee, Jr., 116.

[51] O. R., 29, part 1, p. 831; ibid., part 2, p. 832; Taylor's Four Years, 120; O. R., 51, part 2, p. 788.

[52] O. R., 29, part 2, p. 846.

[53] O. R., 29, part 1, p. 830.

[54] O. R., 29, part 1, p. 898.

[55] Taylor's General Lee, 225.

[56] O. R., 29, part 1, p. 830.

[57] O. R., 29, part 2, p. 847.

[58] Taylor's Four Years, 120.

[59] Taylor MSS., Dec. 5, 1863.

[60] Cooke, 365.

[61] Taylor MSS., Dec. 5, 1863.

True to these chilly predictions, when Lee reached Verdiersville he found no troops there, but down the road, in a thick pine wood, fires were burning and Confederate cavalry outposts were to be seen. After establishing his headquarters at the Rhodes house,[62] Lee walked down the plank road and found Stuart just rising from beside the fire, where he had slept since midnight with only one blanket. "What a hardy soldier!" Lee exclaimed as Stuart approached. The same thing might have been said of Lee himself, for he had cast aside his cape and wore only his uniform.[63]

In a brief conversation with his chief of cavalry, Lee directed him to cover the roads in the direction of Chancellorsville and Spotsylvania Courthouse, as the enemy was believed to be moving in that direction. Not long after Stuart rode off to look for Hampton's division, which had not yet come up,[64] General Early reported in person. Ewell's corps, Early said, was already beyond Verdiersville on the old turnpike, which approximately paralleled the plank road. Lee simply ordered him to continue his advance in the direction of Chancellorsville and to attack any force he encountered.[65]

Early rode off to direct this movement. He soon sent back word that the cavalry pickets had been driven in and that General Hays, who was leading Early's own division, had met Federal infantry at Locust Grove, situated on a ridge about a mile and a half east of Mine Run. Assuming that this was a force thrown out to protect the rear of Federals moving eastward from the nearby fords, Lee did not ride forward to reconnoitre in person, but waited at Verdiersville for the arrival of Hill's corps, which had a long march on the plank road from its encampments.

While Early deployed his men slowly and cautiously, the morning hours passed. Shortly after noon some echoes of action may have reached Lee from the northeast, but the pine forests were thick, and sound did not carry far. Ere long, however, he must have been informed that while Johnson's division was advancing toward Bartlett's Mill, the ambulance train had been fired on from the north.[66] Steuart's brigade had moved out from

---

[62] O. R., 29, part 1, p. 831.
[63] Cooke, 363–64.
[65] O. R., 29, part 1, p. 832.

[64] O. R., 29, part 1, p. 898.
[66] O. R., 29, part 1, p. 862.

the road, the rest of the division had been recalled, and a line of battle had been formed facing the Rapidan.[67] Meantime, Early had completed his dispositions and had put Rodes and Hays in line, opposite what appeared to be a strong force at Locust Grove. Instead, therefore, of having a race for Chancellorsville, with an enemy moving southeastward from the fords of the Rapidan, Lee found the Federals in his front and on his left flank. Still, this situation did not altogether contradict the view that the enemy was advancing toward Fredericksburg or the Richmond and Fredericksburg Railroad. The Federal columns might have been delayed in crossing the fords opposite Lee's front, or the forces that had been encountered by Early might be a heavy rearguard.

About 1 P.M., Heth's division, at the head of Hill's corps, reached Verdiersville. Lee gave the men an hour's rest and then directed that they continue their march up the plank road toward Mine Run.[68] Some time after the last regiment of the division had filed past, Lee himself rode forward with his staff. When he had gone about two miles he found the division halted and heard firing ahead. At length, Heth rode up and reported that when his advance had reached a point between two and three miles from Verdiersville, he had come upon a detachment of Stuart's cavalry skirmishing with Federals along the plank road. Heth had thrown forward skirmishers to support the cavalry, but they had been driven in quickly. Several attempts to drive •off the enemy had been made to no purpose. Might he advance his whole division and feel out the strength of the Federals? Lee consented. and Heth hurried away.[69]

In rear of Heth's line of battle, Lee waited. North of him, where Johnson's division had been fired upon, a hot action was in progress. To the northeast, Rodes's and Early's men were skirmishing briskly. And now Heth was about to engage. It was, to say the least, stiff and extended resistance to be offered by an adversary who was supposed to be hastening toward the railroad below Fredericksburg.

General Hill, who joined Lee about this time, had been of opinion that the enemy had only cavalry in his front,[70] but General Stuart, in a note sent at 2 o'clock, expressed the belief that

[67] O. R., 29, part 1, p. 847.
[69] O. R., 29, part 1, p. 897
[68] O. R., 29, part 1, pp. 895, 897.
[70] O. R., 51, part 2, p. 788.

the enemy was advancing up the Rapidan.[71] Most significant of all was a dispatch from General Thomas L. Rosser, one of Stuart's new brigadiers. He reported that during the morning he had found the ordnance train of the I and V Army Corps on the plank road near Wilderness Tavern. Attacking, he had captured 280 mules and 150 prisoners,[72] and—what was of far greater immediate importance—he had observed that the wagons were headed for Orange Courthouse, not for Chancellorsville.[73]

Was Meade, then, moving against the Army of Northern Virginia, rather than to the Richmond and Fredericksburg Railroad? It seemed probable, but until the purpose of the enemy was more fully disclosed, Lee hardly dared hope that his numerically inferior army would have the opportunity of fighting a defensive battle. When, therefore, Heth returned late in the evening and announced that he had driven the enemy's skirmishers from their advanced position, Lee was unwilling to authorize an advance until he had personally examined the enemy's position and had seen for himself how strongly the Federals were posted.[74] He ordered Anderson's division of Hill's corps to the right and rear of Heth to fill in the gap between Heth's left and Early's right,[75] and after Hill returned from making these dispositions, Lee went with him on a reconnaissance.

By this time he had information that the force which Johnson's division had encountered on its advance was an entire corps, part of which had been driven off, with a Confederate loss of some 545 men.[76] Such additional intelligence as reached Lee confirmed the suspicion formed after the receipt of Rosser's dispatch and led him to conclude that the whole of the Army of the Potomac was in his front.[77] It was not necessary to go in search of the enemy; the enemy was searching for him! For the first time since Fredericksburg the army was to have a chance of receiving the enemy's assaults instead of attacking. As it was now nearly dark, Lee determined not to advance against the strong position of the Federals that evening, but to withdraw to the west bank of Mine

[71] O. R., 51, part 2, p. 788.
[72] O. R., 29, part 1, p. 828. Rosser in his first dispatch (O. R., 51, part 2, pp. 788-89) stated that the captured animals numbered 150.
[73] O. R., 51, part 2, pp. 788-89.
[74] O. R., 29, part 1, p. 897.   [75] O. R., 29, part 1, p. 896.
[76] O. R., 29, part 1, p. 847.   [77] O. R., 29, part 1, p. 896.

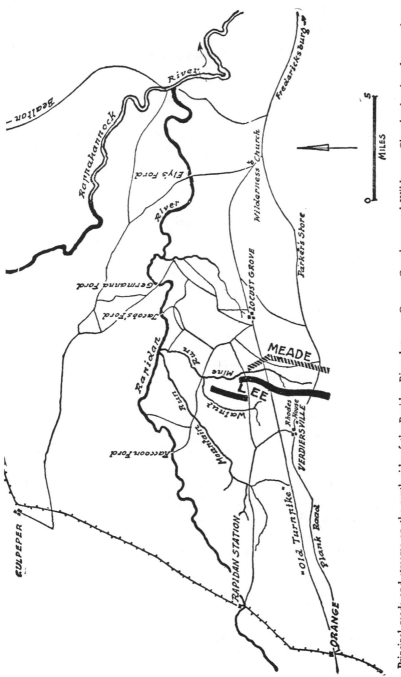

Principal roads and streams on the south side of the Rapidan River between Orange Courthouse and Wilderness Church, showing the opposing positions along Mine Run, Nov. 29, 1863.

Run during the night and to await developments.[78] Early retired behind the run without additional orders and took up a good line there.[79] Hill's corps was recalled during the night.[80]

When Early reported, about daylight on the 28th,[81] Lee instructed him to move his troops still farther westward to an even better defensive position, for if Meade was of a mind to assume the offensive, Lee wished to meet it on the most favorable ground.[82] But before Early could execute this order he found the Federal infantry advancing to Mine Run and, with Lee's permission, he waited to repulse them.[83] A heavy rain began to fall while the army stood ready to resist attack,[84] and this downpour seemed to deter the enemy. Making one or two minor adjustments in his front, to protect it from enfilading fire,[85] Lee ordered earthworks thrown up. As the earth began to fly, he rode or walked among the soldiers with encouraging words. "In an incredibly short time (for our men work now like beavers)," one officer wrote shortly afterwards, "we were strongly fortified and ready and anxious for an attack." [86]

But the enemy did not attack that day, nor the next, though he opened a heavy artillery fire on the 29th and threatened to assault.[87] Lee could not believe that Meade had made elaborate preparations and had moved his whole army for a mere demonstration, so he continued to strengthen his earthworks, while the enemy set to work to emulate him. The day witnessed the strange spectacle of two great armies exchanging occasional cannon shots and contenting themselves, for the rest, with seeing which of them could pile the higher parapets.[88] It chanced to be a Sunday, and the weather was very cold.[89] The men who were not on duty gathered about their fires and, here and there, assembled in prayer meetings incident to the great revival that showed no sign of losing its force. As Lee rode out on a tour of inspection, he, with his staff, chanced to pass one of these gatherings. He promptly dismounted and participated reverently in the service.[90]

78 O. R., 29, part 1, p. 896.   79 O. R., 29, part 1, p. 833.
80 O. R., 29, part 1, pp. 896–97.   81 Early, 322.
82 O. R., 29, part 1, p. 834.   83 Ibid.
84 O. R., 29, part 1, p. 836.   85 O. R., 29, part 1, p. 834.
86 Taylor's Four Years, 120.   87 Taylor's General Lee, 227.
88 Taylor's Four Years, 121.   89 Cf. 4 B. and L., 91; O. R., 29, part 1, p. 836.
90 Taylor's Four Years, 121; Jones, 416; Jones: Christ in Camp, 51.

On the 30th, the weather still very cold, Stuart reported early that the enemy was forming line of battle on the south side of the Catharpin road.[91] But once again expectations were deceived, and no general engagement occurred. Puzzled as Lee was by Meade's lack of action,[92] he was so confident of the outcome of a Federal attack that he notified Davis not to reinforce him with troops that might be needed for the defense of Richmond.[93] He continued to keep a sharp lookout on his flanks, however, especially on his right, where there had been some active cavalry skirmishing on the 29th.[94]

Sometime on the 30th a hurried message arrived from General Stuart, asking Lee to come to him at once. Lee went with the messenger, and found Stuart in the company of Wade Hampton in rear of the left flank of the enemy. Hampton had reached that position unobserved and believed that it was possible to turn the Federal position and repeat Jackson's movement at Chancellorsville. Lee studied the ground carefully and conferred with some of his officers but decided against immediate action,[95] probably because he could not bring the troops into position in time to attack that day, or else because he wished to wait a little longer in the hope that Meade would attack.

When the morning of December 1 came and went with no further sign of any intention on the part of the Federals to press the offensive, Lee lost hope that the Federals would assume a vigorous offensive and he determined to take the initiative himself. "They must be attacked; they must be attacked," he said.[96] Hill was directed to draw Anderson's and Wilcox's divisions of veterans to the extreme right,[97] probably with an eye to moving them to the position Hampton had discovered the previous day, and Early was instructed to extend his right to cover the ground vacated by the two divisions. Lee's plan was to carry Wilcox and Anderson beyond the enemy's left flank and to sweep down it, while Early held the defenses on Mine Run with his own corps and with Heth's division. The weather was so cold that water

[91] O. R., 51, part 2, p. 791.   [92] O. R., 29, part 1, p. 826.
[93] O. R., 51, part 2, p. 790.   [94] O. R., 29, part 1, pp. 901–2.
[95] H. B. McClellan, 398. Neither Hampton nor Stuart mentioned this incident in his report, but McClellan vouched for it. Hampton was in rear of the enemy after dark on the 29th (O. R., 29, part 1, p. 900).
[96] Cooke, 369.   [97] O. R., 29, part 1, p. 896.

froze in the canteens of the men that night,[98] but the movement got under way smoothly and without interruption by the enemy, though there were some evidences of activity within the Federal lines.[99]

Before daybreak on December 2 the whole army was ready; Anderson and Wilcox were in position; the rest of the men were on the alert; the gunners were at their posts. As soon as it was light enough to see, the skirmishers looked eagerly through the woods for the Federal pickets. But they scanned the thickets in vain: The enemy was gone![100] The withdrawal was so unexpected that a staff officer who was sent to order Hampton's division to pursue the foe found the videttes on the watch for an advance by the Federal divisions that were then fast making their way toward the fords of the Rapidan.[101] Informed of the changed situation, the cavalry rode fast and hard,[102] and the infantry followed through woods the retiring enemy had set afire.[103] Meade, however, had a long lead, for he had started during the late afternoon of the 1st, and the chase was fruitless.[104]

"I am too old to command this army," Lee said grimly, when he saw that his adversary had retreated, "we should never have permitted those people to get away." [105] In deep depression of spirits, and indignant at the many evidences of purposeless vandalism,[106] he soon recalled the infantry and moved back toward his camps higher up the stream. When he had cooled down, two days later, he wrote of Meade, "I am greatly disappointed at his getting off with so little damage, but we do not know what is best for us. I believe a kind God has ordered all things for our good." [107]

Except for a troublesome raid by General W. W. Averell against the Virginia and Tennessee Railroad, beginning Decem-

98 *James A. Graham Papers*, 172.   99 *Taylor's Four Years*, 121.
100 *O. R.*, 29, part 1, pp. 829, 896.   101 *Long*, 316.
102 *Cf. O. R.*, 51, part 2, pp. 791–92.   103 *Long*, 317.
104 *O. R.*, 29, part 1, p. 829.   105 3 *B. and L.*, 240; *Cooke*, 269–70.
106 *O. R.*, 29, part 1, p. 830; *Early*, 324–25 n.

107 *R. E. Lee, Jr.*, 116. Meade had crossed in the expectation of attacking Lee and of reaching the Virginia Central Railroad, but he had been delayed in his advance by the tardiness of the III Corps. After he found Lee behind Mine Run, he waited to select the best position for attack and finally decided to make his assault on Nov. 30, but when Major General G. K. Warren of the II Corps examined the ground closely, he became

ber 11,[108] the Mine Run episode marked the end of active operations in 1863.[109] It had been for Lee no such year of victory as
'62. The bloody glory of Chancellorsville had been dimmed by
the defeat at Gettysburg. The limit of the manpower of the
South had almost been reached. The spectre of want hung over
the camps. From the time of the return to the line of the Rappahannock and Rapidan after the Pennsylvania campaign, the army
had met with no major disaster, but it had scored no success.
Taking Bristoe Station, the capture of the Rappahanock bridgehead and the movement to Mine Run as one campaign, Lee's
losses had been 4255 and his gain had been nil.[110]

These casualties, amounting to nearly a whole division, were
not due to recklessness on the part of the men, or to ready surrender. Aside from those killed and wounded in Johnson's division as it marched to Mine Run, virtually the whole of Lee's
losses were attributable to defective leading or to carelessness on
the part of commanding officers. The operations had lacked not
only the dash of Jackson but the tactical skill of Longstreet, as
well, and they must have raised serious misgivings in Lee's mind
as to the future handling of the two corps left him. The im-
petuosity that had marked A. P. Hill ever since the battle of
Mechanicsville cost the army the service of two effective brigades
at Bristoe Station, and along with them the possibility of a substantial victory. Not since McLaws's slow bungling at Salem
Church had there been a worse example of generalship. The
defense at Rappahannock Bridge and at Kelly's Ford on November 7 was unskillful, even though no blame could be fixed. As for

convinced his men would be uselessly slaughtered and thereupon took the responsibility
of not executing his orders. Unwillingly persuaded by this incident that his adversary
was in an impregnable position, Meade reluctantly directed a withdrawal to the north side
of the Rapidan (*O. R.*, 29, part 1, p. 13 *ff.*, *ibid.*, p. 698; 2 *Meade*, 156–58).

[108] *O. R.*, 29, part 1, p. 926 *ff.*; *ibid.*, 29, part 2, p. 867; *ibid.*, 51, part 2, pp. 793,
794 *ff.*, 797, 798; *Taylor MSS.*, Dec. 13, 20, 1863.

[109] *Cf. Taylor MSS.*, Dec. 5, 1863.

[110] The casualties were as follows: Bristoe Station 1381 (*O. R.*, 29, part 1, p. 414);
miscellaneous cavalry actions, 154 (*ibid.*, 414, 454); Kelly's Ford and Rappahannock
Bridge, 2033 (*ibid.*, p. 616); Mine Run, 601 in the infantry (*ibid.*, 838), and twenty-eight
in the cavalry (*ibid.*, 900–901). The figure for Rappahannock Bridge is ascertained by
subtracting from Early's gross loss the number separately reported by Chief Surgeon
Guild. The losses of the cavalry in the miscellaneous actions are established by deducting
from Stuart's report (*ibid.*, 454), the totals for the cavalry shown in Guild's report (*ibid.*,
414). Meade's losses were: Bristoe Station, 2292, including prisoners captured in the cavalry (*O. R.*, 29, part 1, p. 226); Kelly's Ford and Rappahannock Bridge, 461 (*ibid.*, 560–
61); Mine Run, 1653 (*ibid.*, 686); total, 4406.

Ewell, he made no mistake at Bristoe Station and was not present at Mine Run, but he was so enfeebled by his former wounds that Lee was deeply concerned for him.[111] With his quaint language, his aquiline countenance, and his wooden leg, he was a picturesque and appealing figure as he rode gamely among the troops. Every one was puzzled to know how he contrived to stick on his horse.[112] Lee, however, had to ask himself the more serious question of how Ewell could sustain the hardships of an active campaign, and that question had added point, because, in Longstreet's absence, Ewell was ranking lieutenant general. If Lee went down, the command would devolve, temporarily at least, on him. Taylor probably voiced the secret feeling of his chief when he wrote, "I only wish the general had good lieutenants; we miss Jackson and Longstreet terribly."[113] The full weight of the army rested on Lee. He had to give to his corps commanders a measure of direction that had been unnecessary when he had operated with two corps under "Stonewall" and "Old Pete." His might now be the responsibility of fighting the battles as well as of shaping the strategy. It was a heavy burden to be borne by a man whose heart symptoms were becoming aggravated.

The final operations of 1863 marked two new stages in the methods of war employed by the Army of Northern Virginia. They increased, in the first place, the faith of the troops in the great utility of field fortification. Lee's construction of the South Carolina and of the Richmond lines had early demonstrated his belief that the commanding general should provide the maximum cover for his men when they were to be engaged for a long period in defensive operations. His use of field works did not date, as some authorities have claimed, from Mine Run,[114] but from Fredericksburg and, more particularly, from Chancellorsville. After Mine Run, as the declining strength of the army forced it more and more to the defensive, field fortification became a routine. Every soldier was a military engineer.

If the infantry were finally converted to the use of earthworks

---

111 *O. R.*, 33, 1095–96.
112 *W. W. Chamberlaine*, 83, but see Pendleton's comment, *Pendleton*, 277.
113 *Taylor MSS.*, Nov. 15, 1863. Ewell resumed command Dec. 4 (*O. R.*, 29, part 2, pp. 859–60).
114 Cf. 2 *Davis*, 449; *Cooke*, 366–67.

at Mine Run, the cavalry developed, in the second place, an important new tactical method during the last five months of the year. Prior to the Bristoe campaign, the sharpshooters of the cavalry had been organized officially, and during the second battle of Brandy, October 11, they were dismounted by regiments and were effectively employed. In that action, Lomax's whole brigade left their horses in the rear and for a time occupied a line of breastworks.[115] Again, in the "Buckland Races," Fitz Lee used some of his cavalrymen on foot.[116] During the Mine Run operations, when the cavalry had to contend with a thick forest and heavy undergrowth, through which it was impossible for mounted men to pass, these tactics of dismounted action were developed. In the fighting of November 27, and again on the 29th and on the 30th, the troopers were led against the enemy by regular infantry approaches.[117] From that time onward, as the necessities of the service demanded, the dismounted cavalrymen were frequently summoned to support the thinning line of the infantry. It was hard on the troopers but it saved horses, and it prepared the army more fully for the fearful tests that awaited in the campaign of 1864.

[115] *O. R.*, 29, part 1, p. 465.   [116] *Thomason*, 469.
[117] *O. R.*, 29, part 1, pp. 898–99, 900, 902.

CHAPTER XII

A Sacrificed Christmas

LEE came back to his headquarters at Orange Courthouse to find other reason for distress than the escape of Meade unpunished from Mine Run. The public prints were full of alarming news from Tennessee. All that had been achieved at Chickamauga had been undone. Instead of flanking the position at Chattanooga, as Lee had recommended, Bragg had waited in front of the town until he had been driven off by the incredible Federal assaults on Lookout Mountain and Missionary Ridge, November 23–25, 1863. Bragg, the papers reported, had retreated to Dalton, where he had been relieved of command.[1]

So fraught with possible disaster was this sudden turn of events that Lee put aside his habitual reserve and wrote the President on December 3 a serious letter of direct advice. Prefacing his proposals with the statement that his information was based solely on newspaper reports, he pointed out that the enemy might penetrate into Georgia "and get possession of our depots of provisions and important manufactories." As tactfully as he could, he suggested that Beauregard be put at the head of the Army of Tennessee, and that troops be drawn from Mobile, from Mississippi, and from Charleston to strengthen the threatened line of Federal advance. Then he laid down this general strategic policy: "I think that every effort should be made to concentrate as large a force as possible, under the best commander, to insure the discomfiture of Grant's army. To do this and gain the great advantage that would accrue from it, the safety of points practically less important than those endangered by his army must be hazarded. Upon the defence of the country threatened by General Grant depends the safety of the points now held by us on the Atlantic,

---

[1] Bragg had asked on Nov. 29 to be relieved. This had been done on Nov. 30. Lieutenant General W. J. Hardee, ranking corps commander, had been placed temporarily in charge of the defeated army, but had no ambition to succeed Bragg (*O. R.*, 31, part 2, pp. 682–83; *ibid.*, part 3, pp. 764–65).

and they are in as great danger from his successful advance as by the attacks to which they are at present directly subjected." [2] This was a clear forecast of the strategy the Federal Government was to employ in the Southern campaign of 1864, when Sherman's march to the sea sounded the final doom of the Confederacy. Lee plainly saw in December, 1863, the probability of what was to happen in December, 1864, and as far as he could he sought to prevent it by an immediate concentration.

The answer to this letter came in a brief telegram two days later: "Could you consistently go to Dalton, as heretofore explained?" Davis asked. Lee did not want to make the exchange of commands. He did not feel that he had the physical strength to undertake an active campaign with a demoralized army in an unfamiliar country. Something deep within him shrank from facing the bickerings and jealousies that had been inflamed in the Army of Tennessee. He doubted if he would have the co-operation of the corps and division commanders, and he did not believe that his temporary presence with them would yield any substantial result. What was needed was an able, permanent commander who knew the officers and had the vigor to suppress their rivalries. Besides, if he left the Army of Northern Virginia, a new leader would have to be assigned to it, for Ewell was too feeble to direct it. All this Lee set forth frankly on December 7, in a reply to the President. "I hope," he concluded, "your Excellency will not suppose that I am offering any obstacles to any measure you may think necessary. I only seek to give you the opportunity to form your opinion after a full consideration of the subject. I have not that confidence either in my strength or ability as would lead me of my own option to undertake the command in question." [3]

It seemed as if the President were determined to act, for on December 9 Lee received a summons to Richmond. Lee assumed that Mr. Davis would permit him to return to the Rapidan long enough to put his official business in order, but he interpreted the brief message to mean that he was to be ordered to the far South. At that prospect, the affection Lee had formed for the Army of

---

[2] *O. R.*, 29, part 2, pp. 858–59.
[3] *O. R.*, 29, part 2, p. 861. *Cf. Taylor MSS.*, Dec. 5, 1863. Colonel Taylor considered it "just possible" Lee and his staff would be sent to Dalton.

Northern Virginia asserted itself with the pang a man feels when he is forced to tear up his life by the very roots. In a hurried note to Stuart, he bade him seek positions for the cavalry where they could be foraged and would not be too far from the enemy. "My heart and thoughts will always be with this army," he said, but there he stopped. His was not a nature to sentimentalize.[4]

By way of the worn and creaking Virginia Central Railroad, Lee departed that same day, December 9. Arriving in Richmond, he left the train under the shadow of the hill where the Confederate Congress was then sitting, and went up town, through troubled streets, to quarters Mrs. Lee had rented on Leigh Street between Second and Third.[5] They were in a two-story wooden house, a humble place compared with Arlington, but the first home of their own in which the members of the family had been able to gather since the outbreak of the war. As Lee sat down for the first time in this new abode, he must have heard many stories of the wanderings of the family during the exciting months when he could only keep in touch with them by hurried letters that often were delayed and sometimes went astray.

After the sojourn in North Carolina, Mildred Lee remained at school in Raleigh during the winter of 1862–63, and Mary Lee, the eldest daughter, spent most of her time at Cedar Grove, the plantation of Doctor and Mrs. Richard Stuart, in King George County.[6] Mrs. Lee and Agnes went to Richmond that same winter and were the guests of Mr. and Mrs. James Caskie at the southeast corner of Eleventh and Clay. Here General Lee visited them, when he came to the capital, and here he formed the acquaintance of the charming Norvell Caskie, the young daughter of the house, who was one of Agnes's most intimate friends and soon became one of the General's most admired circle.[7] For

---

[4] O. R., 29, part 2, p. 866. The original is in the H. B. McClellan MSS.

[5] Captain R. E. Lee stated (op. cit., 112), that the house was on Clay Street, but in a letter among the Johnston MSS., Agnes Lee mentioned to Fanny R. Johnston, Nov. 21–27, 1863, that the house was at Third and Leigh. John K. Graeme, Asa Johnson, and Gibson Worsham have identified this house as later numbered 210 East Leigh. Mr. Graeme, who remembers seeing Mrs. Lee there, thinks the family boarded with the occupant, Mrs. Roy, but the reference cited in note 14, p. 210 indicates that the Lees were housekeeping.

[6] Mrs. Richard Stuart had been a Miss Calvert of Riversdale, Md., and was a cousin of Mrs. Lee on the Custis side (R. E. Lee, Jr., 356).

[7] D. S. Freeman: "Lee and the Ladies," Scribner's Magazine, November, 1925, p. 467.

Christmas, 1862, most of the family went from Richmond to Hickory Hill. Although Mrs. Lee's arthritis was then severe, she insisted on making the desserts and went into the basement kitchen for that purpose, but without complete success, for Grandfather Williams Wickham, accustomed to bountiful living, privately confided that she had been too sparing with the sugar.[8] From Hickory Hill the family returned to the Caskies in Richmond and remained there until some time after June 9, 1863, when the mother, Agnes, and Mildred went again to Hickory Hill.[9] They were on that fine old estate when the Federal raiders captured Rooney Lee and carried him off to Fort Monroe. The shock of this gloomy affair and the spread of her infection so crippled Mrs. Lee that she could only move about on crutches. In the belief that a visit to the mineral baths would help in restoring her health, plans were made to carry her to one of the Virginia spas. Agnes and Mildred were to accompany their mother; and as Charlotte Wickham Lee was also in bad health, through excessive grief over her wounded husband, it was decided to take her, also, and to let her choose the resort. She selected the Hot Springs in Alleghany County. About July 15, Mrs. Lee journeyed to Ashland, spent two days in the company of her old neighbor, Mrs. John P. McGuire, and then started for the resort in a box car fitted up as a bedroom.[10] The vacation was not successful. Charlotte's condition grew worse and Mrs. Lee's was not bettered. The food was so poor at the springs that the guests entered a formal protest, especially against the bread.[11] After Mrs. Lee came back to Richmond, she took the house on Leigh Street late in October. There was room for Agnes and for Mildred, but space was so limited that Charlotte had to find quarters on Fifth Street, near Cary, half a mile from her mother-in-law. The city council of Richmond took cognizance of the family's embarrassment in the crowded capital and proposed to buy a home and present it to the General, but as soon as he heard of the resolution, he wrote a grateful letter asking that the project

[8] Mrs. A. C. W. Byerly to H. T. Wickham, Jan. 29, 1931, *MS.*, copy of which Honorable H. T. Wickham has graciously placed at the writer's disposal.
[9] Mrs. Chesnut (*op. cit.*, 236), made a note that she visited Mrs. Lee at the Caskies on June 9.
[10] *Mrs. McGuire*, 232.
[11] Mrs. R. E. Lee to Mrs. Williams Wickham, *MS.*, Aug. 7, 1863, *Wickham MSS.*

be dropped and that the city devote to the families of soldiers whatever surplus funds it might have available.[12] Prompt as Lee was to decline this offer, he was nonetheless grateful for it and for the multitude of courtesies shown his family. "The kindness exhibited toward you as well as myself by our people," he wrote Mrs. Lee, "causes me to reflect how little I have done to merit it, and humbles me in my own eyes to a painful degree."[13] In the little house on Leigh Street there was satisfaction over the small comforts the family could enjoy from its own resources, and much pride, at least on Agnes's part, that when company came to dine, there were enough glasses to go around.[14]

But there were griefs enough, too. Mrs. Lee's condition was definitely worse, and though she still talked bravely of what she would do when she could walk again, she could not get about even with the aid of her crutches and had to use a rolling-chair.[15] Rooney's plight was a constant grief to the family, and not least to his father. Lee had viewed the capture of his second son as a dispensation of Providence and had sought to comfort Charlotte with the assurance that her husband would be well cared for.[16] At first, this had been done. Rooney had been placed in the hospital at Fort Monroe and had been allowed liberties on his assurance that he would not attempt to escape while there;[17] but on July 15 he had been ordered into close confinement and had been threatened with death by hanging if the Confederate authorities executed Captain W. H. Sawyer and Captain John M. Flinn. These two Federals had been selected by lot from among the officers confined in Libby prison and were under sentence in retaliation for the killing of Captain T. G. McGraw and William F. Corbin, C. S. A., who had been caught as spies within the Federal lines in Kentucky.[18] Lee never believed in retaliation,[19] but apparently

---

[12] Lee to the President of the city council, Richmond, Va., Nov. 12, 1863; text in *McCabe*, 443-44; *Jones*, 173; *Long*, 321. McCabe added, *loc. cit.*, that the "city authorities . . . secured the amount appropriated for a house, to his family in such a manner as to prevent them from being placed in danger of want." No confirmation of this statement has been found.

[13] Jones, *L. and L.*, 295.   [14] Mrs. A. C. W. Byerly, *loc. cit.*

[15] Mrs. A. C. W. Byerly, *loc. cit.*; Jones, *L. and L.*, 296.

[16] Lee to Charlotte Lee, July 26, 1863, *R. E. Lee, Jr.*, 100.

[17] II *O. R.*, 6, 69.

[18] II *O. R.*, 6, pp. 118, 1127. For Sawyer and Flinn, see II *O. R.*, 5, 691, 702; *ibid.*, 6, 87, 104, 107, 108.

[19] *Cf.* R. E. Lee to G. W. C. Lee, Aug. 7, 1863; *Duke Univ. MSS.*, and Jones, *L. and L.*, 278-79; 2 *R. W. C. D.*, 253.

he made no effort to intervene in Rooney's behalf. The Federal threat, however, had been effective in preventing the execution of Sawyer and Flinn, and that doubtless saved Rooney's life, though he had been kept a close prisoner for some weeks. As all exchanges had been suspended, Lee had no idea when he would be released,[20] but for a time was hopeful of an early exchange.[21] The restraints on Rooney were gradually relaxed until he received so much attention from friends and visitors at Fort Monroe that the authorities decided to send him to Johnson's Island, where he would not be lionized.[22] Fortunately for him, the orders were modified to permit his transfer to Fort Lafayette,[23] for which place he left Fort Monroe on November 13.[24] Lee told his family that this was a gain, inasmuch "as any place would be better than Fort Monroe, with Butler in command." He added: "His long confinement is very grievous to me, yet it may all turn out for the best." [25] While Lee was in Richmond, Rooney was definitely placed on the same status as other prisoners,[26] and the worst was over, so far as he was concerned. But Charlotte's condition became daily more serious. All her vitality seemed to be gone.

There was a third sorrow to the family, one of which few outsiders had more than vague hints. Agnes Lee had a handsome second cousin, named William Orton Williams, son of a West Point graduate, Captain William G. Williams, who had been killed in the battle of Monterey during the Mexican War. Orton, as he was known to his family, had been in the United States army as a lieutenant of the Second Cavalry on the outbreak of hostilities in 1861 and had joined the South. He had been an aide to General Leonidas Polk, and then had served as assistant chief of artillery to General Bragg. At Shiloh he had much distinguished himself.[27] He had come to Virginia at Christmas time, 1862, and had visited Agnes at Hickory Hill. His Christmas presents, a riding whip and a pair of gauntlets, had been among her treasured gifts.[28] They had ridden together, and he had made his addresses to her, but had been rejected. Orton was much too fond of drink, and his failure to win Agnes's hand, coupled with

[20] Lee to Mrs. Lee, Oct. 25, 1863; *R. E. Lee, Jr.,* 111.
[21] R. E. Lee to G. W. C. Lee, Sept. 27, 1863; *Duke Univ. MSS.*
[22] II *O. R.,* 5, 484–85, 495. [23] *Ibid.,* p. 500.
[24] *Ibid.,* 516. [25] *R. E. Lee, Jr.,* 117. [26] II *O. R.,* 5, 706.
[27] *O. R.,* 10, pp. 414, 469. [28] Mrs. A. C. W. Byerly, *loc. cit.*

other disappointments and entanglements, made him reckless. He procured assignment to a secret mission, probably in Canada or in Europe,[29] and to conceal his identity was commissioned colonel of cavalry under the name of Lawrence W. Orton.[30] On June 8, 1863, attended by his cousin, Captain Walter G. Peter, and clad in Federal uniform, he rode into the Union lines at Franklin, Tenn. With forged papers he introduced himself as Colonel Orton and his companion as Major Dunlap. They had come, he said, with special instructions to examine all posts.[31] Although they seemed little interested in the matters that spies would usually study, their actions aroused suspicion.[32] They were detained for the verification of their passes, and when these were declared spurious, they were arrested, tried by drumhead court-martial, and executed early on the morning of June 9, 1863. Before they were hanged, the men confessed their identity,[33] but maintained they were not spies—a statement in which the commandant at Franklin joined. They were, at least, "not ordinary spies," he reported, "and had some mission more important than finding out my situation. . . . Said they were going to Canada and something about Europe; not clear. We found on them memorandum of commanding officers and assistant adjutant generals in Northern states. Though they admitted the justice of the sentence and died like soldiers, they would not disclose their true object. Their conduct was very singular indeed; I can make nothing of it." [34] In the few hours allowed him before he was executed, Williams wrote a brief note to his sister, Martha, known in the family as "Markie." He said: "Do not believe that I am a spy. With my dying breath I deny the charge. Do not grieve too much for me. . . . Altho I die a horrid death I will meet my death with the fortitude becoming the son of a man whose last words to his children were, 'Tell them I died at the head of my column.' . . ." A copy of this message was sent by "Markie" to Agnes. Little was said of the affair in the family, but there was grief at this tragic end of a friend and a kinsman.[35] General Lee had always

---

29 *O. R.*, 23, part 2, p. 416.
31 *O. R.*, 23, part 2, p. 397.
33 *O. R.*, 23, part 2, pp. 415–16, 424 ff.
30 *O. R.*, 52, part 2, p. 451.
32 *O. R.*, 23, part 2, p. 416.
34 *O. R.*, 23, part 2, p. 416.
35 W. G. Beymer, who apparently was unacquainted with Williams's connection with the Lee family, published an interesting account of the case under the title, "Williams, C. S. A.," in *Harper's Magazine*, vol. 119.

been interested in Orton and, at "Markie's" request, in 1853 he had given much thought to the choice of a school for the boy.[36] He was outraged now at the execution of the young man. Although he did not write to "Markie" for fear his letter might raise suspicion against her in Georgetown, where she still resided, he kept her grief in his heart. Three years later he was to say ". . . my blood boils at the thought of the atrocious outrage, against every manly and Christian sentiment which the Great God alone is able to forgive." [37]

Custis Lee was unhappy, too. His brothers and his kinsmen had been in nearly all the great battles of the Army of Northern Virginia; he had occupied a sheltered position as one of the President's aides, a post of honor, yet not to his liking. His great desire was to see field service, but his keen conscience made him feel that he should not undertake it without experience, nor did either he or his father consider that they should ask for a transfer from the President's staff.[38] Custis lived at the time with a group of other staff officers in a large house on Franklin Street, and his constant duties gave him little opportunity of seeing his family, but his state of mind was of course familiar to them and his discontent with his position was a family distress.

Still another shadow hung over the household. Under a law passed by Congress in June, 1862 (as amended February 6, 1863), direct taxes had been levied on real estate "in the insurrectionary districts within the United States" and commissioners had been named to assess and collect these taxes. The commissioners were empowered, in case of default, to sell the property, and as the aim of the act was, in effect, to expropriate the holdings of Southern men in occupied territory, the officials held to the rule that they would only accept payment from the owners in person. On behalf of the Lees, their cousin, Philip R. Fendall, tendered the taxes imposed on Arlington, $92.07 with a penalty of 50 per cent. The commissioners refused to receive the money and were preparing to issue a tax title to the United States. The old home, the

---

[36] *Markie Letters*, 35.

[37] Lee to Martha Williams, Dec. 1, 1866; *Markie Letters*, 71–72.

[38] *Jones*, 183. The rest of the incident that Jones described, as is explained in note 48, p. 226, is apocryphal, but there is no doubt that General Lee and Custis chafed because the younger man was on staff duty, removed from the post of danger.

centre of the life of the family, was about to be lost—for delinquent taxes in theory, by confiscation in fact.[39]

Thus, when Lee came home that evening of December 9 he realized how heavily the war had smitten his family—their home had been lost, Mrs. Lee was almost helpless in her invalidism, one son was in prison, the General's brilliant first-born was unhappy because of his assignment, one daughter was dead in a far-off cemetery, another had been touched by tragedy, and his only daughter-in-law was not far from death. Lee himself, who had entered the struggle in the full vigor of robust manhood, was aging hourly, his hair and beard white, and that sharp, paroxysmal pain intermittently wrenching his left side.

But there was little time to dwell on family woes, even had Lee been of a nature to yield to them. The question that had brought him to Richmond, the question of whether he should undertake a new campaign on strange terrain, had to be discussed in long conferences with the President, and a multitude of details concerning the army had to be handled with railroad officials and with the chiefs of the bureaus of the War Department.[40] Lee remained willing to assume the difficult task in Georgia, if the President thought it proper to send him there. In talking with Senator B. H. Hill, he said simply: "I have no ambition but to serve the Confederacy and do all I can to win our independence. I am willing to serve in any capacity to which the authorities may assign me." [41] But he held to his belief that others could accomplish more with the Army of Tennessee than he could hope to do, and when he found the President indisposed to name Beauregard to succeed Bragg, as he had originally advised, it seems probable that he urged the appointment of General Johnston to the command.[42] There was some delay in a decision, while Mr.

[39] The tax title was passed, Jan. 11, 1864, on a government bid of $26,800, which the treasury simply transferred on its own books. For these and facts on the later history of Arlington, the writer is indebted to Enoch A. Chase of Washington, who has made a comprehensive study of the estate.

[40] Cf. O. R., 33, 1073–74, for a mention of a conference with H. D. Whitcomb, superintendent of the Virginia Central Railroad, who assured Lee that his line would soon be put in order.

[41] Jones, 241.

[42] Neither Davis nor Johnston mentioned Lee's influence in this appointment, but Mrs. James Chesnut, who was usually well informed, noted in her diary on Dec. 21, 1863: "Joe Johnston has been made commander-in-chief of the Army of the West. General Lee has done this, 'tis said."

Davis waited for information from the Southwest,[43] but by about the 15th it was settled that Lee would not be ordered to Dalton.[44] On December 16, Johnston was assigned to the post,[45] with instructions to reorganize the army and to prepare for an offensive as soon as practicable.[46] Lee is not known to have said anything publicly of this appointment, but it undoubtedly was not only a relief to him, but a satisfaction also, for his faith in the ability of Joseph E. Johnston had not been impaired by that officer's failure to relieve Vicksburg. Lee could go back to his beloved army, and Johnston, he trusted, could keep the Federals from invading Georgia.

In the midst of the conferences that led to this conclusion, Lee received as much of attention and of honor in Richmond as his nature would permit. The Confederate House of Representatives passed a resolution inviting him to have a seat on the floor,[47] and when he went to worship at Saint Paul's Church on December 13, a silent ovation must have been given him after the service as he walked slowly down the aisle, bowing to friends and acquaintances, right and left.[48] The President took advantage of his presence to get his judgment on the work recently done on the city's fortifications. With General Elzey and some members of Mr. Davis's staff, they made a tour of inspection on December 15.[49]

General Averell was on another of his raids at the time. Knowing their chief's dislike of unconfirmed rumors,[50] the officers at Lee's headquarters were loath to forward him all the stories that came in concerning the move. Lee learned enough to make him anxious to return to the army and do what he could in trapping the troublesome Union cavalryman, but the Federal contrived to get quickly away after burning the station and the supplies at

---

43 Lee to Walter Taylor, Dec. 12, 1863, *Taylor MSS.*
44 *Taylor MSS.*, Dec. 20, 1863. Taylor did not give a definite date for the decision.
45 *O. R.*, 31, part 3, pp. 835–36.
46 *O. R.*, 31, part 3, pp. 842–43, 856–57; 2 *Davis*, 547–48.
47 Thomas S. Bocock to R. E. Lee, Dec. 16, 1863; *Duke University MSS.* The formal thanks of both branches of Congress were later extended him, under a resolution signed by the President Jan. 8, 1864 (*Journal of the Confederate Senate*, 3, 521; *Journal of the House*, 6, 585, 586, 598; *O. R.*, 27, part 2, p. 326; *ibid.*, 29, part 2, p. 911; *Richmond Enquirer*, Jan. 8, 1864). It will be recalled that a similar resolution had been initiated in the House, Aug. 21, 1863 (*Richmond Examiner*, Aug. 22, 1863), but had not been passed by the Senate before adjournment. See *supra*, vol. II, p. 343.
48 *Mrs. Chesnut*, 264.   49 Bocock to Lee, *loc. cit.*; *Mrs. Chesnut*, 265.
50 *Taylor MSS.*, Dec. 13, 1863; *cf.* Taylor to Ewell, *O. R.*, 51, part 2, pp. 796–97.

Salem, Va.[51] There was, consequently, no special reason why
Lee should hurry back to the Rapidan, and there were numerous personal reasons why he should spend Christmas with his
family—the first time it had been possible since 1859. Robert
had come to Richmond;[52] Charlotte was very ill; the enemy was
quiet on the Rapidan. Why should he not remain?

At Lee's camp, his aides were asking the same question and
were not envious of his good fortune. But they knew the man
and were uncertain whether he would stay at the capital. "It will
be more in accordance with his peculiar character," Major Walter
Taylor confided to his sweetheart, "if he leaves for the army just
before the great anniversary; he is so very apt to suppress or
deny his personal desire when it conflicts with the performance of
his duty."[53] Taylor's judgment was not in error, for the next day,
December 21, Lee appeared in camp.[54] He had deliberately sacrificed his Christmas to set an example of obedience to duty.

It was a gloomy Christmas he had in his tent. Oppressed by
Mrs. Lee's condition and by Charlotte's illness, he was acutely
conscious, also, of the distress of the country people round about
him. When some of the foreign observers came to visit him during
the day, he could not forbear reference to the plight of the poor
families living in the devastated area, and the one touch of feeling that he ever exhibited toward the enemy—his oft-recurring
resentment at the atrocities inflicted on non-combatants—showed
itself as he recounted how the enemy seemed determined to burn
and to harass even when the country was so barren that the Southern army could not hope to draw supplies from it.

Captain Ross, one of the *attachés,* remarked that Arlington had
been treated in the same way.

But Lee interrupted him quickly. "That I can easily understand," he said, "and for that I don't care; but I do feel sorry for
the poor creatures I see here, starved and driven from their homes
for no reason whatsoever."[55]

The news from Charlotte had been somewhat more encouraging, and on the 26th Lee was hopeful that she might recover, but

[51] *O. R.,* 29, part 1, pp. 924–25.
[52] *Mrs. Chesnut,* 265. [53] *Taylor MSS.,* Dec. 20, 1863.
[54] For the date of his return, see Lee to Mrs. Lee, Dec. 22, 1863, *Duke Univ. MSS.*
[55] *Ross,* 207.

216

that evening he received from Custis a telegram announcing her death.[56] Lee's affection for Charlotte was as deep as that for his own children, yet he received the sad intelligence of her death with the spirit of resignation he always displayed. "It has pleased God," he said, "to take from us one exceedingly dear to us, and we must be resigned to His holy will. She, I trust, will enjoy peace and happiness forever, while we must patiently struggle on under all the ills that may be in store for us. What a glorious thought it is that she has joined her little cherubs and our angel Annie in heaven. Thus is link by link the strong chain broken that binds us to earth, and our passage soothed to another world. Oh, that we may be at last united in that heaven of rest, where trouble and sorrow never enter, to join in an everlasting chorus of praise to our Lord and Savior! I grieve for our lost darling as a father only can grieve for a daughter, and my sorrow is heightened by the thought of the anguish her death will cause our dear son and the poignancy it will give to the bars of his prison. May God in His mercy enable him to bear the blow He has so suddenly dealt, and sanctify it to his everlasting happiness!" [57]

With that prayer, he approached the end of 1863 . . . while the bones of the dead bleached on Cemetery Ridge and slow starvation crept along the coast.

[56] *R. E. Lee, Jr.*, 117–18. Captain Lee stated that when the news reached Rooney Lee "at Fortress Monroe" that Charlotte was dying, he asked for a parole of forty-eight hours to visit her, with the assurance that Custis, his equal in rank, would stand hostage for him. "This request," said Captain Lee, "was curtly and peremptorily refused." If Captain Lee was correct in this statement, the correspondence must have been carried on with Fort Lafayette through Fort Monroe, for Rooney Lee had been transferred to the former place on Nov. 13, 1863. See *supra*, p. 208.

[57] Lee to Mrs. Lee, Dec. 27, 1863, *R. E. Lee, Jr.*, 117–18.

CHAPTER XIII

LEE AS A DIPLOMATIST

(THE WINTER OF 1863–64)

THE first three months of 1864 were spent in a routine similar in many particulars to that which Lee had taken up after Burnside's "Mud March" in the winter of 1862–63. From his head-quarters in a wood on the southern slope of Clark's Mountain,[1] Lee rode daily with Major Venable or Major Marshall or both[2] to study some part of his long line of twenty miles.[3] As far as practicable, he kept the infantry in sheltered camps and entrusted the picketing to the cavalry. This was not easy. When forage was at its lowest some of the mounted regiments had to ride forty miles to their posts, but there seemed no other way of protecting the front. Large units of infantry could not be posted at each ford because it would weaken the army too greatly. Small forces, Lee reasoned, could easily be cut off.[4]

On February 6 the Federals crossed in strength at Morton's Ford, remained all day and returned that night to the north bank[5] —a mere demonstration, Lee thought, "only intended to see where we were and whether they could injure us."[6] On February 22, Lee went to Richmond to confer with the President on the military outlook,[7] and while there, breakfasting at the White House, was given a lecture on strategy by an Alabama senator. He "smiled blandly the while," Mrs. Chesnut noted in her diary, "though he did permit himself a mild sneer at the wise civilians in Congress who refrained from trying the battlefield in person, but from afar dictated the movements of armies."[8] Lee spent

---

[1] Cooke, 371. It was one of Lee's idiosyncrasies, Taylor wrote to his sweetheart, "to suffer any amount of discomfort and inconvenience sooner than to change a camp once established" (Taylor MSS., Oct. 25, 1863).

[2] Taylor's General Lee, 221.

[3] Hotchkiss in 3 C. M. H., 428–29.   [4] O. R., 33, 1089.

[5] O. R., 33, 141, 1148, 1169–70; Taylor MSS., Feb. 6–8, 1864, Lee's Dispatches, 136.

[6] Lee to Mrs. Lee, Feb. 14, 1864; Fitz Lee, 323.

[7] Taylor MSS., Feb. 21, 1864.   [8] Mrs. Chesnut, 292.

much time with the President and with General Bragg, who had come to Richmond to act as Mr. Davis' adviser. The visit was interrupted on February 29 by the news that General Kilpatrick and Colonel Ulric Dahlgren had launched a long-expected raid on Richmond.[9] Lee passed up the railroad only a few hours before Dahlgren struck it, and once again he narrowly escaped capture.[10] He immediately organized an expedition into Madison County to meet a diversion incident to the main raid, but this served no other purpose than to expose the men, unsheltered, to freezing weather and to a snowstorm.[11] Dahlgren and Kilpatrick were repulsed at the Richmond defenses, and Dahlgren himself was later killed in King and Queen County. On his body was found an address to his soldiers, directing that the prisoners in Richmond be released, that the city be burned, and that President Davis and his Cabinet be killed. This paper created an immense stir and, later in the spring, prompted General Lee to make formal inquiry of General Meade as to the authenticity of the document.[12]

These were the only operations of importance in northern and central Virginia until Grant opened the Wilderness campaign in May, 1864. Numerous warnings from the lower Peninsula of an expedition against Richmond caused Lee to urge the further

[9] *Taylor MSS.*, March 4, 1864; *O. R.*, 29, part 2, p. 832.

[10] *Taylor MSS.*, March 4, 1864. He found that General Ewell had been miles away when the raid began, that Chilton was out of touch with the situation, and that the order to meet the enemy's advance had been judiciously issued by the faithful Taylor. For the reports of Dahlgren's raid, see *O. R.*, 33, 169 *ff.*; for Lee's correspondence regarding it, *ibid.*, 33, 1200, 1205, and *O. R.*, 51, part 2, p. 823; for the advance on Frederickshall, *Long*, 318–19; for the operations of the Confederate cavalry, *H. B. McClellan*, 399, *G. W. Beale*, 128 *ff.*; for the feeling in Richmond, *Mrs. McGuire*, 255, *Miss Brock*, 283; 2 *R. W. C. D.*, 164; for an interesting account of the enemy's movements in Hanover County, C. S. Anderson in *Locomotive Engineering*, January, 1898, p. 6 *ff.*; for a brief general account, 2 *Davis*, 306–7; and for an excellent, more extended narrative, G. Watson James in 39 *S. H. S. P.*, 71.

[11] *Taylor MSS.*, March 4, 1864; *O. R.*, 33, 1205. The Federal force participating in this demonstration was the VI Corps, which went to Madison Courthouse, and Custer's cavalry, which penetrated almost to Charlottesville but did not succeed in destroying the railroad bridge over the Rivanna (*O. R.*, 33, 169).

[12] *Taylor's Four Years*, 123. E. A. Pollard in his *Third Year of the War*, 243–44 n. gave convincing evidence that the address was found on Dahlgren, though probably a rough draft. Meade forwarded Lee a statement from General Kilpatrick repudiating the incendiary paragraphs, but Meade privately admitted to his wife, "I regret to say Kilpatrick's reputation, and collateral evidence in my possession, rather go against this theory." Meade stoutly went on: "However, I was determined my skirts should be clear, so I promptly disavowed having ever authorized, sanctioned or approved of any act not required by military necessity, and in accordance with the usages of war" (2 *Meade*, 190–91).

strengthening of the defenses of that city and of Petersburg.[1f]
He speculated, also, whether this new, anticipated advance on the
capital would precede or follow the opening of the campaign in
northern Virginia.[14] An abortive advance in North Carolina was
made on New Berne, February 1–2, at the instance of General
R. F. Hoke and with the approval of Lee.[15] After this failure,
Lee was anxious to recall Hoke,[16] but that officer justified delay
by the brilliant capture of Plymouth on April 20, with approximately 2500 prisoners,[17] for which exploit he was promoted major
general.[18]

Insignificant as were these affairs compared with the great battles of the preceding years, there was abundant work for General
Lee at headquarters—work as difficult as that of open campaigning, work that called for qualities the lack of which has made
many an able field commander a mere name in dusty reports.
Lee the strategist had to be Lee the diplomatist. Many of the
best officers were dead, notably Jackson and Pender. Others had
been incapacitated or had sustained crippling wounds. Some had
heart-burnings and a sense of failure. Lack of promotion rankled
the spirits of not a few. In the artillery, Gettysburg had shown
that certain of the older men were incompetent and by their
seniority were blocking the promotion of younger, more scien-
tific gunners. There were in some cases distinct problems of difficult personality or dangerous dislikes. All these were aggravated
by a long, cold winter of idleness. It was Lee's task to remove
the incompetent, to promote the deserving, to humble the arro-
gant, to soothe the sensibilities of the disappointed, and to prepare the command once more for the cruel exactions of what
might be the decisive campaign. The means he employed to these
ends are worthy of examination in some detail.

The assignment of new officers to brigade and divisional command had been under way since the close of the Gettysburg cam-

---

18 O. R., 29, part 2, pp. 719, 750, 778–79, 849; ibid., 33, 1081, 1126–27, 1131, 1273:
ibid., 51, part 2, pp. 810–11, 816, 861, 875–76, 879; Lee's Dispatches, 158–59; 2 R. W.
C. D., 145; Jessie A. Marshall: Private and Official Correspondence of B. F. Butler, 3, 373,
14 Lee's Dispatches, 140 ff.
15 O. R., 33, pp. 47 ff., 1062, 1099, 1102, 1104; O. R., 51, part 2, p. 817; R. E. Lee
to Jefferson Davis, MS., Jan. 2, 1864, Duke Univ. MSS.
16 O. R., 33, 1278.
17 O. R., 33, 296 ff.; O. R., 51, part 2, p. 870.   18 O. R., 51, part 2, p. 874.

paign. The most important position to fill had been that of a successor to General Pender. On August 1, Lee had recommended Brigadier General Cadmus M. Wilcox, whom he described as "one of the oldest brigadiers in the service, a highly capable officer" who deserved promotion.[19] To succeed Pettigrew, he had chosen W. W. Kirkland, who had been colonel of the Twenty-first North Carolina, in Hoke's brigade;[20] and in the place of the fallen Semmes he had selected Goode Bryan, colonel of the Sixteenth Georgia, Wofford's brigade.[21] Perrin had been given Mc-Gowan's old brigade, temporarily;[22] John Pegram had been assigned to that formerly led by William Smith.[23] In the absence of Rooney Lee, the able John R. Chambliss was named to head his command,[24] and in March, 1864, Brigadier General N. H. Harris was designated to handle the brigade of Carnot Posey, who had died on November 13, 1863, of wounds received at Bristoe Station.[25] All these promotions were made without arousing many open jealousies. The only exception of consequence was Colonel Edward A. O'Neal of the Twenty-sixth Alabama. After Rodes's promotion to Major General, a new commander for his brigade had been necessary, and Lee had recommended O'Neal, then the senior colonel.[26] For some reason, O'Neal's commission had been delayed, but he had been in charge of the brigade at Gettysburg, where, on the first day, he had not distinguished himself.[27] Lee did not censure O'Neal or bring him before a court of inquiry, but quietly recommended three other Alabama colonels in preference to him. Colonel Cullen A. Battle was chosen. This much incensed O'Neal, who subsequently applied for the transfer of his regiment to the army under General Polk.[28] That, however, was not the end of the matter. In the spring of 1864, Senator James Phelan of Alabama—the same gentleman who had lectured Lee on strategy at the White House—protested to Mr. Davis that injustice had been done Colonel O'Neal, and Davis forwarded the papers to Lee. Lee prepared a detailed answer, in which he stated that if the military situation permitted, he would like a court of inquiry in the case. Then he went on:

[19] *Lee's Dispatches*, 115–16.
[20] *O. R.*, 29, part 2, p. 701.
[21] *O. R.*, 29, part 2, p. 702.
[22] *O. R.*, 29, part 2, p. 739.
[23] *O. R.*, 29, part 2, p. 783.
[24] *O. R.*, 51, part 2, p. 817.
[25] *O. R.*, 33, 1027.
[26] *Lee's Dispatches*, 49.
[27] See *supra*, p. 77.
[28] *O. R.*, 33, 1133–34.

"I concur with the Honble. Mr. Phelan that Col. O'Neal is a most true, brave and gallant officer. Still I believed that Cols. Gordon, Morgan and Battle gave promise of making better brigade commanders, and therefore recommended them before him. The regiment of Colonel O'Neal . . . has been transferred. . . . I am unable to compare his qualifications with those of the officers of the Alabama regiments mentioned by Mr. Phelan, and . . . cannot say whether he is the best commander that can be selected for a brigade composed of those regiments. If he is, I should be gratified at his promotion." [29] Later on, when O'Neal's troops returned to Virginia and a brigadier's commission for him reached headquarters, Lee sent it back with endorsement of another officer and the simple comment, "Since my first letter to His Excellency I have seen Colonel O'Neal and have made more particular inquiries into his capacity to command the brigade and I cannot recommend him to the command." [30]

In making these and all other promotions, Lee was mindful not only of valor and leadership displayed on the field, but of discipline maintained in camp and on the march. He came one day upon a cavalry brigade halted in a lane adjoining a field of ripe watermelons. All the troopers except those of one regiment were dismounted and were devouring the melons. Lee sent for the colonel of the regiment that had not been allowed to enter the field. Why, he asked blandly, were not those men helping themselves to the melons that were so abundant? "My men, General," the colonel answered, "are not allowed to disobey your orders concerning pillaging." Lee said no more and rode on. As it happened, several of the colonels of that brigade had been recommended for promotion. When the time came to make the award, Lee gave it to the colonel who had obeyed orders. [31] Equal stress he always placed upon the temperance of those who were considered for high command. "I cannot," he said, "place in control of others one who cannot control himself." [32]

The promotions in the artillery caused much concern and called for the full measure of Lee's diplomacy. He seems to have been

---

[29] Lee to Davis, April 6, 1863; *Lee's Dispatches*, 146–48.
[30] Lee to Davis, June 11, 1864; *Lee's Dispatches*, 225.
[31] General T. L. Rosser: "General Robert E. Lee" in *Frank Leslie's Popular Magazine* (cited hereafter as *Rosser*), vol. 43, p. 13.
[32] *Jones*, 170.

guided largely by the judgment of General Pendleton, who prepared a full and lengthy memorandum on the qualifications of the various corps chiefs and battalion commanders.[33] In carrying out Pendleton's recommendations, Lee took good care that older officers like Colonel J. B. Walton of the First Corps should not have their sensibilities offended by transfers,[34] and he was willing to forego the personal convenience of retaining as capable an assistant as Colonel A. L. Long on his staff in order that Long might have higher rank and the Second Corps the advantage of his services as its chief of artillery.[35]

Lee was much embarrassed in many cases by the policy of the administration which yielded to the demand that brigade officers should come from the same states as their troops. Governor Vance of North Carolina, who visited the army in March, 1864, and made a number of speeches that Lee enjoyed greatly,[36] was particularly insistent that his state be "recognized." To satisfy him, Lee put the North Carolina cavalry under General L. S. Baker, removed a Virginia brigadier from the command of a mixed brigade of North Carolinians and Virginians, named a Maryland officer of the old army, George H. Steuart, in his place, and transferred General Iverson from a North Carolina to a Louisiana brigade. When Robert Ransom and Pender had been made major generals, North Carolinians succeeded to their brigades, and when Pettigrew died, Kirkland, of the same state, as already noted, was given his troops.[37] To maintain capable leadership while respecting state pride was an unending problem with Lee.

Holding to good men with the same care he exhibited in promoting the capable,[38] Lee dealt considerately with those who were incapacitated or of weak physique. He felt that an invalid corps should be organized for such officers, both that they might be employed and also that their absence might not be injurious to their command or prevent the promotion of capable subordinates.[39]

[33] O. R., 29, part 2, p. 839; Pendleton, 309.
[34] O. R., 32, part 2, p. 566; ibid., part 3, p. 595.
[35] Long, 303; Long MSS.   [36] James A. Graham Papers, 184.
[37] O. R., 29, part 2, pp. 723–24. Cf. Lee's Dispatches, 119–22, 127–29.
[38] See Lee's unwillingness to part with General Wofford, O. R., 29, part 2, p. 711, and with General Edward Johnson, Lee's Dispatches, 164.
[39] Lee to Davis, Nov. 29, 1863, O. R., 29, part 2, p. 854.

The case of General Ewell did not fall precisely in this category, but there was much doubt in Lee's mind whether that stout-hearted soldier could endure the hardships of open campaigning. In January, 1864, when some question was raised as to the physical ability of General Ewell to keep the field, he asked Lee's opinion regarding an application for an easier post. The answer Lee wrote was characteristic: "I cannot take upon myself to decide in this matter," he said. "You are the proper person, on consultation with your medical advisers. I do not know how much ought to be attributed to long absence from the field, general debility, or the result of your injury, but I was in constant fear during the last campaign that you would sink under your duties or destroy yourself. In either event injury might have resulted. I last spring asked for your appointment provided you were able to take the field. You now know from experience what you have to undergo, and can best judge of your ability to endure it. I fear we cannot anticipate less labor than formerly. Wishing you every happiness, and that you may be able to serve the country to the last . . ." [40] Ewell decided to stick it out, and Lee did his utmost not to overtax his powers of endurance. In February, 1864, when Lee went to Richmond for consultation with the President, he had to leave General Ewell in command, as senior lieutenant general, but he tried to arrange the duties so as to impose the least discomfort on him. At Lee's instance, Major Venable wrote Ewell, "He [General Lee] directs me to say that General Chilton will remain here in the office, and is instructed to consult with you on all matters of importance connected with the army. Should it become necessary, General Lee desires you either to move up to Orange Courthouse or to remove the office to your quarters, as you may think best." [41]

With the indifferent, Lee tried exhortation or satire, and the inexperienced he ceaselessly sought to train in their duties. [42] When he had to remove an incompetent man, he did so as tactfully and as quietly as possible. Not once during the whole war did he initiate court-martial proceedings against an officer, and

[40] *O. R.,* 29, part 2, pp. 1095–96.
[41] *O. R.,* 29, part 2, pp. 1192–93. For another interesting example of Lee's considerate dealing with officers who had become partially disabled for field duty, see 7 *S. H S. P.,* 162.
[42] For an excellent statement of his rule on this point, see *infra,* p. 331.

only in the rarest instances did he call for courts of inquiry. One such case occurred after the New Berne operations of January–February, 1864. On complaint that General Seth M. Barton had failed to do his expected part, Lee forwarded the information to President Davis, with the statement that he hoped the explanation of General Barton would be satisfactory.[43] When the reports failed to clear Barton, Lee promptly asked that a court be convened.[44]

The troublesome case of Brigadier General William E. Jones illustrated how Lee always endeavored to minimize in the Army of Northern Virginia, by diplomacy and effort, the personal differences that arose almost as frequently as in the Army of Tennessee but created far less scandal. He always saw to it the army's soiled linen was washed in camp, not in public. Jones was a professional soldier of undoubted competence and had succeeded Stuart in command of the First Virginia Cavalry. Subsequently he became head of the "Laurel Brigade," which contained many of Ashby's famous troopers. He was accounted the best outpost officer in the army, but he had an unfortunate habit of parading his grievances and won the unhappy name of "Grumbler" Jones. Between him and Stuart, two antagonistic natures, there developed differences that were hopelessly irreconcilable. Jones offered his resignation before the Gettysburg campaign, but Lee withheld it. Subsequently, Stuart brought Jones to a court-martial. Lee sought to transfer him to an infantry brigade to save his services to the army, but when the court-martial findings were confirmed, Lee solved the difficulty and saved Jones's feelings by sending him to southwest Virginia.[45] Colonel Thomas L. Rosser was promoted brigadier general as his successor.[46]

Another Jones caused Lee some vexing hours—Major General Samuel Jones, commanding in southwest Virginia. Jones was a high-minded, generous gentleman in every sense, and he had admittedly a difficult line to defend, but he had so little success in dealing with the repeated raids of Federal cavalry that the people in that section of Virginia became dissatisfied with him. Lee defended him for many months, but concluded at length

---

[43] *Lee's Dispatches*, 136.   [44] *O. R.*, 33, 1186–87.
[45] *O. R.*, 29, part 2, pp. 771–79. Jones was later killed in action (3 *C. M. H.*, 618).
[46] *O. R.*, 29, part 2, p. 788.

that a man who could not make better use of his forces should be transferred somewhere else. When his judgment became fixed, be proceeded directly and without equivocation. Jones was sent to Charleston, S. C., and Major General John C. Breckinridge, former Vice-President of the United States, was named in his stead.[47] Before appointing Breckinridge, Davis was urged by some of his friends to name Custis Lee to the place. The President was fully satisfied of Custis's qualifications and offered him the post, but Custis was not anxious to have it, and his father was disinclined to put an inexperienced staff officer in command of so important a district.[48] Lee was proud of the achievements of his sons and nephews,[49] but sedulously avoided anything that smacked of nepotism. He refused to take Robert on his staff,[50] and when he read that several officers of his name and blood were sponsoring a ball at Charlottesville, he wrote, "There are too many Lees on the committee. I like all to be present at battles, but can excuse them at balls." [51]

Lee's troubles with the Joneses were small compared with those that came to light when the First Corps prepared to rejoin the Army of Northern Virginia in the spring of 1864. Longstreet's high hopes of great achievements in Tennessee had been shattered. Although he retained his full measure of self-assurance in dealing with Lee, he did not distinguish himself after Chickamauga. His disappointment led him to consider retiring, both as commander of the forces in east Tennessee and as head of the First Corps. The War Department had asked Lee if he would consider changing Ewell for Longstreet, but Lee opposed Longstreet's resignation and declined to make an exchange of corps in the belief that both were more effective as they were then organized.[52] Having no one to succeed Longstreet who possessed that officer's

---

[47] O. R., 29, part 2, pp. 767; O. R., 33, 1086, 1106, 1124, 1172–73, 1196, 1211, 1255; O. R., 51, part 2, pp. 813–14, 816.

[48] In General Lee's only published reference to the matter he speaks of the tender to Custis of the "Valley command" (Jones, L. and L., 303). The facts are set forth by President Davis in 11 S. H. S. P., 563. General Echols' version is in ibid., 453. The circumstances, which were not generally known, gave rise to the myth that when Davis was considering the dispatch of Lee to Dalton, he proposed to name Custis his successor with the Army of Northern Virginia (cf. Jones, 183).

[49] Cf. supra, vol. II, p. 305–6; Lee to Mrs. Lee, after a visit from some of his nephews in the autumn of 1863: "As soon as I was alone I committed them in a fervent prayer to the care and guidance of our Heavenly Father" (White, 335).

[50] R. E. Lee, Jr., 119–20.   [51] R. E. Lee, Jr., 121.

[52] O. R., 33, 1074–75.

ability in the field, he was willing to endure his peculiarities for the good of the cause.[53] The contagion of strife in the Army of Tennessee and Longstreet's own bitterness demoralized his command. When he returned to Virginia, to await the opening of the spring campaign of 1864, he had three of his generals, Mc-Laws, J. B. Robertson, and E. M. Law, under arrest or under charges. The cases of Robertson and McLaws did not come under Lee's jurisdiction, as their alleged offenses occurred in another department. Robertson was suspended for misconduct, according to Longstreet's version,[54] and McLaws, found guilty on one minor charge, was ordered off duty for sixty days, but the findings of the court-martial were disapproved by the President, and the officer was restored to field service.[55] He did not return, however, to the Army of Northern Virginia, and when he was subsequently ordered to do so, Lee requested that he be sent elsewhere.[56] That was one of Lee's methods of dealing with men who had failed. So long as they remained with the army, he made the best of them. If they were relieved of command for any reason, and better men took their places, he usually saw to it that they were not again given assignments beyond their capacity. As for General Law, the first charges against him were not entertained by President Davis,[57] but when Law appeared again for duty, Longstreet ordered his rearrest and made representations of such misbehavior by Law in destroying an official record that General Lee acquiesced in Longstreet's recommendation of a court-martial.[58] Mr. Davis, however, reprimanded Longstreet for ordering the second arrest, whereupon Longstreet became incensed and threatened once more to resign unless the charges against Law were examined. The President did not yield and, so far as the evidence shows, Lee did nothing further. Law served with the army during part of the spring operations of 1864 until he was wounded at Cold Harbor. Subsequently he was transferred to South Carolina.[59] Longstreet fell into complete disfavor with the administration

---

[53] Longstreet's grievance was aggravated by the fact that E. Kirby Smith was promoted over him, Feb. 19, 1864, to the full rank of general (*Longstreet*, 524–25).

[54] *Longstreet*, 548. The *Official Records* do not show the disposition of his case. For Longstreet's return to Virginia, see *infra*, p. 266.

[55] *O. R.*, 31, part 1, p. 506. [56] *Lee's Dispatches*, 182, *cf.* 80–83.

[57] *O. R.*, 33, 1291. [58] *O. R.*, 31, part 1, p. 473.

[59] *O. R.*, 31, part 1, pp. 468, 470, 473, 473–74; *Longstreet*, 517 *ff.*, 548–49; *Lee's Dispatches*, 304; 7 *C. M. H.*, 422 *ff.*; 14 *S. H. S. P.*, 548.

as a result of these affairs, and received one of the sharpest censures delivered during the war for making some inquiry as to why General Charles Field had been promoted. He was told that his remarks were highly insubordinate and that his inquiry was a direct reflection upon the executive. That was the end of Longstreet's brief rôle as a confidential adviser of the Secretary of War, except in one instance.[60]

Along with these troublesome questions of promotion and discipline, Lee had to discharge during the winter of 1863–64 the continuous duty of soothing the sensibilities of officers whose minds the weariness of war was disturbing. Nor did this task end with the inactive season. Rather did it increase as the twilight of the Confederacy approached. Even at headquarters he had to mollify some aggrieved officers. Lee never had an adequate personal staff. As an engineer he had not been accustomed to having many assistants, and as the responsible head of an army of declining strength he was unwilling to set a bad example by taking a large number of officers from the combat units. Chilton, Long, Venable, Marshall, and Taylor, five clerks,[61] an indefatigable quartermaster in the person of Major Harman,[62] Bernard Lynch, the mess steward,[63] and Perry, who had remained as Lee's body-servant for a short time after he was emancipated under the Custis will[64]—these were his whole personal entourage from highest to humblest. After Long was promoted chief of artillery of the Second Corps, Lee did not fill his place. His personal staff work fell on four men, and an undue part of it on Major Taylor, the great ambition of whose life was to satisfy the General.[65] There were moments of unhappiness in the dealings of the older man with the rapid, efficient young assistant adjutant general, but Lee would usually relieve these by a kindly inquiry or by a friendly chat in a headquarters tent.[66] "The Tycoon," as his staff officers sometimes irreverently styled Lee,[67] generally used only Major Marshall and Major Venable in the field except during action, and then he pressed into service all of his aides and

---

[60] O. R., 32, part 3, p. 738. See *infra*, p. 260.
[61] *Taylor MSS.*, April 18, 1864. [62] *Taylor MSS.*, March 8, 1864.
[63] Known as "Bryan" to all at headquarters, *Taylor's Four Years*, 221.
[64] Jones, *L. and L.*, 286; *Fitz Lee*, 237. [65] *Taylor MSS.*, Aug. 8, 1863.
[66] *Taylor MSS.*, Jan. 28, Feb. 21, March 20, 1864.
[67] *Taylor MSS.*, Nov. 14, 1863.

the officers of the general staff attached to his headquarters. Major Taylor was left in charge of the "paper-work," though whenever opportunity offered, he continued to indulge himself in daring feats on the field of battle. Colonel Chilton remained titular chief of staff, but either because he was not suited for the post, or else because Lee was his own principal staff officer, Chilton gradually turned over the duties of that office to Taylor and acted as inspector general. The arrangement was not wholly satisfactory and least of all to Chilton, who was thoroughly devoted to the Southern cause. In March, 1864, following some failure on the part of the Senate to commission him at an acceptable date as brigadier general, he asked to be relieved that he might accept appointment with the adjutant general.[68] When Chilton decided to leave, Lee wrote him a friendly, tactful letter, regretting his departure and praising his service, but saying frankly that he believed he would be of more general service with General Cooper than with him. "I shall always feel great interest in your welfare and success," he wrote, "and trust that in your future sphere of action, your zeal, energy, and intelligence will be as conspicuous as in your former." [69] Lee occasionally used other staff officers for short periods of emergency, but he chose no successor to Chilton and during the winter of 1863–64 merely divided the ever-increasing duties among the three who were constantly with him.

He was exacting of his staff officers and in the feeling that they must join with him in subordinating self to duty, he gave them few furloughs and no promotion that was not awarded by act of Congress. They had the greatest respect for him, but did not share the general awe of the army for his presence. They knew that he was a hard taskmaster and that his temper was strong, though usually controlled, and they avoided him when his wrath was aroused or when he was sick and rendered irritable by inability to move about. At such times they dealt with him chiefly through Major Venable, whose age, dignity, and station placed him more nearly on even terms with the General.[70] Except for

68 *Taylor MSS* , Feb. 21, March 4, March 20, March 23, 1864.
69 R. E. Lee to R. H. Chilton, March 24, 1864; *Chilton Papers.*
70 *H. B. McClellan MSS.* Major McClellan served on Lee's staff for some time after the death of General Stuart. See vol. I, p. 642.

occasional misunderstandings, Lee's tact and fairness and the loyalty of his aides combined to assure harmony. No general ever had more devoted service than he received from his personal assistants, but surely no officer of like rank ever fought a campaign comparable to that of 1864 with only three men on his staff, and not one of the three a professional soldier.

Precise justice, like that of Washington, and consideration for their rights and sensibilities as individuals were Lee's first rules in dealing with his officers. He always gave them the benefit of the doubt. He never praised them except when he was sure they deserved it, but he never rebuked them unless he was certain they merited it. His attitude toward General W. N. Pendleton was typical. The chief of artillery, a minister in private life, had a good sense of organization, was a capable reconnaissance officer, and had a sharp eye for artillery positions, but he was not efficient in combat. His behavior in the affair on the Potomac after the Sharpsburg operations had been much criticised. At least one outspoken artillerist had said that Pendleton was "Lee's weakness . . . like the elephant we have him and we don't know what on earth to do with him. . . ." [71] Lee had known Pendleton since their West Point days and had personal attachment for him, coupled with the respect he always had for a clergyman. He cannot have been wholly satisfied with Pendleton, however, because he never gave him real control of the artillery in action and generally left him in charge of the reserve only. During the entire course of the war he never recommended Pendleton for promotion, and when Davis proposed in 1864 to give him a corps in the Army of Tennessee, Lee politely said he "could not select him to command a corps in this army." He added: "I do not mean to say by that he is not competent, but from what I have seen of him I do not know that he is." [72] In the autumn of 1863, Pendleton forwarded Lee a letter in which he mentioned some question that had been raised as to his handling of the artillery defense of Fredericksburg during the Chancellorsville campaign. Lee evidently had his own doubts on the subject, but he saw no gain from agitating them, and in his answer he did what he

[71] *Ham Chamberlayne, Virginian*, 134.   [72] *Lee's Dispatches*, 242.

could to dismiss the matter. "1 think," said he, "the report of my dissatisfaction at your conduct is given upon small grounds, the statement apparently of your courier, upon whom I turned my back. I must acknowledge I have no recollection of the circumstances, or of anything upon which it could have been based. The guns were withdrawn from the heights of Fredericksburg under general instructions given by me. It is difficult now to say, with the after-knowledge of events, whether these instructions could, at the time, have been better executed, or whether if all the guns had remained in position, as you state there was not enough infantry supports [sic] for those retained, more might not have been captured." [73] If that satisfied Pendleton, it did not give the lie to history.

Somewhat similar was the case of General Heth. That officer, whom Lee personally esteemed very highly, had been the most unfortunate of Lee's subordinates during the campaigns of 1863. His whole division had been wrongly blamed for the failure on the third day at Gettysburg; to him had fallen the difficult task of covering the rear when the army had recrossed at Falling Waters; and at Bristoe Station the two brigades that had been uselessly slaughtered were of his command. A. P. Hill very manfully took full blame for Bristoe Station and exculpated Heth for Gettysburg and Falling Waters,[74] but there must have been whisperings in the army that Heth was incompetent. When he went to Richmond during the winter, he sought introductions, perhaps with an eye to putting the facts in their true light before the military committees of Congress. Lee gave him a letter to Senator R. M. T. Hunter, in which he reviewed the circumstances leading to Heth's promotion and said: "At Gettysburg . . . General Heth [was wounded] in the battle of the first day, when he steadily drove the enemy before him. He was unable to take further part in the battles around Gettysburg, but resumed command of his division on the march from Pennsylvania. At Bristoe his division was again engaged and according to the report of Genl. Hill, who was present, performed its duty. I have given you a part of Genl. Heth's military history and refer you to the official reports of the battles named to show you that he is worthy

[73] O. R., 29, part 2, pp. 724-25.   [74] O. R., 51, part 2, p. 811.

of your attention." [75] That was all—just, friendly, and precise, even to saying that, "according to the report of Genl. Hill," Heth had not been to blame at Bristoe. Not having been present himself, Lee would not vouch for more.

During the winter of 1863–64, General Early served for a time in the Shenandoah Valley.[76] He was well-disciplined and devoted but a better strategist than a tactician. At Malvern Hill he had lost himself in the woods and at Bristoe Station he had floundered about. Few, however, were more censorious or more outspoken in criticism of other officers. While directing the operations of General Imboden in the Valley, he so often disparaged that officer that Imboden, in desperation, appealed for a court of inquiry. Early endorsed the application with the statement that Imboden's command was poor in discipline and that he would not like to have to rely on it in an emergency. The papers in due course reached General Lee. He had already heard Early's complaints of Imboden and was inclined to believe them well-founded,[77] but he did not think any good could result from airing the deficiencies of the troops, so he indorsed the papers simply: "General Imboden has been informed by letter today that I do not think a court of inquiry advantageous." Each of the disputants might take that as he pleased: Lee would have none of such a controversy.

In his official reports, Lee was equally careful to respect the sensibilities of his subordinates. The preparation of these documents, which was entrusted to Major Marshall, was rarely undertaken until all the subsidiary reports had been received. Marshall had first to reconcile all discrepancies by personal interviews and then he had to complete a rough draft. Lee went over every line of this with a sharp pencil and a sharper eye, eliminating any superfluous word and softening most of the asperities. "He weighed every sentence I wrote," Marshall stated, "frequently making minute verbal alterations, and questioned me closely as to the evidence on which I based all statements which he did not know to be correct." [78] This method made his reports more

[75] R. E. Lee to R. M. T. Hunter, Jan. 22, 1864; *MS.* in the possession of Julien H. Hill of Richmond, placed at the author's disposal through the kind offices of the late Richard E. Cunningham, of Richmond.

[76] *Cf. O. R.,* 33, 1091.   [77] *O. R.,* 33, 1086.

[78] *Marshall,* 178 *ff.*

nearly accurate than almost any others written on the military operations of the War between the States, but it robbed them of so much of their dramatic interest that Charles Carter Lee, his eldest brother, protested humorously. The government, he said, employed the General to do the fighting but should retain himself to write the reports. "We could then combine," he said, "and be irresistible." [79] On March 8, 1863,[80] General Lee had sent in the report on the Seven Days; that on Fredericksburg was signed April 10, 1863,[81] that covering Second Manassas bore date of June 8, 1863,[82] and that dealing with Sharpsburg was forwarded August 19, 1863.[83] All these he designed to form a continuous narrative.[84] As the report on Gettysburg involved far more questions of personal inefficiency than any of the others, he took infinite pains to make it historically valid without reflecting needlessly on any one. He struck out, as already noted, Marshall's caustic references to Stuart's responsibility for the confusion after the army entered Pennsylvania, he made no criticism of Ewell or of Longstreet, and when he completed the paper, January 20, 1864,[85] there was not a phrase in it to arouse jealousies or to injure the morale of the army. His rule in preparing his reports was to state facts without personal censure, and sometimes, as in the report on Chancellorsville, it was only when he omitted praise that criticism could be implied.[86]

As he was in these reports, so he was in his dealings with all his officers, and not in serious matters only. He took every opportunity of showing them small acts of kindness. Especially if an officer was visited in camp by his wife, Lee saw to it that they had evidence of his good will. When the campaign was about to open in 1864, he issued the usual order of "Women to the rear," but as the enemy showed no signs of moving, the wives of some of the officers lingered unduly. One day, when Lee went aboard a train at Orange Courthouse, he found Captain A. R. H. Ranson

79 *Fitz Lee*, 18.

80 *O. R.*, 11, part 2, p. 489. *Cf. O. R.*, 21, 1113–14 for Lee's statement of his reasons why the reports were delayed.

81 *O. R.*, 21, 550.

82 *O. R.*, 12, part 2, p. 551.   83 *O. R.*, 19, part 1, p. 144.

84 *Ibid.*, and *O. R.*, 29, part 2, pp. 747–48.

85 *O. R.*, 27, part 2, p. 312.

86 This report contained no direct criticism of McLaws's behavior at Salem Church but it did not mention that officer among those whose acts Lee commended.

with Mrs. Ranson. He stopped and said, "Captain Ranson, I wish you to introduce me to Mrs. Ranson."

The young woman arose instantly and began, "Oh, General Lee, I disregarded your order. It was my doing, not my husband's, and I beg you to forgive both of us."

"Pray do not disturb yourself," Lee said. "My order was not intended for you at all. It was intended only for your husband. I intend to get a great deal of work out of him this summer, and he cannot do his work unless his horses are in condition. Every evening for some weeks, about nightfall, I have observed that he mounted his horse behind his camp and galloped off to Orange Courthouse, three miles away, and every morning he came galloping back about sunrise. Now you know this is not good for the horses. By the time I should need his services they would be worn out, and I was obliged to put a stop to it."

Then he sat down by her and talked so agreeably that he made her forget her concern, "but," said Ranson, in recounting the story, "there was in General Lee's little joke a reproof and warning to me, and although my wife's fears were relieved, he let me know that he had his eye on me, and that he knew more of my movements than had been supposed."[87] Lee observed, in fact, the conduct of many an officer who did not realize that he was studying him, and in this way he acquired a surprisingly complete knowledge of the capacity of even his colonels. During the Mine Run operations, when he received a report of a strong demonstration on his right flank, his first question was, "Who commands the regiment?" He knew the answer would tell him what to expect.[88]

Finding one day that Colonel Hilary P. Jones had lost his gauntlets, Lee gave him a pair of his own;[89] when he received a proposal to reorganize the Society of the Cincinnati, he opposed it on the ground that it might arouse jealousies;[90] a statement that the officers were not receiving their pay with regularity led him to make prompt representation to the President[91]—there were scores of such incidents. And there were cases, also, where Lee's

---

[87] A. R. H. Ranson: "General Lee as I Knew Him" in *Harper's Magazine*, vol. 122, p. 329.
[88] *Cooke*, 368.
[89] Letter of V. M. Fleming to the writer, Dec. 16, 1927.
[90] *Lee's Dispatches*, 160–61.   [91] *O. R.*, 29, part 2, p. 769.

humor found expression. He was always threatening to marry off his bachelor generals to girls of his acquaintance. The more indifferent the individual to feminine charms, the more insistent Lee was—at least to the young women—that the officer accept the happy bondage of matrimony. General Edward Johnson was, at the time, a serious gallant, but Lee insisted that General Early was a far more acceptable suitor. To his cousin Margaret Stuart he wrote, "General Early has just returned from a visit home, and is handsomer than ever. He looks high in his new garments, and the black plume in his beaver gives him the air of a gay cavalier"—a description that will be illuminated by any picture of Early.[92]

But when the occasion required, Lee gave remembered counsel or administered unforgettable rebukes. If possible, he was tactful and considerate in this. During the winter a report reached headquarters that the enemy was moving on the extreme right of the Confederate front. Colonel Marshall was at once dispatched to that sector to inform General Ewell and to make proper dispositions. Marshall found that Ewell had already heard the rumor and had discovered it to be without foundation. Naturally, Marshall said nothing about a change in the Confederate front. When he returned and stated the facts, Lee made no protest, but that evening at dinner he called to Marshall from the opposite end of the table. "Major Marshall," said he, "did you know General Twiggs?"

Marshall answered that he knew him only by his reputation in the Mexican War.

"General Twiggs," said Lee, "had a way of instilling instruction that was very effective, and no one ever forgot a lesson taught by him. When he went to Mexico he had a number of young officers connected with his staff who were without experience but very zealous and desirous to do their duty thoroughly. Sometimes they undertook General Twiggs's orders, and would fail to do what he told them to do, or would not do it as the general had ordered it to be done. If General Twiggs remarked upon such liberties being taken with his orders, these gentlemen were always ready to show that they were right and that General

_____
[92] R. E. Lee to Margaret Stuart, March 20, 1864; Jones, _L. and L.,_ 301.

Twiggs was wrong. The general bore this without complaint or rebuke for some time, but one day a young officer came to report his execution of an order General Twiggs had given him, and reported that when he had reached the place where the thing ordered by General Twiggs was to be done, he had found the circumstances so entirely different from what General Twiggs had supposed that he thought that the general would not have given the order had he known the fact, and was proceeding to satisfy General Twiggs that what the young officer had done was the best under the circumstances. But General Twiggs interrupted him by saying, 'Captain, I know that you can prove that you are right, and that my order was wrong; in fact, you gentlemen are always right, but for God's sake do wrong sometimes.' "

Marshall commented: "Although General Lee was satisfied with what I had done on this occasion, he wished to impress the lesson of a literal obedience to orders on my mind, and you may be sure that I never forgot it, when it was possible to refer any doubtful matter back to him for further instructions." [93]

Lee would restrain the vehemence of his subordinates in the same manner. Out reconnoitring one day with a very partisan officer, Lee was shocked when the man exclaimed that he wished all the enemy were dead. "How can you say that, General?" Lee exclaimed. "Now, I wish that they were all at home attending to their own business, and leaving us to do the same." After Appomattox, he confided to a friend that he had never seen a day when he did not pray for the enemy.[94] General Henry A. Wise was the only man, it would appear, who ever had the temerity to joke with Lee on the subject of his prayers. In 1862, Lee had jestingly informed Wise that he had received a complaint that Wise's troops had been guilty of depredation, but he could hardly credit it because his informant had said that Wise had cursed him. Wise is said to have replied, "Well, General Lee, if you will do the praying for the Army of Northern Virginia, I'll be damned if I will not do the swearing." [95]

[93] 23 S. H. S. P., 207–8.   [94] Jones, 196; see also Grayjackets, 103.
[95] This is the version in B. H. Wise, 318–19. In 2 B. and L., 276–77, the circumstances are somewhat differently related and Wise is credited with saying: "General Lee, you certainly play Washington to perfection, and your whole life is a constant reproach to me. Now I am perfectly willing that Jackson and yourself shall do the praying for the whole Army of Northern Virginia; but in Heaven's name, let me do the *cussin'* for one small brigade."

In dealing with laggard officers, and with those who sought to get him to express unfriendly opinions, Lee was usually tactful. Once, later in the war, when an officer's slowness had permitted the Federals to escape, Lee remarked drily, "General, I have sometimes to admonish General Stuart or General Gordon against being too fast. I shall never have occasion to find that fault with you." On another occasion, when an officer tried to make him criticise another general by pointing out his shortcomings, Lee would only say, "Well, sir, if that is your opinion of General Blank, I can only say that you differ very widely from the General himself." [96]

But Lee set limits to his tact. He had a habit, when in camp, of occasionally writing down reflections that somewhat echo Marcus Aurelius, who seems to have been one of Lee's favorite authors. Among these maxims, found in his field valise after his death, was one to this effect: "Private and public life are subject to the same rules; and truth and manliness are two qualities that will carry you through this world much better than *policy,* or *tact,* or *expediency,* or any other word that was ever devised to conceal or mystify a deviation from a straight line." [97] To that rule he held. The same Captain Ranson, whose wife had failed to obey the order to go to the rear, had known General Lee before the war, and was once invited to share with the General the contents of a basket of food that had been sent him. Ranson was late in arriving and in answer to a message that Lee was waiting for him, hurriedly put in an appearance. "Captain Ranson," said Lee gravely, "do you think it right to keep us all waiting in this way?" Ranson tried to apologize and, later in the evening when a bottle of Madeira was passed around, made some feeble joke about the incongruity of drinking such wine from tin cups. His table companions received his jest in cold silence, but Lee remarked that the wine had come from an old lady, a friend of his in Petersburg, and that he was afraid she would not relish the joke. Ranson subsided. "I felt," he confessed later, "as if I would be glad if the earth would open and swallow me up." [98]

Lee was particularly sensitive to greediness, and in dealing with

[96] *D. H. Maury,* 238.   [97] *Jones,* 145.
[98] Ranson, *Harper's Magazine,* vol. 122, p. 328.

it he was not diplomatic. Once, when a corps commander and one of his aides dined with the commander, Lee had on the table a dish of bacon and greens and a solitary slice of beef that some one had sent him. The lieutenant general, when asked what he would have, asked for the vegetables, but when Lee put the same question to the aide, he said he would have some beef. Lee gave him the slice. A little later, Lee chanced to have dinner with the same lieutenant general, who had provided a roast of beef. When his host inquired what he cared to eat, Lee turned smilingly to the same greedy aide: "I will thank you for a piece of that beef, if Captain S—— does not want all of it." [99]

A more vigorous forthrightness is reported to have been displayed after the army had moved to the Richmond line, during the summer of 1864, when Lee happened to meet near the front an officer who was always careful to keep to the rear. "Good morning, General," Lee is alleged to have said, with undisguised sarcasm, "Are you not afraid to trust yourself so far from the city, and to come where all this firing and danger is?"

"Oh, General," said the officer, "I am somewhere upon the lines every day."

"Indeed," said Lee, "I am very glad to learn it, sir. Good morning, General," and he is said to have turned away with something closely akin to scorn.[100]

Once again, during the Spotsylvania campaign, a general of infantry hotly berated the cavalry for permitting Sheridan to break through and destroy a food depot. "And they have captured my cow," he complained, "and I have no milk for my coffee. If I were in command of this army, I would notify General Grant that, inasmuch as he had sent his cavalry to the rear and destroyed our rations, I should not give his prisoners whom we hold a morsel of food, and if he wanted to save them from starvation, he would have to send rations here to them!" Lee passed at that moment. The officer repeated what he had said. Turning impatiently to him, but making no pause as he walked, Lee broke forth: "The prisoners that we have here, General ——, are my prisoners; they are not General Grant's prisoners, and as long as

[99] D. H. Maury, 236-37.
[100] D. H. Maury, 237. General Maury got this story second-hand. It may not be authentic.

I have any rations at all I shall divide them with *my* prisoners." [101]

Except in the case of Longstreet, Lee was usually less disposed to employ his tact in dealing with professional soldiers than with civilians who had taken up arms. He had always been frank with Jackson and he was occasionally plainspoken with Stuart. Among Stuart's scouts was a daring young man, Channing Smith, a kinsman of Governor William Smith of Virginia, successor to Governor Letcher. The chief of the cavalry corps carried on a correspondence with Governor Smith, and sent him, on occasion, reports in which he recounted with praise the exploits of Channing Smith and some of his other scouts. Governor Smith thoughtlessly let parts of these letters be printed. When they came under Lee's eye, he pointed to this paragraph in an early dispatch to Stuart: "From some letters of yours to Governor Smith published in the papers, I consider the lives of Stringfellow, Channing Smith and others greatly jeopardized. They will be watched for, and if caught, hardly dealt by. You had better recall them and replace them by others. I do not consider that I can make my official letters to the department public without the authority and permission of the Secretary of War, or furnish copies to others." [102] The rebuke was as positive as it was delicate.

The self-mastery, and the unfailing consideration displayed toward the fiery men about General Lee, had its effect upon others. As his officers found him quick to reward merit and slow to blame, always just and always generous, ready to instruct the inexperienced and to trust the capable, there developed among them a respect for his character as great as their admiration for his military skill. Slowly he came in their minds not only to represent their cause, but to incarnate it and to idealize it. Proud as was the name of the Army of Northern Virginia, they almost ceased to say that they belonged to that host and spoke of themselves as serving in "Lee's army." And by that more personal name, with all the tribute to Lee that it implied, they usually styled the army in familiar conversation till it had become only the glamorous memory of their waning years.

101 *Rosser, loc. cit.,* 15–16.
102 Lee to Stuart, April 23, 1864; *H. B. McClellan MSS.*

CHAPTER XIV

Can the Army Be Saved for New Battles?

That the Army of Northern Virginia did not decline in morale during the winter of 1863–64 was due, first of all, to its previous record of victories. Soldiers who had triumphed at Second Manassas, at Fredericksburg, and at Chancellorsville refused to regard Gettysburg, Bristoe Station, and Rappahannock Bridge as anything more than a succession of unhappy accidents. Having beaten the enemy often, the men would not believe the Federals had so improved in generalship or in fighting prowess that they could defeat them except when circumstances, the elements, or the superiority of position gave the Army of the Potomac an unassailable advantage.

The adaptability of the individual contributed, in the second place, to the army's morale during the same shivering months. The majority of Lee's soldiers were country boys, many of them only one or two generations from the frontier and nearly all of them accustomed to a primitive life in which every man had to shift for himself. The regiments from the rural districts had shown their resourcefulness early in the war. Those from the cities had quickly "reverted to species" and by the third winter of the war were equally adept in the art of making themselves comfortable wherever they were thrown. The men's ingenuity increased in proportion to their hardships.

Still a third factor was the invincible good cheer of the troops. This probably had its origin in the isolated lives they had led prior to the war. Once the embarrassment of new association had worn off, contact with men from other states was stimulating. Only the most incurable pessimist failed to contribute his part to the merriment of camp, much after the manner of boys who were "showing off." The sternest experience was softened by their jokes, as in the case of the hot and hungry infantryman who came upon a group of commissary officers, seated under a clump of trees and enjoying an ample dinner. The soldier, a North Carolinian, walked up to the fence that surrounded the grove, put his head through the palings, gazed longingly, and then remarked with fine satire, "I say, misters, did any of you ever hearn tell of the battle of Chancellorsville?" [1] Of similar spirit was the sick, straggling Georgia private who was plodding through the woods one day in the fall of 1863, when he was overtaken by a North Carolina bandsman with a great bass drum. The soldiers had made life so miserable for the musicians that this sensitive votary of the Muse had left the road and was making his way quietly forward among the trees to escape the jibes at his music and his valor. He stalked past the Georgian without a word, only to be halted by a plaintive voice: "Mister, oh, mister!" Sympathetically the drummer turned. "What can I do for you?" he inquired. In the same voice, the soldier asked, "Won't you be so kind as to pick a tune on that ar' thing?" [2] An army that ate the meat of mirth could keep its morale even on the rancid bacon and cornbread that often formed its only ration.

Religion was another factor in sustaining the spirit of the soldiers through the long, blusterous months on the Rapidan. The revivals begun the previous year were still sweeping through the camps. Nearly every brigade built itself a log chapel, into which, night after night, the men crowded to hear fervent preachers tell of an everlasting life that robbed the *minié* of its terror. That winter 15,000 men were converted, and many of them were fired with a faith that defied the battle. [3]

Lee himself was a force no less potent in preserving the morale of the army. His methods were as simple as they were effective. They reflected his own character and his interest in the welfare of the men entrusted to him, and in no sense did they bespeak any ordered, calculating analysis of what would or would not inspire soldiers. He rode frequently among the camps, alone or attended by only one or two staff officers. Sometimes the men would cheer him;[4] more often they received him with a silence that was almost reverent. Yet they never hesitated to bring him their complaints, in the knowledge that he would always receive

[1] *La Bree*, 320. [2] *Grayjackets*, 221.
[3] Jones, *L. and L.*, 298; *Gordon*, 230. [4] *Cooke*, 276–77.

them as friends in a common cause. During the Gettysburg campaign, as Lee stood by a road along which a column of half-
exhausted men were marching under a singeing sun, a stout
private broke ranks and approached him. Some of the staff turned
the man back, but Lee told them to let him come to him. "What
is it you want?" he said kindly. The soldier, who was perspiring
in streams, answered quickly, "Please, General, I don't want
much, but it's powerful wet marching this weather. I can't see
for the water in my eyes. I came aside to this old hill to get a
rag or something to wipe the sweat out of my eyes." Lee immediately took out his handkerchief and handed it to him. "Will
this do?" he inquired. "Yes, my Lordy, that indeed!" the man
exclaimed. "Well, then," Lee answered encouragingly, "take it
with you, and back quick to ranks; no straggling this march, you
know, my man." General Sorrel, who witnessed this typical incident, said in comment on it, "Lee's talk and manner with the
soldier were inimitable in their encouraging kindness." [5]

John H. Worsham recalled that after the campaign of 1864
opened, Lee chanced again to be by the roadside, mounted on
Traveller while some of his veterans were on the march. "As
our column approached him," he wrote, "an old private stepped
out of ranks and advanced to General Lee. They shook hands like
acquaintances and entered into a lively conversation. As I moved
on I looked back, and the old man had his gun in one hand and
the other hand on Traveller's neck, still talking." [6]

Lee was as simple with the farmers of the countryside as he
was with his soldiers. On one of the advances of the army, a
farmer rode up to a bivouac where Lee was sitting and addressed
him as "colonel," not guessing his identity. Lee put him at his
ease and chatted with him for some time. At length the planter
told the "colonel" that he had come to the army in the hope of
seeing General Lee and wondered if it was possible for him to do
so. "I am General Lee," his host replied, "and I am most happy
to have met you." [7] While he was on the Rappahannock, a
soldier called at Lee's tent, with his wife. Lee invited the couple
in and soon learned all about them by friendly questions. "She
was from Abbeville district, S. C.," he enthusiastically wrote Mrs.

---

[5] *Sorrel*, 178.   [6] *Worsham*, 300.   [7] *Jones*, 235.

Lee that night. "Said she had not seen her husband for more than two years, and, as he had written to her for clothes, she herself thought she would bring them on. It was the first time she had travelled by railroad, but she got along very well by herself. She brought an entire suit of her own manufacture for her husband. She spun the yarn and made the clothes herself. She clad her three children in the same way, and had on a beautiful pair of gloves she had made for herself. Her children she had left with her sister. . . . She was very pleasing in her address and modest in her manner, and was clad in a nice, new alpaca. I am certain she could not have made that. . . . She, in fact, was an admirable woman. Said she was willing to give up everything she had in the world to attain our independence, and the only complaint she made of the conduct of our enemies was their arming our servants against us. Her greatest difficulty was to procure shoes. She made them for herself and children of cloth with leather soles. She sat with me about ten minutes and took her leave—another mark of sense—and made no request for herself or husband." [8]

With the courtesy he showed this woman, he welcomed all visitors, humble in station or exalted in rank. Only those who came to appeal from the verdict of courts-martial and those who importuned him for promotion found access to him difficult. If an officer wrote him in protest at the elevation of some one else, or in complaint of his failure to receive recognition, Lee would turn the paper over to one of his staff with the request, "'Suage him, Colonel; 'suage him." If he could avoid it without discourtesy, he would not grant an interview to such an officer. Once, after a man with a grievance had insisted on seeing him, Lee came out of his quarters with a flushed face and exclaimed to Colonel Venable, "Why did you permit that man to come to my tent and make me show my temper?" [9]

Lee's respect for the individuality of his men extended to their wants and their duties. He was quick to defend them against discrimination and against imposition. The sutlers who set themselves up at Orange Courthouse during the winter were, in the main, a grasping lot, and they became so exorbitant in their

[8] Lee to Mrs. Lee, Nov. 1, 1863, *R. E. Lee, Jr.,* 112–13.
[9] Venable in 4 *B. and L.,* 240.

charges that the men rose against them and plundered their wares. In plaintive indignation the sutlers hurried to General Lee to ask protection for the future. He heard their protests with his wonted patience and ended by putting this question to them: "You think that the boys treated you badly?" The sutlers were of one mind: "Outrageously, General," they insisted, "outrageously." Lee looked at them: "Had you not, then, better set up shop somewhere else?" They did.[10] On the other hand, he investigated every just grievance, and when a prisoner complained to him that the soldiers had abused and taunted him, Lee was instant in his reproof.[11]

The spiritual needs of his men he supplied, also, as best he could. Some of his generals, less religious in nature than he, fell into the habit of making Sunday a time for reviews and festivities. Two of the chaplains came to Lee and tactfully asked that military duties on the Sabbath Day be reduced to the necessary minimum. Lee made no promises but let the conversation drift to the progress of the revivals. One of the clergymen noted that as they told Lee of what was happening, "we saw his eye brighten and his whole countenance glow with pleasure." [12] When the ministers rose to leave, the spokesman stated, "I think it right that I should say to you, General, that the chaplains of this army have a deep interest in your welfare, and that some of the most fervent prayers we offer are in your behalf." Lee flushed, and tears came into his eyes. He choked for a moment and then, with the directness that would have been cant in a soul less simple than his, he replied, "Please thank them for that, sir. I warmly appreciate it. And I can only say that I am nothing but a poor sinner, trusting in Christ alone for salvation, and need all the prayers they can offer for me." [13] The next day he issued a general order for the better observance of the Sabbath.[14] He went regularly to church,[15] and not infrequently, when his duties did not press too heavily, he attended the chaplains' meetings.[16]

---

[10] *Land We Love,* 163.   [11] *W. W. Chamberlaine,* 86.
[12] Jones: *Christ in the Camp,* 49.   [13] Jones: *Christ in the Camp,* 50.
[14] *O. R.,* 33, 1150; *Jones,* 415–16; 10 *S. H. S. P.,* 91.
[15] *Cf.* W. W. Scott in 6 *William and Mary Quarterly,* 280; *Taylor MSS.,* February, 1864.
[16] *Taylor MSS.,* March 20, 27, 1864. For a letter from Lee to Reverend Moses D. Hoge, acknowledging a Bible that the minister had brought in through the blockade, see P. H. Hoge: *M. D. Hoge,* 196.

His regard for his men was, of course, known to them, and when coupled with their respect for him as a soldier, it produced in them something akin to the idolatry of youth for greatness. After one of his battles, Lee met a soldier who was coming from the front with a shattered right arm. "I grieve for you, my poor fellow," Lee said, "can I do anything for you?" The soldier answered, "Yes, sir, you can shake hands with me, General, if you will consent to take my left hand." Lee grasped his powder-stained hand warmly—with an admiration he made no effort to conceal.[17]

Late in the winter a scout arrived at headquarters with newspapers and reports of a heavy eastward movement of troop trains along the Baltimore and Ohio. The scout, who was only a boy in years, had ridden one horse to death in order to reach Lee speedily and was close to collapse. Lee listened to him and left him for a moment to issue an order. When he returned, he found that the boy had toppled over from his camp-stool and had fallen half on the General's cot, in the deep sleep of exhaustion. Lee covered him, walked out of the tent, tied the flap and left him alone until his cramped position caused him to awaken, two hours later. Then the General supplied him with food and saw to it that he received proper care.[18] Incidents of this sort became known to the army and explain in part why it was that in March, 1864, when he was in Richmond, the men who were waiting at the transportation office heard of his presence in the city and with many a "God-bless-him," inquired where they could see him.[19] But perhaps the best tribute to him was paid one night when some of the infantry were discussing the *Origin of Species,* which had then been published less than four years. Darwinism had its warm advocates, but one soldier refused to accept the arguments. "Well, boys," he said, "the rest of us may have developed from monkeys; but I tell you none less than God could have made such a man as 'Marse Robert.' " [20]

The material wants of the men who gave him this measure of

---

[17] *Jones,* 319.
[18] George Baylor: *Bull Run to Bull Run,* 331 *ff.* Baylor thought this occurred just before the Mine Run campaign, but the reference to the troop trains shows it was subsequent thereto.
[19] *Mrs. McGuire,* 256.   [20] *Jones,* 319.

admiration could not be supplied that winter. Some of the worst wear-and-tear in clothing and footgear had been offset by September, 1863,[21] but as the fall advanced and the weather grew worse, the depletion of Confederate credits abroad and the capture of several ships loaded with quartermaster stores resulted in such a shortage that shoes were worn out faster than they could be replaced.[22] There were thousands of barefooted men in the army before the end of October.[23] After a period of extremely cold weather in January,[24] only fifty men in one regiment were decently shod, and a brigade sent out on picket duty had to leave behind it several hundred men who could not march because of the condition of their shoes.[25] Lee sought to save every hide he could, and to remedy the shortage he undertook to have shoes made in the army, but with indifferent success.[26] He kept the women of his family and all their acquaintances busy knitting warm socks, especially for the men whose homes were within the enemy's lines.[27] It was characteristic of Lee, however, to withhold his requisitions during a part of the winter, in order that Longstreet's troops in the mountains might get shoes.[28] As for blankets, they were to be had only by importation, as the South produced none.[29]

Worse even than the shortage of shoes and blankets was the lack of food for the men. As early as June, 1863, Commissary General Northrop had served warning that the meat supply in the South would not last until the new bacon came in.[30] In July he had notified Lee that he would be compelled to recommend a reduction in the ration,[31] and in his annual report for 1863 he stated that there would not be enough meat in the country during the next twelve months for the people and the army. As the civilians would insist on having meat, he added bitterly that the troops "must bear the brunt of hunger as well as of arms." [32] By December, 1863, the government had only twenty-five days' supply of beef and bacon east of the Mississippi and had no reserve

---

21 *Sorrel,* 180.
22 *O. R.,* 29, part 2, pp. 784–85, 835; *ibid.,* 33, 1094–95; IV *O. R.,* 2, 870.
23 *R. E. Lee, Jr.,* 111.   24 *Welch,* 85.
25 *O. R.,* 33, 1094–95.
26 *O. R.,* 33, 1098, 1131–32, 1146–47, *Rosser, loc. cit.,* 12.
27 Jones, *L. and L.,* 300.   28 *O. R.,* 32, part 2, p. 761.
29 *O. R.,* 33, 1147.   30 IV *O. R.,* 2, 574–75.
31 *O. R.,* 51, part 2, p. 738.   32 IV *O. R.,* 2, 970–71.

whatsoever in Virginia.[33] In January the shortage of cereals was almost as acute.[34] Davis contrived to get 90,000 pounds of meat when it seemed that the army must go without fats,[35] but the daily ration had to be cut to four ounces of bacon or salt pork, with only one pint of corn meal per man.[36] For two days during the winter the men went without any food.[37] One hungry soldier anonymously sent Lee his meat ration, carefully placed between two chips, and wrote sadly that though he had been born a gentleman, hunger had forced him to steal.[38] Another man in the ranks wrote Lee asking if he knew of the want to which the army had been reduced. He added that if the General was aware of conditions, the men would realize there was reason for the shortage. Lee did not answer directly, but the next day he issued an order explaining the situation and exhorting the troops to endure as their forefathers had in the Revolution.[39] The soldiers responded to his appeal loyally and complained little, but as they surveyed their scant allowance of unbolted meal, they started a grim joke which lingered in the army until Appomattox—that the opposing forces were the "Fed and the Cornfed."[40] There were weeks, of course, during which the rations of some of the units were ample,[41] but the periods of want were so frequent and so prolonged that Lee had to inform the administration in the most sombre terms that ruin was threatened if the army was not rationed. On January 22, 1864, he wrote the Secretary of War, "Unless there is a change, I fear the army cannot be kept effective, and probably cannot be kept together."[42] As late as April 12, when the opening of the campaign waited only on the final preparations of the enemy across the Rapidan, Lee told the President, "I cannot see how we can operate with our present supplies."[43]

The reasons for this struggle with starvation were numerous. The Southern states prior to 1861 had been heavy importers of

33 IV O. R., 2, 960.

34 O. R., 51, part 2, p. 808.　　35 O. R., 33, 1064.

36 O. R., 33, 1061; McCabe, 431; W. W. Dame: From the Rapidan to Richmond (cited hereafter as Dame), 26–27.

37 Dame, loc. cit.　　38 3 B. and L., 240; White, 334.

39 R. E. Lee, Jr., 118–19; O. R., 33, 1117.

40 David Macrae: The American at Home (cited hereafter as Macrae), 1, 191. R. E. Lee, Jr., 118.

41 Taylor MSS., Feb. 23, 1863.

42 O. R., 33, 1114.　　43 O. R., 33, 1275.

pork. After the commencement of the dark conflict, the govern‚ ment was slow to contract for adequate supplies of meat from abroad. The management of the commissary had been negligent and inefficient. The railroads were inadequate to the demands made on their worn equipment and tracks.[44] Serious as were these conditions, it was not Lee's nature to content himself with explaining to the administration their inevitable consequences. Through the whole of the winter, he strove himself to correct these conditions. The subsistence of the troops became his first and greatest concern.

What could he do to get food for the men? First of all, as he saw it, the improvement of the railroads and the better use of their rolling stock were essential. At the beginning of the war, the railways had thought they would inevitably be ruined and they had encouraged their operatives to enlist in order to save expenses. Many of them had neglected maintenance and none of them had been able to replace worn-out equipment.[45] Some of the more progressive lines had purchased a few necessities in Europe, and had brought them in through the blockade, but they had received scant encouragement from the government, which, however, had refused to take over the operation of the railways.[46] As a result of all this, the lines deteriorated during the winter of 1863–64, while the demands on them increased steadily, chiefly because the exhaustion of grain in Virginia and North Carolina necessitated the hauling of corn from Georgia to feed the men and horses of Lee's army.[47] By the end of 1863, the Virginia Central Railroad, which was Lee's supply line from Richmond, was so close to a breakdown that when it handled troops it could not deliver provisions or forage.[48] In January, 1864, when Lee moved Hoke's brigade to North Carolina, for the New Berne expedition, he had to dispatch the regiments on separate days in the freight cars that had delivered supplies.[49] In February, Lee was forced to

[44] McCabe, 432 ff.; E. A. Pollard: The Lost Cause, 480–89.

[45] IV O. R., 2, 881; C. W. Ramsdell: The Confederate Government and the Railroads, in 22 American Historical Review, 795.

[46] O. R., 51, part 2, pp. 850–51. IV O. R., 2, 841, 866. The East Tennessee Railroad was an exception, and was put under government operation in January, 1864 (O. R., 33, 1105).

[47] O. R., 32, part 2, p. 762; ibid., 33, 1077, 1178, 1236–37. For the capacity of the railroads see IV O. R., 2, 486.

[48] O. R., 51, part 2, p. 798; ibid., 33, 1073. [49] O. R., 33, 1104.

march Battle's brigade to the Richmond, Fredericksburg and Potomac Railroad and transport the men thence to Hanover Junction because the Virginia Central was unable to move them.[50] By March, the Virginia Central had but eight locomotives in working order.[51] The next month, Longstreet's corps could only be brought back from Bristol at the rate of 1500 a day.[52] Tracks were as bad as the equipment, for no new rails were being rolled in the Confederacy.[53] To complete the railroad from Greensboro, N. C., to Danville, Va., so that Lee might not be cut off from the South in case the Petersburg and Weldon Railroad was broken by the enemy, the Confederacy actually had to take up the rails on the York River Railroad and on six miles of the Charlottesville and Statesville Railroad and replace them on the new line.[54] Lee had long foreseen the danger of a collapse of the railways. One of his first orders after assuming command in March, 1862, had been designed to straighten out a railroad tangle,[55] and now, with the crisis at hand, he conserved his rail transportation with the utmost care. He had previously urged the officials of the Virginia Central Railroad to improve their line,[56] and he made it mandatory that all cars be unloaded and returned promptly.[57] On occasion, he did not hesitate to employ the troops around Richmond in repair work on the railroads.[58] He agreed, if necessary, to release car builders from the ranks, though he believed ship carpenters could be utilized for this purpose.[59] Likewise he joined most earnestly with Northrop in urging that passenger trains be withdrawn from service,[60] in order that the lines should be used only for moving troops and supplies; and he went even further in advocating the evacuation of non-combatants and prisoners from Richmond, where they had to be fed, in part, with transported supplies.[61] In the same spirit, Lee endeavored to prevent

---

[50] *O. R.*, 33, 1181.   [51] IV *O. R.*, 3, 226–27.   [52] *O. R.*, 33, 1286.

[53] *Ramsdell, loc. cit.*, quoting IV *O. R.*, 3, 93, 229, 1092.

[54] *O. R.*, 33, 1864; Eva Swatner: "The Military Railroads During the Civil War," in *The Military Engineer*, July-August, 1929, p. 314; For a history of the Greensboro-Danville road, see *Ramsdell, loc. cit.*, 801. The line was opened May 20, 1864.

[55] *Ramsdell, loc. cit.*, quoting IV *O. R.*, 1, 1010–11.

[56] See *supra*, p. 214.

[57] *Cf.* Lawton to Lee, Feb. 17, 1864: "I sincerely wish they [all the commanding generals] could be as seriously impressed as you are with the injury . . . sustained [by delays in unloading cars]" (*O. R.*, 32, part 2, p. 762).

[58] *O. R.*, 33, 1209.   [59] *O. R.*, 33, 1294.   [60] *O. R.*, 51, part 2, p. 861.

[61] *O. R.*, 33, 1077, 1275, 1276–77; *O. R.*, 51, part 2, pp. 850–51; 2 *R. W. C. D.*, 188.

the wastage of provisions en route to the army.[62] Thanks to this co-operation, the energetic administration of a new quartermaster-general, A. R. Lawton, a former brigadier in the Army of Northern Virginia, kept the wheels turning and prevented the collapse that would otherwise have occurred. In March, 1864, Lawton was able to report that the creaking lines were hauling more than at almost any other period of the war, though it was admittedly a "forced march." [63]

Knowing that the railroads, under the best possible management, could not be relied upon to bring a sufficiency of supplies to the army, Lee's second method of providing food for his men was through raids into western and southwestern Virginia.[64] Many hogs and cattle were procured in this way. At one time, raids became so necessary that Lee was prepared to undertake them in almost any quarter where supplies were to be had in a quantity to justify them.[65] Besides these measures, Lee advocated and prevailed upon the War Department to approve a system of trading with the enemy;[66] he sent off most of the cavalry into country where it could subsist itself;[67] he protested against the practice whereby officers were allowed to purchase food at the various army-posts for their families;[68] he issued strict orders to protect cultivated enclosures;[69] he granted furloughs at the rate of sixteen for each one hundred men, in order that they might not have to be fed at the front, but he was restrained in doing this by the knowledge that if too many furloughs were issued, the railroad trains would be overcrowded.[70] At his own headquarters, he set an example of the utmost frugality. All luxuries that were sent by admirers he dispatched forthwith to the hospitals, and as protests were made against this, he replied simply, "I am content to share the rations of my men." [71] When a plain meal was finished he would sometimes say to Major Taylor, "Well, we are

---

[62] O. R., 33, 1076–77.
[63] O. R., 33, 1236–37. Despite Lawton's efficiency, some of the politicians tried to oust him (IV O. R., 3, 49–51, 318).
[64] For western Virginia, see O. R., 29, part 2, p. 889; O. R., 33, 1061, 1066, 1101, 1142; for southwest Virginia and the country bordering it, see O. R., 33, 1065–66, 1093, 1129–30, 1162.
[65] O. R., 33, 1112–13.
[66] O. R., 33, 1180–81; O. R., 51, part 2, p. 842; IV O. R., 3, 154, 245, 261, 287 ff.
[67] R. E. Lee, Jr., 118.   [68] O. R., 33, 1114–15, 1161.
[69] O. R., 33, 1126.   [70] O. R., 33, 1114–15.
[71] White, 334.

just as well off as if we had feasted on the best in the land; our hunger is appeased, and I am satisfied." [72] A simple vegetable dinner drew forth his warmest praise when he was visiting, [73] and his own mid-day fare was usually cabbage boiled in salt water. [74] Once when he had guests, he ordered middling bacon with the cabbage, but when the diners sat down, the meat was so scant that all of them politely declined it. The next day, recalling that the meat had not been eaten, he bade his steward bring it— only to be met with the confession that there had been no bacon at headquarters and that what he had seen the previous day had been borrowed and had been duly returned to its owner, untouched. [75] On the rare occasions when food was abundant and Lee's table was graced with a piece of beef, or with a joint of mutton, which was one of his favorite dishes, he would always remark, if urged to have a second helping, "I would really enjoy another piece, but I have had my allowance." [76]

All that could be devised to relieve the scarcity of food, Lee undertook diligently—except one thing: He would not resort to indiscriminate impressment of the little that the people in the war zone had for their own subsistence; and in refusing to do this, he had a long, pointed correspondence with the commissary general. [77]

The shortage that Lee sought to ease by these measures extended equally to the feed for the horses. At the end of August, 1863, promises had been made that the army would be supplied with 3000 bushels of corn a day, [78] but before the middle of November, the amount had fallen off so heavily that Lee feared unless more was forthcoming many animals would be lost during the winter. [79] Ere long the daily supply declined to 1000 bushels a day [80] and the hay and fodder were relatively even less. Instead

[72] *Taylor's Four Years*, 222.
[73] 6 *W. and M. Quarterly*, 281.　　[74] *Marginalia*, 233.
[75] *McCabe*, 434–35.　　[76] *Mason*, 225.
[77] *O. R.*, 29, part 2, pp. 837, 838, 843, 844, 862, 1064–65, 1087–88, 1113–14, 1128; IV *O. R.*, 3, 198–99, 249; 2 *R. W. C. D.*, 147. The want of food in the districts south of the Rappahannock had been so grave as early as the autumn of 1863, that Lee had urged Governor Letcher to assist the people with public funds (*O. R.*, 29, part 2, pp. 823–24).
[78] *O. R.*, 51, part 2, p. 761.
[79] *O. R.*, 29, part 2, p. 830; *cf. Pendleton*, 306: "The difficulty of feeding our animals where we have to meet the enemy is almost insuperable."
[80] *McCabe*, 432.

of ten pounds of corn and ten of long forage *per diem,* the horses often got only five pounds of corn and nothing besides. Sometimes only a little hay or unthreshed wheat or dry straw was available. The horses would eat the bark off trees, would gnaw through the trunks of the smaller forest growth and would devour empty bags, scraps of papers and all the small débris of the camp.[81] Lee's love of animals and his dependence on his transport for the execution of his plans alike prompted him to take such drastic relief measures as were in his power. All the forage in a large area was reserved for the army;[82] boards of officers were sent out in search of communities where the mounts could be kept alive;[83] most of the artillery was retired to the line of the Virginia Central Railroad;[84] the cavalry were scattered for miles beyond either flank;[85] detached cavalry forces were moved to more distant points in order that they might not consume forage within hauling distance of the army;[86] the farmers, by Lee's orders, were not allowed to retain more than six months' supply of corn for their animals.[87] Once, when he saw that the saddles of a cavalry command had slipped after the animals had climbed a long hill, he personally had them readjusted and, at the end of the march, sent for the officers and gave them a practical lecture on the care of the horses' backs.[88]

There was no misreading the ominous meaning of this slow starvation of the horses. All the apprehension that Lee had felt the previous winter over the prospective exhaustion of the horse-supply was now sharpened, because it was conceded that if the horses died they could not be replaced. As early as July, 1863, the quartermaster general had advised that 8000 to 10,000 animals were absolutely necessary to replace those killed or worn out,[89] but they could not be found east of the Mississippi. General Pendleton fostered a system of infirmaries[90] and saved many horses that would otherwise have died. The loss through hunger

---

[81] E. L. Wells: *Hampton and His Cavalry in '64* (cited hereafter as *Wells*), pp. 99-101.

[82] *O. R.,* 29, part 2, pp. 835–36.   [83] *O. R.,* 29, part 2, pp. 863–64.

[84] *Long,* 317.

[85] *O. R.,* 33, 1095, 1100, 1112; *R. E. Lee, Jr.,* 118.

[86] *O. R.,* 33, 1140; *O. R.,* 51, part 2, p. 814.   [87] *O. R.,* 51, part 2, p. 859.

[88] *Rosser, loc. cit.,* 12.   [89] IV *O. R.,* 2, 615–16.

[90] *O. R.,* 29, part 2, pp. 643, 697; *ibid.,* 33, 1182–83.

and disease was heavy, nonetheless.[91] Butler's brigade, which had received 2000 horses in a year, could not mount 500 men in February, yet could not be spared from the front to recruit either men or animals.[92] Longstreet had been unable to take all his batteries with him to Georgia for lack of horses to pull the guns,[93] and when the spring approached, General Bragg had to recommend that Lee's artillery be reduced for the same reason. "I have never found it too large in battle," Lee replied, though he expressed his willingness to weaken that arm if it should develop that the horses could not be provided.[94] Half of the animals in Stuart's horse artillery were reported to have died during the winter, and a reduction in the number of his batteries seemed inevitable.[95] Five days before the opening of Grant's offensive, May 4, 1864, Lee reported that he was unable to get the troops together for want of forage.[96]

To the burden of maintaining the army's morale and of finding food for its personnel and horses was added, all winter long, the labor of recruiting the ranks for the coming campaign. Lee accepted as final the statement of President Davis after Gettysburg that he saw no means of raising the army to the strength it had possessed before that battle.[97] The General saw his forces reduced by the departure of Longstreet's corps, then raised to around 48,000 men during the months from October through December by the return of the wounded, and then diminished again by furloughs and detachments to around 35,000 at the middle of February.[98] When conditions were at the worst, the absentees from the Second Corps alone numbered 11,610, including prisoners of war.[99]

---

[91] Cf. O. R., 33, 1174. [92] O. R., 33, 1153, 1154, 1163, 1164.
[93] O. R., 29, part 2, p. 719. [94] O. R., 33, 1285–86.
[95] R. E. Lee to J. E. B. Stuart, April 23, 1864; H. B. McClellan MSS.
[96] Jones, L. and L. 305. [97] See supra, p. 163.
[98] The reports are not complete, but the following are the totals of officers and men present for duty at intervals during the winter: Oct. 20, 37,052 (O. R., 29, part 1, p. 405); Oct. 30, 49,502 (O. R., 29, part 2, p. 811); Nov. 10, 48,586 (O. R., 29, part 1, p. 823); Dec. 10, 49,580 (O. R., 29, part 2, p. 866); Dec. 20, 48,991 (O. R., 29, part 2, p. 884); Dec. 31, 49,127 (O. R., 29, part 2, p. 898); Jan. 10, 1864, 46,908 (O. R., 33, 1075); Jan. 31, 38,614 (O. R., 33, 1135); Feb. 10, 33,991, excluding the artillery of the Second Corps and the troops in the Valley district (O. R., 33, 1157); Feb. 20, 41,395 (O. R., 33, 1191); March 10, 39,634 (O. R., 33, 1216); March 20, 47,405 (O. R., 33, 1233–34); April 10, 52,952 (O. R., 33, 1271); April 20, 54,344 (O. R., 33, 1297–98).
[99] O. R., 33, 1173.

Lee's chief hope of building up his army to effective fighting strength lay, of course, in procuring the return of the detached units, but he deferred any attempt to this end until March, because of the shortage of supplies.[100] His next hope was in a sterner policy of conscription that would bring into the ranks those who were still evading military duty. The second conscription act, which had been approved by the President September 27, 1862, just after the Maryland expedition, had raised the age limit of compulsory military service from thirty-five to forty-five years;[101] but this law had been much weakened by exemptions subsequently voted,[102] and its enforcement had led to a "dual system" under which General Gideon Pillow had undertaken what might be termed "enforced volunteering" for Bragg's army at the same time that the regular conscription officers were scouring the land.[103] By the winter of 1863–64, it was manifest that a more drastic statute and more vigorous enforcement were necessary. Lee threw all his influence on the side of universal compulsory service. "The law," he wrote the President, "should not be open to the charge of partiality, and I do not know how this can be accomplished, without embracing the whole population capable of bearing arms, with the most limited exemptions, avoiding anything that would look like a distinction of classes. The exemptions of persons of particular and necessary avocations had better be made as far as possible by authority of the department rather than by special enactment."[104] He was equally insistent that the law and the practice should be changed to make it impossible for a man subject to conscription to join some easy command and then to claim, tacitly at least, that he could not be sent to the armies that were seeing hard service. Instances of this sort had occurred when some of General Samuel Jones's troops had been dispatched to Lee after the Gettysburg campaign. Desertions among these men had been heavy because they regarded their call to the front as a breach of implied contract. The same reasoning by soldiers in the ranks had weakened Imboden's command. In South Carolina, it was notorious that very large cavalry

---

[100] O. R., 29, part 2, p. 910; O. R., 33, 1175.
[101] IV O. R., 2, 160.   [102] IV O. R., 2, 160–62, 456.
[103] A. B. Moore: Conscription and Conflict in the Confederacy, 191 ff.
[104] Nov. 29, 1863, O. R., 29, part 2, p. 853.

254

regiments had been recruited with privates of this mind, while the volunteer regiments from that state had been depleted by gallant fighting to mere *cadres*.[105]

These conditions were corrected to some extent by the third conscription act, approved on February 17, 1864, which lowered the age-limit to seventeen and raised it to fifty years, with the proviso that the oldest and youngest recruits should be organized for state defense.[106] Much stronger regulations concerning exemptions and disability were put into effect the next month.[107] Substitution was barred by another statute, and those who had hired substitutes were made liable to conscription.[108] There was hope that these measures would bring substantial reinforcements to the army, as it was estimated that 126,000 white men between eighteen and fifty-five years were still available in the South.[109]

Having done his utmost through official channels to have the law made more effective, Lee had to rely, for the rest, on careful administration of the army to increase its combatant strength. His steps to this end, falling into two general categories, showed much resourcefulness and exhibited the inflexible resolution he had displayed in so many other matters, to spare no effort to win Southern independence. His first measures, which took a wide diversity of form, were designed to prevent the wastage of the troops he had. He exercised great vigilance in declining to issue furloughs, except in accordance with the general policy he had laid down to send numbers of his men home in order to relieve the pressure on the commissary. Furloughs were refused to members of the Georgia legislature, who were commissioned officers in the army.[110] When war-worn Florida, Alabama and Texas troops sought permission to visit their native states and to recruit, he declined unequivocally, unless acceptable units, with the same number of men, were sent him in advance.[111] He refused extensions of leave in individual cases, even at the instance of such persuasive young friends as the brilliant Miss Belle Stewart of Brook Hill.[112]

---

105 *O. R.*, 33, 1085–86, 1091–92, 1097.
106 IV *O. R.*, 3, 178 *ff.*; A. B. Moore, *op. cit.*, 308.
107 IV *O. R.*, 3, 217 *ff.* 108 IV *O. R.*, 3, 11–12.   109 IV *O. R.*, 3, 103.
110 *O. R.*, 51, part 2, p. 781; 3 *Confederate Records of Georgia*, 488–89.
111 *O. R.*, 29, part 2, pp. 869–70, 885–86; *ibid.*, 33, 1133; IV *O. R.*, 3, 21–23.
112 R. E. Lee to Miss Belle Stewart, Feb. 27, 1864, *Bryan MSS.* Lee wrote of the application Miss Stewart made for a young friend: "I cannot extend the leave of absence . . . without interfering with the regular furloughs to others. We can only grant a

The policy of keeping down wastage from the ranks Lee applied, in the same way, to all details for detached duty, especially to those that placed soldiers near their homes, where they would be disposed to employ kinsmen as assistants.[113] He declined to detail men because their families had need of them, or because there were many brothers of the same family in the army. "It is impossible," he said, "to equalize the burdens of this war; some must suffer more than others." [114] He stopped promotion to the rank of junior second lieutenant soon after the Gettysburg campaign.[115] During the winter he sent examining boards of surgeons to the hospitals to bring back malingerers and able-bodied men acting as stewards.[116] He prevailed upon Congress to prohibit the formation of new companies of partisan rangers, because these were being recruited secretly from the infantry. When the law became operative, he was disposed to except only Mosby's command from its provisions.[117] Similarly, he protested against a proposal to organize a company of horse-artillery from within the enemy's lines, for use in southwest Virginia, on the ground that this would simply mean taking men from existing commands.[118] As a deterrent to men who sought easy posts, as well as to those who lost hope and courage, he had to maintain a stern policy toward deserters. Wherever possible he saved them from the death penalty, but he refused to deal with any of them until they had returned to the army.[119] Occasionally, he sent out parties to recover deserters.[120]

Direct recruitment and re-enlistment were Lee's second method of internal administration for the maintenance of his armed

limited number of leaves of absence, and a man must return before another can receive one. You see therefore the disappointment that would be created by interrupting the established rules." For examples of the manner in which the men waited for furloughs during the winter of 1863–64, see diary of Captain R. E. Park in 26 *S. H. S. P.*, pp. 28–30.

[113] *O. R.*, 33, 1311.

[114] *O. R.*, 33, 1256.   [115] *O. R.*, 51, part 2, pp. 756–57.

[116] *O. R.*, 33, 1173–74, 1196; IV *O. R.*, 3, 158–59.

[117] *O. R.*, 33, 1081, 1083, 1252; IV *O. R.*, 3, 194; *Lee's Dispatches*, 131 *ff.*

[118] *O. R.*, 33, 1120. To illustrate the seriousness of this situation, Lee told the Secretary of War that he had received the resignation of a captain who retired because only two of the thirty-four men on his roll were present for duty. Fourteen had deserted and three had left to join other commands. Among those who had done this was a lieutenant, absent without leave.

[119] *O. R.*, 29, part 2, pp. 806, 820, *ibid.*, 33, 1187–88; *ibid.*, 51, part 2, pp. 781–82; *Lee's Dispatches*, 149 *ff.*

[120] *O. R.*, 33, 1063, 1269.

strength. Taking care not to interfere with the regular work of conscription, he offered a thirty-day furlough to every private soldier who procured an able-bodied recruit—as great a stimulus as could have been applied.[121] Every voluntary re-enlistment for the war by commands whose time had expired under the law, he commended in general orders.[122] General Hoke and his brigade were retained in North Carolina for a time on recruiting duty;[123] General Imboden was named as chief enrolling officer for a large district, under the conscription law, while discharging his other duties;[124] days were spent in efforts to recruit the cavalry, especially the South Carolina regiments.[125] Everywhere that Lee could find a recruit, he sought to bring him into the ranks. Even the guards at Camp Lee in Richmond were called up, and their places were taken by boys and old men.[126] The only exception he made was in the case of the cadets at the Virginia Military Institute. He declined their tender of service with the statement that he wished them to guard the "western frontier" and would call them if needed—a measure of precaution that ere the campaign was well under way saved the day at New Market.[127] Every soldier in the camps and every dweller in the war zone knew how Lee was searching for men. In the Cole home, which Lee often visited, the little boy of the household, sitting on his knee, announced that he intended to raise a company. Who, asked Lee—it was a familiar question in his mind—who were to be in the company? "I haven't thought of that yet," the lad replied, "will you be one?" "Yes," said Lee, "I'll be glad to." [128]

Labor was ceaseless in keeping up the spirit of the men, in finding food for them, in saving the horses from starvation, and in trying to fill the ranks. No campaign wore on Lee with greater severity than did the cruel winter of 1863–64. Every resource of mind, all his physical energy, and all the character he had built up through his years of self-control he threw into the struggle to keep his army in condition to fight. Reviewing some of his

[121] O. R., 33, 1059; W. S. White in *Richmond Howitzers Battalion*, 239.
[122] *Cf. O. R.*, 33, 1144, 1152, 1173, 1212.
[123] O. R., 33, 1160–61.   [124] O. R., 33, 1281; 2 R. W. C. D., 197.
[125] O. R., 27, part 2, p. 1068; O. R., 33, 1118–19, 1125, 1185–86, 1214, 1231; O. R., 51, part 2, p. 1231; 2 R. W. C. D., 135.
[126] 2 R. W. C. D., 187.   [127] O. R., 51, part 2, p. 875.
[128] C. C. Cole to the writer, Dec. 12, 1932.

correspondence, his son wrote, "One can see from these letters of my father how deeply he felt for the sufferings of his soldiers, and how his plans were hindered by inadequate supplies of food and clothing. I heard him constantly allude to these troubles; indeed, they seemed never absent from his mind." [129] He knew that success depended on calling out the full resources of the country.[130] Determined to do his utmost to that end, he did not permit himself to think what might happen if the country was unwilling to make the necessary sacrifices. That he left to God. Submissive, though determined, he did not quail, even when he read that Lincoln had called for 700,000 new troops in March. Seven hundred thousand . . . and the Army of Northern Virginia could not hope to muster 65,000 when Meade crossed the Rapidan!

[129] *R. E. Lee, Jr.,* 111.   [130] *O. R.,* 29, part 2, p. 1128.

CHAPTER XV

Preparing for the Campaign of 1864

As the end of the winter of 1863–64 approached, Lee began to shape his plan for active operations. He could no longer be guided exclusively by what was desirable in Virginia from the standpoint of strategy. Instead, he had to consider what was practicable with his reduced supplies and weakened transport; and even within these limits he had to adapt his scheme of operations to the increasing threat of a Federal invasion of Georgia. Although nothing of military importance, except a raid on Meridian, Miss., had occurred since Johnston had taken command of the Army of Tennessee, the outlook was dark. Johnston with a badly equipped army was at Dalton, Ga.; Longstreet was cut off from him and was wintering most unhappily in east Tennessee. Opposing these two, the Federals had at hand three strong armies so placed that they could easily be concentrated for an advance into Georgia.

How could this dangerous invasion be prevented? No question troubled the administration more, and on none was there a sharper division of opinion. Johnston did not believe he should take the offensive until he was reinforced and supplied with more transportation.[1] Longstreet, after some weeks of virtual despair, concluded that the Confederate armies must advance or be overwhelmed. The administration was for an aggressive policy but was unwilling to strip other parts of the Confederacy of their defenders in order to swell Johnston's ranks. Lee was too busy with the problems of his own army to make a full study of the strategic involvements in Tennessee, and as General Bragg was now chief military adviser to the President,[2] Lee's inclination

---

[1] A good summary of Johnston's views appears in *O. R.*, 32, part 3, p. 839.

[2] He had been named Feb. 24, 1864, "under the direction of the president" to assume "charge of military operations in the armies of the Confederacy" (*O. R.*, 33, 1196)—the vexatious office that Lee had held from March through May, 1862. From the time Lee took command of the Army of Northern Virginia until the date of Bragg's appointment, the position had been vacant, though Davis considered that Lee was more or less on detached duty and was still his principal adviser (*O. R.*, 51, part 2, p. 750).

against volunteering advice to his superiors was stiffened by military etiquette. Moreover, he had heard nothing directly from Johnston and did not know the exact condition of the Army of Tennessee. His chief contact with the situation was through Longstreet, who wrote him often and at length. Longstreet's first proposal was that he be recalled to Lee, that one corps of the army be mounted, and that it be thrown in rear of Meade.[3] Lee pointed out that this was impracticable, and urged that Johnston and Longstreet attack the Federals.[4] There followed an exchange of letters in which Longstreet asked for sufficient horses to mount his corps and to operate in Kentucky against the Federals' line of communication. Lee thought that an advance into Kentucky would be desirable, but explained that the horses could not be supplied without rendering immobile the other armies of the Confederacy.[5] Longstreet then advanced the remarkable proposal that Lee hold Richmond with part of his troops, take the rest to Kentucky, open an offensive there and leave Johnston free to move to Virginia.[6] At this stage of the correspondence, Lee went to Richmond and there learned that the administration favored joint operations by Johnston and Longstreet in middle Tennessee. Lee had apprehensions whether the country would supply sufficient food and forage for this move, but he commended the plan to the study of Longstreet.[7] A few days later, Longstreet arrived at Lee's headquarters and unfolded still another plan—that Beauregard be sent to join the First Corps and that these forces execute the proposed offensive into Kentucky.

This appealed to Lee as more feasible, and inasmuch as President Davis had written to Longstreet inviting suggestions,[8] Lee urged that Longstreet take train to Richmond and present the proposal to the chief executive. Longstreet, however, argued that he was out of favor with the administration and that his authorship would of itself prejudice the government against his project.[9] It would be far better, he said, if Lee put forward the plan. Lee would

---

[3] *O. R.*, 32, 541.   [4] *O. R.*, 32, part 2, p. 566.

[5] *O. R.*, 32, part 2, pp. 654, 760, 789, 809; *ibid.*, part 3, pp. 582, 594–95.

[6] *O. R.*, 32, part 3, p. 582.

[7] *O. R.*, 32, part 3, pp. 594–95. Lee did not state in this letter that the proposal came from the administration, but the information he gave as to the alleged resources of middle Tennessee could not have been derived from any other source available to him.

[8] 6 *Rowland's Davis*, 199 ff.; *cf. supra*, p. 228.   [9] *Longstreet*, 544.

not, of course, parade another's scheme as his own, but he agreed to go to Richmond with Longstreet and to present the question to the President. He made the journey about March 10,[10] and after a quiet Sunday of church attendance and conversation with his family, he called on the President Monday morning, March 14. For this first interview he went alone, probably because he had not procured in advance the President's permission to bring Longstreet with him. There is no record of what happened at this meeting. After dinner, he returned with Longstreet and discussed the situation in the West in much detail but arrived at no conclusion. Longstreet later wrote an account of this council in which he represented General Lee as much disgusted at the insistence of the President and General Bragg on a campaign into middle Tennessee. Johnston was known to be in opposition, and Bragg himself, after Chickamauga, had pronounced such a movement visionary.[11] It is quite probable that Longstreet's zeal for his own plan led him to exaggerate Lee's disappointment at its rejection, for it is of record that if a way could be found to overcome the shortage of provisions Lee as late as April 2 was in favor of the operation in middle Tennessee.[12] His inclination throughout was to defer to the judgment of General Johnston who was on the ground and, as Lee said, could "better compare the difficulties existing to a forward movement with the disadvantages of remaining quiet." [13]

After these conferences, Lee spent a few days in Richmond with his family.[14] He found Mrs. Lee and her daughters diligently knitting socks for the soldiers. Not content with what the household could do, Mrs. Lee enlisted the service of all her regular visitors. "Her room," Mrs. Chesnut wrote, "was like an

---

[10] He was at headquarters March 9 (*O. R.*, 33, 1212), though a misdated letter in the *Taylor MSS.* stated that he was in Richmond on the 8th. He was certainly there on March 13, for Mrs. Chesnut saw him at church (*Mrs. Chesnut*, 299). She wrongly dated this March 12.

[11] Longstreet, *op. cit.*, 546, wrote that Lee pulled at his beard "nervously and more vigorously as time and silence grew, until at last his suppressed emotion was conquered. The profound quiet of a minute or more seemed an hour. When he spoke it was of other matters, but the air was troubled by his efforts to surrender hopeful anticipations to the caprice of empirics. He rose to take leave of the august presence, gave his hand to the President and bowed himself out of the council chamber. His assistant went through the same forms, and no one approached the door to offer parting courtesy."

[12] *O. R.*, 32, part 3, pp. 736–37.   [13] *O. R.*, 32, part 3, p. 737.

[14] 2 *R. W. C. D.*, 172. Mrs. McGuire, *op. cit.*, 255, noted that he was in attendance at the 7 o'clock morning Lenten services in the basement of St. Paul's.

industrial school: Everybody so busy." [15] The family had more space for these activities, because it had moved from 210 East Leigh to "The Mess," a large house, now numbered 707 East Franklin, that had been used previously by Custis and some of his fellow staff officers.[16] Rooney had at last been exchanged and had come home, almost broken-hearted over Charlotte's death, but not embittered by his imprisonment. He was quick to assert that despite the popular hatred of General B. F. Butler he had received the utmost consideration at the hands of that officer.[17] It took no small effort on the part of General Lee to get his son to pull himself together again and to resume his military duties.[18] Custis's state of mind was much the same: anxious for field duty, he still had scruples about undertaking it without experience. He was offered command of the Department of Richmond, long under the direction of Major General Arnold Elzey, but he hesitated to accept it. His father thought he should do so. "I appreciate the motives," he said. "But until you come in the field you never will gain experience." [19] Finding Custis unwilling to put aside his compunctions, Lee decided to ask for him as chief of engineers of the Army of Northern Virginia; but when he delicately presented two other names besides that of Custis, the Secretary of War passed over Custis and sent him Major General M. L. Smith,[20] a seasoned and very capable officer who was to prove most useful. Custis's own inclination was to come to his father as chief of staff, but the General would not approve. "This would be very agreeable to me," he said, "but more open to all the objections that could be brought against your holding the post of chief of engineers. I presume, therefore, it would not be favorably considered. It is a delicate matter to apply for any one on the staff of another. I am not certain that it is proper to

---

[15] *Mrs. Chesnut*, 292.

[16] The fullest account of life at "The Mess" is that by Mrs. Sally Nelson Robins in *Brock*, 322 *ff*. Mrs. Robins was wrong in the date she gave for the Lees' occupancy of the house but she preserved many charming stories of what happened there. The move from 210 E. Leigh was probably made about Jan. 1, 1864. On Dec. 22, 1863, Lee wrote of the "proposed change of residence" and urged his wife to occupy "Custis's room," presumably the front bed-chamber on the second floor, or the "back room down stairs," known in Virginia as the "back parlor" (Lee to Mrs. Lee, *Duke Univ. MSS.*).

[17] The order for Rooney's exchange was dated Feb. 25, 1864 (II *O. R.*, 6, 991). He was in Richmond before March 14 (2 *R. W. C. D.*, 170). For the case of the men in retaliation for whose treatment he had been threatened with death, see II *O. R.*, 7, 119. Mrs. Chesnut (*op. cit.*, 300) is authority for stating that Butler was kind to Rooney Lee.

[18] *Jones*, 401.   [19] Jones, *L. and L.*, 303.   [20] *O. R.*, 33, 1245, 1265, 2187.

ask for one serving with the President. In addition it is more important that he should have the aid he desires than I should." [21] While careful about Custis's military correctness, General Lee continued, at the young man's expense, to indulge in his favorite jest of marrying him off. In sending a pass about this time to Miss Jennie Washington for herself and her sisters, who had been sojourning at Charlottesville, he assured her: "Custis bears up wonderfully under the circumstances. He hopes he has only to wait until six months after the declaration of peace when all public dues are to be paid." [22]

Back in the sombre camps on the Rapidan, after his stay in Richmond, Lee thought for a few days that the heaviest shock of battle was to come in Tennessee,[23] but by March 28 he concluded that the blow would fall in Virginia.[24] Signs multiplied that the Federals were accumulating a large force in his front,[25] and Longstreet telegraphed from Bristol that the IX Corps was coming eastward.[26] Lee began to call for his detached units, but was willing to have Longstreet remain in Tennessee if there was a chance of an offensive there. As it became increasingly probable that the Unionists were detaching troops from the western army for use in Virginia, Lee reasoned that this might give Johnston a better opportunity for aggressive action, even though Longstreet was recalled to the Army of Northern Virginia.[27] "They cannot collect the large force they mention for their operations against Richmond without reducing their other armies"—such was his calm statement to the President.[28] The administration took his view of the changed situation and on April 7 ordered Longstreet to return from Bristol, Va.–Tenn., to Charlottesville to await Lee's orders, though the lack of rail transportation made it uncertain when his movement could begin.[29]

[21] Jones, L. and L., 304. This was on April 9, three weeks after Lee's return to the army.

[22] R. E. Lee to Miss Jennie Charlotte Washington, April 2, 1864, MS., placed at the writer's disposal through the kindness of Miss Eliza W. Willis, daughter of Mrs. Nathaniel H. Willis, formerly Miss Jennie Washington.

[23] O. R., 32, part 3, p. 595, Lee's Dispatches, 141; Maurice, 226.

[24] Lee to Davis, April 2, 1864, Duke Univ. MSS.; O. R., 52, part 2, pp. 648–49.

[25] R. E. Lee to Margaret Stuart, March 29, 1864, R. E. Lee, Jr., 123; O. R., 33, 1244.

[26] O. R., 32, part 3, p. 720.   [27] O. R., 32, part 3, p. 736; ibid., 1244, 1254–55.

[28] April 5, 1864; O. R., 33, 1260–61.

[29] O. R., 32, part 3, p. 756; ibid., 51, part 2, pp. 1076–77. For the dates of Longstreet's successive movements, see O. R., 36, part 1, p. 1054.

Lee's balancing of the ponderables on the military scales was accurate. He could not realize, and few even in Washington could see, that an imponderable was tipping the beam. That imponderable was the influence of President Lincoln. The Richmond government had discounted his every moderate utterance and had capitalized his emancipation proclamation in order to stiffen Southern resistance. The Confederate people had mocked him, had despised him, and had hated him. Lee himself, though he had avoided unworthy personal animosities and doubtless had included Mr. Lincoln in his prayers for all his enemies, had made the most of the President's military blunders and fears. References to Lincoln in Lee's correspondence and conversation were rare. He was much more interested in the Federal field-commanders than in the commander-in-chief. After the late winter of 1863–64, had Lee known all the facts, he would have given as much care to the study of the mind of the Federal President as to the analysis of the strategical methods of his immediate adversaries. For that remarkable man, who had never wavered in his purpose to preserve the Union, had now mustered all his resources of patience and of determination. Those who had sought cunningly to lead him, slowly found that he was leading them. His unconquerable spirit, in some mysterious manner, was being infused into the North as spring approached.

By April 3, Lee commenced to bring up the strongest horses, to reduce transportation, and to make preparations for meeting the large army the Federals were mustering. The Northern states were responding whole-heartedly to the calls sent out in March for 700,000 men.[30] Ulysses S. Grant, a soldier equipped with abilities that complemented Lincoln's, had been brought from the West, had been named lieutenant general and had been placed in command of all the Union armies.[31] The prospect stirred Lee. "Colonel," he told Taylor, that officer having now been promoted, "we have got to whip them; we must whip them, and it has already made me better to think of it." Taylor added, in reporting this conversation to his sweetheart, that Lee had been "complaining somewhat" and it seemed to do him good to look forward to a test with "the present idol of the North." [32] His

[30] III O. R., 4, 59, 181.
[32] Taylor MSS., April 3, 1864.
[31] 2 Grant's Memoirs, 114.

wish was not immediately gratified, however, for there followed a long rainy spell that transformed the roads into mires. The enemy could not move, of course, until the highways dried, though there was every prospect that as soon as the ground was firm, Grant would cross the river.[33] Meantime, conflicting intelligence reached headquarters as to whether the XI and XII Corps were returning to the Army of the Potomac and if so, whether they were moving directly toward the Rapidan, or were gathering at Annapolis, Md., for some undetermined purpose.[34]

Lee studied with the utmost care the reports that came from his spies during this period of waiting, and on April 16 he was satisfied that three attacks were in the making—a main assault across the Rapidan, a diversion in the Valley of Virginia, and an attack on the flank or rear of the Army of Northern Virginia, probably directed against Drewry's Bluff on James River, so as to expose the water-line of Richmond.[35]

How could this greatest offensive of the war be met? Lee believed that much might still be accomplished by aggressive Confederate action in the West,[36] but from the beginning of the discussion of the next move in Tennessee, he had argued that the alternative to this was an advance in Virginia against Meade.[37] "We are not in a condition," he told the President, "and never have been, in my opinion, to invade the enemy's country with a prospect of permanent benefit. But we can alarm and embarrass him to some extent, and thus prevent his undertaking anything of magnitude against us."[38] His judgment now told him that the prudent course was to bring Beauregard's army to defend Richmond and to hasten the movement of Longstreet's corps, which was moving very slowly from Bristol. This done, he desired to "move right against the enemy on the Rappahannock," as he phrased it to the President. He went on: "Should God give us a crowning victory there, all their plans would be dissipated, and their troops now collecting on the waters of the Chesapeake would be recalled to the defense of Washington."

[33] *Pendleton*, 319, 323; *James A. Graham Papers*, 186; O. R., 33, 1273.

[34] O. R., 33, 1267, 1268–69, 1290–91.

[35] O. R., 33, 1276, 1282–83. O. R., 51, part 2, p. 865. It is scarcely necessary to point out that the plan Lee anticipated was precisely the one the Federals had formulated.

[36] O. R., 33, 1320–21.

[37] O. R., 32, part 2, p. 760; *ibid.*, 33, 1185.   [38] O. R., 33, 1144.

Regretfully he had to add: "But to make this move I must have provisions and forage. I am not yet able to call to me the cavalry or artillery. If I am obliged to retire from this line, either by a flank movement of the enemy or the want of supplies, great injury will befall us. I have ventured to throw out these suggestions to Your Excellency in order that in surveying the whole field of operations you may consider all the circumstances bearing on the question. Should you determine it is better to divide this army and fall back toward Richmond I am ready to do so. I, however, see no better plan for the defence of Richmond than that I have proposed." [39] His confidence in his veterans was not at all shaken by the strength of the Army of the Potomac or by the prestige of General Grant. If the flanking movement against Richmond could be successfully met, he said quietly, "I have no uneasiness as to the result of the campaign in Virginia." [40]

The offensive if practicable, the defensive if inevitable—between these courses the government had to decide, and decide not only according to its judgment of the strategic situation but also according to its ability to supply the army. Johnston was still unprepared to take the offensive in the West; the danger to Richmond from the East was increasing, while the threat against Charleston was neither more nor less formidable than before; the commissary could do little for the soldiers and the quartermaster general even less for the horses. Thus circumstanced, the embarrassed administration had to compromise. Longstreet's slow movement from Bristol to Charlottesville was continued to Gordonsville,[41] so that he would be available as a reserve in case of an attack on Richmond from the east.[42] Beauregard was hurried northward with part of his troops, and was put in charge of all the forces between the James and the Cape Fear Rivers.[43]

On the 18th, Lee issued orders to send back all surplus baggage and to prepare for movement at any time,[44] for there seemed no reason to doubt the earlier conclusion that Grant was only waiting for the ground to dry.[45] Hourly thereafter, ears were strained

[39] O. R., 33, 1282–83. These views he repeated the next day in a similar letter to General Bragg (O. R., 33, 1284–85).
[40] O. R., 33, 1290–91.   [41] O. R., 33, 1286.   [42] O. R., 33, 1326.
[43] O. R., 33, 1307–8; ibid., 35, part 2, pp. 448–49. Beauregard assumed command at Weldon, N. C., April 23.
[44] Welch, 90. For the reduction of baggage, etc., see O. R., 33, 1262.
[45] O. R., 51, part 2, p. 869; Taylor MSS., April 18, 1864.

for the opening gun; but on the 25th Lee decided that for some undiscovered reason the enemy's advance was temporarily held up.[46] He regarded this as an advantage to Southern arms, because in a few days there would be enough grass to supply the animals temporarily and thereby to make a general concentration possible.[47]

Finding the enemy still inactive on the 29th, Lee hurried to Gordonsville and reviewed Longstreet's corps, which, though reduced in numbers and sadly in need of refitting,[48] seemed to have preserved all its old fighting spirit. "General Lee must have felt good in getting the welcome extended to him by those who had been lost to him so long," one private wrote. "The men hung around him and seemed satisfied to lay their hands on his gray horse or to touch the bridle, or the stirrup, or the old general's leg—anything that Lee had was sacred to us fellows who had just come back. And the General—he could not help from breaking down . . . tears traced down his cheeks, and he felt that we were again to do his bidding." [49]

Returning to Orange, he urged the President to send forward those units of his army that were still in the rear,[50] and then he waited quietly for the enemy to cross the river. When the band of the Twenty-sixth North Carolina came to serenade him, he took its colonel into his tent and, as he discussed coming operations, expressed only the hope that he could strike the enemy with his centre so that he could reinforce his attack from either flank.[51]

On the morning of May 2, he climbed once again—and for the last time—to the observation post on Clark's Mountain, and after studying with his glasses the location of the corps spread out beneath him, and the rolling fields of Culpeper, he told his companions that the enemy's crossing would be at Ely's or at Germanna[52]—the fords that led into the Wilderness where the ghost

---

[46] *Lee's Dispatches,* 166–67; *O. R.,* 33, 1320–21.

[47] *Lee's Dispatches,* 166–67.   [48] *O. R.,* 33, 1320–21.

[49] F. M. Mixson: *Reminiscences of a Private* (cited hereafter as *Mixson*), 65.

[50] Lee to Custis Lee, April 30, 1864, 30 *Confederate Veteran,* 124; *Lee's Dispatches,* 167–68. He had called up the First Engineers on April 12 (*O. R.,* 33, 1278). For the discussion over the organization of these troops, see *O. R.,* 27, part 2, pp. 1017, 1020.

[51] G. C. Underwood: *History of the Twenty-Sixth North Carolina,* 97. Lee told Colonel Lane, the regiment's commander, "I don't believe we can have an army without music."

[52] 4 *B. and L.,* 119; *cf.* 3 *C. M. H.,* 431; *O. R.,* 36, part 1, p. 1070; *ibid.,* part 2, pp. 942–43.

of "Stonewall" Jackson walked. The landscape below him was much as it had been when he had first ascended Clark's Mountain in August, 1862, but the military outlook was far different. Then there had been reserves of men and of food behind him; now there were neither. His it had been in '62 to plan how he would fall upon the foe; now he must exert himself to checkmate the enemy's advance. Yet he knew he could count on the valor of those who, since that August day, had fought the bloodiest battles that ever drenched America. The morale of the army, which had been high throughout the winter,[53] was now at its finest fighting pitch. "Never," wrote Colonel Taylor, "was [the army] in better trim than now. There is no overweening confidence, but a calm, firm and positive determination to be victorious, with God's help."[54]

The spirit of the army was the spirit of its leader. He was as surely the captain of his soul that day on Clark's Mountain as ever he had been in his life. "You must sometimes cast your thoughts on the Army of Northern Virginia," he told one of his young cousins, "and never forget it in your prayers. It is preparing for a great struggle, but I pray and trust that the great God, mighty to deliver, will spread over it His almighty arms, and drive its enemies before it."[55] And to his son he wrote: "Our country demands all our strength, all our energies. To resist the powerful combination now forming against us will require every man at his place. If victorious, we have everything to hope for in the future. If defeated, nothing will be left for us to live for. . . . My whole trust is in God, and I am ready for whatever He may ordain."

In that spirit he came down from the mountain.

53 *Cf. Welch,* 86, Jan. 16, 1864: "I believe if we whip the Yankees good again this year they will quit in disgust." *Taylor MSS.,* Feb. 23, 1864: "The army was never in better spirits, its morale is unsurpassed"; *ibid.,* March 20, 1864: "[Grant], if I mistake not, will shortly come to grief if he attempts to repeat the tactics in Virginia which proved so successful in Mississippi"; *ibid.,* April 18, 1864: "We are in a better condition and more hopeful than ever."
54 *Taylor MSS.,* April 24, 1864. Welch, *op. cit.,* 92, noted that the army believed Lee intended to act on the defensive. "It is said that he is full of confidence."
55 R. E. Lee *to* Margaret Stuart, April 28, 1864, *R. E. Lee, Jr.,* 123.

CHAPTER XVI

INTO THE WILDERNESS AGAIN

(MAY 4–5, 1864)

AT 9 o'clock on the morning of May 4, 1864, the flags on the signal station atop Clark's Mountain spelled out the message that was the beginning of the end of the Southern Confederacy: The great sea of tents that had flooded the fields around Culpeper had disappeared, and the enemy was streaming down the road that led by Stevensburg to Germanna and to Ely's Ford.[1] The campaign that many believed would be decisive was opening at last.[2]

As Lee was expecting that the enemy would move at any moment against his right flank, he lost no time in formulating plans or speculating on probabilities. Issuing the usual warning to the army to respect private property, he ordered A. P. Hill to leave R. H. Anderson's division to guard the approaches to the "Gordonsville loop" of the Virginia Central Railroad, with instructions to rejoin his corps as soon as it was certain that the enemy had disappeared from that front.[3] Ewell was directed to have Ramseur's brigade cover the lower crossings of the Rapidan.[4] The rest of Ewell's and Hill's corps, Lee promptly ordered east-

[1] 3 *C. M. H.*, 433; *O. R.*, 36, part 1, p. 1054. It is proper to observe in this first note on the Wilderness campaign that the *Official Records* contain only a small number of Confederate reports for the period from May 4, 1864, to the close of the war in Virginia. No general report by Lee survives, though Jones remarked in 14 *S. H. S. P.*, 568, that such a document was prepared on the operations from the Rapidan to the James, and that the original draft was then in the possession of Colonel Charles Marshall. In the absence of any general narrative by the army commander, the Southern story of the campaign has to be reconstructed from three major sources, viz., Lee's brief telegrams to the President and to the Secretary of War, the few subordinate reports that were filed, and the correspondence in the *Official Records*. Fortunately, the authorities for this period are quite numerous and, in many instances, are of prime historical importance.

[2] *Cf. Taylor MSS.*, May 1, 1864: "I am deeply impressed with the vast importance of success in this campaign. . . . The beginning of the end is, I believe, at hand. . . . Never did matters look so bright for us."

[3] Venable in 14 *S. H. S. P.*, 523. Special attention is directed to Colonel Venable's monograph. Written in 1873 by one of the best-informed of Lee's staff officers, it is perhaps the most valuable brief Confederate account of the long struggle from the Rapidan to the James. For the orders regarding private property, see *O. R.*, 36, part 2, p. 946. These orders were reiterated for the wagon-trains, May 23, *ibid.*, 36, part 3, p. 826.

[4] *O. R.*, 36, part 1, p. 1081.

ward to meet the enemy's advance. Longstreet, who had one division at Mechanicsville, five miles south of Gordonsville, and a second division north of Gordonsville, was told to start at once and to move to Todd's Tavern, where he could form the Confederate right.[5] General Bragg was urged to return Longstreet's other division immediately. This division was Pickett's, then on duty around Richmond.[6]

When the feeble wagons had been packed with the scant baggage and the still scanter supplies of the army, Lee started along the familiar Plank road with Hill's corps. Ewell took the parallel route of the turnpike or "old stone road" nearer the Rapidan.[7] The ranks of neither corps were full. With Anderson left behind, Hill had only two divisions, though both were somewhat larger than most of those in the army. Together they numbered around 14,500 muskets.[8] Ewell lacked no complete division but had two brigades and one regiment on detached service, in addition to Ramseur's brigade.[9] The Second Corps consequently had on the march about 13,500 infantry.[10] Besides these 28,000 men, Lee had in the two corps perhaps 4000 artillery. In scattered units over a large territory, he could count about 8400 cavalry, though it was questionable whether the horses could stand the strain of open campaigning. In case he met the enemy's main force before the arrival of Longstreet or Anderson, he would have only three full divisions of infantry—Heth's, Wilcox's, and Johnson's—and parts of two others, Rodes's and Early's. When Longstreet came up and Anderson rejoined, Lee would muster of all arms between 61,000 and 65,000,[11] with 213 guns.[12] In discipline and experience, the

[5] Cf. Longstreet, 556. Field's division had been moved north to Gordonsville on May 2 to meet a possible Federal advance around the Confederate left (O. R., 36, part 1, p. 1054).
[6] O. R., 51, part 2, p. 887. Pickett's division had been in bad condition (O. R., 29, part 2, pp. 773–74) and had not recovered its old morale as late as May 28 (O. R., 36, part 3, p. 844).
[7] As early as 1834, the author of Letters on the Virginia Springs (Philadelphia, 1835) had found this road "in bad repair and rough, but not dangerous" (p. 12).
[8] Cf. Wilcox in Annals of the War, 493.
[9] R. D. Johnston's brigade of Rodes's division was at Hanover Junction; the Twenty-first Georgia, Doles's brigade, Rodes's division, and Hoke's brigade, Early's division, were still in North Carolina (O. R., 36, part 1, pp. 1069–70).
[10] Ibid.
[11] Webb (4 B. and L., 152) and Humphreys (The Virginia Campaign of 1864 and 1865, p. 14, cited hereafter as Humphreys), put the strength of Lee's army, on the opening of the campaign, at 61,953; Taylor, in his Four Years, estimated it at 64,000; Longstreet (op. cit., 552), figured 65, 405.
[12] O. R., 36, part 1, pp. 1036 ff.

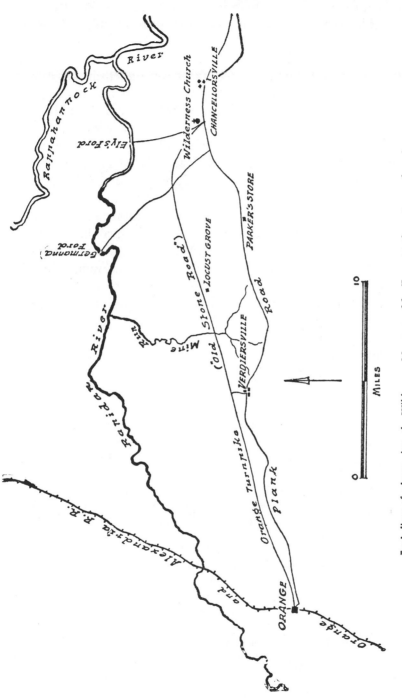

Lee's lines of advance into the Wilderness, May 4–5, 1864 (Longstreet's route not shown).

combat-force was better than it had ever been. Sickness was negligible,[13] despite the fact that the rations barely sufficed to sustain
life.[14] In leadership, it was very different from the army that had
fought at Chancellorsville or at Gettysburg. Both Longstreet's
divisions were led by men who had never served in that capacity
under Lee: At the head of McLaws's old troops was Brigadier
General J. B. Kershaw, of South Carolina, an able soldier, and
over Hood's division was Major General Charles Field. This
officer was to acquit himself creditably, though he lacked the tre-
mendous driving force that had distinguished Hood, now commanding a corps under Johnston. Three of Kershaw's brigadiers
were new, as were two of Field's.[15] In the Second Corps, the three
major generals were the same, Early, Johnson, and Rodes, but
four of the brigadiers had risen to that grade since the Gettysburg
campaign.[16] In the Third Corps, Wilcox was about to fight his
first major battle as division commander in succession to Pender.
The commanders of his brigades were unchanged. Heth, however, had three brigadiers who had not held like rank at Gettysburg, though two of them had shared in the unhappy affair at
Bristoe Station.[17] In Anderson's division there were two new
brigade commanders.[18] Most of these recently commissioned
general officers were capable men, and if some of them were
lacking in experience, Lee had full assurance that their soldiers
were not.

Lee did not know the strength of the adversary against whom
he was advancing. His scouts had reported that the enemy had
75,000 men and would move with 100,000,[19] but Lee did not

---

[13] *Welch,* 91–92.   [14] *Cf.* 3 *B. and L.,* 230.

[15] Colonel John W. Henagan, formerly of the Eighth South Carolina, headed Ker-
shaw's brigade; Barksdale's famous troops had been entrusted to Brigadier General B. G.
Humphreys; over Semmes's brigade, as noted, was Brigadier General Goode Bryan. In
Field's division, the Texas brigade was led by the valiant John Gregg. Micah Jenkins had
a new brigade consisting of the 1st, 2d, 5th, and 6th South Carolina and the Palmetto
Sharpshooters.

[16] John Pegram had William Smith's brigade, somewhat enlarged; Leroy A. Stafford
commanded the Louisiana brigade previously under General Nicholls; Robert D. Johnston had Iverson's former command; and Cullen A. Battle had wisely been assigned to the
Alabama troops with which Rodes had won his fame.

[17] W. W. Kirkland, who had Pettigrew's old brigade, John R. Cooke, and H. H.
Walker, who headed Brockenbrough's troops.

[18] Abner Perrin, who had been given the brigade of Wilcox upon the promotion of
that officer, and N. H. Harris, who, as already stated, had succeeded to Posey's command
after that officer had died of his wounds.

[19] *O. R.,* 33, 1278–79.

think Grant's force exceeded 75,000[20] and he was skeptical concerning the reputed size of the army that was expected to make a flank attack on Richmond while Grant hammered on the line of the Rapidan and Rappahannock.[21] Lee was not certain, either, whether Grant would follow Meade's example, and turn southwest toward the Central Railroad after crossing the Rapidan, or would emulate Hooker and march to the southeast, against the line of the Richmond, Fredericksburg and Potomac below Fredericksburg.[22] If Grant moved toward the southwest, Lee could hold his old lines on Mine Run with a part of his force and manœuvre with the rest.[23] Should Grant advance to the southeast, he would have to pass through the Wilderness of Spotsylvania.

Lee strongly hoped and rather expected that this latter would be his opponent's line of advance.[24] He was conscious of the inferiority both of his numbers and of the weight and range of his artillery. His plan was to catch Grant on the march, where his numerical superiority would mean least. Especially was he anxious to engage the new Union commander in the tangle of the Wilderness, where the fine Federal ordnance could not be employed.[25] For these reasons, and also because it would be difficult to bring up a sufficient force in time to dispute the crossing of the Rapidan, Lee determined to leave Grant alone until he was on the south side of the river. Then he intended to attack him there, as soon as Longstreet came up.[26]

Maturing the details of this plan as he rode forward at the head of Hill's column on the Plank road,[27] Lee bivouacked in the

---

[20] *O. R.*, 33, 1290. Colonel Taylor computed it at 70,000 to 80,000. *Taylor MSS.*, May 1, 1864.

[21] *O. R.*, 36, part 1, p. 943. As a matter of fact, according to Humphreys (*op. cit.*, 14), Grant had 122,146, including the IX Corps, which was within supporting distance. Other estimates of Grant's strength, ranging from 116,886 to 127,247, are cited in *Longstreet*, 552. Fitz Lee (*op. cit.*, 327) pointed out that Grant could have manned a battlefront of thirty miles, two lines deep, whereas Lee could have covered only sixteen miles.

[22] *Lee's Dispatches*, 169 ff.

[23] *Cf. O. R.*, 36, part 2, p. 948, where Lee informed Ewell he would take up the line of Mine Run if the enemy operated in that direction.

[24] *Cf.* Lee to Bragg, *O. R.*, 51, part 2, p. 887, urging that Pickett's division be sent to Spotsylvania Courthouse. Lee would hardly have done this if he had not thought that Grant would move in that direction.

[25] *Lee's Dispatches*, 184; Henderson: *Science of War*, 317; *Maurice*, 228–29.

[26] Lee to W. S. Smith, July 27, 1868, *Jones*, 268; *Long*, 325–26; *O. R.*, 36, part 2, p. 948.

[27] 3 *C. M. H.*, 434.

woods opposite the Rhodes house at Verdiersville, where his headquarters had been during the Mine Run campaign.[28] Heth's division was encamped nearby, and Wilcox was in rear of Heth, having made the long march from a point six miles above Orange

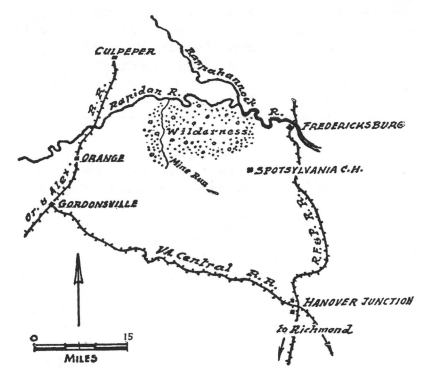

The Wilderness of Spotsylvania in relation to the railroads running to Richmond.

Courthouse.[29] Ewell's corps was at Locust Grove, on the old stone road, his advanced units about six miles northeast of Hill's.[30]

To Lee's camp fire in the woods, during the evening, couriers brought many messages, some encouraging and some disquieting. Davis telegraphed that reinforcements were on the way, though the first of them could hardly arrive within less than four days.[31] In another message, the President announced that a Federal force

[28]   36, part 2, p. 948. See *supra*, p. 196.
[29] Wilcox in *Annals of the War*, 488.
[30] *O. R.*, 36, part 1, p. 1070.   [31] *O. R.*, 51, part 2, p. 886.

GENERAL LEE WITH CERTAIN OFFICERS OF HIS PERSONAL STAFF AND OF THE
GENERAL STAFF OF THE ARMY OF NORTHERN VIRGINIA

After a photograph in the Confederate Museum, Richmond, Va.

LIEUTENANT GENERAL RICHARD STODDARD EWELL, SUCCESSOR TO
JACKSON IN COMMAND OF THE REDUCED SECOND CORPS OF THE
ARMY OF NORTHERN VIRGINIA

LIEUTENANT GENERAL AMBROSE P. HILL, PROMOTED AFTER CHANCEL-
LORSVILLE TO COMMAND THE NEWLY CREATED THIRD CORPS, ARMY
OF NORTHERN VIRGINIA

Hill was then 38, of a nervous temperament, quick and impetuous. He was a handsome man of middle height, with hair a reddish brown.

LIEUTENANT COLONEL WALTER H. TAYLOR

Assistant adjutant-general of the Army of Northern Virginia and, in 1864–65, its chief of staff in all but name. Colonel Taylor was only twenty-six when the war ended.

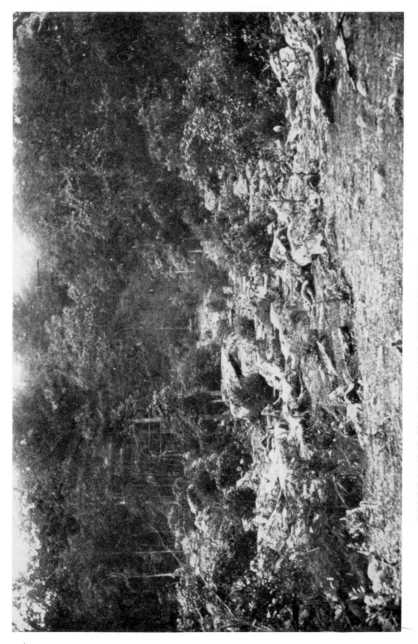

LITTLE ROUND TOP AFTER THE CONFEDERATE ATTACK OF JULY 2, 1863

The dead are almost indistinguishable from the rocks among which they fell.

THE MANNER OF MEN THAT LEE COMMANDED

Flanked on either side by armed Union guards, these prisoners of war were cavalrymen of the Army of Northern Virginia, captured shortly before the beginning of the Gettysburg campaign. Their diversity of apparel, ranging from complete uniform to simple civilian attire, was typical of the entire army after 1862.

WHAT LEE LEFT BEHIND AT GETTYSBURG

In this photograph, taken probably on July 5, after Lee had retreated, most of the dead are Union soldiers. Their shoes have been stripped from them and the pockets of some of them have been rifled.

THE PONTOON-BRIDGE AND FORD AT JERICHO MILLS, NORTH ANNA RIVER, TAKEN JUST AFTER WARREN'S CORPS HAD CROSSED, MAY 23, 1864

THE TOLL OF COLD HARBOR

The Negroes shown in this picture, some of them soldiers and some civilians, were engaged in April, 1865, in the re-burial of Federals killed in the bloody repulse of June 3, 1864.

THE TYPE OF RAILWAY ON WHICH LEE HAD TO RELY FOR SUPPLIES

This photograph was made in April, 1865, and shows Appomattox Station and its spur-track on the Southside Railroad, but nearly all the lines were in virtually the same worn condition as early as 1864.

PART OF THE INTERIOR OF FORT STEDMAN, TEMPORARILY CAPTURED BY THE COMMAND OF GENERAL
JOHN B. GORDON, MARCH 25, 1865

This work was typical of many fortifications on the Union lines around Petersburg. The gabions and fascines, topped with sandbags, were of the usual Federal construction. The chimney in the left centre is that of an officers' "bomb-proof," the nineteenth-century "dug-out." The pile of earth on the right is the cover of a powder-magazine.

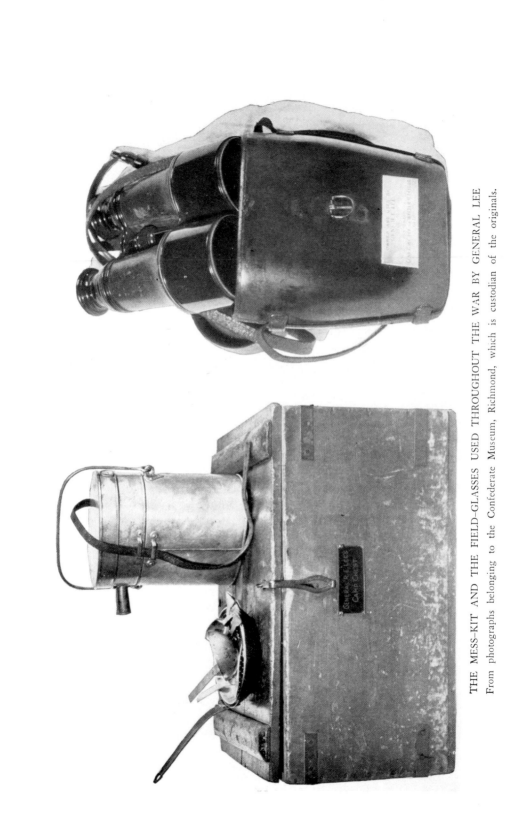

THE MESS-KIT AND THE FIELD-GLASSES USED THROUGHOUT THE WAR BY GENERAL LEE

From photographs belonging to the Confederate Museum, Richmond, which is custodian of the originals.

GENERAL LEE ON TRAVELLER AT THE TIME THE WAR WAS GOING AGAINST HIM

This photograph, taken at Petersburg in 1864, is the only known one of the war period that shows Lee on his most famous horse, though a picture of master and mount, made in 1866, has been widely circulated.

After the original at Washington and Lee University.

TITLE PAGE AND MRS. LEE'S INSCRIPTION IN GENERAL LEE'S PRAYER-BOOK

This book was used from 1846 until 1864 and then exchanged because the type was too small for him to read it easily. The most worn page in the book, marked by a small strip of paper, is that containing the Psalter for the thirtieth day—"Blessed be the Lord my strength: who teacheth my hands to war, and my fingers to fight" (Psalm 144).

From the original in the possession of Dr. Churchill G. Chamberlayne.

WHAT THE WAR DID TO MRS. LEE

This photograph of Mrs. Lee bears a United States revenue stamp of 1865 and probably was taken in Richmond during the winter of 1864–65 when the strain on her was at its worst. She was fifty-six in October, 1864.

"THE MESS," FORMER RESIDENCE OF CUSTIS LEE AND OTHER OFFICERS, USED BY MRS. R. E. LEE AS HER RICHMOND HOME FROM APPROXIMATELY JANUARY 1, 1864, UNTIL THE FAMILY'S DEPARTURE FROM RICHMOND, LATE IN JUNE, 1865

It was to this house that General Lee returned after Appomattox. The property belonged to John Stewart of Brook Hill, who declined, after the collapse of the Confederacy, to accept rent from Mrs. Lee otherwise than in Confederate money, for which it was first leased to the family.

had landed at Bermuda Hundred on James River, close to the railroad that linked Richmond and Petersburg[32]—a move that Lee had anticipated in previous correspondence with the executive.[33] General Imboden reported that a Union force under General Sigel was advancing up the Shenandoah Valley and was probably moving against Lee's left flank.[34] There was new evidence, also, that General Averell was preparing a raid against the Virginia and Tennessee Railroad.[35]

Thus, ere the day was done, Lee was assured that the enemy was simultaneously taking the offensive, as he had expected, in four directions—Grant with the main army overland from the north against Richmond, Butler on the line of the James, Sigel in the Shenandoah Valley, and Averell in the southwest. If Richmond be regarded as Lee's right flank and the Valley as his left, he now had to face an attack on the centre, on either flank and on one of his lines of communication, that with southwest Virginia and Tennessee. Yet Lee's view was not confused by the minor operations. In a letter written before the receipt of the news of the landing at Bermuda Hundred, he told the President, "It seems to me that the great efforts of the enemy here and in Georgia have begun, and that the necessity of our concentration at both points is immediate and imperative." [36] Grant in Virginia and Sherman in Georgia—these were the adversaries who threatened the life of the Confederacy, and they must be met, Lee reasoned, by abandoning the less important fronts so as to bring together all the troops into two strong armies. To strengthen Johnston who was opposing Sherman, he had previously urged that troops be drawn temporarily from Mobile and from the army of General Leonidas Polk.[37] He now recommended that Beauregard, who had already been sent to Weldon, be advanced with all available forces to defend Richmond from Butler's attack.[38] Lee did not neglect the Valley,[39] but he realized that the Army of Northern Virginia would have to bear the brunt of the major offensive of the enemy in the Old Dominion.

[32] O. R., 51, part 2, p. 887.
[33] Lee had not, however, predicted the landing-place.
[34] O. R., 37, part 1, p. 713.
[35] O. R., 37, part 1, p. 707.   [36] Lee's Dispatches, 173.
[37] O. R., 33, 1285, 1321, 1332.   [38] Lee's Dispatches, 173.
[39] Cf. his instructions to Breckinridge, May 4, 1864; O. R., 37, part 1, p. 713.

While assuming that Grant would seek the initiative, Lee was not disposed to yield it to Grant if he could possibly retain it. Longstreet reported during the evening that he would camp between Foust and Brock's Bridge on the North Anna River, and that he hoped to be at Richards' Shop, six miles south of Verdiersville by noon the next day, May 5.[40] On this assurance, Lee determined to attack Grant. Writing to Ewell at 8 P.M., and instructing him to move early the next morning, Colonel Taylor gave him these further directions in Lee's name: "If the enemy moves down the river, he wishes to push on after him. If he comes this way, we will take our old line. The General's desire is to bring him to battle as soon now as possible," [41] as soon, that was, as Longstreet was within supporting distance. In this, Lee acted on his own initiative and judgment, for President Davis had telegraphed him, "you can estimate the condition of things here [in Richmond], and decide how far your movements should be influenced thereby." [42]

Late in the night of May 4–5, General Stuart advised Lee that the enemy still was in the Wilderness.[43] The next morning, when there was no evidence of a Federal movement to the southwest, Lee became satisfied that the enemy intended to pass through the gloomy mazes of the Wilderness in an effort to turn his right flank. As this was precisely what he most desired, the prospect raised Lee's spirits. Unwont as he was to talk of prospective operations in the presence of his staff, he chatted cheerfully of the situation as he ate his breakfast. Grant, he felt, was throwing away much of the advantage of his superior forces by entangling himself in the Wilderness, instead of profiting by Hooker's experience there.[44]

Soon the Third Corps was ready to go forward on the Plank road. Lee rode at its head with Hill, preceded by Stuart and some of his cavalry.[45] Not long after the column entered the Wilderness, Major Campbell Brown of Ewell's staff rode up and

---

[40] *O. R.*, 51, part 2, p. 887.   [41] *O. R.*, 36, part 2, p. 948.
[42] *O. R.*, 51, part 2, p. 887.   [43] *O. R.*, 51, part 2, p. 887.
[44] Venable in 4 *B. and L.*, 240–41; *Long*, 327. For the considerations that led Grant to move against Lee's right, instead of against his left, see *Humphreys*, 9; 4 *B. and L.*, 106–7. Grant had read Lee's signals and had directed his troops to prepare for immediate action (*Longstreet*, 556).
[45] 14 *S. H. S. P.*, 524; *H. B. McClellan*, 406.

reported that the Second Corps was advancing along the old stone road and wished instructions. Lee was anxious to hold the enemy but desirous, of course, that Longstreet should come up before a general engagement began, so he sent back word to Ewell, who was somewhat ahead of Hill, to regulate his advance by that of the Third Corps. While he did not absolutely forbid Ewell to meet the enemy, he expressed his preference that a major battle should not be precipitated until the arrival of Longstreet.[46]

Tramping onward over the route that had been followed in November, the Third Corps passed the sombre works along Mine Run and ere long met a detachment of the enemy's cavalry.[47] Stuart galloped off to the right, where Rosser was soon skirmishing with the Federals, and Kirkland's infantry brigade pushed the rest of the Union cavalry back up the road.[48] Shortly after 11 o'clock, there came another message from General Ewell, an important message: From his position, said Ewell, he could see a column of Federals crossing the turnpike by the route from Germanna Ford and moving on toward the Orange Plank road, in a southeasterly direction.[49] This confirmed the observations of the morning and made it certain that the enemy was in the Wilderness and was seeking to turn the Confederate right, playing, apparently, into Lee's hand. Ewell was again instructed to conform to Hill's movements and not to bring on a battle, if practicable, until Longstreet arrived.

About noon, however,[50] there came from the direction of the old stone road the sound of heavy firing. Hill moved on past Parker's Store and brushed aside a cavalry attack on his right flank.[51] At this stage of the advance, the first tactical obstacle was encountered, an obstacle that played a large part in the fighting that followed: The course of the turnpike or old stone road, and that of the Plank road were diverging, and the space between them was now so wide that there was no contact between Hill's left on the Plank road and Ewell's right on the turnpike. For this reason, Lee could not tell what the firing from Ewell's front indicated, or how the Second Corps was faring in an action that swelled steadily in violence.

[46] O. R., 36, part 1, p. 1070.   [47] Wilcox in *Annals of the War*, 489.
[48] Wilcox, *loc. cit.*, O. R., 36, part 1, p. 1028.
[49] O. R., 36, part 1, p. 1070.
[50] O. R., 36, part 1, pp. 554, 555.   [51] Wilcox, *loc. cit.*, 489.

For two miles, through the scrub growth of the Wilderness, Lee rode on ahead of Heth's division, with no enemy in sight. Shortly before 3 o'clock, he turned aside into a little clearing on the left-hand side of the road. Riding to a grove of trees in an elevated field, whence there was a view down the valley of Wilderness Run, he dismounted with Hill and Stuart to study the ground while awaiting the arrival of the leading division. Nearby was the home of the Widow Tapp, destined ere two days were done, to become a sinister name in American military history.[52]

Lee was concerned at the separation of the two corps, which apparently he had not anticipated. With Ewell seriously engaged, and the enemy in close proximity to Hill's front, there was manifest danger that Grant would find the gap between Hill's left and Ewell's right. The Federals might then pour into the unguarded area and perhaps might turn the exposed flanks of both corps. As if to confirm this fear, a blue skirmish line deployed in a few minutes from the cover of some old-field pines within easy musket range on the left. Hill remained where he was, either from surprise or in the belief that the skirmishers would fall back. Stuart stood up. Lee, rising quickly, hurried off, calling loudly for Colonel Taylor, in order, doubtless, to give instructions for troops to be advanced to drive back the Unionists.[53] Had the Federals pressed on, they might have made the richest capture that had fallen to any soldiers in the war, but they were as surprised at meeting graycoats as the Confederates were at seeing them, and they quickly withdrew without firing a shot. The direction of their advance was ominous, nevertheless. Doubtless other forces were behind them in the gap between Hill and Ewell. As quickly as he could reach him, Lee ordered Wilcox, who was behind Heth, to file off to the left and to establish contact with the right of Ewell's corps.[54]

Wilcox had been gone only a short time, and Heth had scarcely been placed across the Plank road in line of battle, when the Federals attacked furiously down the road and on either side of it. The woods were so thick that the enemy could scarcely be seen

[52] The Tapp house was burned, and now only a shrub or two in a pasture show where it stood.

[53] W. H. Palmer in W. L. Royall: *Some Reminiscences* (cited hereafter as *Royall*), 28; Venable in 4 *B. and L.*, 241; 3 *C. M. H.*, 435.

[54] Wilcox, *loc. cit.*, 492.

at all, but the volume of his fire showed that he was in great strength. Soon Lee realized that Heth's left flank, and perhaps his right, also, might be turned, and that Wilcox might be cut off before he could form junction with Ewell. He determined to recall Wilcox and to form him on Heth's left, for it was better to have a gap between Wilcox's left and Ewell's right than to have Ewell, Wilcox, and Heth all fighting with their flanks in the air. Fortunately, Wilcox had left two brigades behind him to form the right of his line of battle as he extended to the left. These two, Scales's and McGowan's, were at once brought back. Thomas's brigade returned in a short while and was placed on Heth's left, where the enemy threatened to get in rear of the Confederates.[55] Lane was kept for a time in reserve. The enemy's first onslaught was beaten off, largely because of a very gallant counterattack by McGowan; but a second assault followed the first, and a third the second. Still the lines held.

Slowly, now, but perceptibly, the weight of the enemy's attack began to shift to the Confederate right, whither Wilcox reported he could see large masses of troops moving. Lee reasoned that the Federals might be pulling away from Ewell. This might offer the Second Corps an opportunity of getting on the Federals' right and perhaps of reaching their line of supply from across the Rapidan. A message was sent off to Ewell at 6 P.M., with instructions to make this move if possible. In case Ewell met resistance too heavy to be overcome, Lee planned to turn the Federal left, upon the arrival of Longstreet and of R. H. Anderson.[56] As Longstreet's orders were to move to Todd's Tavern, five miles south of the point where Hill was then fighting, Lee sent off Colonel Venable with instructions to Longstreet to change his line of march and to come up in support of Hill along the Plank road.[57]

By the time these messages were on their way, a fourth and a fifth Federal attack had been made. Both had been repulsed, but they had been delivered with as much vigor as the Federals had ever displayed against the Army of Northern Virginia. Two divisions could not stand indefinitely against a repetition of these assaults. Longstreet must be hurried up to reinforce Hill. For this purpose, Lee sent off Major H. B. McClellan of Stuart's staff

[55] Wilcox, *loc. cit.*, 492–93.   [56] *O. R.*, 36, part 2, p. 952.   [57] *Longstreet*, 557.

to find General Field, whose division was heading Longstreet's advance, and to tell him to speed his march.[58]

Night was drawing on when a new fury of fire came to Lee from the extreme right, but this proved to be, in part, from Lane's brigade, which Wilcox had prudently moved to the right to meet a fresh threat there.[59] Lane's, however, was the last brigade that Hill had at his disposal. Just as that grim fact became apparent, word was received from Wilcox, north of the Plank road, that the enemy was again pushing into the gap between his line and the right of Ewell. Reinforcements must be sent— but whence were they to come? Not a man on the line could be moved, for the pressure was heavy on all; not a unit was in immediate reserve. The only troops not actually engaged were about 125 men of the Fifth Alabama battalion, who were guarding the prisoners. As quickly as possible, these Alabamians were hurried to the left of Wilcox. Going in with a yell that must have created a false impression of their numbers, they hurled back the enemy.[60]

That was the last infantry attack. Darkness fell, and the firing died away after 8 P.M. The sky was cloudless, but in the heavy woods nothing was visible beyond a radius of a few feet. Prisoners taken during the engagement represented parts of three corps. Hill's estimate was that his 14,500 men had fought 40,000.[61]

Ewell now sent a report[62] saying that he, too, had been vigorously assailed.[63] Jones's brigade of Johnson's division had been attacked about noon, as it was advancing, and had been thrown back on Battle, whose ranks had been disorganized. Daniel's brigade had been brought up in support from Rodes's division, and Gordon, of Early's division, who had been thrust forward, had delivered a brilliant counterattack. The whole corps had then been put in line of battle and had been instructed to throw up earthworks. The fighting had been so intense that the muskets

---

[58] H. B. McClellan MSS.
[59] Palmer in Royall, 29-30.   [60] Palmer in Royall, 30.
[61] Palmer in Royall, 30. The attacks had been delivered by Getty's division of the V Corps and by nearly the whole of the II Corps, with Major General Winfield S. Hancock in general command (O. R., 36, part 1, pp. 319-20). Toward the end of the fighting, Wadsworth's division and Baxter's brigade of the V Corps were sent to reinforce Hancock, but, said General Meade in his official report, "They did not arrive . . . in time before dark to do more than drive in the enemy's skirmishers and confront him" (O. R., 36, part 1, p. 190).
[62] Dated 8 P.M.   [63] O. R., 51, part 2, pp. 889-90.

of Pegram's brigade had become too hot to handle,[64] but the enemy had suspended his attacks, and the Second Corps would be able, Ewell said, to hold its ground.[65]

It had been, altogether, a hard day's fighting, with heavy losses. The significant fact was that the Federals had not waited to be attacked but had advanced quickly to challenge the oncoming Confederates. The new Federal commander obviously did not intend to allow the Army of Northern Virginia to take the initiative and to assail him on the march. Still, the enemy had been halted in the Wilderness, and Grant's plan of moving around the right flank had been disclosed. That was gain. During the afternoon, Lee had considered attacking the next day from his left, but Longstreet and Anderson could come up more quickly on the right than on the left. Besides, there was more ground for manœuvring on the right. If the three divisions due to arrive during the night could get on the Federal flank south of the Plank road, they might be able to roll up the Union line and to throw Grant back against the fords of the Rapidan. And that would be the end of another "On to Richmond."

As Hill's officers moved about, it became apparent that the lines of Heth and of Wilcox were badly disarranged. Spread through the woods, "they were," in the language of Colonel William H. Palmer, Hill's adjutant general, "like a worm fence, at every angle." [66] If the men ventured even a short distance in front of their positions to get water, they found themselves among the enemy's pickets. Federals were captured who thought they were still within their own lines. It was desirable, of course, to straighten out the front and to establish entrenchments, but in the black darkness, this was almost impracticable with exhausted troops. The simplest course seemed the safest—to leave the men where they were and to relieve them with Longstreet's corps upon its arrival. That could not be long. Field had doubtless received

[64] 33 *S. H. S. P.*, 22.
[65] *O. R.*, 51, part 2, p. 890. For Ewell's report, see *O. R.*, 36, part 1, pp. 1070–71, covering the reports of his subordinates. McHenry Howard gave a very detailed account of the action in IV *M. H. S. M.*, 97 *ff.*, and Gordon, *op. cit.*, 239 *ff.*, explained his part in the engagement on the left. G. W. Nichols, *A Soldier's History of His Regiment*, 141, made it appear that Lee was on this part of the line during the course of the action, but his statement is refuted by Thomas, *op. cit.*, 477–78, and by Gordon, *loc. cit.* Their narratives showed that the conversation alleged to have taken place between Lee and Gordon was actually between Ewell and Gordon.
[66] Palmer in *Royall*, 30; Wilcox, *loc. cit.*, 494.

his orders to hurry on, and he should be up by midnight. Kershaw would follow. So would Anderson. The line could be taken over by comparatively fresh men, that dangerous gap

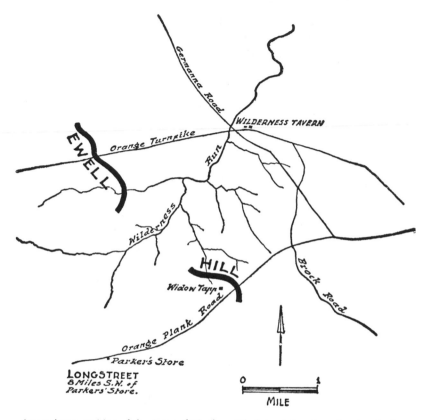

Approximate position of the Army of Northern Virginia at the close of action in the Wilderness of Spotsylvania, May 5, 1864.

between Hill and Ewell could be filled, and the turning movement could be begun at daylight. So, when Heth and Wilcox asked for orders, Lee bade them remain in position, as they were, with the assurance that they would be relieved by 12 o'clock or soon after.[67]

---

[67] Palmer in *Royall*, 30–31; Wilcox, *loc. cit.*, 494–95; Venable in 14 *S. H. S. P.*, 525. Both Venable and Longstreet (*op. cit.*, 560) suggested that there was negligence on the part of Hill and his division commanders in not fortifying their line, but all the evidence indicates that they acted in the belief that they would be withdrawn long before dawn.

Lee had spent most of the afternoon and evening in the field at the Widow Tapp's and there he prepared to bivouac, only a few hundred yards from the line of Hill's infantry and almost under the guns of Poague's battalion, which had been brought up to check the Federal advance but had not been employed during the day.[68] He had just sat down to eat his scant supper when Major H. B. McClellan made his report. With suppressed indignation, the cavalryman told how he had gone to Field's camp, as Lee had directed, and had delivered Lee's instructions for Field to move at once to support Hill. Field, he said, had refused to accept the verbal orders and had stated that he was under instructions from General Longstreet to move at 1 A.M.

This was serious. Instead of arriving by midnight to relieve Heth and Wilcox, the head of Longstreet's corps would hardly reach the lines until daylight, when the enemy would be astir.[69] Realizing the danger to Heth and Wilcox from a delay in the

[68] *Pendleton*, 325; Venable in 14 *S. H. S. P.*, 524.
[69] Longstreet marched about sixteen miles on the 4th before he halted in the vicinity of Brock's bridge (*O. R.*, 36, part 1, p. 1054). On the 5th, instead of reaching Richards's Shop by noon, as he had written Lee he hoped to do, Longstreet did not cover the fifteen miles to that point until 5 o'clock (*Longstreet*, 557). A march of ten miles more that evening would have put the corps in position to relieve Heth and Wilcox by midnight, but Longstreet elected to stop at the shop, to rest the troops for five or six hours, and then to go on. His advance both days was a subject of controversy between Fitz Lee and himself. The former contended that General Lee sent an engineer officer to show Longstreet the route on the 4th, but that Longstreet refused his services, took the wrong road, and lost twenty-four hours in reaching the battlefield (5 *S. H. S. P.*, 184–85; *cf. Fitz Lee*, 330). Longstreet definitely refuted this, in *From Manassas to Appomattox*, 568 ff. On the other hand, Longstreet was very careless in his statement of the time of his various movements in this advance to support the Third Corps. He wrote (*op. cit.*, 556) that it was 1 P.M. on May 4 when he received Lee's orders to start from Mechanicsville. Alexander affirmed, however (*ibid.*, 570), that he was instructed by noon on the 4th to put his artillery in motion. Field (14 *S. H. S. P.*, 542) said that he received his orders from Longstreet at the same hour. The orders sent Field by Longstreet, as printed in *O. R.*, 36, part 2, p. 947, are dated 11 A.M. Longstreet was, therefore, at least two hours wrong as to the time of his start. Instead of moving within three hours after he received his orders, as might be inferred, it was five hours before he had his columns in motion. Again, Longstreet stated that it was 11 P.M. on the 5th when the guide arrived who was to conduct the army through the woods to the Plank road, and he left the reader to conclude, perhaps, that if the guide had arrived sooner, the start would have been made earlier. The fact is that Major McClellan had taken the guide with him to Field's headquarters and was back at Lee's bivouac by 10 P.M. The guide was probably at the disposal of Longstreet's leading division by 9 P.M. Longstreet may have been culpable for not pressing on during the late afternoon of the 5th but it is probable that he used good judgment. In the absence of specific information of a crisis, it may have been better to rest his men so as to have them ready for hard fighting on the 6th. There seems to be no basis in fact for the claim of White (*op. cit.*, 356), that Lee expected Longstreet early on the afternoon of May 5. The case of Field may be a little different. He was, of course, under Longstreet's orders and, as a new division commander, hesitated to accept verbal orders from a cavalry staff officer he scarcely knew. His men had probably rested four hours, however, when McClellan arrived. Had he then moved to the front as Lee intended, the near-disaster on the morning of May 6 might have been averted.

arrival of Longstreet, Major McClellan volunteered to ride back with written orders, which General Field must perforce obey. But Lee would not have it so. Without the slightest show of impatience at what McClellan considered the insubordination of Field, General Lee explained: "No, Major, it is now past 10 o'clock, and by the time you could return to General Field and he could put his division in motion, it would be 1 o'clock; and at that hour he will move." [70] Whatever the risks, they had now to be taken, whether on the front where Heth's and Wilcox's weary men waited, or in the gap between Hill and Ewell. And if the dangers of the dawn could be overcome, then the Army of Northern Virginia should show its old offensive power once more and Grant be borne down as Hooker had been in those same grim tangles of the Wilderness.

[70] *H. B. McClellan MSS.*

CHAPTER XVII

History Fails to Repeat Itself

(MAY 6–7, 1864)

When Lee learned from Major McClellan that Longstreet could not arrive until nearly daylight on May 6, he did not communicate that fact to Wilcox or to Heth. He probably reasoned that as the First Corps and Anderson of Hill's corps would come on the ground before the enemy would attack, nothing was to be gained by arousing the apprehension of the tired commanders. Nor did he order the front of the Third Corps fortified, because he intended Longstreet's men, upon their arrival, to take up and to entrench a line that had been drawn early the previous evening a short distance in rear of Wilcox and Heth.[1]

At 3:30 a.m., however, Wilcox became alarmed over the non-arrival of the expected reinforcements. He sent a summons to the rear for all the corps pioneers to come forward and to entrench. Before they could reach the front, day had broken, and by the time they started felling timber, they were visible to the enemy and were quickly driven from their work. Sunrise found the men of the Third Corps still scattered through the Wilderness, with little semblance of a line and with no cover except that afforded by the young trees.[2] At 5 o'clock, almost with the sun, the Federal infantry opened fire at close range and soon was attacking hotly in front and on both flanks. The Confederates made such resistance as they could—here good and there feeble—and contrived for perhaps half an hour to retard the enemy. To their calls for assistance, Lee sent back an urgent appeal that they hold on until Longstreet was at hand. Soon stragglers began to leave the front; their number multiplied; presently Wilcox's line began to give ground; then it went to pieces, except directly on the road, and men came pouring to the westward. Some were running. Others

[1] Wilcox, *loc. cit.*, 495.   [2] Wilcox, *loc. cit.*, 495.

walked swiftly to the rear with never a look at the enemy. A few loaded and halted and fired and moved on. It was a sudden crisis of a sort the army had never known except at Sharpsburg. The minds of the weary men were in flux. In a minute they might be in a mad panic.

One glance showed Lee that the fate of the day and the control of the army were in the balance. Swiftly he ordered Taylor to gallop to Parker's Store and to prepare the wagon train for instant retreat in case the corps could not be halted. Then out into the road he hurried to help rally the retreating soldiers. He found himself in the midst of McGowan's South Carolinians who so often had proved their valor.

"My God, General McGowan," he cried in a loud voice to their commander, "is this the splendid brigade of yours running like a flock of geese?"

"General," answered McGowan, "these men are not whipped. They only want a place to form, and they will fight as well as they ever did." [3]

Still Wilcox's men were rushing down the road and across the fields. A little more and the whole divisional front would be bare. The enemy would sweep on—and what was there to stop him? Only the hope that Longstreet would come up at that moment! If the old luck of the Army of Northern Virginia held, and reinforcements arrived before actual rout began, all would be well. But if Longstreet were delayed much longer, then . . . here was General Wilcox telling of the break and asking for orders.

"Longstreet must be here," Lee told him, his voice anxious, and the strain showing plainly now in his face, "go bring him up!"

Wilcox turned and made off. Lee rode back into Mrs. Tapp's field. There were still some Confederates east of the house, though the number was small—wounded men mostly. Should the artillery wait until these troops passed, or should it open now and try to keep off the Federals who were gathering thickly, there where vision ended in that maze of green boughs and blue coats? Not one minute longer, said Hill, could the artillery delay! If it did, the guns would all be captured.

Open, then, Colonel Poague, with your valiant old batteries—

[3] *Alexander,* 503.

give them grape! Poague's guns were already loaded; the command rang out; twelve belching pieces filled the woods with fire. Another round, and then another, Colonel Poague, if there's time; the enemy is still 200 yards away.[4]

Around Lee the choking smoke and the excited cannoneers; behind him a wild scene of confusion, officers shouting and waving their sabres, soldiers numbed with exhaustion or with fear, scarcely conscious of the orders given them. A long, agonizing minute of this, and then, through the smoke, twenty or more ragged soldiers running with their muskets in their hands—not to the rear but into the space where Poague's guns were still vomiting grape.

"Who are you, my boys?" Lee cried out as he saw them gathering.

"Texas boys," they yelled, their number multiplying every second.

The Texans—Hood's Texans, of Longstreet's corps, just at the right place and at the right moment! After the strain of the dawn, the sight of these Grenadier Guards of the South was too much for Lee. For once the dignity of the commanding general was shattered; for once his poise was shaken.

"Hurrah for Texas," he shouted, waving his hat; "Hurrah for Texas."

In rising excitement, he yelled to them to form line of battle at once. As the willing veterans sprang into position, a brigade of them now, he rode to the left of the line. He would lead them in the countercharge. The line started forward. He spurred frantic Traveller through an opening in the gun pits, and was on the heels of the infantry men.

Then, for the first time they realized what he intended to do. "Go back, General Lee, go back!" they cried. He paid no heed to them. They began to slacken their pace: "We won't go on unless you go back!" He did not hear them. His face was aflame and his eyes were on the enemy in the front. General Gregg tried to head him off; a tall sergeant seized his bridle rein; nothing stopped him until Colonel Venable arrived. Longstreet was at hand, Venable shouted into the General's ear; had he not better

[4] *O. R.*, 36, part 1, pp. 1054–55, 1063; *Pendleton*, 325–26; Palmer in *Royall*, 31; Wilcox, *loc. cit.*, 496.

turn aside and give Longstreet his orders? For a moment there was a hard conflict between the impulse of the warrior and the commander's sense of responsibility. Then, like a man coming out of a trance, Lee slowly pulled back his horse, his glare still to the front; he waved his hat to the onrushing Texans and went back to Longstreet—to be told bluntly that he should go farther behind the lines.[5]

While Lee had been rallying Hill's men and cheering the Texans, the First Corps had been forming, Kershaw on the right and Field on the left of the Plank road. The retreating troops of Heth and of Wilcox had reached Longstreet's men just as the First Corps had established its line, but it had opened ranks, had allowed the fugitives to pass through, and then, in perfect order, had begun its advance.[6] As soon as these veterans moved forward, Lee regained his poise. He left Longstreet to direct the counter-movement and busied himself with providing the slight artillery support that could be used in that tangled terrain.[7] Quickly, too, he began reforming Wilcox and Heth on the left of Longstreet. This was not a difficult task, for McGowan's statement proved correct. Most of the troops of the Third Corps retreated only some 300 yards and now were ready to fight again. As soon as they were organized, Lee sent them to fill the gap between their flank on the Plank road and Ewell's on the turnpike.[8]

[5] The facts of this, the first of the four incidents of "Lee to the rear," are singularly difficult to establish in their sequence, chiefly because most of those who recorded his meeting with the Texans did so long afterwards, when much telling had put a robe of rhetoric over the actual happenings. The writer has followed the account of Colonel Venable, who was with Lee through the whole episode, and wrote of it in 1873. See 14 S. H. S. P., 525–26. In *Pendleton*, 326, there is an account that has some claim to authenticity because it, too, was written early, but it was penned in the old age of the author and probably for a lecture. Its climaxes seem a little too theatrical. For other accounts, see *Longstreet*, 560, where the chronology is almost certainly confused; W. H. Palmer in *Royall*, 32; *Taylor's General Lee*, 234, which agrees with Venable's account; Polley, *Hood's Texas Brigade*, 231, which is very dramatic and not accurate in detail; *Sloan*, 84–85; *Jones*, 316; *Grimes*, 52; "R. C. of Hood's Texas Brigade," in 5 *Land We Love*, 481–86, the most florid of all accounts by an eye-witness; J. C. Wheeler in 11 *Confederate Veteran*, 116–17; A. C. Jones in the Lexington, Va., *Gazette*, May 20, 1880.
[6] *O. R.*, 36, part 1, pp. 1054–55, 1061, 1063; *Longstreet*, 560; *Alexander*, 503. Cf. *Sorrel*, 235: "I have always thought that in its entire splendid history the simple act of forming line in that dense undergrowth, under heavy fire and with the Third Corps men pushing to the rear through the ranks was perhaps [the First Corps's] greatest performance for steadiness and inflexible courage and discipline."
[7] *Pendleton*, 326.
[8] MS. *report of General C. M. Wilcox on the operations of 1864*, among the *Lee Military MSS.* (cited hereafter as *Wilcox's MS. report*), 34; Venable in 14 *S. H. S. P.* 525.

Not long after Hill had set off to the northward with his troops, his adjutant general, Colonel William H. Palmer, came galloping back to Lee to report that Hill had found a force of the enemy in the gap between the Second and Third Corps and wished the loan of a brigade of Anderson's division, if Anderson had arrived, in order that he might have enough men to capture the Federals who had ventured so far to the front. Anderson[9] had found Longstreet ahead of him on the Plank road and had been compelled to wait until Longstreet had cleared it. Lee had already given orders for Anderson to report to Longstreet and he was loath, now, to detach any part of the division without the knowledge of its temporary chief.

"Well," said Lee when Palmer asked for the brigade, "let's see General Longstreet about it."

They rode together through the copses, to the swelling accompaniment of a violent fire on a lengthening front, and reached Longstreet just as Anderson's division was reporting, about 8 A.M.[10]

"General Hill," said Lee, "wants one of Anderson's brigades."

Old Pete was in his glory then. His troops were all in position and were advancing faultlessly. He answered with the ease of a confident victor. "Certainly, Colonel," he said, addressing himself to Palmer, "which one will you take?"

"The leading one," said Palmer, with the inference that all brigades of the Third Corps were equally good.

As quickly as he could, Palmer led the troops off, and Lee returned to the field on the left of the road to follow the furious fighting up the Plank road.[11] The counterattack of Longstreet's veterans had halted the Federals and now was forcing them back slowly toward temporary works from which they had advanced against Hill earlier in the morning.[12] Kershaw, in particular, having favorable ground on the right of the road, organized a charge, dislodged the enemy, and hurled him back to a second line.[13] These gains were made by sheer valor, for the Federals fought with the magnificent determination that had been observed the previous day.

---

[9] Who had camped for the night of May 5–6 at Verdiersville (*Longstreet*, 559).
[10] *Longstreet*, 561; *Alexander*, 504. [11] W. H. Palmer in *Royall*, 34.
[12] *O. R.*, 36, part 1, p. 1055. [13] *O. R.*, 36, part 1, p. 1061.

The ground was incredibly difficult. It was bad enough at any time, with its endless mazes of low-spreading pines and its stunted oaks, many of them only an inch or two in diameter; but now, as one witness has put it, almost every bush "had a bullet through it, causing these white oak runners to bend down from being top heavy. These bullets all seemed to go through about the height of a man's waist. In tumbling down, [the bushes] made almost an impassable barrier. Together with this obstacle the dead and the dying were so thick that we could not help stepping on them." [14] Through this treacherous tangle, Field and Kershaw continued to press forward, but with heavy casualties. The Texans lost nearly two-thirds of their numbers,[15] and the other brigades suffered heavily.

Before 10 o'clock the first stage of the battle was over. The Federal attack on Hill had been beaten off; the enemy on the whole of the Confederate right flank had been driven back beyond the positions he had occupied at the opening of the engagement; the front was momentarily stabilized.

What next? Lee had planned the previous evening to turn the Union left south of the Plank road. It had been with this in view that he had directed the march of Longstreet and of Anderson on his right flank. Doubtless he had communicated his general plan to Old Pete. Now, while Lee was still working to effect a junction between Hill and Ewell, General Wofford suggested to Longstreet that he use Anderson and part of his own

---

[14] *Mixson,* 70. The most familiar description of the Wilderness is perhaps that given in General Hancock's report (*O. R.,* 36, part 1, p. 325): "It was covered by a dense forest, almost impenetrable by troops in line of battle, where maneuvering was an operation of extreme difficulty and uncertainty. The undergrowth was so heavy that it was scarcely possible to see more than 100 paces in any direction. No movements of the enemy could be observed until the lines were almost in collision; only the roar of the musketry disclosed the position of the combatants, to those who were at any distance. . . ." McHenry Howard's description in 4 *M. H. S. M.,* 97, referred more specifically to conditions on the left and was equally accurate: "It is in places level and marshy, or with numerous wet spring-heads, but for the most part rugged or rolling, with very few fields of thin soil, easily washing into gullies, and still fewer houses scattered here and there. The woods, which seem to stretch out interminably, are in some places of pine with low spreading branches, through which a horseman cannot force his way without much turning and twisting, but generally the oak predominates. In many places the large trees had been cut down in years past and a jungle of switch had sprung up ten or twenty feet high, more impenetrable, if possible, than the pine. A more difficult or disagreeable field of battle could not well be imagined. There is no range for artillery. It is an affair of musketry at close quarters, from which one combatant or the other must soon recoil, if both do not construct breastworks, as they learned to do with wonderful rapidity."

[15] 14 *S. H. S. P.,* 544; *Reagan,* 189.

corps to get on the left flank of the Federals and roll up the line while the rest of the infantry attacked in front.[16] Longstreet was agreeable. General M. L. Smith, the new chief engineer of the army, had reported to Longstreet, under Lee's orders, and was now sent off to see if there was a route through the woods by which the turning movement could be executed.[17] He had not gone far to the south of the Plank road when he found the cut of an unfinished railroad from Orange to Fredericksburg,[18] similar in nearly all respects to that which had formed Jackson's line of defense on part of his front at Groveton. This railroad cut was not on the map issued for the campaign and its location was not known, apparently, until Smith came upon it.[19]

As soon as General Smith returned, about 10 A.M.,[20] Longstreet ordered his adjutant general, Lieutenant Colonel Moxley Sorrel, to conduct three brigades to the railroad cut, under Smith's direction, and to throw them against the enemy's flank which, Smith said, extended only a short distance south of the Plank road. Lee was of course apprised and was willing for the manœuvre to be made, but as usual he left the execution entirely to the corps commander. He had completely recovered his composure by this time, and had none of the excitement he had displayed when the enemy had broken through Hill's lines. When a courier brought him a message from Anderson and sat on his weary, panting animal after he had delivered the paper, Lee rebuked him sharply: "Young man," he said, "you should have some feeling for your horse; dismount and rest him." Without another word, he

---

[16] *O. R.*, 36, part 1, pp. 1061–62. This is the only reference to General Wofford's authorship of this historic move, but as it was made specifically by General Kershaw, who was in a position to know the facts, there is no reason to question it.

[17] *Longstreet*, 561; *O. R.*, 36, part 1, p. 1055.

[18] This railroad, of narrow gauge, was subsequently completed and was styled the Piedmont, Fredericksburg, and Potomac. It is still in operation and is known as the Virginia Central, after its famous neighbor to the southward, which is now a part of the Chesapeake and Ohio.

[19] Although good for the country both to the east and to the west, the Confederate map of Orange and Spotsylvania showed only the main roads through the Wilderness. Had the map been more accurate and detailed, Lee doubtless would have ordered Longstreet to advance up the line of the unfinished railroad on his move from Parker's Store. A copy of this map is among the *Lee Military MSS.* The lines of the railroad and of most of the lesser roads of the Wilderness are crudely traced in pencil. This would indicate that they were inserted on the field, for if these data had been available at headquarters before the opening of the campaign, they would almost certainly have been entered in ink. General Stuart's copy, now in the Confederate Museum, and unquestionably used by him during the Wilderness campaign, lacks the pencilled lines on Lee's copy.

[20] *Alexander*, 504.

reached into the saddle-bag on Traveller's back, took out half a buttered biscuit and gave it to the courier's mount.[21]

Presently an officer came back from the front of Wilcox's division. Lee quizzed him closely. What was the meaning of the

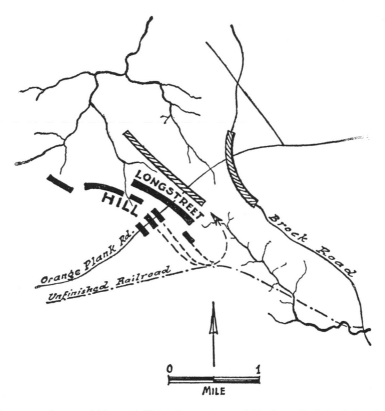

Manœuvre of parts of First and Third Corps, Army of Northern Virginia, designed to turn the left flank of the Army of the Potomac in the Wilderness of Spotsylvania, May 6, 1864.

firing in that quarter? Had Wilcox found the right of Ewell's corps? Had the enemy been located in front of the division? When the officer explained that he had seen the wood where Wilcox's flank was said to rest, and had observed the glint of the sun on the rifles of the enemy, Lee pondered. He evidently was in doubt as to whether this indicated that the foe was planning to drive a wedge between Ewell and Hill. If so, then obviously

21 Walter B. Barker in 12 *S. H. S. P.,* 329.

a delay in launching the attack against the Federal left might throw the army back on the defensive. To the officer Lee only said, "Those bullets keep coming this way," [22] but he must have counted the seconds and weighed the very *miniés* that continued to fly from the Federal left toward the centre.

At length, about 11 o'clock,[23] there swelled from the Confederate right the sudden roar of a new attack. Led by Colonel Sorrel, four brigades had moved to the railroad cut, and now were advancing northward against the left of Meade's army. Soon the joyful news was received that the enemy's line was being rolled up. Some of the Union brigades were already routed. The victorious Confederates were close to the Plank road; a general advance of the whole right wing was ordered. Longstreet had sufficient men—five of the brigades at his disposal had not yet gone into action. With their help and that of the troops already in line, Longstreet believed that Grant's army could be hurled back, a broken and confused mass, against the fords of the Rapidan. A triumph, Longstreet thought, akin to that which might have been won the previous year, if Jackson had not fallen, was now awaiting the army.[24] A tragic morning was trending to a glorious noon!

And now Longstreet's troops started forward again, some for a new flanking movement,[25] some driving eastward to find the Federals who had retreated from the weakened front along the Plank road. Lee hurried over to that highway and hastened toward the battle-line, in order to sustain Longstreet's attack with Hill's corps and with the artillery, if the advance carried the army where the guns could be employed. When he reached the front, the eastward advance up the Plank road had already carried the troops opposite the point where the four brigades had attacked northward from the railroad cut. The two columns thus formed a right angle. A few units of the flanking column, in fact, had already crossed the Plank road. Lee paused to see that some logs were cleared away, so that the artillery could pass;[26] Long-

[22] *W. W. Chamberlaine*, 94–95.

[23] For the varying statements as to the time of Longstreet's attack, see *O. R.*, 36, part I, pp. 353, 489, 493.

[24] *O. R.*, 36, part 1, pp. 1055, 1062, 1090; *Longstreet*, 561–63; *Sorrel*, 236 ff.; Wilcox, *loc. cit.*, 498; 14 *S. H. S. P.*, 544 ff.; 20 *ibid.*, 69; *Alexander*, 504–6.

[25] *Alexander*, 505.   [26] 14 *S. H. S. P.*, 545.

street, confident, almost exuberant, was just setting off with his
entourage to follow the wild, cheering troops. If Lee looked after
his senior lieutenant, there might have flashed before him, for
an instant, the picture of Jackson as he, too, had ridden out of
sight into the devouring shadows of that same Wilderness, on his
way to turn the flank of Hooker. The atmosphere was the same,
the atmosphere of victory. McClellan and Pope, Burnside and
Hooker, Meade and Grant—all were one when the Army of
Northern Virginia got under way!

Only an instant for reflection, and then a rattle of small arms
up the road, a strong voice frantically crying "Friends," the sound
of maddened horses galloping off, staff officers calling for surgeons . . . the Confederate troops parallel to the road evidently had
fired on their own comrades advancing up it . . . some one had
been hit. In a few seconds the evil tidings were passed to Lee.
The Erinyes were still pursuing! Whenever a decisive victory had
been in the making, rain or accident or death had snatched it
away. And now, at what had seemed the most hopeful moment
in the opening battle of the decisive campaign, Longstreet, the
most experienced and the ablest of the surviving corps leaders,
had been wounded! It was the fate of the Confederacy![27]

Colonel Sorrel came quickly to give Lee the facts and to say
that Longstreet, coughing blood at every breath, urged Lee to
continue the manœuvre, which he had entrusted to General Field
as ranking division commander of the corps. Lee paused long
enough to make solicitous inquiry about the nature of Longstreet's
wound[28] and then he rode up to the temporary commander. He
did not take the battle from Field's hands, but remained nearby,
where the acting chief of the corps had the good sense to consult
him.[29]

It was immediately apparent that the advantage had been
pushed to the limit and that Longstreet had been wrong in
assuming that he could hurl the enemy back to the Rapidan
without disposing his troops anew. "My division and some others
probably," Field wrote, "were perpendicular to the road and in

---

[27] A Virginia regiment that had crossed the road had been returning to its brigade,
had been mistaken for the enemy, and was fired upon; the volley struck the horsemen
who had been going forward. General Jenkins was killed (*Longstreet*, 564–65).

[28] *Sorrel*, 238, 239.　　　　　　　　[29] Field in 14 *S. H. S. P.*, 547.

line of battle, whilst all those which had acted as a turning force were in line parallel to the road, and the two were somewhat mixed up. No advance could possibly be made till the troops parallel to the road were placed perpendicular to it, otherwise, as the enemy had fallen back down the road, our right flank would have been exposed to him. . . . Our two bodies being on the road at the same point, one perpendicular and the other about parallel to it, neither could move without interfering with the other." [30]

In the Wilderness jungle, where the smoke from burning leaves was adding to the confusion, the recall of the flanking column and the drawing of a new line of battle were exasperatingly slow tasks. Meantime, of course, the enemy was recovering from his near-panic and was bracing himself in strengthened works along the Brock road to meet a new assault. When Longstreet's troops were all in position, and the offensive could be renewed, it was 4:15, and the Federals could not be shaken.[31]

Finding that nothing further could be achieved on the right, Lee rode over to the left, where, at 5:30 P.M., he found Ewell in consultation with Early and with John B. Gordon, commander of one of Early's brigades. Little had been accomplished all day by the Second Corps, except to beat off a few minor attacks.[32]

"Cannot something be done on this flank," Lee asked, "to relieve the pressure upon our right?"

Ewell and Early had nothing to propose, but Gordon, after listening silently for a few minutes, said that he had found the extreme right of the Federal army exposed. He had asked permission to attack it but had not been allowed to do so. Early had been arguing against the proposal ever since Gordon had made it before 9 o'clock, and now he insisted once more that the enemy's flank was not "in the air"—that the IX Corps was in support.

At Lee's instance, Gordon explained. He had reconnoitred in person, he said, and had been several miles in the rear of the flank of the opposing force, which was the VI Corps. His con-

[30] 14 S. H. S. P., 545.
[31] 14 S. H. S. P., 545–46; Alexander, 507; O. R., 36, part 1, p. 1062. Longstreet (op. cit., 565) sought to leave the impression that Lee delayed from overcaution, and that if he had not been wounded a complete victory could have been won.
[32] O. R., 36, part 1, p. 1071.

viction was fixed that no troops were in support of the weak Federal right. On this statement of fact, Lee sided with the brigade commander. "His words were few," Gordon wrote at a later

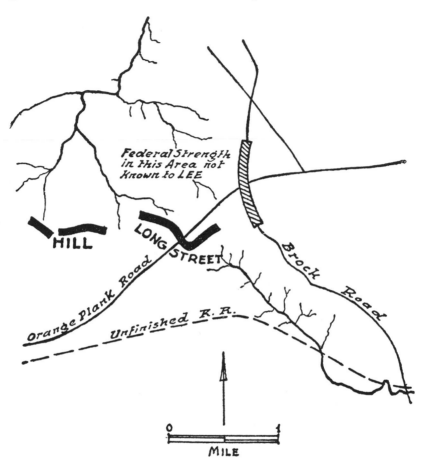

Approximate position of the Confederate right and right centre, about noon, May 6, 1864, after Longstreet's advance.

time, "but his silence and grim looks while the reasons for that long delay were being given, and his prompt order to me to move at once to the attack, revealed his thoughts almost as plainly as words could have done." [33] Gordon immediately went forward with the impetuous ardor of youth—he was not yet thirty-two.

[33] *Gordon,* 258.

Having Robert D. Johnston's brigade in support,[34] he swept a mile of the front of Sedgwick's corps, cut off the Army of the Potomac temporarily from its base across the Rapidan, and captured some 600 prisoners.[35] But twilight caught the Confederates on the Union trenches and forced them back, with only their prisoners, their scant booty, and their tale of another lost opportunity. If Lee had elected that day to remain on the left, rather than on the right, where he had projected his turning movement, the attack on Sedgwick's flank might have come in the forenoon instead of close to sunset, and a different record might have been written. As Lee rode glumly back to headquarters at the Tapp house, he must have lamented anew that fatal volley in the battle of Chancellorsville, which had taken the Second Corps from the masterly hands of Jackson, and had led him, in the absence of a better choice, to entrust that magnificent body of fighting men to Ewell.

Night now fell on the confused field, yet such a night as even the Army of Northern Virginia, in all its desperate adventures, had rarely known before. The woods were now on fire in many places. Distant flames cast weird shadows. Choking smoke was everywhere. And from the thickets came the cries of the wounded, frantic lest the flames reach them ere the litter-bearers did.[36] It was war in Inferno.

The situation, in other respects, was not gloomy. Lee's casualties during the day had been severe, but, judging from the dead on the ground, those of the Federals had been much heavier.[37] The enemy had attacked with greater ferocity than ever before, but he

[34] Johnston had arrived that day from Hanover Junction. *Cf.* 14 *S. H. S. P.*, 523, where his starting-point is wrongly given as Hanover Courthouse.

[35] *O. R.*, 36, part 1, pp. 1071, 1077–78; *Gordon*, 258; *Taylor's General Lee*, 237. Early maintained (*op. cit.*, 348) that Burnside's corps was not moved until after Gordon had advocated an attack on the flank of the VI Corps. Gordon (*op. cit.*, 258 *ff.*) refuted this, but, oddly enough, used only a small part of the evidence. Burnside's report, Hancock's and those of the division commanders of the IX Corps (*O. R.*, 36, part 1, pp. 321, 906, 927, 928, 942) make it plain that from the beginning of the day's fighting, only the 4th Division of the IX Corps was on the Federal right. This division, consisting principally of new Negro troops, was not in support of the VI Corps, but was spread out on guard duty all the way to the Rapidan (*O. R.*, 36, part 1, p. 988). There can be no question that Early had been completely deceived as to the strength and dispositions of the enemy in his front. Ewell, as he did all too often, accepted Early's view.

[36] *Cf. Sorrel*, 244.

[37] Grant's losses, May 5–7, 1864, were 17,666 (*O. R.*, 36, part 1, p. 133). Alexander (*op. cit.*, 508) gave the correct figures for killed, wounded, and missing. The Confederate losses, on the same basis, would have been approximately 7600.

had been halted in his advance, repulsed on his centre, defeated on his left, and roughly handled on his right.

In like circumstances, and with losses no greater, Hooker had retreated the previous year: Would Grant do so now? Would history repeat itself? Stuart and Fitz Lee reported the Federal cavalry withdrawn, as if concentrating on Chancellorsville.[38] That might indicate either a retreat or a movement down the Rappahannock, but the first of these alternatives did not seem probable to Lee. He felt that there was at least one day's more fight in the Army of the Potomac. It would be well to strengthen the Southern lines and to invite attack. Then, if the enemy were repulsed, a chance might come to destroy him.[39]

The Confederates of the right wing built themselves stout entrenchments during the night of May 6–7, in anticipation of Grant's assaults, and by the morning of the 7th, they had a strong front.[40] But they did not receive their expected reward at dawn. No attack came. In contrast to the roaring desperate action of the preceding day, the forenoon was so quiet that it seemed bewildering. Hours passed with only an exchange of picket fire. Nowhere was there a sign of impending action. More than that, from the extreme left of the Confederate line, General Early reported that the Union troops had abandoned their ground opposite his division and for part of the front of Johnson's command.[41]

This was significant news to Lee. It meant that Grant had severed his line of communications via Germanna. And that implied, of course, that he was not contemplating a retreat, at least not at that point. History was failing to repeat itself. Grant was not willing to withdraw incontinently across the Rappahannock, as Burnside and Hooker had done when they had been defeated. He had, however, to move before he exhausted the supplies in his wagons. If he was about to march, in what direction was Grant going? Obviously, either eastward toward Fredericksburg, or southeastward in the direction of Spotsylvania Courthouse. If his purpose was to open a new line of supply, he

---

[38] *O. R.*, 51, part 2, p. 894.

[39] *Taylor's Four Years*, 129; for the bivouac of the army, see 14 *S. H. S. P.*, 546. Grant was overwhelmed at his failure. He "went into his tent, and throwing himself face down on his cot, gave way to the greatest emotion." Charles Francis Adams said: "I never saw a man so agitated in my life" (Eben Swift: "The Military Education of Robert E. Lee," 35 *Virginia Magazine of History and Biography*, 149).

[40] Palmer in *Royall*, 34–35.   [41] *Early*, 350.

would logically go to Fredericksburg; but if he intended an advance on Richmond, the direct road to Spotsylvania Courthouse
was less than half as long as that by way of Fredericksburg.

Besides, Spotsylvania was of strategic importance, in the angle
between the Richmond, Fredericksburg and Potomac and the

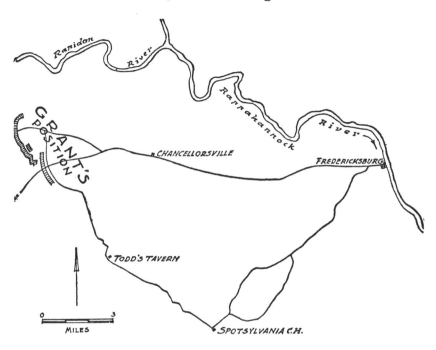

Alternative routes to Spotsylvania Courthouse from Grant's position in the Wilderness,
May 7, 1864.

Virginia Central Railroad. The place was an excellent approach
to Hanover Junction, where the two railroads met. An adversary
seeking to drive the Army of Northern Virginia back on Richmond, by cutting off its supplies, would almost certainly strike for
the junction.

It was likely, for these reasons, then, though it was not yet
certain, that when Grant moved it would be toward Spotsylvania.
The army must be ready to meet him there. As a first step, Lee
directed General Pendleton to cut a way southward through the
forest from the Plank road to the highway running from Orange
Courthouse to Spotsylvania. This would give the Confederates an

299

inner line, roughly parallel to that which the Federals would probably follow.[42] Longstreet's corps, then on the extreme right, would naturally be the first to march over the new route to meet an advance on Spotsylvania. But who was to lead that corps?

The approaches to Hanover Junction from the Wilderness-Spotsylvania front.

The news from Longstreet was that his wound in the throat and shoulder would not necessarily be fatal,[43] but, if he escaped Jackson's fate, months would elapse before he could resume his duties. It was no light matter to choose even a temporary successor to the senior corps commander. Three men in the army were entitled by service and ability to be considered for the post—Early, Edward Johnson, and "Dick" Anderson. In choosing among them, much depended on the preference of the men of the First Corps: they must have the chief under whom they would fight best. To ascertain their sentiments, Lee sent for Longstreet's dapper and

[42] O. R., 36, part 1, p. 1041. The road struck the Orange-Spotsylvania highway in the vicinity of Shady Grove Church. See 3 C. M. H., 445, which reference, however, confused the Po with the Ny River.
[43] O. R., 51, part 2, p. 893.

capable adjutant general, the same Colonel Sorrel who had led the flanking column so brilliantly the previous day.

"You have been with the corps since it started as a brigade," Lee said when he had explained the case, "and should be able to help me."

Sorrel answered candidly that Early probably was the ablest of the three under consideration, but would certainly be the most unpopular with Longstreet's men. "His flings and irritable disposition had left their marks," Sorrel subsequently recorded, "and there had been one or two occasions when some ugly feelings had been aroused while operating in concert."

"And now, Colonel," Lee went on, "for my friend Ed. Johnson; he is a splendid fellow."

"All say so, General, but he is quite unknown to the corps. His reputation is so high that perhaps he would prove all that could be wished, but I think that some one personally known to the corps would be preferred."

That, of course, brought the conversation around to "Dick" Anderson. "We *know him,*" Sorrel said, "and shall be satisfied with him," mindful of the days of victory when Anderson had led a division of the First Corps, ere he had been transferred to the Third.

"Thank you, Colonel," Lee concluded. "I have been interested, but Early would make a fine corps commander." He probably preferred Early,[44] but he could not ignore the considerations Sorrel urged, and later in the day he announced the temporary appointment of Anderson, with Mahone to command Anderson's division.[45] He took pains, however, during the operations that followed, to keep a close eye on Anderson and to give him a measure of direction he never exercised in dealing with the more experienced corps commanders.[46]

After his conference with Sorrel, Lee rode across to the Confederate left. In the company of General Gordon he went over the scene of that officer's attack on the evening of the 6th, and talked with less restraint than usual of the enemy's probable

---

[44] *Cf.* 14 *S. H. S. P.,* 453.

[45] *Sorrel,* 242–43; 14 *S. H. S. P.,* 546; *O. R.,* 36, part 2, p. 967.

[46] His letters to Anderson in *O. R.,* 36, part 3, are much more numerous than those to any other officer, except perhaps Breckinridge, after that officer joined him from the Shenandoah Valley.

movements. "Grant is not going to retreat," he said. "He will move his army to Spotsylvania."

Gordon had not studied the larger strategy of the campaign and he asked in some surprise if there were any evidence that Grant was moving in the direction of the courthouse.

"Not at all, not at all," Lee answered, "but that is the next point at which the armies will meet; Spotsylvania is now General Grant's best strategic point." [47] Bidding farewell to Gordon, Lee rode back to the right. He examined the line closely as he went and found his men ready and confident. Nowhere was any action in progress more serious than a "feeler" or a minor demonstration.

The news that began by this time to sift in from the outposts was in part contradictory but was rather specific as to the presence of the enemy's cavalry at Todd's Tavern on the road from Grant's position to Spotsylvania Courthouse.[48] During the early afternoon, Lee cautioned Stuart to study the roads in the direction of Spotsylvania,[49] and then, for the second time that day, he rode over to visit General Ewell's lines.[50] Returning, he halted for a conference at Hill's headquarters. While he was there, Colonel Palmer came down from the attic of the house to report that a large park of heavy guns had been set in motion from the opposite hill, where Grant's headquarters were believed to be located. The guns had started toward the Confederate right—in the direction of Spotsylvania.[51]

Lee, of course, had been studying closely every intelligence report on Grant's probable movements. All day the evidence had been cumulative that his adversary's objective was Spotsylvania. This final item of confirmation proved decisive. Without further

[47] *Gordon*, 268–69. The account of this interview well illustrates the difficulties of historical criticism that arise in using General Gordon's *Reminiscences*. General Gordon had General Lee add to the quotation given in the text: "I am so sure of his [Grant's] next move that I have already made arrangements to march by the shortest practicable route, that we may meet him there." As it was early morning when this conversation occurred, it is historically demonstrable that Lee had not "made arrangements" beyond ordering Pendleton to cut a road. The writer has often been perplexed, as in this instance, to know where General Gordon's memory ended and where his imagination began, the more so as there was never the slightest question as to that splendid gentleman's desire to state the facts accurately.

[48] *O. R.*, 36, part 2, pp. 969–71; *ibid.*, 51, part 2, pp. 897–98.

[49] *O. R.*, 36, part 2, pp. 969–70. It has long been assumed, doubtless on the authority of Long (*op. cit.*, 334), that Stuart gave Lee his first definite news that the Federals were moving on Spotsylvania. This may have been the case. It is proper to note, however, that at 3 P.M. on May 7 (*O. R.*, 51, part 2, pp. 897–98), Stuart informed Lee that "the enemy is not advancing toward Spotsylvania Court House on the Brock road."

[50] *O. R.*, 36, part 2, p. 970.   [51] Palmer in *Royall*, 35.

inward debate, he sent Anderson orders to withdraw the First Corps from the line after dark and, when it had been rested, to put it in motion for the courthouse. Hill and Ewell were directed to follow Anderson as soon as the situation in their front justified that course.[52]

Word somehow reached the men in the works that Grant was on the move and they interpreted this to mean that he had given up hope of taking Richmond by the overland route. Confident and rejoicing, they raised the rebel yell in Anderson's corps and took it up along the whole line. At a given point, one could hear it on the right, then in front and then dying away in the distance on the left. "Again the shout arose on the right—again it rushed down upon us from a distance of perhaps two miles," one officer wrote, "—again we caught it and flung it joyously to the left, where it ceased only when the last post had huzzahed. The effect was beyond expression. It seemed to fill every heart with new life, to inspire every nerve with might never known before. Men seemed fairly convulsed with the fierce enthusiasm; and I believe that if at that instant the advance of the whole army upon Grant could have been ordered, we should have swept [him] into the very Rappahannock." [53]

With the sound of that great demonstration in his ears, Lee sent off Colonel Venable and Colonel Taylor to notify Stuart that Anderson was to move that night to Spotsylvania Courthouse. As the two rode together through the dark forest, they talked of their chieftain, and of the new operation he was launching. They had faith that he was right in weakening his front and in marching off two of his eight divisions, but how did he know Grant's purpose? The enemy seemed as strong on the front as he had been since the battle opened: by what process had he concluded that the morning would find the enemy gone? They asked, they pondered, they wondered, but they could not answer.[54] Behind them, undismayed, Longstreet's veterans were waiting, their faces toward the South.

[52] Palmer in *Royall*, 35; *O. R.*, 36, part 1, pp. 1041, 1071; *ibid.*, part 2, p. 968. For the details of Anderson's orders, see *infra*, p. 306, note 7.

[53] *History of McGowan's Brigade*, 135–36. *Cf.* G. C. Underwood: *History of the Twenty-Sixth North Carolina*, 81.

[54] *Taylor's General Lee*, 238.

CHAPTER XVIII

THE BLOODY CLIMAX OF A HURRIED RACE

(SPOTSYLVANIA, MAY 8-12, 1864)

STEALTHILY the Confederate skirmishers wormed their way through the shell-torn Wilderness on the morning of May 8. Cautiously the infantry peered over the rough entrenchments. Anxiously at the Tapp house, Lee waited for word from the outposts. It came quickly. The Federals were gone from the Confederate left and centre—gone, and not in the direction of the Rapidan. At first, the reports indicated that the Federals had moved down the river toward Fredericksburg. Lee so advised the War Department,[1] but soon he received a dispatch from General Hampton stating that Channing Smith, one of the most daring and reliable of his scouts, had just returned from a ride within the enemy's lines and was quite positive that the V Corps was on the road toward Todd's Tavern.[2] As that resort was on the road to Spotsylvania Courthouse, Lee at once set out for the courthouse and dispatched orders to Ewell to move the Second Corps to Shady Grove Church.[3]

On his way Lee learned that A. P. Hill had become so sick overnight that it would not be possible for him to continue in command. That was no small addition to the burden of the commanding general at a moment when his adversary was seeking to outflank him. Longstreet badly wounded on the 6th, Hill incapacitated on the 8th—two of the three corps passing into the hands of new men, and Ewell himself apt to collapse at any time!

[1] O. R., 36, part 2, p. 974.
[2] W. B. Hackley: *Little Fork Ranger,* 56–58, contains Smith's narrative. On the basis of Lee's telegram to the War Department, General Grant based the claim (2 *Memoirs,* 212, 215) that Lee on the morning of May 8 had not "become acquainted" with his move toward Spotsylvania. It is manifest, however, that Lee could only have been for an hour or so under the impression that Grant was marching toward Fredericksburg, because Smith's report was received soon after sunrise.
[3] O. R., 51, part 2, p. 902.

It seemed as if the high command was to be destroyed in the face of the enemy, for in addition to the disabled chiefs of corps, General J. M. Jones and General Micah Jenkins had been killed, General L. A. Stafford had been mortally wounded, and Generals

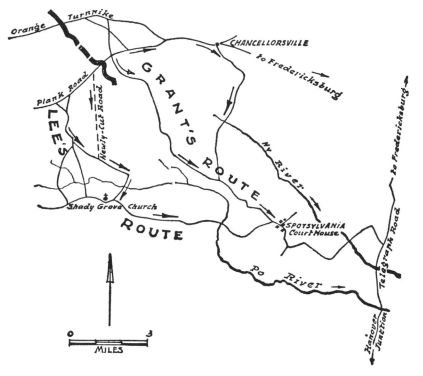

Routes of the opposing armies from the Wilderness to Spotsylvania Courthouse, May 7–9, 1864.

John Pegram and Henry L. Benning had been seriously hurt.[4] There could, of course, be no delay in filling Hill's place. Lee designated Early to act in his stead and arranged it that General John B. Gordon, who had so distinguished himself on the 6th, should have command of Early's division.[5]

[4] *O. R.*, 36, part 1, p. 1028.

[5] *O. R.*, 36, part 1, p. 1071, *O. R.*, 36, part 2, p. 974; *O. R.*, 51, part 2, p. 902; *Early*, 351. Hays's brigade was shifted from Early's to Johnson's division, to be consolidated with Stafford's brigade. Johnston's command of Rodes's division was transferred to Early to compensate. General Hill was very loath to leave his troops, and though he was for the time unable even to sit up, he insisted on being transported in an ambulance with his troops and had the vehicle parked immediately behind the line (14 *S. H. S. P.*, 532).

Probably by the time Lee reached Shady Grove Church, he learned that his expectation of a Federal move to Spotsylvania Courthouse had been realized, and more than realized: Anderson had reached that point and was already engaged hotly in defending it. Lee pressed on when he heard this. Leaving behind him Ewell's troops, who were marching wearily through the dust and smoke of the burning forest, he reached the vicinity of the courthouse before 2:30 p.m.[6] He then discovered that there had been a race between his army and Grant's for Spotsylvania, and that Anderson had won, though by the narrowest of margins. General Stuart had covered the route of Anderson's advance and had guarded the roads by which the Unionists would move toward the courthouse. Fitz Lee had been attacked by infantry on the road leading to Spotsylvania from Todd's Tavern, and Rosser, with one brigade, defending the courthouse proper, had been assailed by a mounted Federal division. Both Fitz Lee and Rosser had fought stubbornly during the early morning of the 8th, but they had been pushed slowly back and had been close to disaster when the head of Anderson's corps had come up on the double-quick and had relieved them. Subsequent Federal assaults had been beaten off with heavy loss to the enemy. It was a close escape from a turning movement that would have cost the Army of Northern Virginia dearly. Anderson deserved high credit, because he had started early and had pushed on vigorously. It was, perhaps, his greatest single service to the Confederate cause.[7] Stuart had directed the defense around Spotsylvania with the utmost skill. But behind these reasons for deliverance lay the conclusion of Lee on the afternoon of the 7th that Grant would

[6] O. R., 36, part 1, pp. 1028–29.

[7] It should be observed that Lee's orders to Anderson had been to withdraw his men as soon after dark on the evening of May 7 as possible. They were to retire a safe distance from the line and then were to rest before starting for Spotsylvania Courthouse over the road cut that day. Anderson duly moved his men out of the trenches, but as he subsequently wrote, "I found the woods in every direction on fire and burning furiously and there was no suitable place for rest." Besides, he explained, "The road by which I was conducted was narrow and frequently obstructed so that at best the progress of the troops was slow and the guide having informed me that it preserved the same character until near Spotsylvania I determined to continue the march until I should be within easy reach of that place" (undated letter of R. H. Anderson, in C. Irvine Walker, 162). General Pendleton stated in his report (O. R., 36, part 1, p. 1041), that Anderson's orders were to march by 3 a.m. of the 8th. Anderson himself did not mention the time-limit set for his departure from the Wilderness. In the diary of the First Corps (O. R., 36, part 1, p. 1056), there is an account of this move, but it is marred by a hiatus that makes it almost unintelligible.

move toward Spotsylvania. Had Lee not reasoned that his adversary would march in that direction, Grant would have outgeneralled him.[8]

There was a lull in the fighting after Lee arrived. The Federal cavalry withdrew; Spotsylvania Courthouse was in the hands of Anderson; and the infantry who had attacked him appeared to have been well beaten. Prisoners said the force was the whole of the V Corps. As the anxious afternoon wore on, however, signs of a new effort to destroy Anderson began to multiply. The VI Corps was reported to have come up to join the V in a sharp new assault. At 5 o'clock the storm broke. Over the fields and through the woods, the long, heavy clouds of bluecoats swept. But Confederate artillery was in position now, the infantry of the oft-tried First Corps was confident, and the attacks were not pushed on a wide front. Only on Lee's extreme right did danger develop. There, the Federal left overlapped for some distance and seemed in a fair way of enveloping the Confederate flank. But Lee's logistics did not fail him. Ewell had been told to hurry on, as Anderson might need support,[9] and now, precisely at the moment it was needed, the head of the Second Corps appeared on the road from Shady Grove. Rodes's division was leading and was at once thrown in on Anderson's right. It speedily broke up the enemy's flank attack, drove him back some distance, and put an end to the day's fighting.[10] Johnson's division formed on the right of Rodes, and, as night was coming on, was placed in a body of oak timber with instructions to throw up works. With direction indicated chiefly by the Federal camp fires stretched out in front of them, the men dug with much zeal and, ere morning, had a line they steadily strengthened.[11] Gordon's division was held in reserve. The Third Corps, which had been the last to leave the Wilderness position, bivouacked for the night northwest of Todd's Tavern.[12]

On the safe assumption that Early would arrive promptly with this corps, General Lee would have his whole force again in front

[8] O. R., 36, part 1, pp. 1028–29, 1042, 1056; 14 S. H. S. P., 527, 547; *Alexander*, 510–11; *Taylor's General Lee*, 239–40.
[9] O. R., 51, part 2, p. 902.
[10] O. R., 36, part 1, pp. 1029, 1042, 1056, 1071–72; Venable in 14 S. H. S. P., 527–28.
[11] 21 S. H. S. P., 232–33; 33 *ibid.*, 20–21.
[12] *Early*, 351–52; O. R., 36, part 1, p. 1095.

of the Army of the Potomac on the morning of May 9. The movement from the Wilderness was being completed without difficulty or serious loss. The army still stood between Grant and Richmond. That meant much. At the same time, the enemy was in immense strength and seemed determined to break through and to bear down all opposition. The whole demeanor of the Unionists was far different from what it had ever been in Virginia during any previous campaign. More than that, the other offensives in the state were becoming serious. General B. F. Butler had landed in force on the south side of James River between the Appomattox and Drewry's Bluff and had cut the Richmond and Petersburg Railroad.[13] A cavalry column had burned a railroad bridge at Stony Creek, between Petersburg and Weldon,[14] where it would certainly delay Beauregard's army, which was coming up slowly from the Carolinas. In the Shenandoah Valley, General Sigel was still at Winchester,[15] but could be expected to move at any time. Two forces of cavalry in the southwestern area were threatening the Virginia and Tennessee Railroad as well as the mines on which the state relied for nearly all its salt.[16] Nowhere was there any sign that the pressure exerted by the enemy was lightening. Everything, on the contrary, indicated that General Grant intended to fight on.

A long campaign was thus in prospect, with scant hope of reinforcements. It was more necessary than ever to conserve the strength of the Army of Northern Virginia. Lee did not intend to abandon offensive strategy, if the enemy gave him an opening, but as long as Grant continued to attack where he could be repulsed without heavy Southern losses, it obviously was to Lee's advantage to maintain the defensive. Provided the enemy could be held at a distance from Richmond and from the vital lines of communication, this course was as safe as it was profitable. "We have succeeded so far," Lee wrote Davis on May 9, "in keeping on the front flank of [Grant's] army, and impeding its progress, without a general engagement, which I will not bring on unless a favorable opportunity offers, or as a last resort. . . . With the blessing of God, I trust we shall be able to prevent Gen. Grant from reaching Richmond, and I think this army could render no

13 Cf. O. R., 36, part 2, p. 972.   14 O. R., 51, part 2, p. 903.
15 O. R., 37. part 1. p. 407.   16 O. R., 37, part 1, pp. 10, 723 ff.

more effectual service. . . . We could not successfully resist a larger force than that to which we are opposed, and it is of the first moment that we should have timely information of any increase." [17]

To prepare the ground for this defensive, Lee was up and was eating his breakfast by 3 A.M. on May 9. Longstreet's absence and Hill's illness put upon him such a burden of work that he had to make this his regular hour of rising during the campaign. He was usually occupied, with little or no opportunity for rest, until 9 or 10 or even later in the evening.[18]

Heavy as were the demands on his physique and on his intellect, the line he drew when Early brought up Hill's corps on the 9th, showed that his engineering skill and military judgment were unimpaired. Spotsylvania Courthouse lies on a ridge between the Po and Ny Rivers, two of the small streams that contribute their waters and their names to the Mattapony. This ridge is about three and a half miles wide at Spotsylvania and is a well-secured military position, because the rivers, though they are not wide, are "deep," to quote General Grant, "with abrupt banks, and bordered by heavily wooded and marshy bottoms . . . and difficult to cross except where bridged." [19]

To cover the courthouse and the three important roads that led southward from it, Lee drew a crude semicircle with the Po as its diameter. Several nights were spent in extending this front. When the line was completed the extreme right was a trifle more than three miles from the extreme left, and the whole position was compact and thoroughly defensible, except for a long salient on the left centre. This was occupied by Johnson's division of the Second Corps and was to play a gloomy part in the conflict. Lee's front, Colonel Henderson wrote, "was exactly adapted to the numbers he had at his disposal; in order to turn the position his adversary would have to cross one of the streams, and so divide his army, giving him an opportunity of dealing with him in detail, and his line was far stronger than that which he had held in the Wilderness." [20] Part of the front had open ground in the

[17] *Lee's Dispatches*, 176–77.   [18] 3 *B. and L.*, 242; 14 *S. H. S. P.*, 529.
[19] 2 *Grant's Memoirs*, 218.
[20] G. F. R. Henderson: *The Science of War*, 322. Both Grant (*op. cit.*, vol. 2, p. 218 *ff*.) and Humphreys (*op. cit.*, 72 *ff*.) pointed out the strength of the Confederate position. Humphreys gave a very detailed description of the ground.

direction of the Federal advance. Elsewhere the chief weakness of the position was that the woods came close to the line. As far as practicable, abatis were set. The artillery was located with

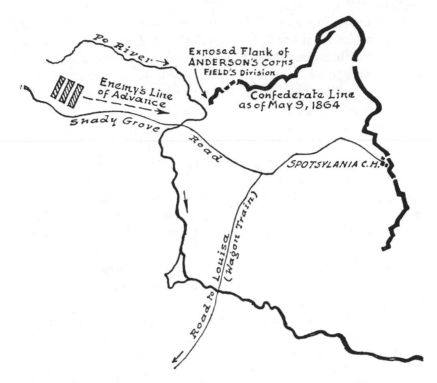

Situation along the Po River as reported to General Lee on the afternoon of May 9, 1864.

much care. Anderson held the left, Ewell the centre, and Early, when he came up on the 9th,[21] occupied the right, which was gradually extended southward.[22] The strength of the line was the more remarkable when it is remembered that it was not laid out at leisure but was started from the positions taken up by the infantry on May 8 and was then developed to make the most of the natural advantages of the adjacent terrain. "It was not only the entrenchments," said Henderson, "but the natural features of the ground also on which Lee relied in his defensive tactics. His eye for ground must have been extraordinary." [23]

[21] *Early,* 353.   [22] The course of the line is sketched on p. 323.
[23] Henderson: *Science of War,* 333.

Before Lee's field fortifications were carried as far as he desired, either on the right or on the left, he had need of them. On the afternoon of the 9th, the enemy's skirmishers felt out Anderson's lines with some vigor.[24] A little later in the day a strong force was reported on the south side of the Po in the direction of the Shady Grove road. If this force advanced to the bend of the river it would be able to enfilade the extreme left of the Confederate line on the other side of the stream. And, again, if the enemy continued to press eastward, south of the Po, he would reach the highway from Spotsylvania to Louisa Courthouse, along which Lee had placed his wagon train.[25]

The move, however, placed a relatively small part of the Federal army in a position where it could be attacked before it could be reinforced. Lee made the most of this. First, he ordered Early to send one of his divisions from the extreme right to the extreme left, so as to extend the left flank of Field's division and to protect it from an enfilade.[26] At the same time Lee instructed Early to dispatch another division south of the Po and to assail the enemy advancing eastward on the Shady Grove road. Heth's division, chosen for this purpose, moved early on the morning of May 10, found Federals in the vicinity of Waite's Shop that afternoon, and proceeded to attack. The Unionists at once began to withdraw, but some of the force held their ground and repulsed several very hard assaults by Heth. In the end the Federals retired across the Po, leaving one gun and some prisoners in Confederate hands.[27]

Meantime, north of the Po, interest shifted to the point where the right of the First Corps joined the left of the Second. This part of the front had given Lee no little concern. On the 9th, General Lee had seen its weakness and, at the instance of General

---

[24] *O. R.*, 36, part 1, p. 1056. [25] *Early*, 353.

[26] Early sent Mahone's division for this purpose. It occupied the crossing of the Shady Grove road over the Po.

[27] *Early*, 353. The Federals were the entire II Corps, but before they could all be deployed for action, General W. S. Hancock, their able commander, was ordered to avoid battle south of the Po and to send back two of his three divisions to the north bank, to be utilized in an attack on General Warren's front. Barlow's division was left to cover the withdrawal of the other units. Having repulsed Heth, Barlow followed the rest of the corps. The Confederates mistook this voluntary withdrawal for a retreat. It was, perhaps, fortunate for Early that the Federals were recalled when they were, because Heth's division was at a distance from any support, except for some of Hampton's cavalry, and doubtless would have fared badly in a fight with the whole of the II Corps, which was then the best in the Army of the Potomac.

Ewell, had consented to its extension farther to the northward to include some high ground from which it was believed the Federal artillerists could have dominated the Confederate position if they had been allowed to remain there.[28] The inclusion of this elevation made that sector a great, irregular angle, with the apex to the north.[29] Its average width was about half a mile and its depth

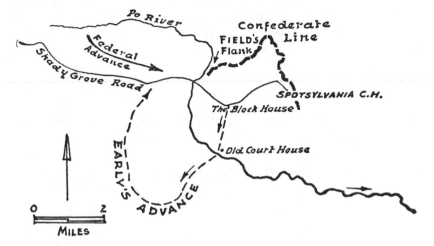

Advance of Early, May 10, 1864, to meet the Federal manœuvre south of the Po River.

approximately one mile. The soldiers promptly dubbed it the "Mule Shoe." [30] Lee contemplated the construction of a second line, across the base of the angle, and is said to have issued orders to have the work started.[31] This, however, was a rather large undertaking because the greater part of the interior of the angle was wooded. Either the woods had to be cleared, or else the base line had to be located where the enemy would have cover under which to approach unobserved.[32] Artillery had been placed at the apex of the angle and the entrenchments had been so strengthened that many officers felt the position could be held until there was leisure to prepare the line in rear of it.[33] Nonetheless, Lee was

[28] O. R., 36, part 1, p. 1071.   [29] See sketch, p. 323.
[30] O. R., 36, part 1, p. 1067; 21 S. H. S. P., 239; 33 ibid., 19–20; 3 C. M. H., 447.
[31] 3 C. M H., 447.
[32] Taylor's Four Years, 130; 33 S. H. S. P., 23.
[33] Statement of Colonel Thomas H. Carter, in charge of the artillery in the salient,
21 S. H. S. P., 239.

studying the terrain closely and that afternoon had his headquarters within the angle, some 150 yards in rear of Doles's brigade, of Rodes's division. This brigade occupied a position about
midway the northwest face of the salient,[34] and had a battery of
the Richmond Howitzers battalion supporting it. In front of
Doles's works were abatis and in rear of them was a partially
completed second line. The only condition that made his position
especially vulnerable, from the Confederate point of view, was
that thick, low-hanging pine woods came within 200 yards of the
works.[35]

During the day several attacks against Anderson's lines were
beaten off.[36] As the hot afternoon passed[37] there were signs of
Federal activity nearer the centre. Toward 6 o'clock, heavy guns
began to bombard the western face of the salient. On the hour,
the firing ceased. In about ten minutes there was a wild cheer,
followed quickly by the opening of hot infantry fire.[38] Soon a
courier hurried up to Lee with the startling news that Doles's
lines had been broken, that the howitzers had been captured, and
that the enemy was pouring into the salient.[39]

Lee at once mounted and started forward to rally the men, but
his staff officers protested that he must not go where the fire
would almost certainly be fatal. When at length they dissuaded
him from rushing directly into the action, he said, "Then you
must see to it that the ground is recovered."[40] Colonel Taylor
flung himself on his horse and galloped into the fury of the fight.[41]
Colonel Venable hurried off to bring part of Johnson's division
to the left.[42] Lee sought out the nearest battery and instructed
its commander, Captain A. W. Garber, to leave his guns and to
take his men forward to serve the captured howitzers, which he
was sure the Confederates would recover in a few minutes.[43]

The fire by this time was as violent as any that had ever been
heard in the battles of the Army of Northern Virginia,[44] but the
Southern troops on either side of the gap began to close in, and

[34] Venable in 14 *S. H. S. P.*, 528.   [35] *O. R.*, 36, part 1, p. 667.
[36] *O. R.*, 36, part 1, p. 1029; *O. R.*, 51, part 2, pp. 910–11.
[37] Waldrop in 3 *Richmond Howitzers*, 51.
[38] *O. R.*, 36, part 1, p. 668.   [39] *Taylor's General Lee*, 240.
[40] *Taylor's General Lee*, 240. This is usually regarded as the second "Lee to the
rear."
[41] Statement of C. C. Taliaferro, April 25, 1895, *Taylor MSS.*
[42] 14 *S. H. S. P.*, 528.
[43] 33 *S. H. S. P.*, 342.   [44] *Welch*, 97.

those who had been driven out reformed on the second line. Taylor, seizing a flag and still mounted, led the men onward,[45] in company with other officers. The Federals, who were admirably handled by Colonel Emory Upton, resisted with the utmost determination. They received no reinforcements, however, and were slowly pushed out of the works. By nightfall the danger was past, and the line had been restored. The Confederate loss was subsequently estimated at 650, but was probably higher.[46] That evening, as if to expiate the butchery, a Confederate band played "Nearer, My God, to Thee," and a Union band answered with the Dead March from "Saul." [47]

To the end of the third day at Spotsylvania, then, the attacks of the enemy had been repelled with heavy casualties. The margin of safety had been a little narrower than usual, to be sure, but there had been nothing to indicate any decline in the prowess of the army. The veterans who stood behind their earthworks and mowed the enemy down, suffered far less than did the Federals. Still, it was now a week since the three corps had left their cantonments on the Rapidan—and the enemy showed no disposition to suspend his costly assaults. More than that, ugly news came from the rear. The Federal cavalry, now under a new commander, Major General Phil H. Sheridan, had slipped around the flank of the Confederate army, and on the 9th had struck the Central Railroad at Beaver Dam Creek, where two locomotives, three trains of cars, most of the reserve stores of the army and 504,000 rations of bread and 904,000 of meat had been destroyed. The railroad had been torn up and culverts had been demolished for some distance.[48] Then the Union horse had moved on toward Richmond, while Stuart, gathering his scattered units, pushed the endurance of weary men and hungry mounts to the absolute limit in an effort to get between Sheridan and Richmond.[49] Lee was accustomed to Federal raids by this time and expected from them

---

[45] Taliaferro statement, *loc. cit.*

[46] *O. R.*, 36, part 1, p. 1072. *Ibid.*, part 2, p. 983. Some intimate details of the recovery of the trenches are given in *Richmond Howitzers Battalion*, 246.

[47] *Thomas*, 479.

[48] The loss of transportation was even more serious than the damage to the track, because the Central at this time had only eight engines and 108 cars in running order (*O. R.*, 51, part 2, p. 903).

[49] *O. R.*, 36, part 1, pp. 777, 790; *ibid.*, 51, part 2, p. 909.

a measure of annoyance without serious injury to the army; but in this instance he saw the fulfillment of all the fears he had felt during the winter concerning the cavalry. If the horses did not hold out, so that Stuart could at least protect the scant supplies that were reaching the army, then anything might happen!

May 11 dawned dark. Heth was moved back from the south side of the Po to the vicinity of Spotsylvania, while Mahone remained to guard the extreme left of the First Corps.[50] General Lee spent part of the morning examining carefully the rear of Rodes's lines, against which the attack of the previous evening had been directed.[51] He was accompanied by General M. L. Smith, chief engineer, and was convinced that the "Mule Shoe" could be held with the help of the artillery. General Edward Johnson, who commanded at the apex of the salient, went out beyond the skirmish line and failed to find the enemy. Lee, however, gave instructions that if the enemy should attack any part of the front in the vicinity of the salient, Gordon should at once advance Early's division in support without waiting for further orders.[52]

During the early afternoon the rain began to fall heavily,[53] and the enemy, who had been silent all morning,[54] began to bestir himself. There were renewed demonstrations on the left, as if the Federals were planning to cross the Po again. Lee promptly ordered Early to send troops to the south of the river and told him to occupy Shady Grove.[55]

Before Early began his move with two brigades of Wilcox's division, surprising dispatches arrived at general headquarters from Rooney Lee, who was in rear of the enemy's left flank. He reported that the Federal wounded had been sent to Belle Plain and that their wagons had been underway all night.[56] It was impossible to tell, from the information Rooney forwarded, whether the move was southward in the direction of the Annas, or northward in retreat to Fredericksburg.[57] In either case, the informa-

---

[50] *Early*, 354.   [51] McHenry Howard: *Recollections*, 292.   [52] 14 *S. H. S. P.*, 529.
[53] Waldrop in 3 *Richmond Howitzers*, 52; 3 *B. and L.*, 170. Ewell (*O. R.*, 36, part 1, p. 1072) stated that "it rained hard all day" but all the other authorities agree that the downpour came late and that the temperature fell after dark.
[54] 33 *S. H. S. P.*, 22.   [55] *Early*, 355.   [56] *O. R.*, 51, part 2, pp. 916–17
[57] Ewell (*O. R.*, 36, part 1, p. 1072) stated the enemy's withdrawal was reported to be toward Fredericksburg. Taylor in his *General Lee*, 242, said the information was that the enemy was moving to the Confederate right.

tion was so circumstantial that Lee felt he should prepare the army for instant movement. Many of the batteries were in advanced positions and would be very difficult to withdraw during the darkness. Lee directed that all guns so situated should be brought off before nightfall, to prevent delay in case of sudden orders to begin the march.[58] At the Harrison House, within the "Mule Shoe," Lee conferred with General Ewell and with General Long, corps chief of artillery, and particularly ordered the artillery of Johnson's division withdrawn from the salient, as it had to come through thick woods by a single narrow and winding road.[59] It is not certain Lee had subsequent intimation from any quarter that Johnson protested against the withdrawal of these guns, and later notified General Ewell that the enemy was becoming active on his front.[60] The suspicions of none of the commanders within earshot seem to have been aroused by the unusual fact that the enemy's bands struck up about 11 o'clock and continued to play, in the rain and darkness, for hours on end.[61]

The music had scarcely died away, and the black of the night was just beginning to change to the gray of a cold, wet fog, when there came to Lee's headquarters the rattle of heavy infantry fire from the salient. The General had arisen, as usual, at 3 o'clock, and lost no time in mounting Traveller.[62] Riding to the front through woods still so deep in shadows that a line of troops could not have been seen a hundred yards away, he soon encountered men running toward the rear. Without attempting to get from

58 O. R., 36, part 1, p. 1044.
59 O. R., 36, part 1, pp. 1044, 1086, 1088–89. 7 S. H. S. P., 535 ff.
60 21 S. H. S. P., 240; 33 ibid., 336; O. R., 36, part 1, pp. 1079–80; Venable in 14 S. H. S. P., 529. In his paper on this campaign, published in 4 M. H. S. M., 113, McHenry Howard stated that after he had been released from prison General Ewell, or the adjutant general of that officer told him that General Lee was notified of the threat on Johnson's front. Lee is also said to have observed, "See, gentlemen, how difficult it is to have certain information, or how to determine what to do. Here is a dispatch from General Johnson stating that the enemy are massing in his front, and at the same time I am informed by General Early that they are moving around our left. Which am I to believe?" Captain Howard cited Colonel Marshall as authority for General Lee's remark. He added that despite the uncertainty, General Lee ordered the artillery replaced at daybreak. On the other hand neither Ewell, Johnson, nor Long, in their respective official reports, affirmed or even suggested that Lee was informed of Johnson's apprehensions. Long recorded, moreover (O. R., 36, part 1, p. 1086), that he received at 3:30 A.M. on May 12 an order from General Johnson, endorsed by General Ewell, to send back the artillery. Had that paper been referred to General Lee, his endorsement probably would have been noted also. The evidence is thus in conflict, and the question has to be left in the measure of doubt expressed in the text.
61 21 S. H. S. P., 252.   62 Venable in 14 S. H. S. P., 529.

them the story of what had happened, he began to rally them. Taking off his hat so that he might be recognized, he exhorted them to halt. "Hold on!" he cried. "We are going to form a new line. Your comrades need your services. Stop, men." [63] Some heeded him and halted; others ran wildly past him. "Shame on you men, shame on you," he called out in his deep voice. "Go back to your regiments; go back to your regiments!" [64]

In a few moments, out of the salient, rode Major Robert W. Hunter, of the staff of General Edward Johnson. Hunter was mounted on an artillery horse, and shouted his message in his excitement: "General, the line is broken at the angle in General Johnson's front!"

Lee's expression changed instantly. Remembering that he had ordered General Gordon to move his division forward to any point of the salient that might be threatened, he reined Traveller in. "Ride with me to General Gordon," he said, [65] and turned to the left and rear. Perhaps on the way, Hunter had breath to tell him more of what had happened—how Johnson had been on the *qui vive* all night, how the enemy had suddenly burst over the lines held by the Louisiana brigades and by the remnant of J. M. Jones's Virginians, how some of the infantry had found their charges useless because of the rain, how artillery that had been ordered back had arrived just in time for full twenty pieces to fall into the enemy's hands, how General Johnson, hobbling along on a stick, had tried to keep the men together, and how the enemy had captured him and General George H. Steuart and most of the division. There were thousands of bluecoats in the salient; the lines of the army were split in twain. [66]

Two hundred yards brought Lee to the point where the left of Pegram's brigade was hurriedly forming. Still farther to the left was Gordon's brigade, under Colonel Clement A. Evans. [67] These troops, and Johnston's four regiments, formed the whole of Early's division, which Gordon was temporarily commanding. The three

[63] Major E. M. Williamson to the writer, June 4, 1932; same author in Danville, Va., *Register*, May 14, 1930.
[64] Robert Stiles: *Four Years under Marse Robert* (cited hereafter as *Stiles*), 259.
[65] 33 *S. H. S. P.*, 339.
[66] *O. R.*, 36, part 1, pp. 1044–45, 1072–73; 1079–80; 21 *S. H. S. P.*, 240–41, 242–43; 33 *ibid.*, 252, 338; *LaBree*, 164–65.
[67] 33 *S. H. S. P.*, 339; *O. R.*, 36, part 1, pp. 1078–79.

brigades had been scattered when Gordon had ordered them forward to support Johnson, but already Gordon had boldly thrown out the men of Johnston's entire brigade as skirmishers and had ordered them to advance, in the hope that they could hold off the enemy till the other units were ready to charge.[68] A few minutes after Lee reached the flank of Pegram's brigade Gordon himself came dashing along the line. Meeting Lee, he pulled up his horse on its haunches and saluted: "What do you want me to do, General?" he asked.[69]

Lee, of course, approved the dispositions the Georgian had already made and directed him to proceed with the counterattack. His manner was far calmer than it had been on the morning of May 6, when he had witnessed the break in the lines of Heth and Wilcox in the Wilderness, but the battle-blood was surging in his veins. As Gordon turned to complete his arrangements, Lee rode to the centre of the line, between the Fifty-second Virginia of Pegram's brigade[70] and the Thirteenth Georgia of Gordon's.[71] His hat was still in his hand and he quietly turned Traveller's head to the enemy.[72]

By this time a searching fire was penetrating the woods where the graycoats were taking position. Gordon himself had just escaped death from a bullet that grazed his coat, not an inch from his spine,[73] but when he saw Lee's position, he realized that the General was preparing to join in the charge and he broke out dramatically, "General Lee, this is no place for you. Go back, General; we will drive them back. These men are Virginians and Georgians. They have never failed. They never will. Will you, boys?"

"No, no," cried every man within hearing distance.

"General Lee to the rear; Lee to the rear!"

"Go back, General Lee, we can't charge until you go back!"

"We will drive them back, General!"

Gordon and some of his officers placed their mounts between him and the enemy, whose fire had come nearer and had in-

---

[68] *Gordon,* 276; Venable in 14 *S. H. S. P.,* 529–30.
[69] 21 *S. H. S. P.,* 246.   [70] 8 *S. H. S. P.,* 34.
[71] G. W. Nichols: *A Soldier's Story of His Own Regiment,* 151.
[72] *Gordon,* 278. *Cf. Long,* 341, for a refutation of the contemporary claim that Lee sought death in this charge because he despaired of success.
[73] *Gordon,* 277; 21 *S. H. S. P.,* 246.

318

creased ominously during the few seconds of delay. A minute more and the enemy would be upon them. Gordon did not wait on military etiquette. Leaning forward, he caught hold of Traveller's bridle, but in the crowding of the flanks of the two brigades, which were now ready to advance, Gordon was pushed behind Lee. Thereupon a sergeant of the Forty-ninth Virginia seized Traveller by the reins and jerked his head to the rear.[74]

As Lee rode unwillingly back a few paces, he heard the clear voice of Gordon above the roar of the musketry: "Forward! Guide right!"[75]

Lee turned to young Robert Hunter, the officer who had brought him the first news of the break on Johnson's front. "Major Hunter," said he, "collect together the men of Johnson's division and report to General Gordon."[76]

Almost before Lee could say even this, Gordon's line of battle had disappeared in a dense growth of old field pines. There was a wild burst of firing—next, a hoarse, quavering, rebel yell, and then comparative silence as the two lines came to grips, too close together to load and fire.[77] To his immeasurable relief, as daylight came, Lee saw that Gordon was driving the Federals up the salient, but he discovered, almost simultaneously, that Gordon's lines were not long enough to cover the whole front on which the enemy was pressing. Others, fortunately, observed this before Lee could issue orders. On the right of the salient, Lane's North Carolinians had already rushed forward and had halted the advance.[78] On the left, Rodes threw Ramseur's brigade into action.[79] Daniel supported Ramseur. Together they held back the flood for a time, but they were so inferior in number that Rodes began to call for reinforcements. Lee immediately dispatched Colonel Venable to General Mahone, with instructions

---

[74] 32 *S. H. S. P.*, 203. There is much confusion as to the exact sequence of events during this familiar episode. The writer has followed chiefly the account of W. W. Smith, who was close at hand, young at the time, and apt to remember (*cf.* 8 *S. H. S. P.*, 35; 32 *ibid.*, 212). Another excellent contemporary account, from *The Richmond Sentinel*, is reproduced in *Marginalia*, 229. For other accounts see 14 *S. H. S. P.*, 530; 21 *ibid.*, 246; 32 *ibid.*, 200 *ff.*; Gordon, 278 *ff.* The sergeant who led Lee to the rear is said to have been William A. Compton, of Front Royal, Va. (32 *S. H. S. P.*, 203). There is some disagreement whether the episode occurred in front of the Forty-ninth or of the Fifty-second Virginia (*cf.* 8 *S. H. S. P.*, 34, and 32 *ibid.*, 212). Both regiments claimed that Lee was led back through their ranks.

[75] 21 *S. H. S. P.*, 246–47.

[76] 33 *S. H. S. P.*, 339.

[77] 21 *S. H. S. P.*, 247.

[78] 14 *S. H. S. P.*, 530.

[79] *O. R.*, 36, part 1, p. 1082.

that one brigade of Mahone be left to cover the crossing of the Po on Field's left flank and that the rest of the division be dispatched forthwith to aid Rodes. It was a dangerous thing to do, for the battle was now spreading along the front, but the salient must be held, and, if possible, the lines must be restored.[80] Lee did not concern himself, for the moment, with reinforcing the right of the salient, for he knew that the two brigades of Wilcox's division, which had been sent to the south of the Po the previous day, had found no enemy there, had returned, and would soon be available to strengthen Lane's gallant defense.[81]

Gordon's troops were fighting like men possessed, and by this time were masters of the centre of the salient. Soon Scales and Thomas of Wilcox's division were with Lane on the right and were pushing the enemy back toward the apex of the angle.[82] By 6:30 o'clock it was apparent that the Federals were being held, and more than held, except on the left, in front of Ramseur and Daniel. There the battle was doubtful, for the Federals were still throwing in more and more troops, as if their reserves were inexhaustible. Rodes must have help—and quickly.

To provide it, Lee rode off in search of Mahone's division, which was moving up from the right. Not far from the courthouse, he found Harris's brigade resting by the side of the road. In a few words Lee ordered Harris forward to support Rodes, and took his place by that officer's side to speed the march. The column started briskly forward toward the salient and soon came under artillery fire from long-range Federal batteries that were playing on the approaches to prevent the dispatch of reinforcements. Traveller became excited as shells burst around him, and he began to rear wildly. Lee kept his seat, and sought to quiet his mount. Once more Traveller reared, and as he did so, a round shot passed under his girth only a few inches from Lee's stirrup. If the horse had not been in the air at the moment, the General would almost certainly have been killed. It was the narrowest escape from death that he had experienced since that day, seventeen years before, when the sentinel had fired on him as he and Beauregard had come out of the covered way at Vera Cruz.

Harris's veterans knew and loved Lee well, for they had fought

---

[80] 8 S. H. S. P., 107.   [81] Early, 355.   [82] Wilcox MS. report, 39.

many times under his eye, when Carnot Posey had been their leader. They were quick now to see his danger. "Go back, General," they yelled, "Go back! For God's sake, go back!" And some of them tried to get between him and the enemy's fire, or to turn him to the rear. His anxiety was apparent to all who saw him that day,[83] but his battle-ire was aroused, and if he was not personally to have a hand in repelling the enemy from the salient, he must have guarantee that it would be done. So, simply but but stubbornly, he answered their appeal. "If you will promise me to drive those people from our works, I will go back." The men shouted their agreement and started on more vigorously than ever. Lee told Colonel Venable to guide them to Rodes's position, and after watching them for a moment with admiring eye, he turned his horse toward Early's lines, on the right of the salient. Harris's men did not arrive a moment too soon. Just as they reached Rodes at the doublequick, an aide galloped up from General Ramseur to say that he could hold his ground only a few minutes longer unless help was forthcoming.[84]

Before 9 o'clock McGowan's brigade was sent to support Harris. It gave Rodes enough rifles to halt the Federal advance and to stabilize the fighting on the left side of the salient.[85] Then, gradually, as Gordon and Wilcox pressed them on the centre and right of the salient, the Federals were forced back to the apex and ere long were driven over the parapet. In front of this they rallied once more and refused to be moved. The second phase of the battle was ended. The enemy had attacked successfully; the Confederate counterattack had cleared the salient.

What next? Should Lee permit the enemy to remain on the outer side of the parapet, separated from his own men only by the length of a bayoneted gun? He was, said Fitz Lee, "very sensitive about his lines being broken. It made him more than ever personally pugnacious." [86] All his impulse prompted him to force the enemy back to the woods. Sound tactics dictated the same course. He could not afford to leave the enemy at his para-

[83] *Sorrel*, 246.
[84] This account of the fourth "Lee to the rear" is paraphrased from a letter written to General N. H. Harris, Nov. 24, 1871, by Colonel Charles S. Venable, who was a witness to the whole scene (8 *S. H. S. P.*, 107).
[85] *Wilcox's MS. report*, 39; *O. R.*, 36, part 1, pp. 1093–94.
[86] *Fitz Lee*, 336. Cf. Rosser, *loc. cit.*, 14: "Of all things, General Lee most disliked to lose ground after taking his position for battle."

pet, if it was possible to drive him out. For the Federals, from that position, would certainly renew the assault when they found an opening, and then they might sweep down the salient again. In the face of their attack, it would be impracticable to complete a line in rear of the salient, or to withdraw in daylight to it. At the very least, the men must hold on until they could be brought during the night to the gorge of the salient.[87]

Word was passed to Gordon and to Rodes to keep their men at the parapet, to contest every new attack, and to hurl the enemy back if they could. Gallantly enough they held to their task while Lee hastily examined the rest of the front to see what he could do to aid Ewell's men. He decided very soon that he could not accomplish anything on his left. The Federals were already attacking there. Anderson beat them off, thanks to Alexander's readiness with his artillery,[88] but he could not attempt an offensive.[89] On the centre and right of Hill's corps, Lee found that no assaults had been delivered. The enemy seemed absorbed in the operations against Ewell. Already Wilcox's work was over, and his part of the line was restored. Both his division and Heth's were available for a counterstroke, for which the ground seemed favorable. On the front of the line of Hill's corps, south of the "Mule Shoe," was a projection styled Heth's salient. Troops moving from the right side of this salient would be unseen by the Federals in front of the "Mule Shoe," and if they reached an oak wood in front of their lines, they would be on the flank of the Federals.

"Captain Nicholson (commanding sharpshooters) of Lane's brigade," General Wilcox subsequently reported, "had explored the woods in front of the right face of the salient on Heth's front and ascertained that the enemy were in line facing the left face of the salient, the right resting in the woods in front of the former face."[90] Lane filed quietly into the woods opposite the right face

---

[87] *Alexander*, 525.

[88] Instead of withdrawing his batteries on the evening of May 11, in accordance with general instructions to prepare for a move, Alexander "had his ammunition chests in the trenches mounted on the caissons, and [had the] gun carriages taken to the vicinity of their guns, but retained the latter in position as the safest course" (Pendleton in *O. R.*, 36, part 1, p. 1044. *Cf. ibid.*, part 1, p. 1057; *Alexander*, 518).

[89] Irvine Walker, *op. cit.*, 169, said that after the battle Lee sent R. H. Anderson a letter "thanking him for the masterly handling of his corps and commending his men for their gallantry."

[90] *Wilcox's MS. report*, 40.

of the salient and soon had his line at right angles to the enemy's front. Mahone's brigade under Colonel Daniel A. Weisiger was in support. The situation was promising.

Before the two brigades could strike, the Federals, who proved

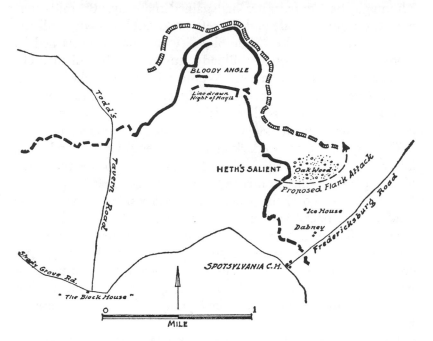

The Bloody Angle near Spotsylvania Courthouse, showing particularly the terrain and direction of the proposed flank attack on the Federals from Heth's Salient, May 12, 1864.

to be of Burnside's IX Corps, advanced to attack the left face of Heth's salient. Lee watched them come forward. Hill's artillery opened upon them at once, the infantry fired as soon as they could bring down their mark, and Lane, of course, hit the Federals in flank.[91] As the front of the advancing line shifted somewhat, Lee rode forward under a hot fire and directed that the artillery change its range. The officer who was to deliver the order to other batteries started out immediately by the route over which Lee had come. "Have that officer take a road nearer the rear of

[91] *Wilcox's MS. report*, 40; *Early*, 356; Lane's report, which is not printed in the *Official Records* appears in 9 *S. H. S. P.*, 145 *ff*. This has been the least understood incident of the battle of Spotsylvania Courthouse, but Wilcox's report, which is very clear and explicit, made plain the exact nature of what was planned and executed.

the line of guns," he said rapidly, "it is a safer way." He seemed quite oblivious to the fact that he had done what he did not wish another to attempt.[92]

Burnside's attack was quickly repulsed in what was the clearest advantage the Confederates had gained that day. By mid-afternoon the right was safe and the left could hold its own. Still the fight raged around the "Mule Shoe," which had now earned its more familiar name of the "Bloody Angle." Successful in itself, the counterattack by Lane and Weisiger failed to shake the grip of the Federals on the outer side of the parapet. From every vantage-point, the Federal artillery, rising to unprecedented violence,[93] poured its fire into the salient and plastered Anderson's lines.

The fog gave place to dark clouds that emptied themselves at intervals in violent showers. The Federals held to the outer side of the parapet; the Confederates challenged their grip on it. Men were pulled over the parapet from either side and were made prisoner. Bayonets were thrust through the logs.[94] Both forces fought as had their frontier fathers at the stockades. The loss of life was staggering; some of the brigades, wet, bleeding, and decimated, were close to exhaustion. As soon as the attacks on Anderson slackened, Lee called for Humphreys's brigade and for Bratton's[95] and sent them from Anderson's lines to support Ewell.[96]

Then Lee determined to make another effort to force the Federals from the parapet of the Bloody Angle by an advance from Heth's salient. Sending for General Lane, he complimented the conduct of that officer's sharpshooters earlier in the day. He was loath, he said, to send them into action again, but he wished to ascertain the enemy's position on the Fredericksburg road and would be glad if those "fine soldiers" would undertake it. Lane replied that however tired the men might be, he knew they would go wherever Lee ordered them. "I will not send them unless they are willing to go," Lee answered. When Lane

<hr>

[92] *W. W. Chamberlaine*, 100. Lee exposed himself so often during the course of the campaign that he drew many protests from the general officers as well as from the men in the ranks. "I wish," he said, in answer to one such protest, "I knew where my place is on the battlefield; wherever I go some one tells me it is not the place for me" (Jones, *L. and L.*, 317).
[93] 3 *C. M. H.*, 453; *Fitz Lee*, 355; *Welch*, 97.   [94] *O. R.*, 36, part 1, p. 1094.
[95] Bratton had succeeded the able Micah Jenkins, killed in the Wilderness.
[96] *O. R.*, 36, part 1, p. 1057.

introduced Captain Nicholson, Lee repeated what he had said to Lane. The sharpshooters were at once brought forward and greeted Lee with cheers as they passed him.[97] They soon discovered, however, that the Federals had entrenched positions in front of Early. Two brigades were then thrown out—only to uncover a still stronger line that would bar any large-scale flanking operation from the Confederate right.

The possibilities had now been exhausted. The battle had to be fought out at the parapet of the salient until the defenders could be withdrawn to the gorge. Lee directed that the line at that point be completed forthwith,[98] and late in the evening he went there in person to encourage the men. In Ewell's company he walked among the tired troops as they felled trees, carried them into position and piled earth on them.[99] It was 800 yards to the point where the battle was raging.[100] If the line could be completed and occupied safely, there would be little danger of another irruption of the enemy.

Long after darkness had engulfed the rear of the salient, the flash of rifles, the roar of the Federal guns, and the appearance of weary, dazed, and bloody men from the front told of the fidelity with which the veterans of the Second Corps were obeying Lee's orders to hold the parapet. They had been fighting now for sixteen hours and more, with no rest, no food. The enemy, still two or three to one, fired ceaselessly through every opening in the parapet, or hurled bayoneted guns, like spears, down on the heads of the Confederates. The dead were so numerous that they filled the ditch and had to be piled behind it in a ghastly parados. The survivors waded in mud and gore, slipping now and then over the mangled bodies of their comrades. In all the bloody story of that mad, criminal war there had not been such a hideous ordeal. When it seemed that the remnant of the brigades could not endure even fifteen minutes longer, word would come that they must hold on—that the line at the gorge of the salient was not yet finished. Then, with a grim setting of jaws, they would bite new cartridges, ram home the charges, fire over the parapet

[97] 9 S. H. S. P., 156.   [98] Cf. O. R., 51, part 2, p. 922.
[99] John O. Casler: Four Years in the Stonewall Brigade, 323–24. Casler stated that Lee remained on the line all night, but he may have been mistaken in this.
[100] O. R., 36, part 1, p. 1073.

and drop back into the muck of the ditch to do the same thing over again, with trembling fingers and numbed arms. At last, about midnight, when the enemy was as weary as they, Lee sent them orders to fall back slowly to the new line. Even then their discipline was perfect. At a whispered command, one unit would slip away, those on either side would close in, and the fire would be kept up. Had "old Jack" seen them there in the midnight, even his iron countenance would have melted at their misery, but his eyes would have fired in admiration of their valor.

It was nearly dawn on the 13th[101] when the last of them passed through the gorge of the salient to new security—but security bought at a ghastly price. Never before, save in the charge of Pickett and Pettigrew at Gettysburg, had as many soldiers of the Army of Northern Virginia been captured as in that salient. Lee did not attempt to give any estimate of their number when he sent a brief report to the President at the end of the day.[102] Ewell subsequently put down the number at 2000,[103] but the Federals claimed to have taken over 3000.[104] The casualties among the commanding officers had been terrific. Major General Edward Johnson and Brigadier General George H. Steuart had been captured, Brigadier General Abner Perrin had been killed, Brigadier General Junius Daniel had been mortally wounded, and Brigadier Generals James A. Walker, Samuel McGowan, R. D. Johnston, and S. D. Ramseur less seriously injured.[105] In nine days' fighting, five general officers had been killed or mortally hurt, nine had been wounded and two had been captured.

And this doleful list did not tell the whole story of that dreadful day. In the midst of the battle, when the whole army had been wrestling with the blue thousands that had streamed over the parapets, a messenger had arrived with news of Stuart's movements to head off Sheridan's raid before it reached Richmond. Spurring their worn mounts, the anxious Southern troopers had

101 3 C. M. H., 454.
102 O. R., 36, part 1, p. 1030.   103 O. R., 36, part 1, p. 1072.
104 O. R., 36, part 1, pp. 14, 192. The report of General M. R. Patrick, provost marshal general, showed that from May 1 through May 12, the number captured was 7078 (ibid., p. 280). So heavy had Lee's losses been that all the survivors of Johnson's division were united after the battle into one small brigade, which Colonel William Terry was later promoted to command. In this consolidation the remnant of the "Stonewall Brigade," Jackson's first command, lost its identity (O. R., 36, part 3, p. 813; 21 S. H. S. P., 237).
105 O. R., 36, part 1, pp. 1030, 1073, 1079, 1082, 1094.

intercepted the Federals at Yellow Tavern, seven miles north of Richmond and had given battle there. Stuart himself, as always, had been in the fullest of the fight, and, just as the Unionists had turned off to try to force a way into Richmond by some less-contested route, he had been shot through the body by a dismounted blue cavalryman. That had been on the afternoon of the 11th. The wounded Stuart had been borne into Richmond, and, when the dispatch was sent Lee, was believed to be dying.[106]

Stuart dying! The "eyes of the army" about to be destroyed. It was the worst calamity that had befallen the South since that May day, just a year previously, when "Stonewall" had breathed his last. Lee was surrounded by a number of young officers when he finished reading the dispatch, and he had to steel himself as he announced the news. "General Stuart," he said, as he folded up the paper, "has been mortally wounded: a most valuable and able officer." He paused a moment and then he added in a shaken voice, "He never brought me a piece of false information."[107] Later in the night, while the battle had still been frenzied, another message brought the dreaded word: With the cheerful composure that marked all his acts, Stuart had died after 8 P.M. that evening. Lee put his hands over his face to conceal his emotion, as he heard that his great lieutenant was dead, dead in the crisis of his beloved army's life, dead at the age of thirty-one and before the fullness of his powers had been realized.[108] As quickly as he could, Lee retired to his tent to master his grief, and when one of Stuart's staff officers entered, a little later, to tell him of Stuart's last minutes, Lee could only say, "I can scarcely think of him without weeping!"[109] To Mrs. Lee he wrote, "A more zealous, ardent, brave and devoted soldier than Stuart the Confederacy cannot have."[110] Jackson dead, Stuart dead, Longstreet wounded, Hill sick, Ewell almost incapacitated—the men on whom he had most relied were going fast! He had to walk alone.

Still another woe that black night brought. In his raid on Rich-

---

[106] 7 S. H. S. P., 107 ff., 140 ff.

[107] W. Gordon McCabe, an eye-witness, in R. E. Lee, Jr., 124–25.

[108] 37 S. H. S. P., 95.

[109] Cooke, 403; 3 B. and L., 243 n. It is apparent from the latter reference that Lee did not receive the news of Stuart's wounding until the 12th.

[110] R. E. Lee, Jr., 125. The formal announcement to the army of the death of Stuart appears in O. R., 36, part 3, p. 800.

mond, Sheridan had cut the Richmond, Fredericksburg and Potomac Railroad precisely as, on the 9th, he had torn up track on
the Central. The army's communications with Richmond were
thus interrupted. South of Petersburg, on May 7, General Kautz
had broken in two places the Petersburg and Weldon Railroad on
which both the commissary and the quartermaster general relied
for the transportation of grain.[111] No supplies were arriving either
for the men or for the animals.

The wagon trains had several days' short rations of bread and
meat. If this gave out, the soldiers could be counted on to tighten
their belts and to endure hunger until the railroads could be repaired. But what of the horses? If they were not fed the guns
could not be moved. There seemed no recourse save an uncertain
one suggested in a message from the quartermaster general—to
appeal to patriotic farmers behind the battle-front to lend the
army corn, on Lee's personal pledge that it would be repaid
promptly in kind.[112]

All this load of death, disaster, and threatened hunger was put
on Lee's shoulders that dreadful 12th of May; yet he bore it with
so stout a heart that even those who knew him best did not
realize that in its agonizing demands upon him the day of the
Bloody Angle was second only to the final day at Gettysburg. He
did not admit the imminence of ruin or lament the things he
could not control. Unafraid, with faith in God, he faced the
doubtful morrow.

[111] *O. R.*, 36, part 1, p. 172.   [112] *O. R.*, 36, part 2, pp. 989–90.

CHAPTER XIX

A Merciful Rain and Another March

(spotsylvania, may 13–22, 1864)

The rain that had drenched the struggling shoulders of the Army of Northern Virginia on the day of the grapple for the Bloody Angle seemed a mercy on the morning of May 13. It had, to be sure, contributed to prevent the recovery of four of the captured Confederate guns that the enemy was said to have left in the salient on the 12th,[1] but now it gave the weary army rest. As the downpour swelled the streams and filled the roads with water, the outposts could relax, and the men who sat by the fires in the deep woods had assurance that, for the hour at least, their lives were their own.

The desperate character of the previous day's fighting was more apparent now that the scene could be surveyed when it was free of smoke and mist. Many amazing stories were told of what had happened, among them that two great forest trees had been hewn down by *minié* balls. Lee was loath to believe this, when he heard it from a member of Ewell's staff. "Captain," he said to his informant, "can you show us those trees?" Later on, when the site was accessible, the officer led him to it. One of the trees was an oak with a diameter of twenty-two inches, chipped away to an unsustaining splinter, as if beavers had gnawed it. The other was only two inches smaller across the centre.[2] Had not the survivors been nearby in the woods, it would have seemed incredible that men had held their ground in such a fire as felled those trees.

The blessed rain continued with a few intermissions until May 17—four full days after the end of the battle of the Bloody Angle.[3] Large-scale operations were at a standstill. For the soldiers in the ranks, the needed rest was continued; to Lee, "rest" was a euphe-

[1] *O. R.*, 36, part 1, p. 1073; 7 *S. H. S. P.*, 535–38.
[2] *Wilcox's MS. report*, 41; *O. R.*, 36, part 1, p. 1093; 33 *S. H. S. P.*, 18–19.
[3] *Pendleton*, 332; 2 *Meade*, 195; C. A. Dana in *O. R.*, 36, part 1, pp. 69–72.

mism. He still rose at 3 A.M. daily and, for long hours of toil, was so busy in correcting the confusion caused by the protracted operations that he was glad to snatch a few minutes' sleep on a plank with one end raised on a rail.[4]

Consolidating the decimated brigades of Johnson's old division, Lee named John B. Gordon major general, with rank from the date of his great struggle to recover the Bloody Angle.[5] Until Lee could decide on a new commander of the cavalry corps, for there could be no successor to the unique Stuart, he directed the separate divisions to report directly to army headquarters;[6] and because he was well satisfied with the manner in which the divisions of the First Corps were being handled, he requested the cancellation of orders issued by the War Department for the return of Major General McLaws to his old command.[7] Making such temporary arrangements as he could for the brigades whose leaders had been killed or wounded, he exerted himself to keep the morale of the army from weakening under strain.[8] By assuming the blame for the capture of the Bloody Angle, he avoided all recrimination over the loss of Johnson's division, precisely as he had for the failure at Gettysburg.[9] The cause of the disaster, he said, was the withdrawal of the artillery from the salient, and he was responsible for this because he had permitted himself to be misled by false reports of a new movement on the part of the enemy.[10]

Lee taught Hill a most important lesson on May 15, when he shifted Anderson from the left to the right of the line to cover Snell's Bridge, across the Po on the road to Richmond.[11] To secure this position it was necessary to clear a commanding hill in front of the lines. Wright's brigade of the Third Corps was assigned to this task, but was mishandled. Harris had to be sent in, and some needless casualties had to be sustained before the manœuvre to the right could be completed. Lee himself went to the scene and joined General Hill in rear of a nearby church. Hill,

---

[4] Lieutenant R. J. Washington in *G. W. Beale*, 142.

[5] *O. R.*, 36, part 3, p. 814; 14 *S. H. S. P.*, 533.

[6] *O. R.*, 36, part 2, p. 1001. *Taylor's General Lee*, 250. Irvine Walker (*op. cit.*, 173) stated that Lee offered the general command of the cavalry to Major General R. H. Anderson, but that Anderson declined. The writer has not found any confirmation of this in any other authority.

[7] *Lee's Dispatches*, 182.

[8] *Cf. O. R.*, 51, part 2, p. 925.   [9] See *supra*, p. 146.

[10] 33 *S. H. S. P.*, 24.   [11] *O. R.*, 36, part 1, p. 1057.

who had not yet resumed command, was furious at Wright's blundering tactics and vowed he would have a court of inquiry. In answer to him, without premeditation, Lee made a statement that sums up, more perfectly than any other utterance of his whole career, his theory of handling the untrained officers on whom he was forced so largely to rely: "These men are not an army," he said, in his simple, earnest way; "they are citizens defending their country. General Wright is not a soldier; he's a lawyer. I cannot do many things that I could do with a trained army. The soldiers know their duties better than the general officers do, and they have fought magnificently. Sometimes I would like to mask troops and then deploy them, but if I were to give the proper order, the general officers would not understand it; so I have to make the best of what I have and lose much time in making dispositions. You understand all this, but if you humiliated General Wright, the people of Georgia would not understand. Besides, whom would you put in his place? You'll have to do what I do: When a man makes a mistake, I call him to my tent, talk to him, and use the authority of my position to make him do the right thing the next time." [12]

Still again, about this time, during the course of a ride directly in rear of the lines, a six-gun Federal battery opened on Lee and the staff officers with him. One shell, striking the ground nearby, ricochetted over the heads of the party. "Our horses," Major H. B. McClellan wrote, "soon became excited and quickened their pace until it became a gallop. This did not suit General Lee. Traveller was curbed and punished into a walk, when the General remarked that he did not wish to have the appearance of being nervous under fire in the presence of his men." [13]

In reality, Lee need have had no concern on this score, for the spirit of the men, in the words of General Pendleton, was "wonderful." He added: "Everything is braved and borne not only with resolute determination but with the most cheerful good humor." [14] Colonel Taylor admitted that the loss of guns at the

---

[12] Colonel William H. Palmer to the writer, June 25, 1920. Colonel Palmer, on whose memory Lee's words were indelibly imprinted, thought that this occurred on May 18 Lee to Davis, May 15, 1864 (*Lee's Dispatches*, 181–82), makes it almost certain that the incident occurred on the 15th. The late Richard E. Cunningham had the same story from Colonel Palmer and made a detailed memorandum of it, which he generously gave the writer.

[13] *H. B. McClellan MSS.*   [14] Pendleton, May 17, 1864, *op. cit.,* 332.

Bloody Angle hurt the pride of the army, "but," he hastened to write, "we are determined to make our next success all the greater to make amends for this disaster. Our men are in good heart and condition, our confidence, certainly mine, unimpaired. Grant is beating his head against a wall." [15] For himself, Lee could only say, "I grieve over the loss of our gallant officers and men, and miss their aid and sympathy. . . . Praise be to God for having sustained us so far."

The gaunt spectre of want was repulsed temporarily during these days of rest. When the Federal cavalry raids had interrupted communications with the South, Colonel Northrop, grumbling much over the loss of provisions at Beaver Dam, had protested that he could not feed the army ten days longer unless the railroads were repaired.[16] Lee appealed to the nearby farmers and must have received some help from them,[17] for on the 14th he still had three days' rations on hand.[18] The next morning both the Central and the Richmond, Fredericksburg and Potomac were running normally.[19] The supplies that were now laid down at his advanced bases, Lee distributed in larger quantities, to the great satisfaction of the men. As he stopped at a bivouac fire and inquired how the mess was faring, one cheery veteran answered that he feared the army would grow fat and lazy, because they were getting two-thirds of a pound of meat daily, though their ration during the winter had been only a quarter of a pound.[20]

Yet these heartening incidents could not change the gravity of the situation. Casualties to date, though never fully reported, must have been well in excess of 15,000, and not a single regiment had arrived, except Johnston's brigade on May 6,[21] to make good the losses. General Grant was believed to be receiving large reinforcements.[22] If the Army of Northern Virginia was to continue to stand between the Federals and Richmond, it must be strengthened. But how and whence? Lee had read on the 12th that the X and XVIII Union Corps had been recalled from the south At-

---

[15] *Taylor MSS.*, May 15, 1864.   [16] 2 *R. W. C. D.*, 208.

[17] *Cf. O. R.*, 37, part 1, p. 737; *ibid.*, 51, part 2, p. 926.

[18] *Lee's Dispatches*, 177–78.

[19] 2 *R. W. C. D.*, 211. These two lines probably were restored on the 13th.

[20] *H. B. McClellan MSS.*

[21] 14 *S. H. S. P.*, 523.   [22] *Cf. Lee's Dispatches*, 187.

lantic seaboard and had been sent to Butler, and he had asked the President if Confederate troops could not be brought from that territory. Mr. Davis had answered regretfully that he had already stripped the coast states and knew of no organized units from which he could draw, except perhaps a few in Florida.[23]

There were fourteen brigades, large and small, in the defenses of Richmond, Drewry's Bluff, and Petersburg, with one brigade of cavalry and an abundance of artillery;[24] but Sheridan's cavalry was just below Malvern Hill, undefeated,[25] Butler was pressing on toward Drewry's Bluff from the south side of the James,[26] and Kautz's cavalry was now on a raid against the Richmond and Danville Railroad.[27] Breckinridge had two brigades and one battalion of infantry in the Valley of Virginia and had called to him the cadet corps of the Virginia Military Institute, which Lee had held for just such an emergency. All that Lee thought he could get at the time was Hoke's old brigade, which had reached the Richmond line from North Carolina,[28] and even this was denied him for the moment.

President Davis, whose courage was never higher and whose head was never clearer than in this dark crisis, did not believe it was safe to release any troops from around Richmond until Beauregard had launched against Butler an attack that Davis and Bragg were urging him to deliver. General Beauregard, for his part, was developing a succession of sketchy plans whereby Lee should withdraw to the Chickahominy and reinforce him in routing Butler, after which happy consummation Beauregard's army was to join with Lee's in crushing Grant.[29] The administration did not look with favor on these proposals and, so far as the records show, did not present them in detail for Lee's consideration. "I dare not promise anything now," Davis told Lee. "If possible, [I] will sustain you in your unequal struggle, so long and nobly maintained." [30] He suggested that Lee summon to him the troops in the Shenandoah Valley, but Lee considered this too risky.[31] With a single protest against the detachment of any

23 *O. R.*, 51, part 2, p. 922. 24 *O. R.*, 36, part 2, pp. 207–10.
25 *O. R.*, 36, part 1, p. 792; *ibid.*, 51, part 2, p. 941.
26 *O. R.*, 36, part 1, p. 20. 27 *O. R.*, 36, part 1, p. 21.
28 *O. R.*, 51, part 2, p. 925. 29 *O. R.*, 36, part 2, pp. 1021, 1024.
30 *O. R.*, 51, part 2, pp. 926, 933.
31 *O. R.*, 51, part 2, p. 929; *Lee's Dispatches*, 180.

cavalry,[32] Lee accepted the inevitable and continued to face Grant with his diminished forces.

On the 14th, while the rain was still falling and the roads were almost beyond travel by the most venturesome, the Union forces evacuated the tip of the Bloody Angle.[33] That day and the next and on the 16th there were confused movements and feints on the enemy's part, with a suggestion that Grant was preparing to move southward, but with no renewal of the general offensive.[34] Lee was concerned, almost depressed, at his inability to ascertain the inwardness of these manœuvres. "Ah, Major," he said to H. B. McClellan, who had been assistant adjutant general of the cavalry corps, "if my poor friend Stuart were here I should know all about what those people are doing." [35]

Then, perhaps unexpectedly, there came the sunshine of good news almost at the very time the clouds broke away in brighter weather.[36] On the 15th, at New Market, Breckinridge met Sigel and with the assistance of the battalion from the Virginia Military Institute, which fought with a valor that would have added lustre to Saint Cyr, he drove the invaders down the Valley. It was a rout reminiscent of Jackson's operations of two years previously. Lee was immensely pleased that the upper Valley was cleared and that, at a single blow, one of the most serious threats against his flank had been relieved. He hastened to send his congratulations to Breckinridge and urged him to pursue the enemy into Maryland, or, if that was not practicable, to join the Army of Northern Virginia at once.[37] An advance into Maryland he considered more fruitful of potential results, but if that was beyond Breckinridge's strength, then he hoped to have at least temporary reinforcement by two brigades of infantry.

Scarcely had the soldiers realized the importance of the success in the Valley than the telegraph and the Richmond newspapers[38]

[32] *O. R.*, 51, part 2, p. 937.   [33] 14 *S. H. S. P.*, 533.
[34] *O. R.*, 36, part 2, pp. 1011, 1012, 1015, 1030; *ibid.*, 51, part 2, pp. 929, 933; *Lee's Dispatches*, 181–82. *Cf.* 2 *Meade*, 195, letter of May 15: "I think we have gained decided advantage over the enemy; nevertheless, he confronts us still, and, owing to the strong positions he occupies, and the works he is all the time throwing up, the task of overcoming him is a very difficult one, taxing all our energies."
[35] *H. B. McClellan MSS.*   [36] May 17; *O. R.*, 36, part 1, p. 72.
[37] *O. R.*, 37, part 1, pp. 737–38. For Lee's brief instructions to Breckinridge, whom he left largely to exercise his sound discretion, so long as that officer was in the Valley, see *ibid.*, 712, 713, 722, 728.
[38] *O. R.*, 36, part 2, p. 1015.

reported an even finer victory: On the 16th, Beauregard attacked Butler below Drewry's Bluff and hurled him back to Bermuda Hundred Neck, where, in General Grant's expressive phrase, he was "as completely shut off from further operations directly against Richmond as if [he] had been in a bottle strongly corked." [39] This created a situation that was to play so large a part in subsequent operations that it is sketched on page 336.

Butler's predicament is readily seen. So long as he remained in Bermuda Neck, while Beauregard's line was a "cork," his powers of doing mischief were small. More than that, as the mouth of the "bottle" was only four miles wide, a very small force of infantry, supported by ample artillery, would suffice to hold him there. Lee, being confident of this, at once asked that some of Beauregard's troops be sent to him. [40] He saw in Butler's distress the one opportunity, in all the Southland, of giving his army substantial reinforcements.

Almost simultaneously with the news of Beauregard's success came reports that Sheridan's raid against Richmond had ended, that Kautz had given up his attacks on the Richmond and Danville Railroad, and that Crook and Averell had started back into western Virginia from their operations against the Virginia and Tennessee. [41] As if by a miracle, the widespread offensives that had attended the opening of the campaign had resolved themselves into the major thrust of Grant against Richmond, with the "bottled" Butler a continuing nuisance but not an immediate danger. Finally, on the 18th, as if to give a final dramatic climax to the changed situation, an attempted general assault through the Bloody Angle was broken up so quickly and so easily that the army scarcely realized General Grant had planned another 12th of May. [42]

Relieved though he was by the repulse of this assault and by

[39] *O. R.*, 36, part 1, p. 20. For the reports, see *O. R.*, 36, part 2, p. 196 *ff.* The victory would have been far more nearly complete but for the failure of General W. H. C. Whiting, who was wrongly accused of being drunk but who was guilty of gross mishandling of his troops. See *Walter Harrison*, 126–27; *O. R.*, 36, part 2, p. 1026; *ibid.*, part 3, pp. 811, 822, 824–25, 845.

[40] *Lee's Dispatches*, 187.   [41] *O. R.*, 36, part 1, pp. 21, 23, 792.

[42] *O. R.*, 36, part 1, pp. 1046, 1073, 1087; *ibid.*, part 2, p. 1019; 33 *S. H. S. P.*, 332–33; *Alexander*, 527–28. *Cf.* 2 *Meade*, 197: ". . . on advancing, we found the enemy so strongly entrenched that even Grant thought it useless to knock our heads against a brick wall, and directed a suspension of the attack."

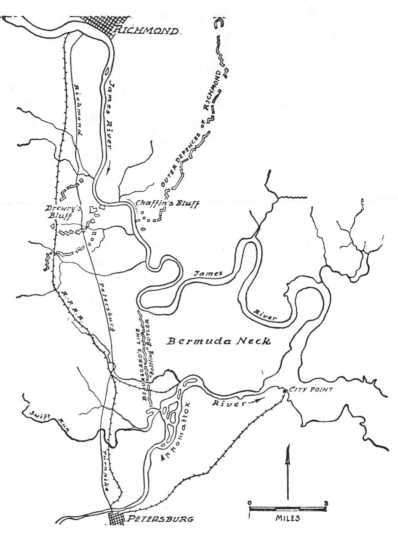

Sketch illustrating how Butler's Army of the James was "bottled" in Bermuda Neck, May 16, 1864.

the failure of all the minor offensives in Virginia, Lee was not for a moment misled as to the magnitude of the danger that still confronted him. He knew, by the evening of the 18th, that Breckinridge had decided against an advance down the Shenandoah Valley and was preparing to entrain for Hanover Junction

336

with 2400 infantry,[43] but he had as yet no assurance that any of the troops from the Richmond-Drewry's Bluff line would be sent him. In a lengthy confidential dispatch to the President on the 18th, Lee thus summarized his view of the situation: "[Grant's] position is strongly entrenched, and we cannot attack it with any prospect of success without great loss of men which I wish to avoid if possible. The enemy's artillery is superior in weight of metal and range to our own, and my object has been to engage him when in motion and under circumstances that will not cause us to suffer from this disadvantage. I think by this means he has suffered considerably in the several past combats, and that his progress has thus far been arrested. I shall continue to strike him wherever opportunity presents itself, but nothing at present indicates any purpose on his part to advance. Neither the strength of our army nor the condition of our animals will admit of any extensive movement with a view to drawing the enemy from his position. I think he is now waiting for reenforcements. . . . Other reports represent that General Grant . . . has been assured . . . that he shall have all he requires. . . . The importance of this campaign to the administration of Mr. Lincoln and to General Grant leaves no doubt that every effort and every sacrifice will be made to secure its success. A Washington telegram . . . states that it is reported that the 10th and 18th army corps now south of the James will be called to General Grant, as they are not strong enough to take Richmond, and too strong to be kept idle. The recent success of General Beauregard may induce the fulfilment of this report, if the idea was not previously entertained. It is also stated that the troops from General Sherman's Dept. under General Smith . . . have been ordered back, it may be to join Genl Sherman or to be brought East. The defensive position of Genl. Johnston which I doubt not is justified by his situation, may enable the enemy to detach a portion of the force opposed to him for service here. I trust that no effort will be spared to prevent this, or should it occur, to give timely notice of it. From all these sources General Grant can, and if permitted will repair the losses of the late battles, and be as strong as when he began operation. I deem it my duty to present the actual, and what I consider the

---

[43] O. R., 51, part 2, p. 943; Lee's Dispatches, 189.

probable situation of affairs to your Excellency, in order that your judgment may be guided in devising the means of opposing the force that is being arrayed against us. I doubt not that you will be able to suggest the best means to be taken, and that all the emergency calls for will be done as far as it is in your power." [44] Later in the day, Lee summarized these representations by telegraph and again gave the warning that more than once had induced the President to send him troops even when Richmond had seemed to be threatened: "The question," he said, "is whether we shall fight the battle here or around Richmond. If the troops are obliged to be retained at Richmond I may be forced back." [45]

Abundant evidence was forthcoming on May 19 of the determination Lee credited in these dispatches to his stubborn adversary. On the Confederate right the enemy seemed as strong as ever, but on the left, which Ewell had held alone since Anderson had been shifted on the 14–15, there were indications that the enemy might be withdrawing. This suggested the possibility that the Union troops opposite the Confederate left were being moved to the other flank. The turning movement that Lee had been suspecting since May 15 might be under way.

To ascertain the facts, Lee ordered Ewell to demonstrate during the afternoon in front of his lines, but Ewell asked to be allowed to undertake a circuitous manœuvre that would put him in rear of the Federal right flank. Lee gave the permission and, as usual, left the details to Ewell. Not long after the Second Corps had started, Lee found to his consternation that Ewell had sent back his artillery because of the badness of the roads. [46] Realizing that this was inviting disaster, [47] Lee sought to extend Early's left to cover Ewell's front. Very soon rapid firing announced that Ewell had encountered the foe. As his object was merely to discover whether Grant had abandoned that part of the front, Ewell prepared to withdraw, but before he could do so the Federals attacked him with much vigor. Happily, General Hampton, who had screened Ewell's operation, had carried a battery of his horse artillery along with him, and he quickly disposed this to check the enemy. The onrush of the Federals was, however, so vigorous

[44] *Lee's Dispatches*, 183–86.   [45] *Lee's Dispatches*, 186–87.
[46] *O. R.*, 36, part 1, p. 1088.   [47] 14 *S. H. S. P.*, 533; *O. R.*, 36, part 1, p. 1046.

that General Ramseur became fearful that Ewell's 6000 would be routed. Without waiting for orders, he delivered a vigorous counterattack with his brigade. When forced to suspend this, because both his flanks were in danger of envelopment, Ramseur fell back some 200 yards. In a short time the troops on the left of Rodes's division gave way, and Ramseur had to retire to the position from which he had started his counteroffensive. There Pegram's brigade came up on his left and rectified the line, which Ramseur was able to hold until nightfall. The corps then returned as it had come, and without molestation, but it left about 900 killed, wounded, and missing in the enemy's lines—a heavy price to pay for the information that the enemy had not denuded his right.[48] The affair was badly managed except for the gallant action of Ramseur and Pegram, and it probably raised anew in the mind of General Lee a doubt as to the physical ability of General Ewell to handle his troops when quick decision and prompt action were required in the face of a vigilant, aggressive foe.

Grant, in any case, had not moved. That was the situation at dark on the 19th. Whether he had slipped away during the night, or would march the next day, or would use his reinforcements for a new attack on the Spotsylvania line, was still undetermined on the morning of May 20. There was, however, encouragement for Lee in a telegram received from Mr. Davis early in the day. The President announced that he had ordered Pickett's division and Hoke's brigade to march to Lee, though Beauregard was loath to give up the troops and was still contending that Lee should fall back to the line of the Chickahominy for a better concentration of the defending forces.[49] Wherever and whenever Grant moved, Lee would have five more brigades to employ against him. "Am fully alive," he telegraphed the President, "to the importance of concentration and being near base. The latter consideration may impel me to fall back eventually. Will do so at once if deemed best. My letters gave you my views. The troops promised will be

[48] *O. R.,* 36, part 1, pp. 1073, 1082–83; 14 *S. H. S. P.,* 533; *Taylor's General Lee,* 243; *Alexander,* 528.
[49] *O. R.,* 51, part 2, p. 945. For the movement of these units from the south to the north side of the James, and for the re-disposition of those left on the Richmond and Drewry's Bluff sectors, see *O. R.,* 36, part 2, p. 1022; *ibid.,* part 3, pp. 799, 807; *ibid.,* 51, part 2, pp. 947, 948, 951; 2 *Davis,* 514.

advantageous in either event. I have posted Breckinridge at [Hanover] Junction to guard communication, whence he can speedily return to Valley if necessary. . . ." [50]

Scarcely had this message been dispatched than signs multiplied of an impending southward movement by the Federals. Lee at once transferred the Texas brigade to the south of the Po to protect some guns he placed there to cover the crossing;[51] and when he advised Ewell of the indications of a Federal shift, he urged him to strike the enemy's rear if he found an opening.[52] This was in accordance with the broad strategic policy Lee had kept in mind since the beginning of the campaign—to resume the offensive if he could catch the enemy in motion. By evening, he was so well satisfied Grant was changing position that he told General Ewell to move to the right at daylight the next morning unless some good reason developed for not doing so.[53]

Before 9 A.M. on May 21, General Lee knew that the enemy was moving toward Bowling Green and Milford. He had already concluded that Grant's new base would be at Port Royal, on the Rappahannock River,[54] and he now had Ewell's corps in position along the Po, prepared to move at the tap of a drum.[55] The rest of the army was made ready to leave the Spotsylvania lines as soon as the Federals disappeared from in front of Early and of Anderson, who held the left and the centre, respectively, after Ewell moved from the vicinity of the Bloody Angle.[56]

But where should the army seek to interpose itself between Grant and Richmond? That was the question Lee had to answer. Obviously the enemy had the lead—how much of a lead, it was impossible for Confederate headquarters to say with assurance, though the cavalry was sending in reports through the signal stations every fifteen minutes.[57] Obviously, too, Grant would

[50] *Lee's Dispatches*, 188–89.   [51] *O. R.*, 36, part 3, p. 801.
[52] *O. R.*, 36, part 3, p. 801.   [53] *O. R.*, 36, part 3, p. 801.
[54] Even before final orders to that effect had been given by General Grant, Lee reasoned that this would be done (*O. R.*, 36, part 3, p. 77).
[55] *O. R.*, 36, part 1, p. 1058.   [56] *O. R.*, 36, part 1, p. 1058.
[57] *R. L. T. Beale*, 120. The II Corps, which led the Union advance, received instructions to move at 2 A.M. on the morning of May 21. At the instance of General Hancock the orders were changed to permit him to start at dark on the 20th, in order to pass the Confederate signal stations before daylight. Hancock was somewhat delayed in getting off, because of the slow arrival of the cavalry. He did not state the exact hour of departure in his report (*O. R.*, 36, part 1, pp. 340–41), but the corps headquarters memoranda (*ibid.*, 362) indicate that the column got under way at 11 P.M. Grant, in short, commenced to move only six hours before Lee began to conform, and this despite all

make for Richmond as fast as he could, and he must be met as far from the city as possible. A siege of the capital must, if possible, be avoided. For the moment, that part of the Federal host moving by way of Bowling Green was behind the Mattapony, safe from attack. If Grant kept beyond that river for any considerable distance, Lee realized that he might not be able to meet him again until the Army of the Potomac was south of the Pamunkey.[58] The reason for this was purely geographical, and will be apparent from the sketch of the course of the two rivers shown on the next page.

The advance on Richmond, in short, might readily be from the northeast, especially as the Federal command of the sea made it possible for Grant to establish a base at any point on any of the rivers, to the very head of navigation. At the same time, one Federal column was certainly on the Milford road, whence it could move to attack Richmond from the north, via Hanover Junction, and, in doing so, could sever communication with the Valley by seizing the Central Railroad.

Which would it be—an advance from the northeast or from the north? Lee could not say, as yet, but he decided very quickly to move back to the North Anna River. If the enemy struck from the north, he would have a river line from which to defend Hanover Junction and the Central Railroad. In case the enemy continued down the Mattapony, the Army of Northern Virginia could easily move from the North Anna to a new position behind the Pamunkey.[59] There was but one objection to making this stand on the North Anna: It was only twenty-three miles from Richmond—dangerously close. Lee would have preferred to bring north of the river the troops at Hanover Junction, and to give battle as far from Richmond as possible. But he reasoned that if he tried to operate between Spotsylvania and the North Anna, or followed the enemy eastward, some part of Grant's force might slip by and get between him and Richmond.[60] The North Anna was the nearest position of strength that he could take up and

fact that he was operating in a wooded country, where concealment should have been easy. It does not seem to have been pointed out by critics of the campaign, but General Grant may properly have been censurable for sending off so large a part of his cavalry under General Sheridan that he was unable to keep his march from being observed by Confederate spies and outposts.

[58] O. R., 36, part 3, p. 812.   [59] *Pendleton*, 335.   [60] *Pendleton*, 335.

be sure that his adversary would not easily slip around his flank. His solicitude for Richmond, rather than his wishes, shaped his strategy.[61]

Hanover Junction it was, then! He telegraphed instructions for

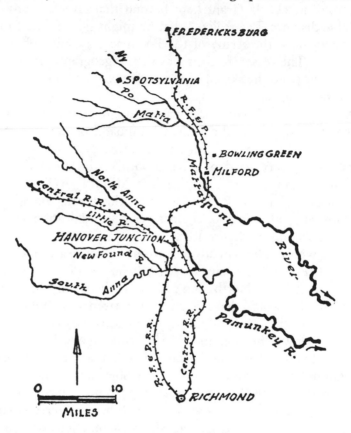

Sketch showing how the Pamunkey River covered Grant's advance of May, 1864, toward Richmond.

the waiting troops to remain there and to defend the place against raiders.[62] The wagon trains he started southward by roads west of those on which the army was to move.[63] Not long after noon, Ewell was put in motion for Mud Tavern and the Telegraph

[61] *Cf. infra,* p. 349.   [62] *O. R.,* 36, part 3, p. 815.
[63] The route was New Market, Chilesburg, and Island Ford (*O. R.,* 36, part 1, p. 1056).

342

road,[64] on the way to the Junction. Orders were given General Early to sweep his front and, if he found that the enemy had departed, to prepare to march.[65] Similar directions went to Field.[66]

Lee himself moved his headquarters to the Southworth house, on the right bank of the Po, and there he remained, somewhat impatiently, to hear the outcome of the reconnaissance north of that river. While he waited, General Hill rode up and reported. Prompted no doubt by the feeling that he should not place upon another the responsibility of directing his corps in a new and perhaps critical movement, he informed his chief that he was well enough to take up his duties again. Lee at once restored him to command and ordered Early to resume the leadership of his division under Ewell.[67]

Early was of opinion that only skirmishers were in his front, but they resisted so vigorously a reconnaissance by General Wilcox that two brigades were sent after them and were soon engaged in a stiff fight. A very violent storm came up as the action progressed, but it did not halt Wilcox's veterans, who advanced some distance.[68] Field, too, encountered some opposition on his sector. He was so slow in getting away that he provoked a sharp message from Lee: "Unless we can drive these people out, or find out whether they are all gone," Lee wrote Anderson, "we are detained here to our disadvantage." [69] Soon, however, Anderson was convinced that only a rearguard remained on the line, and he followed Ewell.[70]

---

[64] There is some confusion as to the hour of Ewell's departure. Hotchkiss stated (3 C. M. H., 458) that Ewell left about noon, but he was certainly wrong in saying that Lee rode off at that hour with him, unless he mistook Lee's departure for the Southworth house as his start for the North Anna. The dispatches in O. R., 36, part 3, pp. 814–15, though not conclusive, indicate that Lee was some distance from Spotsylvania during the afternoon. Early stated (op. cit., 359) that Ewell left "on the afternoon of the 21st." Ewell himself (O. R., 36, part 1, p. 1074) gave no hour for the movement. Anderson (ibid., 1058) established nothing more than that his corps, preceded by Ewell, began its march "in the afternoon." The sequence of events in the text is believed to be substantially correct.

[65] O. R., 36, part 3, pp. 814–15.   [66] Ibid.

[67] O. R., 36, part 3, p. 814; Early, 358. Hill probably should have waited several days longer, for his handling of his troops on the line to which the army was hurrying was not that of a man physically at his best.

[68] Wilcox's MS. report, 42–43.   [69] O. R., 36, part 3, pp. 814–15.

[70] Anderson was certainly on the march before 6:40 P.M., as evidenced by a dispatch in O. R., 36, part 3, p. 824. That dispatch, wrongly dated May 22, manifestly was written May 21.

As the evening drew on, several of Lee's general officers joined him at the Southworth house for instructions. Hill was there, and Early. Anderson lingered for a while, and Rooney Lee came up. To all of them Lee gave his final verbal orders. He told Hill to withdraw his last units at 9 P.M. from the bloody Spotsylvania line, unless the enemy left before that time. The Third Corps was then to move by roads west of and parallel to the route Ewell and Anderson were to pursue.[71] When Early asked if he should guard the right bank of the Mattapony, Lee informed him that Hancock had been at Milford since morning, that he had possession of the hills on the south side of the river, and that he had fortified them.

One by one, their orders understood, the officers rode off. Lee remained alone with his staff and a few guides who had been assigned him that day by reason of their familiarity with the roads of the nearby counties. Presently, with no more ceremony than if he were departing for an evening ride, Lee said to his companions, "Come, gentlemen." Mounting silently, he touched the reins of Traveller and turned his head southward.[72]

The great battles of Spotsylvania were now at an end. How many they had been and how desperate! Each year of the war, from the time Lee had taken command of the Army of Northern Virginia, the course of the conflict had brought him into Spotsylvania, and not once had he been defeated there. In Fredericksburg stood the wall from which the incautious Burnside had been bloodily repulsed; across the county ran the narrow, mysterious roads over which the Second Corps had hurried to the flank of Hooker's host; in a shell-torn thicket, no stone marked the spot where Jackson had fallen. Still bare in the woods near Hamilton's Crossing was the site on which Lee had planned the invasion of Pennsylvania. But never again were the thickets to echo the wild rebel yell. To the thousands of shallow graves in the forests none were to be added. The barricades might rot and the trenches wash away. The trumpet vine might climb the gaunt, scarred trees, and the honeysuckle cover the ruin of the shell-

---

[71] *O. R.,* 36, part 1, p. 1058.
[72] *Cooke,* 400; E. C. Moncure: *Reminiscences of the Civil War* (cited hereafter as *Moncure*), p. 1.

swept homes. Spotsylvania's sacrifices were complete. No more was to be exacted of her. The fields and the forests that had witnessed the high noon of the Confederacy were to be spared the night of a waning cause.

CHAPTER XX

A Vain Invitation to Attack

(THE NORTH ANNA, MAY 22-27, 1864)

WITH Eustis Moncure by his side as a guide, and with Colonel Taylor and W. G. Jesse, another guide, immediately behind, Lee rode through the night toward Traveler's Rest, midway between the Po and Ta Rivers. He had little to say, but he inquired the names of his youthful companions and reassured himself as to their knowledge of the roads. When they reached Traveler's Rest, they turned to their left and came into the Telegraph road at a humble place bearing the uneuphonious name of Mud Tavern. Here Moncure remarked that some of the enemy were a mile farther to the eastward, on the road to Guiney's Station.

"How do you know?" asked Lee.

When Moncure explained that his cavalry command had been there about noon and had been forced back, Lee halted for a moment and told Colonel Taylor to instruct General Anderson to send a regiment down the road toward Guiney's to protect the passing column. Riding on, he soon overtook the artillery of Ewell's corps, where the weary drivers were hurrying the weak horses onward through the mud. Ere long he came in the darkness to the crossing of the Ta River at Jerroll's Mill. Half a mile beyond the river he rode into a jam of broken wagons, crowded guns, and swearing soldiers. Lee wormed his way through them, speaking to the officers and men as he passed and giving directions for clearing the road. The soldiers could not see him but they seemed to sense who he was, and, in a few minutes, they had the wheels turning again. Pressing on, Lee and his little cavalcade reached the junction of the Bethany, Welch's, and Bowling Green roads. For the second time Moncure spoke up to warn his com-

346

mander that the enemy were only a mile away to the eastward. As before, Lee asked why he knew, and again Moncure answered that he had been there on a reconnaissance that afternoon. Lee had Taylor leave a courier at the crossroads to instruct Anderson, upon arrival, to protect his flank.

Having covered fifteen miles, Lee was on the rear of Ewell's infantry, who were struggling on through the darkness toward Hanover Junction. By the roadside stragglers were encountered, some of them asleep and some of them resting, before they set out to overtake their commands. In characteristic tone, Lee addressed them: "I know you do not want to be taken prisoner," he said, "and I know you are tired and sleepy, but the enemy will be along before or by daybreak and if you do not move on you will be taken."

There was grumbling from the roadside and a few tart answers from soldiers who were safe from identification in the blackness of the night. "Well you may order us to 'move on, move on,'" one of them retorted, "when you are mounted on a horse and have all the rations that the country can afford!"

Lee made no answer and needed to make none, for some of the men nearest to him peered into his face, half-suspecting who he was.

"Marse Robert!" they exclaimed.

The effect was instantaneous. The soldiers got up as if they had never known weariness, and gave him a shout. "Yes, Marse Robert," they said, "we'll move on and go anywhere you say, even to hell!"

Thanking them and bidding them good speed, Lee trotted on and about 2 A.M. on the morning of the 22d came to the quaint little house by the roadside, whence Doctor Joseph A. Flippo ministered to the ills of the countryside. A light was burning in the house, for the good doctor sought no sleep that night, with the army tramping by and the enemy likely to come up when the last gray brigade had passed. Lee paused to rest his mount and to chat with Flippo, and then went on once more. When he reached the north side of Stevens' Mill pond, four miles north of Mount Carmel Church, he found his headquarters tents erected, with Ewell's troops resting nearby. Here he halted, but before he

347

went to his own cot, which the faithful "Bryan" had set up for him, he inquired if his young guides had any rations. Moncure hesitated to answer, for he did not wish to impose on the General's scanty larder, though he and his companion were quite without provisions. Guessing the reason for the soldier's embarrassment, Lee told him and Jesse to tie their horses, to get some feed from the nearest quartermaster, and then to go into his headquarters tent and eat. If the men had visions of a hearty early morning breakfast of substantials, they were soon disappointed, for when they presented themselves, all "Bryan" could give them was two very bad biscuits each and a cup of coffee that was a satire on the name.

Lee rested for an hour or two and then, before dawn, summoned Moncure and sent him off with an open dispatch to General Hampton, advising him of the army's progress and instructing him to hold the enemy in check and to fall back slowly toward Hanover Junction.[1]

The troops of the Second Corps were now stirring. They had covered the seventeen miles to Dickinson's Mill almost without a halt, and they had relaxed only an hour or two, but they must reach the North Anna before the enemy, and to do that they must press on. The first news that reached Lee, as he prepared to ride on with the van of the corps, was that Hoke's unattached brigade and Barton's brigade of Pickett's division were at hand, and that Corse's and Kemper's, also of Pickett's division, had reached the vicinity of Milford the previous evening. Four brigades—and with Breckinridge's two, a total of a division and a half! Approximately a third of the wastage of the campaign had been repaired. In announcing to the President the arrival of these troops, Lee had his first opportunity of explaining his withdrawal from Spotsylvania. He said: ". . . in a wooded country like that in which we have been operating, where nothing is known beyond what can be ascertained by feeling, a day's march can always be gained. . . . I should have preferred contesting the enemy's

---

[1] *Moncure*, 1–3. This narrative is of great simplicity but of singular dramatic force. It has here been paraphrased but the pamphlet merits a reading by all who are interested in General Lee's dealings with his men. It should be noted that Moncure is one day in error in his chronology. The events he described as of May 22–23, occurred on the 21st–22d.

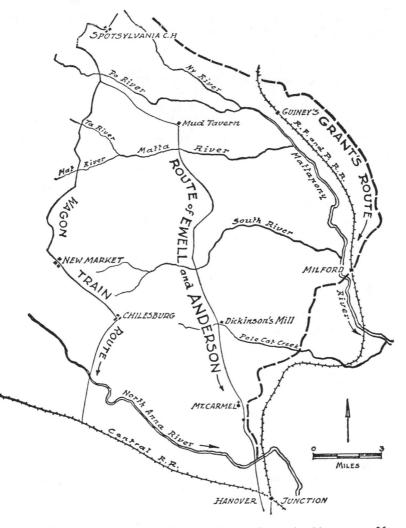

Lines of advance to the North Anna River by the opposing armies, May 21–23, 1864. The route of the Third Corps of the Army of Northern Virginia is not shown. It lay to the west of that followed by Ewell and Anderson.

approach inch by inch; but my solicitude for Richmond caused me to abandon that plan." [2]

Proceeding with the troops, Lee was soon joined by Major Jed Hotchkiss, the capable topographical engineer of the Second Corps. Together they talked of the battles of Spotsylvania and of

[2] *Lee's Dispatches,* 192. *Cf. supra,* p. 342.

the struggle for the Bloody Angle. "We wish no more salients," Lee remarked grimly.[3] Soon they reached the hills that look down on the crossings of the North Anna. The railroad bridge to the left and Fox's Bridge on the Telegraph road were both intact. A small Confederate garrison held the works that had been erected to protect the wooden spans.[4] The race to the new position had been won. If Grant was headed in that direction, he would find the stream between him and the Army of Northern Virginia.

Lee left orders for Ewell and Anderson to pass to the south bank and to take position there, without destroying the spans or evacuating the bridgeheads. With his staff he went on to Hanover Junction, three miles southward, and there he established headquarters in the southwest angle of the crossing of the Richmond, Fredericksburg and Potomac and Central Railroads.[5] At 9:30 A.M. he had the satisfaction of telegraphing to the Secretary of War that the Second Corps was arriving, that the First was close up, and that Hill was expected to come in on the right.[6] The day was hot, but the breeze was pleasant,[7] and as the troops came up they were loosely disposed in the fields on the south

---

[3] *White,* 380.

[4] Although mentioned frequently in the dispatches as Taylor's Bridge, the wagon crossing was properly Fox's Bridge. It had been destroyed in 1862 and had not been rebuilt when the artillery had been sent back to the North Anna after the battle of Fredericksburg. Lieutenant J. Thompson Brown of the artillery had received orders and a detail of men to reconstruct it. Brown had never had any experience in such work but he had promised the men two weeks' furlough if they made a bridge. He had very ingeniously weighted one end of each long timber so that it would sink into position, and had used this as his foundation. The bridge served every purpose. It stood a short distance west of the present North Anna Memorial Bridge on the Richmond-Washington highway (*Letter of General Jo Lane Stern to J. F. Howison,* July 14, 1926). General Stern had lived as a boy in the neighborhood and had been an interested observer of Lieutenant Brown's engineering.

[5] *Stern to Howison, supra.*

[6] *O. R.,* 36, part 3, p. 823. General Stern, in the *Richmond Times-Dispatch* of Jan. 20, 1907, published an interesting account of delivering a telegram to the General in his headquarters by unceremoniously entering his tent under the raised flap and touching the General on the shoulder. "He was very courteous," General Stern wrote, "as if it were an everyday occurrence for boys to punch him on his shoulder."

[7] *Pendleton,* 336. Moncure, *op. cit.,* 4, stated that about noon on May 23 he returned to Lee's headquarters and found the General in consultation with men who, he was told, were Davis, Seddon, and Breckinridge. If Moncure was in error in his chronology for the day of May 22, as he was for the night of May 21–22, then this meeting occurred on May 22 and not, as he put it, on the 23d. There is no other reference to such a conference, though there is nothing in the published correspondence of the 22d to prove that it could not have occurred. If, again, Moncure gave the correct date, May 23, then he must have been misinformed as to at least one of the persons he saw in Lee's tent, for there is in *O. R.,* 36, part 1, p. 1030, a dispatch from Lee to Seddon that would hardly have been written if Lee had seen Seddon that day.

bank, Ewell on the right and Anderson opposite the bridges. It was the first time since May 4 that the army had not been in sight of the main body of the enemy.[8]

The afternoon of the 22d passed without the appearance of any Federal force on the north side of the river, but Hampton reported that the Army of the Potomac was marching by Milford and that its objective seemed to be Hanover Junction. Lee hoped that it was. Now that he had occupied the Junction, he felt himself in position to move after Grant, whatever his adversary's line of march. He was anxious for Beauregard to join him, if possible, for an attack on the Army of the Potomac, because, as he wrote President Davis, "it seems to me our best policy to unite upon [Grant's army] and endeavor to crush it." At the same time, he did not think it sound strategy to permit the enemy to reach the Chickahominy before the Army of Northern Virginia was reinforced by Beauregard. It was as easy, he thought, to assail Grant after he had crossed the Pamunkey as to take the offensive on the Chickahominy. "His difficulties," he said of Grant, "will be increased as he advances, and ours diminished, and I think it would be a great disadvantage to us to uncover our railroads to the west, and injurious to open to him more country than we can avoid." [9] In short, if he could meet Grant where the larger numbers and the superior artillery of the enemy did not make the offensive hopeless, it was still his intention to attack—and as far from Richmond as practicable. Perhaps he recalled, as he planned, Napoleon's memorable analysis of just such a problem as confronted him then. "Manœuvre incessantly," Napoleon had said, "without submitting to be driven back on the capital which it is meant to defend or shut up in an entrenched camp in the rear." [10]

Carefully, on the morning of May 23, Lee reconnoitred the ground on the south side of the river, opposite the bridges.[11] He did not fortify extensively, probably because he did not believe the enemy would attack,[12] or because he wished to keep contact with the north bank as he had at Rappahannock, or else because he knew he could not long retain a position close to the river,

8 *Taylor MSS.*, May 23, 1864; *Taylor's Four Years*, 132.
9 Lee to Davis, May 23, 1864, *Lee's Dispatches*, 194–97.
10 See *supra*, vol. 1, p. 354.   11 Stern to Howison, *supra*.
12 *Cf.* Henderson: *Science of War*, 327.

inasmuch as the south bank was dominated by the high ground on the north side of the stream.[13] The army, however, was where it could manœuvre on either flank. Ewell was continued on the right, Anderson was left where he was, and Hill, who reached Hewlett's on the Central Railroad at noon on the 22d, was moved down the railroad to Anderson's Station and was bivouacked in woods nearby.[14]

The Confederate cavalry outposts withdrew and bluecoats began to appear on the left bank of the North Anna about noon on the 23d. Soon it was apparent that the enemy was moving up in great force, probably with his entire army. Once again Lee had reasoned rightly concerning his opponent's objective; once again the Army of the Potomac had marched straight to a wall of waiting bayonets. Lee made ready for whatever might come, but he did not recall the small Confederate commands remaining in the bridgeheads, as it was believed the Southern batteries could protect them until it was apparent whether Lee would have need of the bridges, in case the enemy moved up or down the north bank of the river.

Ere long the enemy's artillery opened against the bridgeheads, and the Confederates answered. General Lee happened at the time to be in the yard of Ellington, the home of the Fox family, overlooking the river. The owner, W. E. Fox, came up and invited the General into the house. Lee thanked him and said that he would be there only a few minutes. Mr. Fox thereupon pressed him to take some refreshment. Again the General declined, but seeing that Mr. Fox's hospitality was offended, he added that if Mr. Fox had any buttermilk, he would be glad to have a glass. Mr. Fox insisted that the General take a seat on the porch, and hurried off to bring the milk and some stale bread, which was all he had. He brought the pitcher and the plate and set them before Lee. The General poured out the milk and was in the act of drinking it when a Federal battery, whose commander evidently had seen a uniform on the porch, fired a round shot. It passed within a few feet of the General and imbedded itself in the door-

[13] *Cf.* Lee to Davis, May 25, 1864: "We have been obliged to withdraw from the banks of the North Anna, in consequence of the ground being favorable to the enemy, and the stage of the water such that he can cross at any point" (*Lee's Dispatches,* 200).

[14] *Wilcox's MS. report,* 44–45. Hill had started his march from Hewlett's at 7 A.M. on the morning of the 23d, moving on a road that ran parallel to the railway. *Ibid.*

frame, where the marks may be seen to this day. To Mr. Fox's amazement, the General finished his milk as if nothing had happened, thanked his host and then rode quickly away, lest his presence provoke a bombardment of the house.[15]

Opposite the railroad crossing and Fox's Bridge there now were signs of Federal activity in ravines that could not be reached by the Southern guns. Nearly two miles upstream,[16] at Ox Ford, Union troops gathered in large numbers but made no attempt to cross. From a point beyond the left of the position A. P. Hill had occupied, there had come the sound of artillery firing which had caused some excitement at corps headquarters. To ascertain the situation there, Lee determined to make personal reconnaissance, and as he felt weary and unwell, he procured a carriage and rode westward. He found some of the horse artillery in position with cavalry support, throwing up a light fortification of fence rails. Across the North Anna, on the skirt of a wood, the Federals were visible. Lee took out his glass and studied them carefully. Then he turned to the courier who had accompanied him. "Go back and tell General A. P. Hill to leave his men in camp," he said, "this is nothing but a feint; the enemy is preparing to cross below." [17] He had scarcely returned to Hanover Junction before his prediction was fulfilled. General Wilcox, under orders from General Hill, had gone forward to examine the ground somewhat east of the artillery position where Lee had been. There was a bend in the river at this point, opposite Jericho Mills, which was three miles above Ox Ford. About 3 o'clock General Wilcox found that the enemy had crossed at the mill and was advancing southward through a densely wooded country.[18] He galloped back and reported to General Hill, who at once ordered him to advance his division and to attack.

Moving up the road directly south of the Central Railroad and parallel to it, General Wilcox formed his line opposite Noel's Station, with Lane on the right, McGowan on the left of Lane,

---

15 *Statement of the late Judge R. H. Cardwell,* July, 1926. Judge Cardwell had the story, many years previously, from the lips of Mr. Fox.

16 Measuring the distance by the river.

17 *Neese,* 274–75. Lee made his reconnaissance from Neese's gun position.

18 The first crossing had been at noon but was not discovered for three hours (*cf.* *O. R.,* 36, part 1, p. 568). The ford at Jericho Mills, now reverting to a wilderness, is one of the most picturesque spots on all the battlegrounds of Virginia.

and Thomas on the left of McGowan. Scales's brigade was placed
in rear of Thomas, with instructions to march around Thomas's

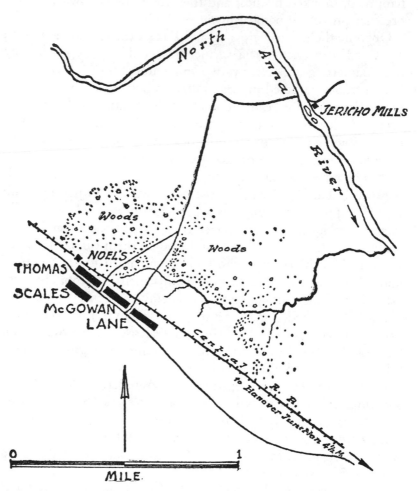

Order of battle and line of advance of Wilcox's division in the action against the V Corps,
Army of the Potomac, May 23, 1864, near the North Anna River.

left and to assail the enemy in flank and rear if it should be found
that Thomas's flank extended beyond that of the enemy. Lane
and McGowan had to advance over open ground, down to a
boggy little stream, and then upward to a thick wood, where the
enemy was believed to be. Thomas's advance from the first was

to be through the woods. The action opened briskly. Lane and McGowan reached the forest in their front and swept into it. Thomas quickly drove the enemy backward. In a short time, however, Thomas gave way at the very moment that the enemy in his front did the same thing. McGowan's left was thrown "in the air" on Thomas's withdrawal and a gap was created. One of Lane's regiments broke twice, but the remaining three pressed on. Scales's brigade found the enemy's flank but for some reason did not press it. By nightfall the division was glad to withdraw— in the unhappy knowledge that the troops in its front, which proved to be the V Corps of Warren, were still on the south bank and were entrenching rapidly. It was a badly managed affair, and no credit either to Hill or to Wilcox. Heth's division had been brought up during the afternoon but had not been successful in driving the enemy.[19]

The action on Hill's front might mean that the enemy was preparing to cross the North Anna with his entire army, for Grant would hardly have thrown so large a force to the south side simply to feel out the Confederates. On the opposite flank, about 7:15 P.M.,[20] in the midst of a furious rainstorm,[21] there was another move that might indicate a determination on Grant's part to force a crossing. From the ravines beyond the bridgeheads, the enemy swarmed forward and overwhelmed the small garrison. Between 100 and 200 men, who could not run the gauntlet over the bridges in the gathering darkness, were captured.[22]

Was all this a ruse? On the theory that it might be, Lee directed Anderson, at the end of the day, to pack his wagons and to be ready if necessary to move the next morning.[23] To prepare for the larger probability of an attack by the enemy on the front where the Army of Northern Virginia then stood, Lee decided to change his lines. He could not keep the enemy from moving to the south side opposite the bridges, for after he burned these the enemy could easily ford the river, where the water was then low.[24]

---

[19] Federal reports in *O. R.*, 36, part 1, pp. 542 *ff.*; Pendleton's, *ibid.*, 1047; *Wilcox's MS. report*, 45 *ff.*; Lane's report in 9 *S. H. S. P.*, 241–42; *History of McGowan's Brigade*, 153 *ff.* These are the only Confederate accounts, hence the uncertainty as to Heth's movements. General Wilcox merely stated in his report that he saw Heth's division marching by a flank along the railroad in rear of his division.

[20] *O. R.*, 36, part 1, p. 467.

[21] *O. R.*, 36, part 1, p. 432.

[22] *O. R.*, 36, part 1, pp. 193, 341.

[23] *O. R.*, 36, part 1, p. 826.

[24] *Lee's Dispatches*, 200.

Neither could Lee fight close to the river, on his right, because the
Federal guns, already in battery on the higher ground on the
north bank, dominated the position he occupied. If, then, the
Federals could cross opposite his right, as they already had opposite his left, they might hope to turn either flank, or both. But
there was one point where the ground favored Lee. That was in
the centre, near Ox Ford. There the Confederates held the elevation and could prevent a Federal crossing. Lee accordingly determined on a novel system of defenses. He drew back Ewell and
the right of Anderson to the southeast; he kept the left of Anderson opposite Ox Ford; and he directed that as soon as Hill's men
were rested, they were to run a line from Ox Ford southwestward
to Little River. Thus Lee would have his front a very wide
inverted "V" with its apex to the north and both flanks well
secured—the left by Little River and the right by swampy ground
east of Hanover Junction. As Henderson well phrased it, Lee
"shut up his line like one closes an umbrella," [25] as the sketch shows.
He was now in position where he could easily reinforce one wing
from the other, and as long as he held Ox Ford he could compel
Grant to fight with his wings separated. Thus favorably situated,
Lee was sanguine. His communications were shorter,[26] and his
strength was raised, at last, some 8500 by the arrival of all of
Pickett's division, Hoke's old brigade, and Breckinridge's command.[27] The opportunity for which he had been waiting might
come the very next day. But before it developed, Lee was attacked
by a violent intestinal complaint, brought on, no doubt, by bad
food and long hours.[28] He was loath, as always, to yield to sick-

[25] *Science of War*, 328.
[26] *Cf.* Lee to Mrs. Lee, May 23, 1864: "We have the advantage of being nearer our
supplies and less liable to have our communications, trains, etc., cut by his cavalry, and he
is getting farther from his base. Still, I begrudge every step he takes toward Richmond"
(*Fitz Lee*, 338–39).
[27] Pickett was attached temporarily to the Third Corps (*O. R.*, 36, part 1, p. 1058).
Hoke's brigade returned to Early's division, from which Evans's, formerly John B. Gordon's brigade, was transferred to Gordon's, previously Johnson's division (*Early*, 359).
Breckinridge's two brigades were not formally attached and were under the direct orders
of Lee. They were assigned position between the First and Second Corps, on the right
centre (*O. R.*, 51, part 2, p. 957). Alexander's estimate of the strength of all these reinforcements was 9000 (*op. cit.*, 530), but his figures are slightly high.
[28] 14 *S. H. S. P.*, 535. The date of this illness can be fixed with reasonable certainty.
He was not sick when he was at the Fox house, and as that was on the day the Federal
artillery reached the river bank, it must have been the 23d. Pendleton, *op. cit.*, 336, noted
that Lee was "quite unwell" on the 25th. The malady must, therefore, have showed itself on the night of the 23d–24th or on the 24th.

ness, and on the 24th he tried to transact army business as usual. Early in the day he rode over to the left flank and learned the details of Hill's failure the previous evening. Morning reports showed that in Wilcox's division alone the casualties had been

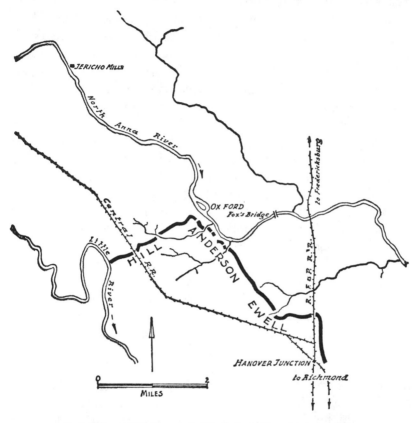

Lee's "inverted V" line on the North Anna River, May 24, 1864.

642—entirely too many men to be lost to no purpose.[29] Lee's temper was least under control in his rare periods of sickness, and when he saw General Hill he is said to have asked him abruptly, "Why did you not do as Jackson would have done—thrown your whole force upon these people and driven them back?"[30]

[29] *Wilcox's MS. report*, 48.
[30] 3 *C. M. H.*, 460. White (*op. cit.*, 381), without citing his authority, quoted Lee as saying, "General Hill, why did you let these people cross the river? Why did you not drive them back as General Jackson would have done?"

There was no answer to the question, and no remedy for the situation that had developed on that flank, except to put Hill to work digging his part of the "V" line,[31] in the hope that the enemy might make some blunder and offer an opening. The Federals on that sector, however, took no chances. While Hill's men dug, they too threw up dirt, and soon had a line which crossed the Central Railroad two-thirds of a mile northwest of Anderson's Station.[32] This, of course, meant that communications with Staunton would once more be interrupted, and that a part of the track of the Virginia Central would be torn up again.[33]

On the right, opposite the bridges, the Union forces crossed to the south bank as soon as they discovered that the Confederates had drawn in their lines.[34] This put the enemy precisely where Lee wanted him: If Grant tried to reinforce the right from the left, or *vice versa,* he would have to cross the river twice. The Confederate centre held stubbornly to Ox Ford. An attempt by Grant to force a crossing at that point and to connect the Federal left and right in a continuous line south of the river was easily defeated.[35] For a few hours opportunity beckoned, and if Lee had been well enough to organize a strong and immediate attack on either flank, he might perhaps have crushed the II Corps on his right or the V on his left; but hourly, as the Union entrenchments rose, his chances of success grew less.[36]

Lee was worse on the 25th and confined to his tent,[37] but he insisted on receiving reports and he carried on his official correspondence, in which there was not even a hint that he was sick. Some of his staff were disposed to think that he should not have vexed himself with duty when he was almost incapacitated. But what could he do? Beauregard's hands were full at Bermuda Hundred, and to whom else could he turn over the command? To Ewell, senior corps chief, who was himself scarcely able to keep the field? To Hill, who had just failed on the left? To Anderson, who had been in corps command scarcely more than a fortnight? As long as he was able to direct operations, Lee had no alternative. He must endure the pain and the debilitating symptoms. In his

---

[31] *History of McGowan's Brigade,* 156. [32] Now called Verdon.
[33] The actual work of destruction began May 25 (*O. R.,* 36, part 1, pp. 582, 592).
[34] Part of the II Corps made this move (*O. R.,* 36, part 1, p. 341).
[35] *O. R.,* 36, part 1, pp. 918, 1030–31.
[36] *Maurice,* 239; *Humphreys,* 132–33. [37] *Pendleton,* 336; 14 *S. H. S. P.,* 535.

dispatches he was able to keep his measured tone. Writing to the President of the heavy reinforcement of Grant, he again urged joint operations by his army and Beauregard's, and at whatever point most advantageous to Beauregard. His phrases were as considerate and as self-controlled as if he had been at his best.[38] In his tent it was different. As he felt opportunity slipping away, his grip on himself weakened, and he had a violent scene with Colonel Venable, who argued some point with him. When Venable emerged from the General's tent, he was, Major McClellan remembered, "in a state of flurry and excitement, full to bursting, and he blurted out, 'I have just told the old man that he is not fit to command this army, and that he had better send for Beauregard.' "[39] Lee could not, would not give up, but he broke out vehemently: "We must strike them a blow—we must never let them pass us again—we must strike them a blow!"[40] To Doctor Gwathmey he said of Grant, "If I can get one more pull at him, I will defeat him."[41]

The opportunity was gone, however. The Unionists were too strong to be attacked and too cautious to assault the lines with their forces divided. The 25th passed with nothing more serious than a few demonstrations.[42] To procure more rest than was possible at Hanover Junction, Lee moved his headquarters three miles down the Richmond, Fredericksburg and Potomac Railroad to Taylorsville.[43] He had the satisfaction of knowing that the troops were rested, and that their morale was still high.[44] No concern whatever did he have as to their willingness and ability to fight, but he dreaded the numerical superiority of the enemy, particularly in the cavalry.[45]

[38] *Lee's Dispatches*, 198 *ff*.
[39] *H. B. McClellan MSS.* The date of this episode is not fixed.
[40] Venable in 14 *S. H. S. P.*, 535. [41] *Cooke*, 404. [42] *O. R.*, 36, part 1, pp. 8, 78.
[43] His dispatch of May 26, received at 8:30 P.M. was dated from Taylorsville (*O. R.*, 36, part 3, p. 834).
[44] There was division of opinion among the Southerners whether the Union troops were as stiff adversaries as they had been at the opening of the campaign (*Taylor MSS.*, May 23, 1864; *Taylor's Four Years*, 133; *Memoir of Capt. C. Seton Fleming*, 97; *Pendleton*, 336). Some of the Federals thought the Army of Northern Virginia was losing confidence. *Cf.* C. A. Dana, May 26: "Rebels have lost all confidence, and are already morally defeated. This army has learned to believe that it is sure of victory. Even our officers have ceased to regard Lee as an invincible military genius. On part of the rebels this change is evinced, not only by their not attacking, even when circumstances seem to invite it, but by the unanimous statements of prisoners taken from them" (*O. R.*, 36, part 1, p. 79).
[45] Lee to Seddon, May 26, 1864: "The enemy's superiority in Cavalry will, I fear, enable him to do us much injury" (*O. R.*, 36, part 1, p. 834).

The Federals did not wait long in the difficult position where Lee had placed them by drawing his inverted "V." On the 26th there were heavy demonstrations along the river, and reports that the enemy was moving up the left bank. Lee ordered the enemy's lines felt out, and he began to suspect that instead of

Sketch showing how Grant's move from the North Anna River to Hanovertown on the Pamunkey shortened the distance between the front and Richmond.

sliding his left flank southward, Grant might be preparing to move on Richmond by the Union right flank.[46]

This suspicion was disproved at dawn on the morning of May 27. The enemy was found to have evacuated the south bank of the North Anna, and was marching down the north bank. Grant had declined the challenge to battle and was preparing to try again. Almost at the same time, cavalry outposts that Lee had prudently placed far on his right reported that the Federals were

[46] O. R., 36, part 3, p. 834, three dispatches; *ibid.*, 51, part 2, p. 960.

crossing at Hanovertown on the Pamunkey River.[47] The Pamunkey is formed by the junction of the North and South Anna Rivers, and its course is from northwest to southeast. When Grant started down the North Anna for the Pamunkey he had the cover of a river and, at the same time, was getting eight miles nearer Richmond, for the distance from Richmond to the North Anna is about twenty-three miles north to south, while Hanovertown is fifteen miles by air northeast from the Confederate capital.

General Lee must have had the possibility of this manœuvre in mind when he wrote on May 21 that he doubted if he could strike Grant until after the Union army had passed the Pamunkey.[48] He did not waste an hour now in hurrying to intercept his adversary in this new effort to reach Richmond. Ewell's corps was immediately set in motion down the Richmond, Fredericksburg and Potomac Railroad toward Ashland, and Anderson, with Breckinridge, was ordered to follow him. Hill was to form the rearguard and was to leave the North Anna that evening.[49]

The operation on the North Anna was not accounted a success because it did not compel Grant to give battle. Strategically, it accomplished far more than Lee could then foresee. It forced the Federal commander to abandon a direct movement on Richmond from the north, and that, as the event proved, was to leave Lee in command of communications with the Valley of the Shenandoah. This, in turn, not only gave him an opportunity for offensive operations there but assured him such supplies as western Virginia could yield. No achievement of the entire campaign from the Rapidan to the James meant more in prolonging the struggle. Five months later Meade was to write of the Virginia Central, "Until that road is destroyed, we cannot compel the evacuation of Richmond." [50]

But now Lee saw the battle brought back, close to the fields where he had taken command not quite two years previously. Two years only! It seemed an æon of anxiety.

---

[47] O. R., 36, part 3, p. 836; *ibid.*, 51, part 2, pp. 962, 964.
[48] See *supra*, p. 341.
[49] *Wilcox's MS. report*, 48.   [50] Oct. 22, 1864; 2 *Meade*, 236.

CHAPTER XXI

MANŒUVRE ON THE TOTOPOTOMOY

(MAY 27–30, 1864)

PAST scattered farmhouses, where the women waved their hand-kerchiefs as bravely as when every march had been northward, Lee rode[1] with Ewell's corps toward Richmond on the morning of May 27. He made good speed, for the Second Corps could always outmarch any other large unit in the Army of Northern Virginia. About mid-day he learned from the cavalry that the enemy seemed to be advancing from Hanovertown on the Pamunkey to Haw's Shop, an important crossroads ten miles northeast of Mechanicsville on the way to Richmond. This was of course familiar terrain to Lee. He remembered that there was a fine defensive position on the ridge between Totopotomoy and Beaver Dam Creeks, the same ridge he had ordered Stuart to reconnoitre at the beginning of the famous "ride around McClellan." The columns were ordered in that direction, to intercept Grant and, if might be, to give him battle there.[2]

Continuing down the Telegraph road, Lee came in the afternoon to the vicinity of the Chickahominy River, just west of the upper waters of the Totopotomoy. There he received reports that only cavalry had been seen in the vicinity of Haw's Shop and that a column of infantry was vaguely said to be moving along the south bank of the Pamunkey from Hanover Courthouse to Hanovertown. This information was much too indefinite to justify Lee in throwing the whole army to the northeast of Richmond, for this would leave open to the enemy the direct road from the north, via Ashland. Consequently, Lee decided to halt the columns for the night north and northwest of Atlee's so that they could be moved in whichever direction the advance of the enemy

---

[1] Probably in a carriage.
[2] *Lee's Dispatches*, 202; 3 *C. M. H.*, 463; *Early*, 361; *O. R.*, 36, part 3, pp. 837, 838–39; T. Roberts Baker in 3 *Richmond Howitzers*, 12.

might develop.[3] Lee opened his headquarters at the Jenkins house, a few hundred yards from the Telegraph road,[4] near the point where the road to Atlee's leaves the main highway. The Second Corps was immediately to the eastward and southeastward. General Ewell established himself slightly more than a mile east of Lee at Satterwhite's. The leader of the Second Corps had

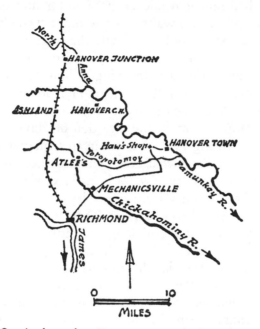

The terrain of Grant's advance from Hanovertown on the Pamunkey, May 28, 1864.

been suffering, like his chief, from an intestinal malady, had ridden all day in an ambulance, and by evening was so ill that he had to turn over the command of the troops temporarily to General Early, who was at the nearby Hughes house.[5]

Lee was now only nine miles by road from Richmond. He could have wished the distance ten times as great, and he was determined, by engaging Grant as soon as practicable, to avoid a second siege of the capital.[6] But proximity to the city, along with

---

[3] *Lee's Dispatches,* 202–3; *Early,* 361; *O. R.,* 36, part 3, pp. 838, 841; *ibid.,* 51, part 2, pp. 962–64.
[4] This old home remains substantially as it was in 1864. Visitors are still shown the back porch on which Lee rested.
[5] *O. R.,* 36, part 1, p. 1072; part 3, p. 838.   [6] *Lee's Dispatches,* 203.

its dangers, was not without some advantages. For one thing, of course, it shortened his communications and lengthened those of his adversary. For another, it gave him the promise of the assistance of the 5700 troops in the garrison of Richmond when he was close enough for the two forces to be consolidated.[7] And, thirdly, he was now near the line of the Chickahominy, on which General Beauregard had said it would be possible for him to unite with Lee in an offensive. Lee was willing to move even closer to Richmond if Beauregard would designate the place where he would find it most convenient for the two forces to unite.[8]

Still uncertain in the early morning of May 28 whether Grant's advance would be down the Telegraph road or from the Pamunkey, Lee ordered the cavalry to make a forced reconnaissance across the Totopotomoy, in the direction of Haw's Shop, and to ascertain if the strong Federal horse in that quarter had infantry behind it. He was somewhat better circumstanced for a vigorous employment of his cavalry now, for he had received the Fourth and part of the Fifth South Carolina Cavalry and had the assurance that the Sixth would soon arrive. These were the large, well-mounted commands that had long been idle in South Carolina, while Lee had been pleading for them.[9]

A little later in the day he moved his headquarters to the Clarke house near Atlee's.[10] He was so unwell by the hour he arrived there that he had to accept a room from the hospitable owner and transact army business indoors. It was the first time since the opening of the campaign that headquarters had not been under canvas.[11] Sick as he was, Lee proceeded to dispose his troops with the greatest care. He advanced the head of Early's corps to the vicinity of Pole Green Church on the south bank of the Totopotomoy, five miles due east of Atlee's. Anderson he put in rear of Early, and Hill he stationed west of Anderson, near Shady

---

[7] O. R., 36, part 3, p. 861. The department of Richmond was then under Major General Robert Ransom, Jr.

[8] Lee's Dispatches, 203.

[9] O. R., 36, part 3, pp. 831, 852; Wells, 153 ff. The scattered cavalry commands around Richmond were organized into a brigade under Brigadier General P. M. B. Young (O. R., 36, part 3, pp. 812, 841).

[10] O. R., 36, part 3, pp. 844, 846; Taylor's General Lee, 246. The Clarke house, now the home of T. Ellett Clarke, is in the southwest fork of the crossroads, between the old highway and the station.

[11] 4 B. and L., 244.

Grove Church.[12] If Grant attempted to cross the Totopotomoy,
Lee could easily move the other corps into line of battle with
Early; and if the enemy's march was down the Telegraph road,
the column could readily be reversed, for Shady Grove was only
five miles from the Telegraph road, thus:

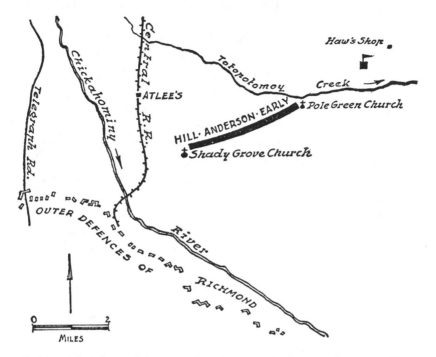

Position of the infantry of the Army of Northern Virginia, forenoon of May 29, 1864.

The day passed without incident at headquarters, but in front
of Haw's Shop the cavalry had a vigorous fight with Sheridan's
command. The Confederates threw the enemy back against his
supports, captured prisoners from the V and VI Corps, and
thereby established the fact that Grant had much infantry south
of the Pamunkey. But the gray troopers were greatly outnumbered and had to face the fire of the Spencer repeating carbine,
which was just coming into use. In the end, they were compelled

[12] Breckinridge's small command, which is not noted on the sketch, was between Anderson and Hill (O. R., 36, part 3, p. 844).

365

to give ground. The newly arrived South Carolina regiments behaved like veterans.[13]

Lee pondered the report the cavalry brought back. If Grant had two corps east of Haw's Shop, it was fairly certain that his main attack would not be down the Telegraph road.[14] He had, however, three routes to Richmond from Haw's Shop. He could march northwestward, avoid the Totopotomoy,[15] and strike for the Central Railroad at Peake's Turnout, or, secondly, he could move directly westward against Atlee's, or, thirdly, he could turn south, across the Totopotomoy, enter the Old Church road, and make for Mechanicsville.

There was manifest advantage to the enemy in seizing the Central Railroad. At one stroke, Grant could again sever Lee's communications with western Virginia and re-establish for himself a rail line of supply from the Rappahannock. Lee applied his maxim that it was always well to expect the enemy to do what he should do, and he anticipated an advance by "Route One" or "Route Two" on the map.[16] He accordingly shifted the left of his line somewhat to the northeast, and closer to the Totopotomoy. To cover the whole front of possible advance he made the most of an almost impenetrable area on his right centre, between Early's corps and Breckinridge's command. He left this ground practically unoccupied, though Anderson's corps was within supporting distance. Ewell was on the right along the Shady Grove road; Anderson was at an angle behind Ewell's left; then came Breckinridge; on the extreme left was Hill, covering the point where the road from Shady Grove to Hanover Courthouse crossed the Totopotomoy.[17] Nothing happened during the day to test the wisdom of these dispositions. In mid-afternoon, Federals appeared in some force on the south side of the Totopotomoy, in

13 O. R., 36, part 1, pp. 793, 1031; Wells, 154 ff.; Alexander, 533–34. Lee was of opinion that the South could not manufacture or transport enough ammunition to supply repeating rifles, even if the Confederacy could supply the weapons. "We want a rifle," he said, "the loading of which takes a certain amount of time: That makes the man to value his shot, and not to fire till he is sure of his aim" (T. M. Maguire, The Campaigns in Virginia, 32).

14 O. R., 36, part 3, p. 843.

15 The lower stretch of the Totopotomoy is locally called Pony Swamp, but to avoid confusion, only one name is used here.

16 O. R., 36, part 3, pp. 846, 848; ibid., 51, part 2, pp. 967, 968.

17 O. R., 36, part 3, pp. 845, 846, 847.

the direction of Ewell's left, but they did not progress far and contented themselves with sharp skirmishing.[18]

Lee watched these movements with care and put Anderson on

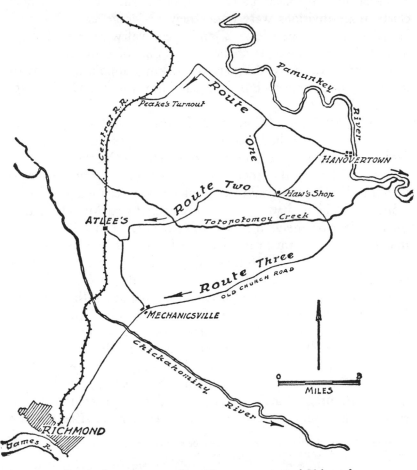

Grant's alternative routes from Hanovertown toward Richmond.

the alert to support Ewell,[19] but he had additional concern on the 29th. General Ewell's condition had become more serious and, in Lee's opinion, necessitated rest at a distance from the army. Early was left in charge and Ewell was given leave of absence,[20] in the

---

[18] *O. R.,* 36, part 3, p. 846. This advance was by Griffin's division of the **V Corps** (*O. R.,* 36, part 1, pp. 194, 543).

[19] *O. R.,* 36, part 3, p. 846.   [20] *O. R.,* 36, part 3, p. 846.

hope that he could resume his duties when operations were less active.[21] The high command had changed most alarmingly since the campaign had opened. With Lee himself so unwell that he could hardly leave headquarters, two of the three corps had new chiefs, three divisions were under new major generals, fourteen brigades had changed leaders, and the cavalry were without a head.[22] Lee was anxious about the leading of some of his brigades[23] and was very desirous of making appointments with temporary rank under a bill then pending before the Confederate Congress.[24]

A still greater concern on the 29th was the attitude of Beauregard. That officer had become alarmed over the activity of Butler on the Bermuda Hundred front, and on the 27th had been uncertain whether the enemy was preparing to advance or to withdraw.[25] He was convinced that he was occupying twice as many troops as he had, and he so far convinced Mr. Davis that the President on the 28th hinted to General Lee that Beauregard might be doing as much good where he was as he could accomplish with the Army of Northern Virginia.[26] Davis sent one of his aides to Beauregard for further details, only to learn that in Beauregard's opinion 4000 soldiers, but no more than that, had left Butler to reinforce Grant. "My force is so small at present," he said, "that to divide it for the purpose of reinforcing Lee would jeopardize the safety of the part left to guard my lines, and would greatly endanger Richmond itself."[27] Mr. Davis went out to Atlee's during the afternoon to discuss the situation,[28] and, in the evening, Beauregard arrived. He maintained in a lengthy discussion that he could spare none of his 12,000 men. Lee did not

[21] For General Ewell's brave protests that he was able to return to duty on June 1, see O. R., 36, part 1, p. 1074.

[22] Early's division passed to S. D. Ramseur, who was promoted major general. William Mahone was leading Anderson's old division, and Gordon was in command of Edward Johnson's. The number of new brigade commanders would have been seventeen had not Hays's brigade been consolidated with Stafford's, while the Stonewall Brigade, Steuart's and J. M. Jones's had been placed under Brigadier General William Terry, as noted. Three other brigades were soon added to this list when Generals James H. Lane and E. M. Law were wounded and Brigadier General John Finegan, a newcomer, took charge of the united Florida troops.

[23] Cf. O. R., 36, part 3, p. 851.

[24] IV O. R., 3, 457, 496; O. R., 51, part 2, pp. 973–74.

[25] O. R., 36, part 3, p. 842.

[26] O. R., 51, part 2, pp. 965–66.   [27] O. R., 36, part 3, p. 849.

[28] John ——— to Roane ———, June 4, 1864, MS., copied by B. E. Case of Hartford. Conn., and typescript loaned the writer by Doctor Lyon G. Tyler.

attempt to gainsay him, much as he desired reinforcement.[29] The conference ended amicably, but without result. Lee had grimly to telegraph the President, "If Gen. Grant advances tomorrow I will engage him with my present force."[30] The best he could hope for the moment was that with Beauregard on the south of the James and the Army of Northern Virginia immediately in front of Grant, the President could spare him some of Ransom's garrison of Richmond.[31]

But the situation was changed over night. Early on the morning of the 30th the enemy began to disappear from the Confederate left, where A. P. Hill and Butler's cavalry were on guard, and almost simultaneously there were signs of a new shift by Grant on the right of the Confederate line. Lee's most reliable scout reported that the Federals, in his opinion, were moving along the road to Old Cold Harbor.[32] Putting all this information together, Lee concluded that the Federals would fortify a line along the Totopotomoy and then, "will probably make another move by their left flank toward the Chickahominy," as he expressed it to Anderson. He added: "This is just a repetition of their former movements."[33]

Pending developments, the only practical step seemed to be to strike at that part of Grant's army on the south side of the Totopotomoy, in front of the Second Corps. That corps, though much reduced in number, was in a good position, and had already constructed two crossings over the fields to the Old Church road, on which the enemy was demonstrating with cavalry near Bethesda Church.[34] When Early proposed to develop this situation by a vigorous attack, Lee at once approved, subject to Early's discretion.

Rodes was moved to the right and the action was opened. The burden of it fell on Early's old brigade. This command had been

---

[29] *Lee's Dispatches*, 208–9. ". . . I am unable to judge," he told the President in a letter the next day, "but suppose of course that with his means of information, his opinion is correct."

[30] *Lee's Dispatches*, 204.   [31] *Lee's Dispatches*, 209.

[32] *O. R.*, 36, part 3, pp. 850–51; U. R. Brooks in *Butler and His Cavalry*, 224, quoting Charles Marshall to M. C. Butler, 8:00 A.M., May 30, 1864. For Hill's position, see *O. R.*, 51, part 2, p. 969.

[33] *O. R.*, 36, part 3, p. 851.

[34] *O. R.*, 36, part 3, p. 854. Early, *op. cit.*, insisted that the corps could count only 9000 muskets, but his figure may have been a little low.

led by Brigadier General John Pegram until that officer had been wounded, and then by Colonel Edward Willis of Georgia.[85] As these veterans went forward, Lieutenant Colonel C. B. Chris-

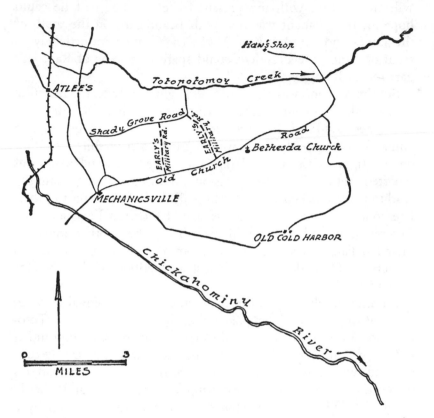

The terrain of the Totopotomoy-Chickahominy watershed, to illustrate the action of May 30, 1864, at Bethesda Church.

tian of the Forty-ninth Virginia, which had lost nine color bearers since the opening of the campaign, observed that his regiment was not displaying its flag.

"Orendorf," said Colonel Christian to a tall, thin boy from Amherst County, "will you carry the colors?"

"Yes, Colonel," Orendorf answered, "I will carry them. They

[85] Colonel Willis is said to have been recommended for promotion to brigadier general, but died before his commission reached him. He was a very young officer of great merit (6 *C. M. H.*, 452; 14 *S. H. S. P.*, 160 ff.; 33 *ibid.*, 57 n.; Sorrel, 252–53).

killed my brother the other day; now, damn them. let them kill me, too." [36]

As the line went forward, the Union cavalry quickly withdrew. Rodes's men passed into a broad field, swept back an opposing brigade and immediately came under a very heavy fire. Their lines were torn by every round, for the Union gunners had the exact range. They charged desperately on, almost to the artillery position, and then, before the eyes of watching remnants, were repulsed with slaughter. Orendorf was torn to bits by a cannon ball, as he defiantly waved his flag not twenty feet from the enemy.[37] The failure of the attack was complete, though the loss in three of the brigades was comparatively light.[38]

During the afternoon, while Early was engaged at Bethesda Church, evidence began to accumulate that reinforcements from Butler were moving to Grant, via the White House on the Pamunkey River. Beauregard had forwarded reports on the 26th of suspicious activity in the Federal shipping on the James,[39] though he held to his contention that only some 4000 men had left Bermuda Hundred.[40] Now the signal officer on the lower James reported that seventeen transports had passed down the river, carrying at least 7000 men.[41] General Ransom informed General Bragg that a newspaper correspondent had been captured near Tunstall's Station, and that letters found on him indicated the man's belief that Smith's XVIII Corps was at the White House.[42] This corps was known to have been with Butler. Lee's own scouts had it that Butler's fleet, conveying the same corps to Grant, would be at West Point on the 30th.[43]

On the basis of this information, and to save time that might be lost in transmitting the request through Richmond, Lee called directly on Beauregard for reinforcements. When that officer

---

[36] 33 *S. H. S. P.,* 59.   [37] *Ibid.*

[38] *Ibid., Early,* 362; *Alexander,* 534. In his account of this "battle of Bethesda Church," Alexander made the serious mistake of saying that Lee in person ordered the attack. The *Official Records* plainly show that General Lee was not present, that the proposal originated with General Early, and that the orders, as repeated to General Anderson, made the attack discretionary (*O. R.,* 36, part 3, pp. 851, 854). It is only fair to remember, however, that Lee favored an offensive that day, as, indeed, he did whenever he saw an opening during the progress of this campaign. Early contended that the attack failed because Anderson did not support him (*O. R.,* 51, part 2, p. 975).

[39] *O. R.,* 51, part 2, p. 961.
[40] *O. R.,* 36, part 3, p. 849.   [41] *O. R.,* 51, part 2, p. 971.
[42] *O. R.,* 51, part 2, p. 971.   [43] *Lee's Dispatches,* 207.

answered about nightfall that the War Department would have to decide what troops should be sent, Lee lost patience. "The result of this delay," he telegraphed the President, "will be disaster. Butler's troops (Smith's corps) will be with Grant tomorrow. Hoke's division, at least, should be with me by light tomorrow." [44]

When Lee used that grim word "disaster," the wheels of the War Department turned swiftly. Beauregard was ordered to dispatch Hoke by trains that would be sent him immediately; but before the call reached Beauregard, he, too, had concluded that the risk to Richmond was greater than that on his own line and he advised the department that Hoke's command was to start at once and was to be followed by Bushrod Johnson's division as soon as the movements of the enemy in Beauregard's front would permit. Before midnight, Lee had assurance from the President that every effort would be made to have Hoke's four brigades with the Army of Northern Virginia the next day. [45] This was a good division of more than 7000 officers and men. [46] Adding it to the reinforcements already received, Lee had now made good approximately 70 per cent of the losses he had sustained since the opening of the campaign, and he was more than ever determined, if he found an opening, to take the offensive in what he told Anderson was "the grand object, the destruction of the enemy." [47]

[44] *O. R.,* 36, part 3, p. 850.
[45] *O. R.,* 36, part 3, pp. 850, 857; *ibid.,* 51, part 2, p. 969.
[46] *O. R.,* 36, part 3, pp. 817–18. The division consisted of Martin's and Clingman's North Carolina, Hagood's South Carolina, and Colquitt's Georgia brigades.
[47] *O. R.,* 36, part 3, p. 828. This passage occurs in a misdated dispatch.

CHAPTER XXII

And Still Grant Hammers

(cold harbor, may 31–june 3, 1864)

Now began the last great manœuvres in the campaign from the Rapidan to the James, the manœuvres that were to change the character of military operations in Virginia and substitute siege tactics for field strategy.[1]

By dawn on May 31 the right, under Early, had been extended beyond the Old Church road, which led from the Federal position to Mechanicsville and thence to Richmond. The line crossed the road about a mile west of Bethesda Church and four miles east of Mechanicsville. Thence the Confederate front extended irregularly to the north and northwest for a distance of seven and a half miles. The left rested on the Chickahominy swamp, west of Atlee's Station.[2] The whole line had been well fortified and, if well supported by artillery, could be held by a comparatively small force of infantry. The works admirably covered the approaches to Richmond from the upper Pamunkey, as will appear from the sketch on the next page.

But if Grant was moving by the left flank, as Lee believed, it would be possible for him to swing around to the Chickahominy River and force the Army of Northern Virginia to stand siege in the Richmond defenses. That was the one thing above all others that Lee most desired to avoid, for he knew it could end only in defeat.[3] He must, then, extend his flank to save himself from being chained to Richmond. Fitz Lee's cavalry was already well

---

[1] It is perhaps in order to note that the Confederate correspondence for the operations of May 31–June 3 is fragmentary and that the positions and movements of the troops have to be established by piecing together bits of information. Much that should be said with precision has to be qualified. There is, however, no justification for accepting the view, tacitly admitted in many of the Southern narratives, that the details of what happened at Cold Harbor are hopelessly confused.

[2] O. R., 36, part 1, p. 1058; ibid., 51, part 2, p. 974; Early, 362.

[3] See infra, p. 398.

beyond Early's exposed flank, holding the crossroads at Old Cold Harbor, the strategic importance of which Lee had learned in the campaign of the Seven Days. To support Fitz Lee, the commanding general directed that Hoke's division, which was be-

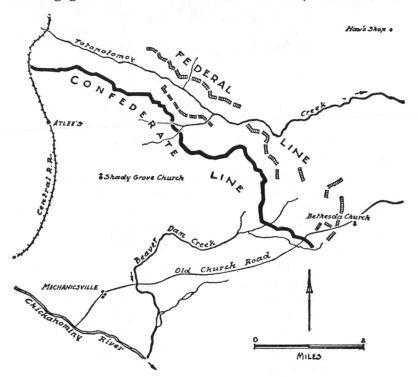

Positions of the opposing armies on Totopotomoy Creek, May 31, 1864.

ginning to detrain in Richmond, should move toward Cold Harbor.

The morning of the 31st passed without any development of consequence, but in mid-afternoon, Fitz Lee reported from Old Cold Harbor that the enemy was half a mile from that place and was advancing on it, though only cavalry had been discovered at that hour. Fitz Lee said that he was preparing to dispute the enemy's progress where he stood, but he asked if the van of Hoke's division, which was then between Mechanicsville and Cold Harbor, should not be ordered to him.[4]

[4] O. R., 36, part 3, p. 858.

General Lee did more than this. Being almost certain that Smith's corps was moving from White House to join Grant, and reasoning that Grant's army would be strung out on the march, he thought he saw an opportunity for striking the blow he had so long wished to deliver. If he could attack the enemy at Cold Harbor, before the Federal left was in position, he might double it up. To this end, Anderson was taken from his position between Breckinridge and Early and was shifted during the later afternoon into Early's position and beyond it. Breckinridge extended his line somewhat to the right and Early to the left to fill the gap made by Anderson's departure. Anderson was then quietly moved by the right flank until he was close to Beulah Church, which was about one mile northwest of Old Cold Harbor. Kershaw was in position early in the night; Pickett and Field were on the road behind Kershaw.[5] Hoke's brigades were to file in on Anderson's right. The situation then would be as shown on page 376.

Fifteen thousand Confederate infantry would be in the vicinity of Cold Harbor by daylight. That force, well handled, should be sufficient to turn Grant's left flank and to create a confusion during which the other corps might attack. The great day might be at hand.[6] What had seemed possible on May 6, when Longstreet had struck the enemy's left in the Wilderness, might be achieved.

About 7 o'clock on the evening of May 31, not long before Anderson reported the arrival of his van near Beulah Church, a significant message came from Fitz Lee. The enemy's cavalry, he said, had attacked his troopers and Clingman's brigade of infantry at Cold Harbor and had driven them from the crossroads. Fitz Lee was not sure, but he thought Federal infantry were in his front.[7]

---

[5] *O. R.*, 36, part 1, p. 1058; *ibid.*, 51, part 2, p. 974; *Early*, 362; *Alexander*, 535–36.

[6] It must be explained that the points of junction of the various commands at daybreak June 1 cannot be established with certainty. Early, who was the only authority on the position of his corps, simply wrote that Rodes was withdrawn to the west side of Beaver Dam Creek, but he did not specify which branch of the creek (Early, *op. cit.*, 362). The diary of the First Corps (*O. R.*, 36, part 1, p. 1058) stated that Anderson took over the whole of Early's line. Wilcox (*MS. report*, 48) said that he was moved to the right to a station "near Pole Green Church," but he did not explain whether he was on the right of Breckinridge or whether he was separated from the rest of the corps. The question is not material, but as it cannot be determined, the sketch shows no lines of division between any two corps.

[7] *O. R.*, 36, part 3, p. 858. There are no Confederate reports of this action. The account by the Federal commander, Brigadier General A. T. Torbert, appears in *ibid.*, part 1, pp. 805–6.

Infantry! Evidently, then, there was a race for Cold Harbor just as there had been for Spotsylvania Courthouse, and the Confederate infantry, by odd chance, were led by the man who had

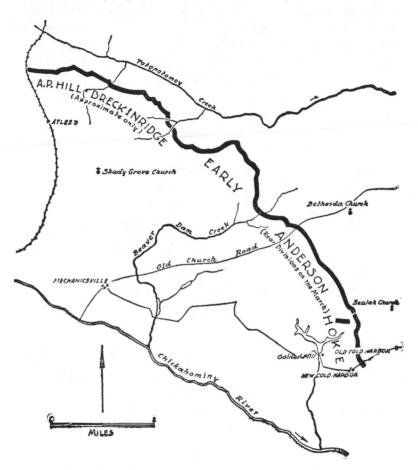

Approximate front of the Army of Northern Virginia, 1 A.M., June 1, 1864.

won before. Lee at once took the precaution of placing Hoke under Anderson, and directed that Hoke's rear brigades be hurried to Cold Harbor.[8] Lee doubtless wished to go himself, so that he could himself direct the turning movement, but while he was physically much better, he was still so weak that he had to ride

[8] *O. R.*, 36, part 3, p. 858.

376

in a carriage.[9] The most he felt justified in doing was to advance his headquarters to Shady Grove, where he would be nearer the centre of operations in case Anderson's attack made a general offensive possible.[10]

Hope might well have beaten high in the heart of Lee when he retired at Shady Grove on the evening of May 31. His plans had been well laid and the opportunity at Cold Harbor was great. When he arose on the morning of June 1, and strained his ears vainly for the sound of battle from his distant right, he had every reason to believe that the first courier from Anderson would bring great news. The 1st of June was a memorable date in his military career. Two years before, in a house not many miles away, he had assumed command of the Army of Northern Virginia: Was Anderson about to send him, as an anniversary gift, a report of a stunning victory at Cold Harbor?

It was far otherwise. The dispatch that finally reached him told a humiliating story of failure. Anderson attacked at dawn, in accordance with instructions. The advance was led by Kershaw's veteran brigade. Lee had been aware that the brigade was without a regular commander and had urged Anderson to name one.[11] Anderson had delayed, or else had been unable to find a suitable man overnight, and he sent the brigade into action on the morning of June 1 under its ranking colonel, Lawrence M. Keitt of the Twentieth South Carolina, a green regiment that had recently joined the army. Keitt was a distinguished ante-bellum politician and orator who had come to Virginia only a short time previously and had never been in close action. He knew little of the methods of fighting then in vogue in the Old Dominion, and the men of the other regiments were fearful he would make some blunder. He dashed boldly forward, mounted on his charger, and was killed at the first onset. His raw regiment broke

9 General Lee's opposition to the use of alcoholics showed itself during this illness. Doctor Lafayette Guild, medical director of the army, prescribed port wine and sent the General a case of it, but Lee would not use it (J. W. Fairfax to J. T. Parham, May 21, 1897. *Fairfax MSS.*). Jones (*op. cit.,* 169) stated that a friend in April, 1861, gave Lee two bottles of whiskey which he carried in his headquarters' wagon for medicinal use. At the end of the war they had never been opened.

10 One dispatch on the morning of May 31 is dated from "Near Coleman's, on road from Shady Grove Church to Mechanicsville" (*O. R.,* 36, part 3, p. 858), and a dispatch on the morning of June 1 (*ibid.,* 865), is dated "Shady Grove Church."

11 *O. R.,* 36, part 3, p. 851.

and forced the seasoned troops to give ground.[12] Liaison between Anderson and Hoke was incredibly bad; Hoke did nothing; the attack failed and perhaps the greatest opportunity presented the army after May 6 was thrown away.[13]

Bitterly as Lee must have been disappointed, he lost no time in repining. If he could not roll up the Army of the Potomac from his right, he must strengthen that flank to keep Grant from tying him down to the Richmond defenses. By doing that, while holding his position on the left, opposite the Totopotomoy, he might yet find an opening.

Breckinridge was at once ordered to Cold Harbor to strengthen and to extend the right,[14] and Lee himself prepared to go there in person. As it happened, Breckinridge was absent from his headquarters when the order reached him, and Heth's division of the Third Corps was changing position. Ere long, an attack developed on Heth's front which, of course, held Breckinridge temporarily where he was and forced Lee to defer his own start for Cold Harbor. Cooke's brigade and Kirkland's, however, easily beat off the enemy. A little later, Breckinridge and Mahone cleared up the ground in their front and took about 150 prisoners. Almost at the same hour the cavalry that was covering the Confederate left met an advance by the Federal horse and drove it back in the dashing style of 1862.[15]

These three isolated attacks, if designed to alarm Lee for his left, entirely failed of their purpose. He took them to be mere demonstrations to distract his attention, and some time after 4 o'clock he started for Cold Harbor.[16] On his arrival he opened headquarters, probably in the field on the right of the Cold

[12] *History of Kershaw's Brigade,* 366 ff.; Johnson Hagood: *Memoirs of the War of Secession* (cited hereafter as *Hagood*), 257; *O. R.,* 36, part 1, p. 1049.

[13] In commenting on this abortive affair, Alexander (*op. cit.,* 536) said: "Unfortunately, Hoke's brigade [division] had not been put under Anderson's command, so neither felt full responsibility." The fact is precisely the contrary. Early in the evening of May 31, as noted in the text, Lee wrote Anderson: "General Hoke will, whilst occupying his present position relative to you, be under your control. He was directed to see you and to arrange for co-operation tomorrow" (*O. R.,* 36, part 3, p. 858).

[14] *O. R.,* 36, part 3, p. 863.   [15] *O. R.,* 36, part 1, pp. 1031–32.

[16] He was certainly at Shady Grove as late as 4 P.M. (*O. R.,* 36, part 3, p. 865). Alexander (*op. cit.,* 536) stated that Lee was "not upon the ground in the early hours of the day" of June 1, with the inference that he came later. The statement that he went there during the evening of the 1st rests primarily upon the *H. B. McClellan MSS.,* in which Major McClellan explained that Lee went to Mechanicsville on the morning of June 2 to look for Breckinridge. Obviously Lee would not have known that Breckinridge had not come up if he had not been near Cold Harbor himself.

Harbor road, just west of the crossing of Powhite Creek at Gaines's Mill.[17] He found that important events had happened during the afternoon. Fitz Lee, who had been in advance of Hoke's right, had been forced back by superior numbers. This so threatened Anderson's right that he ordered Hoke to extend his flank southward beyond Old Cold Harbor to the terrain won by D. H. Hill in the battle of Gaines's Mill nearly two years before.[18] The key to this position was Turkey Hill. Knowing its strength, Lee had given particular instructions that it should be occupied fully,[19] but Hoke did not extend his flank any great distance.[20] He might have intended going farther in that direction, but immediately after he made the movement, the enemy attacked with vigor north of the road between New and Old Cold Harbor.[21] The force of the Federal assault broke the lines between the left of Hoke and the right of Anderson.[22] Clingman's brigade of Hoke's division gave way and Wofford's of Kershaw's division had to fall back, but Kershaw threw in two regiments and regained some of the ground. Hunton's brigade of Pickett's division was thereupon sent to Hoke. Working along the left flank of Hoke, the brigade

[17] Postmaster General Reagan, who visited Lee on June 3, said (op. cit., 193), that the headquarters were near the mill in an open field, a few hundred yards in rear of which was a wood of some fifteen or twenty acres, surrounded by clear ground. The spot, he said, was within artillery range. The site indicated in the text is the only one nearby that corresponds to this description, though it was not within range of guns of less than 20 pounds.

[18] O. R., 36, part 1, p. 867; Hagood, 255.   [19] Reagan, 193.

[20] This seems a proper point at which to note the tradition, long current in North Carolina, that Lee said during the campaign that if he were incapacitated by his diarrhœa, he desired General Hoke to succeed him. There is not the slightest hint of this in any contemporary narrative and its improbability is so great that it may be dismissed as pure fable. General Hoke, though a capable, hard-hitting soldier, had but recently been promoted to divisional command and at this time was handling his division for the first time in action. Lee had not seen him in many months and, except for giving general supervision to the successful minor operation at Plymouth, N. C., had never dealt with him otherwise than as a colonel and a brigadier general. It is inconceivable that Lee would have dreamed of putting Hoke over A. P. Hill, Anderson, or Early, to say nothing of major generals like Rodes, Kershaw, and Gordon. It is futile to speculate on what Lee would have advocated if his illness had disabled him, but in the writer's opinion he would probably have recommended that Beauregard assume command.

[21] This road, across which the Confederate lines ran, is to be mentioned so frequently in the following pages that it will for convenience often be designated simply as the "Cold Harbor road."

[22] Positions at Cold Harbor are very difficult to establish with accuracy. On the map there are two points that conform to the general description of the break, but the detailed accounts given in the History of Kershaw's Brigade, 371, and in Alexander, 537–38, make it practically certain that the rupture was in the ravine 600 yards north and 400 yards east of New Cold Harbor crossroads. The position was in advance of the heavy Confederate lines still preserved in that part of the Richmond battlefield park. The existing lines at the ravine were drawn and fortified after the operations of June 1.

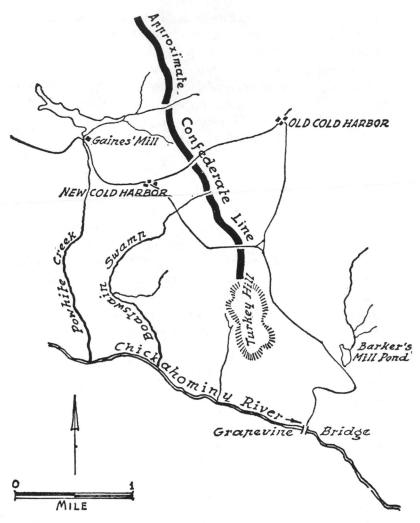

Position of the Confederate right, afternoon of June 1, 1864, to illustrate the strategic importance of Turkey Hill.

almost closed the gap. The enemy withdrew after nightfall,[23] but contact between Hoke and Anderson was practically lost, and no little confusion prevailed at Anderson's headquarters.[24] Anderson's final dispatch of the day, received by Lee at his new headquarters, was to the effect that he had to be reinforced or his

[23] *O. R.*, 36, part 1, p. 662.   [24] *O. R.*, 36, part 1, p. 1059; *ibid.*, 51, part 2, p. 976.

lines would be broken.[25] Lee had already anticipated this need. Breckinridge, as far as Lee knew, was well on the way and should arrive in time to meet the new attack that Lee expected the enemy to make at daylight.[26]

But Lee had to look beyond his own army for the strength with which to resist the enemy on a longer line. Writing to the President during the day, he reported a rumored advance of the enemy up the York River Railroad,[27] and he began to question whether Grant might not be making for James River. If so, it was desirable for Beauregard to bring his troops north of the river and to take position on the right of the Army of Northern Virginia. Lee had been trying for days to effect joint action with Beauregard, and he had consistently failed, except for procuring Hoke's division. On June 1 he tried diplomacy anew. First he telegraphed Beauregard of Grant's shift toward the James, adding that he was ignorant of the situation on Beauregard's front and did not know whether it was in his power to leave the Bermuda Hundred line.[28] Beauregard answered that he could not evacuate the south side of the James, prior to the departure of the Federals from that quarter, unless the government was willing to abandon communications between Richmond and Petersburg. In Lee's opinion that was not desirable, "but," he told Beauregard, in an appeal to that officer's known ambition, "as two-thirds of Butler's force has joined Grant, can you not leave sufficient guard to move with the balance of your command to [the] north side of James River and take command of right wing of army?"[29]

At dawn on the 2d Lee awaited two developments—the arrival of Breckinridge and the resumption of the attack; but he looked in vain for Breckinridge and, when he did not hear from him, was relieved that the Federals withheld their assaults. Anxious regarding Breckinridge, he set out for Mechanicsville, feeble though he still was. He covered the entire distance before he found the Kentuckian at the village with his troops eating breakfast. It was explained that the column had not started until after

---

[25] O. R., 51, part 2, p. 976.   [26] H. B. McClellan MSS.
[27] O. R., 36, part 1, p. 1031. This dispatch caused Humphreys (op. cit., 170), and Alexander (op. cit., 535), to state that Lee was unaware of the presence of Smith's XVIII Corps with Grant's army until after it had attacked at Cold Harbor on the 1st. This was not the case. Lee, it will be remembered, had told Davis on the night of May 30 (O. R., 36, part 3, p. 850): "Butler's troops (Smith's corps) will be with Grant tomorrow."
[28] O. R., 36, part 3, p. 865.   [29] O. R., 36, part 3, p. 864.

10 P.M. from the Confederate left and had then been so weary from its day's fighting that the men had to rest every half hour, Major McClellan, who was acting as guide, had no map, and in his ignorance of the country, led the troops by a long route. Lee said nothing at the time and contented himself with hurrying the march.[30]

Probably while he was at Mechanicsville, Lee learned that the Federals had disappeared from opposite a part of the front of the Third Corps. Reasoning that this meant a still heavier concentration around Cold Harbor, Lee ordered Mahone and Wilcox to march at once for the right and to take position beyond Breckinridge, who was to form south of Hoke, between Old Cold Harbor and the Chickahominy.[31]

Lee did not stop with this manœuvre. If Grant was throwing division after division to the Cold Harbor sector, he might readily be weakening his right; and if that was the case, then there might be a chance to turn that flank and thereby to upset Grant's plans at Cold Harbor. With this in view, Lee gave discretionary orders to Early to attack if he found a favorable opening,[32] and then he rode once more to the scene of his first victory at Gaines's Mill. He found no change in the situation when he arrived. All was quiet for the time, but a battle was brewing. The very prospect of it seemed to stimulate him perceptibly, and he was almost himself again physically, though his staff had noticed for several days that he was more disposed to remain quiet and to direct operations from a distance. "If he had competent lieutenants," Taylor said, "'tis the course he might always pursue." [33]

At last Breckinridge arrived and moved into position. When Major McClellan returned after his unsuccessful adventure as a guide, Lee sent word for him to come to his quarters. McClellan is the best witness to what happened then:

---

[30] H. B. McClellan MSS.

[31] The time of the shifting of Breckinridge, Mahone, and Wilcox to the right has been one of the obscure points in the Cold Harbor campaign, but so far as Breckinridge is concerned, it can be cleared up without much difficulty from the H. B. McClellan MSS. and from the History of McGowan's Brigade, 157. Wilcox stated in his MS. report, 48, that he moved on the morning of June 1 and reached the Confederate right at 3 P.M., but the text of this report shows several errors and corrections of dates, and all the other available sources are unanimous in saying that Wilcox moved on the morning of the 2d (Lane's report, 9 S. H. S. P., 244; History of Thirty-third North Carolina in 2 N. C. Regts., 574; History of McGowan's Brigade, 157).

[32] O. R., 36, part 1, p. 1032.   [33] Taylor MSS., June 1, 1864.

"With a sinking heart I obeyed. The General was seated on a camp stool in front of his tent, an open map spread out on his knees. When I was in position before him, he traced a road with his index finger, and quietly remarked, 'Major, this is the road to Cold Harbor.'

" 'Yes, General,' I replied, 'I know it now.'

"Not another word was spoken, but that quiet reproof sunk deeper and cut more keenly than words of violent vituperation would have done." [34]

Mahone and Wilcox were now on the road, struggling with heat and dust and thirst. To new troops, the discomforts of the march would have been intolerable; but to the wiry veterans of the Third Corps these things were part of the price they had to pay to beat the enemy, and they were endured with only the casual grumbling and swearing that were their cherished prerogatives.

After Mahone came up he probably went in support of Breckinridge.[35] Wilcox arrived at 3 P.M. and took ground to the right and rear of Hoke, where his men began immediately to entrench themselves.[36] Lee was not satisfied with the position of his right wing. The enemy to the east had better ground and dominated much of Turkey Hill, which Lee had especially enjoined the commanders on the Confederate right to occupy. He had only awaited the arrival of reinforcements to correct this, and he now ordered Breckinridge to prepare for action. Soon, with the support of two of Wilcox's brigades, Breckinridge was thrown forward and the enemy was cleared from the hill.[37] This advance gave Lee artillery control of the bottom-land near the Chickahominy and secured his right against any turning movement, but to make that flank invulnerable he extended Wilcox on the right of Breckinridge until he was within half a mile of the river.[38]

While making these dispositions, Lee was hopeful that Early had found opportunity of striking a blow on the Confederate left.

34 *H. B. McClellan MSS.*

35 This cannot be stated positively, as the references to Mahone's division are singularly few in the reports of the later phase of the campaign from the Rapidan to the James.

36 *Wilcox's MS. report*, 48; Lane in 9 *S. H. S. P.*, 244; *History of McGowan's Brigade*, 157–58.

37 *Wilcox's MS. report*, 48; *History of McGowan's Brigade*, *loc. cit.*; *Reagan*, 193.

38 *Wilcox's MS. report*, 48.

His first intelligence of what had happened there probably magnified the success, for Lee telegraphed the Secretary of War that Early ". . . drove the enemy from his intrenchments, following him until dark." [39] Actually, as Lee subsequently learned, Rodes had attacked, with Gordon on the right and Heth on his left, and had brushed aside a strong skirmish line but had been halted in front of heavy works thrown up northwest of Bethesda Church.[40] Here the action ended. Whatever was to be accomplished as a next move must be undertaken on the Confederate right.

It was now the end of the thirtieth day since Lee, from the observation tower on Clark's Mountain, had watched the Federals among their last camps in Culpeper. Never before had the Army of Northern Virginia been so long engaged with the enemy. A week of fighting had sufficed to drive McClellan to Harrison's Landing. A fortnight's offensive operations had hurled Pope's demoralized troops into the Washington defenses. The Maryland expedition had been a matter of twelve days. Fredericksburg and Chancellorsville had been still briefer chapters. Even the ordeal of Gettysburg, from the crossing of the Potomac till the army was safely back on Virginia soil, had lasted but eighteen days. Now, after a month, the persistent Federals were still aggressive, and apparently were as strong as when, on May 5, the first skirmishers had met in the Wilderness. This hammering was having its effect. The morale of the army appeared to be excellent, though the losses had been heavy, the weather oppressive, and rations of the meagrest;[41] but the same grim question was rising in many minds: Would the battle never end? Would the enemy continue forever to move around the right flank? Killing Federals, the wags of the army were saying, was like fighting mosquitoes: where one was caught, two would appear.[42] On the defensive, the Army of Northern Virginia was as valiant as it had ever been, but on the offensive, though Lee was almost daily planning some new stroke, the operation was never carried through quite as he had hoped. Was the fault that of the commanding officers, or was war weariness beginning to show at last in those superb brigades?

[39] O. R., 36, part 1, p. 1032.   [40] Early, 363.
[41] O. R., 36, part 1, p. 87; C. A. Page, 92, 4 B. and L., 143, 231.
[42] 14 S. H. S. P., 537; cf. 4 B. and L., 231.

Had it become a struggle of endurance—a test of whether the Army of Northern Virginia would be destroyed before Grant would have enough of the slaughter and would quit?

Lee did not ask himself these questions. Save in shaping his strategy and in seeking men and supplies, he never looked into the future, for the future belonged to God; but he knew the limits of endurance, even of his soldiers, and he was struggling hourly to find reinforcements and to outwit his stubborn antagonist so that he could relieve those weary, loyal soldiers who were lying that night in the shallow trenches they had thrown up along the road where they had stopped.[43]

There would assuredly be another bloody engagement on the morrow: could Beauregard spare as much as one brigade to help in winning a victory on that old battleground of flaming memories? It seemed doubtful, doubtful even whether Lee could retain all of the thin divisions he had. For here, on the evening of June 2, was a telegram from General Imboden at Mount Crawford, saying that General Hunter, who had succeeded Sigel, had the previous day forced him from Harrisonburg in the Shenandoah Valley.[44] Breckinridge had been brought from the Valley because Sigel had been driven back. If Hunter was moving up the Shenandoah again, it might be necessary to send Breckinridge back with the two little brigades that were now occupying a critical sector south of the road between the two Cold Harbors. Could the army hold its own if it were weakened still further?

A heavy rain had begun to fall before 4 o'clock on the afternoon of the 2d and continued to pour down during the night of the 2d–3d. It was in refreshing contrast to the heat and dust of the previous day, but it made duty in the trenches disagreeable, particularly for those men stationed in the bogs created by the little streams that lost their way in wandering westward from the watershed around Old Cold Harbor.[45]

And a long line it was on which the soldiers waited for the dawn. Across the Chickahominy, Fitz Lee's cavalry watched the

[43] *Cf.* 2 *Meade,* 201: "How long this game is to be played it is impossible to tell; but in the long run, we ought to succeed, because it is in our power more promptly to fill the gaps in men and material which this constant fighting produces."
[44] *O. R.,* 51, part 2, p. 981.   [45] *O. R.,* 36, part 1, p. 87; *Hagood,* 259.

crossings to report either an advance on Richmond from the York River Railroad or a movement on Grant's part toward the James.[46] North of the river and within half a mile of it was the right of Wilcox's division. On the left of Wilcox lay Breckinridge, with Mahone in support. Beyond him, northward, was Hoke, his right south of the Cold Harbor road and his left not quite so much extended as it had been when it had been broken on the afternoon of the 1st. Hunton, of Pickett's division, was between Hoke and Kershaw, with Anderson's, Law's, and Gregg's brigades of the First Corps in support. Pickett was on the left of Kershaw, and Field who was beyond him, connected with Early. Ramseur, leading Early's old division, was either on Early's right or in reserve. Then came Gordon. Rodes was on the left of Gordon, and Heth, of the Third Corps, was on the extreme left. The sketch on the opposite page can only approximate the points of junction of the different units.[47]

All along the front, when the rain ceased and the shadows began to gray on the morning of June 3, the ragged veterans manned the trenches and stood on the alert. In exposed positions, the guns were charged and primed. Everywhere the feeling was the same: The enemy was surely coming! Why not? That thin, sprawling line was all that stood between him and Richmond. At headquarters, Lee was astir with the dawn, busily considering where he should locate his artillery south of the Chickahominy, in case the enemy moved in that direction.[48] Circular orders were issued for the recall of the last man on extra duty.[49] Every rifle would be needed behind the parapet that day.

Suddenly, at 4:30, there was a roar of cheers and a crash of musketry, beginning on Lee's right and spreading all along the line. An instant after, the thunder of guns swelled from the heights of the Chickahominy far over to the Confederate left. A general assault was on, a determined effort, backed by all the might of the Army of the Potomac, to break through, everywhere,

[46] Cf. Lee's Dispatches, 212–13.

[47] The exact positions can never be established unless there exists some evidence not now available, though the order of battle, except for Ramseur's division, is determinable. Major Jed Hotchkiss, topographical engineer of the Second Corps, whose maps are invaluable guides to troop positions, seems, unfortunately, to have left no map of Cold Harbor operations.

[48] O. R., 36, part 1, p. 1051.   [49] O. R., 36, part 3, pp. 869–70.

anywhere—and to take the road into the city that woke from sleep, startled at the loudest firing it had ever heard.[50]

Lee could only listen to the din and speculate whether it would come closer, for he had not a single regiment in general

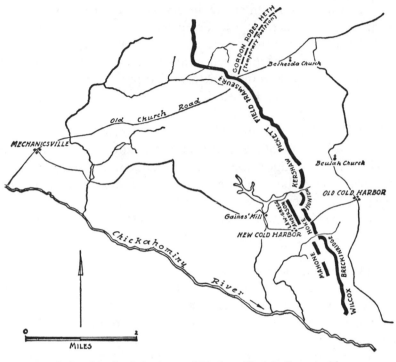

Order of battle of the Army of Northern Virginia, June 3, 1864.

reserve, and until he could ascertain where the Federal assaults were heaviest, he could not weaken one part of the line to strengthen another. The army had to repel the attacks or be destroyed. For five minutes, for ten, the noise was so overwhelming that it was impossible to tell anything except that the whole front was furiously engaged. Through the smoke that hung heavily over the flat country, nothing was to be seen of retreating, routed columns. Now the firing fell away, now it rose again, as if a new assault was being delivered. Shells were falling by this time in the field where Lee's headquarters were located, and soon

[50] 2 R. W. C. D., 224; Mrs. McGuire, 275.

the wounded began to come back from the front, but they were not numerous. Stoutly, in that inferno, the lines must be holding. The grand assault must be failing—but what of the details?

At a word, couriers and staff officers rode off to find the commanding generals on the line and to get reports. As Lee awaited their return, listening intently, the fire on some parts of the line began to slacken perceptibly. From the right, south of the road to Old Cold Harbor there were cheers, Federal cheers, and then, ere long, the sound of increased infantry fire, as if new troops had been thrown in. Like a thunderstorm that passes quickly but roars as it passes, the artillery was less furious, though every battery seemed still to be engaged.

In half an hour the first of the messengers returned. On the front of Wilcox, no attack had been delivered.[51] The enemy had reached Breckinridge's line and had broken through a bit of swampy ground, but Mahone had sent in Finegan[52] and the old Maryland battalion and was restoring the front.[53] Hill had shown to Lee's courier the dead lying on one another where Grant had vainly assaulted. "Tell General Lee," he said, "it is the same all along my front." [54] Hoke reported that the slain and wounded literally covered the ground and that, up to that time, he had not lost a single man in his division.[55] On the sector held by the right of Kershaw, where the enemy had entered the works on the afternoon of June 1, successive assaults had been pushed with vigor but had been beaten off with ease.[56] Like favorable reports came from the centre and from the left, when later messengers returned.[57]

[51] *Wilcox's MS. report*, 48.

[52] Brigadier General John Finegan had recently been sent from Florida by General Patton Anderson with two battalions of infantry, which, as noted on p. 368, had been consolidated at once with the remnants of Perry's brigade. The whole was placed under Finegan (*O. R.*, 36, part 2, p. 1013; part 3, pp. 836, 843).

[53] *O. R.*, 36, part 1, p. 1032; *ibid.*, 51, part 2, p. 983. This break occurred at a point where, said Long, "a portion of the Confederate line occupied the edge of a swamp of several hundred yards in length and breadth, enclosed by a low semicircular ridge covered with brushwood." Long explained: "On the previous night the troops assigned to this part of the line, finding the ground wet and miry, withdrew to the encircling ridge, leaving the breastworks to be held by their picket-line. The attacking column quickly carried this part of the line, and advanced through the mud and water. . . ." The site of this was about 900 yards east, 20 degrees south of New Cold Harbor.

[54] *Cooke*, 406.   [55] 2 *Davis*, 524.

[56] *O. R.*, 36, part 1, p. 1059. Law in 4 *B. and L.*, 138; *Alexander*, 539-40.

[57] Colonel William Preston Johnston, of the President's staff, who had come out to observe the battle, hurried back to Richmond from Lee's headquarters and was probably the first to carry the news to the President (*Lee's Dispatches*, 223).

On the front of the First Corps, attack followed attack with so much vigor that Anderson by 8 o'clock had counted fourteen.[58] From the Confederate works the Federal officers could be heard commanding their men to advance, but as the bloody morning hours passed, the only response to each new order would be a volley from the ground. The men realized it was futile to go on.[59] By 11 o'clock, though the artillery were still thundering and the infantry were exchanging furious volleys, the assaults on all parts of the line seemed to be suspended, for the moment at least. Lee, alone at headquarters, except for a single orderly, was beginning to think of the next phase of the great contest when Postmaster General Reagan rode up. He had come out from Richmond with Judge Meredith and Judge Lyons and had heard the desperate fire. Was not the artillery very active? he asked with the curiosity of the civilian.

"Yes," said Lee, "more than usual on both sides. That does not do much harm here." But, he added, waving his hand toward the line where, Reagan said, the sound of the musketry was like the tearing of a sheet, "It is that that kills men."

"General," said the Texan, "if he breaks your line, what reserve have you?"

"Not a regiment," Lee answered, "and that has been my condition ever since the fighting commenced on the Rappahannock. If I shorten my lines to provide a reserve, he will turn me; if I weaken my lines to provide a reserve, he will break them."

Then, taking advantage of the presence of one who was powerful in the civil councils of the Confederacy, Lee explained the exhaustion of his army and its physical deterioration for lack of vegetables. He had urged the men, he said, to dig and eat the roots of the sassafras and the wild grape, but these were a poor substitute. When Reagan returned to Richmond would he see the commissary general and urge him to send potatoes and onions to the army? "Some of the men now have scurvy," Lee added sadly.

Reagan promised and changed the conversation to something

[58] O. R., 36, part 1, p. 1059.

[59] This led Swinton to assert that the Union troops refused to attack, after the first repulse, but MacMahon (4 B. and L., 218) and Gordon (op. cit., 298) are authority for stating, from opposite sides, that there was no mutinous refusal. The men simply could not push their assaults home in the face of the fire from the Confederate works.

389

more personal. There was uneasiness in Richmond, he explained, because of reports that Lee was exposing himself unduly. Could he not discharge his duties equally well by keeping out of danger?

Lee answered that he had to be close to the front, though he had sent back the stores and the wagons. "I have as good generals as any commander ever had," he went on, "and I know it, but still it is well for me to know the position of our lines. To illustrate this, in forming my right, I directed that it should cover Turkey Hill, which juts out on the Chickahominy Valley so as to command cannon range up and down the stream. In forming the line, however, this was not done, and on yesterday afternoon I had to direct General Breckinridge to recover that position by an assault which cost us a good many men." [60]

Reagan rode off and Lee turned to the grim task of seeing if he could replace the men who were still falling along the lines under the Federal fire. Hoke had reported that he had captured prisoners that morning from the XVIII Corps, which had joined Grant from Butler's army. This was what Lee had been expecting since the evening of May 30 and it proved, beyond further quibble, that the force in front of Beauregard had been greatly reduced. [61] Beauregard on the previous day had telegraphed Lee that the Federals still opposed him in strength and that he could not further reduce his troops. [62] Lee now put the facts before the President and added, "No time should be lost if reinforcements can be had." [63] The administration was of the same mind and, in a terse exchange of messages, ordered Matt Ransom's brigade from Beauregard to Lee. [64]

After 1 P.M. it was apparent that the enemy had abandoned all hope of successful general assaults. The Confederate wounded could now be brought out, and the lines could be put in order. On Breckinridge's front the works had been recaptured without heavy loss, so that the whole position was now intact. Desultory firing continued until about nightfall. Then, as Breckinridge and Finegan were establishing their skirmishers, the enemy delivered

---

[60] *Reagan*, 192–93.
[61] *Lee's Dispatches*, 212 ff.
[62] *O. R.*, 36, part 3, p. 868.
[63] *Lee's Dispatches*, 214.
[64] *O. R.*, 36, part 3, pp. 870, 871–72; *Calendar of Confederate Papers*, 59–60.

a final attack, but was beaten off easily.[65] The pickets kept up their nervous dispute and at intervals the artillery would open, but the battle was over. "Our loss today," Lee was able to write the President at 8:45, "has been small, and our success, under the blessing of God, all that we could expect." [66]

That was the most he had to say of the ghastly day that will always cause a shudder whenever the name Second Cold Harbor is mentioned. Lee might have written much more, for while his own casualties had not exceeded 1200 to 1500 on the six miles of front,[67] more than 7000 of Grant's men crowded the field hospitals or lay, in every attitude of agony, on the open ground, in the ditches and among the slashed trees. Their agonized cries rose in a tragic chorus, but the sharpshooters were busy everywhere, and the suffering Northerners could not be relieved from the Confederate lines. No flag of truce came from the Federal side asking for permission to remove the wounded and to bury the dead.

The repulse had been an incredible success. Although the Confederates did not know it at the time, the planned major assaults had been broken up within eight minutes after the advance had begun.[68] One observant Confederate brigadier on the left of Hoke's division subsequently confessed that the worst was over before he realized that any serious attack had been delivered.[69] It was, Colonel Venable recorded, "perhaps the easiest victory ever granted to the Confederate arms by the folly of the Federal commanders." [70]

In the night of misery that covered at last the woods and the trenches, Lee was of course unaware of the effect this final, costly repulse was to have on Grant's strategy, and equally unaware—was it fortunately so?—that he had won his last great battle in the field.

[65] O. R., 51, part 2, pp. 982–83.
[67] Alexander, 542.
[69] Hagood, 260.

[66] O. R., 36, part 1, p. 1032.
[68] 4 B. and L., 217.
[70] 14 S. H. S. P., 536.

CHAPTER XXIII

The Crossing of the James

The cries of the wounded were fainter on the morning of June 4, but all day long the same pitiful plea, "Water, water, for God's sake, water!" could be heard within the Confederate lines. No attack was made that day over the ground covered by these agonized men, but no request came from the Union side for a truce to succor them. Lee, of course, dispatched no flag, because virtually none of the casualties in front of his trenches had been among his own men. It was June 5 when Grant sent any message, and then he merely proposed that each army be privileged to put out relief parties when no action was on.[1] Lee had to say, in answer to this unusual proposal, that it would lead to "misunderstanding and difficulty," and that when either army desired to remove the victims of battle, it should follow the normal procedure and ask for a suspension of hostilities. "It will always afford me pleasure," he said, "to comply with such a request as far as circumstances will permit."[2] Grant could not bring himself to make this tacit admission of defeat until late in the afternoon of the 6th.[3] The subsequent slow exchange of official communications through the lines delayed the execution of the truce until the evening of June 7.[4] By that time all except the ambulant wounded had died or had been removed at night by comrades.

The period of this correspondence and the five days that followed the burial of the Union dead—eight days altogether—were marked by no general action. The skirmishing, however, was constant, and several minor attacks were delivered by Lee, only to be halted before they reached the formidable Union positions.[5] On the 6th Early prepared a second sweep down the Federal lines from the Confederate left to the right, but found it impossible to

---

[1] O. R., 36, part 3, p. 600. [2] Ibid.
[3] O. R., 36, part 3, pp. 638–39. [4] O. R., 36, part 3, pp. 666, 667.
[5] O. R., 36, part 1, pp. 1033, 1034; ibid., 51, part 2, p. 984.

392

progress through the trench system of the enemy.[6] The Northerners, for their part, remained on the defensive. Some of the Confederates took this to mean that the Union high command had at last seen the futility of frontal assaults. "Grant," said General Pendleton, "has been so shaken in the nerves of his army, if not in his own, that apparently he must get some rest." [7] Lee held a more cautious view, because of other operations undertaken by the enemy. On June 7 most of Sheridan's cavalry corps started for a raid up the Virginia Central Railroad.[8] Lee at once detached Hampton and Fitz Lee with 4700 troopers in pursuit, leaving with the army only Rooney Lee's small division and Gary's mounted brigade of the Richmond garrison—a very serious division of force. It was an inevitable countermove but it was to prove most costly. Lee observed that Sheridan started about the same time that Sigel's successor, Major General David Hunter, began moving up the Shenandoah Valley. Lee assumed that these two advances were connected, and he reasoned that Grant might be waiting on the outcome, rather than halting because of exhaustion.[9]

Lee did not, however, adopt the assault tactics his antagonist seemingly had abandoned temporarily. General Matt W. Ransom's brigade had been sent over from the Bermuda Hundred front to strengthen the department of Richmond and indirectly had made good the losses at Cold Harbor.[10] As long as Grant remained north of the Chickahominy, the Confederate front was quite secure. But the front of action was so restricted, the Federal commander was guarding all the approaches so closely, and the Confederate cavalry was so reduced, that Lee did not think he could drive Grant out except by an assault on the Federal fortifications, and this he was anxious to avoid if possible.[11]

As the armies watched each other, neither willing to take the offensive, Lee had his first opportunity of fixing the status of the officers who had been named to succeed those who had fallen

---

[6] *Lee's Dispatches*, 219. On the evening of the 8th a surprise attack was projected for dawn of the 9th but was abandoned (*O. R.*, 36, part 3, p. 880).

[7] *Pendleton*, 340. *Cf.* 2 *Meade*, 201: "I think Grant has had his eyes opened, and is willing to admit now that Virginia and Lee's army is not Tennessee and Bragg's army."

[8] *Lee's Dispatches*, 221 *ff.* Sheridan's report is in *O. R.*, 36, part 1, pp. 795 *ff.*

[9] *Lee's Dispatches*, 221 *ff.*

[10] *Cf. O. R.*, 36, part 3. p. 874.   [11] *Lee's Dispatches*, 219.

between the Wilderness and Cold Harbor. Under the new law permitting appointments with temporary rank, Anderson was promoted lieutenant general and Early was elevated to the same grade.[12] Ewell, naturally, was displeased at being supplanted, and made formal application to be returned to duty, but Lee did not think he could stand the hardships of active service and slated him to take charge of the department of Richmond.[13] Major General Robert Ransom, whom Ewell was to succeed, when able to do so, was sent to head the cavalry in western Virginia. His troops were placed under Custis Lee until Ewell could take charge.[14] In this way Custis at last had opportunity of active combat, with his father near enough at hand to guide him. Mahone was given temporary rank as major general to direct Anderson's division, and Ramseur was awarded the same honor with Early's division. Kershaw was formally designated as successor to Mc-Laws in the First Corps, and a number of new brigadiers were named, some with permanent and some with temporary rank.[15] Lee was acutely conscious of the shortage of good material but careful, as always, to select the best men available.[16]

While these officers were adjusting themselves to their duties in the trenches around Cold Harbor, the men were dodging the Union sharpshooters and were enjoying what was to them the sumptuous fare of fat Nassau bacon and onions, with the luxury of sugar and coffee.[17] Their spirits rose with their rations. "Old U. S. Grant is pretty tired of it—at least it appears so," Colonel Taylor wrote his sweetheart. We are in excellent trim—men in fine spirits and ready for a renewal of the fight whenever the signal is given." [18] The assurance that prevailed in the army was reflected in Richmond. "I have been struck very forcibly," Richard W. Corbin wrote his father in Paris, "by the sense of security which seems to prevail here among all classes. . . . Such is the unbounded confidence of the people in Lee and his noble army,

[12] *O. R.*, 36, part 3, p. 873.
[13] *O. R.*, 36, part 3, pp. 863, 897; *ibid.*, 40, part 2, p. 646. *Lee's Dispatches*, 242–43. It was Lee's expectation at the time to restore Ewell to duty when, as he said, "the present occasion for extraordinary exertion shall have passed" (*O. R.*, 36, part 3, p. 898).
[14] *O. R.*, 51, part 2, p. 1006.   [15] *O. R.*, 36, part 3, pp. 873–74, 883.
[16] *Cf. O. R.*, 40, part 2, p. 650, for the case of Major General Arnold Elzey. *Cf.* also *O. R.*, 51, part 2, p. 993.
[17] 14 *S. H. S. P.*, 537; *O. R.*, 36, part 3, p. 888. The meat ration, raised to one-half pound, was again reduced to one-third pound on June 11 (*ibid.*, 899).
[18] *Taylor MSS.*, June 9, 1864.

that you hear them talking not only of driving the enemy but of gobbling him up." [19]

On the sectors around Cold Harbor the men saw more of their commanding general. He rode among them often, for now he could discard his carriage, and his garb was almost as simple as theirs—blue military breeches with boots, a short linen sack coat, no waistcoat or suspenders, a soft felt hat and buff gauntlets. Traveller was always faultlessly groomed, but Lee at this time usually carried neither sword, pistol, nor fieldglasses.[20] Rarely was he attended by more than one orderly.[21] Wherever he went, he always was quick to return the salutations of his veterans. To a feeble-minded soldier who greeted him with an unmilitary "Howdy do, dad," he returned a kindly "Howdy do, my man." [22] There were some "croakers" in Richmond who said Lee had lost much of his influence with President Davis because an anti-administration congressman had proposed that he be named dictator in case constitutional government was set aside;[23] and others maintained that at last he had met a foeman who could match his steel, even if he was not worthy of it;[24] but his influence over his troops was undiminished. Once, during the Cold Harbor campaign, a noisy column was passing along a Hanover road, with banter and clatter, when some of the men observed Lee resting under a tree. Word was instantly passed that "Marse Robert" was asleep, and the men immediately became as silent as if they had been skirmishers, taking position within earshot of the enemy.[25]

Anything was a relief after the ghastly fighting of the preceding month, but nothing of the hilarity of winter quarters prevailed in those scorching trenches, under the June sun, there in the sands and swamps of Hanover. The sharpshooting was worse than it had ever been, owing to the nearness of the opposing lines. Vicious artillery fire broke out at intervals. Demonstrations were frequent. More serious, on every count, was a slow, daily shifting of the Federal line to the left in Grant's favorite manoeuvre.[26] This kept Lee's army constantly on the alert, lest the Federals slip by its right flank.[27]

---

[19] *Letters of a Confederate Officer*, 30.
[20] *Hagood*, 304.
[21] *Ibid.*   [22] *Figg*, 204.
[23] 2 *R. W. C. D.*, 230.
[24] *O. R.*, 51, part 2, p. 993.
[25] 35 *Confederate Veteran*, 287.
[26] *O. R.*, 36, part 1, p. 1033.
[27] *Cf. O. R.*, 36, part 3, p. 877.

Simultaneously, bad news came from the Shenandoah Valley. Hunter's column, which had begun its march when Sheridan started on his raid up the Virginia Central Railroad, was reported to be strong and aggressive. At Piedmont, above Staunton, on June 5, Hunter fell on the Confederate cavalry under Brigadier General W. E. Jones, killed him, routed his small force, and took 1000 prisoners.[28] The next day Hunter occupied Staunton, where the Virginia Central crossed the Valley. Toward him, from Lewisburg, Brigadier General George Crook was moving along the railway, destroying it as he advanced. General Averell was following Crook with his cavalry. Rumor put the combined strength of these invaders at 20,000[29]—a force large enough to do much mischief. Lee, anxiously consulted by the President,[30] did not lose his strategical perspective. "It is apparent," he said, "that if Grant cannot be successfully resisted here we cannot hold the Valley— If he is defeated it can be recovered." He thought, on the whole, however, that the Southern cause would best be served by returning Breckinridge and his command to Lynchburg, whence the troops could be moved according to Hunter's line of advance.[31] Breckinridge left on or about June 7, and reduced Lee's strength by approximately 2100.[32] Hill took over the lines Breckinridge vacated. Heth's division, which had been brought from the left,[33] was moved up in immediate reserve.

The situation now became complicated. Lee was satisfied that the X Corps from General Butler, as well as the XVIII, was in his front, and that the force opposing Beauregard was very small.[34] Beauregard, on the other hand, was becoming more and more alarmed. He interpreted Grant's shift to the left as designed to bring the Army of the Potomac to the James, and he was concerned over the appearance in the river of a large pontoon bridge.[35]

---

28 *O. R.*, 37, part 1, pp. 95, 150.

29 *O. R.*, 37, part 1, p. 151. Their real number was around 17,500 (*O. R.*, 37, part 1, pp. 96, 571).

30 *O. R.*, 51, part 2, p. 990; *Lee's Dispatches*, 215; Lee to Davis, MS., June 5, 1864, *Duke Univ. MSS.*

31 *Lee's Dispatches*, 216–18, 219 ff.   32 *Lee's Dispatches*, 217.

33 *Early*, 363. Heth had marched on the 4th.

34 *Lee's Dispatches*, 218. Lee was misled by the fact that two divisions of the X Corps had been incorporated in the XVIII as its third division (*O. R.*, 36, part 1, p. 179).

35 *O. R.*, 36, part 3, pp. 878, 878–89; *O. R.*, 51, part 2, pp. 986, 996.

A movement across the James had, indeed, become such a distinct possibility that Lee had now to reckon on four threats:

1. Grant was within nine miles of Richmond and might continue his hammering. To oppose him, with part of the Confederate cavalry detached, Lee had less than 45,000 men of all arms and could use the garrison of Richmond of about 7400.[36] Grant's strength was assumed to be as great as at any time during the campaign—a minimum of 100,000.

2. Grant might cross the James and crush Beauregard's 7900 men either at Bermuda Hundred, at Petersburg, or on both sectors.[37] In any such operation Grant could utilize Butler's command—small, in Lee's opinion, formidable in the judgment of Beauregard.

3. Hunter might sweep the Valley and then move eastward with his force, which was now estimated at 15,000, instead of 20,000.[38] To defeat him, Breckinridge would have 9000 when he reached the foot of the Blue Ridge, though hardly more than 5000 of these could be counted as combat troops.[39]

4. Sheridan might cut the Virginia Central Railroad and join Hunter or, having devastated midland Virginia and having destroyed Lee's communications with the Valley, might return to Grant. Sheridan's strength was unknown but was understood to be much greater than that of the 4700 that Lee had sent after him in Hampton's and Fitz Lee's divisions.[40]

In short, with 73,000 men in four areas of action, Lee was facing 125,000 to 130,000.[41] These were odds of which Lee was not unmindful, but in his view, nothing that could happen in west-

---

[36] This estimate of Lee's strength assumes 25,000 casualties from the Wilderness through Cold Harbor and 15,000 replacements, not counting temporary additions to the Richmond garrison, subsequently returned to Beauregard. The V. M. I. cadets, who had been listed with the Richmond garrison, had left the city (O. R., 36, part 3, p. 861). Their place was taken by Matt Ransom's brigade of 1800 (ibid., 819). This raised the Richmond garrison for a few days to the figure given in the text. Of this number, 2500 were artillerists serving the guns in the Richmond defenses.

[37] O. R., 51, part 2, p. 999. The probability that Grant would cross the James was generally conceded in Richmond and was openly discussed in The Richmond Examiner on June 7, 8, and 9.

[38] O. R., 37, part 1, p. 159.   [39] O. R., 37, part 1, p. 758.

[40] E. L. Wells, 189. Sheridan had about 9000 men.

[41] To recapitulate, Lee had about 49,000 men in the Army of Northern Virginia, counting his absent cavalry. Breckinridge had 9000, as noted, Beauregard 7900, and 7400 were in the Richmond defenses. These figures are no better than approximations, owing to the absence of reports, but if they err they overstate Lee's numbers. There are no reports of the strength of the Army of the Potomac on June 10. Grant had 103,-

ern Virginia or even, for the time being, at Petersburg, was as important as inflicting a defeat on the Army of the Potomac. No diversion clouded his vision. "We must destroy this army of Grant's before he gets to James River," he told Early. "If he gets there, it will become a siege, and then it will be a mere question of time." [42] It was the first time he had ever hinted at such an outcome.

On the afternoon of June 9 Lee received a message from General Bragg announcing that a surprise attack had been delivered that morning against Petersburg. Beauregard had sent to the beleaguered city all the troops he could spare from the Bermuda Hundred line and said that if he were not reinforced by Lee he would have to choose between losing Petersburg and abandoning the railway between Richmond and that city. [43] Lee did not believe that Grant had detached troops from the Army of the Potomac, or that he could send a force across the James from the position he then occupied without being observed. He regarded the move against Petersburg as a reconnaissance and nothing more. [44] Nevertheless, Lee set Matt Ransom's brigade in motion for the Confederate pontoons at Drewry's Bluff [45] and Bragg ordered Gracie's brigade to the same crossing. [46] As it developed, neither was required immediately at Petersburg. For, when the Federals had appeared in front of the defenses of the city, the district commander, Brigadier General Henry A. Wise, had mustered the few troops at his disposal and had manned that part of the extensive works facing the enemy. In Petersburg the tocsin had been sounded and the reserves in the city, men over forty-five and boys in their middle 'teens, had been called to defend the works that Wise could not cover. Major Fletcher H. Archer, a veteran of the Mexican War, who commanded these poorly armed civilians, had posted them judiciously and had told them

875 on June 1 (*O. R.*, 36, part 1, p. 209), exclusive of the XVIII Corps. His casualties of the next three days were around 13,000. Listing the X and XVIII Corps as part of the Army of the James, Butler's strength was at least 20,000. Add 15,000 for the columns under Hunter and the total is 125,000, to which should be added an undetermined number of replacements between June 1 and 10.

[42] Early, quoted in *Jones*, 40.   [43] *O. R.*, 36, part 3, p. 884.

[44] Lee to Beauregard, June 9, 2:30 P.M., in 2 *Roman*, 566. It was the statement of Lee concerning Grant's inability to cross the James without being detected that drew the sarcasm of D. H. Hill mentioned in note 52, p. 400.

[45] *Lee's Dispatches*, 223–24; cf. *O. R.*, 51, part 2, p. 997.

[46] *O. R.*, 36, part 3, p. 885; *ibid.*, 51, part 2, p. 997.

they must die before they let the Unionists seize their town. A Negro band from the city had sallied out under Philip Slaughter to play inspiring airs and to give the impression that ample troops were at hand. Even the prisoners in the jail had been released at their own request to share in the city's defense, and had been hastily organized as the "company of penitents." On the left, facing Wise, the Federal infantry had done little more than make a demonstration, but on the right, Kautz's cavalry had attacked with vigor. The old men and the boys had beaten off one attack and had held up a second until they had been almost surrounded. Then the survivors had been compelled to retreat, but they had gained enough time for Beauregard to hurry up reinforcements. Graham's battery had gone through the town at the gallop, followed by Dearing's cavalry. Before the dust from their passing had settled, Graham had been shelling the enemy. Kautz had quickly retreated, Dearing had followed him up, and the battle had been over—perhaps the unique battle of the entire war.[47]

What did this attack portend? Was it merely a bold raid against Beauregard's flank, or was it the preliminary of a movement to transfer the campaign to the south side of the James? There was, as yet, no way of ascertaining the answer; but on June 11, after Beauregard transmitted a rumor that a column had crossed the river and was planning a new advance on Petersburg,[48] Gracie's brigade was sent him as a precaution.[49] It was common talk in Richmond that if Beauregard was wrong that day about the appearance of Grant's troops on the south side, he would soon be right. The movement of the Army of the Potomac over the James was taken for granted by many,[50] especially as reports continued to come in of pontoons moving up the river,[51] presumably to afford Grant a crossing either on the lower Chickahominy or on the James. Beauregard's friends were exhorting him to tell the War Department that in his critical situation he

[47] Reports in *O. R.*, 36, part 2, pp. 273 ff.; 4 *B. and L.*, 535 ff.; 35 *S. H. S. P.*, 6 ff.; Mrs. Campbell Pryor's *MS. Memoirs*; F. H. Archer in George S. Bernard: *War Talks of Confederate Veterans* (cited hereafter as *Bernard*), 107 ff.; *MS. Address* by P. H. Drewry, M.C., June 9, 1927. The last-named is the fullest account. Some facts supplementing General Wise's congratulatory orders in *O. R.*, 36, part 2, pp. 316–17, appear in 2 *Roman*, 224–25. Much picturesque matter will be found in 1 *Macrae*, 167 ff.
[48] *O. R.*, 36, part 3, p. 889.
[49] *O. R.*, 36, part 3, p. 896; *ibid.*, 51, part 2, pp. 1003, 1004.
[50] Corbin: *Letters of a Confederate Officer*, 30; *O. R.*, 51, part 2, p. 1005.
[51] *O. R.*, 40, part 2, p. 653.

had either to sacrifice the Bermuda Hundred line or Petersburg, as he could not hold both.[52]

Lee, however, had to consider all the other possibilities, along with that of a general movement of Grant's army to the south side of the James. In the face of Grant's persistent efforts to bludgeon his way into Richmond, Lee could not afford to weaken his front north of the Chickahominy on the assumption that his adversary had suddenly changed his strategy and his tactics. Nor could Lee overlook the chance that Grant might shift to the south of the Chickahominy and besiege Richmond between that stream and the James, as McClellan had essayed to do in 1862. Finally, Lee had to consider the likelihood that Grant would return the troops taken from Butler and would undertake simultaneous operations up both banks of the James. Next only to the preservation of his own army, Lee's first assigned duty was to defend Richmond. That had to be put above another temporary break in communications between Richmond and Petersburg, above even the safety of so important a railroad centre as Petersburg.

At his disposal were only two methods of resolving the dilemma that Grant's proximity to the James presented: Either Lee had to attack, or else he had to concentrate on his right and prepare to move after Grant as soon as his adversary marched southward from the Cold Harbor line. Much as Lee desired to take the initiative, the first course was impracticable. "To attack [Grant] here," Lee told the President, "I must assault a very strong line of entrenchments, and run great risk to the safety of the army." [53] He could only prepare for the next stage of the campaign by concentrating on his right. This he did by bringing Early from the left, where he now faced abandoned works, and putting him in rear of A. P. Hill.[54] To reduce the chances that Grant could make an orderly withdrawal unobserved, Lee had, since the battle of Cold Harbor, bombarded the Federal lines heavily about 9 P.M. every evening.[55]

Early took his new position on the 11th.[56] The previous day

---

[52] In writing Beauregard to this effect, General D. H. Hill remarked that it was "arrant nonsense for Lee to say that Grant can't make a night march without his knowing it" (O. R., 36, part 3, p. 896). Lee had said nothing of the sort but, on the contrary, early in the campaign, had told the President that in a wooded country, Grant could always get one march ahead of the defending army. See *supra*, p. 348.

[53] O. R., 51, part 2, p. 1003.   [54] *Early*, 364.   [55] 4 *B. and L.*, 219.   [56] *Early*, 364.

General Breckinridge had arrived at Blue Ridge tunnel, west of Charlottesville, and had telegraphed that Hunter was moving up the Valley, either toward Lexington or toward the mountain gaps that led to Lynchburg. General Bragg was of opinion that the Valley should be cleared; Davis passed on the message to Lee without suggestion. Lee answered on the 11th that it was desirable to expel the enemy from the Valley, but that this would require him to detach a corps. "If it is deemed prudent," he said, "to hazard the defense of Richmond . . . I will do so." But, he added, "I think this is what the enemy would desire. A victory over General Grant would also relieve our difficulties." [57] The next day the news was that Hunter had occupied Lexington on the 11th. He was now free to cross the Blue Ridge and, with the Valley under his control, to harry midland Virginia and then to reinforce Grant. This was too great a risk to take. Hunter must be stopped. Without further debate on the subject, Lee promptly changed his mind. He ordered Early to break camp and to start on the morning of the 13th with his artillery and his 8000 infantry for the Shenandoah Valley to meet Hunter. [58] Coupled with the previous detachment of Breckinridge, this meant that Lee was losing 20 per cent of his entire force or approximately one-fourth of his infantry at a time when his adversary was engaged in the most menacing manœuvre he had thus far undertaken. Yet if the thing had to be done, Lee determined to make the most of the necessity. With good generalship, Early would have enough men to dispose of Hunter. Then Lee planned that Early should march down the Shenandoah Valley and make a new demonstration against Washington and Baltimore. This, Lee hoped, would either compel Grant to attack the Army of Northern Virginia in an effort to make Lee recall Early, or else force Grant to detach troops for the defense of the capital and thereby give Lee some prospect of a successful offensive against the reduced Army of the Potomac. [59]

By one of those coincidences that place the history of the Army

[57] *O. R.,* 51, part 2, p. 1003.

[58] *Early,* 364. Writing to W. H. Taylor, April 29, 1867, General Early remarked that he was sure none of Lee's staff officers knew anything of Lee's orders to him during the time he was in corps command, "for," said he, "I received all orders of importance from the General in person, or by letter in his own handwriting" (*Taylor MSS.*).

[59] *O. R.,* 37, part 1, p. 346; *ibid.,* 40, part 2, p. 667; *Early,* 371, 380.

of Northern Virginia among the most dramatic stories in the annals of war, Lee's skirmishers brought back the long-expected word at the very hour when the men of Early's corps were turning their faces westward: The long trenches in front of Cold Harbor were empty; Grant was gone. Either toward the James or toward the lower stretches of the Chickahominy, the Army of the Potomac had marched away so quietly that the Confederate pickets had not observed its departure. When they advanced a mile or two beyond the old Federal lines the skirmishers still failed to find the enemy.[60]

Immediately the order was given to take up the pursuit. Wasting no time in choosing easy routes, Lee threw both corps across the Chickahominy, struck for the Charles City road and moved down it toward Riddell's Shop, which had been just within the Federal lines at the battle of Frayser's Farm.[61] The day was very hot and straggling was serious, but the columns were kept closed and rapid speed was made.[62] The Confederate cavalry outposts which had been stationed at Riddell's Shop were met during the march and reported that Federals, advancing up the Long Bridge road from the direction of the Chickahominy, had driven them pack. This quickened the pace of the infantry. Late in the afternoon contact with the enemy was established by Hill's corps and he was forced steadily eastward. All the prisoners proved to be cavalrymen, though there was some suspicion that Federal infantry had been in support.[63] Nightfall found the army extended southward from the White Oak Swamp. Hill was on the left, with his right flank near Riddell's Shop, and 'Anderson held the right, bivouacked on the battlefield of June 30, 1862. The cavalry occupied the Willis Church road and Malvern Hill.[64] Lee was thus covering the approaches to Richmond between the lower Chickahominy and the James, and at the same time had his right flank within ten miles of the pontoon bridge at Drewry's Bluff, in case Grant moved across James River. The situation had changed so abruptly and might involve so great an extension of front that President Davis asked whether it might not be wise

[60] *O. R.*, 36, part 1, p. 1035.
[61] *O. R.*, 36, part 3, pp. 1059–60; *Wilcox's MS. report*, 49.
[62] *History of McGowan's Brigade*, 160.
[63] *O. R.*, 36, part 1, p. 1035; *Wilcox's MS. report*, 49.
[64] *O. R.*, 36, part 1, pp. 1052, 1060; *Lee's Dispatches*, 239–40.

to recall Early. Lee did not favor it. "I do not know that the necessity for his presence today is greater than it was yesterday," he said. "His troops would make us more secure here, but success in the Valley"—success in marching on Washington—"would relieve our difficulties that at present press heavily upon us." [65]

As the exact strength of the Federal force on the Long Bridge road was not determined when darkness ended the pursuit on the evening of the 13th, Lee intended to attack there with Hill's corps, but on the morning of June 14 he found that before the skirmishers advanced at dawn the enemy had departed.[66] Whither had Grant moved? In the absence of Hampton and Fitz Lee, no cavalry operations, on a large scale, could be attempted to ascertain where Grant was reconcentrating, but everywhere that Lee's scant cavalry units could operate close to the front they were sent out to uncover the enemy. In some instances the scouting parties were so numerous that they interfered with one another.[67] Before noon their reports began to arrive. Grant was said to have crossed Long Bridge from the north bank of the Chickahominy with nearly the whole of his army;[68] the base at White House had been broken up; the enemy was believed to be at Harrison's Landing; captured stragglers asserted that he intended to pass over the James at that point.[69]

It was impossible, however, with certainty to ascertain the position or movements of the Federals. There were few county roads in that part of Charles City County whither Grant had moved, and those few ran in rough quadrilaterals. By maintaining strong guards at the crossroads, Grant could screen his army as effectively as if he had taken ship and vanished down the James. For the first time since the opening of the campaign Lee was out of touch with his adversary. His cavalry was too scanty to make a reconnaissance in force, and the infantry both too distant and too weak to attempt an advance. It is worth while to sketch the terrain to show how the land favored Grant by making complete concealment possible within the area he had blocked.

---

[65] *Lee's Dispatches*, 240. This letter is marked June 15, but the internal evidence fixes June 13 as the correct date.

[66] *Lee's Dispatches*, 229; O. R., 36, part 1, p. 1035.

[67] *Lee's Dispatches*, 230; O. R., 51, part 2, p. 1016.

[68] O. R., 51, part 2, p. 1016.   [69] O. R., 51, part 2, pp. 1013, 1017.

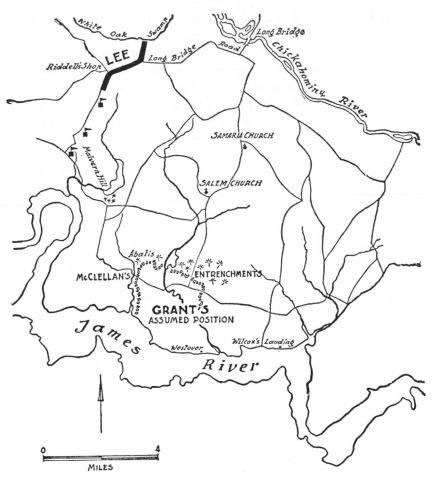

Terrain between the Chickahominy and James Rivers, east of the line White Oak Swamp-Malvern Hill, showing how command of a few crossroads concealed Grant's position after leaving Cold Harbor, June 13, 1864.

Weighing all the probabilities suggested by such reports as he had, Lee wrote the President at 12:10 P.M. June 14:

". . . I think the enemy must be preparing to move South of James River. . . . It may be Gen. Grant's intention to place his army within the fortifications around Harrison's landing, which I believe still stand, and where by the aid of his gunboats, he could offer a strong defence. I do not think it would be advantageous

404

to attack him in that position. He could then either refresh it or transfer it to the other side of the River without our being able to molest it, unless our ironclads are stronger than his. It is reported by some of our scouts that a portion of his troops marched to the White House, and from information derived from citizens, were there embarked. I thought it probable that these might have been their discharged men. . . . Still I apprehend that he may be sending troops up the James River with the view of getting possession of Petersburg before we can reinforce it. We ought therefore to be extremely watchful and guarded. Unless I hear something satisfactory by evening, I shall move Hoke's division back to the vicinity of the pontoon bridge across James River in order that he may cross if necessary. The rest of the army can follow should circumstances require it." [70]

Lee had received intelligence of Forrest's success at Brice's Crossroads, Miss., on June 10, and the still more welcome news that Hampton had met Sheridan at Trevillian's Station, near Gordonsville, on June 11–12, had defeated him handsomely and had removed the threat of a junction between Hunter and Sheridan.[71] This was most substantial relief, and evidence to Lee's believing eyes that the South was not forsaken by "a gracious Providence." He added, "We have only to do our whole duty and everything will be well." [72]

Within three hours after this letter was written information accumulated that Grant was on the James and that part of his forces were at Wilcox's Landing, below Westover, where the stream was narrow. Lee made his contemplated disposition of Hoke and promptly explained to the President: "I see no indication of [Grant's] attacking me on this side of the river, though of course I cannot know positively. As his facilities for crossing the river and taking possession of Petersburg are great, I have sent Gen. Hoke with his command to a point above Drewry's Bluff

[70] *Lee's Dispatches*, 227–232.
[71] *O. R.*, 36, part 1, pp. 1095–98; U. R. Brooks: *Butler and His Cavalry*, 236 *ff.*; E. L. Wells, 190 *ff.*
[72] *Lee's Dispatches*, 232. *Cf.* Lee to Reverend T. V. Moore, n. d. (summer of 1864): "I thank you especially that I have a place in your prayers. No human power can avail us without the blessing of God, and I rejoice to know that, in this crisis of our affairs, good men everywhere are supplicating Him for his favor and protection" (Jones, *Christ in the Camp*, 52).

in easy distance of the first pontoon bridge above that place. He will execute any orders you may send to him there."[73]

The cumulative result of the successive detachments that culminated in these orders was about as follows:

Effective Infantry strength, June 4 42,000
Less Breckinridge, June 7 2,100

Total, June 8 39,900
Less Early, June 13 8,000

Total, June 14, A.M. 31,900
Less Hoke, June 14 6,000

Total, June 14, P.M. 25,900
Margin of error, 10 per cent . . . . 2,590[74]

28,490

The Richmond garrison, by the return of Gracie to Beauregard, was reduced to 6400.

Before Hoke had moved to the pontoon bridge, the Confederate cavalry had pushed on to Harrison's Landing, where it had encountered the enemy. The First and Third Corps had spent the day on substantially the line taken up on the evening of the 13th. But if Grant was going to cross the James there was no point in holding a position so far advanced. On the contrary, if the Army of Northern Virginia was to be called upon to defend both the north and the south sides of the river, it was desirable to retire closer to the Richmond defenses.

The cavalry were withdrawn accordingly,[75] and Lee was planning on the afternoon of the 14th to move the infantry nearer the Richmond entrenchments[76] when messages from General Beauregard raised a new doubt whether Grant was actually contemplating an early crossing of the James. Beauregard announced that transports were moving upstream. Further, he quoted his

---

[73] Lee's Dispatches, 233. Cf. ibid., 234.
[74] These figures, independently computed, agree closely with Venable's estimate, 14 S. H. S. P., 538, that Lee had from 25,000 to 27,000 infantry after detaching Hoke.
[75] O. R., 36, part 1, p. 1035.   [76] Lee's Dispatches, 236.

scouts as saying that a pontoon train which had gone down the James several days before had returned part of the way. As it had not passed Coggin's Point, which is opposite Harrison's Landing, it might have gone up the Chickahominy.[77] A little later Beauregard telegraphed that deserters said Butler had been reinforced by the XVIII and part of the X Corps, previously sent to Grant.[78] Could it be, then, that Grant had simply used the pontoons to cross the Chickahominy, that he had returned Butler's troops, and that he was planning to operate against Richmond, between the Chickahominy and the James, while Butler resumed the offensive south of the James? The suggestion that Butler's troops were being restored to him fitted in with the reports from the White House that Lee had forwarded earlier in the day to President Davis.[79] Grant's march down the river might simply have been undertaken to give him a more convenient base on deep water.[80] For these reasons Lee decided not to draw back to the fortifications of Richmond on the night of the 14th. Instead, he kept his headquarters at Riddell's Shop and remained with his right flank in the direction of Malvern Hill.[81]

The next morning, June 15, opened one of the most difficult periods in the history of the Army of Northern Virginia, a crisis that put Lee's military judgment to the supreme test. Very early his cavalry reported Federal troopers in their front, on the road from Salem Church, and at Malvern Hill.[82] A. P. Hill wrote that the enemy was active on his front, also, but that, as late as 9 A.M., he had encountered only cavalry.[83] The ease with which the Federals were driven back[84] indicated that there was no great strength behind them and renewed Lee's doubts whether Grant intended to attack on the north side of the James. As that, in turn, increased the probability of an attack on Petersburg, Lee

[77] O. R., 51, part 2, p. 1012.   [78] O. R., 40, part 2, p. 653.
[79] O. R., 36, part 1, p. 1035; ibid., 51, part 2, p. 1013.
[80] Cf. Lee's Dispatches, 231.
[81] O. R., 36, part 1, p. 1052. For the location of his headquarters, see Lee's Dispatches, 239, 240.
[82] O. R., 36, part 1, p. 1035. Salem Church was five miles north of Westover. The main route from Salem Church westward entered the road leading from Richmond to Harrison's Landing, at a point two miles southeast of Malvern Hill. Needless to say, the Federal horse had been thrown out on these roads to screen Grant's movement. Their position illustrated what was said on p. 403 concerning the ease with which Grant's new base could be protected.
[83] O. R., 51, part 2, p. 1017.   [84] O. R., 36, part 1, p. 1035.

felt that he should not hold Hoke any longer at the pontoon bridge but should send him forthwith to support Beauregard. He issued orders accordingly.[85]

Shortly after Hoke was ordered to move, Colonel Samuel B. Paul, one of Beauregard's aides, arrived at Lee's headquarters with a full statement of the strength and disposition of Beauregard's troops. Lee was busy at the time and not disposed to go fully into the papers, saying that he knew Beauregard was weak, but that he would have to make the best of the force he had. When Paul insisted, Lee reviewed the situation with him. The General explained that he had already ordered Hoke to Beauregard, and expressed the belief that Beauregard was mistaken in saying he was confronted with troops from Grant's army, though it was probable he soon would be. Those that had returned, Lee contended, were Butler's men who had been with Grant. After some discussion, Colonel Paul stated that Beauregard believed he would be safe, both at Petersburg and at Bermuda Hundred, if all his original command were restored to him. The only troops of Beauregard's army still north of the river were the 1800 men of Matt Ransom's brigade in the Chaffin's Bluff defenses. These were not under Lee's orders, but he promised to ask that they be returned to Beauregard, even if their place had to be taken by local defense units from Richmond. He assured Paul that if Beauregard were seriously threatened, he would send aid and, if need be, would come himself.[86] With friendly personal messages to General Beauregard, he sent the anxious officer on his way.

Almost in the tracks of Colonel Paul's departing horse, a courier arrived with dispatches from General Bragg. These covered telegrams from General Beauregard received prior to 8:45 that morning. The latest of them was probably one written at 7 A.M. This set forth that the return of Butler's forces and the arrival of Grant at Harrison's Landing rendered Beauregard's position "more critical than ever." Beauregard said: "If not reinforced immediately, enemy could force my lines at Bermuda Hundred Neck, capture Battery Dantzler, now nearly ready, or take Petersburg, before any troops from Lee's army or Drewry's Bluff could arrive

---

[85] *Lee's Dispatches*, 235. Hoke received his instructions before 11:30 A.M. and set his troops in motion at once (*O. R.*, 40, part 2, p. 658).

[86] For the evidence on this controverted interview, see Appendix, III—5.

in time." He concluded, "Can anything be done in the matter?"[87]

There was nothing in this, or in any other of the dispatches, to indicate that Beauregard thought any of Grant's troops were already on the south side of the James. Beauregard's immediate concern was over the smallness of the force with which he confronted Butler's restored army. Lee had already anticipated Beauregard's need by dispatching Hoke, and now, answering Bragg at 12:30 P.M., he urged that Ransom be returned to Beauregard.[88] Pending further developments, he decided to keep the remainder of the army, now reduced to six divisions, on the lines it then occupied.

The cavalry that had followed the enemy during the morning returned late in the afternoon and reported that all their prisoners were Federal troopers. No infantry had been encountered.[89] That probably was all the news Lee had, for, so far as the records show, he received no further advices from Richmond that day. Perhaps General Bragg reasoned that as Lee had sent Hoke's division to Beauregard and was dispatching Matt Ransom after Hoke, Beauregard would have sufficient strength to meet the new movements of the enemy in front of Petersburg that he reported in a series of dispatches to Bragg during the day.[90] Beauregard's files show no telegrams to Lee, though copies of two messages to Bragg were directed through Richmond to be forwarded to Lee. One of these telegrams, marked 1 P.M., said that Hoke would be sent to Petersburg, that Johnson's division might have to be moved there from Bermuda Hundred to support Hoke, and that another division should be dispatched to the south side. The second telegram to Bragg, 9:11 P.M., announced that the enemy had penetrated the lines at Petersburg. Johnson would be sent there to aid Hoke, Beauregard said, and Lee would have to look to the defense of Petersburg and of Bermuda Neck.[91] The evidence is strong, though circumstantial, that these two messages had not reached Lee when he was awakened by a staff officer at 2 A.M. on the morning of June 16 and was handed this telegram:[92]

[87] O. R., 40, part 2, p. 655.
[88] Lee's Dispatches, 235–36, 242–43. [89] O. R., 51, part 2, p. 1017.
[90] O. R., 40, part 2, pp. 654–56. [91] O. R., 40, part 2, p. 656.
[92] Lee wrote Davis from Drewry's Bluff at 7:30 P.M., on the 16th: "I received at 2 A.M. a dispatch from Genl. Beauregard stating that he had abandoned his lines on Ber-

Petersburg, Va., June 15, 1864, 11:15 P.M.

General R. E. Lee,
  Headquarters Army of Northern Virginia:
  I have abandoned my lines of Bermuda Neck to concentrate all my force here; skirmishers and pickets will leave there at daylight. Cannot these lines be occupied by your troops? The safety of our communications requires it. Five thousand or 6,000 men may do.

G. T. BEAUREGARD,
  General.[93]

That and no more. Manifestly, no soldier of Beauregard's distinction would be abandoning the Bermuda Hundred line and concentrating on Petersburg unless the enemy was likely to capture that city. But was it Grant or Butler, and in what strength? If Lee had received copies of all the telegrams Beauregard had sent Bragg that day, he would not have been able to say whether the attacking troops were Grant's or Butler's. There had been one hint in a dispatch from Brigadier General James Dearing, commander of Beauregard's cavalry, that the IX Corps was south of the James,[94] but, for the rest, General Beauregard had only mentioned a Federal force, first estimated at four regiments of cavalry and four of infantry, and then as three brigades of infantry with cavalry support.[95] Who, besides these, were now menacing Petersburg? Being wholly in the dark, Lee could only act on the information Beauregard gave him. As that officer asked for 5000 or 6000 men to occupy a critical sector that he was about to abandon, Lee did what he had done wherever Beauregard had made a call for troops in the face of an immediate threat: He sent them. Although the act would reduce his mobile force on the north side of the James to something between 21,000 and 24,000 infantry, plus the doubtful strength of the immobile Richmond garrison, he unhesitatingly summoned Pickett's division from the vicinity of Frayser's Farm and directed it to cross the river at Drewry's Bluff and to occupy the lines.[96] Anderson was in-

muda Neck . . ." (*Lee's Dispatches*, 243). If Lee had received copy of Beauregard to Bragg, 9:11 P.M., June 15, he would almost certainly have acted on it and would have mentioned that message to the President.
  [93] *O. R.*, 40, part 2, p. 657.
  [94] *2 Roman*, 570.   [95] *O. R.*, 40, part 2, pp. 655, 656.
  [96] *Lee's Dispatches*, 244. Pickett then had around 4500 men.

structed to proceed at once to Bermuda Hundred, in person, with the head of the column, and to take charge on the exposed front. Beauregard was requested, if he could, to keep his skirmishers in position until these reinforcements arrived.[97] It was only a request, for in dealing with Beauregard, Lee did not exercise the power, if indeed he knew it had been given him the previous day by the President, to direct the operations of all separate commands in Virginia and North Carolina—a definite if belated recognition of the need of a unified command.[98]

One brigade of Pickett's division was speedily under way; the others were slow in taking the road. It was nearly 8 o'clock when the first brigade crossed the James on the pontoon bridge, and 9 before the rest of the division was over.[99] Anxious to see the situation for himself, and doubly anxious because his information was so scanty, Lee broke up his headquarters at Riddell's Shop and followed the first troops. Shortly before 9:40 A.M., on the morning of June 16, he was south of the river.[100] He turned aside, soon after he crossed, and knelt by the roadside, in the dust, while a minister prayed for Divine guidance in the new operations he was about to undertake.[101] Then he rode on to Drewry's Bluff. This move brought him midway between his own army and Petersburg, where he could supervise operations on the Bermuda Hundred front; but it did not put him in closer touch with Beauregard and it separated him from the cavalry on the north side of the river. He had to rely on the telegraph for communication with Beauregard and on a line of couriers to Malvern Hill and beyond.

His first act on arriving was to advise Beauregard of his position and to inform him of the arrival of Pickett's division, with a request for what he needed most—intelligence as to what the enemy was doing.[102] Before Beauregard could receive this message, one was handed Lee from Petersburg. It was filed at 9:45 and read as follows:

"The enemy is pressing us in heavy force. Can you not send forward the re-enforcements asked for this morning and send

97 *Lee's Dispatches*, 244.
99 *Lee's Dispatches*, 244.
101 Jones, *Christ in the Camp*, 51.
98 *O. R.*, 40, part 2, p. 654.
100 *O. R.*, 40, part 2, p. 659.
102 3 *S. H. S. P.*, 296.

to our assistance the division now occupying the trenches lately
evacuated by Johnson's division, replacing it by another division?

G. T. Beauregard." [103]

Evidently Beauregard had sent earlier dispatches that had not
been received, dispatches in which he had asked for reinforcements; but now he explained nothing except that he was being
pressed and needed help. Not one word had yet reached Lee
from him indicating or even intimating that Grant had crossed
the James.[104] For all Lee knew, the troops attacking Petersburg
might be those that were known to be returning to Butler from
Grant. To bring another division from the northside would
be to reduce the troops there to 20,000–23,000 infantry, including
the diminished Richmond garrison. Counting Pickett, the force
on the south side of the James already was 19,600 infantry, with
about 1900 cavalry.[105] In the absence of specific information as
to Beauregard's situation, Lee at 10:30 A.M. could only telegraph
him in answer:

"Your dispatch of 9:45 received. It is the first that has come to
hand. I do not know the position of Grant's army, and cannot
strip north bank of the James. Have you not force sufficient?" [106]

While Lee was waiting for an answer to this, the head of
Anderson's column was moving down the Petersburg pike.
Shortly after 1 o'clock Lee heard from Anderson that he had
encountered the enemy at a point about opposite Chester and was
driving the Union skirmishers back. "It is to be presumed," wrote
Anderson, "that he has possession of our breastworks opposite
Bermuda Hundred." The commander of the First Corps went
on: "I have not been able to communicate with our troops near

[103] O. R., 51, part 2, p. 1078.

[104] This is an essential point in explaining Lee's dispositions on June 16. Beauregard
had telegraphed at 7:45 that a prisoner had been taken that morning who said that he
belonged to Hancock's corps, and that it had crossed on the 14th and 15th (O. R., 51,
part 2, p. 1078). This message doubtless had been sent to Lee via Richmond and had
not yet been forwarded to Drewry's Bluff.

[105] Pickett, 4500; Hoke, 6000; Wise, 2200; Bushrod Johnson, 5100; Ransom, 1800;
Cf. 5 M. H. S. M., 149–55.

[106] O. R., 40, part 2, p. 659.

Petersburg. If I find difficulty in clearing the road it will be impracticable for General Pickett to reach Petersburg." [107]

A new complication, this! Regardless of how badly Beauregard might need reinforcements, if the road to Petersburg was blocked they could not be sent there speedily. More than that, as he would have to follow roundabout roads, Lee feared it would be a slow and costly business to "bottle" Butler again and to reopen the Petersburg turnpike. [108] So, without delay, Lee ordered Field's division to cross at Drewry's Bluff and directed that Kershaw march his division to the north end of the pontoon bridge and await orders there. [109] When Field arrived, the disposition of the joint forces would be as follows: At Petersburg, Wise's brigade and Bushrod Johnson's and Hoke's divisions, with a few minor units; on the south side of the James between Drewry's Bluff and the Appomattox, Pickett's and Field's divisions; on the north side, at the pontoons, Kershaw's division; on the line from Malvern Hill to Riddell's Shop, A. P. Hill's three divisions, with one division and one brigade of cavalry in support; at Chaffin's Bluff, a few regiments of second-line infantry and some heavy artillery; at Drewry's Bluff, a small battalion of marines and a few other gunners. Leaving the heavy artillery and the cavalry out of account, the comparative strength of the forces defending Richmond and those on the Drewry's Bluff-Petersburg front would be: north side, 20,000 to 23,000; south side, 22,600. [110]

Beauregard's next telegram contained nothing to justify a change in these dispositions. Beauregard explained, instead, that Pickett had not reached his line at Bermuda Neck by 10:30 and that, at that hour, his pickets still held the second line, under orders to maintain it as long as practicable. [111] Lee's information did not indicate that the pickets were still in position, and at 1:15 he telegraphed Beauregard that he feared their withdrawal had caused the loss of the line in front of Bermuda Neck. He explained Anderson's movements and his plans to repossess the lines

---

[107] *O. R.*, 51, part 2, p. 1079. *Cf. Lee's Dispatches*, 244; *O. R.*, 40, part 1, p. 760.
[108] *Lee's Dispatches*, 244–45.   [109] *Lee's Dispatches*, 240; *O. R.*, 40, part 1, p. 760.
[110] This assumes that Field's division numbered 3000. If it were larger, the force on the southside would be increased by the excess.
[111] *O. R.*, 51, part 2, p. 1078. The text of this telegram is not marked with the hour at which it was written, but its opening sentence shows it was sent after 10:30. It fits into the day's chronology at this point, and at no other.

and concluded: "What line have you on your front? Have you heard of Grant's crossing James River?" [112]

Soon it was 3 o'clock. Anderson was driving back the Federal skirmishers and was preparing to attack the second Confederate line, which had been abandoned that morning, when Lee received a reassuring answer from Beauregard, written at 12:45 P.M.:

"Your dispatch of 10:20[113] received. We may have force sufficient to hold Petersburg. Pickett will probably need re-enforcements on the lines of Bermuda Hundred Neck. At Drewry's Bluff at 9 A.M. or later no news of Pickett's division." [114]

Still not a word about the troops opposing Beauregard! Measurable assurance that he had sufficient strength at Petersburg, and apparently more concern for Bermuda Hundred Neck than for the city to which he had been asking that reinforcements be sent! It was an odd telegram, to which Lee replied with a broad hint for more specific information and with a frank statement that he himself had no positive knowledge on Grant's crossing the river:

"Dispatch of 12:45 received. Pickett had passed this place at date of my first dispatch. I did not receive your notice of intended evacuation till 2 A.M. Troops were then at Malvern Hill, four miles from me. Am glad to hear you can hold Petersburg. Hope you will drive the enemy. Have not heard of Grant's crossing James River." [115]

In answer to this message, Beauregard only stated that the signal corps reported the movement of forty-two transports up the James in recent days.[116] Lee had every reason to believe that the transports were returning Butler's troops from the White House, and at 4 o'clock he so advised Beauregard. He added now a specific inquiry on the all-important question: Had Grant been seen crossing the James?[117] In other words, was Beauregard sure that the troops opposing him had come from Grant, rather than from Butler?

[112] 2 *Roman*, 571.
[114] *O. R.*, 51, part 2, p. 1078.
[116] *O. R.*, 51, part 2, p. 1078.
[113] The correct hour was 12:30.
[115] *O. R.*, 40, part 2, p. 659.
[117] *O. R.*, 40, part 2, p. 659.

This time the answer was slow in coming. Down the Petersburg pike, Anderson's troops manœuvred for the second line occupied that morning by the Federals and took the left of it without difficulty about 6 P.M.[118] At Drewry's Bluff, Lee sat down to
write the President of the day's events. After telling him of the
troop movements, he expressed the fear that it would be difficult
and costly to recapture the first line occupied by the Federals
after Beauregard had been forced to call its defenders to Petersburg. Lee then wrote: "I have not learned from General Beauregard what force is opposed to him in Petersburg, or received any
definite account of operations there, nor have I been able to learn
whether any portion of Grant's army is opposed to him." [119]

As Lee was finishing this letter, another telegram arrived from
General Beauregard, but this contained only the information that
he had countermanded the order for the withdrawal of his pickets
from the Bermuda Hundred line and that they had held on until
10:15 A.M., but had then been compelled to withdraw. In justice
to Beauregard, who had clearly done his utmost to maintain the
front until the arrival of Pickett, Lee added this information to
his letter to the President.[120]

At last, at the end of the long, tense day there came a somewhat
more specific telegram from Beauregard, written at 7 P.M. and
reading thus:

"There has been some fighting today without result. Have
selected a new line of defences around city, which will be occupied
tomorrow, and hope to make it stronger than the first. The only
objection to it is its proximity to city. No satisfactory information
yet received of Grant's crossing James River. Hancock's and
Smith's corps are however in our front." [121]

Lee must have held that sheet a long time in his hand and
must have read it again and again: "Some fighting . . . a stronger
line. . . . No satisfactory information yet received of Grant's
crossing James River"—nothing in that to hint of disaster or even

---

[118] *O. R.*, 40, part 1, p. 760. F. A. Osborn in 5 *M. H. S. M.*, 199; *Walter Harrison,*
130.
[119] *Lee's Dispatches*, 244–45.
[120] *Lee's Dispatches*, 245.   [121] *O. R.*, 51, part 2, p. 1079.

of acute danger. Smith's corps was there, and Smith belonged to Butler's army. But Hancock's corps, of course, was of the Army of the Potomac. Was Lee to conclude that only this corps from Grant was across the James? Was the remainder of the main Federal army still on the northside?[122] It was a portentous question with which to close a day of doubt. Small wonder he wrote in a letter on the same 16th of June, "Our existence depends upon everyone's exerting themselves at this time to the utmost."[123]

The first news that reached Lee at Drewry's Bluff on the morning of June 17 was altogether encouraging. At 11 o'clock the previous night Pickett's men had recaptured the first Confederate line on the left, from the Howlett House to Clay's Farm.[124] The troops went to work at once to re-establish Battery Dantzler, where the guns and carriages which had been buried by Beauregard's orders, were found uninjured.[125] From Petersburg, Beauregard reported that he had repulsed two attacks during the night and had captured 400 prisoners, though he had not entirely regained his first position.[126] For the time it seemed as if the situation was stabilized, with every prospect that Petersburg would be held, that the Bermuda Hundred front would be recovered in its entirety, and that the four divisions on the north side of the James would not be needed south of the river. Lee telegraphed Beauregard his congratulations and urged him to restore his lines, not knowing to what point Beauregard had retreated or whether he was fighting at a disadvantage. Once again he inquired: "Can you ascertain anything of Grant's movements? I am cut off now from all information."[127]

Ordering the immediate repair of the Richmond-Petersburg Railroad, a part of which had been broken by Butler's advance,[128] Lee watched the operations to regain the southern end of the first line on Bermuda Hundred Neck, kept Beauregard advised of his progress, and made a personal examination of Trent's Reach on the James, where the Federals had sunk a number of vessels in

---

[122] In a telegram to Bragg, Beauregard limited still further his reference to the troops from Grant. "They belong," he said, "to First Brigade of Hancock's corps" (O. R., 40, part 2, p. 660).

[123] Lee's Dispatches, 247.

[124] Lee to Davis, 3 S. H. S. P., 298.

[125] Ibid.; 2 Roman, 231, 575.

[126] 3 S. H. S. P., 298.

[127] O. R., 40, part 2, p. 664.

[128] 3 S. H. S. P., 297–98.

the hope of preventing the descent of the Confederate ironclads from Richmond.[129] All was going well when, shortly before noon, Lee received this message from Beauregard, written at 9 A.M.:

"Enemy has two corps in my front, with advantage of position. Impossible to recover with my means part of lines lost. Present lines entirely too long for my available forces. I will be compelled to adopt shorter lines. Could I not be sufficiently re-enforced to take the offensive [and] thus get rid of the enemy here? Nothing positive yet known of Grant's movements." [130]

This message had to be read carefully. Written in the characteristic manner of one who was always fashioning some bold design, it did not state that reinforcements were necessary to maintain the new lines Beauregard announced that he was preparing to draw. His request was for reinforcements with which to take the offensive. He stated that he was faced by two corps and, inferentially, by only two. Nor could he affirm that any more of Grant's army was in his front than the II Corps, which was one of those he had mentioned the previous evening as opposed to him. The other, of course, was the XVIII. Manifestly, if Beauregard had only that force against him, the rest of Grant's army either had not crossed or had not reached the Petersburg lines. Lee could only answer: "Until I get more definite information of Grant's movements I do not think it prudent to draw more troops to this side of the river." [131]

Presently, Beauregard telegraphed for information as to the movements of the V Corps. He suggested that it had probably gone to meet Early and that the Petersburg line might be suddenly reinforced and the enemy in his front crushed.[132] This did not look as if Beauregard were *in extremis*. Lee replied with such scanty facts as he had concerning the movements of the V Corps to June 14;[133] and, as it seemed impossible to get any detailed facts from Beauregard concerning Grant's operations, he turned

---

129 Dispatches in 3 *S. H. S. P.*, 298–99. The message to Davis, as there printed, improperly gives the name of the Reach as "French's." Trent's Reach is the southern side of the bend that was to be eliminated by the digging of Dutch Gap Canal. It is about one and one-quarter miles in length.

130 *O. R.*, 51, part 2, p. 1079.   131 *O. R.*, 40, part 2, p. 664.
132 *O. R.*, 51, part 2, p. 1079.   133 *O. R.*, 40, part 2, p. 664.

again to the north bank to see if the cavalry that had been left there could find out where the V, VI, and IX Corps were.[134]

Anderson by this time held all the Confederate second line and most of the first line, except for a stronghold on Clay's Farm. During the early afternoon, Pickett on the left and Field on the right were made ready to assault this central position so as to restore the front as Beauregard had held it prior to the morning of the 16th. Just as the assault was about to be made, the engineers reported that a line could be drawn around that part of Clay's Farm in such a fashion as to make an assault unnecessary. Orders were immediately sent to Pickett and to Field to abandon plans for attacking. These orders reached Field, but they did not arrive at Pickett's headquarters until his men were on the move. Not knowing that Field had been ordered to remain where he was, Pickett informed Gregg's brigade of Field's division that he would need its support on his right flank. Gregg conformed and, in doing so, gave warning to the next brigade on his right that his flank would have to be guarded. As Pickett moved up the high ground in his front, Gregg began to manœuvre to cover him. Soon the men began to pour out from Field's trenches to share in the assault, and ere long, despite orders, the whole left of Field's division was sweeping forward with Pickett. The Federals made only a feeble resistance. Shortly after 4 o'clock the Confederate flag was again flying along the whole of the front opposite Bermuda Neck.[135] Lee had not witnessed the assault in person and he thought that it had been made exclusively by Pickett's division. In admiration for the achievement he wrote Anderson a message of congratulation which is interesting not only because it is almost the only instance in which Lee displayed his sense of humor in an official dispatch of this sort, but also because it exhibits his unshaken faith in his army. The paper read:

"General: I take great pleasure in presenting to you my congratulations upon the conduct of the men of your corps. I believe that they will carry anything they are put against. We tried very

[134] O. R., 40, part 2, p. 663.
[135] Venable in 14 S. H. S. P., 538–39 and in 4 B. and L., 245; O. R., 40, part 2, p. 665; ibid., 51, part 2, pp. 1019–20; Lee's Dispatches, 247.

hard to stop Pickett's men from capturing the breastworks of the enemy, but couldn't do it. I hope his loss has been small." [136]

The road to Petersburg was now out of range of the enemy, and the railway would soon be repaired. This had not been done a moment too soon. For while the men of Anderson's corps were mounting the hill on Clay's Farm, Beauregard was forwarding new and alarming dispatches. The enemy, he said, that morning had carried another of the weak points on his old line and was concentrating on his right centre. He was collecting all available troops to resist until nightfall, when he hoped to take up new lines. "We greatly need re-enforcements to resist such large odds against us," he concluded. "The enemy must be dislodged or the city will fall." [137] In another dispatch, which was received just prior to 4:30 P.M., Beauregard reported that a large number of troops from Grant's army crossed the James above Fort Powhatan on the 16th and that a prisoner affirmed 30,000 were on the south side marching to join those in front of Petersburg. [138]

There was nothing specific, even yet, as to what troops remained on the northside and what units had crossed to Petersburg, but Lee felt that Beauregard's situation was now serious, despite his previous assurance and talk of a counter-offensive. Lee at once ordered A. P. Hill, if he had no contrary news of the enemy, to move to Chaffin's Bluff. [139] To Beauregard he telegraphed: "Have no information of Grant's crossing James River, but upon your report have ordered troops up to Chaffin's Bluff." [140] Kershaw, about the same time, was directed to move from Chaffin's Bluff to the Bermuda Hundred line. [141]

Lee had moved his headquarters on the forenoon of the 17th to the vicinity of the Clay house, [142] and there during the evening

[136] Walter Harrison, 130–31.   [137] O. R., 51, part 2, p. 1079.

[138] O. R., 51, part 2, p. 1080. Cf. O. R., 40, part 2, p. 665.

[139] O. R., 40, part 2, p. 662. A second undated message to Hill, contingent in its terms, may have been sent earlier in the day (ibid.).

[140] O. R., 40, part 2, p. 665.

[141] The hour of Kershaw's move is doubtful. In the History of Kershaw's Brigade, 380, the statement is made that the march began at midnight and continued until the next day; but in the diary of the First Corps (O. R., 40, part 1, pp. 760–61), Kershaw's arrival at Perdue's, opposite Chester, is recorded on the 17th and his departure for Petersburg at 3 A.M. on the morning of the 18th is noted. General Lee, writing at 10 P.M., indicated that Kershaw was then on the march and had selected his bivouac for the night (O. R., 40, part 2, p. 665).

[142] Three miles southeast of Chester and east of the Petersburg pike.

he awaited developments. Vague indications began to point to a reduction in the Federal forces on the Bermuda Hundred sector.[143] The Confederate troops were disposed for a shift to Petersburg if that, as now seemed probable, should be the next turn of the wheel of fortune: Hoke was already with Beauregard; the First Corps was, or soon would be, entirely on the Bermuda Hundred front; the Third Corps was marching toward Chaffin's Bluff. If Beauregard found that the whole of Grant's army was on the south side of the James, part of the First Corps could easily be moved to Petersburg the next morning, and Hill could be sent on before the 18th was out, leaving the remainder of Anderson's troops on the Bermuda Hundred line. If, again, Grant should be contemplating a surprise attack on Richmond, Hill was still on the north bank and close enough to the outer defenses to man them against assault.

The next telegram from Beauregard—what a flood of them there had been during the last two days!—had been written at 5 P.M. and read thus:

"Prisoners just taken report themselves as belonging to the Second, Ninth and Eighteenth Corps. They state that the Fifth and Sixth Corps are coming on. Those from Second and Eighteenth came here by transports and arrived first; others marched night and day from Gaines' Mill and arrived yesterday evening. The Ninth crossed at Turkey Bend where they have a pontoon bridge. They say Grant commanded on the field yesterday. All are positive they passed Grant on the road several miles from here." [144]

Until that hour, on the evening of June 17, it must be remembered that Lee had been told only that the Federal force on Beauregard's front was large, and that the II and XVIII Corps had been identified. Now, it appeared, the whole army was there or close at hand, except for part of the X Corps, which, of course, was on the Bermuda Hundred line. Even strength of that command now seemed definitely diminished.[145]

If all this were true, a clear course of action was marked out.

143 *Lee's Dispatches*, 251.   144 *O. R.*, 51, part 2, p. 1080.
145 *O. R.*, 51, part 2, p. 1080; *Lee's Dispatches*, 251.

But was it true? Lee had a poor opinion of the information given by prisoners and by untried scouts, and with the fate of Richmond at stake he was not prepared to trust everything to this telegraphic summary of the examination of miscellaneous prisoners by an unidentified officer. At the same time, if the information was correct, then there was every reason to expect an overwhelming assault on Petersburg as soon as the Army of the Potomac could be disposed in Beauregard's front. Lee concluded that the weight of probability was much on the side of Beauregard's information and that the greater part of Grant's army was on the south side of the river,[146] but he did not feel himself justified in altogether abandoning the possibility of an attack on Richmond by an adversary whose command of the river made it easy for him to move swiftly large bodies of men.

He did not have to wrestle much longer with his perplexities. Before 10 o'clock this message from Beauregard, written at 6:40 P.M., was handed him:

"The increasing number of the enemy in my front, and inadequacy of my force to defend the already much extended lines, will compel me to fall within a shorter one, which I will attempt to effect tonight. This I shall hold as long as practicable, but, without reinforcements, I may have to evacuate the city very shortly. In that event I shall retire in the direction of Drury's Bluff, defending the crossing at Appomattox River and Swift Creek." [147]

If Beauregard was reduced to this plight, and faced as long odds as his previous telegram had indicated, then some further chance had to be taken that Richmond might be captured by a surprise attack, or else Petersburg would be lost. So, at 10 o'clock, Lee ordered Kershaw to march early the next morning to reinforce Beauregard in Petersburg[148] and simultaneously he instructed A. P. Hill to continue to Chaffin's Bluff, to cross the pontoon bridge, to move to the Petersburg pike and there to await further orders.[149] If needed in Petersburg, he could hurry thither; if required on the north side of the James, he could return.

---

146 *O. R.*, 36, part 3, p. 901.
147 2 *Roman*, 234–35.   148 *O. R.*, 40, part 2, p. 665.
149 *O. R.*, 40, part 2, p. 663; 4 *S. H. S. P.*, 190.

About the time these orders were issued, Captain A. R. Chisolm of Beauregard's staff arrived at the Clay house with the first full details Lee had yet received of the battle that had been going on at Petersburg since the beginning of the Federal offensive. The story was enough to stir Lee's martial blood: Dearing's 1900 cavalry had been driven back on the morning of June 15 to the lines that had been erected in a crude half circle on the south side of the Appomattox River, in front of Petersburg. These works were manned by three thin regiments of Wise's fine brigade, with twenty-two field guns and some heavy pieces. A few weak and scattered units of infantry supported Wise, whose total effective strength, Dearing included, was 2738.[150] Wise spread out this little force on nearly six miles of the Petersburg defenses and awaited attack. The enemy advanced from the east and skirmished briskly until 7 o'clock that evening.[151] Shortly after that hour the enemy broke through the line just south of the City Point Railroad and could undoubtedly have marched straight into Petersburg had he pressed on. As it was, he delayed long enough for Wise's absent regiment to come up. It was followed soon by Hagood's brigade, the advance of Hoke's division, sent by Lee. These troops took a position in rear of the break in the line, and, by the morning of the 16th, when all of Hoke's division had arrived, were able to present a more formidable front to the enemy. Three brigades of Bushrod Johnson's division also arrived from the Bermuda Hundred line a few hours later and gave Beauregard more confidence. During the afternoon a general assault was delivered. This gained some advantage for the Federals, though it brought them no decision. Beauregard himself was on the ground by this time and, with the assistance of Hoke and Bushrod Johnson, put up an almost flawless defense. At intervals the Confederates counterattacked as if they had abundant strength,[152] and on nearly the whole of the line they held the Federals at bay. No attempt whatever was made by the Union troops against the extreme right of the Confederate position, which was virtually undefended.[153] On the 17th the Federals

---

[150] 2 *Roman*, 567. General Wise stated that his actual combat strength was only 2200. Federal critics credit him with 4000. See 5 *M. H. S. M.*, 150.

[151] Wise in 25 *S. H. S. P.*, 13, and in 2 *Roman*, 568.

[152] *Cf.* Ropes in 5 *M. H. S. M.*, 165.

[153] *Cf.* Beauregard to Wilcox, June 9, 1874, 5 *M. H. S. M.*, 121.

renewed their attacks with vigor and soon penetrated a gap in the front of Johnson's division. They did not develop this, however, and failed in every assault until nearly the hour Captain Chisolm left Petersburg. Then about sundown they smashed through the right centre of Johnson's division and doubtless would have doubled up the whole of Beauregard's line but for the arrival, at that very moment and at that precise point, of Gracie's brigade, which had formed the picket line General Beauregard had left at Bermuda Hundred when he had withdrawn the rest of Bushrod Johnson's division.[154] Gracie immediately counter-attacked, closed the gap, and halted the enemy. As Chisolm was describing this to Lee, Beauregard was drawing back to a new line, well-sighted but unpleasantly close to Petersburg.[155]

Chisolm's visit and Beauregard's telegram, with its hint of a possible evacuation of Petersburg, determined Lee to send Field's division after Kershaw's, as a further reinforcement to Beauregard. The outlook brightened momentarily, after this was ordered, for a later message from Beauregard told of a successful repulse of the last assaults of the enemy; but the next dispatch, dated 12:40 A.M. contained a new warning:

"All quiet at present. I expect renewal of attack in morning. My troops are becoming much exhausted. Without immediate and strong reinforcements results may be unfavorable. Prisoners report Grant on the field with his whole army." [156]

Soon two other staff officers from Beauregard reached Lee's headquarters and confirmed all this. One of them, probably Major Giles B. Cooke, told Lee that Beauregard said: "Unless reinforcements are sent before forty-eight hours, God Almighty alone can save Petersburg and Richmond." The language was not pleasing to Lee. He answered, simply and reverently, "I hope God Al-

---

[154] Beauregard to Wilcox, loc. cit., p. 121. Ransom had been ordered to relieve Gracie. Singularly enough, Colonel Roman (op. cit., 2, 232) affirmed that Gracie's brigade came from Chaffin's Bluff, "whence," he said, "at last, the War Department had ordered it to move."

[155] O. R., 40, part 2, p. 666; Beauregard to Wilcox, loc. cit., 122; Ropes in ibid., 166 ff.; Hagood, 266 ff.; 2 Roman, 233 ff.; W. Gordon McCabe in 2 S. H. S. P., 269 ff. The best map of the Petersburg defenses at this period of the operations is that in O. R., Atlas, Plate XL.

[156] O. R., 40, part 2, p. 666.

mighty will." [157] Before morning, and perhaps before these officers arrived, Lee learned that his cavalry on the northside had reached the vicinity of Wilcox's Landing on the afternoon of the 17th and had gained positive information that the last of Grant's army had crossed over to the south of the James on a pontoon bridge at that point.[158]

By 3:30 A.M., on June 18, the situation was clear for the first time since the enemy had disappeared on the morning of June 13. Lee proceeded at once to shift the remainder of his force to the new front. The undamaged part of the Richmond-Petersburg Railroad was utilized to expedite the troop movement;[159] A. P. Hill was instructed to continue the march of his corps to Petersburg, leaving one division north of the Appomattox, in case it might be recalled to defend Richmond; Rooney Lee was ordered to Petersburg with one brigade of his cavalry, while the other remained north of the James;[160] General Early was acquainted with the situation and was told to strike the enemy and return to Petersburg as soon as practicable, or else to carry out the original plan and make a diversion toward the Potomac.[161] Finally, Lee himself broke up headquarters at the Clay house and rode swiftly after Anderson's troops toward Petersburg.[162]

---

[157] 2 *Roman*, 576–77. As narrated by Colonel Roman in 1874 this incident might create the impression that Lee was cynical in his answer. Lee never was that, nor was he ever otherwise than reverent in his use of the name of God. Colonel Roman was one of the two officers to go to Lee's headquarters. He stated that he was unable to see the General but was told by a staff officer whom he thought was Colonel Walter Taylor, that Beauregard was mistaken as to the force in his front. Further, Colonel Roman said he was told that General Lee was confident the greater part of Grant's army was still on the north side of the James. Major Giles B. Cooke, according to Colonel Roman, insisted on seeing General Lee and received much the same impression. Major Cooke's diary, which Colonel Roman quoted, is not explicit on the point at issue, and Major Cooke himself is now (1934) unable to recall the details. The contention must, therefore, rest on Colonel Roman's statement. In the light of the facts given in the text, one of two things is apparent: either the officer who talked to Colonel Roman was himself misinformed, or else Colonel Roman's memory was at fault when he wrote in 1874. General Lee could not have said that he was sure Beauregard's information was erroneous and that the major part of the Army of the Potomac was still in front of Richmond. Lee had stated to Beauregard that he was without information as to Grant's positions, and when he did receive intelligence during the night of June 17–18 it was to the effect that Grant was across the James.

[158] W. H. F. Lee to R. E. Lee, June 17, 1864, 4 P.M. (*O. R.*, 51, part 2, p. 1080). This dispatch should have reached Lee's headquarters in a maximum of eight hours.

[159] *O. R.*, 40, part 2, p. 668.

[160] *Lee's Dispatches*, 249–50, 251–52. For the arrival of Hill's troops in Petersburg, see 1 *Macrae*, 193.

[161] *O. R.*, 40, part 2, p. 667.

[162] A critique of the movement across the James will be found on pp. 438 *ff.*

At 7:30 that morning, as the exhausted troops of Beauregard's command put aside their spades and took up their muskets on the new line they had constructed during the night, they saw the glint of the bayonets of Kershaw's division coming through a ravine near Blandford cemetery, and it was to their weary eyes the fairest sight of the entire war.[163] Field's division arrived at 9:30 A.M.;[164] Hill's divisions were spread out on the Petersburg pike, fighting dust and thirst and marching at a furious pace.[165] When they arrived, which would not be before night, they were to take position on the extreme right and were to extend the front well beyond the railroad that led from Petersburg to Weldon.[166]

Lee reached Petersburg about 11 o'clock[167] and rode out at once to join Beauregard. Together they went over the line that had been drawn the previous night. It was so close to Petersburg that when the enemy organized his front the city could be bombarded. Otherwise, Lee had no fault to find with it. Colonel D. B. Harris, Beauregard's brilliant chief engineer, had excelled himself in selecting the best available ground when he had scarcely a moment to spare. Beauregard was so elated at the safe withdrawal to this line, and so reassured by the arrival of Kershaw and Field, that he proposed an instant attack against the enemy's flank. Lee immediately rejected the idea, in the conviction that the troops were too much exhausted for combat.[168] It was no day to waste troops in futile counterattacks. It was, instead, a time to watch every move, to consider every step, and to conserve every life. For the great and bloody campaign from the Rapidan to Petersburg had now ended in something closely akin to what Lee had most desired to avoid. He could not have forgotten, that June morning, what he had told Early: If Grant reached James River, "it will become a siege, and then it will be a mere question of time."[169] With communications still open and the troops on the north side of the James well outside the Richmond defenses, it was not yet a siege, but that, too, was only a question of time.

[163] MS. Memoirs of W. B. Freeman.   [164] O. R., 40, part 2, p. 668.
[165] History of McGowan's Brigade, 162.   [166] Wilcox's MS. report, 51.
[167] Venable stated in 14 S. H. S. P., 539, that Lee arrived with "the van of his army, Kershaw's division"; Beauregard's telegram of 11:30 A.M. to Bragg (O. R., 40, part 2, p. 668) stated that Lee had just arrived. Lee advised the War Department (O. R., 40, part 2, p. 667): "Kershaw's and Field's division preceded me."
[168] 2 Roman, 247.   [169] See supra, p. 398.

CHAPTER XXIV

"RAPIDAN TO PETERSBURG" IN REVIEW

THE burdens that Lee took up at Petersburg on June 18 occupied him daily. Except for brief visits to Richmond, he was rarely away from the sound of the firing. Visitors' horses were always at his hitching post. Mountains of military papers had to be reviewed. Each morning brought so much of anxiety that the evening found him weary. The crowded present gave him little time to think of the past. Yet there must have been rare hours when he could look back on the bloody wrestle from the Rapidan to Petersburg and would ask himself whether anything that he might have done, or might have left undone, after May 4, could have saved his army from the ordeal of the long and ghastly siege.

Students of military history have been raising the same question ever since and have reviewed the campaign from many angles. Rarely, however, has it been considered adequately for what it fundamentally was—on the one side an example of the costliness but ultimate success of the methods of attrition when unflinchingly applied by a superior force, and, on the other side, an even more impressive lesson in what resourcefulness, sound logistics, and careful fortification can accomplish in making prolonged resistance possible, even on a limited field of manœuvre, by an army that faces oppressive odds.

Lee's object from the hour Grant started his columns down the Rapidan was clear: He would seek to catch his adversary on the march and to destroy him, or, if that was impossible, to keep him from reaching Richmond. The capital must be saved, and that meant it must be saved from siege.

In seeking to attain his object, Lee was as heavily handicapped as a general well could be: His numbers were scarcely more than half those of his opponent; he had no prospect of any large reinforcements; his artillery was inferior in weight of metal and in range to that of the enemy; the mounts of his cavalry could not endure hard service and could not be replaced when worn out; because of casualties and illness during the campaign, he had to change the commanders of two of his three corps and the senior officers of more than a third of his brigades; for eleven of the most critical of the forty-five days of the campaign he was himself almost incapacitated; he was once cut off from his base of supplies, lost his reserve food supplies, and, during the early stages of the campaign, had to subsist his men and feed his horses on rations that barely sustained life. At the very crisis of Grant's offensive, Lee was compelled to detach two brigades and then an entire corps. Save for a major disaster in the field, virtually everything happened to him that could operate to prevent the fulfilment of his mission.

When the campaign opened, half of Longstreet's infantry and most of his artillery were distant about twenty miles, a long day's march, from the south bank of the Rapidan, where the army was in contact with the enemy. Lee has been criticised for thus disposing the First Corps. The argument is that this prevented his throwing the whole strength of his army against Grant as soon as he encountered him in the Wilderness.[1] Manifestly, it would have been better if Longstreet had been with Lee on the afternoon of May 5. It must be remembered, however, that Longstreet was being held on the Virginia Central as a reserve, to be employed either with the Army of Northern Virginia or against an enemy that might attack Richmond from the east or south. Further, Gordonsville was Lee's intermediate base and was a railroad junction of great importance, connected both with Lynchburg and with the Shenandoah Valley. There was as much probability that Grant would march straight for Gordonsville as there was that he would move by his left flank and cross the Rapidan and the lower fords. Such an advance on Gordonsville was seriously considered by Grant.[2] If it had been undertaken, or even if formidable demonstration had been made against the town, Lee would properly have been subject to criticism for exposing Gordonsville and the railroad.

[1] *Alexander,* 498.   [2] *Humphreys,* 9–10, and *supra,* p. 276, note 44.

When it was certain that Grant intended to cross the Rapidan in the vicinity of Germanna Ford, Lee decided not to dispute his passage of the river but to wait until the Army of the Potomac was spread out in the Wilderness. This undoubtedly was the course of wisdom. Grant's artillery was almost useless in the battle of May 5–6, and his cavalry could do little. That his great superiority of numbers was offset by Lee's manœuvre is shown by the fact that in the first day's fighting, Lee with less than five divisions forced Grant to stop and give battle, when it was to Grant's advantage to hurry out of the Wilderness and into open country. The delay cost Grant 17,666 casualties, or at least 10,000 more than Lee sustained. It is true that if Longstreet had been in line on the afternoon of the 5th, Grant would have lost still more heavily and might have been forced back across the Rapidan. But a complete concentration, in all the circumstances, was beyond Lee's power. As it was, Grant lost more men in the Wilderness than Hooker did in 1863. Had casualties been the only measure of success, the battle of the Wilderness would have been a greater victory than Chancellorsville.

Lee's handling of his army in the Wilderness involved four debatable acts. First of all, during the afternoon of the 5th and until about midday of the 6th, he fought one battle on the Plank road while Ewell fought another on the turnpike. The two were not correlated. A gap of nearly a mile remained between the right of Ewell and the left of Hill. This was, of course, a dangerous situation, though the nature of the ground on Grant's centre made it somewhat less serious than it would appear to be on the map. Lee had to take chances in concentrating along the main highways because the Wilderness was almost impenetrable.

Lee undoubtedly made a mistake in not withdrawing or fortifying the line of the Third Corps during the night of May 5 when Wilcox's and Heth's men lay on a broken irregular line in the Wilderness, having the foe, so to say, within bayonet thrust. To be sure, the two divisions were exhausted, and Lee had every reason to assume that Longstreet would arrive before daylight on the 6th and would relieve Hill; but the fact remains that by this, the second debatable act in his conduct of the battle, he left tired troops in a most exposed position under commanders who were

428

not of the first class. Heth and Wilcox could easily be surprised and might be demoralized, and if they were, then the enemy might readily turn both flanks of the Third Corps. Such incaution on Lee's part can only be explained on the ground of compassion for the weary soldiers of Heth and Wilcox. But if Longstreet had been even an hour later in coming up, compassion might have entailed slaughter.

Beyond doubt, in the third place, Lee lost an opportunity because he was unaware earlier on May 6 that Grant's right was "in the air" between Germanna Ford and the turnpike. Gordon's fine attack was delivered so late that it could not be fully developed. For this, however, the fault rests on Ewell rather than on the commanding general. On the morning of the 6th, Lee had his hands full until Longstreet delivered his attack. He might then have started for the Confederate left, though Longstreet and Hill worked so poorly together that his presence on the right was most desirable at a time when a co-ordinated advance by the two corps seemed to hold out the promise of a victory. Even if Lee had galloped off to Ewell's front he would have been recalled immediately by the news that Longstreet had been wounded. He was compelled to entrust the left to Ewell until late afternoon. Had Jackson been in Ewell's place, one can imagine how quickly he would have investigated Gordon's report that the flank of the enemy was exposed. Instead of doing this, Ewell deferred to the opinion of Early, who insisted that the Federal right was not "in the air" because it should not have been.

The other act of Lee's in the Wilderness that has been criticised adversely was his failure to continue the flank movement immediately after Longstreet was wounded. On this point, his critic was Longstreet, who naturally wished to put his last great service to the Confederacy in its brightest light. Field's statement of actual combat conditions[3] is a sufficient answer to Longstreet. With that wing of the army already forming a right angle, the advantage had been pushed to the limit at the moment Longstreet fell. The course Lee took in straightening out his front before resuming the attack doubtless saved the Federals from some casualties but it probably saved the Confederates from still

[3] See *supra*, pp. 295-96.

more. If Lee had continued to advance up the Plank road while another column was parallel to it, flank fire of the sort that brought Longstreet from his saddle would have killed many men.

From the Confederate point of view, the whole of the battle of the Wilderness presented a succession of dangers and difficulties. If they were met by Lee in such a manner as to leave no just ground for criticism except for his failure to fortify or to withdraw from the line of Heth and Wilcox on the night of the 5th, then the result manifestly is a credit to Lee's generalship. But that is not all. When an army that is numerically to its enemy as six to ten is able to inflict losses that are in the ratio of fourteen to seven, then a question is raised as to the skill with which the larger army is handled. Especially is this the case if most of the fighting occurs outside field fortifications. Once again it must be said that it is beyond the function of a biographer of Lee to criticise the skill of his opponents. But in reaching a fair appraisal of Lee's place as a soldier, the shortcomings of his adversaries must sometimes be taken into account. In this instance, the student of war is apt to ask himself, How was it that Grant exposed his right as he did on the 6th of May? With so large an army at his disposal, why did he not more adequately cover his left flank south of the Plank road? One of three conclusions seems inevitable: General Grant was less skillful in this battle than his previous achievements would have led one to expect, or he was carelessly contemptuous of Lee, or else he relied on his great superiority in numbers to the neglect of the finer qualities of leadership.

The transfer of the First Corps from the Wilderness to Spotsylvania on the night of May 7–8, to anticipate Grant's move to that point, has always been regarded as one of Lee's most brilliant achievements. Colonel Taylor cited the order for this march as an evidence that Lee possessed "the faculty . . . of discovering, as if by intuition, the intention and purpose of his opponent." [4] The quality of fathoming his antagonist's next move Lee undoubtedly displayed many times, but it came from close observation, from careful analysis of his intelligence reports, and from clear reasoning on the general strategy, not from some vague "intuition." On

[4] *Taylor's General Lee,* 238.

May 7 the evidence of a move was cumulative from early morning, when it was found that Grant's communications with Germanna Ford had been abandoned. In piecing all his information together, and in deciding that Grant was making for Spotsylvania, Lee did no more than he had done on a dozen occasions. The act was spectacular because the results were. He deserves as much credit for the speed with which he ordered Ewell to follow Anderson as for his decision to send the First Corps to Spotsylvania. A close study of his logistics on May 7–8 will show them to have been flawless.

Lee's dispositions after he reached Spotsylvania are interesting to soldiers in two particulars. First, as Henderson has pointed out,[5] he most admirably adapted his position to the troops at his command. The student of war who is interested in econcmy of force can hardly find a better field exercise than to go to Spotsylvania and try to locate, in the face of an imaginary enemy, a stronger line, except for the "Mule Shoe," than Lee drew. At Spotsylvania, as fully as anywhere else, the modern soldier will appreciate the point of the tribute paid to Lee by General R. L. T. Beale of the cavalry, when he said that a pencilled order given him by Lee "showed a familiarity with the topography of the country extending not only to by-roads but even to paths." [6] Thanks largely to the activities of Captain A. H. Campbell of the topographical engineers Lee then had better maps of some parts of Virginia than had previously been available to him, but for Spotsylvania he had only a poor sketch that showed none of the elevations. He must have relied heavily on quick field observation and must have employed the aptitude for collecting data that he had developed long before in Mexico. He was repaid in 1864, and, indeed, throughout the war, for the long hours he had spent in questioning natives and in tracing roads at General Scott's instance.

The ground around Spotsylvania Courthouse is interesting to the soldier, again, because field fortification was there fully developed for the first time in America. Thrown on the defensive with a smaller force, Lee sought to protect his men and to increase the effectiveness of their fire by giving them the full benefit of

[5] See *supra*, p. 309.　　　　[6] *R. L. T. Beale,* 119.

431

temporary earthworks. What had been done at Fredericksburg after the battle of December 13, 1862, on the left in the initial stage of the Chancellorsville campaign, in the forest along Mine Run, and in the Wilderness was done more elaborately across the fields and through the woods around Spotsylvania. The field fortifications used in this campaign were often started on piled-up fence rails or felled trees and were raised with great rapidity. When the works were constructed under fire the dirt was always thrown up toward the enemy, so that what would be "the ditch" in more recent warfare was the defending position. Similar defenses, constructed at leisure, had the ditch in front. The infantry works were co-ordinated most carefully with those for the artillery. On occasion, as at the "Mule Shoe," prior to May 12, light ordnance was placed in advance of the infantry fortifications, and, where the ground permitted, it sometimes was located immediately in rear of the trenches. There is a sector at Cold Harbor[7] where the infantry were almost directly under the muzzles of the guns. It is impossible to say how much of the credit for these field fortifications belongs to Lee and how much to General M. L. Smith of the engineers. There was a marked improvement in fortification after General Smith joined the army, but this may have been due to the changed nature of operations and not to the initiative of General Smith, who had learned much and had made many innovations at Vicksburg.

Turning to the details of the battles around Spotsylvania Courthouse, it must be written down that Heth's battle south of the Po on May 10 was not well fought, and that Ewell's advance on the 19th was not well planned. Lee's own shortcomings during this period of the campaign were confined to two things—his acquiescence in the inclusion of the "Mule Shoe" in the Confederate line, and his withdrawal, during the night of May 11-12, of Johnson's artillery from that salient.

In permitting the occupation of this bad position, Lee was over-influenced by Ewell. He, in turn, was probably led to exaggerate the elevation of the salient by the height of the great trees in it. As operations after May 12 showed very plainly, the ground

___

[7] On the front of the First Corps and between the first and second ravines north of the Cold Harbor road.

around the McCool house did not dominate the line as much as Ewell thought it did. Nothing material would have been lost if the salient had never been taken up.

Lee's decision to withdraw Johnson's batteries from the "Mule Shoe" was a plain instance of his being misled by inaccurate reports of a new movement on the part of the enemy. The case is the more personal if, as seems likely, those reports emanated from Rooney Lee, who was usually careful and undeniably capable. The circumstances have, of course, to be taken into account. Grant had remained but three days in the Wilderness. It was reasonable to assume that he would not waste time by lingering at Spotsylvania after he found Lee entrenched across his front. When the scouts affirmed that the enemy was again on the march, the intelligence fitted in with the probability. If the spies were right, then it was important that the pursuit should not be delayed by the slow withdrawal of the artillery along the narrow roads in the woods. But the scouts were wrong, and the responsibility for accepting erroneous reports falls on Lee. It cannot even be established, though it is probable, that he was uninformed during the night of suspicious activities in front of Johnson's position. If he was not advised of this, the blame is still in some sense his. He should have seen to it that he was notified of all developments, for at that time nothing was more important to headquarters than to know what Grant was doing. Of course, the extreme inclemency of the weather and the uncertainty that usually prevails when wind and rain distort every sound in the darkness are factors fairly to be weighed, but they do not absolve Lee of a mistake of judgment.

At Spotsylvania, as in the Wilderness, Lee was materially helped by the methods his antagonist applied. Grant did not hold literally to his boast, "I never manœuvre." He did manœuvre, but he did not manœuvre well. It is difficult to say how large a success he might have attained if, during the night or at dawn, instead of in the afternoon, he had moved Hancock to the south side of the Po, opposite Anderson's right flank. Lee had taken pains to draw his front in such a way as to permit the quick shifting of his troops from one flank to the other. Hancock might not have been able to shake Lee if he had continued to operate on the right bank of the river, but his effort was certainly made with the minimum of skillful direction from general headquarters. It is likewise difficult to understand why Grant did not operate against Lee's right flank, which was not extended far to the south of Spotsylvania for several days after both armies were in position. To be sure, the ground on that sector was not altogether favorable, but if the pertinacity shown in fighting for the Bloody Angle had been displayed on the Confederate right, Lee might have been compelled to fall back on the Louisa road. That would have been a serious matter, as Grant might then have been able to seize Hanover Junction.

The chief criticism that must be made of the Federal operations at Spotsylvania, however, is the manner in which Grant on May 12 continued to hurl troops into the Bloody Angle until the captured position was so crowded with men that they got in one another's way. If the front of attack had been extended farther southward, to engage the Third Corps at a time when there was every reason to assume that Lee would weaken other parts of his line in order to reinforce the Bloody Angle, the Confederate commander might have been hard pressed to resist. Of course, Grant had to throw enough force behind the surprise attack to make it effective; but when it is remembered that he outnumbered Lee almost two to one, the situation on the flank of the IX Corps, as uncovered by Lane's reconnaissance, seems scarcely believable.[8]

The transfer of the Army of Northern Virginia from Spotsylvania Courthouse to the North Anna was in some respects an even finer military performance than the move from the Wilderness that halted Grant at Spotsylvania. Within six hours after Grant began his march toward Bowling Green, Lee was shifting the left wing of his army to the right. Then followed the careful sweeping of the lines in front of Early and Anderson, and then the rapid, orderly retirement to the North Anna.

Lee's reasons for taking that position have been given in full and need not be repeated here, but they involved more than placing the Army of Northern Virginia once more between Grant and Richmond. By moving to the North Anna, and then fortifying so strongly that his opponent did not even attack him there,

---

[8] See *supra*, p. 323.

Lee deflected to the eastward the line of Grant's advance on Richmond. As has already been pointed out,[9] that was strategically of the greatest consequence, because it meant that the Virginia Central Railroad remained in Confederate hands. Communications with Staunton could be reopened. Co-operation between Grant and Sigel's successor was rendered more difficult. A drive against the Federals in the Valley was facilitated, and the roads for a new invasion of Maryland were restored to the Confederacy. The grand strategy of Grant's advance, to be sure, was based on the sound principle that his mission was to destroy Lee's army, not to capture or to hold any given point; but that mission could have been more readily and quickly performed if he had placed within his lines the most direct route to the Shenandoah Valley. He could then have made himself master of all western Virginia and would have deprived Lee of large supplies. As it was, Grant cut the railroad, but during the whole of the operations on the North Anna and on the Totopotomoy, he was almost within sound of the whistles of the trains on the Virginia Central, and was powerless to hold the streaks of rust that bound Richmond and the Valley together. It is not too much to repeat that Lee's arrival at the North Anna ahead of Grant prolonged the war by saving a large part of Virginia to the Confederacy for another six months.

On the North Anna the only offensive operation that the Army of Northern Virginia could undertake, that of Wilcox north of Noel's Station on the afternoon of the 23d, was undeniably a failure. Hill's handling of the Confederate left, in fact, was at that time far from brilliant. But Lee's choice of the "V" front made his left as impregnable as the right. Concerning this line, the only criticism ever made was that the position was so strong as to discourage Grant from attacking it—a singular tribute, surely, to Lee's engineering.

Confederate authorities have often said that if Lee had not been stricken ill on the North Anna he would have defeated Grant there. This view is hardly justified by the facts. Lee's insistent cry from his tent, "We must strike them a blow," [10] doubtless echoed his well-established purpose to take the offensive whenever and wherever he found an opening; but even if he had been in

[9] See *supra*, p. 361. [10] See *supra*, p. 359.

full strength, it is doubtful if he could have accomplished anything on the North Anna, once the Federals had crossed to the right bank and had fortified there. Had he attacked on his left, he would have found that Warren had ample room for manœuvre. The result might have been to carry the battle up the Central Railroad, which was not desirable, for reasons already given. If, again, Lee had attacked from his right on the North Anna, he would soon have come under artillery fire from the left bank and would have been stopped before he could win a decision, just as Jackson had been at Fredericksburg on the afternoon of December 13, 1862. Lee's position, in short, was defensively ideal, but it could only serve to force Grant to another movement by his left flank.

When that movement was made on May 27, Lee was promptly informed. He had suspected such a manœuvre and had his cavalry disposed far down the Pamunkey to warn him of any advance in that direction. This employment of his cavalry was a part of Lee's defensive routine. Whenever he was guarding a river line, in a position that could be turned, he always spread his cavalry for a great distance on either flank, twice as far, probably, as most generals would have thought necessary.

Being quickly advised of the appearance of the enemy at Hanovertown, Lee encountered no difficulty in making the move from the North Anna to the Totopotomoy. He was then in familiar country, for which he had a new and excellent map,[11] and he placed his army where he could meet an attack either from the Pamunkey or down the Central Railroad. Nothing of great moment happened until Grant made his shift to Cold Harbor. Whether this was better than a drive for the Central Railroad need not be argued here. Both lines of approach offered advantages. Once Grant had started for Cold Harbor, Lee's task was to reach that point in sufficient strength to thwart Grant's turning movement and, if possible, to double up his left. The only question that arises here is whether Lee concentrated at Cold Harbor on June 1 as heavily as he should have.[12] It is to be noted, in

[11] Campbell's admirable map of April 26, 1864, printed as Plate XCII in the *Atlas* of the *Official Records*. A reference by Early in *O. R.*, 51, part 2, p. 997, makes it plain that this map had been issued by the time the army reached the Totopotomoy.
[12] The late Doctor Hartwell Macon of Ingleside, Hanover County, related that General Grant rode into his yard, dismounted and sent off his staff officers and couriers on

answer to this, that Lee's projected line, as of June 1, extended from the vicinity of Atlee's, thence to the right in front of the Totopotomoy, on across the Old Church road and southeast to Cold Harbor, a distance of nine miles. To defend this line he had not more than 46,000 men, including Hoke's division, which was just arriving from the south side of the James. This gave Lee a density of only 5000 infantry a mile, whereas his opponent, who had the initiative, could dispose 10,000 men per mile. Lee had more than 10,000 infantry and about 2000 cavalry within striking distance of Cold Harbor by the early morning of June 1. That was all he could do, and he could not have done that much if he had not insisted on the dispatch of Hoke from Beauregard.

The actions at Cold Harbor on June 1 were poorly directed on the Confederate side. The fiasco in the early morning was a discredit both to Anderson and to Hoke. The surprise in the afternoon at the ravine between Hoke and Kershaw may have been excusable. Throughout the day the hand of a master was lacking. Anderson was a new corps commander; Hoke was inexperienced at the head of a division; the shock troops were led by a gallant amateur in the bitter business of war. At no time during the campaign did Lee feel more heavily the losses he had sustained among his general officers in the Wilderness and at Spotsylvania. Grant may have owed his escape from a serious defeat that day to the recklessness with which Longstreet and others had exposed themselves during the fighting in May.

From the time Lee himself arrived on the Cold Harbor front the battle was well-ordered. He anchored his right on the high ground above the Chickahominy and located his support lines opposite the weakest points in his front. Then he simply waited. When Grant attacked, the Union lines were mowed down with a slaughter worse than that inflicted on Pickett and Pettigrew at

---

various missions. The doctor, who was crippled and unable to do military duty, though he was an ardent Southerner, walked out and invited the General indoors. Grant declined and walked to and fro in the yard. At length he pulled out his watch and said, more to himself than to Doctor Macon, "If I don't hear his guns in fifteen minutes, I've got the old fox now." As Doctor Macon waited, the minutes seemed interminable, but before a quarter of an hour had elapsed, the echo of artillery came across the fields from the direction of Old Cold Harbor. Grant mounted without a word and rode off. There is no reason to doubt the authenticity of this story, but it is impossible to fix the exact time, though the incident doubtless occurred on May 31. It shows by how narrow a margin of time Lee was able to protect his right flank.

Gettysburg. Grant later went on record as saying that he always regretted making the last assault. "At Cold Harbor," he wrote, "no advantage whatever was gained to compensate for the heavy loss we sustained."[13] The repulse, in his opinion, impaired the morale of his army and raised that of the Confederates.[14] He undoubtedly was correct. The prospect, however, was not so forbidding on June 3 as it seemed in retrospect. He was within nine miles of Richmond, as the crow flies. For a month he had been hammering at an adversary who could not continue to replace his losses, whereas the Army of the Potomac could draw indefinitely on resources that were, in comparison, almost limitless. Besides, the strength of the Confederate position was deceptive. On that part of the front where the Federal losses were heaviest the approaches were through woods. In rear of the Confederate lines the ground was open, with no trees to give a measure of the elevation. Grant apparently thought, as most historians since his day have assumed, that the whole of the ground of attack was a plain. On the right centre this was true only of the front immediately on either side of the Cold Harbor road. To right and to left, the little streams flow through boggy ravines that offer some exceedingly formidable artillery positions, from which a cross-fire can be directed on an attacking force. It is not remarkable that Grant was deceived as to the strength of Lee's lines or that he was repulsed. It would have been remarkable if he had broken through.

The success of Grant in crossing the James unhindered and the failure of Lee to reinforce Petersburg more quickly and more heavily, after the attack of June 15, have been very generally regarded as the most serious blemishes on Lee's military record, with the possible exception of his order for Pickett's charge at Gettysburg. There was disappointment at the time in Richmond because Grant was not assailed while in motion.[15] Later critics have had much praise for General Grant, because they have credited him with keeping Lee in the dark as to his position and plans until the Army of the Potomac was in front of Petersburg. General Humphreys cited Lee's dispatch of 3 P.M., June 16 to Beauregard—". . . Have not heard of Grant's crossing the James"

[13] 2 *Grant's Memoirs,* 276.   [14] *Ibid.,* 276–77.   [15] *McCabe,* 504.

—as if the whole shift to the south side of the James had been unsuspected, and he added, "at that hour only the VI Corps and Wilson's cavalry remained on the north bank."[16] Colonel Thomas L. Livermore went so far as to affirm: ". . . not only was the movement so orderly, silent, and well covered that the enemy did not attack, but the strategy also was so complete that from the 13th, when it began, until the 17th, General Lee did not venture to quit his intrenchments at Cold Harbor."[17] In summarizing the operation General Alexander wrote: "It must be said that Grant successfully deceived Lee as to his whereabouts for at least three days, and thus, at the most critical period of the war, saved himself from a second defeat, more bloody, more signal, and more undeniable than Cold Harbor. For if Beauregard alone, with only 14,000 men, was able to stop Grant's whole army even after being driven by surprise into temporary works, what would Lee and Beauregard together have done from the strong original lines of Petersburg?"[18]

It is easy, of course, to point out the errors in these criticisms,[19] but, *prima facie,* the basis of this contention appears valid. Grant began ferrying his army over the James on June 14. He soon completed a superb pontoon bridge from Wilcox's Landing to Windmill Point. Bringing the XVIII Corps by water back from White House to Bermuda Hundred, by daylight of June 15 he had 45,000 to 47,000 on the south side of the James.[20] That force was hourly increased. With the exception of a part of the cavalry corps, the whole of the Federal army, some 110,000 to 113,000, was south of the river before Lee was sure that any part of it, other than the II and XVIII Corps, was there. This looks as if Lee, for once, was outgeneralled.

Much evidence, however, that was not available when these early critics wrote of the campaign has since been published,[21]

---

[16] *Humphreys,* 214. Humphreys forgot, incidentally, that the 4th Division of the IX Corps had not crossed.

[17] 5 *M. H. S. M.,* 47. [18] *Alexander,* 557.

[19] Livermore, needless to say, was mistaken in almost all his assertions. Instead of not venturing "to quit his intrenchments" at Cold Harbor until June 17, Lee left there early on the 13th and, on the evening of June 17, was south of the river, having with him all but 27,800 of the troops he could utilize. Included in the 27,800 were his cavalry and the garrison of Richmond.

[20] Including the troops that had remained with Butler.

[21] *Lee's Dispatches* was not printed until 1915 and was not available to General Alexander. General Humphreys and Colonel Livermore did not even have *O. R.,* 51,

439

and this reverses the verdict. Instead of appearing as the most serious instance during the war when Lee was outwitted, the operations of June 14–18 constitute a most informative example of how a limited force may be defensively employed to defend two widely separated positions when a stronger adversary is so placed that he can move unobserved, as must occasionally happen even in modern warfare, though a commander can now utilize aerial observation.

The evidence on the issue has been given in detail in the previous chapter, without breaking the narrative to analyze it in relation to the larger question of Lee's generalship as compared with Grant's. It must now be reviewed briefly in the light of the conditions that confronted Lee. These conditions were:

1. In a country as heavily wooded as that below Richmond, Grant, or any other competent general, could steal one march on his opponent.

2. Lee was weakened by the absence of two of the three divisions of his cavalry, which he had been compelled to send off in order to meet Sheridan's raid up the Central Railroad. This was one of the many prices Lee had to pay for declining man-power and diminished horse-supply. His cavalry, which once had been greatly superior to his adversary's, was now inferior in every respect other than in actual hand-to-hand combat.

3. Lee's mobile infantry and artillery, as distinguished from the small force of second-line reservists and heavy artillery in the Richmond defenses, had been reduced by the departure of Breckinridge and of Early to less than 32,000. These detachments were most regrettable, but in a strategical sense they were inevitable. If troops had to be sent to the Shenandoah Valley, it was wise to dispatch them in sufficient numbers to make a demonstration against Washington. The hard subtraction of these troops, however, made it impossible for Lee to take the offensive against the Army of the Potomac which, exclusive of cavalry, numbered at least 93,000 and perhaps more.

4. Lee's first assigned duty was to keep Grant from Richmond.

part 2, which was issued in 1897. It is not certain that General Alexander used the very important telegrams in this volume to fill the gaps in *O. R.*, 40, and it is altogether likely that he overlooked certain messages in the supplement to *O. R.*, 51. part 2, which clear up several obscure points.

The permanent severance of communications with the south would, of course, involve the fall of the city in a very short time;[22] but if the choice lay between the loss of Richmond and the risk of a temporary break in communications, Lee could not hesitate in deciding to defend his capital. It is debatable whether the Confederate administration was right in insisting that Richmond be held at any price, but there can be no disputing the fact that in the summer of 1864 this was the fixed policy of the government. Lee was forced to subordinate everything to that or else should have resigned his commission.

These were the controlling circumstances with Lee when Grant withdrew from the Cold Harbor front and moved by rapid, well-executed marches to Wilcox's Landing. In doing this the Union commander put twenty-two miles of road between himself and Lee. Grant's choice of a place for throwing his pontoons was, perhaps, his best single stroke of the entire campaign. Especial pains were taken to select a point on the river beyond observation by Lee, as it was assumed that the Confederate leader would use his inner lines and would reinforce Beauregard quickly if Grant attempted to construct a bridge at a nearer and more convenient point, such as the flats below Malvern Hill.[23] Lee could not reach Grant at Wilcox's Landing. He could not prevent the return of the XVIII Corps from the White House by water. Nor could he stop the transportation of the advanced units of the II Corps by ship from Wilcox's Landing to Windmill Point.

Three facts, however, are now definitely established, and they cancel most of what has been written about this aspect of the movement:

1. Lee expected Grant to cross the James.

2. He knew the approximate position of his adversary by the early afternoon of June 14.

3. He had ordered Hoke's division to the Confederate pontoon bridge at Drewry's Bluff eight hours before Grant's bridge at Wilcox's Landing was finished.[24]

Lee was ready, in short, to begin the reinforcement of Beaure-

---

[22] Cf. 2 Davis, 640. [23] Humphreys, 198–99.

[24] Hoke's orders were issued before 4 P.M. (Lee's Dispatches, 234); the Federal pontoon bridge was not completed until midnight of the 14th (Humphreys, 203).

gard before Grant had done more than utilize his available transports to strengthen Butler's army.

When new troops began to appear in front of Petersburg on June 15, Lee naturally was forced to rely on Beauregard for information as to their number and identification. Unfortunately, many of the reports that he received from Beauregard were belated, vague, and well-nigh equivocal. This was not altogether Beauregard's fault. That officer had set up what he considered an efficient signal system on the James,[25] but he had no spies and his intelligence service was so rudimentary that even the examination of prisoners seems to have been delayed.[26] He was preoccupied with the defense of a long line and was unable to determine whether the troops that assailed the Petersburg defenses were Butler's or Grant's.

However excusable all this was, it proved a handicap to Lee. The first concern expressed by Beauregard was that he might not be able to hold both Drewry's Bluff and Petersburg. Then he stated that if he had the whole of his original command he would be safe on both sectors. Lee promptly restored it. Beauregard next voiced the opinion that if 5000 or 6000 men were sent to the southside, they would suffice to cover Bermuda Neck while he reconcentrated at Petersburg. Lee forthwith sent Pickett's division of 4500 men and rode with it himself to the Petersburg pike, where Butler had seized Beauregard's abandoned lines. On the afternoon of that same day, June 16, Lee brought over Field's division.

Beauregard was an experienced officer whose rank and judgment were to be respected. He was presumably the best judge of his needs. Not one request for men did he make with which Lee did not comply, from the time of the first threat until Beauregard, becoming optimistic, asked for reinforcements to undertake a counteroffensive that the judgment of Lee did not approve. All this is a most material consideration in determining whether Lee did everything that could have been expected of him.

The substance of all Lee's information from Beauregard on the 16th and during the forenoon of the 17th of June was that he was confronted at Petersburg by the II and XVIII Corps. In answer

[25] 2 *Roman*, 244–45.   [26] *Cf.* 2 *Roman*, 575–76.

to repeated inquiries whether more troops of the Army of the Potomac were south of the James, Beauregard could make no positive answer. Lee knew that these two corps, plus the other forces under Butler, could not exceed 51,000 to 53,000 men. To combat them, 27,000 Confederates were then on that bank of the river. The odds against the Confederates there were no longer than those to which Lee was accustomed during the whole of the campaign. He had, in fact, already sent more reinforcements to Beauregard than he had made available for Ewell when that officer had been holding the base of the Bloody Angle against the concentrated attack of three corps.[27]

It was after 4 P.M. on the afternoon of June 17 when Lee was told by Beauregard for the first time that he was faced by practically the whole of the Army of the Potomac, as well as by part of Butler's Army of the James. Within twelve hours thereafter, Lee had on the southside, or on the march thither, all his mobile troops except Hampton's cavalry and two battalions of artillery under Colonel Thomas H. Carter.[28] The table on page 444 will exhibit the strength of the opposing forces north and south of James River from June 13 to the morning of June 18. In the last column is Beauregard's estimate of the strength of the enemy in his front.[29] Included are all the cavalry.[30]

Beauregard's troops made a splendid fight in front of Petersburg, and were handled by him with great skill and boldness. Nobody could have done better, favored though he was by some curious delays and by a most singular division of authority among the Federal commanders.[31] He was aided, too, by good initial positions and by a strong force of well-employed artillery. It must be said, however—and in no derogation of his generalship—that the excellence of Beauregard's battle grew as the story was told. Es-

---

[27] 4 *B. and L.*, 246.   [28] *Lee's Dispatches*, 251.

[29] It should be emphasized once more that these figures are approximations, as the exact strength of neither army can be established.

[30] Sheridan of the Army of the Potomac and Hampton and Fitz Lee, of the Army of Northern Virginia, it will be remembered, were detached at the time. Lee had W. H. F. Lee's division and Gary's brigade, the latter being part of the Richmond garrison; Grant had Wilson's division with him; Butler had Kautz's.

[31] *Cf.* 5 *M. H. S. M.*, 77 *ff.*, 159 *ff.* The latter reference is to a paper done in the candid manner of the distinguished J. C. Ropes. See also *Alexander*, 548–49; 552 *ff.* Grant prepared the orders for the attack by Smith's XVII Corps on June 15, but did not notify Meade of the time of its march, with the result that Meade could not coordinate the attack of the II Corps. Hancock could easily have been in position to sup-

APPROXIMATE FORCES NORTH AND SOUTH OF JAMES RIVER, JUNE 13–18, 1864
(ooo omitted)

	NORTHSIDE		SOUTHSIDE		BEAUREGARD'S ESTIMATE OF THE FEDERAL STRENGTH ON THE SOUTHSIDE
	Confederate	Union	Confederate	Union	
June 13....	44.7 to 47.6[32]	104 to 111	11.3[33]	15 to 17	
June 14, evening ..	44.7 to 47.6	74 to 81	11.3	45 to 47	25 to 27
June 15, morning..	36.9 to 39.8	74 to 81	19.1	45 to 47	"large increase," c. 11 A.M.
June 5, evening ..	36.9 to 39.8	68 to 74	19.1	51 to 53	
June 16, morning .	36.9 to 39.8	56 to 62	19.1	63 to 65	35
June 16, evening ..	28.9 to 31.8	31 to 37	27.1	88 to 90	7 P.M., 51 to 53
June 17, morning..	28.9 to 31.8	25 to 31	27.1	94 to 96	11:15 A.M., intimating V Corps was not in his front[36]
June 17, evening ..	24.9 to 27.8	7.5	31.1	111 to 113	4:30 P.M., 81 to 83
June 18, morning..	9.8[34]	7.5	47.2 to 51.1	111 to 113	5 P.M., "whole army"

pecially after Colonel Roman began the preparation of his military biography of Beauregard, the repulse of the Federal attacks on June 15–17 was glorified into something akin to a rescue of Lee from certain ruin by his comrade on the south side of the James. This view was generally credited by the participants, because many of the troops that shared in the actions had not, until that time, been acquainted with the close and desperate combat by which the Army of Northern Virginia sustained itself in the field.

port Smith by noon on June 15, but he was not at hand until evening. Smith's attack on the evening of the 15th could have been pushed through to Petersburg, but was delayed by the unauthorized action of his chief of artillery in sending back the horses to be watered. They were hurriedly returned and the assault was launched, about 7 P.M., but General Smith did not think himself safe in continuing the pursuit after dark. On the 16th and 17th the Federals seem to have had no plan of utilizing their vastly superior numbers against the Confederate right, though it could readily have been turned. From the Federal point of view, the actions of June 15–17 were as much mismanaged as any that Grant ever fought in Virginia.

32 Including Richmond garrison, 6400.

33 Including Drewry's Bluff garrison, 365.

34 W. H. F. Lee, with about 1000, was moving to the southside, but his precise whereabouts on the morning of June 18 are not determinable (cf. Lee's Dispatches, 249).

35 At 7:45 A.M., Beauregard reported the II Corps on the southside, but Lee did not receive this telegram.

36 O. R., 51, part 2, p. 1079.

A soldier's first hard battle is usually his worst—in memory, at least. On the other hand, Lee, his staff, and his veterans were so accustomed to fighting against long odds that they took them as a matter of course. Lee did Beauregard the compliment of assuming that his men could fight equally well and against like odds. A commander who had seen Cooke at Sharpsburg, Jackson at Second Manassas, Barksdale at Fredericksburg, Pickett at Gettysburg, and the Second Corps at the Bloody Angle could hardly become so excited over the attacks on Petersburg that he would risk the capture of Richmond, strip the north bank of the James, and increase a force of 27,000 in order to resist an attack by a force that Beauregard put down at two corps. Lee had heard the cry of "Wolf-wolf" so often from the southside during May that he may have been a little skeptical of Beauregard's reports. No special concern did he have for the safety of Petersburg until Beauregard acquainted him on the afternoon of June 17 with the newly discovered fact that the whole of the Army of the Potomac was confronting him.[37]

This is the record. It speaks for itself. Lee unavoidably lost contact with Grant on June 13–14, but he did not misread the intention of his adversary. He reasoned that Grant would cross the James, precisely as he had reasoned that McClellan would reinforce Pope, Burnside move to Fredericksburg, and Grant reconcentrate on Spotsylvania. He was not outgeneralled nor taken by surprise. If he did not reinforce Beauregard heavily at Petersburg until the strength of the attacking force became known, he gave Beauregard in every instance the help that general asked

[37] It is significant that Colonel Walter H. Taylor, who usually kept his sweetheart informed of all important operations, seemingly regarded the operations of June 15–18 as little more than routine campaigning. On June 15 he remarked there was "nothing of importance today." On the 18th, instead of describing the struggle for Petersburg as a crisis of the Confederacy, he allowed himself the luxury of a love-letter in which the fighting was not even mentioned (*Taylor MSS.*, June 15–18, 1864). General Pendleton viewed the whole operation as a normal phase of an unhappy war, and in a letter of June 18 he dismissed it in two sentences: "Grant has taken all his army to the south side. We go to meet him as usual" (*Pendleton*, 342). The Federals, for their part, had become so accustomed to being repulsed that they accepted the frowning fortifications as a warning against staking too much on an assault. There is, perhaps naturally, no hint in Grant's official report of the operations of June 16–18 to indicate that he thought the Petersburg defenses inadequately manned on those days (*O. R.*, 36, part 1, p. 25). When he came to write his memoirs he modified this judgment (*op. cit.*, 2, 296), possibly after reading Roman. Meade wrote: "We find the enemy, as usual, in a very strong position, defended by earthworks, and it looks very much as if we will have to go through a siege of Petersburg before entering on a siege of Richmond . . ." (2 *Meade*, 205). He attributed failure on June 18 to the "moral condition of the army" (2 *ibid.*, 207).

for defense, though his own forces were then dangerously small. He had to be guided by Beauregard's information, which was limited and slowly accumulated, but he sent enough troops to Petersburg to hold it, without neglecting his major mission, that of insuring the safety of Richmond.

To summarize now the entire campaign from May 4 to June 18, the only three serious shortcomings that can be charged against Lee would seem to be, first, that he did not withdraw Heth and Wilcox or strengthen their lines on the night of May 5; second, that he ordered Johnson's artillery from the "Mule Shoe" at Spotsylvania during the evening of May 11; and, third, that he lost contact with Grant on June 13–14, in the absence of the greater part of his cavalry, and risked the capture of Petersburg until Beauregard got accurate information as to the presence of Grant's army in front of that city. Against these three errors, if they are to be so considered, may be set down his sound decision to give battle in the Wilderness, the swift move to Spotsylvania, the selection of an admirable line there, the shift to the North Anna, the deflection of Grant's advance on Hanover Junction by the construction of an excellent system of field fortifications, the transfer of operations to the Totopotomoy, the concentration at Cold Harbor, the repulse of Grant's general assault there, the relief of Petersburg, and—as a final gauge of the ferocity of the Confederate defense—the infliction of approximately 64,000 casualties, with a loss of about 30,000 men.[38] The Federals lost more men before the guns of Lee's army, with the stout assistance of Beauregard's troops on June 15–18, than Lee had in the Army of Northern Virginia when the campaign opened.

[38] Two different totals of the Federal losses are given, one of 63,966 (*O. R.*, 36, part I, pp. 133 *f.*), and the other of 64,216 (*ibid.*, 195). Neither of these included the losses in the Army of the James on June 15–18. Inasmuch, however, as the figures cover the period to June 20, instead of to June 18, it is probable that subtractions about offset additions. Included are the casualties inflicted by the Confederates of Beauregard's command on June 15–18, because these cannot be separated from those attributable to the Army of Northern Virginia. Butler's losses of 6215, prior to June 15 (*O. R.*, 36, part 2, pp. 18, 19) are excluded. The estimate for the Confederate forces assume 5000 casualties in the Petersburg and Bermuda operations of June 15–18, and 25,000 in the Army of Northern Virginia prior to that time. These figures are based chiefly on a comparison of returns after the operations with the strength of the army at the beginning of the campaign, making proper allowance for reinforcements. The figures may slightly overstate the Confederate losses but they are believed to be approximately correct, though precision, in the absence of official returns of casualties, cannot be claimed for them.

The balance of achievement, then, is to Lee's credit, overwhelmingly. So far as general strategy and headquarters tactics could influence the result, his generalship had never been finer, if, indeed, it had ever been quite so good. Wherever Grant advanced, there he found Lee's bayonets closing the road to Richmond. Yet even before the crossing of the James, time and numbers were having their effect. Lee did not lose the battles but he did not win the campaign. He delayed the fulfillment of Grant's mission, but he could not discharge his own. Lee found few opportunities of attacking the enemy in detail or on the march, and in every instance where he assumed the offensive, except in the turning movement of May 6, he failed to achieve the results for which he had hoped. This was not because the Army of Northern Virginia fought less well than before, but because the Army of the Potomac was relatively stronger and fought better. "Lee's Miserables" never behaved with greater gallantry than in the Wilderness on May 5 and in recovering the Bloody Angle on May 12; but their numbers were smaller, and in some subtle fashion General Grant infused into his well-seasoned troops a confidence they had never previously possessed. There was, likewise, an ominous decline in the standard of Confederate corps, divisional, and brigade command. Too many of the ablest officers had been killed and were replaced by soldiers less skillful. After Longstreet was wounded, every corps commander failed badly, at least once. Two excellent new divisional commanders were developed in Kershaw and Gordon. Ramseur and Mahone showed promise. But some of the others did not fulfill expectations, and a few more were definitely mediocre. The same thing was true of the brigade commanders. There was no remedy for it and there could be no blame on Lee because of this, but the sombre fact remained: troops were no longer led as they had been in the period from Second Manassas through Chancellorsville. In the largest sense, only Lee and the men in the ranks still made the army terrible in battle.

CHAPTER XXV

LEE'S MOST DIFFICULT DEFENSIVE

WHEN General Lee went to church in Petersburg on June 19, 1864,[1] the day after he reached the city, the military problem in the solution of which he sought divine guidance was as grave as any he had ever faced. The front of battle was now twenty-six miles in length—from the cavalry outposts at White Oak Swamp, to Chaffin's Bluff, thence on the south side of the James from Drewry's Bluff past Bermuda Hundred Neck to the Appomattox, and over that stream, southward and westward in front of Petersburg, to a point beyond the Jerusalem plank road. The whole of this line had at all times to be held. Lee was required, in the second place, to prevent the enemy from seizing ground that would force the Confederate army back into the Richmond defenses;[2] thirdly, he had to cover the capital against surprise attack at any point not protected by his lines; and fourthly, he had to keep open the railroads, on which he was dependent for supplies.

In performing this task, for what assistance could he hope? Early might be able to change the gloomy outlook. Lee was satisfied that officer could drive back Hunter,[3] and, indeed, on the second day at Petersburg, he received news that Hunter had retired from in front of Lynchburg.[4] Perhaps, as Lee had planned ere he detached him, Early could advance down the Shenandoah Valley, spread terror in the North and thereby force General Grant either to detach a large part of his army for the defense of Washington, or else to attack Lee in the hope of compelling him to recall Early. Again, by some miracle, a great victory might be

[1] 1 *McCrae*, 173.
[2] *Cf.* Lee to a corps commander, in a letter undated and without address, but presumably written on June 21 or about that time, printed in 9 *S. H. S. P.*, 137, and in *O. R.*, 40, part 2, p. 702: "We shall be obliged to go out and prevent the enemy from selecting such positions as he chooses. If he is allowed to continue this course we shall at last be obliged to take refuge behind the works of Richmond and stand a siege, which would be but a work of time."
[3] *Lee's Dispatches*, 254.   [4] *O. R.*, 37, part 1, p. 765.

won in the far South that would release troops from that section to reinforce the Army of Northern Virginia; but a miracle it would have to be, because Johnston had fallen back from Dalton to Kennesaw Mountain and was as hard beset by Sherman's hammering tactics as Lee had been by Grant's.[5]

For the rest, Lee had to rely on his own army and Beauregard's, plus such conscripts as might be brought in and such convalescents as might return. Valiant as his army was, the limits to its possible accomplishments were manifest. Although there was abundant reason for believing that the Federals were dispirited after the severe repulses they had sustained,[6] Lee's own force had been so reduced by casualties and detachments that he had small chance of undertaking a sustained offensive unless Grant should be guilty of some serious blunder and present an opening. "General Grant," he told the President, "will concentrate all the troops here he can raise, from every section of the United States. . . . I hope Your Excellency will put no reliance in what I can do individually, for I feel that will be very little. The enemy has a strong position, and is able to deal us more injury than from any other point he has ever taken. Still we must try and defeat him. I fear he will not attack us but advance by regular approaches. He is so situated that I cannot attack him." [7] Lee believed, however, that he could defend Richmond from a direct assault delivered on the northside, provided he could keep the Richmond-Petersburg Railroad in running order for the transfer of troops in an emergency.[8]

The one advantage of the Confederate commander was this: Grant had approached Petersburg from the east. His lines ran north and south and had not yet been extended to the southwest or to the west. Lee's own lines, on the Confederate left, paralleled Grant's, but as Lee had to protect Petersburg fully, he drew his lines north and south and then to the west. On the sector east of Petersburg, little distance separated the trench systems that sweating thousands were now throwing up under the June sun; but from the point where Lee's line curved to the westward, while

---

[5] Cf. Henry, 384.

[6] Colonel Taylor noted on June 21 that many of the enemy surrendered without firing a gun (Taylor MSS.). Cf. Anderson in O. R., 51, part 2, p. 1025 and 2 Meade, 206.

[7] Lee's Dispatches, 254–55.   [8] Lee's Dispatches, 251.

Grant's continued southward, the space between the two fronts widened gradually until it became as much as two miles. The extreme Confederate right, which was lightly held, quite overlapped the Federal front there. This situation gave Lee a certain

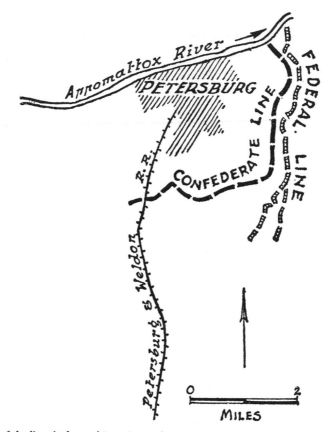

Sketch of the lines in front of Petersburg, after June 18, 1864, showing how the extension of the Confederate right placed it at so great a distance from the Federal front that Lee could hold it lightly and use part of its defenders as a general reserve.

freedom of manœuvre on his right. He availed himself of this very promptly and employed his right division as a general reserve to strengthen the sector to the east, as occasion required, or to be moved across the James and aid Custis Lee in defending Richmond.

The question of subsistence was more serious than the prospect of being pinned to the Richmond-Petersburg defenses. Lee was almost entirely dependent on the railways to feed his army. These roads were four in number. Close to the Richmond defenses lay the long-contested Virginia Central. Directly south from Peters-

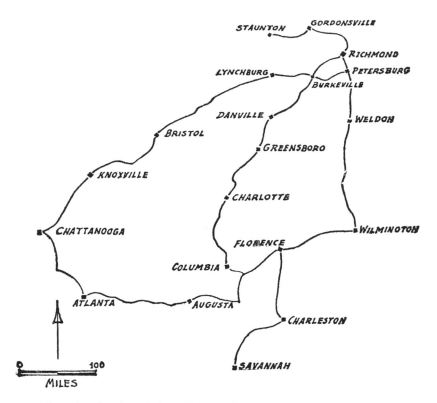

The main railroad supply-lines of the Confederate army in front of Richmond.

burg ran the Petersburg and Weldon Railroad, which was a link in the main coastal route leading to Wilmington and Charleston and thence to Atlanta. Southwestward from Richmond was the track of the Richmond and Danville. This was connected at Danville with the new Piedmont Railroad, leading to Greensboro, N. C. General Lee, it will be recalled, had been very anxious to have the Piedmont completed, in anticipation of a possible loss of the Petersburg and Weldon. Now that the Piedmont was at last open, though wretchedly constructed, it gave Richmond a

451

second, if a slow and devious, connection with the rich corn belt of northwestern Georgia. Besides these lines, Lee had to defend the Southside Railroad, which led by way of Lynchburg to Bristol, on the Virginia-Tennessee border. This railroad was of

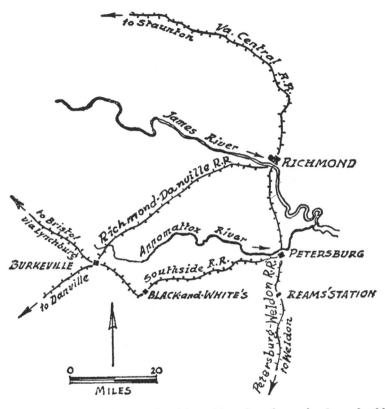

The open railroad supply-lines on the Richmond-Petersburg front, after June 18, 1864, showing how cars of the Richmond and Danville and of the Southside railroads could be switched at Burkeville.

no mean importance because it crossed at Burkeville the track of the Richmond and Danville. Supplies arriving by way of Greensboro and Danville and intended for the army could be transferred to the Southside road at Burkeville and could be sent immediately to Petersburg. This will be plain from the sketch shown above.

Surveying these lines of communication, Lee was satisfied that it would be almost impossible to hold permanently the Petersburg

452

and Weldon, the northern end of which was less than three miles from the left flank of the Federals. His aim was to keep the enemy from that railway, if possible, until the harvest in Virginia, or as long as he could do so without heavy loss. Meantime, he urged that the Southside, the Richmond and Danville, and the Piedmont be supplied with ample rolling stock and defended by the second-line reserves, so that these lines could supply the army when the Petersburg and Weldon fell into the enemy's hands. "If this cannot be done," he told the Secretary of War, in as plain words as he had ever employed, "I see no way of averting the terrible disaster that will ensue."[9]

He soon had evidence that the dangers to the railroads were as immediate as they were serious. On the 21st of June outposts reported an extension of the Federal lines toward the Weldon tracks. Simultaneously, the Union cavalry was found to have started on a raid farther down the same road. The only large mounted unit that Lee then had on the south side of the James was Rooney Lee's division, for Hampton was still watching Sheridan north of the river. Rooney's troops, who had skirmished with the enemy on the 21st were sent in pursuit of the raiders. Wilcox's division was moved out to take the place of the cavalry, but it found the enemy's infantry retiring.[10] The next day, when Lee rode to the Confederate right, he learned from Mahone that the Federal infantry was again advancing.[11] Mahone thought he saw an opening for a flank attack and asked permission to deliver it. With Lee's approval, he led off three brigades from the Confederate right, found that a gap had been carelessly left between the II and VI Corps, and quickly rolled up two strong Federal divisions.[12] He skillfully drew back before nightfall with more than 1600 prisoners, four guns and eight flags.[13] Still more might have been accomplished had Wilcox co-operated with Mahone,

[9] O. R., 40, part 2, p. 690. Cf. ibid., pp. 671, 682, 683, 684, 686–87; ibid., 51, part 2, p. 1023.

[10] Wilcox's MS report, 51.

[11] Grant had abandoned his drive to the railroad and was moving as if to envelop the Confederate right.

[12] This action was near the Johnson house, three-quarters of a mile due south of what later became the Confederate Fort Walker.

[13] O. R., 40, part 1, p. 750; ibid., 51, part 2, p. 1026. The Federal reports are in ibid., 40, part 1, pp. 325 ff. The best account of the action is that of W. Gordon McCabe in 2 S. H. S. P., 273–74.

but as Wilcox's orders from Hill were contrary to Mahone's plan, Wilcox held to his instructions and did little.[14]

Encouraged by the evident low morale of the Federal infantry in this engagement, Lee at once projected an offensive against the Federal right near the Appomattox. As most of the participating troops belonged to Beauregard, that commander prepared the plan of operations. A heavy force of artillery was placed at Hancock's Hill, on the north side of the Appomattox, and was directed to open on the morning of the 24th. Hoke's division was then to advance and was to storm the Federal line. Field was to follow, and the two were to sweep down the Union works. On the designated day, Lee rode out to the hill and joined Beauregard to witness the action. It opened brilliantly but ended abruptly when the advance of Hagood's brigade of Hoke's division was not supported. Hoke apparently thought that Field did not execute his part of the operation, but Lee was of opinion that Field could not have moved forward until Hoke had cleared the lines. "There seems to have been some misunderstanding," he said, "as to the part each division was expected to have performed"---and he dropped both the move and all criticism of it.[15]

This fiasco of the 24th offset the success of the 22d. The net advantage of current operations depended on the outcome of the cavalry raid undertaken by the Federals simultaneously with the advance of their infantry on the 21st. Union horse reached the Weldon Railroad at Reams Station, some eight miles south of Petersburg, tore up several miles of track there, and then started out in two columns, one to destroy the line of the Southside in the vicinity of Black-and-White's[16] and the other to wreck the junction at Burkeville.[17] Rooney Lee followed the former column and soon engaged it. His father was provoked that Hampton had lingered so long on the north side of the James and seemingly to so little purpose in dealing with Sheridan. On the 25th he sent the South Carolinian a rather sharp call for reinforcements.[18] On the previous day, however, Hampton had redeemed himself

---

[14] *Wilcox's MS. report,* 52.

[15] *O. R.,* 40, part 1, p. 799. For reports, see *ibid.,* pp. 796 *ff.* See also, Field in *S. H. S. P.,* 550; Venable in *ibid.,* 540; *Hagood,* 271. The last-named officer was very critical of the handling of Anderson's brigade of Field's division.

[16] Now Blackstone.   [17] See map, p. 452.   [18] *Lee's Dispatches,* 258.

by a handsome victory over Gregg at Nance's Shop,[19] and speedily sent part of his command to the Petersburg sector.

Pending its arrival, Lee followed anxiously the news of the raiders. Those who had moved to the Southside Railroad were driven from Black-and-White's, after doing some damage there, and then were hurried off to join the other column, which was destroying the Richmond and Danville. The joint force then made for the bridge across Staunton River, in the hope of burning the span, but it was repulsed valiantly on June 25 by a handful of reserves under Captain L. B. Farinholt, a young soldier whose whole military career had been one gallant adventure.[20] On the 27th Lee's information was that the column was returning to the Federal lines by a southerly route, chosen to bring the Federals back to the Weldon Railroad in the vicinity of Stony Creek, where further wreck might be wrought.[21]

When General M. C. Butler reached Lee's headquarters that day, bringing cavalry reinforcements from the northside, the commanding general received him with flattering attention, in part, perhaps, to atone for his criticism of Hampton on the 25th. As he so often did when he wished to show his appreciation of a visitor's service, he offered him some delicacy that had been sent him. "I only wish," he said, "that I had enough to divide with your gallant soldiers who have distinguished themselves so nobly." [22]

With Butler at hand, and the rest of Hampton's command coming up, Lee swiftly set a trap for the railroad wreckers. Butler was to place himself between the returning Federals and the Weldon Railroad. Hampton was to join him there. Mahone was moved out of the Petersburg lines and was advanced to Reams Station. Fitz Lee was to support him at that point with his division of cavalry, as soon as it arrived from the northside.

The plan worked out perfectly. Butler and the rest of Hampton's division formed a junction with Rooney Lee. Together they drove the enemy on the 28th and headed him for Reams Station, which the Federal commander thought was in Union hands.

[19] Sometimes called "the engagement at Samaria Church" (O. R., 40, part 2, pp. 686, 688).
[20] For Farinholt's report, see O. R., 40, part 1, p. 765.
[21] U. R. Brooks, *Butler and His Cavalry*, 272–73.   [22] *Ibid.*, *loc. cit.*

When the weary Federals approached that place on the 29th, Hampton pressed their rear, Mahone met them in front, and Fitz Lee struck their flank. The result was an utter rout, involving heavy Federal casualties, 1000 prisoners, thirteen guns, the wagon train and all the loot and Negroes that had been seized on the raid.[23]

This brilliant action gratified the army, and, though Lee did not know it, their heavy losses led the Federals to conclude that they no longer had a numerical superiority in cavalry.[24] There was much jest in Confederate camps when Mahone's returning infantry and the tired cavalrymen told of the speed with which the retreating Federal commander, who proved to be Brigadier General James H. Wilson, had hastened back to the security of the Union lines. The favorite gag was that Wilson had eagerly "torn up" the roads to break Lee's communications, and then, with like alacrity, had "torn down" the roads to escape his pursuers.[25] To Lee, however, the fact that Wilson had destroyed parts of two railways meant more than that he had scattered the dust of the country byways in returning to the Federal camps. There was a bad break on the Southside and a much worse one on the Richmond and Danville Railway that could not be repaired for weeks. Lee redoubled his efforts to strengthen his cavalry and to guard these lines of communication.[26] Meantime he hauled supplies around the gaps and pushed the work of replacing the ruined rails.[27] Writing to the President during the progress of the raid, he reaffirmed his belief that the shortage of supplies was his most serious concern, and hinted that this might compel him to attack Grant in his fortified position, dangerous as that would be.[28]

As continuous hot, dry weather forced a virtual suspension of large-scale operations toward the end of June, while the men labored to strengthen the lines,[29] the only cheer in the army was over the good news of Early's advance down the Shenandoah Valley. Hunter had retreated westward and not northward as

[23] O. R., 40, part 1, p. 752; ibid., 51, part 2, p. 1028; 9 S. H. S. P., 107; W. Gordon McCabe, an eye-witness, in 2 S. H. S. P., 274–77.
[24] 2 Meade, 209–10.   [25] 2 S. H. S. P., 277.
[26] Lee's Dispatches, 268–69, 273 ff.
[27] O. R., 40, part 2, pp. 695, 697, 697–98, 700, 701, 709. It was not thought the Richmond and Danville could be repaired before July 25 (O. R., 51, part 2, p. 1029).
[28] O. R., 37, part 1, pp. 766 ff., 769.
[29] Lee to Mrs. Lee, June 26, 1864, Fitz Lee, 354; 2 Meade, 208; Pendleton, 354.

Lee had feared,[30] but as there was at least a possibility that Hunter might return, Lee reasoned that Early's best method of dealing with that invader would be to march for the Potomac.[31] When Early approached New Market, and seemed to have a clear road to Harpers Ferry, Lee hoped for a time that his plan would work out —that a farther advance on Early's part might lead Grant to attack the Petersburg lines, in the hope of compelling him to recall the expedition.[32] And if Grant could be induced to attack, another Cold Harbor would be awaiting him!

In the respite allowed the Army of Northern Virginia by the hot weather and by the inability of the enemy to undertake a new movement,[33] Lee made many new acquaintances and renewed old friendships in the pleasant city of Petersburg. He had established his headquarters on the lawn of Violet Bank, the home of the Shippen family, just north of the Appomattox, and close to the Richmond-Petersburg turnpike.[34] It was a pleasant house, with an inviting rear balcony, and was set in a grove of trees.[35] The mistress of Violet Bank was an invalid,[36] but she was unremitting in her kindness to General Lee, as were the people of the town. They sent him many presents of food, nearly all of which he distributed in the hospitals for the comfort of the sick and wounded.[37] From Petersburg people and from friends in Richmond came also more clothing than Lee could use. "If they are not gray," he said about one lot of garments, "they are of no use to me in the field." [38] Despite the tenders of the Shippens, he kept his quarters in the old tent he had used since the West Virginia campaign of 1861, a tent now so leaky and battered that in July he had to ask that it be replaced.[39] From this tent he wrote to Mrs. Lee on the anniversary of their wedding day: "Do you recollect what a happy day thirty-three years ago this was? How many hopes and pleasures it gave birth to! God has been very merciful

[30] O. R., 51, part 2, p. 1025; Jones, 241.   [31] O. R., 37, part 1, pp. 766, 769.
[32] O. R., 37, part 1, p. 769. For Early's advance to New Market. see O. R., 51, part 2, p. 1029.
[33] Taylor MSS., July 3, 1864.
[34] Taylor's General Lee, 252; R. E. Lee, Jr., 133.
[35] Taylor MSS., July 10, 1864.   [36] R. E. Lee, Jr., 133.
[37] R. E. Lee, Jr., 132.
[38] Lee to Mrs. Lee, June 19, 1864; Fitz Lee, 353.
[39] Lee to the Q. M. G., July 21, 1864; 11 Confederate Veteran, 531.

and kind to us, and how thankless and sinful I have been." [40]
From this tent, also, he went out into the grove on Sundays for
morning worship conducted by General Pendleton, or by Reverend William H. Platt, rector of Saint Paul's, whose church in
Petersburg was under fire and had been temporarily closed.[41] At
first the bombardment had alarmed the people of the town, but
as it continued with only an occasional casualty, they became
accustomed to it and went calmly about their duty and their
pleasure. The weird sound of the passing shells became as
familiar as the whistles of their tobacco factories.[42] One day, near
the town, Lee encountered a little girl at a gate, caring for a baby.
A shell had just fallen in a nearby field, but the girl had paid no heed
to it. He drew rein: "Whose children are these?" he asked.

"This is Charles Campbell's daughter," said the girl, "and this
is General Pryor's child."

"Run home with General Pryor's baby, little girl, away from
the shells. My love to your father. I'm coming to see him." And
he rode on.[43]

It is not of record whether he found opportunity of calling on
Campbell, the historian, but he entered cheerfully into the social
life of the place, as he always did when his headquarters remained
long in one community. When he had the leisure he would often
ride into town—sometimes for a meal, more often for a call, and
not infrequently to condole with a family that had recently lost
a son or a father in battle. Hearing that Norborne Banister of
Chelsea had been killed, he went to the fine family mansion. The
funeral of the boy was in progress at the time, so Lee remained
outside till the obsequies were over, and then he quietly disappeared. The next day he returned and soon was coming almost
every Sabbath, on invitation, to dine and to talk with the family.
The usual Lord's Day fare, it is remembered, was Irish potatoes,
one slice of bacon for each person, corn bread, "coffee" made of
parched sweet potatoes, and dried apricots sweetened with sor-

[40] June 30, 1864; R. E. Lee, Jr., 133.
[41] Pendleton, 359; R. E. Lee, Jr., 134–35; Taylor's General Lee, 254. For the identification of this clergyman, the writer is indebted to Reverend G. MacLaren Brydon, his-
toriographer of the diocese of Virginia.
[42] Cf. Lewellyn Shaver: History of the Sixtieth Alabama Regt., 59.
[43] Mrs. Roger A. Pryor: My Day, 209

ghum—as sumptuous a meal as patriotic city folk could allow themselves in that famished year.[44]

If there was quiet on the Petersburg sector that permitted these social amenities, there were alarums and anxieties, hopes and forebodings on other fronts of the hard-beset South. General Early's name was on every tongue late in June, and his prospects were discussed in every council and at every bivouac. He was advancing down the Valley and soon would be in position to threaten Washington. Lee continued to hope that Grant would meet this thrust by taking the offensive. "It is so repugnant to Grant's principles and practice to send troops from him," Lee told the President, "that I had hoped before resorting to it he would have preferred attacking me."[45] Grant's talent and strategy, he wrote Custis, consisted in accumulating overwhelming numbers.[46] But, to his disappointment, Grant did not fulfill Lee's hope. Instead, signs multiplied that the Federal commander was making detachments, and as Lee was confirmed in his belief that he could not advantageously attack Grant in positions that were now exceedingly strong, he began by July 11 to consider the dispatch of troops to strengthen Early. It was a dangerous venture; perhaps it was desperate, for the Army of Northern Virginia, including Beauregard's forces, now numbered only 55,000 men of all arms.[47]

Many schemes for giving effectiveness to Early's advance were proposed. One was to organize a movement for the liberation of the prisoners at Point Lookout, so that they could join Early. Lee canvassed this thoroughly and sent his son Robert as a special courier to Early to explain his part in a projected enterprise to this end.[48] Another suggestion was to dispatch an artillery expedition against Washington. Lee deemed this scarcely practicable.[49] Still another plan was to conceal Lee's presence at Petersburg and to create the impression that he was personally leading

---

[44] Mrs. Campbell Pryor's MS. Memoirs, p. 3.

[45] O. R., 37, part 2, p. 593.

[46] Lee to G. W. C. Lee, July 24, 1864; Duke Univ. MSS.

[47] O. R., 37, part 2, pp. 594, 595, 598; cf. Lee to Davis, MS., July 23, 1864, Duke Univ. MSS. For the strength of the army on June 30, see O. R., 40, part 2, p. 707.

[48] R. E. Lee, Jr., 131; Early, 385; Lee's Dispatches, 269 ff.

[49] O. R., 37, part 2, p. 599.

the army in the Valley, as if it were engaged in a major offensive.[50]

Opinion varied in the army as to the outcome of Early's operations. Some were optimistic. Colonel Taylor wished that Jackson might have been in command,[51] and was satisfied that the blessing of Heaven would not be on a man as godless as Early.[52] Beauregard was aggrieved that the leadership had not been entrusted to him.[53] Early soon settled all doubts and vindicated Lee's confidence in him. For a time he made a continent hold its breath. By July 4 he was at Harpers Ferry; on the 6th he crossed the old battlefield of Sharpsburg; the 9th saw him on the Monocacy, where he defeated a Federal force under Major General Lew Wallace; on the 11th he was within range of the forts defending Washington. His column, however, was too feeble to venture an assault, and he had to withdraw on the 14th to Virginia soil, by way of White's Ford, above Leesburg.[54] Lee was delighted at Early's audacity and much amused at the panic his appearance created,[55] but he was not disappointed at Early's return. He had not expected him to be able to capture Washington. His view of the potential results was conservative. Before Early turned back, Lee wrote the President that the expedition might serve a useful purpose in compelling the enemy to keep troops near the Potomac.[56] He did not believe President Lincoln would willingly consent to the return to Grant of the forces sent to guard Washington;[57] but he held no high expectations unless Early was strong enough to cross the Potomac a second time, and he anticipated that the Second Corps might be forced to return to the upper Valley if Hunter's column was not called to Maryland.[58] In an effort to make it sure that Hunter would be occupied on Federal soil, Lee urged that Brigadier General John H. Morgan be sent on a raid into Pennsylvania,[59] but he argued in vain for this. Early continued to demonstrate vigorously, despite his lack of support, and on July 28 he was able to announce that he had again

[50] 2 *R. W. C. D.*, 248; *O. R.*, 51, part 2, p. 1031; P. G. T. Beauregard to W. H. Taylor, *MS.*, July 8, 1864, *R. C. Taylor, Jr. MSS.*, for the use of which letter the writer is indebted to its owner.

[51] *Taylor MSS.*, July 10, 1864: "Oh! if Jackson was only where [Early] is."

[52] *Taylor MSS.*, July 25, 1864.   [53] 2 *Roman*, 273.

[54] *Early*, 384 *ff.*; reports in *O. R.*, 37, part 1.   [55] *Lee's Dispatches*, 279–80.

[56] *Lee's Dispatches*, 279.   [57] *O. R.*, 37, part 2, p. 599.

[58] Lee to Davis, July 23, 1864, *Duke Univ. MSS.*

[59] *O. R.*, 37, part 2, pp. 601 *ff.*

forced the enemy across the Potomac and was himself at Kerns-town.[60]

The outlook in the South became gloomy while Early's advance was raising hope in some hearts. General Johnston was ma-nœuvred from his strong position on Kennesaw Mountain and fell back close to Atlanta. There were hints that he intended to abandon Atlanta, also, and he was most reticent in his communi-cations with the War Department. President Davis had discovered in the winter of 1861–62 the proclivity of General Johnston for retreating,[61] but he was slow now to give ear to the clamor that arose from Georgia for the removal of that officer.[62] Lee must have known that a change of commanders was being considered, but he was not prepared for a crisis when he received on July 12 a cipher telegram from the President announcing that it was necessary to remove Johnston and asking what he thought of Hood as a successor.[63] Lee always had cherished a high opinion of Johnston, though he was quite familiar with the peculiarities of his friend "Joe." He knew little of the immediate reasons for the contemplated action of the President, but he knew the limita-tions of Hood, at least to the time the beloved Texan had left the Army of Northern Virginia. He accordingly wrote the chief executive this characteristic reply, which Colonel Taylor coded:

"Telegram of today received. I regret the fact stated. It is a bad time to relieve the commander of an army situated as that of Tenne. We may lose Atlanta and the army too. Hood is a bold fighter. I am doubtful as to other qualities necessary." [64]

Later in the day he wrote the President more in detail:

"I am distressed at the intelligence conveyed in your telegram of today. It is a grievous thing to change commander of an army situated as is that of the Tennessee. Still if necessary it ought to be done. I know nothing of the necessity. I had hoped that Johnston was strong enough to deliver battle. We must risk much to save Alabama, Mobile and communication with the Trans-

---

[60] O. R., 37, part 1, p. 347.   [61] Cf. O. R., 2, 977.   [62] Cf. 2 Davis, 556.
[63] This telegram has been lost. Its content has to be reconstructed from Lee's an-swer, Lee's Dispatches, 282.
[64] Lee's Dispatches, 282.

Mississippi. It would be better to concentrate all the cavalry in Mississippi and Tennessee on Sherman's communications. If Johnston abandons Atlanta I suppose he will fall back on Augusta. This loses us Mississippi and communication with Trans-Mississippi. We had better therefore hazard that communication to retain the Country. Hood is a good commander, very industrious on the battlefield, careless off, and I have had no opportunity of judging of his action when the whole responsibility rested upon him. I have a high opinion of his gallantry, earnestness and zeal. General Hardee has more experience in managing an army.

"May God give you wisdom to decide in this momentous matter." [65]

This was as reserved as his counsel to the administration usually was in everything that did not pertain to supplies, recruitment, and the operations of his own army. Reading between the lines, it was plain that he doubted the wisdom alike of removing Johnston and of naming Hood. His judgment of the strategy required in the South was plainly put: Johnston, he thought, should send his cavalry against Sherman's communications and accept the risks of battle. A few days after Lee expressed these views, Secretary Seddon visited him, told him that the removal of Johnston had been decided upon, and asked his advice, as Davis had, concerning a successor. There is no record of Lee's reply other than that he declined to give positive counsel and expressed his regret at the necessity felt by the administration for a change of commanders.[66] He must have had no little misgiving when he learned on July 18 that Johnston had been ordered to turn over the army to Hood.[67] If Hood succeeded, there was hope for the South. But if he failed, only the dwindling Army of Northern Virginia stood between the Confederacy and ruin.

[65] *Lee's Dispatches*, 283–84.   [66] 2 *Davis*, 561 and note.
[67] *Cf. Gordon*, 132, though the author was mistaken as to the time of his conversation with Lee. For Taylor's comments on Lee's advice to Davis regarding the proposed removal of Johnston, see his *Four Years*, 139; *Norfolk Virginian*, Aug. 22, 1874, with Taylor's annotations, *Taylor MSS*. It is worthy of remark that though Taylor never saw the text of Lee's telegram to Davis after he put it in code, the original of that message, when subsequently discovered in the De Renne papers, bore out Taylor's description of its contents, almost to the very language. This is to be remembered in appraising statements by Taylor concerning events of which he was the only historical witness. He was remarkably accurate.

CHAPTER XXVI

LEE ENCOUNTERS A NEW TYPE OF WARFARE

("THE CRATER," JULY 30, 1864)

WEARILY, along lines that were now becoming very formidable earthworks, the survivors of Lee's many battles awaited the next move of their adversary. An hour before dawn every man was aroused and stood at arms to repel attack. After daylight, one man in two could sleep as best he might under the summer sun. The other 50 per cent of each command had to remain constantly on the alert, weapons in hand. Half an hour before dusk the whole of each regiment mounted the fire step and remained there until dark. Then those who had slept during the day went on duty.[1] Two men of each company were required to keep up infantry fire from dawn till night. Each fired once in five minutes —twenty shots to a regiment every ten minutes.[2]

The sharpshooters became so proficient on both sides that momentary exposure of the person was almost certain to result in a serious wound, if not in death. There was always, too, the danger of an exchange of mortar shells. The Federals had put these weapons into action at the beginning of the investment of Petersburg. The Confederates began to employ them on June 24.[3] It was seldom that the artillerists of either army got the exact range of the trenches, but they fired steadily, sometimes furiously, and forced the men to keep under cover, especially when in rear of the works. In hot weather the heat, the flies, and the stench of the latrines made existence a torture. When a long June drought ended and thunderstorms became frequent, the water was often two feet deep in the trenches and sometimes eighteen inches on the banquette.[4] Drainage was very slowly installed. Those who

[1] *Hagood*, 283–84.
[2] Shaver: *History of the Sixtieth Alabama Regt.*, 64.
[3] *Alexander*, 560.   [4] *Hagood*, 287.

sickened under this ordeal were scarcely better off than those who contrived to "stick it out"; for many of the field infirmaries were for a long time in wretched condition.[5]

Often, as the weary men listened in moments of silence, they thought they heard the sound of picks at work, far underground. As early as July 1, General Alexander, who was going home for a short leave on account of a wound, reported to General Lee his conviction that the enemy was mining.[6] Countershafts were sunk at intervals along the lines, and listening galleries were run out, but the engineers failed to encounter the Federal miners.[7] Suspicion was strongest that the enemy was striking for a position known as Elliott's salient, located one and five-eighths miles south of the Appomattox and nearly three-quarters of a mile southeast of Blandford Cemetery. This was, in reality, more of a re-entrant than a salient, and was a somewhat weak point, closer to the Federal works than almost any other part of the front. In rear of it a second and part of a light third line were constructed.[8]

Perhaps the precautions against the explosion of a mine were not so thorough as they might have been, because the Confederates did not believe a tunnel could be run for the 500 feet that lay between the lines. Francis Lawley, the correspondent of *The London Times,* who happened to be at Lee's headquarters when Alexander reported his suspicions, maintained that 400 feet was the absolute limit of length for such a tunnel, because ventilation could not be had for a greater distance. The men in the ranks took the talk of a mine as something of a joke and told newcomers that Grant was trying to mine all the way under Petersburg, so as to take the army in reverse. Already, they said, the Federals had carried their tunnel as far as Sycamore Street, the main thoroughfare of the town, and had installed a train. A conscript was assured that if he listened carefully, he could hear the roar of the engine, and if he looked he could see the smoke from it, rising through the spaces among the cobblestones of the roadway.[9]

All the signs of mining operations on the Petersburg front

[5] *Hagood,* 285. For Lee's efforts to remove out of range the wounded in the Petersburg hospitals, see J. H. Claiborne: *Seventy Five Years in Old Virginia,* 204 *ff.*
[6] *Alexander,* 564.
[7] *Alexander,* 565; *cf.* O. R., 40, 1, 783. *Cf. ibid.,* part 3, p. 797.
[8] *O. R.,* 40, part 1, p. 778; *ibid.,* part 2, p. 714.
[9] *Taylor MSS.,* July 25, 1864.

General Lee followed with care, but he had equal anxiety for the north side of the James River. General Ewell, who had now gone on duty, had only a small force there, consisting chiefly of the heavy artillerists at Chaffin's Bluff. In the emergency created by the movement to Petersburg, the local defense forces of the capital had been called out, and had remained on the line below Richmond until the end of June.[10] Lee also had kept two brigades of infantry at Chaffin's Bluff, though on July 4 he had to warn General Ewell that he could not count on these troops permanently.[11] In his correspondence with Custis, the General often discussed the organization of troops for any sudden attack north of that sector.[12] General Ewell, he reasoned, would be on the alert and could give a measure of protection on the water front by the use of his 20-pounder Parrott guns,[13] but Lee was convinced that he could not get early warning of any sudden advance on Richmond from the landside.[14] His apprehension was heightened by the knowledge that General Grant enjoyed the great advantage of inner lines, for the Federals had thrown a double pontoon bridge across the James at Deep Bottom, whereas Lee's pontoons were above Chaffin's Bluff.

On July 23 there were reports that Union troops had crossed to the northside. Lee thought it likely that they were intended for nothing more serious than to interrupt Confederate operations on the James, but as a precaution he ordered Kershaw's division to Chaffin's Bluff.[15] When he learned that the Federals were entrenching opposite Deep Bottom, Lee directed Kershaw to drive the enemy back and, if possible, to destroy the pontoon bridges.[16] Before Kershaw could accomplish anything, Lee discovered on the morning of July 27 that the II Corps had crossed the James, apparently for a surprise attack on Richmond. He at once dispatched General Anderson to Chaffin's Bluff, followed by Heth's division of the Third Corps. As these troops encountered both

---

[10] O. R., 40, part 2, pp. 686, 696, 711.

[11] O. R., 40, part 2, p. 713. Two brigades of Heth's division had been on the northside. McGowan's and Lane's brigades of Wilcox's division had relieved them on June 25 (Wilcox's MS. report, 54).

[12] E.g., Lee to Custis Lee, July 24, 1864; Duke Univ. MSS.

[13] O. R., 51, part 2, p. 1033.

[14] Cf. Lee's Dispatches, 272: "It is very difficult for me to get correct information here."

[15] O. R., 40, part 3, pp. 794-96. [16] O. R., 40, part 3, p. 796.

infantry and cavalry in considerable numbers on the 28th and had the worst of a skirmish with them, Lee ordered Rooney Lee's cavalry across, together with reserve artillery, and on the 29th he sent Field's division and Fitz Lee's cavalry.[17] The south-

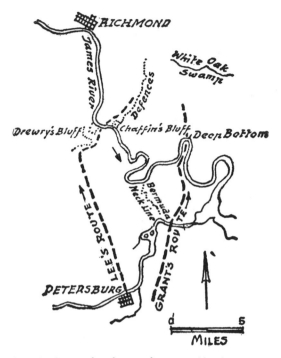

Sketch showing how, in the transfer of troops from one side of James River to the other, Grant enjoyed the advantage of a short route and in effect had the "inner lines."

side was almost denuded by these transfers. Pickett was on the Bermuda Hundred line. In front of Petersburg were only Hoke's and Johnson's divisions of Beauregard's command, Mahone's[18] division of the Third Corps and part of Wilcox's command, altogether about 18,000 infantry. To risk the very existence of this small force was to purchase security for Richmond at a heavy price. Perhaps it was at this time, when he was strained to the

---

[17] *O. R.,* 40, part 1, p. 762; *Pendleton,* 356. Alexander (*op. cit.,* 566–67) was badly mixed in his chronology of this operation. For the correct sequence of events, see Hancock's report, *O. R.,* 40, part 1, pp. 308 *ff.* Lee's display of force led the Federals to abandon what was a serious attempt to capture Richmond and to destroy the Virginia Central Railroad by a quick movement (Hancock's report, *loc. cit.*).

[18] Formerly Anderson's.

utmost to defend so long a line, that Lee began to doubt whether it was wise to attempt indefinitely to hold Richmond with his weakened army.

Late in the night of July 29–30, after reading the dispatches from the northside, Lee became satisfied that the enemy was merely making feints at other points and was preparing to attack on the Petersburg sector. At 2 A.M. on the 30th, a general warning was sent down the trenches.[19] It found Hoke on the Confederate left, defending nearly a mile of the front southward from the Appomattox. Next to Hoke, toward the right, was Bushrod Johnson's division—from left to right, Ransom's, Elliott's, Wise's, and Colquitt's brigades.[20] This was the part of the line on which the evidence of mining by the Federals had been strongest. Johnson's right rested at Rives's Salient, about a fourth of a mile northeast of the point where the Jerusalem plank road passed through the line. West of Rives's Salient, on the right of Johnson, where the Federal lines were at a greater distance, were Mahone's and half of Wilcox's divisions. The men of the Third Corps were veterans, of course, but the greater part of the defenses were in the keeping of Beauregard's army. This was in accordance with a decision that Lee had reached but naturally had never announced, to leave the less-experienced troops on the line and to employ the more seasoned units in open operations when it became necessary to draw men from the thinly held trenches. Before another twelve hours passed, Lee was to have evidence that in a crisis Beauregard's men could be as readily trusted as his own.

At 4:44 on the morning of July 30[21] there came across the Appomattox to Violet Bank the sound of a distant but mighty explosion, somewhere to the southeast of Petersburg. Was it the mine of which there had been so much speculation, or had a great magazine been fired accidentally? Lee and his staff made ready. At 6:10 a galloping officer arrived from General Beauregard.[22] On the front of Elliott's brigade, he said, the enemy had blown up the Confederate line, and under cover of a wild tornado

---

[19] McCabe, 519; 32 S. H. S. P., 359.

[20] Colquitt belonged to Hoke's division but had been assigned temporarily to Johnson, in place of Gracie, who had been detached (O. R., 40, part 1, p. 787, History of Kershaw's Brigade, 393). Colonel Roman stated (op. cit., 2, 261–62) that Johnson's left rested on the Appomattox, but he overlooked the presence of Hoke.

[21] O. R. 40, part 1, p. 557.   [22] 2 S. H. S. P., 289.

of fire had thrown forward heavy columns into the crater formed by the upheaval of hundreds of tons of earth. The Federals were already in the works and at the moment might even be advancing

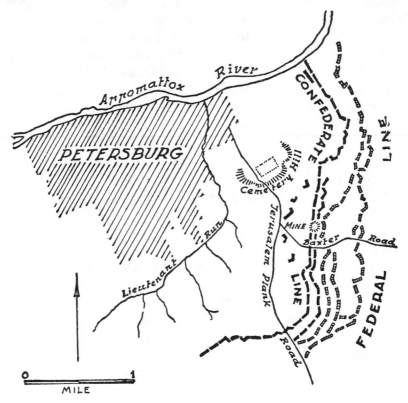

Sketch showing the relation of the Federal mine, exploded on July 30, 1864, to the Confederate defenses around Petersburg.

straight on Cemetery Hill, a sinister name, surely, in the memory of Gettysburg.

Lee's orders were given almost as soon as the message was delivered. The line must be restored at once, or Petersburg would be lost. Colonel Venable was to ride forthwith to General Mahone's headquarters and was to tell him to draw two brigades out of the line, unobserved by the enemy, and to hurry them to a position in rear of the gap in the fortifications.[23] The other

[23] *Taylor's General Lee*, 257; Lee to Mrs. Lee, July 31, 1864, *R. E. Lee, Jr.*, 135-36.

staff officers were assigned instant duty. Lee himself mounted Traveller and, unattended, hurried toward the front. At Hill's headquarters he found that officer's assistant adjutant general, Colonel W. H. Palmer, who told him that Hill had ridden off, a few minutes after the explosion, to bring up Mahone. Lee said he would go in person to expedite the movement. By a short route to the left of Halifax Street and along Lieutenant Run, he hurried with Palmer toward Mahone; but before they reached the house where Mahone was lodged they found his troops under way.[24] Lee turned at once, rode out into the open, and when he reached a point whence the break in the lines was clearly visible, he drew rein, took out his glasses and surveyed it carefully. Smoke was rising thick above it; the whole sector was aflame with bursting shell and flashing infantry fire.

How many Federal flags, he asked, could Palmer count on the works?

The young colonel took his glasses and scrutinized the whole of the captured position. Eleven, he answered.

Eleven regiments, at the least—virtually three brigades—a heavy force, not easily to be driven out!

Lee wheeled Traveller again and rode back to Mahone's column as the two brigades of Weisiger and Wright moved down Lieutenant Run.[25] Seeing that the men of the Third Corps were pressing steadily onward, Lee hastened to General Johnson's quarters, northwest of Blandford Cemetery.[26] Here he found General Beauregard, who had been forward to the Gee house, some 500 yards in rear of the crater formed by the mine. After a few words, they went on to Gee's and, from its upper windows, got an excellent view of the action that was now at white fury.[27]

The explosion had occurred about the middle of Elliott's front,

[24] 20 S. H. S. P., 203; W. H. Stewart: A Pair of Blankets, 154. Mahone's troops were on the Willcox Farm, approximately on a prolongation of Adams Street (18 S. H. S. P., 3). The ground in their rear was visible to the enemy, so they slipped back, one at a time, as if they were going to a nearby spring. The Federal commander on that part of the front, General G. K. Warren, did not know the line had been weakened, and testified as late as December, 1864, that the force opposing him had not shared in the battle (W. Gordon McCabe in 2 S. H. S. P., 289 and n., quoting 1 Report of Comm. on the Conduct of the War, 1865, p. 7).
[25] 20 S. H. S. P., 204.
[26] The location of this house was "on the crest of the hill a short distance from the northwest corner of Blandford Cemetery and near the road leading southwardly up the hill to the cemetery" (18 S. H. S. P., 6).
[27] 2 Roman, 264.

some 200 yards north of the Baxter road.[28] It had destroyed the
front line for a distance of 135 feet and had left a crater some
thirty feet deep, with a breadth, from front to rear, of ninety-
seven feet.[29] Nine companies, forming part of two South Carolina
regiments, had been blown up, together with the men of Pegram's
four-gun battery, which was stationed between the main earthworks and the cavalier trench.[30] Two of Pegram's pieces had been
left intact; the others had been hurled high in the air, and one
of them had landed in front of the wrecked fortification. A great
clod of clay, almost as large as one of the Negro cabins around
Petersburg, had been lifted from the crater and was poised on the
rim nearest the enemy.[31]

As he looked over the ground, Lee could see that the enemy
had crowded men into the crater by the thousand, and had captured about thirty yards of the line to the right of it and some
200 yards to the left.[32] Union flags floated also from the second
line, though none of the Federals were yet over its parapet. Lee
learned that Elliott's men had been demoralized by the explosion
for a few minutes only. Those who had fled from the works had
rallied quickly.[33] On the left of the crater, in the ditches, and
behind the traverses that led from the first line to the second,
they were keeping the Federals at bay. On the right, a fragment
of Elliott's brigade had the support of Wise's men, who held a
sector from which they could pour a fire into the crater and across
the field leading to it. These two brigades, almost unaided, had
met the first onslaught and had prevented the enemy from extending his front along the trenches.[34] To them, first of all, was
due the credit for saving Petersburg.

Lee thankfully observed, also, that the artillery had gone into
action quickly, and was pouring a blasting fire into the crater.
On Wise's front, Davidson's battery had two guns in a fixed

---

[28] O. R., 40, part 1, p. 787.   [29] O. R., 40, part 1, p. 788; 4 B. and L., 548–49.
[30] Ibid., and Captain Geo. B. Lake, in History of Kershaw's Brigade, 413.
[31] 4 B. and L., 561.
[32] 2 Roman, 266. The Federals claimed to have seized approximately 150 yards to
the right, but they admitted that they held this ground only a very short time (4 B. and
L., 555). "Right" and "left," in this description, are from the Confederate position,
looking toward the enemy.
[33] Cf. the statement of their commander, Colonel F. W. McMaster in 10 S. H. S. P.,
120, and in History of Kershaw's Brigade, 395.
[34] O. R., 40, part 1, p. 789.

position, looking down a shallow ravine.[35] Only one of these could bear on the enemy and this one had been abandoned for a short time by its crew, but it had been manned by Wise's troops, some of whom had been trained as artillerists, and it was now firing fast and with the deadliest precision.[36] Apparently the Federals could not locate it, though many of their field pieces were searching for it with their shells.[37] In rear of the left of the crater, where a hill rose above the covered way that ran from the right of Ransom's brigade, was Wright's battery of four 12-pounder Napoleons.[38] The elevated position of this battery gave it a clear field of fire, virtually at point-blank range into the crater.[39] When Lee turned his glasses in that direction, Wright was firing as fast as his men could serve the pieces. The enemy's shot broke about them till the very ground was pockmarked, but this seemed only to spur them to greater speed.[40] From the Jerusalem plank road, almost directly in rear of the crater, Flanner's North Carolina battery was plastering the Federals in the second line, undeterred by the ceaseless fire directed against it.[41] Some nearby mortars were sending their shells into the chasm on high, graceful arcs. The approximate position of each of these Confederate artillery units is shown in the sketch on page 473.[42]

Evidently the enemy was stopped, but for how long? With his superior artillery to cover his infantry, he might force his way up and down the trenches or dash straight forward to Cemetery Hill,[43] which was undefended. The Federals must be driven out: it might be bloody work but there was no way of avoiding it.

Where were Mahone's two brigades? Moving up the covered way, their commander said. A third brigade had been ordered to join them. Were any other reinforcements available? None, General Johnson assured Lee, except one regiment that Hoke was sending from the left, and a few of Elliott's men, who had been

[35] 10 S. H. S. P., 123.   [36] O. R., 40, part 1, pp. 760, 789.
[37] Cf. General H. J. Hunt's comments, O. R., 40, part 1, p. 281.
[38] Manned by soldiers from Halifax County, Virginia.
[39] 10 S. H. S. P., 126–27.
[40] The battery used between 500 and 600 rounds during the engagement (10 S. H. S. P., 127).
[41] 5 S. H. S. P., 247–48.
[42] Artillery subsequently brought into action does not appear. A post-bellum map, giving much more topographical detail, appears in Bernard, 321.
[43] See map, p. 468.

placed in a sheltered ravine between the lines and the Jerusalem plank road. Mahone, then, must charge with what he had— and as quickly as he could file his men into the depression where the South Carolinians were waiting. Calmly Lee directed his subordinates to prepare for the assault; carefully he counselled where the officers should place the Third Corps reserve artillery that was now arriving.[44]

The infantry fire had slackened somewhat by this time—it was now after 8—or else the ears of the combatants had been deadened to its rattle,[45] but the artillery bombardment increased in violence every moment. From across the distant Appomattox, Captain William D. Bradford began to send shell from his 20-pounder Parrotts as far south as the Hare house, in a grim warning to the enemy not to extend the front of attack.[46] Colonel John Haskell, on the Plank road, stirred his gunners to still more brilliant practice; Ellett's and Brander's pieces, under their brilliant battalion chief, Colonel William Pegram, were in battery and added their salvos to the din.[47] Fourteen Union flags were visible now; Federal officers could be seen on the parapet of the second line, waving their swords and urging their men to come out of the ditch and charge up Cemetery Hill.[48]

How much more time would be required to get all the men out of the covered way and into the ravine? Daniel Weisiger, the senior colonel of Mahone's old Virginia brigade, was working furiously to make ready; General Mahone's aide, Captain Victor Girardey, was everywhere; Mahone himself, with encouraging words, was hurrying late-comers into place. The Georgia brigade of Wright, which had marched on the heels of the Virginians, was gathering on their right. At last the word was given for the men to move out of the ravine and to crouch in the open as they formed their line. Only one special instruction was given—that the troops should not fire till they were on the enemy.[49]

At the Gee house, Lee knew that Mahone was forming, and he must have watched with anxious eyes the gray regiments spread themselves along the ravine; but still more anxiously must he have

44 Cf. Pendleton, 359: "General Lee as usual directed with consummate judgment."
45 McMaster in History of Kershaw's Brigade, 399–400.
46 10 S. H. S. P., 127.   47 2 S. H. S. P., 285, 289.
48 History of Kershaw's Brigade, 401.   49 2 S. H. S. P., 291.

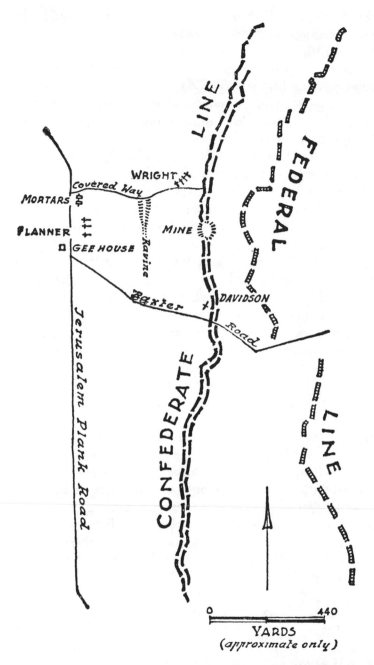

Position of certain Confederate batteries employed in the counterattack of July 30, 1864, for the recovery of that part of the line occupied by the Federals after the mine explosion.

looked to the occupied line to see if the Federals would advance before the Confederates were ready for them.

Soon a Federal officer on the parapet seized a flag, called once more to his men to charge, and sprang down toward the open ground between him and the Confederates. Out from the works came his followers, their number swelling every second.[50]

Girardey saw them leaping over the parapet, and cried out, "General, they are coming!"

"Tell Weisiger to move forward," said Mahone on the instant.

But Weisiger had not waited for orders. He had shouted "Forward" at the same instant that Girardey had called to Mahone, and his 800 men, with some of the Georgia troops and a fragment of Elliott's brigade, raised the old rebel yell and started up the hill.[51]

As Lee saw the valiant gray line spring up from the ground at the very instant the Federals started their charge, he must have had some of the exhilaration he had felt that day at Fredericksburg when he had told Longstreet it was well war was so terrible or they would grow too fond of it.[52] Up the hill the line swept, its ragged battle flags flying, with the fire of all the Confederate batteries redoubled as if in applause. Soon it was apparent that the right of the Georgia brigade had not started with the rest. The front of attack was too short to cover all that part of the line held by the Federals. Perhaps, too, the men unconsciously obliqued to the left, for when they approached the second line, their right was perhaps 100 yards to the left of the crater.[53] "No quarter!" some foolish Federal cried, as they leaped into the rear work. They answered with one volley, jumped over the parapet and fought it out with bayonet and clubbed musket.[54] Only a few minutes of this and then, their lines irregular but unbroken, they rushed for the front trench. Thrust and counterthrust there, and soon, through the smoke, the red of their flags could be seen on the main parapet.[55]

---

[50] 2 *S. H. S. P.*, 291.

[51] A controversy echoed for years over the question of whether Weisiger or Mahone ordered the charge. The conclusion here reached is practically that to which the chief protagonist of General Mahone arrived in 28 *S. H. S. P.*, 220.

[52] See *supra*, vol. II, p. 462.   [53] 28 *S. H. S. P.*, 205–6.

[54] W. H. Stewart: *A Pair of Blankets*, 155–56.

[55] 2 *S. H. S. P.*, 291–92; 28 *ibid.*, 205–6. It must be remembered that when the

Most of the ground on the left was recovered in this charge; the gap was narrowed; Haskell's mortars were brought close up, where they could drop their shells into the crater with so light a charge of powder that the gunners had to smile;[56] gleefully Mahone's men collected the hundreds of muskets the enemy had dropped.[57] Now for the right! Those of the Georgia brigade who had not assaulted with Weisiger were ordered forward to take the second line, immediately behind the crater. At 10:30 they advanced, but met so heavy a fire that they, too, drifted to the left and only reached the rear position where it was already occupied by their comrades.[58] Still the enemy held the crater, a section of the main line on either side of it, that part of the second line just in rear of it, and some scattered rifle pits. On the left of the chasm, Mahone's and Elliott's troops steadily drove the Federals back along the front line until they were almost to the edge of the crater, and on the right Wise's brigade pushed the foe to the very rim.

One more effort must be made, this time by the third brigade of Mahone's division, Saunders's Alabamians, who had been summoned from the right before the first advance. Arriving at 11 o'clock, they were disposed with care. The order was that when they went forward, the other infantry commands on either side the crater, and Colquitt's brigade on the right of Johnson's division, were to co-operate with every musket and every man. Saunders's troops were told to stoop low as they went up the grade, until they reached the point where they could see the enemy. Then they were to break into the doublequick and were not to halt until they reached the crater. Lee sent word to Saunders that he had no more troops available. If the Alabamians did not take the crater on the first assault, he said, he would re-form them and would lead them in person.[59] The thing *had* to be done and done by Saunders. The remainder of the line had been stripped almost bare to supply troops for the counterattacks. On the front from which Mahone had been drawn there was only one man every twenty paces.[60]

Federals held these works, which the Confederates had constructed, "parapet" and "ditch" were in reversed position: the "ditch" was nearest the attacking Southerners, and Federals were where the outer side of the Confederate "parapet" had been.

[56] 2 *S. H. S. P.*, 292.
[57] 2 *S. H. S. P.*, 292.
[58] 2 *S. H. S. P.*, 292.
[59] 25 *S. H. S. P.*, 84.
[60] 33 *S. H. S. P.*, 364.

As Saunders's brigade gathered in the ravine for this grim business, a soldier covered with dirt and powder came up to Captain James C. Featherstone. "Captain," he said, "can I go into this charge with you?"

"Yes," said Featherstone hurriedly. "Who are you?"

The man gave his name, which unfortunately has been lost, and explained that he belonged to one of the South Carolina regiments that had been blown up. "I want to get even with them," he said. "Please take my name, and if I get killed inform my officers of it."

"I have no time for writing now," Featherstone answered. "How high did they blow you?"

"I don't know," the man replied, "but as I was going up I met the company commissary officer coming down, and he said, 'I will try to have breakfast ready by the time you get down.' " [61]

The spirit of this brave fellow was that of the Alabama troops whom he had joined, for the brigade had been Wilcox's, and among its 628 survivors were some who had distinguished themselves in their most renowned battle, that of Salem Church. They were ready now. It was 1 o'clock. On the second, the order "Forward!" went down the line, and the men began to creep out from the ravine and up the hill. The artillery roared anew; the shells screamed over their heads like frightened birds. Soon all were in the open, where the enemy's fire began to tell on their ranks. But this time there was no obliquing. Directly up the incline they went, straight for the crater. Lee watched them, now hidden in smoke, now visible, and saw them reach the second line, from which the enemy had fled. They waited there only long enough to catch their breath and were about to dash into the crater when, at one point, a white flag was raised and the Federals surrendered. At another place on the crater rim the fighting kept up. By direction of Colonel J. H. King, some of the Alabama troops lifted their caps on their ramrods just over the rim of the crater. A hundred bullets tore them to tatters, and the volley that was meant for the men was wasted. Immediately the Alabamians sprang into the crater,[62] followed by soldiers from the other brigades of the division. The mêlée was like a battle of de-

[61] 33 S. H. S. P., 362. [62] 33 S. H. S. P., 364.

spairing demons. One captain fell dead with eleven bayonet thrusts.[63] The sight of Negro troops, whom they now encountered in close action for the first time, seemed to throw Mahone's men into a frenzy. Bewildered by the onslaught, all the Federals who could do so fell back into a smaller pit, in front of which the explosion had raised an earthen barrier. The Confederates were preparing to follow them there, when there were wild cries, shouts, uplifted hands, frantic appeals, and a final surrender.[64] Meantime, thousands of the Federals had scurried across the open ground toward their abatis, preferring the chance of falling before Confederate bullets to the certainty of long confinement in Southern prisons.

The "Battle of the Crater" was over. As quickly as it could be done, an earthwork was run around the edge of the pit and the line was restored. At 3:25, Lee was able to report to the War Department, "We have retaken the salient and driven the enemy back to his lines with loss." [65] Mahone counted 1101 prisoners[66] and Johnson's division had a lesser quota. Twenty flags were taken.[67] The price paid by the Confederates was about 1500, of whom 278 lost their lives or were captured when the mine exploded.[68]

Lee was much gratified that so serious a threat had been repulsed with such unequal losses, and he said of the action, "Every man in it has today made himself a hero." [69] He at once had Mahone regularly promoted to command of the division he had been temporarily heading,[70] and he raised both Colonel Weisiger and Captain Girardey to the rank of brigadier general.[71] The camps rejoiced and told incredible tales of what had happened, but the full horror of the struggle in that inferno of man's own making was not apparent until August 1, when many of the Confederates entered the crater during a truce declared at the request of General Meade.[72] "The sight," wrote Colonel Taylor,

[63] Richard Lewis: *Camp Life of a Confederate Boy*, 57.
[64] 2 *S. H. S. P.*, 293; 33 *ibid.*, 364.   [65] *O. R.*, 40, part 1, p. 752.
[66] *Alexander*, 572.   [67] *O. R.*, 40, part 1, p. 753.
[68] *O. R.*, 40, part 1, p. 788. The Federal casualties, prisoners included, were 4008 (*Alexander*, 572).
[69] W. H. Stewart: *A Pair of Blankets*, 168.   [70] *O. R.*, 42, part 2, pp. 1156–57.
[71] Marcus J. Wright: *General Officers of the Confederate Army*, 123; 6 *C. M. H.*, 421.
[72] *O. R.*, 40, part 3, pp. 691, 821.

". . . was gruesome indeed. The force of the explosion had carried earth, guns, accoutrements and men some distance skyward, the whole coming down in an inextricable mass; portions of the bodies of the poor victims were to be seen protruding from immense blocks of earth. . . . The bottom of the pit . . . was covered with dead, white and black intermingled, a horrible sight." [73]

[73] *Taylor's General Lee,* 258. The proposal to mine the Confederate works was made by Lieutenant Colonel Henry Pleasants, a mining engineer, whose regiment consisted largely of coal diggers. General Burnside, commanding the IX Corps, approved the plan. Work was begun on June 25 and was pushed vigorously by Pleasants. The main gallery was 510 feet long, with two laterals. The eight magazines, after completion on July 23, were filled with a total of 8000 pounds of powder. The high command of the Army of the Potomac was skeptical of success, but it sanctioned the assault (4 *B. and L.,* 545; 2 *Meade,* 217). The attack was delivered by Ledlie's 1st Division of the IX Corps, followed by parts of the other three divisions of that command. The failure of the enterprise was the subject of a court of inquiry, the testimony before which is printed in *O. R.,* 40, part 1, pp. 42 *ff.* The reasons were defective co-ordination, tardiness on the part of some of the units, and, fundamentally, the crowding into the crater of too many troops. This last condition, in turn, was attributable to bad leading, to the effort of new troops to seek shelter, and to the practical difficulty of getting the men out of the crater, once they had entered it (*cf.* 5 *Correspondence of B. F. Butler,* 1 *ff.*). Some picturesque details of the battle, not given in the text, or in the authorities cited *supra,* will be found in Bernard, *op. cit.,* and in *MS. Memoirs of W. B. Freeman.*

CHAPTER XXVII

The Loss of the Weldon Railroad

BLOODY as had been the repulse of Grant at the Crater, Lee expected him to continue mining[1] and he pressed the work of driving countershafts.[2] While watching this, he learned on August 4 that General Grant was moving troops down James River. "I fear," Lee wrote the President, "that this force is intended to operate against General Early, and when added to that already opposed to him, may be more than he can manage. Their object may be to drive him out of the Valley and complete the devastation they [had] commenced when they were ejected from it."[3] The Confederate commander realized Grant had so entrenched himself that he could now send off troops to dispose of Early and still hold his lines. Lee felt that he could release only two divisions, at most, and in doing that would not have a single unit outside the trenches. But he concluded that if it were Grant's intention to overwhelm Early, it would be better to detach troops than to risk the loss of Early's little army and of the Virginia Central Railroad.

Once Lee reached a decision to send reinforcements to any point, he considered that promptness was half of advantage; so, on August 6, he went to Richmond and held a conference with President Davis and General Anderson.[4] The conclusion reached at this council was to dispatch Kershaw's division of infantry and Fitz Lee's cavalry to northern Virginia under General Anderson. The plan was that Anderson should not join Early at once, but should take position in Culpeper, where he could menace the flank and rear of the Federals in case they advanced up the Valley against Early.[5] The troops moved the same day,[6] and when re-

[1] Lee to Mrs. Lee, July 31, 1864, *R. E. Lee, Jr.*, 135–36; *O. R.*, 42, part 2, p. 1161.
[2] *O. R.*, 42, part 1, pp. 883, 884, 887, 888; *ibid.*, part 2, pp. 1155, 1158, 1162–63, 1208; *Pendleton*, 367.
[3] *O. R.*, 42, part 2, p. 1161.
[4] *O. R.*, 42, part 1, p. 873; *Taylor MSS.*, Aug. 7, 1864.   [5] *O. R.*, 43, part 1, p. 996.
[6] *History Kershaw's Brigade*, 417. No reports of the date of Fitz Lee's departure are available, but Federal reports indicate that he was in northern Virginia not later than Aug. 10 (*O. R.*, 42, part 2, p. 144).

ports multiplied of further detachments from Grant—though Lee was not persuaded that the reports were true as to infantry[7]—he prepared to send to Anderson the rest of the cavalry corps, except Rooney Lee's division.[8] His hope was that Anderson might employ the troopers north of the Potomac or east of the Blue Ridge, and prevent too heavy a concentration against Early.[9] Had Lee been able to carry out this plan the course of the war might have been affected by it, for Sheridan might not then have been free to throw his whole strength against Early.[10]

On August 11 Lee went across Bermuda Neck, by this time known in the army as the Howlett line,[11] in order to observe the Federal activities at Dutch Gap. General Butler was reported to be digging a canal at that point, an operation Lee sought to interrupt, because, if it succeeded, the enemy might turn the left of the Howlett line. Again on the 13th General Lee visited that sector to observe the artillery fire.[12] The next day, August 14, the enemy attacked with vigor on the north side of James River. Major General Charles W. Field was in actual command there, though General Ewell headed the department. Field's division of the First Corps and the Chaffin's Bluff garrison occupied an advanced line that ran from the bluff to New Market Heights and thence past Fussell's Mill to the Charles City road. This line, however, was so long that from the mill to the Charles City road the works were merely patrolled by Gary's small brigade of cavalry.

The Federals seized the works near Fussell's Mill early on the 14th, but were met by two regiments of dismounted cavalry, and

---

[7] O. R., 42, part 2, pp. 1161, 1170; *ibid.*, 43, part 1, p. 993.

[8] O. R., 42, part 2, pp. 1170–71, 1171–72.

[9] O. R., 43, part 1, p. 996; *ibid.*, 51, part 2, p. 1034.

[10] Meade remarked on Aug. 13 that the Army of the Potomac would make an effort the next day to test Lee's strength and force him to recall the troops sent to northern Virginia. "Should this fail," said he, "we will be obliged to go up there and leave Richmond" (2 *Meade*, 222).

[11] After the Howlett family that had two homes close to the Confederate positions. On this visit, or another during the summer, Lee rode out with General Eppa Hunton and found the Federal pickets very close to the Confederate lines. "Who are those people out there?" Lee asked. Hunton told him. Lee inquired: "What are they doing there? We are in the habit of believing this country belongs to us. Drive them away, sir; drive them away!" That night Hunton did so. (*Autobiography of Eppa Hunton*, 171.)

[12] O. R., 42, part 2, pp. 1172, 1176; *cf. ibid.*, 1169, 1290 *ff.*; R. E. Lee, Jr., 136; G. Wise: *History of the Seventeenth Virginia*, 194. Mr. Wise was in error by twenty-four hours as to the date of Lee's two visits.

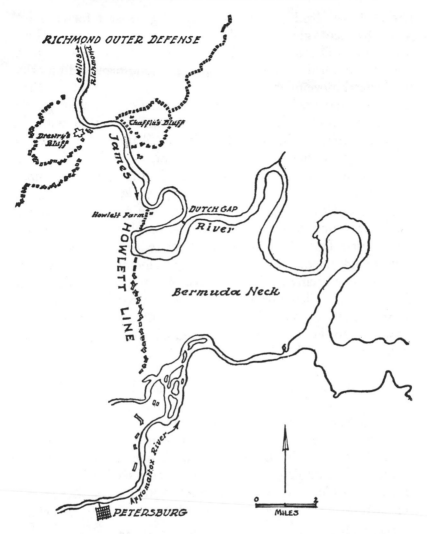

Sketch of the Confederate defenses on the Drewry's Bluff-Howlett line sector, showing how the completion of the Dutch Gap canal might make it possible for the Federal fleet to turn the Howlett line.

when Field brought up a brigade of infantry, the enemy was flanked and forced to retire.[13] The news of this reached General

[13] 14 *S. H. S. P.*, 551–52. This narrative is by General Field and is almost the only adequate account of a very interesting series of engagements.

Lee at Violet Bank, as he was preparing to start for church.[14] With Kershaw gone and all the cavalry except Rooney Lee's division and Dearing's brigade on the way to northern Virginia, Lee of course had no troops to spare. His judgment told him that the Federal move might be a feint, but after assurance from Field that it was serious,[15] he ordered two brigades of infantry from the Petersburg front.[16] At the same time, and doubtless with the deepest regret, he directed Hampton to abandon his march to join Anderson and to hurry back to assist Field.[17] Once again, the initiative enjoyed by the numerically superior enemy upset Lee's strategy.

Going to Chaffin's Bluff in person on the morning of August 15,[18] Lee found that except for some cavalry fighting on the Confederate left[19] the Federals had not renewed the action that day, though they were manifestly very numerous and were fortifying.[20] The enemy's delay gave Lee time to bring up the troops that had been ordered from the southside, together with a scratch brigade from Pickett's division.[21] The infantry were extended somewhat to the left of Fussell's Mill, and Rooney Lee's cavalry took position on the Charles City road. The situation was then about as shown on page 483.[22]

While in the vicinity of Chaffin's Bluff, during the forenoon of the 16th, Lee heard from Field that the Federal cavalry had driven Rooney Lee's pickets from White Oak Swamp and were moving in force up the Charles City road toward White's Tavern.[23] This was ominous news, for Field's line ran at a wide angle to the Richmond defenses,[24] and the Federals were thus already in rear of his left and on a direct road to Richmond. Lee at once sent a message to President Davis asking that the local defense

---

[14] R. E. Lee, Jr., 136.   [15] O. R., 42, part 2, p. 1177.

[16] Probably Harris's and Girardey's; see 14 S. H. S. P., 553.

[17] O. R., 42, part 2, p. 1177.

[18] Taylor MSS., Aug. 15, 1864; Taylor's General Lee, 261; 14 S. H. S. P., 554; Richmond Howitzers Battalion, 271.   [19] O. R., 42, part 2, p. 1189.

[20] 14 S. H. S. P., 552.   [21] Loehr, 53.

[22] It is impossible to draw the line with accuracy, especially on the Confederate left beyond Fussell's Mill, as the works northeast of that point were much changed after General Longstreet returned to duty in October. The sketch in the text has, however, been corrected on the ground by Kenneth A. Tapscott of the United States Park Service and is believed to be substantially accurate.

[23] O. R., 42, part 2, p. 1180.

[24] Field said (14 S. H. S. P., 551) that the lines were perpendicular, but this could only have been an approximation.

troops be called out to man the outer line around the city, and he prepared to take Field's left brigades and to throw them against the flank of the force on the Charles City road.[25] For that

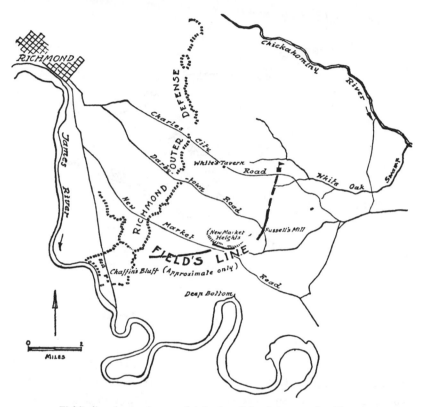

Field's line (approximate only) in the affair of August 16, 1864.

purpose Lee rode along the advanced line, toward Field's position near Fussell's Mill. But before he could reach that point, and long before the tocsin was sounded in Richmond, the enemy had approached within fifty yards of the light Confederate works, to the left of the mill. Then, with a rush and a cheer, the Federals charged. Two Southern brigades broke, and a gap was torn in Field's front.[26] The situation is shown on page 484.

But most of Field's men were tested veterans of many a battle. At the call of their commander, they shifted to the left and

[25] *O. R.,* 42, part 2, p. 1180.   [26] 14 *S. H. S. P.,* 553-54.

opposed a line to the Federals, who, fortunately, did not realize the magnitude of their advantage. Then, in a quick counterattack, Field's division pushed the Union troops back and speedily re-

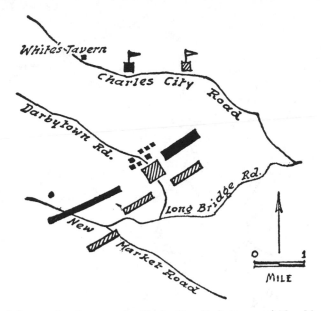

Position of the opposing forces on the Charles City, Darbytown, and New Market roads in the affair of August 16, 1864.

covered the works. A little later, on the Charles City road, more by chance than by fine logistics, the van of Hampton's returning division arrived to support Rooney Lee. Together these troopers ran the enemy across White Oak Swamp.[27] The crisis ended as quickly as it had arisen.

In the midst of the pursuit of the Federals, while Lee was giving orders to hurrying staff officers and couriers, a characteristic incident occurred. One of a group of prisoners came boldly up to him and complained that a Confederate private had taken from him a soldier's most-prized possession, his hat. Lee at once suspended what he was doing, had the Federal point out the man, saw that the hat was returned, and then, without even a shadow of annoyance at the interruption, turned back to his task as if the recovery of captives' headgear were part of his daily duty. "I

[27] 14 S. H. S. P., 554; O. R., 42, part 2, pp. 1180, 1181, 1189.

wondered at him taking any notice of a prisoner in the midst of battle," wrote another Union soldier who was captured that day. "It showed what a heart he had for them." [28]

As the enemy did not renew the battle on August 17, Lee prepared a cavalry operation for the 18th to clear his left flank along the Charles City road. This was measurably successful,[29] but before it was fully developed Beauregard telegraphed that a Federal column in front of Petersburg was moving toward the Weldon Railroad. Having no reserves outside the trenches, Beauregard asked reinforcements.[30] Subsequently, he sent a reassuring message that the column appeared to be small and that he had sent some infantry to support General Dearing's cavalry, who were opposing the enemy's advance.[31] Lee, however, did not relish the prospect of having only one brigade of cavalry on the right of the Petersburg sector and he ordered Rooney Lee to proceed to the southside at once.[32] By the morning of the 19th it developed that at least three divisions of Federal infantry were on the Weldon Railroad, in the vicinity of Globe Tavern, three and a half miles south of the Confederate right at Petersburg. Beauregard stated that he was moving out against these troops with four brigades of infantry and with the cavalry that Lee was sending. Although he telegraphed, "Result would be more certain with a stronger force of infantry," he did not renew his appeal for reinforcements.[33]

Later in the day of the 19th indications pointed to a return to the southside of part of the troops that had been operating on Field's front.[34] That same afternoon, A. P. Hill struck the enemy's column near Globe Tavern, and captured 2700 prisoners.[35] Lee did not gamble on this advantage. In order that Beauregard might have sufficient troops for his offensive, Lee quickly dispatched to the Petersburg sector all the infantry that had been sent to Field's relief.[36] The Federals, however, kept their grip on the Weldon Railroad and could not be dislodged with the force that Beauregard had employed.

[28] John E. Davis to Charles Marshall, n. d., 17 *S. H. S. P.*, 242.
[29] *O. R.*, 51, part 2, pp. 1035–36.   [30] *O. R.*, 42, part 1, p. 857.
[31] *O. R.*, 42, part 1, p. 857.   [32] *R. L. T. Beale*, 141.
[33] *O. R.*, 42, part 1, p. 858.   [34] *O. R.*, 42, part 2, p. 1190.
[35] *O. R.*, 42, part 1, p. 940.   [36] 14 *S. H. S. P.*, 554–55.

485

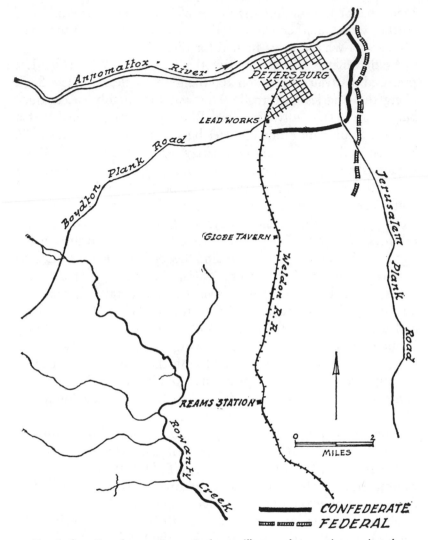

Terrain from Petersburg to Reams Station, to illustrate the operations against the Petersburg and Weldon Railroad.

If the battle was to be renewed, it was plain that still more troops had to be used. Lee urged this on Beauregard.[37] On the morning of the 21st he ordered Hampton to move his division south of the Appomattox, and after a time he directed Field to

[37] Lee's messages of Aug. 20 are missing, but their purport can be gathered, in part, from Beauregard to Lee, *O. R.*, 42, part 2, p. 1192.

send two of his brigades, if the enemy had reduced force north of the James.[38] He decided, also, to go to Petersburg and to see for himself the situation on the Weldon Railroad. He arrived on an excessively hot afternoon,[39] in time to witness a gallant but futile attack by Mahone in front of Globe Tavern. During the course of this fight, through misunderstanding on the part of Hill and Mahone, General Hagood threw his brigade into a re-entrant in the Federal lines and had to lead back the survivors under a heavy fire.[40] Mahone reconnoitred again and told Lee that if he were given two more brigades he would guarantee to drive the Federals from the railroad. Lee assented and sent for the reinforcements, but when they failed to arrive in time[41] he concluded that the enemy had too firm a hold on the railroad to be shaken.[42]

The contingency Lee had anticipated from the time he took up the Petersburg line was at hand: The northern end of the Weldon Railroad from Rowanty Creek to Petersburg was definitely lost. The defense of the capital and the subsistence of the Army of Northern Virginia had now to depend on the full employment of the Southside and of the Richmond and Danville Railroads. There were murmurings in Richmond that the Weldon line need not have been lost if Beauregard had met the first advance with a larger column,[43] but Lee knew both the limitations under which Beauregard fought and the inevitability of the capture of the road by the enemy. With the simple assertion that "the smallness of the attacking force prevented it from dislodging" the foe,[44] he devoted himself to making the most of the lines of supply left him.

The loss of the Weldon Railroad came, unfortunately, at a time when there was no corn either in Richmond or at the army depots around Petersburg.[45] Lee at once set wagon trains to hauling supplies over the twenty miles of road that lay between Petersburg and Stony Creek, which was on the Weldon Railroad line

---

[38] *O. R.*, 42, part 2, pp. 1192–93.   [39] 1 *N. C. Regts.*, 680.

[40] *O. R.*, 42, part 1, pp. 858, 936; *Hagood*, 288 ff.; W. V. Izlar: *Edisto Rifles*, 84–85; *History of McGowan's Brigade*, 164–65; 4 *B. and L.*, 568 ff.; *McCabe*, 524 ff.; Mahone and Hill manfully assumed responsibility for the disaster to Hagood.

[41] W. Gordon McCabe in 2 *S. H. S. P.*, 296 n.   [42] *O. R.*, 42, part 2, p. 1194.

[43] *O. R.*, 42, part 2, p. 1198.   [44] *O. R.*, 42, part 2, p. 1194.

[45] *O. R.*, 42, part 2, p. 1195.

below the point where it had been torn up by the Federals. He believed that by the diligent use of these trains, and of the remaining railroads, with perhaps some importation of grain by way of Wilmington, it would be possible to subsist the army until the Virginia corn crop was harvested.[46] In a wider view, with an eye to the presidential campaign in the North, where McClellan was opposing Lincoln, Lee believed that the failure of the Federals to drive the Confederates from Petersburg, after so much sacrifice, would have a dispiriting effect on the people of the United States.[47] Seddon, seeing the immediate problem, and knowing more of politics, was not optimistic. He felt acute concern because Lee's army and that of Hood were now drawing corn from the same territory.[48]

Four days after Lee decided to abandon the effort to recover the Weldon Railroad, there came a dramatic epilogue. With Rooney Lee's division and his own, now under M. C. Butler of South Carolina, General Hampton was operating west of the railway and in front of the Confederate right. A reconnaissance in force toward Reams Station, some four and a half miles south of Globe Tavern, showed Hampton that the Federals were tearing up the railroad near that point. He found that they were not well placed and he asked the assistance of the infantry in making an attack.[49] It was desirable, of course, that the enemy should not be left free to destroy the railroad indefinitely to the southward, for this would increase the distance between Petersburg and that part of the railroad still in Southern hands. In the political situation, also, every defeat would tend to discredit the war party in the North. With these considerations in mind Lee read Hampton's proposal sympathetically and decided to adopt it. But the mistake of attacking with insufficient force was not to be repeated. Two brigades of Heth's division, two of Mahone's, and three of Wilcox's were ordered to move for Reams Station; Hampton's old division of cavalry and Rooney Lee's were both to

---

[46] O. R., 42, part 2, p. 1195; Lee's Dispatches, 289. Cf. Taylor MSS., Aug. 28, 1864: . . . "and really whilst we are inconvenienced by [the loss of the railroad], no material harm is done us" (cf. 2 Davis, 647).

[47] O. R., 42, part 2, p. 1195. In this reference "unsuccessful" is manifestly a lapsus pennae for "successful."

[48] O. R., 42, part 2, pp. 1195, 1198, 1199.

[49] E. L. Wells, 277; U. R. Brooks: Butler and His Cavalry, 303 ff.

be employed.⁵⁰ Besides the two brigades that Field had been ordered to bring to Petersburg,⁵¹ it would appear that he was now directed to send a third.⁵²

On the afternoon of August 24⁵³ the infantry brigades were

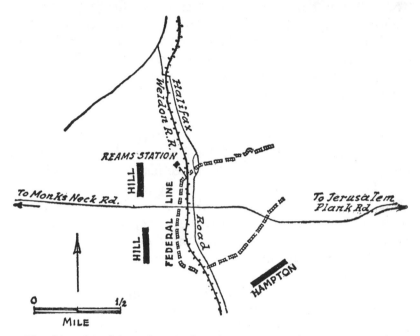

Disposition of Confederate forces in the action at Reams Station, August 24, 1864.

quietly moved beyond the right of the Confederate trenches and were marched by roads that led toward Reams Station from the west. The next morning, with Hampton clearing the way, they advanced eastward through a wooded country. They found Hancock's II Corps in front of some feeble works at Reams Station, entirely separated from the V Corps of Warren, which was farther up the railroad. An assault during the early afternoon by two of the brigades under Wilcox was repulsed. After a brief delay, part of his division and some of Heth's troops attacked

---

⁵⁰ *Cf.* 19 *S. H. S. P.,* 114.   ⁵¹ *O. R.,* 42, part 2, p. 1193.

⁵² This is inferential and is based on the fact that Lee's orders (*O. R.,* 42, part 2, p. 1193) covered only two brigades, whereas Field stated subsequently that he sent three (14 *S. H. S. P.,* 555).

⁵³ *Wilcox's MS. report,* 55.

farther to the left. They were brilliantly supported by Pegram's artillery and quickly stormed the right of the Federal lines. Simultaneously, Hampton worked his way around to the Federal left and, dismounting his men, threw them against the enemy. The victory was immediate and decisive, for the raw recruits in Hancock's corps behaved badly. Some 2000 of them were captured, along with nine guns, and the attempt of the Federals to destroy more of the railroad was abandoned. The Confederate infantry brought off their wounded, buried their dead, and returned the same night to Petersburg.[54]

Like almost every other Confederate reverse during the investment of Petersburg, the loss of the Weldon raid had its origin in the disparity of forces with which Lee had to defend so long a line. His diminished army was not strong enough to meet quickly all the blows that Grant could deliver by shifting his attack from one side of the James to the other. Then, too, Grant's strategy was far better than it had been at any stage of the operations since he had taken command in the East. His drive against Field on August 14–16 had not been, as Lee thought, a major attempt to seize Richmond,[55] but had been intended primarily to destroy the Virginia Central Railroad and in that way to prevent the dispatch of reinforcements to Early.[56] As the attack on the northside had developed, Grant's strategy had changed somewhat. He had initiated the advance to Lee's right merely as a flank movement that might afford him an opening for an attack in the vicinity of the lead works,[57] and he had not considered that Lee had reduced his force sufficiently to justify any large-scale operation in that

[54] There are no detailed Confederate reports of the battle of Reams Station except that of Hampton (O. R., 42, part 1, p. 942) and that of Wilcox, in MS. The Federal reports appear in O. R., 42, part 1, pp. 222 ff. Perhaps the best Confederate narrative is that of Charles M. Stedman in 19 S. H. S. P., 113 ff. See also E. L. Wells, 277 ff., and U. R. Brooks: Butler and His Cavalry, 303 ff.; History of McGowan's Brigade, 180–81. The Federal casualties, prisoners included, were 2742 (O. R., 42, part 1, p. 131). The Confederate losses are not reported fully but in Wilcox's command they amounted to "over 300" (Wilcox's MS. report, 61), and in the cavalry corps they were 94 (E. L. Wells, 283). The total, on this basis, could hardly have exceeded 600.

[55] O. R., 42, part 2, p. 1194.

[56] These reasons are set forth much more explicitly in O. R., 42, part 2, pp. 132 and 148, with their reference to O. R., 40, part 3, p. 437, than in 2 Grant's Memoirs, 321.

[57] O. R., 42, part 2, p. 411. The lead works were located on the Halifax road, just beyond the southeastern end of the city, about three-fourths of a mile northwest of Battery Pegram (see the map p. 486).

quarter. The thrust at the Weldon Railroad had been almost an afterthought and had been undertaken by Grant as a reconnaissance in force, though with the ultimate object of compelling Lee to recall troops from Early, so that Sheridan might strike a blow.[58] Throughout the attacks of August, Lee moved his troops skillfully from right to left, with the soundest judgment and the greatest promptness; but Grant was both lucky and successful, not precisely in the manner he had hoped, but probably in a larger measure than he expected. His operation on the northside did not reach the Virginia Central Railroad, but it spelled the doom of Early because it forced Lee to bring back Hampton, then on his way to oppose Sheridan. The move to the Weldon Railroad was very costly in life and it did not compel Lee to summon immediately to Petersburg any part of Early's infantry, but it did place Grant where he could farther extend his left and bring the Confederate line one notch nearer the strangulation of a formal siege. The fortunes of war, which in this case were but another name for numerical inferiority, were running strongly against Lee. He saw plainly that Grant's operations were designed to starve him out,[59] and for this last, dreadful struggle he prepared himself as best he could with his ever-dwindling resources.

[58] *O. R.*, 42, part 2, p. 244.   [59] *O. R.*, 42, part 2, p. 1194.

CHAPTER XXVIII

Götterdämmerung

After the close of the battles for the Weldon Railroad, Lee returned to Chaffin's Bluff. Neither to his staff nor to the other soldiers he met on his daily rounds did he disclose any of the deep concern he must have felt. He had been a bit irritable at head-quarters, where his staff had now been reduced to three,[1] but on the lines he was as cheerful as ever and seemed in good health and spirits.[2] One day, during the operations on the north side of the James, he was standing on the steps of the Libby house when he saw a small and very fat dog come wandering around the corner of the building. His risibles were stirred. Turning to Colonel Thomas H. Carter's courier, Percy Hawes, a youngster whose scant hundred pounds covered the heart of a lion, he said in his gravely jesting voice, "Percy, don't you think he would make good soup?"[3] During the same engagements, he guyed Colonel Carter with great satisfaction because he encountered that intrepid officer's body-servant going to the rear with much equipage and jangling utensils of cookery, having served the colonel his breakfast on the line.[4] It was about this time also, when he was in an exposed position, under hot shell-fire, that Lee found an excuse for sending his companions to shelter and then stepped out into the open to pick up a tiny sparrow and to return it to the tree from which it had fallen.[5]

He must have needed all his self-mastery to maintain his cheer-fulness and his calm, for each day seemed to bring new anxieties and new perplexities, personal and official. Robert had been wounded in action on August 15, though not seriously;[6] Custis's

---

[1] *Taylor MSS.*, Aug. 14, 15, 1864. Major H. B. McClellan, who had been serving with Lee since the death of Stuart, had rejoined the staff of the cavalry corps.

[2] *Cf.* Richard Lewis: *Camp Life of a Confederate Boy*, 95: The General was "looking remarkably well," Sept. 17, 1864.

[3] Major Henry C. Carter to Percy Hawes, *MS.*, Aug. 12, 1925.

[4] *Long*, 386–87.　　　　[5] *Jones*, 164.　　　　[6] *R. E. Lee, Jr.*, 137.

health was so uncertain that Mr. Davis was unwilling to assign him to duty in the Shenandoah Valley, where there was a vacancy in the cavalry;[7] Mrs. Lee's condition was as bad as ever.

The wear of war was showing on every arm of the service. For a hundred days, Lee told President Davis on August 29, there had not been one without casualties.[8] In the midst of loss, alarms, and exhausting duty, Lee had to take up the old task of reorganization once again. Hampton had shown so much energy and ability that he had been given command of all the cavalry on August 11.[9] He made several excellent suggestions for its betterment,[10] despite the fact that he could do nothing to improve its horses, which were so hard-ridden and so cruelly fly-bitten that they could not fatten, even where they had good pasturage.[11] Hampton, moreover, took a hint from Lee that he might advantageously organize an expedition in rear of Grant's base at City Point,[12] and from this he developed a plan for a raid that, on September 14, was brilliantly executed. It brought 2486 steers to the Confederate commissary at a time when there was only a fifteen-day supply of meat in Richmond for Lee's army.[13]

This raid served, also, to divert the attention of the army from disasters that now began to fall on other fields of battle. A fine Federal fleet under Admiral Farragut on August 5 had destroyed the feeble Confederate craft in Mobile Bay, and, at the end, had shot away the rudder chains of Admiral Buchanan's unwieldy ram *Tennessee,* thereby forcing him to surrender. This action had sealed that port and, to Lee's mind, presaged an early attack on Wilmington.[14] He had not taken over-seriously the gloomy forecasts of the pessimistic Whiting,[15] who still commanded on the North Carolina coast, but he now dispatched Beauregard to Wilmington to ascertain the real state of affairs there. Beauregard's report was, on the whole, favorable to Whiting, who had been much criticised by Governor Vance.[16]

[7] *O. R.,* 43, part 1, p. 992.   [8] *Reagan,* 195.
[9] *O. R.,* 42, part 2, p. 1171.   [10] *Ibid.,* 1173–74, 1174–75.
[11] *Cf. O. R.,* 42, part 2, p. 1275.   [12] *O. R.,* 42, part 2, p. 1235.
[13] IV *O. R.,* 3, 653. For details of "Hampton's beef-raid," see *O. R.,* 42, part 2, pp. 1242, 1247; Hampton's report, *ibid.,* part 1, p. 944; U. R. Brooks, *Butler and His Cavalry,* 314 ff.; E. L. Wells, 287 ff.; 22 *S. H. S. P.,* 147 ff.
[14] *O. R.,* 42, part 2, p. 1206.   [15] *Lee's Dispatches,* 262–63.
[16] For affairs at Wilmington, as Lee was concerned in them, see *O. R.,* 42, part 2, pp. 1209, 1235, 1246; *ibid.,* 51, part 2, p. 1039; 2 *Roman,* 274–75; R. E. Lee to G. W. C. Lee, MS., Sept. 18, 1864; *Duke Univ. MSS.*

In Georgia, as in Alabama, the Southern cause was losing. On September 3 the telegraph announced that Hood, after a series of bloody and imprudent offensives, had been compelled to evacuate Atlanta the previous morning. When this grievous news arrived, Lee was on his way to Richmond to confer with the President, and he doubtless advised with him as to the next move by Hood's defeated army.[17] There is, however, no record of their conversation. Hood's retreat depressed the mind of the public and even of the armed forces. Those who had demanded that the President dismiss Johnston now denounced him for having done so.[18] The men in the ranks of the Army of Northern Virginia had never approved of the change of commanders.[19]

Mobile Bay closed, Atlanta lost—and, now, disaster to Early. That commander had remained north of the Potomac only a few days on his second invasion of Maryland. Upon his return, Lee for a time had not anticipated that Early could do more than keep Sheridan out of the Shenandoah Valley.[20] There had been some question in Early's mind as to how he could co-operate with Anderson east of the Blue Ridge, for though Anderson advanced no claim to the command, he was Early's senior. Sensing this, and needing Anderson to direct the First Corps, Lee ordered him back. Lee then suggested to Early that he reorganize his command,[21] and that he consider alternatives—either to undertake an offensive with the aid of Kershaw's division, which had been sent to northern Virginia on August 6, or else, if he thought a defensive wiser, to return Kershaw secretly to the Richmond front.[22] Before Early could make any decision, as between the two plans, Sheridan attacked him near Winchester on September 19 and, after a hard-fought action, used the powerful Union cavalry to force Early back two miles. In this, the last battle of Winchester, General Rodes was killed and Fitz Lee was badly wounded.[23] As soon as Lee learned of this disaster he directed Kershaw to march

---

[17] *Taylor MSS.*, Sept. 4, 1864; *Taylor's General Lee*, 262.

[18] *Mrs. McGuire*, 303.

[19] *Cf.* U. R. Brooks: *Butler and His Cavalry*, 291–92, quoting John C. Calhoun to Miss M. M. Calhoun, July 22, 1864.

[20] *O. R.*, 43, part 1, p. 1006.   [21] *O. R.*, 43, part 2, p. 874.

[22] *Irvine Walker*, 183, 186–87; *O. R.*, 42, part 2, pp. 1257–58; *ibid.*, 43, part 2, p. 873.

[23] The clearest account of the battle is in *Early*, 420 *ff*. The official reports are in *O. R.*, 43, part 1, pp. 46 ff., 552.

at once to Early's support.[24] Ere Kershaw could reach the Valley from the eastern side of the Blue Ridge, Early sustained another defeat on the 22d at Fisher's Hill.[25] Losing twelve guns and sustaining severe casualties, he was forced to retreat up the Valley. "My troops are very much shattered," Early wrote in deep gloom, "the men very much exhausted, and many of them without shoes." [26] Lee encouraged Early all he could, sent him Rosser's brigade of cavalry and, lacking a better man for his place, declined to relieve him of command in answer to a clamor akin to that which had arisen against Johnston.[27] The only criticism Lee made was a direct one, to Early himself, that he seemed to have operated more with divisions than with his full command.[28] Even this mild censure did not take into account the immense odds against which Early fought. He was credited by Sheridan with 27,000,[29] but certainly had less than 15,000.[30] Lee did not believe that Sheridan had more than 12,000 infantry[31] when, in reality, he had 32,646, exclusive of the Harpers Ferry force.[32] Lee never made as great a mistake in computing the strength of an opposing force.

But if Lee underestimated Sheridan's numbers, he did not and could not misread the warnings of coming calamity, as written at Mobile, in front of Atlanta, and in the Shenandoah Valley. He did not urge on the government the evacuation of Richmond, for when its defense was his chief mission, his sense of discipline precluded any discussion of the subject. He knew how indispensable the city's munition works were to the Confederacy. Yet it seems probable that he was beginning to consider the advisability of abandoning Richmond and Petersburg, of shortening his communications by retiring to the Staunton River, and of undertaking operations in an open country where he would have a wide field

[24] *O. R.*, 43, part 2, p. 878.

[25] *Early*, 429 *ff.*; *O. R.*, 43, part 1, p. 552.

[26] *O. R.*, 43, part 1, p. 558.   [27] *O. R.*, 43, part 2, pp. 880, 893 *ff.*

[28] *O. R.*, 43, part 2, p. 880.   [29] *O. R.*, 43, part 1, p. 23.

[30] John W. Daniel to Walter H. Taylor, *MS.*, Dec. 17, 1904, maintained that Early mustered only 12,000 (*Taylor MSS.*). In *O. R.*, 43, part 1, p. 1002, the strength of the infantry was given as 8269, without counting Wharton's division, which, according to a note in *O. R.*, 43, part 1, p. 1011, could not have numbered less than 1500. The strength of the cavalry with Early is doubtful, but it probably was around 3000. This would make his total strength around 12,700, to which the artillery should be added.

[31] *O. R.*, 43, part 1, p. 559.

[32] *O. R.*, 43, part 1, p. 61. His total "present for duty," infantry, artillery, and cavalry, was 40,672, of whom 6465 were cavalry.

of manœuvre.[33] It is possible, also, that Lee was influenced by the views of his father. "Light-Horse Harry" had contended that in defending Virginia against an enemy who controlled the sea, an army might best withdraw inland from the navigable streams.[34]

Many of Lee's officers who had been wounded in the early stages of the campaign were now returning to duty[35] and were ending what the chief inspector declared to be the "source of almost every evil" in the army—"the difficulty of having orders properly and promptly executed." [36] But attrition and exhaustion were daily becoming more serious. Finegan's and Hagood's brigades, for example, had come to Virginia as recently as the spring

[33] Cf. Long, 370, 403; Taylor's Four Years, 145; De Leon, 348–49; personal statements to the writer by Colonel Walter H. Taylor and Colonel T. M. R. Talcott. The late Captain W. Gordon McCabe, a most accurate authority, stated to the writer that Colonel Charles Marshall and Colonel C. H. Venable likewise were of opinion that Lee desired the evacuation of Richmond long before it was ordered. Colonel Marshall (op. cit., 182) stated that Lee reached this conclusion when he found it was no longer possible to deliver a counterstroke from the Shenandoah Valley. General Long (op. cit., 266) recorded that Lee "had been heard to say that Richmond was the millstone that was dragging down the army." As these officers based their views on inference, rather than on anything Lee specifically said, it is impossible to fix a date, or even an approximate time, when he decided that the defense of Richmond was hopeless. Lee may have reached this conclusion in October, after the battle of Cedar Creek, instead of after the battle of Fisher's Hill. Evacuation of Petersburg did not imply any intention on his part to end the war. He told "a Southern senator that he was determined to die rather than yield" (Jones, 294), and, toward the close of the fighting around Petersburg, he said to the President, "With my army in the mountains of Virginia, I could carry on this war for twenty years longer" (Jones, 295). Subsequently, according to Colonel Venable, "one night when [Lee] was groaning about the difficulties and dangers attending the holding of his long line with his small force, I unwisely ventured to ask why he did not abandon it. He turned on me sharply and said that to do so would be to be a traitor to his government, or strong words to that effect" (C. S. Venable to W. H. Taylor, MS., March 29, 1878. Taylor MSS.). Still later, at some indeterminable date, he realized that the struggle was hopeless. After the war, about 1868, he was riding with a guest of his daughters, Miss Belle Stewart, later Mrs. Joseph Bryan. She asked, "Why are you so depressed?" He answered, "I am thinking about the men who were lost after I knew it was too late." His brilliant young companion inquired, "Why didn't you tell them?" The old General shook his head: "They had to find it out for themselves." (Statement to the writer by John Stewart Bryan.)

[34] On Nov. 5, 1929, Major George Taylor Lee told the writer that he once asked his father, Charles Carter Lee, what General Lee thought about defending Richmond. He said Charles Carter Lee did not make a positive answer, but remarked that when they were children Henry Lee used to talk to them about defending Virginia, and told them that when an enemy that controlled the sea attacked a land force, the enemy, when defeated, could always retreat by using its ships. Henry Lee said the best way to deal with such an enemy was to draw him into the interior of the country where his ships would be of little value. In describing conditions in Virginia, Henry Lee said that the ideal would be to draw the enemy at least fifty miles beyond Tidewater.

[35] McGowan on Aug. 18, 1864 (O. R., 42, part 2, p. 1185); Archer on Aug. 19 (ibid., 1189); Kirkland, the same day (ibid., 1190); Lane, Aug. 29 (ibid., 1207). The return of the army for Aug. 31 (ibid., 1214 ff.) showed so many temporary officers that the old brigades could hardly be recognized, but by Oct. 31 (ibid., part 3, p. 1187 ff.) the roster took on something of its old form.

[36] O. R., 42, part 2, p. 1276.

of 1864, but both were now reduced by two-thirds.[37] On the Howlett line, a couple of artillery companies that had a roster-strength of 252 had only 40 men present for duty.[38] Johnson's division had been kept in the trenches, with scarcely any rest,[39] and not only was being worn down but was showing signs of incipient scurvy.[40] The firing on the front was heavier. One small regiment used 36,000 rounds of ammunition in a month.[41] The local defense troops were being called out so often at Richmond that their absence interfered with the flow of munitions and the transaction of governmental business, yet in an emergency they could cover only a short sector of the defenses.[42] Desertion, too, was disgracing and weakening the army. Old commands like Law's[43] and Corse's brigades[44] reported men leaving their posts. In a single Alabama regiment, one lieutenant and twenty-four men quit and went home.[45] From Johnson's front, where the opposing pickets were close together, men began to slip away almost every night and to go over to the enemy.[46] Meade estimated that an average of ten Confederates a day were coming into the Union lines.[47] Morale was definitely declining. The strength of the force from White Oak Swamp to the extreme Confederate right, including the Richmond garrison and Beauregard's command, hardly exceeded 50,000 men[48] at the beginning of the autumn. "I get no additions," Lee told Bragg on September 26. "The men coming in do not supply the vacancies caused by sickness, desertions, and other casualties."[49] So great was the need for every private who could carry a musket that Lee could not even furlough the Jewish soldiers for their religious observances.[50] With a few thousand conscripts placed in the strongest parts of his line, Lee believed he could use his veterans advantageously against the enemy,[51] but "as matters now stand," he explained to Mr. Davis, "we have no troops disposable to meet movements of

[37] *O. R.*, 42, part 2, p. 1188; *Hagood*, 289. [38] *O. R.*, 42, part 2, p. 1188.
[39] *O. R.*, 42, part 2, pp. 1252–53. [40] *O. R.*, 42, part 1, p. 895.
[41] Shaver: *History of the Sixtieth Alabama Regt.*, 111.
[42] *Cf. O. R.*, 42, part 2, p. 1293; *ibid.*, 51, part 2, p. 1040, and *infra*, p. 516.
[43] *O. R.*, 40, part 1, p. 761. [44] *O. R.*, 42, part 2, pp. 1290–91.
[45] *O. R.*, 42, part 2, pp. 1175–76. [46] *O. R.*, 42, part 1, pp. 890 *ff.*
[47] 2 *Meade*, 228. [48] *Cf. O. R.*, 42, part 2, p. 1213.
[49] *O. R.*, 42, part 2, p. 1292. [50] *Jones*, 444.
[51] *O. R.*, 42, part 2, p. 1200.

the enemy or strike when opportunity presents, without taking them from the trenches and exposing some important point. The enemy's position enables him to move his troops to the right or left without our knowledge, until he has reached the point at which he aims, and we are then compelled to hurry our men to meet him, incurring the risk of being too late to check his progress and the additional risk of the advantage he may derive from their absence." [52]

For the dark emergency these conditions so tragically disclosed, Lee saw but one major policy the government could employ. That was the vigorous enforcement of the conscription act of February 17, 1864. This law had restricted the exemptions from service and had extended the age limit for military duty to include every able-bodied white man between the ages of seventeen and fifty. All from eighteen to forty-five who were then in the ranks were accounted liable for service until the close of the war. Those between seventeen and eighteen and those between forty-five and fifty, who elected to do so, could organize as volunteer reserves or "minute men," and if they did this they were not subject to call for duty outside their state. [53] Lee urged that this statute be applied to the letter[54] and he called attention to the statement of General Kemper that in Virginia alone 40,000 were exempt, were on detail, or had applied for detail and had not then been refused. [55] Urging that every man who was physically fit be brought into the field, [56] he pleaded for the speedy organization of the reserves. [57] In dealing with North Carolina, where difficulty had been encountered in getting out the "minute men," [58] he carried on direct correspondence with General Vance, who was on bad terms with the administration. [59] He advocated a general review of the entire conscription service and a consolidation of its activities with those of organizing the reserves. [60] He wanted to be sure, also, that where reservists were given clerkships they were taking the place of able-bodied men who were being sent into the field. [61]

[52] O. R., 42, part 2, p. 1228.
[53] Text of act in IV O. R., 3, 178 ff.; history and analysis of the law in A. B. Moore: *Conscription and Conflict in the Confederacy*, 308 ff.
[54] O. R., 42, part 2, 1157, 1199–1200, cf. *ibid.*, 1203–4.
[55] *Lee's Dispatches*, 297–98.
[56] *Ibid.*
[58] *Lee's Dispatches*, 280.
[60] *Lee's Dispatches*, 293–95.

[57] O. R., 42, part 2, p. 1230.
[59] O. R., 42, part 2, p. 1242.
[61] O. R., 42, part 2, pp. 1245–46.

In his letters he exhibited none of the deep feeling of the army at the injustice of exemptions,[62] but nothing that he could say to speed up conscription before it would be too late, did he leave unsaid. More vigorously than ever he waged his perennial war on the slackers who sought easy posts, close to home. Besides asking for 5000 Negro laborers to build roads and fortifications,[63] he recommended that Negroes serve as teamsters and perform all possible labor that would release white men for combat service.[64] To discourage desertion by men who wanted to get into new independent companies that would not be likely to see hard service, he prevailed on the Secretary of War to revoke the permits to organize such units.[65] He even intimated, in one appeal, that leniency would be shown deserters who returned to their duty,[66] and he encouraged desertion from the Federal ranks by emulating the Union commanders in promising immunity and transportation to all who came into his lines from the enemy.[67]

Exerting himself, in these ways, to the very limits of his official authority, in order to build up his army and to offset attrition, Lee began to speak very plainly, from the time of the seizure of the Weldon Railroad, concerning the inevitable results of unchecked attrition. His views, of course, were expressed only in confidential letters to the administration and were carefully concealed even from his staff and his corps commanders, but they give more than a hint that he believed the Southern cause was becoming hopeless. On August 23 he told the Secretary of War: "Without some increase of strength, I cannot see how we can escape the natural military consequences of the enemy's numerical superiority," [68] and on September 26, writing General Bragg of his failure to receive enough men to make good his losses, he said: "If things thus continue, the most serious consequences must result." Unless Negroes were sent him, promptly, to replace teamsters, cooks, and hospital attendants, "it might be too late." [69]

Scarcely had this warning been written than it was emphasized

[62] Cf. Taylor MSS., Sept. 25, 1864.   [63] O. R., 42, part 2, pp. 1256, 1260, 1269.
[64] O. R., 42, part 2, pp. 1205, 1260, 1292–93; 2 R. W. C. D., 277.
[65] O. R., 42, part 2, pp. 1175–76, 1183.
[66] O. R., 42, part 2, pp. 1167, 1169.
[67] O. R., 42, part 2, pp. 1182, 1200, 1204, 1210.
[68] O. R., 42, part 2, p. 1200.   [69] O. R., 42, part 2, p. 1293.

by a tragedy on the north side of the James, a tragedy that might have become a catastrophe. Lee had long been apprehensive of a heavy attack on that part of the defenses, where at the time he had barely 2000 men, including only two very small brigades of

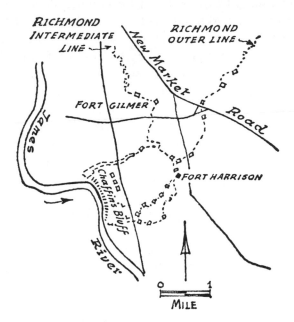

Sketch of the Confederate defenses on the Chaffin's Bluff-Fort Harrison sector, as of September 29, 1864.

veterans, Johnson's Tennesseeans and Gregg's Texans.[70] He instructed Colonel W. Proctor Smith to build a new line of fortifications there, and on September 28 he ordered General Anderson to move north of the James and, under the direction of General Ewell, to assume command.[71] The next morning, early, Lee received a telegram from Ewell announcing that the Federals had made a surprise attack on Fort Harrison and had captured it.[72] As this was one of the most important positions on the outer line of Richmond, and was close to the fortifications of Chaffin's Bluff, its loss was serious in itself and might open the road to the capital.

---

[70] I *S. H. S. P.*, 439.   [71] *O. R.*, 42, part 2, p. 1298.
[72] *O. R.*, 42, part 2, p. 1302. A *MS.* account of the seizure of this fort, written by the commander of its garrison, Major R. C. Taylor, is in the hands of his descendants in Norfolk, Va.

Lee forthwith notified Bragg and directed him to call out the local defense units and all other troops that could be assembled.[73] Telegraphing Ewell to recover the fort,[74] he sent at the same time for General Field, whose troops were on the southside, told him what had happened, and ordered him to cross the James at once.[75] A little later he sent similar instructions to Hoke, whose division, in fine new uniforms, he had reviewed only three days previously.[76] To facilitate Hoke's march, he ordered a special pontoon bridge laid as far down the river as practicable.[77] Four regiments from Pickett were also rushed to the northside. Rooney Lee was directed to move his division over,[78] and six field batteries were given similar orders, with the specific instruction that General Alexander go with them to command all the guns used in stopping the enemy's advance.[79]

As soon as these movements were under way, Lee went in person to the front.[80] He found that Ewell had skillfully employed Gregg and the Tennessee brigade in gallant support of Hardaway's battalion of artillery, and had managed to retain most of that part of the line lying between Fort Harrison and Fort Gilmer.[81] Benning's and Perry's brigades of Field's division had arrived in time to help these troops beat off a violent attack on Fort Gilmer.[82] Field was for attacking Fort Harrison immediately, but Lee saw that the outer line had been stormed, that the defenders were near exhaustion, that only two brigades of the reinforcements were up, and that a precipitate counterattack was for these reasons dangerous. He accordingly told Field to wait.

Soon, Bratton's and Anderson's brigades came up to complete Field's organization. Part of Hoke's men arrived, as did the regiments from Pickett.[83] With this force available Lee seems, for a time, to have considered a night attack, but either because of its difficulties or else because he did not wish to assault until all

---

[73] *O. R.*, 42, part 2, p. 1302.

[74] *O. R.*, 42, part 2, p. 1303.   [75] 14 *S. H. S. P.*, 555.

[76] *Hagood*, 303; for the new uniforms see James Morris Morgan: *Recollections of a Rebel Reefer*, 208. This delightful book, one of the most captivating of Confederate personal narratives, is cited hereafter as *Rebel Reefer*.

[77] *Rebel Reefer*, 208.   [78] *O. R.*, 42, part 1, p. 947.

[79] *Ibid.*, p. 859.   [80] *O. R.*, 42, part 2, p. 1301.

[81] A very graphic narrative of this phase of the defense, by Charles Johnston, will be found in 1 *S. H. S. P.*, 439 *ff*. See also *O. R.*, 42, part 1, p. 935.

[82] 14 *S. H. S. P.*, 555–56.   [83] *O. R.*, 42, part 1, p. 876.

Hoke's division and ample artillery were available, he deferred operations until the morning of the 30th.[84] Before darkness, as he rode alone behind the lines, he met a very youthful soldier who was some distance behind his command.

"What are you doing behind, my little fellow?" he asked.

The boy explained that he had stopped at a well to fill his company's canteens.

"Well," said Lee, "hurry and catch up; they will need you by daylight." The youngster dutifully struck out down the road, and, when he overtook his comrades, announced to them, in a free interpretation of the General's remarks that "Marse Robert" had told him they would have "hell by daylight."[85]

The soldier was wrong as to the hour, but right as to the character of the fighting that occurred on the morning of September 30. It was past noon when Hoke was in position to attack from a point slightly west of north, while Field was drawn up on a front northwest of the fort. Then the artillery opened a concentrated fire on the work for about half an hour. Field had about 500 yards to go, whereas Hoke could form in a ravine close to the towering earthworks the Federals held. For this reason, as the attack was to be on a brigade front, Field threw out Anderson's brigade, which was to lead his attack, with instructions to advance as close as possible to the Federal position and then to lie down and wait until he saw that he and Hoke's troops would reach the works at the same moment. Anderson, however, did not tell his men they were to halt, and when they got orders to advance, they thought they were to drive their charge home.[86] Seeing them rushing forward, Field had to send Bratton's and Perry's brigades forward in support. When the hot, concentrated fire of the fort forced Anderson back, Bratton and Perry were thrown into confusion, and the whole attack by Field's division soon collapsed, though some of Bratton's men got close to the enemy's new parapet.[87] Hoke must have realized that Field was attacking prematurely, but he waited until the agreed time and then delivered an assault, with the understanding that Bratton was to renew his

---

[84] 14 S. H. S. P., 556. [85] F. M. Mixson, 101–2. [86] 14 S. H. S. P., 557.
[87] O. R., 42, part 1, p. 880. The fort seems originally to have been open in the rear but was fortified by the Federals, probably beginning on the night of Sept. 29.

attack at the same time.[88] But co-ordination was not on the cards that day. Hoke was so quickly repulsed that Bratton did not make another attempt.

At this moment Lee arrived on the ground and rode along the

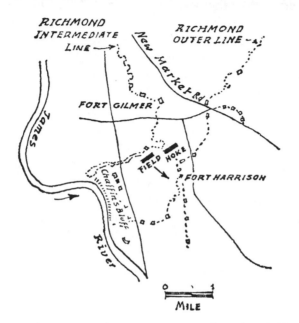

Plan of counterattack on Fort Harrison, September 30, 1864. It is probable, though not certain, that an early work which linked the two lines where "Hoke" appears on this map had been levelled in part by the Federals during the night of September 29–30, 1864.

ranks of Hoke's division as it formed again. Astride Traveller, he seemed oblivious to the fire, exposing himself recklessly.[89] His hat was in his hand; his gray hair was shining in the afternoon light. A mighty cheer went up from the North Carolinians when they recognized him. He urged them to the charge. Fort Harrison was an important part of the defenses, he said, and he was sure the men could storm it if they would make one more earnest effort. They shouted their willingness to try, and, at the order, rushed out again—only to be repulsed a second time, in greater disorder and with heavier losses than before. But Lee persisted. "I had always thought," one young observer wrote, "General Lee

[88] *O. R.*, 42, part 2, p. 880. [89] 2 *R. W. C. D.*, 297.

was a very cold and unemotional man, but he showed lots of feeling and excitement on that occasion; even the staid and stately 'Traveller' caught the spirit of his master, and was prancing and cavorting while the General was imploring his men to make one more effort to take the position for him." [90] They did not refuse. As courageously as before, they went forward, but when they were repulsed and hurled back, they were not far from panic, and they did not halt until they had reached cover.[91] Fortunately the enemy did not attempt to follow the repulsed troops or to exploit his success.

Gloomily Lee rode back to Chaffin's Bluff; regretfully he had to report to the War Department the failure to recapture Fort Harrison;[92] sadly, he answered General Pemberton when that officer, during the evening, ventured to ask if Lee would not take the fort, cost what it might. "General Pemberton," he said, "I made my effort this morning and failed, losing many killed and wounded. I have ordered another line provided from that point and shall have no more blood shed at the fort unless you can show me a practical plan of capture; perhaps you can. I shall be glad to have it." Some of those who heard this answer thought that Lee meant to silence Pemberton with an unforgettable rebuke, but Lee doubtless meant exactly what he said when he affirmed he would be glad to get a better plan. No general more heartily welcomed suggestions at any time and from any source.[93]

While Lee was vainly trying to recapture Fort Harrison, Hampton was checking a Federal advance that might have carried the Federals to the Southside Railroad. On the 29th, Butler's cavalry, in advance of the Confederate right flank below Petersburg, had been attacked and driven back, but Rooney Lee's division, which was under orders to march to the northside, arrived opportunely

[90] Rebel Reefer, 210.
[91] Ibid. cf. O. R., 42, part 1, pp. 859, 938, 947; Hagood, 305; 5 Correspondence of B. F. Butler, 192, 197, 197–98, 201. The fullest study of the action at Fort Harrison is that of Major Charles J. Calrow: Battle of Chaffin's Bluff, the MS. of which its distinguished author has obligingly placed at the disposal of the writer. To Major Calrow's careful reconstruction of the battle of Sept. 30, the writer owes the data for the map on p. 503. A comparison of this map with the earlier one, p. 500, will show that Major Calrow assumes that the Federals during the night of Sept. 29 levelled the works linking Fort Harrison with the intermediate line just south of Fort Gilmer. This cannot be asserted as a fact but it is a probability. The action was confused, the Confederate reports are very meagre, and the positions of the attacking columns cannot be established with absolute certainty.
[92] O. R., 42, part 2, p. 1306.   [93] See supra, p. 16.

and reversed the situation. The next day, September 30, when the Federals again advanced, Heth's division was brought up to support the cavalry. The combined attack of horse and foot repulsed the enemy. On October 1, however, a new advance on Hampton's part was balked by a false report that the enemy was in his rear. Before he could organize a heavy movement, the enemy "dug in."[94]

To give Hampton sufficient infantry backing, it had been necessary to spread Johnson's division to the right and to leave scarcely more than a picket line on part of the Petersburg defenses. "If the enemy cannot be prevented from extending his left," Lee warned Hampton, "he will eventually reach the Appomattox and cut us off from the south side altogether."[95] Dutifully, Hampton began drawing a line that would extend to Hatcher's Run and would remove, for the time at least, any serious danger that the Federals would envelop Petersburg.[96] This, however, meant still more attenuation of force. By October 7 Johnson's division was holding a front previously occupied by that command, by Hoke's division, and by two brigades of Mahone.[97] In an emergency that arose before the end of the month, his division, plus two brigades and one battalion, occupied the whole of the Petersburg defenses from the Appomattox to Battery 45, a distance of nearly six miles.[98]

Lee saw early and plainly what this endless extension of line involved.[99] Ere the line to Hatcher's Run had been started, or even his plan for operating on the northside after the capture of Fort Harrison had been drafted, he wrote the Secretary of War a new appeal for men. In this, for the first time, he spoke of the fall of Richmond as a possibility. He said:

"I beg leave to inquire whether there is any prospect of my

[94] Hampton's report is in *O. R.*, 42, part 1, pp. 947–48; Meade's in *ibid.*, 31. See also U. R. Brooks: *Butler and His Cavalry*, 325 *ff.*; E. L. *Wells*, 318 *ff.* This movement was undertaken as a major operation, simultaneous with the attack on Fort Harrison, in the hope that Petersburg might be taken or the Southside Railroad occupied (*O. R.*, 42, part 2, pp. 1046–47). The Confederates on both sides the James, Sept. 29–Oct. 1, 1864, captured 2226 prisoners (*O. R.*, 42, part 1, p. 870).

[95] *O. R.*, 42, part 3, p. 1133.

[96] *O. R.*, 42, part 3, p. 1146. The line was completed on Oct. 23 (*ibid.*, 1159).

[97] *O. R.*, 42, part 3, pp. 1140, 1143.   [98] *O. R.*, 42, part 3, p. 1180.

[99] The sketch represents new positions taken during the whole of October, and not during the first week only. See *O. R.*, 42, part 1, pp. 166 *ff.*, 436, 546.

obtaining any increase to this army. If not, it will be very difficult
for us to maintain ourselves. The enemy's numerical superiority
enables him to hold his lines with an adequate force, and extend
on each flank with numbers so much greater than ours that we
can only meet his corps, increased by recent recruits, with a di-

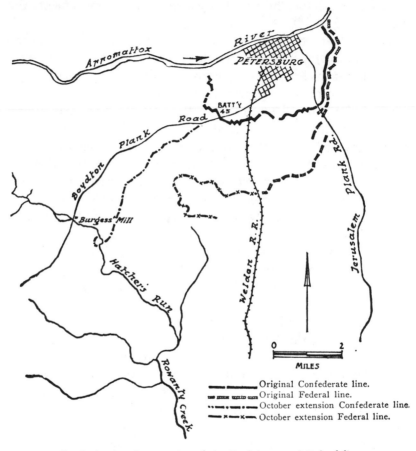

Sketch showing the extension of the Confederate and Federal lines
southwest of Petersburg, October, 1864.

vision, reduced by long and arduous service. We cannot fight
to advantage with such odds, and there is the gravest reason to
apprehend the result of every encounter. . . . The men at home
on various pretexts must be brought out and be put in the army
at once, unless we would see the enemy reap the great moral and

material advantages of a successful issue of his most costly campaign. . . . If we can get out our entire arms bearing population in Virginia and North Carolina, and relieve all detailed men with negroes, we may be able, with the blessing of God, to keep the enemy in check to the beginning of winter. If we fail to do this the result must be calamitous. The discouragement of our people and the great material loss that would follow the fall of Richmond, to say nothing of the great encouragement our enemies would derive from it, outweigh, in my judgment, any sacrifice and hardship that would result from bringing out all our arms bearing men." [100]

The army was beginning to feel even more than Lee expressed in this letter. Colonel Taylor, with the optimism of youth, argued that the capture of Fort Harrison was a negative gain for the enemy, but he had to admit that in the attempt to recover that position "matters were not executed as well as they were planned," and he wondered if all was well with the morale of the army. Perhaps he was not aware of the full import of his words when he wrote his fiancée: "Though our men have not altogether the old spirit, there still are many who will do anything to be expected of mortals; and if this fraction is properly supported, all is well." [101] Truth was that while conscripts were not arriving in sufficient quotas to strengthen the army materially in numbers, enough of them were being sent in to impair the morale and to destroy the old-time confidence of the commanders in the invincibility of their men.

This was grimly illustrated early in October when Lee undertook a movement to recover the exterior line held by the Federals above Fort Harrison as an alternative to the construction of a retrenchment between it and the line to the west. He called out the local defense troops and put them in the works. Thus set free for an attack, Field and Hoke were moved up the line, and Gary's cavalry and Perry's brigade were marched beyond its northern end. The plan was that Gary's men, dismounted, and the infantry of Perry's brigade were to sweep down in rear of the line. Field was then to assault from the west and, if successful in

[100] O. R., 42, part 3, p. 1134.   [101] Taylor MSS., Oct. 6, 1864.

crossing the works, was to join the troops already on the outer side of the exterior line; Hoke was thereupon to attack from the inner side. The whole of the line was to be recovered as far to the southward as the close artillery range of Fort Harrison.

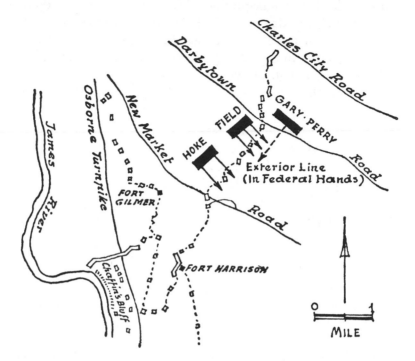

Plan of operations against exterior Richmond line north of Fort Harrison, October 7, 1864. Here again, there is some doubt concerning part of the line. It is known that by October 16, 1864, work was underway on the fortifications that appear as a dotted line bisecting the Chaffin's Bluff enclosure, but it is not clear whether this line had been begun as early as October 7. For the doubt regarding a small part of the line north of Fort Harrison, see the sketch on page 503.

On the 6th Lee had a conference with the President at Chaffin's Bluff[102] and on the morning of the 7th he rode up to Field's front to see the action open. After a while, he inquired of one of his staff if the troops were ready to go forward.

"None but the Texas brigade, General," the officer replied.

"The Texas brigade is always ready," Lee commented, half-proudly, half-sadly.[103]

[102] *Taylor MSS.*, Oct. 6, 1864.   [103] Polley, *Hood's Texas Brigade,* 257.

Soon the advance began. Gary and the little remnant of the Florida brigade pushed forward, turning the works; Field quickly cleared the line and, pursuing the Federals, came upon them in a strong position, well covered by abatis.[104] At this stage of the advance Hoke was to join in the attack from the western side of the exterior line, but for some reason, never explained, he either misunderstood his orders, was deterred by the obstacles in his way, or was held back by the artillery fire of the enemy. Field attacked again, but at doleful cost, for the valiant Gregg fell, killed by a ball through the neck.[105]

As Lee was watching the struggle, a boy of eighteen or nineteen, his uniform all bloody, came up to him.

"General," he said, "if you don't send some more men down there, our boys will get hurt sure."

"Are you wounded, my boy?" Lee inquired.

"Yes, sir."

"Where are you wounded?"

"I'm shot through both arms, General, but I don't mind that, General! I want you to send some more men down there to help our boys."

Lee placed the boy in charge of one of his staff, to be carried to a surgeon, and turned to see what could be done.[106] But it was too late. Struggling through a jungle of small timber, Field was repulsed while Hoke waited.

So it was, time after time, in the battles of the late summer and autumn. On every field there were individual exploits as fine as those of '62. The veterans were as valiant as ever. But, somehow, the old machine was not working as in earlier days![107]

Lee was convinced by this affair, by the operations of October 1–2 on the right at Petersburg, and by the reports of his scouts, that the Federals were planning a further extension of their lines on both flanks, and on the 10th of October he issued a general warning. "We must drive them back at all costs," he told his

---

104 14 S. H. S. P., 557.

105 14 S. H. S. P., 558. Corbin in his *Letters of a Confederate Officer*, 79, stated that Lee regarded Gregg as the best brigadier in the army and was considering him as a successor to Rodes.

106 F. W. Dawson, 127.

107 O. R., 42, part 1, pp. 878, 938. Federal reports in *ibid.*, 703 *ff.*; 14 S. H. S. P., 558; Hagood, 307.

corps commanders,[108] but to General Cooper he confided, in an explanation of Grant's anticipated movement, "I fear it will be impossible to keep him out of Richmond."[109] Abandoning all hope

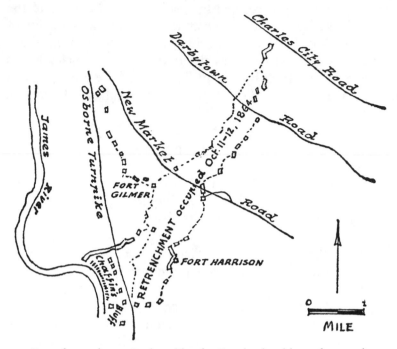

Retrenchment drawn, October 1864, after Lee abandoned hope of recapturing Fort Harrison.

of recovering Fort Harrison on the exterior works, he drew a retrenchment that cut off the fort and secured the front.[110] The day this was done he had the satisfaction of seeing Field repulse the enemy's repeated attacks from his new position.[111]

It was, however, an immense relief to Lee on the 19th to be able to welcome Longstreet back and to place in his experienced hands the defense of the north side, where, it had to be admitted, Anderson had not distinguished himself.[112] Anderson was assigned command of Hoke's and of Johnson's divisions, which were informally organized as a separate Fourth Corps.[113] Long-

108 O. R., 42, part 3, 1144–45.   109 O. R., 42, part 3, p. 1144.
110 Hagood, 310.   111 14 S. H. S. P., 558.
112 For Longstreet's return, see Longstreet, 574; O. R., 42, part 1, p. 871.
113 Irvine Walker, 103.

street was still unable to use his right arm, but he had learned to write with his left hand[114] and was fully capable of resuming command of his old corps. Characteristically, he at once asked that Lee bring together his three divisions on the northside,[115] and he went vigorously to work strengthening his front.[116] In Longstreet's eyes, Lee "seemed worn by past labor, besides suffering at seasons from sciatica, while his work was accumulating and his troubles multiplying to proportions that should have employed half a dozen able men." [117] Yet for a part of the month of October, Lee had only two members of his personal staff on duty. Both Colonel Venable and Colonel Marshall were sick.[118]

To the burdens that Longstreet described, the next sun after that officer's return put a new load of anxiety on the weary shoulders of Lee. Following the battle of Fisher's Hill, General Early had retired up the Valley as far as Waynesboro,[119] but hearing that Sheridan had reduced force, he had again advanced northward. Lee had urged Breckinridge to reinforce Early, if possible, so that Kershaw could be recalled,[120] and on the 12th of October he sent Early a lengthy letter of instructions, cautioning him not to employ his cavalry recklessly. "If [Sheridan]," he wrote, "should remain in the lower Valley, and send reinforcements to Grant, you can reinforce me correspondingly, and watch him with the rest of your troops. It is impossible at this distance to give definite instructions; you can only proceed on the principle of not retaining with you more troops than you can use to advantage in any position the enemy may take and send the rest to me. I have weakened myself very much to strengthen you. It was done with the expectation of enabling you to gain such success that you could return the troops if not rejoin me yourself. I know you have endeavored to gain that success, and believe you have done all in your power to insure it. You must not be discouraged, but continue to try. I rely upon your judgment and ability, and the hearty co-operation of your officers and men still to secure it. With your united force it can be accomplished. I do not think Sheridan's infantry or cavalry numerically

---

[114] *Sorrel*, 265.
[116] *O. R.*, 42, part 3, p. 1182.
[118] *Taylor MSS.*, Oct. 6, 1864.
[120] *O. R.*, 43, part 2, p. 885.

[115] *O. R.*, 42, part 3, pp. 1155, 1185.
[117] *Longstreet*, 573.
[119] *Early*, 435.

as large as you suppose; but either is sufficiently so not to be despised and great circumspection must be used in your operations. Grant is receiving large reinforcements, and building up his army as large apparently as at the beginning of the campaign. This makes it necessary for me to draw to me every man I can." [121]

In the exercise of the discretion thus given him, Early decided to assume the offensive, and on the 19th he attacked Sheridan near Cedar Creek. The battle was his during the forenoon, but in the afternoon some of his infantry broke, the enemy's cavalry outflanked him and he was forced into a disorderly retreat, with the loss of twenty-three guns and about 3000 men. [122]

This meant, of course, that all prospect of a diversion in the Valley of Virginia was at an end. Grant need have no further concern for Washington. Lee's old game of playing on Lincoln's fears for the safety of the capital could not be tried again. More than that, it was doubtful whether Early, with the 12,000 men left him, [123] could keep the enemy from completing the destruction of the food supplies in the Valley, or even prevent his marching eastward over the mountains. Sheridan could reduce force to assist Grant; Lee could not weaken Early except at great risk. A dark autumn was growing blacker.

On his own front, Lee became apprehensive of a new attack, especially as the Federals were digging furiously on Dutch Gap Canal, where some Confederate prisoners were kept under fire in retaliation for alleged forced labor by Negro soldiers the Confederates had captured. Lee put an end to this through correspondence with Grant. [124] Doing what he could to procure the co-operation of the navy in preventing an advance up the river, [125] he remained at Chaffin's Bluff, busy with preparations to meet the next shock.

On October 25–26, there were signs of an increase in the Federal force on the north side of the James, [126] and on the morning

[121] O. R., 43, part 2, pp. 891–92.
[122] Early, 437 ff., 450; O. R., 43, part 1, pp. 553, 561; ibid., part 2, p. 901.
[123] O. R., 43, part 2, p. 911, assuming that Early's cavalry, after Cedar Creek, was temporarily reduced to 1000. If it were larger, Early's total strength would be greater by that excess.
[124] II O. R., 7, pp. 1010 ff. 5 Correspondence of B. F. Butler, 264.
[125] O. R., 42, part 3, pp. 1174 ff.   [126] O. R., 42, part 1, p. 871.

of the 27th the enemy attacked vigorously on the whole front from the New Market to the Charles City road. Simultaneously, Lee received reports that the Union troops had crossed Hatcher's Run on the right of the Petersburg front and were moving toward the Boydton plank road. Taylor remarked, "It looks like a sure enough advance," [127] and Colonel Marshall, in more formal phrase, notified the Secretary of War, "There . . . appears to be a simultaneous movement on both flanks." [128] The administration was profoundly alarmed and called the last available reserves, the munition workers and the cadets, to the defenses. [129]

Counter-operations on the southside had, of course, to be left to the judgment of Hill and of Hampton. On the northside, Lee left the dispositions to Longstreet. And never did he have better reason to trust the military judgment of "Old Pete." The front opposite Fort Harrison had been carefully planted with subterra shells or "land mines," after the capture of that earthwork, [130] so Longstreet had nothing to fear on that sector, which the Chaffin's Bluff garrison manned. He concentrated Hoke and Field on the front of attack, and soon became convinced that the attack there was merely a feint. Shrewdly reasoning that the Federals might be preparing to turn the upper end of the outer line, which was undefended, he boldly moved his infantry as far northward as the Williamsburg road and sent Gary's cavalry to occupy the fortifications on the Nine-Mile road. In the course of a few hours he completely repulsed the enemy and captured some 600 prisoners and 11 flags. No drive on the northside, during the whole of the investment of Richmond, had been broken up so readily. [131]

On the southside the Federals crossed Hatcher's Run at Armstrong's Mill, and Rowanty Creek at Monk's Neck Bridge. Their numbers were large [132] and their advance was rapid. Hampton

---

[127] *Taylor MSS.*, Oct. 27, 1864.   [128] *O. R.*, 42, part 3, p. 1178.

[129] *O. R.*, 42, part 3, p. 1178; 2 *R. W. C. D.*, 316.

[130] *O. R.*, 42, part 3, pp. 1181, 1219. For the marking of the location of these shells, see *History of Kershaw's Brigade*, 471.

[131] *O. R.*, 42, part 1, p. 871; 14 *S. H. S. P.*, 559 *ff.* In *Longstreet*, 576, its author asserted that Lee did not approve but did not forbid the shift to the Williamsburg road, which statement probably means neither more nor less than that Lee let Longstreet fight his own battle.

[132] Hancock operated with two divisions of the II Corps, Warren with the whole of the V, and Gregg with his cavalry division. Parke, in command of the IX Corps, was co-operating on the Federal right.

met them by shifting his attack from road to road with a skill
and a speed that would have done credit to Stuart himself. Hill
hurried Heth and Mahone from the line, where they had been
on a quiet sector.[133] This left Johnson to defend the front from
the Appomattox to Battery 45 with six brigades and one battalion, while three of Wilcox's brigades covered the right of the
new line from Battery 45 to Hatcher's Run.[134] The enemy reached
Burgess's Mill, on Hatcher's Run, but as the two strong Federal
corps failed to co-operate, the combined attacks of the Confederate infantry and cavalry drove the Union troops back in confusion. It was in a spectacular charge during this fighting along
the Boydton plank road[135] that Hampton had one of his sons
killed and another seriously wounded. Despite this personal affliction,[136] he proposed to renew the action at dawn. Hill, however, was unwilling to leave the Petersburg line so thinly held,
especially as there was a surprise attack that evening on Johnson's
front, near the Baxter road.[137] The morning of October 28 found
Hill back in position, the Federals withdrawn to their lines, and
Hampton in possession of the field.[138]

Thus ended the most ambitious of the Federal attempts in the
autumn of 1864 to outflank the Richmond-Petersburg line. It
closed with substantial Confederate victory. Some began to hope
that it was the last great effort of the year, because the weather,
which had been mild and open in October, became uncertain with
the opening of November, "good and bad by turns," as General
Hagood said.[139]

[133] *Longstreet,* 576.

[134] For Johnson's position, see *supra,* p. 505; for Wilcox's, see his *MS. report,* 68.
Thomas's brigade was north of the Appomattox and had been there since July 4 (Wilcox, *loc. cit.*).

[135] The action took that name.

[136] General Lee wrote him Oct. 29: "I grieve with you at the death of your gallant
son. So young, so brave, so true. I know how much you must suffer. Yet think of the
great gain to him, how changed his condition, how bright his future. We must labour
on in the course before us, but for him I trust is rest and peace, for I believe our Merciful
God takes us when it is best for us to go. He is now safe from all harm and all evil, and
nobly died in the defence of the rights of his country. May God support you under your
great affliction, and give you strength to bear the trials he may impose upon you. Truly
your friend . . ." (*MS.* copy, through the kindness of Mrs. Preston Hampton Haskell,
of Richmond, Va.).

[137] *O. R.,* 42, part 1, p. 906.

[138] *O. R.,* 42, part 1, pp. 853, 860, 944 *ff. McCabe,* 538 *ff.,* contains perhaps the
best narrative. See also *E. L. Wells,* 326 *ff.*

[139] *Hagood,* 312, 313.

514

Satisfied that the northside was temporarily safe, Lee started back on November 1 for Petersburg.[140] He made the journey something of a tour of inspection and that day covered the whole of the front from Chaffin's Bluff along the Howlett line to the city.[141] On reaching Petersburg he went to new headquarters. A change from Violet Bank had become necessary, for, with the fall of the leaves, that pleasant place was in plain view of the enemy's batteries across the Appomattox.[142] Lee had approved a move and Taylor had selected the comfortable Beasley house on High Street.[143] The General, however, allowed himself only a single night's rest before starting out to examine the new line on the right.[144] Next he went down as far as Rowanty Creek, where he joined Rooney and Robert, then on outpost duty. It was as happy a meeting as the times would allow. Both boys were well and cheerful. Robert's wound had healed and Rooney had new laurels, won in Hampton's battle on the Boydton plank road.[145]

Remaining on the extreme right several days, Lee found that most of the soldiers in the trenches were in good health,[146] though the men who were doing fatigue duty, in the endless labor of constructing or strengthening fortifications, were beginning to show physical weakness because of the poor ration.[147] Sometimes their food was fairly abundant;[148] more often the third of a pound of "Nassau bacon" that was issued with the daily pint of corn meal was so bad that the facetious affirmed the enemy let it pass the blockade in order to poison the army.[149] Once, when transportation was interrupted, there was only a single issue of meat in four days.[150] Firewood was scarce and green;[151] soap was not to be had.[152] Dirty and cold, the men dug themselves small caves in rear of the trenches, caves that were popularly known as "rat-holes" and officially styled "bomb-proofs," despite the oft-repeated

---

[140] O. R., 42, part 3, p. 1198.
[141] Lee's Dispatches, 305–6; G. Wise, 204.   [142] Taylor MSS., Sept. 4, 1864.
[143] Taylor's Four Years, 141.   [144] O. R., 42, part 1, p. 908.
[145] Long, 398.   [146] Welch, 141.
[147] "Some men dug and shovelled well; but the majority, even of those who looked strong and healthy, would pant and grow faint under the labor of half an hour. This was most strikingly the case when our meat ration failed" (History of McGowan's Brigade, 196).
[148] James A. Graham Papers, 196.   [149] Sorrel, 271.
[150] O. R., 42, part 3, pp. 1156–57.
[151] Taylor MSS., Sept. 4, 1864; History of McGowan's Brigade, 197.
[152] Lee's Dispatches, 288–89.

experience that they were not "proof."[153] The troops were beginning to lack even the means of defense. Percussion caps were running low, though most of the stills in the South that had been dedicated to Bacchus had now been sacrificed to Mars.[154] The Confederates in the advanced rifle-pits were limited to eighteen rounds per man, while the Federal pickets who fraternized with them between the lines complained that each of them was required to expend 100 rounds every twenty-four hours.[155]

The distress of his soldiers wrung the heart of Lee, and the scantiness of their numbers gave him the deepest concern for the future. After his first day of inspection, he wrote the President, "the great necessity I observed yesterday was the want of men," [156] and on every rod of the line he visited after his return to his Petersburg headquarters he read the same warning. With all the troops on the works he could present, at best, only one man every four and a half feet.[157] H. H. Walker's brigade was diminished before the end of November to such feebleness that it was disbanded, and Johnson's Tennessee brigade, which had fought so well at Fort Harrison, was consolidated with Archer's.[158] In Early's command, Terry's brigade contained the fragments of thirteen regiments, and York had the remnants of ten regiments in his brigade.[159] Desertion grew as ominously as a cancer. Johnson's reports told almost daily of men who had been unable to endure the ceaseless vigil of the freezing trenches and had crossed over the lines to safety, if to infamy.[160] Usually, the deserters were new conscripts, but sometimes they seduced older soldiers from their allegiance.[161] Among the local defense troops, on the Richmond front, forty-five desertions occurred in a short time because these reservists feared they were to be retained permanently in the army.[162] Lee hurried the munition workers back to Richmond, both because of their low morale and also because the men were needed in the plants, but the exigencies were such that they were soon put in the trenches again.[163] Lee had to be

153 Shaver, *History of the Sixtieth Alabama Regt.*, 82.
154 *Alexander*, 585.
155 *O. R.*, 42, part 1, p. 918. 156 *Lee's Dispatches*, 306.
157 Shaver, *History of the Sixtieth Alabama Regt.*, 83.
158 *O. R.*, 42, part 3, p. 1235. 159 *O. R.*, 42, part 3, p. 1246.
160 See Johnson's reports in *O. R.*, 42, part 1, pp. 908 *ff.*
161 *James A. Graham Papers*, 199. 162 *O. R.*, 42, part 3, p. 1179.
163 2 *R. W. C. D.*, 326.

stern in the face of the steady loss of men, but if he were not sure that justice had been done a deserter, he would personally see to it that the man had the benefit of the doubt. On one occasion he got up at 2 A.M. and intervened with the President because he was afraid that a German deserter might not have understood the published orders.[164]

It probably was in connection with desertion that Lee had distressing evidence during November that the exhaustion which was threatening the army was wearing down the sensitive nerves of the President. Longstreet's adjutant general reported that General Pickett had about 100 men in his guard-house charged with desertion. "He explains this state of the things," the letter read, "by the fact that every man sentenced to be shot for desertion in this division for the past two months had been reprieved." A little earlier, Lee had been disposed to deal leniently with deserters who returned to the army, but he forwarded this document to the War Department with the endorsement: "Desertion is increasing in the army notwithstanding all my efforts to stop it. I think a rigid execution of the law is [best] in the end. The great want in our army is firm discipline." Through channels, this reached the President. It touched him on the old, sore spot of his constitutional prerogative. He wrote tartly, in a tone he rarely employed with Lee, familiar though it unhappily was to some of the other Confederate leaders: "When deserters are arrested they should be tried, and if the sentences are reviewed and remitted that is not a proper subject for the criticism of a military commander."[165] Lee made no reply.

To meet the losses due to attrition and desertion, it was now apparent that the reservists would be of little value. The only hope lay in conscription and in the substitution of disabled soldiers and Negroes for the able-bodied white men who were on detail. For a while in October there had been hopeful signs of replacements from farmers who had harvested their crops,[166] but before the end of that month Lee had been forced to tell Hampton, "The only source we have to depend upon is the conscription now going on."[167] Lee continued to urge the organization

---

[164] 1 Macrae, 181 ff.
[165] O. R., 42, part 3, p. 1213.   [166] 2 R. W. C. D., 307.
[167] O. R., 42, part 3, p. 1176; cf. ibid., p. 1144.

of Negroes in the service of supply[168] and in this he had the warm support of the President, who asked the approval of Congress.[169] Detailed men were slow in arriving, conscripts were few. From Early, when it was apparent that Sheridan did not intend to follow up his victory at Cedar Creek, Lee recalled Kershaw's division about November 14,[170] but that shattered unit of the old First Corps, which he placed north of the James, was all he felt he could as yet safely detach from the Valley. There was some increase in the cavalry,[171] but the shortage of horses was so great[172] that of the 6200 troopers with Lee, about 1300 were dismounted.[173] For all the efforts of Lee, the President and the War Department, the maximum strength of all arms reached in the return of November 30 was 60,753, exclusive of the Richmond garrison of something less than 6000.[174] This was a gain, but not enough, in Lee's opinion, to give him any prospect of victory. "Unless we can obtain a reasonable approximation to [Grant's] force," he wrote the President early that month, "I fear a great calamity will befall us." [175]

While Lee was thus vainly using all his prestige and all his influence to bring the Army of Northern Virginia up to fighting strength in November, Grant undertook no offensive operations on a large scale. In the Valley of the Shenandoah, Early waited, with his reduced force, gloomy and uneasy. Off Wilmington, whither Bragg had been sent in general command, subject to Lee's control, there was as yet no increase in the blockading fleet to indicate an early attack, though Lee expected that port or Charleston soon to be assailed. He urged that the garrison at either place be ready to assist that of the other.[176]

In the far South were direful developments. Largely at Lee's instance, General Beauregard had been slated to assume charge

[168] IV *O. R.,* 3, p. 838.
[169] IV *O. R.,* 3, p. 797.
[170] *O. R.,* 43, part 1, p. 584.
[171] *O. R.,* 43, part 2, p. 926.
[172] *O. R.,* 42, part 3, pp. 1134, 1198, 1228.
[173] *O. R.,* 42, part 3, p. 1236.
[174] *O. R.,* 42, part 3, pp. 1236, 1248. One brigade of cavalry was not reported.
[175] *Lee's Dispatches,* 306. Grant's and Butler's combined force at this time, exclusive of troops at Fort Monroe and in North Carolina, was 102,342 (*O. R.,* 42, part 3, pp. 765–66).
[176] *O. R.,* 42, part 3, p. 1177. For the dispatch of Bragg to Wilmington, see *O. R.,* 42, part 3, pp. 1142, 1160, 1163, 1207, 1209. Bragg took command on Oct. 22. For Lee's effort to reinforce and victual Wilmington, see Jones, *L. and L.,* 341; *O. R.,* 42, part 3, pp. 1171, 1185, 1215, 1217.

of the department where Hood was operating.[177] Beauregard had bidden Lee an affectionate farewell about September 23[178] and had gone first to Charleston. Then he had been assigned to his new post of duty, but he had no real authority. Hood made his own plans, with the acquiescence of the President. After sending Forrest on a brilliant raid against Sherman's railroad communications, Hood decided to attempt to force Sherman out of Georgia by marching his army into Tennessee. This was, perhaps, the fatal military decision of the war. If Lee was consulted regarding it, there is no record of the advice he gave.[179] On November 16, while Hood tramped toward Nashville, Sherman boldly abandoned his communications with Tennessee and started on his march across Georgia to the sea.[180] For two weeks there was suspense; then, on November 30, Hood met Schofield at Franklin, Tenn., and in a wild, reckless, and wasteful battle threw him back on Nashville, where George H. Thomas was concentrating force in a determination to destroy Hood and to leave Sherman free to move on Savannah.[181]

These events sent a shiver down the spine of every Confederate. Could anything be done to check Sherman's advance? Would Lee be able to send troops to oppose him? Feverishly the question was debated. It probably was the subject most anxiously discussed at a conference between the President and Lee on the 22d of November[182] and it was not easily answered. For Grant seemed to be co-operating shrewdly with his lieutenant in Georgia. Lee's information was that the Army of the Potomac had received twelve days' rations and was preparing a flank movement in an effort to keep him from detaching troops against Sherman. Lee at once made ready to attack Grant, and on November 21 even considered abandoning the Valley and concentrating everything for one final thrust; but Grant's anticipated movement did not occur, and the weather temporarily put a stop to operations.[183]

---

[177] O. R., 39, part 2, p. 1259; 2 Roman, 274–75; T. R. Hay: Hood's Tennessee Campaign, 207.

[178] 2 Roman, 275.   [179] T. R. Hay, op. cit., 70.

[180] 2 Sherman Memoirs, 178.

[181] Cf. Henry, 429 ff., a brief but very effective account.

[182] O. R., 42, part 3, p. 1222; ibid., 51, part 2, p. 1053.

[183] O. R., 42, part 3, pp. 1222–23, 1227, 1229. For the weather, see James A. Graham Papers, 198.

Bragg was forthwith sent southward from Wilmington with half the forces there, in the hope that he might organize a small army at Augusta, Ga., to check Sherman.[184] No decision was made, and none could be reached, as to a detachment from Lee's army, because Grant speedily became most active again. On the 29th there were signs of a new shift of troops to the north side of the James.[185] The next week, when the fickle weather changed again for the better,[186] all the signs pointed to another outflanking movement. "I think we are ready," Taylor wrote, "and hope with God's help for success." [187] Lee made no predictions, but watched every move and studied carefully every spy's report. On December 5 the scouts brought in dark news: The well-led VI Corps, which had been fighting against Early in the Shenandoah Valley, had rejoined Grant.[188]

Heavier odds against the weary Army of Northern Virginia, increased probability that Grant would try once again to swing around one flank or the other, virtual certainty that the Army of Northern Virginia could not detach even a regiment to help in holding back Sherman—could Lee do anything to offset this turn of affairs? There was only one move he could make on the chessboard of war: As Grant had recalled part of his troops from Sheridan, Lee might bring back part of the Second Corps without subjecting Early to the threat of immediate destruction. Accordingly, Gordon's division was ordered to start for Petersburg as soon as Lee was sure of the return of the VI Corps to Grant. Early's division, now under John Pegram, followed it at once.[189] On Longstreet's assurance that the northside was measurably safe,[190] Lee prepared to transfer Hoke to the southside again and to turn over his lines to Kershaw.[191] When Gordon arrived from the Valley, he was marched through Petersburg and was placed on the extreme right.[192] This hurried reconcentration did not counterbalance the return of the VI Corps to Grant, but it

184 O. R., 42, part 3, pp. 1228, 1233.   185 O. R., 42, part 3, p. 1232.
186 James A. Graham Papers, 200.   187 Taylor MSS., Dec. 4, 1864.
188 The VI Corps reached City Point, Dec. 4 (O. R., 42, part 1, p. 68).
189 O. R., 42, part 3, p. 1256; ibid., 43, part 1, p. 587; ibid., part 2, p. 936.
190 O. R., 42, part 3, p. 1256.
191 It is possible that the orders to Hoke, which appear in O. R., 42, part 3, p. 1258, were issued on the receipt of news that the Federals had started the Belfield raid, but it is manifest from O. R., 42, part 3, p. 1262, that Hoke was held on the north bank.
192 Gordon, 376.

made the odds less serious. Moreover, it relieved the cavalry and left A. P. Hill's corps available for employment in meeting new flank operations.

Before Gordon got into position, the Federals, on December 7, undertook a raid down the Weldon Railroad. Lee interpreted this to be an attempt to occupy Weldon[193] and he at once sent Hill to support Hampton, who had put his men on the march at the first report of the enemy's move.[194] Longstreet was ordered to attack on the northside, if possible, to keep the enemy from further enterprises.[195] The weather co-operated, for once, by turning discouragingly cold on the 8th.[196] The enemy got as far as Belfield, but could not cross the Meherrin River to Hicksford[197] or destroy the bridge in the face of the batteries that had been constructed to protect the crossing.[198] When the Federals were forced to turn back, their rations being near exhaustion, Hampton's cavalry skirmished hotly on their flanks and took some prisoners. Hill, however, could not overhaul them, and they returned unpunished. A simultaneous demonstration on Hatcher's Run amounted to little.[199] The enemy had torn up more of the track of the Weldon Railroad than Lee had thought—sixteen miles instead of six—but had done little additional military damage. There was some disappointment in the army that Hill had not engaged the Federal infantry.[200]

Sherman's march to the sea was, meantime, progressing ominously, and the question of detaching troops from the Army of Northern Virginia became even more pressing. Lee considered it likely that Sheridan would reinforce Grant, and that an attempt might be made to break the Confederate centre through the Dutch Gap Canal, which was now nearing completion. For this reason it was dangerous, he thought, to weaken his forces. In the emer-

[193] O. R., 42, part 3, p. 1259.   [194] O. R., 42, part 1, p. 950.
[195] O. R., 42, part 3, p. 1260.   [196] Hagood, 315; Taylor MSS., Dec. 12, 1864.
[197] Belfield was on the north and Hicksford on the south bank of the Meherrin. Together, they now form the town of Emporia.
[198] O. R., 42, part 1, p. 444; map, ibid., 448–49. For the armament at Hicksford, see ibid., part 3, p. 1322.
[199] The Federal force consisted of the V Corps, Mott's division of the II Corps, and Gregg's cavalry. One division of the IX Corps was sent to cover Warren's withdrawal. The demonstration against Hatcher's Run was made by Miles's 1st Division of the II Corps (O. R., 42, part 1, p. 260). Warren's report is in ibid., 443 ff.; Meade's in ibid., 27–38, and Lee's are in ibid., 855 and ibid., part 3, p. 1271. Hampton's is in ibid., part 1, p. 950. See also R. E. Lee to G. W. C. Lee, MS., Dec. 13, 1864, Duke Univ. MSS.
[200] Pendleton, 379.

gency, however, he felt that he could detach a division if Grant were not reinforced by Sheridan, and, as always, he expressed willingness to do more if the administration so directed. Davis, in a quandary, left the decision to Lee. When he heard that the snow was six inches deep in the Shenandoah Valley, Lee, on December 14, ordered Rodes's division to return to Petersburg. This stripped Early of nearly his whole command, but it gave Lee some guarantee that if he had to dispatch a force to Georgia, he could replace a part of it.[201]

With its gallant commander left behind in his grave in the Valley, Rodes's division reached Petersburg on December 18.[202] But the telegraph that told of his approach also brought dread tidings: On the 15th and 16th, Hood had met Thomas in front of Nashville and had been hopelessly routed.[203] On the 19th a great armada from Hampton Roads, eighty-five steamers altogether, arrived off Wilmington.[204] The same day Beauregard announced from Savannah that Sherman was approaching and had demanded the surrender of the place. "The city," he said, "must be evacuated [as] soon as practicable. The loss of Savannah will be followed by that of the railroad from Augusta to Charleston, and soon after of Charleston itself. Cannot Hoke and Johnson's divisions be spared for defence of South Carolina until part of or whole of Hood's army could reach Georgia?"[205]

Davis could not bring himself to believe that Beauregard's forecast was correct, but he turned to Lee for counsel, with the old, old question: What reinforcements could Lee send south? And should they go to Wilmington or to South Carolina?[206] As calmly as he weighed every other question, and without any evidence of the profound anxiety he must have felt, Lee concluded that the danger to Wilmington was more imminent, and, for all the odds on his own front, he ordered Longstreet to send a division to the North Carolina port. Longstreet selected Hoke's.[207] On the

201 *O. R.*, 42, part 3, pp. 1271, 1272, 1272–73, 1278.
202 *Grimes*, 93; *cf. O. R.*, 42, part 3, p. 1277. General John B. Gordon subsequently assumed command of the three divisions of the Second Corps when they were reassembled on the Petersburg front, and in his capacity as senior division major general, acted as lieutenant general, but there is no record that he was ever commissioned at that rank.
203 *Henry*, 432–33.
204 *O. R.*, 42, part 3, pp. 1278–79, 1283.
205 *O. R.*, 44, 966.
206 *O. R.*, 42, part 3, p. 1280.
207 *O. R.*, 42, part 3, p. 1280.

morning of December 20 Lee conferred with Longstreet and with Hoke, and started one of the latter's brigades for Wilmington, over the long route via Danville and Greensboro.[208] The railroad equipment was now near collapse. Cars were few and locomotives were scarcely able to crawl over the worn tracks. It was the 22d before the last of Hoke's men left Richmond.[209] Kershaw and Field took over their lines,[210] and Rodes's division was temporarily sent to Longstreet on the northside.[211] At this juncture, on December 22–23, from a front that was dangerously thin,[212] Longstreet had to detach two brigades to meet a raid on Gordonsville, but they were lucky enough to drive the enemy off, and returned so promptly that their absence had no serious consequences.[213]

The movement of Hoke's division southward from Danville was incredibly slow, so slow that suspicion of treachery on the part of the Piedmont Railroad was widespread in the army.[214] By Christmas Day only the leading brigade had reached Wilmington, and by the afternoon of December 26 scarcely 400 of the next brigade had arrived.[215] For a time it looked as though the delay would be fatal, but, as it happened, the attack was abortive. Union troops were landed and a powder ship was blown up in the mistaken belief that the concussion would destroy Fort Fisher, the main defense of the town.[216] As no damage was done, the land forces returned to their ships,[217] and on the 28th the fleet steamed away.[218] This was, of course, a relief to Lee and to the administration, but the good news that Wilmington was still open to the blockade runners meant little compared to the baleful tidings that on December 21 Sherman had marched into Savannah.

Hood's army a wreck; Georgia and the Gulf states cut off from Virginia; Sherman soon to be ready to march up the coast and to capture Charleston; the Army of the Potomac every day more powerful and better able to outflank Lee, no matter what his

---

208 *O. R.*, 42, part 3, pp. 1280–81.
209 *O. R.*, 42, part 3, pp. 1282, 1287.   210 *O. R.*, 42, part 3, pp. 1281, 1287.
211 *O. R.*, 42, part 3, pp. 1291, 1301.   212 *Cf. O. R.*, 42, part 3, p. 1288.
213 *O. R.*, 42, part 3, pp. 1289, 1290, 1293, 1295, 1301; *ibid.*, 43, part 2, p. 941. General Bratton's report of the engagement in front of Gordonsville is in *ibid.*, 42, part 1, pp. 882–83.
214 *Hagood*, 316; *O. R.*, 42, part 3, pp. 1305, 1334, 1344.
215 *O. R.*, 42, part 3, p. 1334.   216 2 *Grant's Memoirs*, 390–91.
217 *O. R.*, 42, part 3, p. 1323.   218 *O. R.*, 42, part 3, pp. 1334, 1343

vigilance, or what his strategy; Sheridan free to return with his overwhelming cavalry—surely, when the last December sun of 1864 set over the Petersburg defenses it brought the twilight of the Confederacy.

CHAPTER XXIX

THE WINTER OF GROWING DESPAIR

ANXIOUS as had been the months of November and December, 1864, there had been some hours when Lee could think of other things than troop movements, and after the repulse of the attack on Fort Fisher, while Sherman waited in Savannah, there came a brief respite.[1] Fortunately, Lee's health continued good, though he looked much older.[2] He rarely showed any sign of his gnawing anxiety and was ceaselessly active.[3] After he had completed his inspection of the lines on the right, early in November, he had returned to Petersburg, and then, about November 25, had decided to move headquarters farther toward the right, whither Grant seemed perpetually to be extending his flank in his efforts to reach the Southside Railroad. Lee had wished to remain in a tent, where his visitors would be no disturbance to others,[4] but Mrs. Lee and Walter Taylor between them had prevailed on him to accept the invitation of the Turnbull family and to establish himself at their home, Edge Hill, which was about two miles west of Petersburg, on a healthy, convenient, and accessible site. "After locating the General and my associates of the staff," Taylor wrote at the time, "I concluded that I would have to occupy one of the miserable little back rooms, but the gentleman of the house suggested that I should take the parlor. I think that the General was pleased with his room, and on entering mine he remarked: 'Ah, you are finely fixed. Couldn't you find any other room?' 'No,' I replied, 'but this will do. I can make myself tolerably comfortable here.' He was struck dumb with amazement at my impudence, and soon vanished." [5] The quarters were, indeed, the best Lee had ever

---

[1] Taylor had concluded on December 20 that the enemy would not again become aggressive during the winter. *Taylor MSS.*

[2] *Sorrel*, 258; 2 *R. W. C. D.*, 360; *James A. Graham Papers*, 199; *Long*, 396–97; 3 *N. C. Regts.*, 381. Surgeon Monteiro remarked of Lee in October: ". . . I have never looked into such eyes as his. . . . There was a deep meaning in his steady gaze that I have never seen in any other eyes than his" (A. Monteiro: *War Reminiscences* . . ., 14–15).

[3] *Cooke*, 428–29.   [4] *R. E. Lee, Jr.*, 140.   [5] *Taylor's Four Years*, 141.

had during his campaigning,[6] a fact which probably caused him some inward twinges, for Taylor believed the General was never so well satisfied as when he was living like a Spartan.[7] But if the rooms were pleasant, headquarters fare was of the scantiest. When General Ewell visited him, Lee insisted that his guest have his lunch, which consisted of two cold sweet potatoes.[8] An Irish M. P. who came to Edge Hill remarked to Mrs. Pryor, who had furnished him a room, because Lee could not, "You should have seen 'Uncle Robert's' dinner today, madam! He had two biscuits and he gave me one!" Another day the Irishman reported, "What a glorious dinner today, madam! Somebody sent 'Uncle Robert' a box of sardines." [9]

Lee's chief recreation, during many unoccupied hours, was entertaining children. The Federals had ceased bombarding the town during November, but on the 28th they had opened fire again,[10] deliberately, Lee thought, for, as he remarked to Reverend Henry C. Lay, "whenever a house was set on fire, we saw the fire of the enemy increased and converging on that point." [11] Lee was distressed that the bursting of the shells kept his young friends from playing in the city streets and occasionally he would send in a wagon and bring them out to headquarters, where they could frolic, free of danger. One day he was riding back to town with a party of youngsters, when a young guest began to whip the mules to make them go faster. "Don't do that, my little child," he said. The girl forgot after a few minutes and struck the beasts a second time. "Anne," he said, sternly but sadly, "you must not do that again. My conscience is not entirely at ease about using these animals for this extra service, for they are half fed, as we all are." [12] Once he spent a few spare moments playing with a child who was sick abed,[13] and on a Sunday when he entered a crowded chapel and found a plainly dressed little miss vainly looking for a seat, he escorted her to the pew that was reserved for him, and had her remain at his side during the service.[14]

[6] *Taylor MSS.*, Dec. 12, 1864.
[7] *Taylor's Four Years*, 141.
[8] *Jones*, 171.
[9] Mrs. Roger A. Pryor: *My Day*, 235.　　[10] *O. R.*, 42, part 3, p. 1231.
[11] Lay's memoirs in *Atlantic Monthly*, March, 1932, p. 340.
[12] *Mrs. Campbell Pryor's MS. Memoirs*, p. 6.
[13] *Jones*, 410.　　　　　　　　　　[14] *Ibid.*, 410.

"Yesterday afternoon," he wrote Mrs. Lee in January, "three little girls walked into my room, each with a small basket. The eldest carried some fresh eggs, laid by her own hens; the second, some pickles made by her mother; the third, some popcorn grown in her garden. . . . I have not had so pleasant a visit for a long time. I fortunately was able to fill their baskets with apples, which distressed poor Bryan, and I begged them to bring me nothing but kisses and to keep the eggs, corn, etc., for themselves." [15]

Another recreation, though rare, was that of reading a new book. He lingered affectionately, no doubt, over the life-story of that admiring old friend and chief from whom, in April, 1861, he had found it so difficult to part. "I have put in the bag General Scott's autobiography, which I thought you might like to read," he wrote Mrs. Lee late in the winter. "The General, of course, stands out prominently, and does not hide his light under a bushel, but he appears the bold, sagacious, truthful man he is." [16]

His rides into Petersburg and his visits to Richmond were a comfort to him, of course. In Petersburg he called often on Mrs. A. P. Hill, the young and lovely wife of the commander of the Third Corps. "Gen. Lee comes very frequently to see me," Mrs. Hill wrote her mother, all in a breath, "he is the best and greatest man on earth, brought me the last time some delicious apples." [17] When the General "went home" to Richmond, it was always to find Mrs. Lee more and more a cripple, though she was interested in everything and kept her needles busy knitting socks for the soldiers. [18]

The capital was more crowded than ever, dejected[19] and negligently dilapidated.[20] Sometimes, from the sad seniors, Lee would turn away to the children. "I don't want to see you," he would

---

[15] R. E. Lee, Jr., 142–43. It was characteristic of Mrs. Lee that she began a correspondence with these generous girls, whose mother, Mrs. Nottingham, had "refuged" to Petersburg from the vicinity of Eastville, Northampton County, Va. Photostats of three letters to Miss Fanny Nottingham, one of the trio, are in the collection of the Virginia Historical Society.

[16] R. E. Lee, Jr., 147.

[17] Magill MSS., n. d. but evidently of the winter of 1864–65 as the letter was written from Petersburg.

[18] Cf. R. E. Lee, Jr., 141. Among the Richmond visits that have not been mentioned in the text was one on Sept. 12–14, 1864 (Taylor MSS., Sept. 12, 1864; 2 R. W. C. D., 282), and one at the end of December, 1864 (O. R., 51, part 2, p. 1055).

[19] Cf. 2 R. W. C. D., 372, 384.   [20] Miss Brock, 315.

say half in jest and half in reproof, "you are too gloomy and de-spondent; where is —?" and he would name the little girl of the family.[21] The young belles of the town were much in doubt whether it was proper to have dances at so dark a time, and a committee of them asked his advice, with the assurance that if he disapproved, they would not dance a single step. "Why, of course, my dear child," he answered. "My boys need to be heartened up when they get their furloughs. Go on, look your prettiest, and be just as nice to them as ever you can be!"[22]

At Christmas time, when Savannah had fallen and the fate of Wilmington seemed to hang by a thread, he went to Richmond to see his family,[23] but he could not stay more than a day. On his return he learned that some of his friends had sent him a saddle of mutton to brighten the mess at Edge Hill. It went astray, how-ever, and never reached him. "If the soldiers get it," he said, simply, in reporting its non-arrival, "I shall be content. I can do very well without it. In fact, I should rather they should have it than I."[24] At a Yuletide dinner in Petersburg he was no little embarrassed because he wanted to save his portion of turkey so that he could carry it to one of his staff officers who, as he ex-plained, had been very ill and had "nothing to eat but corn bread and sweet-potato coffee."[25] When a barrel of turkeys arrived for himself and his staff he ordered his fowl sent to the hospital, and he announced his purpose in such a tone that the other officers sadly repacked the barrel and sent all its contents to the scanty mess of the convalescents.[26] He discouraged personal gifts as far as he could. Daily, for three months after he came to Petersburg, the wife of Judge W. W. Crump, a distinguished jurist of Rich-mond, sent fresh bread to his mess by a special messenger. "Al-though it is very delicious," he felt constrained to write her, "I must beg you to cease sending it. I cannot consent to tax you so heavily. In these times no one can supply their families and fur-

21 Mrs. Mary Pegram Anderson, in *Richmond Times-Dispatch*, Jan. 20, 1907.

22 *Mrs. Burton Harrison*, 150. For some pathetic and often amusing glimpses of Lee in Richmond during the last months of the war, see 19 *S. H. S. P.*, 382–83; 20 *Confederate Veteran*, 279–81; *Harpers Magazine*, vol. 122, p. 333.

23 J. P. Smith in *Richmond Times-Dispatch*, Jan. 20, 1907.

24 *R. E. Lee, Jr.*, 142.

25 *Mrs. Campbell Pryor's MS. Memoirs*, p. 5; Mrs. Roger A. Pryor: *My Day*, 234.

26 *Harpers Magazine*, vol. 122, p. 333.

nish the Army, too. We have a plenty to eat and our appetites are so good that they do not require tempting." [27]

There was much to be done, during this period and throughout the winter, in maintaining the morale of the officers, for many of them now regarded the Southern cause as lost. In their private speculations as to how long the Confederacy could survive, few affirmed that even the Army of Northern Virginia could resist the enemy longer than July, 1865.[28] Carelessness increased, drinking became worse. Lee had constantly to be stirring some of his subordinates to vigilance. Occasionally he would snub a man whom he thought had been needlessly absent;[29] sometimes he would present his coldest mien to those he found loafing at headquarters;[30] if an officer seemed to be too dainty about his food, Lee would chaff him with exaggerated attention.[31] When a man complained of injustice on the part of his superiors, Lee would urge him to his full duty and not to fear the consequences.[32] The sick officer was always his special care.[33] To the family of wounded or captured men, as well as to the kin of one who was killed, he was quick to send his condolence.[34] Furloughs he had to decline, even in a case so pathetic as that of General Pendleton, who wished to go home to baptize the posthumous child of his son "Sandie," who had been killed in Early's Valley campaign.[35]

So far as circumstances permitted, Lee continued to give encouragement and to administer rebukes by tactful suggestion.[36] Riding out one day in January, 1865, he inquired of General John B. Gordon and of General Heth concerning the progress being made on two heavy redoubts that were under construction on Hatcher's Run. Gordon assured him that his fort was nearly finished. Heth said, with some embarrassment, "I think the fort on my side of the run also about finished, sir."

[27] R. E. Lee to Mrs. [W. W.] Crump, Sept. 21, 1864, MS., for a photostat of which the writer is indebted to Miss Henrietta B. Crump, to whose assistance, in a hundred other ways, this book bears witness.

[28] History of McGowan's Brigade, 198.

[29] Taylor MSS., Dec. 18, 1864.   [30] W. W. Chamberlaine, 110.

[31] F. W. Dawson, 125.

[32] Cf. the case of General E. M. Law in Lee's Dispatches, 304.

[33] General Grimes, op. cit., 100, related that when he went to G. H. Q. on March 13, 1865, Lee observed that he was ill and insisted that he drink a glass of wine—one of the few instances where he ever offered even mild stimulants.

[34] Cf. Mrs. Roger A. Pryor: My Day, 216.

[35] Pendleton, 380-81.   [36] Cf. Sorrel, 269-70.

Lee decided to go with them and to see for himself. Gordon's works were in the conditions described. On Heth's front, the digging had scarcely begun.

"General," said Lee, "you say this fort is about finished?"

"I must have misunderstood my engineers, sir."

"But you did not speak of your engineers. You spoke of the fort as nearly completed."

Heth was riding a very spirited horse that had been presented to his wife, and in his humiliation he must have tugged at the reins, for the animal began to prance about excitedly.

"General," said Lee, in his blandest manner, "doesn't Mrs. Heth ride that horse occasionally?"

"Yes, sir."

"Well, General, you know that I am very much interested in Mrs. Heth's safety. I fear that horse is too nervous for her to ride without danger, and I suggest that in order to make him more quiet, you ride him at least once a day to this fort." That was all, but it was a rebuke that sank into the heart of Heth.[37]

One evening the General came upon a group of young officers who were working over a bit of mathematics, drinking all the while from two tin cups that were replenished at the mouth of a jug that had a guilty, bibulous look. Lee solved their problem for them and went his way with no reference to their refreshment; but the next morning, when one of the group began to recount a very curious dream of the night, Lee quietly observed, "That is not at all remarkable. When young gentlemen discuss at midnight mathematical problems, the unknown quantities of which are a stone jug and two tin cups, they may expect to have strange dreams."[38] He was always careful, however, never to rebuke an officer of rank in the presence of others. On a tour of inspection with Gordon he found some earthworks that had been very badly located, and he said so in plain words. Turning, however, he noticed some young officers within earshot; so he added

---

[37] The version here followed is that of Gordon (*op. cit.*, 379–80), the only other auditor of this famous colloquy. Gordon did not mention Heth's name, but as he said the officer in question was in temporary command of Hill's corps during the illness of the lieutenant general, only Heth could have been meant. Other versions of the incident appear in *Jones*, 243, and *Long*, 388.

[38] *Jones*, 243; *Long*, 400.

works were laid out by skilled engineers, who
r business better than we do." [39]

asion to admonish officers during that dread-
vise had occasion to be grateful to some of
more than to Brigadier General Archibald
Gracie for an act of a kind that Lee best appreciated. One day in
November he had been on the lines with Gracie, who commanded
a brigade in Johnson's division. Being perhaps unfamiliar with
the deadliness of the sharpshooting on that part of the front, Lee
carelessly stood up on the parapet. Gracie, without a word, instantly interposed his body between that of Lee and the enemy.
Both were pulled back over the works before either was hit, but
Lee never forgot the spirit Gracie exhibited. A few weeks later,
on December 3, Gracie was killed by a fragment of shrapnel at
a point on the fortifications where there was not supposed to be
any danger. [40]

Through these anxious days, as always, Lee's reliance was on a
Power which, as he wrote Mr. Davis at the time he recalled
Rodes's division from the Valley, "will cause all things to work
together for our good." [41] Again he told Mrs. Lee: "I pray daily
and almost hourly to our Heavenly Father to come to the relief of
you and our afflicted country. I know He will order all things
for our good, and we must be content." [42] The type of his prayer
book having become too small for his vision, he mentioned the fact
one day to Mrs. Churchill J. Gibson, wife of the rector of Grace
Church, Petersburg, and said that he intended to give it to some
soldier. He remarked, as he spoke, that the volume was the one
he had used during the Mexican War. Mrs. Gibson at once
offered to give him several new copies of the prayer book in
exchange for so interesting a memento. Lee gladly agreed and
distributed the new books through one of his chaplains to men
who asked for them. In each copy he inscribed a line of presen-
tation. [43] Yet, faithfully as he used his new book of devotion, with

[39] Jones, 287.
[40] Alexander, 586; Owen, 356; other versions in 3 N. C. Regts., 381; 17 Confederate
Veteran, 160. For Lee's experience with Gracie at West Point, see supra, vol. I., pp.
337–38.
[41] Dec. 14, 1864; O. R., 42, part 3, p. 1272.
[42] "Early in January, 1865," R. E. Lee, Jr., 143.
[43] Statement of Doctor Churchill G. Chamberlayne, July, 1933; affidavit of Mrs.
Mary W. Chamberlayne in his possession. An incorrect version of this appears in Jones,
Christ in Camp, 53.

the humility that marked his every act, he doubted if his
prayers would avail. In an exchange of letters with General
Pendleton, during the autumn, when Pendleton explained that
he had omitted to say grace at the General's table because he did
not know his chief had asked him to do so, Lee said "[I] am
deeply obliged to you for your fervent prayers in my behalf. No
one stands in greater need of them. My feeble petitions I dare
hardly hope will be answered." [44]

A nation's prayers, and not an individual's only, were needed
as January, 1865, passed. Hourly along the line of thirty-five miles
from the Williamsburg road to the unstable right flank on
Hatcher's Run the pickets kept their rifles barking, and the sharpshooters watched the embrasures on the reddish-yellow parapet
across the fields. Nightly the fuse of each bomb could be traced,
like giants' fireworks, from the mouth of the mortar through the
high trajectory and back again to earth. Never was there silence,
never a day without casualties; yet from the time of the raid on
Belfield in December, 1864, until February, 1865, there was no
large action on the Richmond-Petersburg front, largely because of
the condition of the roads. [45] Elsewhere, calamity followed on the
heels of disaster. Before the middle of January it became apparent
that Sherman would soon start his advance from Savannah toward
Charleston. [46] There were only scattered forces to oppose him.
Kershaw's old brigade, now under General James Conner, was
immediately ordered to Charleston. [47] Cavalry was much needed
there. After conference with President Davis, Lee dispatched
Butler's division to the Palmetto State and authorized General
Hampton to go thither, also, in the hope that his great reputation
in South Carolina would bring new volunteers to the colors. [48]
In retrospect, Lee regarded this as the great mistake he made
during the campaign, because it crippled him in dealing with

---

[44] *Pendleton*, 375–76.

[45] ". . . now [January 13] the roads are worse than I ever saw them before"
(*James A. Graham Papers*, 206).

[46] *Cf.* Sherman in *O. R.*, 47, part 1, p. 17.

[47] *O. R.*, 47, part 2, p. 997; *History of Kershaw's Brigade*, 501; *Lee's Dispatches*
315–17; R. E. Lee to Jefferson Davis, MS., Jan. 15, 1865, *Duke Univ. MSS*.

[48] *E. L. Wells*, 388 *ff*.

subsequent Federal operations against his right flank.[49] When the movement was ordered there seemed no alternative to it, unless Sherman was to be permitted to advance unhindered up the coast.

Before Butler's cavalry could get under way for South Carolina, a great Federal fleet again appeared off Wilmington, convoying an infantry force on transports. This time there was no delay and no experimentation with powder boats. Under the direction of General Alfred H. Terry, the troops were thrown ashore and on January 13 a bombardment of Fort Fisher was begun. Before the early winter's sun had set, two days later, the Union flag was flying over the shattered works, and the last port of the Confederacy was closed.[50]

With Wilmington lost and Sherman about to march northward, the alarm in Richmond grew into a frenzy. Davis was blamed, as the executive of a waning cause always is, both for what he had done and what he had failed to accomplish. Some of those who had been so insistent on a rigid interpretation of the Federal Constitution in 1860 now began to clamor for a dictator. Lee was to be the man. The President must step aside and place all power in the hands of the one person who had the genius to save the South. Longstreet had hinted at something of the sort in December, and Lee had ignored it.[51] To his mind, the very suggestion was abhorrent and a reflection on his loyalty as a soldier and a citizen. So far as the record shows, nobody ever presumed to mention the subject to him personally. At length, as a sort of desperate compromise with Congress, the President consented to the appointment of a general-in-chief.

As it happened, the nearest approach to an open break between General Lee and the President had occurred only a few days before. Late in January or early in February[52] there was an ex-

[49] See R. E. Lee to Wade Hampton, Aug. 1, 1865: "The absence of the troops which I sent to North and South Carolina was, I believe, the cause of our immediate disaster. Our small force of cavalry was unable to resist the united cavalry under Sheridan . . ." (E. L. Wells, 361–62).

[50] Terry's report is in O. R., 46, part 1, pp. 394 ff.; Bragg's appears in ibid., 431 ff. The unfortunate Whiting, grievously wounded, fell into the hands of the Federals, as did Colonel William Lamb, who had been in immediate command of the fort.

[51] O. R., 42, part 3, pp. 1286–87; Jones, 223–24; 2 R. W. C. D., 372. Lee had previously stated, in answer to urging, that if the South won its independence, he would not be Mr. Davis's successor. "That I will never permit," he said. "Whatever talents I possess are military talents" (Jones, loc. cit.).

[52] Cf. IV O. R., part 3, pp. 1066–67.

change of correspondence regarding the destruction of tobacco in the warehouses of Richmond, to prevent its falling into the hands of the enemy. President Davis telegraphed Lee, in effect, "Rumor said to be based on orders given by you create concern and obstruct necessary legislation. Come over. I wish to have your views on the subject." Lee replied in cipher, which Davis had employed, that it was difficult for him to leave Petersburg. "Send me the measures," his telegram concluded, "and I will send you my views." This made Davis very angry. He replied at some length, and ended: "Rest assured I will not ask your views in answer to measures. Your counsels are no longer wanted in this matter." Lee received this in silence when it was decoded, then quietly ordered his horse, rode to the railroad and took the train to Richmond. When he returned he said nothing of what had passed between the President and himself.[53] Evidently, however, all misunderstandings were cleared up for, on February 6, Davis named Lee to the newly created office.[54] The appointment came just at the time when the negotiations for peace at the so-called Hampton Roads conference had failed[55] and when the Federals were active on Lee's right flank. He had his hands full, more than full, and was under no illusions as to what he could do in general command. He wrote characteristically:

"I know I am indebted entirely to your indulgence and kind consideration for this honorable position. I must beg of you to continue these same feelings to me in the future and allow me to refer to you at all times for counsel and advice. I cannot otherwise hope to be of service to you or the country. If I can relieve you from a portion of the constant labor and anxiety which now presses upon you, and maintain a harmonious action between the great armies, I shall be more than compensated for the addition to my present burdens. I must, however, rely upon the several commanders for the conduct of the military operations with which they are charged, and hold them responsible. In the event of their neglect or failure I must ask for their removal."[56]

He did not attempt to do more than he indicated in this letter

[53] C. S. Venable to W. H. Taylor, MS., March 29, 1878, Taylor MSS.
[54] O. R., 46, part 2, p. 1205.
[55] O. R., 46, part 2, p. 446.   [56] O. R., 51, part 2, pp. 1082-83.

and he did not consider that his appointment conferred the right to assign generals to command armies. "I can only employ such troops and officers," he said, "as may be placed at my disposal by the War Department. Those withheld or relieved from service are not at my disposal." [57] It was all he could do to watch Grant, to conserve the strength of his dwindling army, and to combat the dark forces of hunger and disintegration that had long been at work. In December the shortage of provisions had become more acute than ever. No salt meat was available in the depots, and none was arriving from the South.[58] In the emergency the navy lent the army 1500 barrels of salt beef and pork,[59] but the commissary general confessed himself desperate,[60] and a special secret report to Congress bore out his dark view of the South's resources.[61]

In January heavy rains temporarily broke down transportation on the Piedmont Railroad, which linked Lee's army with the western Carolinas. About the same time floods cut off supplies from the upper valley of the James River. Lee then had only two days' rations for his men[62] and already had scoured clean the country within reach of his foragers. In this crisis, at the instance of the War Department, which fell back in every emergency on the magic of his name and on the compelling power of his appeal, he asked the people to contribute food for the army.[63] Almost before he could ascertain whether appreciable results would follow this call, he had to march a heavy column to the extreme right to meet new Federal demonstrations on Hatcher's Run. This was on February 5, the eve of the very worst weather of a bad winter.[64]

---

[57] Letter to sundry congressmen, Feb. 13, 1864, in answer to their request that he name Johnston to command the Army of Tennessee (Mrs. D. Giraud Wright: *A Southern Girl in '61*, pp. 235 ff.).

[58] *Lee's Dispatches*, 307–8.   [59] *O. R.*, 51, part 2, p. 1054.   [60] IV *O. R.*, 3, p. 930.

[61] McCabe, 568 ff. W. L. Royall (*op. cit.*, 43–44) stated on the authority of Major Lewis Ginter, of the staff of General A. P. Hill, that after a tour of inspection in North Carolina, Major Ginter reported to Lee that there was an abundance of supplies in the territory he had visited. Major Ginter urged Lee to seize the trains and to collect supplies. Lee is said to have walked up and down the floor for a while and then is alleged to have answered, "No, Major, I can't do that. It would be revolutionary. If the administration chooses to starve the army, it will have to starve." There is no confirmation of this story from any other source, but the words and sentiments are such as Lee might well have voiced.

[62] 2 *R. W. C. D.*, 384.   [63] *O. R.*, 46, part 2, pp. 1035, 1040, 1075.

[64] Lee was in church in Petersburg on Feb. 5 when he received news of this advance. He waited quietly until communion, then, contrary to his custom, went with the first group to the chancel. He received the communion and, taking up his hat and gloves

The military results were negligible, but for three nights and three days a large part of the Confederate forces had to remain in line of battle, with no meat and little food of any sort.[65] The suffering of the men so deeply aroused Lee that he broke over the usual restraint he displayed in dealing with the civil authorities. "If some change is not made and the commissary department reorganized, I apprehend dire results," he wrote the Secretary of War. "The physical strength of the men, if their courage survives, must fail under this treatment." He did not demand the resignation of the grumbling Northrop, the commissary general of subsistence, but his reference to the necessity of a change was not lost on President Davis. "This is too sad to be patiently considered," Davis endorsed on Lee's dispatch, "and cannot have occurred without criminal neglect or gross incapacity." [66] Within a few days, Northrop was quietly relieved of duty and was succeeded by Brigadier General I. M. St. John, who had much distinguished himself by his diligent management of the mining and nitre bureau.[67] St. John was most reluctant to take the post,[68] but he immediately organized a system by which supplies were to be collected from the farmers, hauled to the railroad and dispatched directly to the army, without being handled through central depots.[69] Lee welcomed the change,[70] and was encouraged by it to believe that if communications could be maintained, the army would be better fed.[71] The people, he reasoned, "have simply to choose whether they will contribute such . . . stores as they can possibly spare to support an army that has borne and done so much in their behalf, or retain those stores to maintain the army of the enemy engaged in their subjugation." [72] This view was at once made the basis of an ingenious appeal for food, addressed to the people of Virginia by a special committee of Richmond ministers and other citizens. A plan was outlined by which a farmer

from the pew, left immediately (*Pendleton*, 389, *Taylor MSS.*, Feb. 5, 1865). He hurried to the right, where the troops were already engaged. Finding some new recruits in excited disorder, he rode out and endeavored to rally them. One frightened man raised his hands in terror and exclaimed, "Great God, old man; get out of the way! You don't know nothing!" (Sloan, *op. cit.*, 110). For the reports, see *O. R.*, 46, part 1, pp. 253 *ff.*: 9 *S. H. S. P.*, 81.

65 *O. R.*, 46, part 2, pp. 1206, 1210.　　66 *O. R.*, 46, part 2, p. 1210.
67 1 *C. M. H.*, 622.　　68 3 *S. H. S. P.*, 104-5.
69 1 *C. M. H.*, 622.　　70 *O. R.*, 46, part 2, pp. 1246, 1247.
71 *O. R.*, 46, part 2, p. 1250.　　72 *O. R.*, 46, part 2, p. 1246.

could ration a soldier for six months—much as money was raised in America during the war with Germany to feed Belgian babies and Armenian orphans.[73]

Anxiously, agonizingly, Lee awaited the response of the people. When he was asked early in March for an appraisal of the military situation, he postulated everything, in his reply, on transportation and on the willingness of the people to make further sacrifices. "Unless the men and animals can be subsisted," he said, "the army cannot be kept together, and our present lines must be abandoned. Nor can it be moved to any other position where it can operate to advantage without provisions to enable it to move in a body. . . . Everything, in my opinion, has depended and still depends upon the disposition and feelings of the people. Their representatives can best decide how they will bear the difficulties and sufferings of their condition and how they will respond to the demands which the public safety requires." [74]

The representatives of Virginia in the Congress were brought together to answer Lee's question. He was present and told them of lengthened lines and thinning forces, of the privations the soldiers had to meet, and of the scarcity of food for them and for the horses. The Virginians replied that the people of the state, with loyalty and devotion, would meet any new demand made on them,[75] but they seemed to General Lee to content themselves with words and assertions of their faith in their constituents. They proposed nothing; they did nothing. Lee said no more—the facts were warning enough—but he went from the building and made his way to his residence with distress and indignation battling in his heart. When dinner was over, Custis sat down by the fire to smoke a cigar and to read the news, but Lee paced the floor restlessly. "He was so much engrossed in his own thoughts," wrote a silent young observer, years afterwards, "that he seemed to be oblivious to the presence of a third person. I watched him closely as he went to the end of the room, turned and tramped back again, with his hands behind him. I saw he was deeply troubled. Never had I seen him look so grave.

[73] Printed copy in *Lee MSS., I.* For the classification of General Lee's military papers, see the Bibliography.
[74] *O. R.,* 46, part 2, p. 1295.
[75] John Goode in 29 *S. H. S. P.,* 179. Practically the same account appears in his *Recollections,* 93, 94.

"Suddenly he stopped in front of his son and faced him: 'Well, Mr. Custis,' he said, 'I have been up to see the Congress and they do not seem to be able to do anything except to eat peanuts and chew tobacco, while my army is starving. I told them the condition the men were in, and that something must be done at once, but I can't get them to do anything, or they are unable to do anything.' . . . there was some bitterness in his tones. . . .

"The General resumed his promenade, but after a few more turns he again stopped in the same place and resumed: 'Mr. Custis, when this war began I was opposed to it, bitterly opposed to it, and I told these people that unless every man should do his whole duty, they would repent it; and now' (he paused slightly as if to give emphasis to his words) 'they will repent.' " [76]

It was on this visit to Richmond, or on another about the same time, that he was chatting with a group of gentlemen at the President's house when one of them said: "Cheer up, General, we have done a good work for you today. The legislature has passed a bill to raise an additional 15,000 men for you." Lee, who had been very silent and thoughtful, bowed his acknowledgments. "Yes," he said, "passing resolutions is kindly meant, but getting the men is another matter." He hesitated for a moment, and his eyes flashed. "Yet," he went on, "if I had 15,000 fresh troops, things would look very different." [77]

Outraged as Lee was by the apparent incapacity of Congress, he warmly encouraged General St. John to do his utmost in applying the same methods of direct appeal the new commissary general had used with notable success in collecting nitre; but as Lee sought to find food for his men he saw new military difficulties added to those of transportation, weather, distress, and growing public despair. The danger of the destruction of all lines of communication with the South and the occupation of the only terri-

---

[76] G. T. Lee in 26 *South Atlantic Quarterly*, July, 1927, 236–37. It may have been at this conference that Lee was inwardly outraged at the action of a Virginia congressman, John Goode, in presenting him a numerously signed petition from Bedford County, asking that the furlough of a miller be extended. The document, passing through channels, finally reached the Secretary of War and then the President, both of whom approved it. When it reached Lee he wrote on it, "Col. Taylor, give him five days," an extension that must have seemed to the miller a very poor return for all the political pressure he had exerted (C. S. Venable to W. H. Taylor, *MS.*, March 29, 1878—*Taylor MSS.*).

[77] *Life and Reminiscences of Jefferson Davis*, by Distinguished Men of His Time, p. 233.

tory from which he was now drawing supplies were daily brought nearer and nearer. "The perils and privations of the troops," in the opinion of an observant colonel who saw him often, "were never absent from his thought." [78]

Bound up, now as always, with subsistence for the men was the old, tragic question of provender for the horses during a winter when there was no pasturage. It was the experience of 1862–63 and 1863–64 more poignantly repeated. Many of the army wagons were used, during most periods of quiet, to collect food and bring it to the railroad. When the army was in a country that had not been stripped of food the wagons could gather enough to make up for the deficiencies of the regular supply from the depots. [79] Now, the territory around Petersburg having been swept of the last provisions, such horses as were not too feeble and too ill-fed to be sent out, had to be used at a long distance from the army, in North Carolina and in western Virginia. [80] Those that remained had then to be fed at places where inability to employ them in foraging made the army wholly dependent on what came by railroad. The familiar "vicious circle" thus was rounded more speedily than ever, and the mobility of the army and its range of vision were hourly decreased. There was danger that the troops might remain where they were until, in a literal sense, they had no horses to move their trains. Yet Lee could not circumvent this by an early departure from Petersburg, because the mud was so heavy the teams could not pull the wagons. He had to wait until the roads were better, even if he had to risk immobility then. [81]

What was true of the wagon trains applied also, of course, to the artillery. The horses had to be taken from most of the guns and scattered through the countryside, at a distance from the line, in order to keep them alive. As late as March 20 it had not been possible to call in even the animals of the horse artillery. [82] Many commands had to be consolidated and reorganized because there were not enough horses for all the batteries. [83]

The cavalry suffered with the wagon train and with the artil-

[78] 29 S. H. S. P., 93.
[79] O. R., 46, part 2, p. 1295; MS. report of Lt.-Col. Thos. G. Williams, assistant commissary general, Lee MSS.—L.
[80] O. R., 46, part 2, p. 1247.   [81] 2 Davis, 648.   [82] O. R., 46, part 3, p. 1328.
[83] Sundry communications on this subject, written by General Pendleton, will be found in O. R., 46, parts 2 and 3.

lery. No substantial force could be kept close to the infantry. When Butler's division was sent off, the horses were subsisted in North Carolina.[84] Two other divisions were scattered in small units because supplies could not be transported to the places where the troops should have been concentrated. At the time of the operations against Hatcher's Run, in February, W. H. F. Lee's division had to be brought forty miles, by roundabout roads, from Stony Creek, where forage was being delivered.[85] Early in March, when it was necessary to send out cavalry on a forced reconnaissance, five days elapsed before Fitz Lee could get his men together and start after the enemy.[86] Rooney Lee, called up at a critical hour, had to be returned to Stony Creek on the very day Lee thought that Grant's cavalry was being heavily reinforced.[87] Before the end of the winter Lee was uncertain whether he would be able to maintain even a small cavalry force around Richmond.[88] There was virtually nothing he could do to maintain the arm of service on which he had to depend not only for early information of the enemy's movements but also for the protection of his communications and for the safety of his right flank from a sudden turning movement. He urged the government to new endeavor in procuring horses,[89] and when it was reported that animals could not be had for lack of money, he frankly advocated the seizure of cotton and tobacco, their sale for gold and the purchase of horses with this medium.[90] Nothing coming of this, he was compelled to extemporize new tactics. Infantry were to be stationed as close as practicable to any point whence the enemy was expected to start a raid, and were then to be moved rapidly to support the thin cavalry that might be thrown forward—a scheme that seems to have been proposed by Longstreet.[91] This meant, of course, that the defensive line had to be weakened, and the danger of a break increased by this detachment of infantry,[92] even when

[84] O. R., 46, part 2, p. 1100. [85] O. R., 46, part 2, p. 1210.

[86] The orders were issued March 2 (Lee MSS.); he moved March 7 (O. R., 46, part 2, pp. 1277 ff.).

[87] March 17; O. R., 46, part 3, p. 1319.

[88] O. R., 46, part 3, p. 1319. [89] O. R., 46, part 2, pp. 1190, 1208.

[90] O. R., 46, part 2, p. 1243. Previously he had urged formal government trading with the enemy for needed supplies (Lee's Dispatches, 318. Cf. Cole to Lawton, IV O. R., 3, 1087–89).

[91] O. R., 46, part 3, p. 1329.

[92] Cf. Lee to Hampton, Aug. 1, 1865, E. L. Wells, 362.

troopers who had no horses were put in the trenches. It was a grim plight for an army that once had boasted a Stuart and stout squadrons of faultlessly mounted boys who had mocked the awkward cavalry of McClellan as they had ridden around his army.

Desertion continued to sap the man-power of the army. After Christmas, when the winter chill entered into doubting hearts, and every mail told the Georgia and Carolina troops of the enemy's nearer approach to their homes, more and more men slipped off in the darkness. Desertions between February 15 and March 18 numbered 2934, nearly 8 per cent of the effective strength of the army.[93] From Pickett's division alone, a command that had won the plaudits of the world, 512 soldiers deserted about the middle of March, during the progress of a single move.[94] There was suspicion that men from different brigades were communicating with one another and were arranging rendezvous.[95] When they left, taking their arms with them,[96] they usually went home, but not a few of the weaker-spirited joined the enemy. From one division, a good one at that, 178 were reported to have "gone over into the Union," in the language of the trenches.[97] Conditions became so bad that when it was necessary to move one of Pickett's brigades through Richmond, Longstreet's adjutant general did not think it safe to let the men wait long in the streets.[98]

The reasons for this wastage in an army that had been distinguished for nothing more than for its morale were all too apparent —hunger, delayed pay, the growing despair of the public mind, and, perhaps more than anything else, woeful letters from wives and families telling of danger or privation at home.[99] Lee noted with much distress that the largest number of desertions were among the North Carolina regiments, which previously had fought as gallantly as any troops in his command.[100] The army was melting away faster than was the snow.

Lee had been able to do little about subsistence and the sup-

---

[93] O. R., 46, part 2, pp. 1254, 1265, 1293; O. R., 46, part 3, p. 1353.

[94] O. R., 46, part 3, p. 1353. For another typical record of desertion, see History of McGowan's Brigade, 198.

[95] O. R., 46, part 2, p. 1261.   [96] O. R., 46, part 2, p. 1254.

[97] O. R., 46, part 2, p. 1265.   [98] O. R., 46, part 3, p. 1343.

[99] James A. Graham Papers, 210–11.

[100] O. R., 46, part 2, pp. 1143, 1254, 1265. For the tone of soldiers' letters from home, see Alexander, 585.

ply of horses, but desertion and the conditions it brought about were military problems. He faced them. After offering amnesty,[101] he had to enforce very sternly the law for the execution of deserters who were recaptured, and when clemency was shown in a case where a court-martial had decreed the death penalty, he telegraphed: "Hundreds of men are deserting nightly, and I cannot keep the army together unless examples are made of such cases."[102] He sent a large detachment to western North Carolina to bring back deserters, and he felt compelled to take from his insecurely held trenches a whole brigade to guard the crossings of the Roanoke River.[103] The articles of war on desertion and the regulations forbidding any man to propose such a course, even in jest, were read throughout the army for three days.[104] Longstreet issued an order in which he announced that he would recommend for commission with the proposed Negro regiments any man who thwarted the attempt of another soldier to desert.[105]

Despair had not entered every heart. If hundreds deserted, there were thousands who had resolved that neither hunger nor cold, neither danger nor the bad example of feebler spirits could induce them to leave "Marse Robert." Many of them "came to look upon the cause as General Lee's cause, and they fought for it because they loved him. To them he represented cause, country and all."[106] The soldiers' letters of this dark period present a hundred contrasts. One Marylander wrote in January: "There are a good many of us who believe this shooting match has been carried on long enough. A government that has run out of rations can't expect to do much more fighting, and to keep on in a reckless and wanton expenditure of human life. Our rations are all the way from a pint to a quart of cornmeal a day, and occasionally a piece of bacon large enough to grease your palate."[107] A young North Carolinian, in precisely the opposite mood, expressed his regret that the people of his state were despairing because of the loss of Fort Fisher. "If some of them could come up here," he wrote, "and catch the good spirits of the soldiers, I think they

[101] O. R., 46, part 2, pp. 1229-30.   [102] O. R., 46, part 2, p. 1258.
[103] O. R., 46, part 2, p. 1265.   [104] O. R., 46, part 3, p. 1357.
[105] O. R., 46, part 3, p. 1361. For the plan to employ Negroes as soldiers, see *infra* p. 544.
[106] Colonel Charles Marshall, quoted in *R. E. Lee, Jr.,* 138.
[107] 29 S. H. S. P., 290.

would feel better." [108] Lee understood the fears of the faint-hearted as much as he valued the courage of those who, knowing the cause to be hopeless, determined to sustain it to the end. In his appeals to all his men, he spoke now as a father to his sons.[109] The little that he could do for their comfort, he did with warm affection. One winter's day, as he and his staff were riding along, he met four private soldiers plodding through the mud toward the lines. Stopping, he asked where they were going, and when they explained that they had been to Petersburg and were afraid they would not reach their posts before roll-call, he had some of his officers take the men up behind them on their horses and carry them to the trenches.[110] When a sergeant of the fine old Fourth South Carolina came to Lee's headquarters and asked for transportation on a furlough he had earned, the General was distressed that the railroad pass had not been issued with the furlough. "They ought to have given you transportation without putting you to this trouble," he said.[111] He was accessible to all his men, even to the cooks. When one Negro attendant presented himself at Edge Hill, Lee had him admitted.

"General Lee," the man began, "I been wantin' to see you for a long time. I's a soldier."

"Ah," Lee answered, "to what army do you belong—to the Union army or to the Southern army?"

"Oh, General, I belong to your army."

"Well, have you been shot?"

"No, sah, I ain't been shot yet."

"How is that?" Lee inquired. "Nearly all of our men get shot."

"Why, General, I ain't been shot 'case I stays back whar de generals stay." Desperate as were the times, Lee found delight in that answer and repeated it more than once to his lieutenants.[112]

Of the men to whom the heart of Lee went out, the wounded always came first. One day he was journeying over to Richmond for an interview with the President. As the train neared the city a crippled soldier got up and struggled to put on his overcoat.

[108] *James A. Graham Papers,* 207; Jan. 15, 1865.
[109] *Cf.* his warning against depredations, Dec. 12, 1864, in *O. R.,* 42, part 3, p. 1270.
[110] 17 *Confederate Veteran,* 603.
[111] J. W. Reid: *History of the Fourth South Carolina Volunteers,* 129.
[112] *Gordon,* 383.

Nobody in the crowded car did anything to help him. Observing this Lee rose and assisted the veteran.[113]

After he had seen that he could not count on the employment of the reserves, Lee had exerted himself in the early winter to organize the local defense troops in Richmond, but he found it progressively more difficult to get them out as the weather grew worse.[114] He had sought, also, to retain the Negro laborers over the Christmas holidays.[115] Although he had previously had a low opinion of the fighting quality of Negro troops, he saw now that the South must use them, if possible. After the beginning of 1865 he declared himself for their enlistment, coupled with a system of "gradual and general emancipation." [116] Congress hesitated and debated long, but at last, on March 13, the President signed a bill to bring Negroes into the ranks, though without any pledge of emancipation, such as Lee had considered necessary to the success of the new policy.[117] Bad as was the law, Lee undertook at once to set up a proper organization for the Negro troops.[118] While Congress had argued, Virginia had acted in providing for the enrollment of Negroes, slave and free, in the military service. On March 24 Lee applied for the maximum number allowable under the statute of the commonwealth.[119] "The services of these men," he said, "are now necessary to enable us to oppose the enemy."

He urged on his lieutenants new economy of force and he strengthened his lines against sudden attack.[120] Personal appeals were made to returned prisoners of war to waive the usual furlough and to rejoin their commands;[121] all able-bodied men were

---

113 1 *Macrae*, 175; *Jones*, 162.
114 *O. R.*, 42, part 3, pp. 1268, 1310; 2 *R. W. C. D.*, 363.
115 *O. R.*, part 3, p. 1267.
116 IV *O. R.*, part 3, pp. 1012, 1013, 1175. Lee's previous view was casually expressed in *O. R.*, 29, part 2, p. 736. On Negro enlistments generally, see Edward Spencer in *Annals of the War*, 554 ff. For the view that the enlistment of the Negroes hastened the demoralization of the army, because it was interpreted as a formal admission by the government that the Southern cause was hopeless, see *History of McGowan's Brigade*, 201. "War Clerk" Jones on Jan. 25, 1865, noted in his diary that a prominent Richmonder expressed the opinion that Lee "was always a thorough emancipationist." Jones added: "If it is really so, and if it were generally known, that Gen. Lee is, and always has been opposed to slavery, how soon would his great popularity vanish like the mist of the morning" (2 *R. W. C. D.*, 398).
117 Text in IV *O. R.*, 3, p. 1161.
118 *Cf. O. R.*, 46, part 2, p. 1356.
119 *O. R.*, 46, part 3, p. 1339.
120 *O. R.*, 46, part 2, p. 1227.
121 2 *R. W. C. D.*, 435.

taken from the bureaus;[122] all "leaves" for officers were suspended;[123] new combat rules and revised marching instructions were issued to meet changed conditions.[124] All that Lee had learned in nearly four years of war, all that his quiet energy inspired, all that his associates could suggest or his official superiors devise—all was thrown into a last effort to organize and strengthen the thin, shivering, hungry Army of Northern Virginia for the last grapple with the well-fed, well-clad, ever-increasing host that crowded the countryside opposite Lee's lines.

[122] 2 R. W. C. D., 379.   [123] James A. Graham Papers, 230.
[124] O. R., 46, part 2, p. 1249.

APPENDIX III—1

Stuart's Instructions for the Gettysburg Campaign

The absence of the greater part of the Confederate cavalry had so disastrous an effect on Lee's operations in Pennsylvania that the reasons why it did not sooner rejoin the infantry were naturally discussed at the time. Criticised for allowing himself to be separated from Lee when the commanding general needed all his mounted troops to establish the positions of the Federals, Stuart vigorously defended his conduct.[1] During the long controversy over Gettysburg, provoked in 1877 by the request of the Comte de Paris for information on the campaign, and given at length in *S. H. S. P.*, vols. 4–7, Stuart's failure to arrive promptly on the flank of Ewell was repeatedly mentioned as one of the causes of Lee's failure to accomplish what he hoped, but little effort was made to analyze fully the orders under which Stuart acted and the reasons that prompted him to make a complete circuit of the Federal army. The criticisms of Stuart gradually increased in severity with successive biographers until 1896, when Longstreet printed his *From Manassas to Appomattox* and Colonel Charles Marshall delivered an address on Stuart's movements.[2] Colonel John S. Mosby replied hotly to both.[3] In 1908 he published his *Stuart's Cavalry in the Gettysburg Campaign,* an intemperate book, in which he tried to demonstrate the inaccuracy of General Lee's two reports on Gettysburg. This provoked replies by Colonel T. M. R. Talcott and Doctor R. H. McKim, whom Mosby answered.[4] The most recent word in the argument was the publication of Colonel Marshall's critique of Stuart in *An Aide de Camp of Lee,* edited by General Sir Frederick Maurice, a chapter which contained so much special pleading that one is led inevitably to conclude that Marshall considered he was subject to censure for the form of Lee's letters of June 22 and 23 to General Stuart.

For the purposes of this biography it is not necessary to consider all the arguments advanced in this controversy. The battle has raged

[1] *Marshall,* 214–16; Stuart's report, *O. R.,* 27, part 2, pp. 692, 707–8.
[2] 23 *S. H. S. P.,* 205 *ff.*   [3] *Ibid.,* 238 *ff.,* 348 *ff.*
[4] 27 *S. H. S. P.,* 210 *ff.,* 369 *ff.*: 38 *S. H. S. P.,* 184.

chiefly over the question whether or not Lee intended to instruct Stuart to cross the Potomac *immediately* east of the mountains. The writer believes that the sequence of events set forth in the text proves that this was not the case. Certainly the claim would not have been advanced with so much assurance or defended so positively if those who entered the controversy had based their arguments on the information that Lee and Stuart possessed at the time, instead of confusing what those officers then knew with what they subsequently learned.

The essential fact is that when Lee sent his final letter to Stuart on June 23 he had information from at least two sources that Hooker was preparing to cross the Potomac at Edwards' Ferry. That of necessity involved so heavy a concentration between Leesburg and the ferry, and from the ferry for some miles southward that it would have been a physical impossibility for Stuart to ride around the rear of Hooker's army and then cross "immediately east of the mountains" without doubling back on his tracks and making a journey twice as long as that which seemed to be open to him by crossing between Hooker and Washington. Lee frankly stated both in his preliminary and in his final report that Stuart had discretion to cross either east or west of the mountains.[5] When Marshall put into the draft report a criticism of Stuart for disobedience to orders, Lee struck it out and said he could not adopt Marshall's conclusions or charge Stuart with the facts as Marshall had stated them, unless they were established by court-martial.[6]

Little time need be spent over the claim of Colonel Marshall put forward in this language: "This explicit order [for Stuart to 'move on and feel the right of Ewell's troops'] precluded any movement by Stuart that would prevent him 'from feeling the right of Ewell's troops' after crossing the Potomac. So that under these restrictions he was practically instructed not to cross the Potomac east of the Federal army, and thus interpose that army between himself and the right of General Ewell." [7] This is a manifest *non sequitur*. If Lee had meant that Stuart should not cross east of the mountains in order to reach General Ewell he could readily have said so. Colonel Marshall must himself have felt this, because while he included this charge in the manuscript he left unpublished and unrevised at the time of his death, he did not advance it as an argument in his address of 1896.[8]

---

[5] *O. R.,* 27, part 2, pp. 306, 316.

[6] D. G. McIntosh, quoting Marshall, in *Review of the Gettysburg Campaign* (cited hereafter as *McIntosh*), 37 *S. H. S. P.,* 95.

[7] *Marshall, op. cit.,* 210.   [8] 23 *S. H. S. P.,* 205 *ff.*

APPENDIX

Doctor McKim claimed[9] that when Hill and Longstreet had crossed the Potomac there was no further hope that Lee's movement could be concealed, and that, in consequence, Stuart should have crossed west of the mountains and passed over the Potomac at Shepherdstown. Doctor McKim overlooked three facts. Under Lee's instructions, Stuart was not to move at all until the First and Third Corps were beyond pursuit from the south side of the Potomac. Secondly, Lee was solicitous that nothing should be done by the cavalry until this movement was safely under way. Thirdly, when this movement was in progress Stuart had a minor mission to perform in annoying and delaying the enemy.

Colonel McIntosh asserted[10] that when Stuart had crossed the river and found Hooker on the north side, he should have turned back, gone up the south bank and recrossed at Shepherdstown. But an examination of the map will make it plain that this would have more than doubled Stuart's march to Ewell's right flank, which was the most important part of his movement.

The claim that Stuart delayed unduly after crossing the Potomac in seeking to put himself on Ewell's flank[11] will be considered in Appendix III—4. The serious charge of Colonel Mosby that General Lee gave an improper record of Stuart's achievements in his two reports is trivial and has already been answered effectively by Colonel Talcott in 37 *S. H. S. P.*, 22–28.

There remains but to answer this very important question: If Lee gave Stuart discretion to pass around Hooker's army, knowing that this would almost certainly force Stuart to cross the Potomac east of Edwards' Ford, who was to blame for what followed? The answer will be clear from a narration of the facts.

Stuart received his final orders "late in the night" of June 23–24th.[12] The next morning Major Mosby returned from a scout east of the Catoctin Mountains and reported that he had ridden freely among the Federal corps which, he said, were quiet. There was no sign of a movement.[13] Under Lee's orders, Stuart had no discretion to undertake a ride around the Federal army unless it was moving northward. He sent off a dispatch to General Lee, however,[14] reporting what Mosby had discovered. Then, instead of preparing to withdraw through the mountains westward to Lee, as contemplated by his orders in case he found the Federals inactive, he made ready to move east-

---

[9] 37 *S. H. S. P.*, 224. [10] 37 *S. H. S. P.*, 92–93.
[11] Doctor McKim advanced this view in 37 *S. H. S P.*, 221.
[12] H. B. *McClellan*, 316.
[13] Mosby, *Stuart's Cavalry*, 78, 81. [14] *Ibid.*, 81.

ward. He doubtless reasoned that even if the Federals were inactive when Mosby passed among their camps on the 23d, they might be moving northward on the 24th. It was Stuart's duty to ascertain that fact.

He construed his orders to mean that he was not to begin his march until "after" the 24th.[15] He did not wait an hour thereafter. At 1 A.M. on the morning of the 25th he started eastward with three brigades so as not to be observed in daylight by the enemy's lookout on the Bull Run Mountains.[16] The troops he took with him were Fitz Lee's, Hampton's, and Rooney Lee's brigades, the last-named under command of Colonel John R. Chambliss. Those he left were Robertson's and Jones's. Stuart's protagonists say he made this selection because Jones was the best outpost officer he had and because his was the largest brigade in his corps. Jones, however, was junior to Robertson, and would not command the force. Robertson's brigade consisted of only two regiments and was so small that it offset the strength of Jones's. Stuart could only justify in one way the contention of his friends that this was an equitable division of force:[17] he would have to count with Jones and Robertson the brigade of Jenkins, which was in advance of Ewell in Pennsylvania. And the strength of this brigade did not approximate the 3800 men credited to it. Stuart's selection, in all probability, was due to his desire to have veteran troops with him, under co-operative commanders. He did not like Jones, who returned this feeling in kind with interest,[18] and he had no high opinion of Robertson. Had he been able to rejoin Lee quickly in Maryland or in Pennsylvania, this selection of veteran troops for a difficult raid would have been a wise arrangement, but as it eventuated, Lee was served in the Gettysburg campaign by the less-experienced cavalry commanders, men who had never worked closely with him before. It was an unfortunate condition and was in part responsible for the difficulties Lee encountered.

When Stuart reached Hay Market, on the road to Centreville, he encountered Hancock's corps, *and it was moving north.* Stuart's underlying orders were that he should take position on Ewell's right as soon as he found the enemy crossing the Potomac. Apparently he did not regard Hooker's northward movement as necessarily indicating a crossing. He did, however, feel that the direction of the Federals' advance gave him the discretion he certainly desired to make a raid around the enemy's army instead of tamely following the First Corps

[15] The orders of the 23d read: "the sooner you cross into Maryland, after tomorrow, the better" (*O. R.*, 27, part 3, p. 923).
[16] *O. R.*, 27, part 2, p. 692.   [17] *H. B. McClellan*, 318–19.   [18] See *supra*, p. 225.

across the river under shelter of the Blue Ridge. Mosby, who had originally suggested the operation to Stuart, had proposed that Stuart "pass through the middle of Hooker's army," which Mosby believed to be camped by corps with intervals of at least ten miles between each two.[19] Such a dash appealed to Stuart. But Lee's orders did not permit him to ride *through* the Federal army. All Lee's consideration had been based on the advantage of attacking the *rear* of the Federals, and he had specified that Stuart was to ascertain whether he could *"pass around their army without hinderance."* [20] When Stuart found himself confronting Hancock's corps, and not the rear of the army, he encountered "hinderance" of the most serious sort. His restraining orders then applied. He should have turned back and proceeded northward when he believed the mountain passes safe. But enthusiasm and his desire to perform another dazzling feat carried him on. He had discretion up to a certain point; Lee must take whatever blame is attached to allowing it; but, with the best intentions in the world, Stuart misused that discretion by violating the essential proviso. Instead of starting westward as soon as he found his road by Hay Market blocked, he blazed away with his artillery at a Federal corps and forced it to extend a line of battle. Then he withdrew to Buckland,[21] sent off a brigade to reconnoitre and, with the remainder of his command, spent the day grazing his horses, for he had no forage.

On the 26th he moved to Wolf Run Shoals, but had to make a halt there to feed his mounts. The next day the march of some of his men was slowed down by the proximity of the Federal horse and by uncertainty as to the positions of the enemy. By violating the one and only condition imposed in his orders—by pushing on in the face of opposition—he was so delayed that he could not cross the Potomac until the night of the 27–28th.[22] Lee had been anxious for him to enter Maryland as soon as possible after the 24th. As it was, Stuart took from 1 A.M. on the 25th, or three whole days, to cross the Potomac.

The facts convey the judgment: Stuart was innocent of most of the charges made against him, but he disregarded his principal mission of moving promptly to the right flank of Ewell and he was guilty of violation of orders when he encountered material "hinderance" and did not turn back. Lee hoped that Stuart could attack the Federal wagon trains and disorganize the Federal advance to the Potomac, but he neither anticipated nor authorized any such operation as Stuart conducted.

[19] Mosby, *Stuart's Cavalry*, 76.
[21] *O. R.*, 27, part 2, pp. 692–93.

[20] *O. R.*, 27, part 3, p. 923.
[22] *O. R.*, 27, part 2, p. 693.

APPENDIX III—2

THE HOUR OF LONGSTREET'S ARRIVAL, JULY 2, 1863

The time of the arrival of Longstreet's corps on Seminary Ridge on the morning of July 2, 1863, is of great importance for two reasons: First, if it had arrived early and had attacked promptly, Lee might have been able to drive the Federals from Cemetery Ridge on the morning of July 2 and might have won a victory or, at the least, might have been spared the slaughter of July 3. The question is of importance, further, because the earlier Longstreet's men arrived, the less the excuse of their commander for the long delay before he had them in position to attack. In defending himself against the charge that he was late in arriving, General Longstreet entirely overlooked the fact that he was thereby indicting himself for not attacking until about 4 P.M.

Longstreet issued his orders for the advance of his troops on the road to Gettysburg at 5:30 P.M. on the afternoon of July 1, subsequent to his conversation with General Lee.[1] These orders were that his troops were to march as far as practicable toward Gettysburg that night without distressing the men and animals. Under these orders, Kershaw's brigade, which led McLaws's division, got within two miles of the town and halted at midnight.[2] The rear of the division seems to have stopped on Marsh Creek about four miles from Gettysburg, on the Chambersburg road.[3] Hood was immediately behind McLaws. Law's brigade was still at New Guilford and started at 3 A.M. for Gettysburg.[4] Orders to McLaws were to move at 4 A.M. but the time was changed to sunrise.[5]

Longstreet gave three specific and one general statement as to the time he joined Lee on Seminary Ridge. (1) He wrote Colonel Walter H. Taylor, April 25, 1875: "My two divisions nor myself did not reach General Lee until 8 A.M. on the 2nd."[6] (2) In *Annals of the War*, 422, he asserted: "I went to General Lee's headquarters at daylight." (3) In 3 *B. and L.*, 340, he affirmed: "On the morning of the 2nd I joined General Lee." (4) In *From Manassas to Appomattox*, 362, he maintained: "The stars were shining brightly on the morning of the 2nd when I reported at General Lee's headquarters and asked for orders."

[1] *O. R.*, 51, part 2, p. 733. [2] *O. R.*, 27, part 2, p. 366.
[3] 7 *S. H. S. P.*, 67; *O. R.*, 27, part 2, p. 358.
[4] 3 *B and L.*, 319.
[5] *O. R.*, 27, part 2, p. 366; 7 *S. H. S. P.*, 67.
[6] *Taylor's General Lee*, 198; the original is in the *Taylor MSS.*

APPENDIX

Quite obviously, in the face of these contradictions, one must look to other witnesses. Hood said [7] that he arrived "shortly after daybreak . . . and during the early part of the same morning, we were both engaged in company with Generals Lee and A. P. Hill in observing the position of the Federals." He mentioned, however, that General Lee "walked up and down in the shade of the large trees nearby," which would of course place this part of the interview well after sunrise. General McLaws simply stated [8] that his orders were to move at sunrise and that his command reached Seminary Ridge "early in the morning." Doctor Cullen said that Longstreet left his camp at 3 A.M. and rode to General Lee's headquarters, "where I found [Longstreet] sitting with [Lee] after sunrise." Colonel Fremantle found Lee and Longstreet in conference after 5 A.M. [9] Ross [10] wrote that he was aroused while it was still dusk, that he ate breakfast with Longstreet, that they rode five miles and that Lee was on Seminary Ridge when they arrived.

This is all the evidence, and it scarcely justifies any conclusion that cannot be assailed with citations no less weighty. Longstreet was certainly in error when he said he arrived while the "stars were burning brightly" and probably was no less wide of the mark in saying that he did not arrive until 8 A.M. As the sun rose at Gettysburg on July 2 at 4:32, it probably is approximately correct to say that Longstreet joined Lee on Seminary Ridge at 5:15 or about that time.

The time of Longstreet's own arrival is less important than that of the appearance of his men. And here, again, the evidence is not conclusive. Hood's march began about 3 A.M., and as the distance his troops had to cover was an average of five miles, the head of his column should have been at the ridge by 5:30 A.M. The whole of it could have been there by 7 or 7:30. Hood himself gave no time for its appearance, simply stating that he arrived "before or at sunrise," and that his division "soon commenced filing into an open field." [11] It is apparent, however, from the report of Lieutenant Colonel W. S. Shepherd that the division was not immediately deployed but remained strung out along the road by which it had moved. [12] McLaws's division did not begin to move until after sunrise [13]—how long after that time it is not easy to say. Dickert noted casually [14] that when Kershaw's brigade was aroused "the sun had long since shot its rays" over Gettys-

---

[7] *Hood*, 56–57.
[8] *7 S. H. S. P.*, 68.
[9] *Fremantle*, 257.
[10] *Ross*, 49.
[11] *Hood*, 56–57.
[12] *O. R.*, 27, part 2, p. 420.
[13] McLaws in *7 S. H. S. P.*, 68; *O. R.*, 27, part 2, p. 366; *3 B. and L.*, 358.
[14] *History of Kershaw's Brigade*, 233.

burg. As the road was little obstructed at that time,[15] the head of Mc·Laws's column was probably on the field by 6 A.M. That command, however, does not seem to have been well closed, and the other division was probably not in position until 8 or 8:30. Hood and McLaws were trustworthy in their statements, but they rode ahead of their troops and probably confused the time of their own arrival with that of the appearance of their troops.

One of the best witnesses is Alexander. He stated[16] that his artillery reached a point one mile west of Seminary Ridge about 7 A.M., and in his official report he recorded the fact that he arrived—presumably on the ridge—at 9 A.M.[17] Ordinarily, in Pennsylvania, the artillery marched between the divisions, but in this instance, as the position of the enemy was known, the artillery probably followed the rear division. When the artillery was at hand, the whole of the corps was up, except for Pickett's division and Law's brigade.[18]

Summarizing the whole case, then, it may be said that Longstreet probably had one division, less one brigade, in rear of Seminary Ridge by 7 or 7:30 A.M., a second division there by 8 to 8:30, and his artillery on the ridge by 9 A.M. It took him, therefore, approximately four and a half hours to bring his corps an average of five miles, and at the end of that time he had not begun his deployment. His troops were simply crowded together, on the ridge and to the rear, without an extension opposite the left flank of the enemy.

This delay in bringing up the First Corps was fatal to the success of Lee's plan. At sunrise on the 2d the Federals had in position on the field only the I, XI, and XII Corps, and almost all these troops were defending Cemetery Hill and Culp's Hill. The II Corps began to arrive at 7 A.M.,[19] the III Corps came up at the same hour and started to take position on Cemetery Ridge,[20] and the V Corps arrived about 8 A.M.[21] Before 7 A.M., the Federals had scarcely 20,000 unwounded men on the ground, but by 9 A.M. the number had been increased to 58,000.

APPENDIX III—3

The Handling of Anderson's Division on July 2, 1863

After the War between the States, when General Lee hoped to prepare a history of the campaigns of the Army of Northern Virginia, he asked

[15] O. R., 27, part 2, p. 366.
[16] 3 B. and L., 358.
[18] 3 B. and L., 319.
[20] O. R., 27, part 1, pp. 482, 531.
[17] O. R., 27, part 2, p. 429.
[19] O. R., 27, part 1, p. 369.
[21] O. R., 27, part 1, p. 592.

General Cadmus M. Wilcox, among others, for copies of his reports. General Wilcox prepared a full copy, which he corrected with his own hand. To his account of Gettysburg Wilcox wrote this interesting addendum, which is attached to the original among General Lee's MS. military papers:

"With reference to this battle of July 2 I beg to state (though too late to do any good) that when I sent my Adjutant General back to the Division commander asking that he send me re-enforcements, that my Adj't Gen'l. returned and reported that General Anderson said, 'Tell Gen'l. Wilcox to hold his own, that things will change'; that he found Gen'l. A. back in the woods which were in rear of the Emmitsburg road several hundred yards in a ravine, his horse tied and all his staff lying on the ground (indifferent) as tho' nothing was going on, horses all tied. I am quite certain that Gen'l. A. never saw a foot of the ground on which his three brigades fought on the 2nd July. Mahone and Posey's brigades were not engaged at Gettysburg, had they been pushed forward when I made my request I am certain that the enemy's line would have been pierced. Captain Shannon, Aide to Gen'l. A, told me, that he did (however) go to Gen'l Mahone with an order from Gen'l A. to advance, and that Gen'l Mahone refused to move, stating that Gen'l A. had told him to hold that position, but says the aide, I am just from Genl A. and he orders you to advance. No, says Mahone, I have my orders from Genl A. himself to remain here, and did not move.

"After recrossing the Potomac letters appeared in Georgia papers commenting severely on Genl A for not supporting Wright, Wilcox and Perry and that his strongest brigades had not fired a shot. Letters were published by Mahone and Posey, the former quite lengthy, in which he states the orders in Anderson's division to be 'to advance by brigades from the right (when McLaws should advance) that is, if the success should warrant it.' I was on Anderson's right and got the order three times during the day, 'to advance when the troops on my right advanced and to report it promptly to the Division commander in order that the other brigades might advance in succession.' I never had any conditional orders, 'if the success should warrant it' but believed that I was required and expected to contribute to the (winning of) success, which I did. I know not what were the orders beyond the Division, but I do know that I received orders three times during the day as stated above, and Genl. Wright informed me that such were his orders. The Florida brigade in good faith advanced with my brigade. I may wrong Genl A, but I always believed that he was too indifferent to his duties at Gettysburg. Wright never liked him afterwards. I really thought that

I should have made some report or complaint against him, but I did not, lest my motives might have been misunderstood, for I had from discontent (whether justly or not it does not matter) on two different occasions asked to be relieved from duty with the Army of Northern Virginia, once in the fall at Culpeper C. H. 1862, and again at Fredericksburg in May 1863."

APPENDIX III—4

STUART IN PENNSYLVANIA

After his belated crossing of the Potomac at Seneca on the night of June 27–28, Stuart lost some time breaking a lock gate and waylaying canal boats on the Chesapeake and Ohio Canal. Then he moved on to Rockville, near which place he encountered a Federal wagon train eight miles in length. Chasing some of the rear wagons back toward Washington, he burned those that were broken or overturned and decided to take the remaining 125 with him. He was further encumbered by some 400 prisoners until he paroled them. On the 29th he struck the Baltimore and Ohio Railroad, burned the bridge at Sykesville, and tore up the track at Hood's Mill. That afternoon he reached Westminster and on the morning of the 30th he arrived at Hanover. His general direction now was to the Susquehanna, where he reasoned the right column of Ewell's corps had arrived by this time. After passing Dover he moved on to Carlisle, and there he received Lee's orders to rejoin at Gettysburg. He was greatly slowed down in his march by his determination to retain his booty, and he lost much time in minor excursions when he should have been hastening to the flank of the army, concerning whose position he heard nothing whatever until after he had reached Dover.[1] When Stuart at length arrived and reported to Lee, the commanding general is reported to have said: "Well, General Stuart, you are here at last!"[2] Stuart felt the rebuke and was conscious of the very general criticism his absence evoked. In his report[3] he sought to justify himself by explaining that his operations had kept the enemy's cavalry from troubling Lee's advance. In submitting this document, through Marshall, he argued that if he had placed himself on the flank of the army, he would have attracted the Federal cavalry.[4] The balance of historical criticism since the war

[1] See his report, *O. R.*, 27, part 2, pp. 693–97.
[2] *Thomason*, 440.
[3] *O. R.*, 27, part 2, p. 707 *ff.*   [4] *Marshall*, 215 *ff.*

has been against this claim. His operations from June 25 to July 1, 1863, have generally been regarded as the least creditable chapter in his career.[5]

APPENDIX III—5

BEAUREGARD'S CALL FOR REINFORCEMENTS, JUNE 15, 1864

Colonel Samuel B. Paul's account of the interview with General Lee on June 15, 1864, regarding the reinforcement of Beauregard for the defense of Petersburg, appears in 2 *Roman,* 579–81. Written in 1874, at the request of General Beauregard, the material passages read as follows:

"On the morning of Tuesday, June 14th, 1864, you sent for me to come to your headquarters—we were then at Dunlop's, on Swift Creek. . . . You detailed to me with some minuteness the evidence of a large increase of strength to the enemy immediately in your front, and stated that a considerable force had been thrown across the river to the south side of the James, below City Point, the mouth of the Appomattox. . . . After giving me these details of fact you directed Colonel Otey to have a statement made in detail of your force and its distribution on your lines; and ordered me to proceed with the same to General Lee, to place before him the facts of the situation, to express to him your conviction that the enemy would commence operations at Petersburg in a short time, and request that he should send you back Hoke's division, and aid you with such other forces as would be adequate to the gravity of the situation. The papers were finished in the Adjutant-General's office by about 2 A.M. on the morning of Wednesday, 15th, and I started to General Lee's headquarters. These were difficult to find, but I reached them at about 12:30 o'clock, and saw Colonel Taylor, who secured me an interview with General Lee some half-hour afterwards. About 1 P.M.—my notes say—General Lee declined to permit me to open the papers, stating that he knew we were weak, but that we would simply have to accomplish all we could with what we had. At first I feared that I would be dismissed without further attention, and an intimation was made that I should return at once to you with that answer. The General seemed much preoccupied. I told

[5] For Stuart's movements in Pennsylvania and for the reasons that prompted them, see *H. B. McClellan,* 321 *ff.;* Fitz Lee in 5 *S. H. S. P.,* 166; *G. W. Beale,* 110 *ff.* Alexander, *op. cit.,* 378, pointed out that Stuart made another error in leaving Robertson instead of Hampton in command in Virginia. Robertson, according to General Alexander, did not understand his instructions and remained in Virginia until ordered by Lee to join him, as noted in the text, p. 62.

557

him that it was but a small part of my instructions to show him your weakness, the importance of your lines to his own safety, and the possibility of disaster to you, but to show the fact that attack was imminent. Gradually his interest seemed to increase, and he stated that he had ordered Hoke's division to rejoin you before my arrival. He then stated that you might rest assured that you were mistaken in supposing that the enemy had thrown any troops to the south side of James River; that a few of Smith's corps had come back to your front—nothing more—and that it was probable the enemy would cross the James, though, he reiterated, no part of his force had yet done so, because he could do nothing else, unless to withdraw altogether, as had been done by McClellan, which he did not believe General Grant thought of. He then said you might be assured that if you were seriously threatened he would send you aid, and, if needed, come himself. With some kind messages to you he then dismissed me."

This statement contains two errors and has one very important omission.

1. Colonel Paul stated that Beauregard told him "on the morning of Tuesday, June 14th, 1864," at his headquarters at Dunlop's, that there was a large increase in the strength of the enemy on his front "and that a considerable force had been thrown across the river to the south side of the James, below City Point."[1] The impression might be created by the words "thrown across" that General Beauregard knew at that time of the crossing of the James by a part of Grant's army. From this, the inference might be drawn that General Beauregard, in ordering Paul to confer with General Lee, intended to give notice to Lee that Grant's van was across the James. The facts justify no such inference. Birney's division of the II Corps, which led the movement across the James, did not begin to embark on the transports until 11:10 A.M. on the morning of June 14.[2] The division landed at Windmill Point, eight miles by signal line below City Point. Beauregard, at Dunlop's "on the morning of June 14," could not have known of the arrival of Birney at Windmill Point. The first transports could hardly have arrived until early afternoon. Beauregard's telegrams to General Lee and to General Bragg on the 14th are confirmatory proof that when Beauregard talked with Paul he did not know that any part of the Army of the Potomac had crossed from the north side. On the contrary, all his appeals for troops on the 14th[3] and until after 7 A.M. on the morning of June 15[4] were based on the theory, not that he was facing Butler *and* Grant,

---

[1] 2 *Roman*, 579.
[3] *O. R.*, 40, part 2, pp. 652–53.

[2] *O. R.*, 40, part 2, p. 316.
[4] *Ibid.*, 653.

but that he was confronting the whole of Butler's army, with the probability that Grant was to cross. The record will show that Beauregard had no certain knowledge until the morning of the 15th that any of Grant's troops were over the James. As Colonel Paul left at 2 A.M. on the 15th to visit Lee, he manifestly could not quote his chief in a matter of which his superior was not then informed. If, therefore, he told Lee that Grant was across the James, what he said was based on Beauregard's supposition of what *would* happen and not on any positive information of what *had* happened.

2. Colonel Paul was in error as to the time of his visit. He said that he interviewed General Lee at 1 P.M. on June 15. Lee's letter of 12:20 to Bragg[5] shows that Paul had been to see him before that hour. This shows that Colonel Paul, though a man of high standing, is not to be accepted as a meticulous witness where the time element is involved. And the time of the different happenings is of the utmost importance in the record of the crossing of the James.

3. Colonel Paul nowhere mentioned that he told Lee, as the latter wrote Bragg an hour or so afterwards,[6] that "the General [*i.e.,* Beauregard] was of opinion that if he has his original force he would be able to hold his present lines in front of Gen. Butler and at Petersburg." Needless to say, this was an assurance of the utmost importance to Lee in disposing his troops. If he sent Beauregard on the 15th all the troops that Beauregard thought he would need to maintain his front, then, obviously, if those forces did not suffice, the error of judgment was Beauregard's, not Lee's. Reference was made to these facts more fully on page 442 ff.

[5] *Lee's Dispatches,* 235.   [6] *Lee's Dispatches,* 235–36.